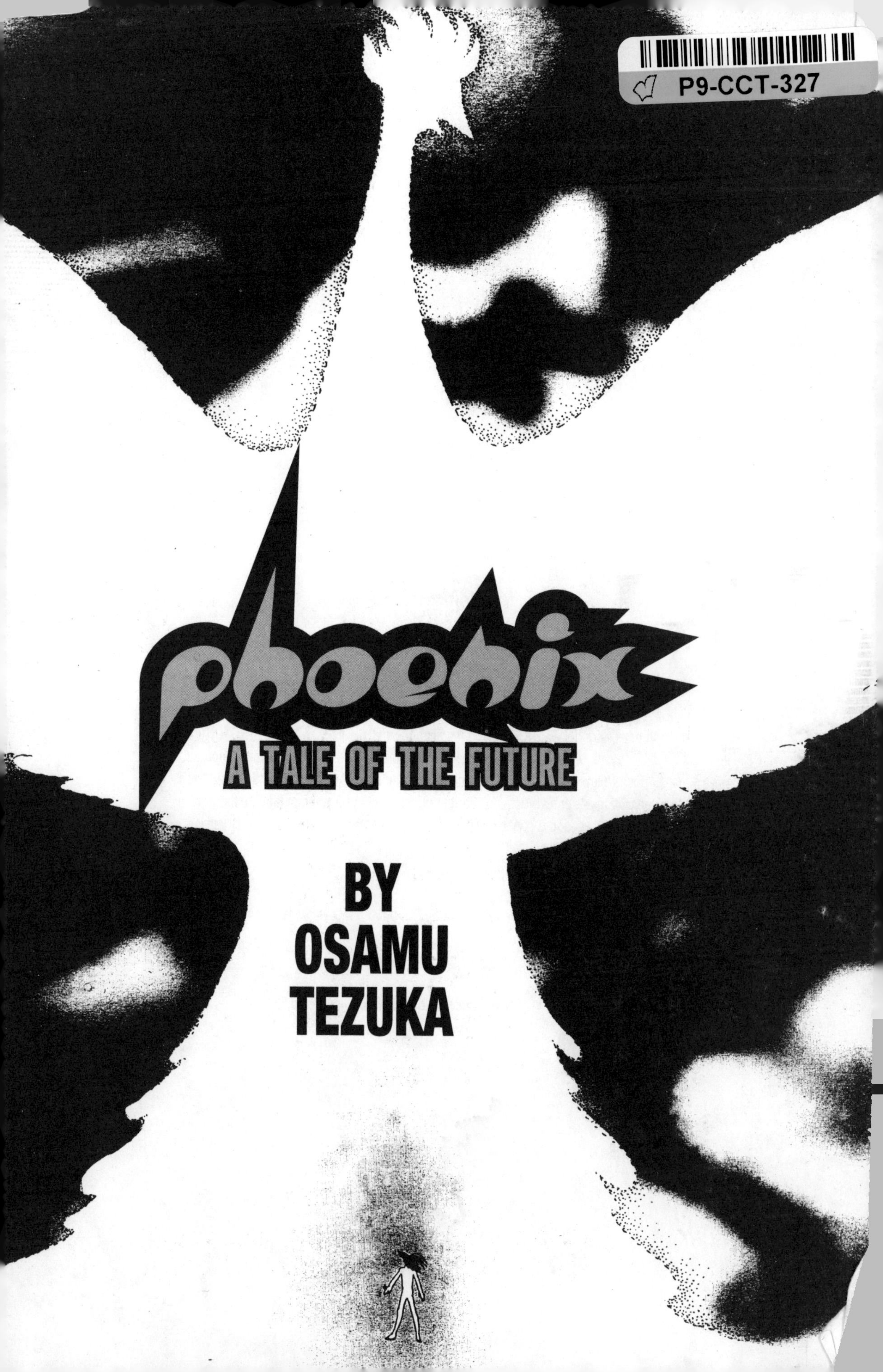
phoenix
A TALE OF THE FUTURE
BY
OSAMU
TEZUKA

PHOENIX: A TALE OF THE FUTURE

STORY & ART BY OSAMU TEZUKA

ENGLISH TRANSLATION BY DADAKAI
Jared Cook, Shinji Sakamoto, and Frederik L. Schodt

Touch-Up Art & Lettering/Susan Daigle-Leach
Book Design/Izumi Evers
Editor/Alvin Lu

Managing Editor/Annette Roman
V.P. of Sales & Marketing/Rick Bauer
Director of Editorial/Hyoe Narita
Publisher/Seiji Horibuchi

Printed in Canada

Published by Viz Communications, Inc., P.O. Box 77010, San Francisco, CA 94107

First printing, May 2002

Visit **www.viz.com** and **www.pulp-mag.com**

Also by Osamu Tezuka available from Viz Comics:

Adolf: A Tale of the Twentieth Century
Adolf: An Exile in Japan
Adolf: The Half-Aryan
Adolf: Days of Infamy
Adolf: 1945 and All That Remains

Black Jack, Volume 1
Black Jack: Two-Fisted Surgeon

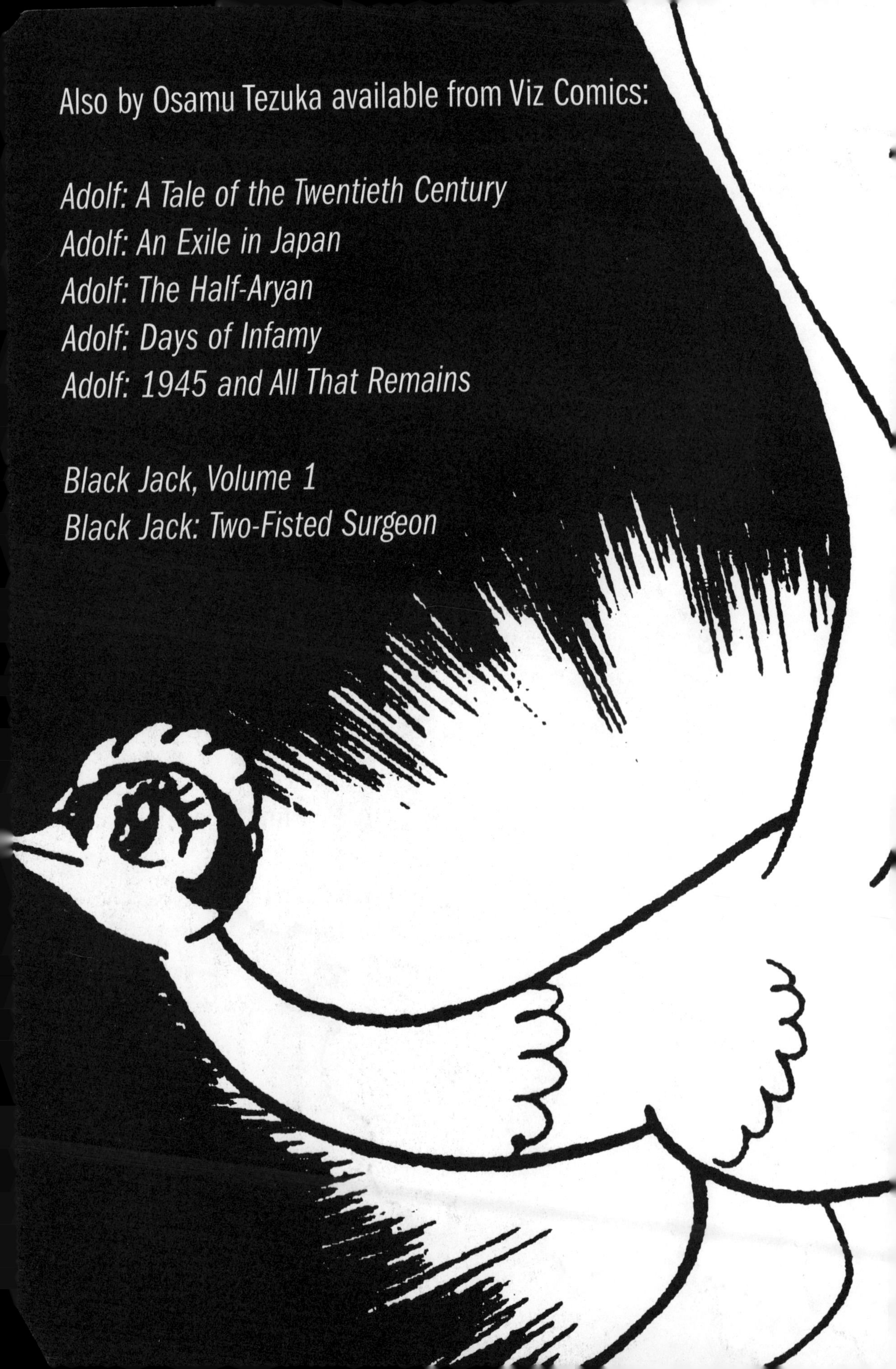

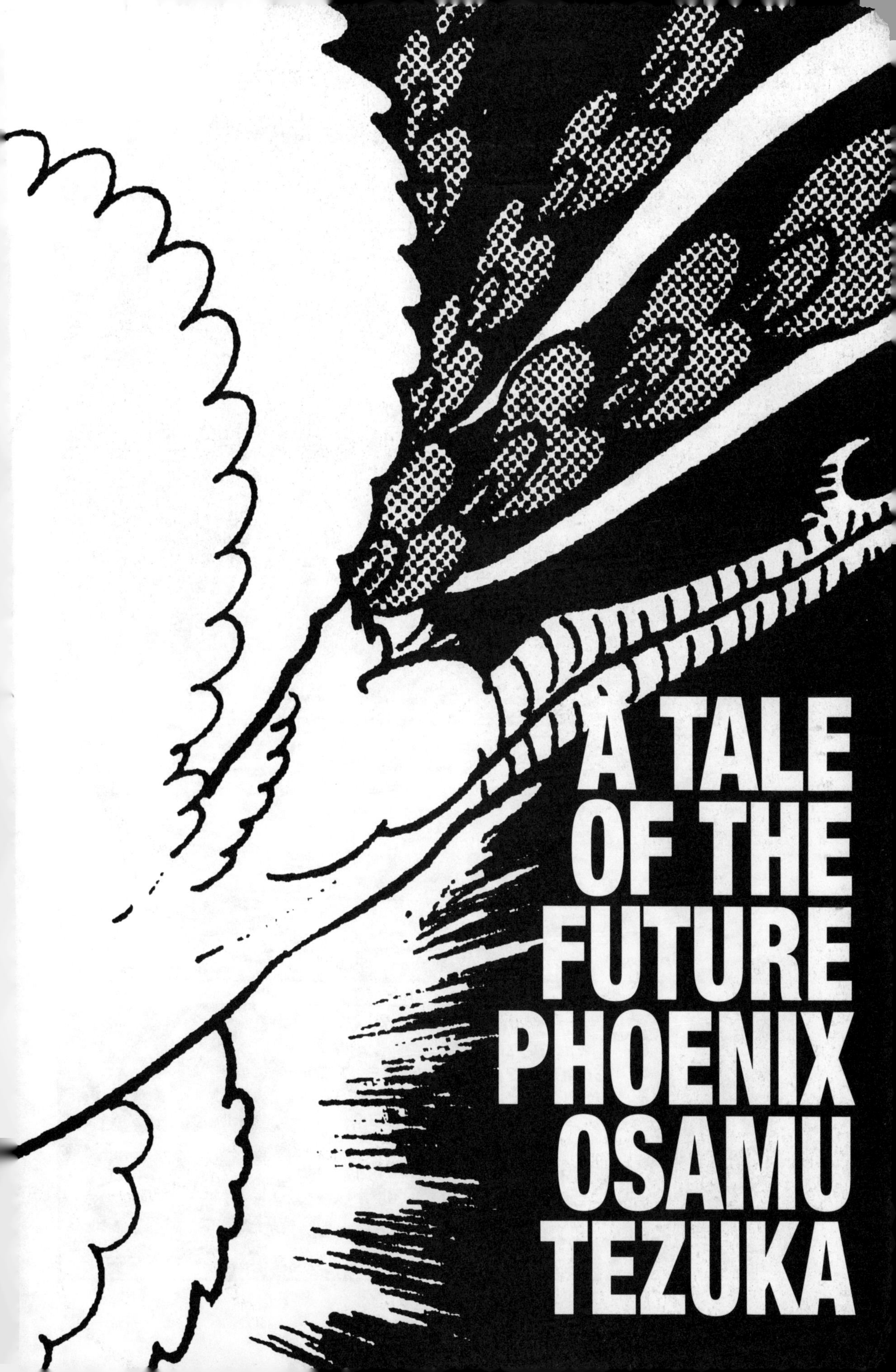

A TALE OF THE FUTURE
PHOENIX

OSAMU TEZUKA

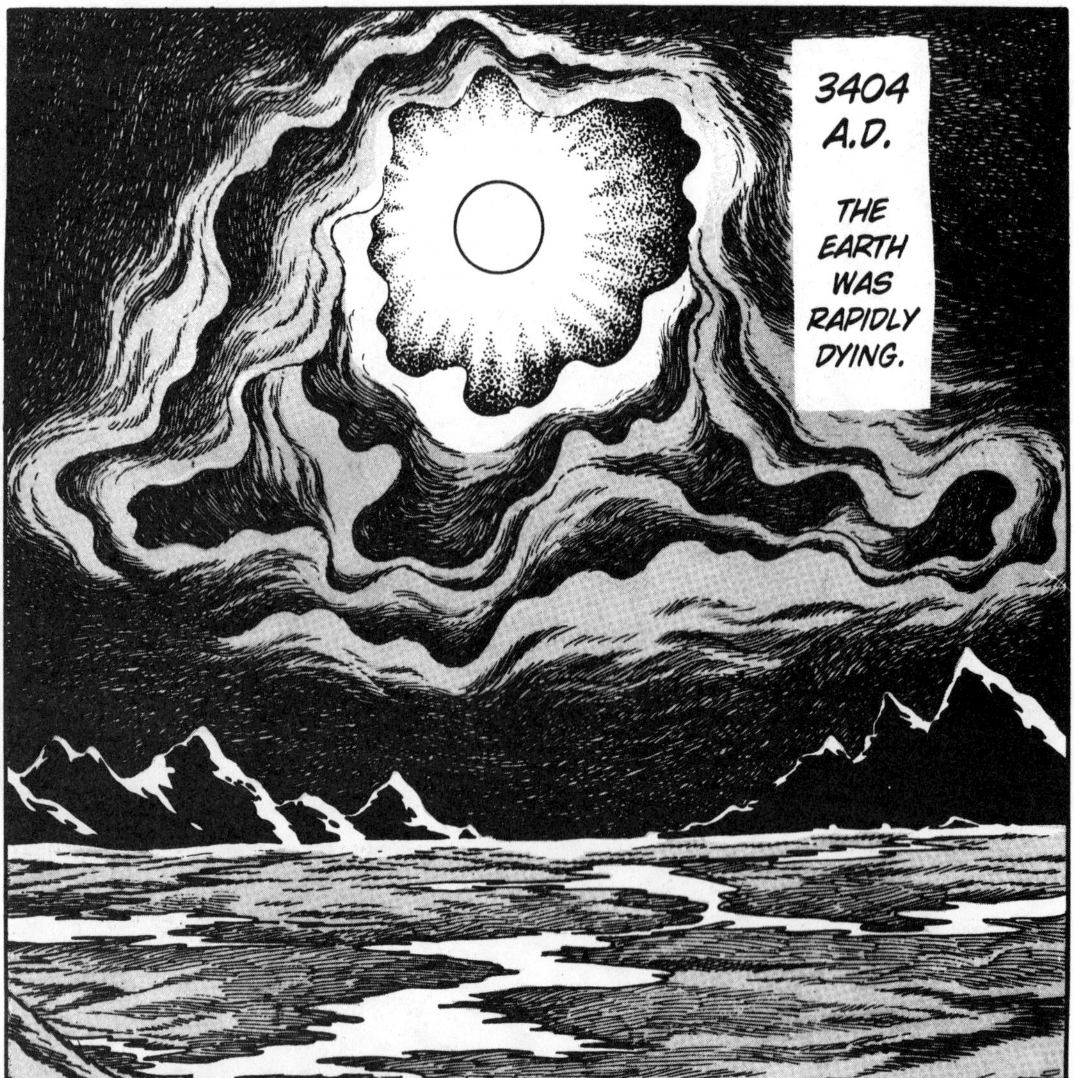
3404 A.D.
THE EARTH WAS RAPIDLY DYING.

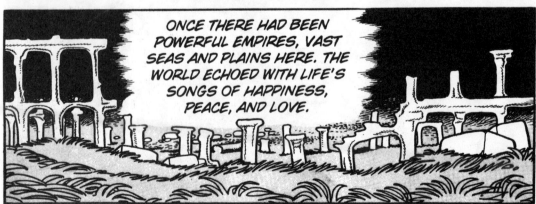

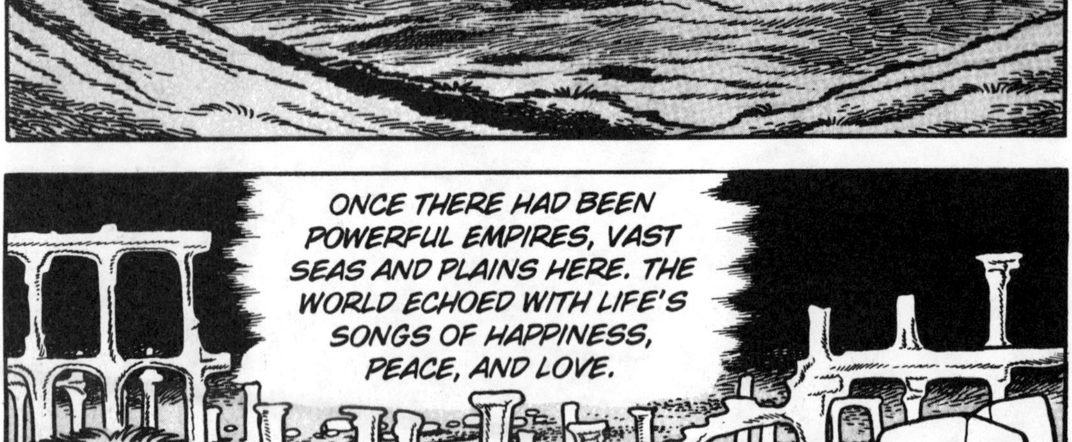
ONCE THERE HAD BEEN POWERFUL EMPIRES, VAST SEAS AND PLAINS HERE. THE WORLD ECHOED WITH LIFE'S SONGS OF HAPPINESS, PEACE, AND LOVE.

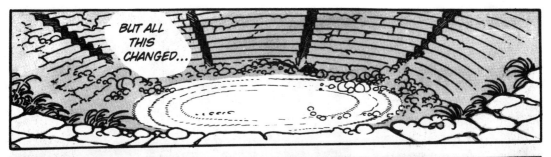

BUT ALL THIS CHANGED...

AND WHAT REMAINED WERE ONLY A FEW SCATTERED SWAMPS...

AROUND WHICH CLUSTERED LISTLESS ANIMALS...

...AND BARREN PLAINS OF WITHERED GRASS.

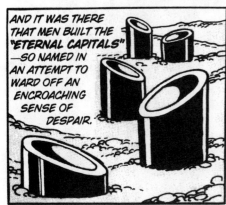

AND IT WAS THERE THAT MEN BUILT THE "ETERNAL CAPITALS" —SO NAMED IN AN ATTEMPT TO WARD OFF AN ENCROACHING SENSE OF DESPAIR.

MAN HAD TAKEN EVERYTHING WITH HIM UNDERGROUND —AND THAT REMAINED HIS LAST FORTRESS.

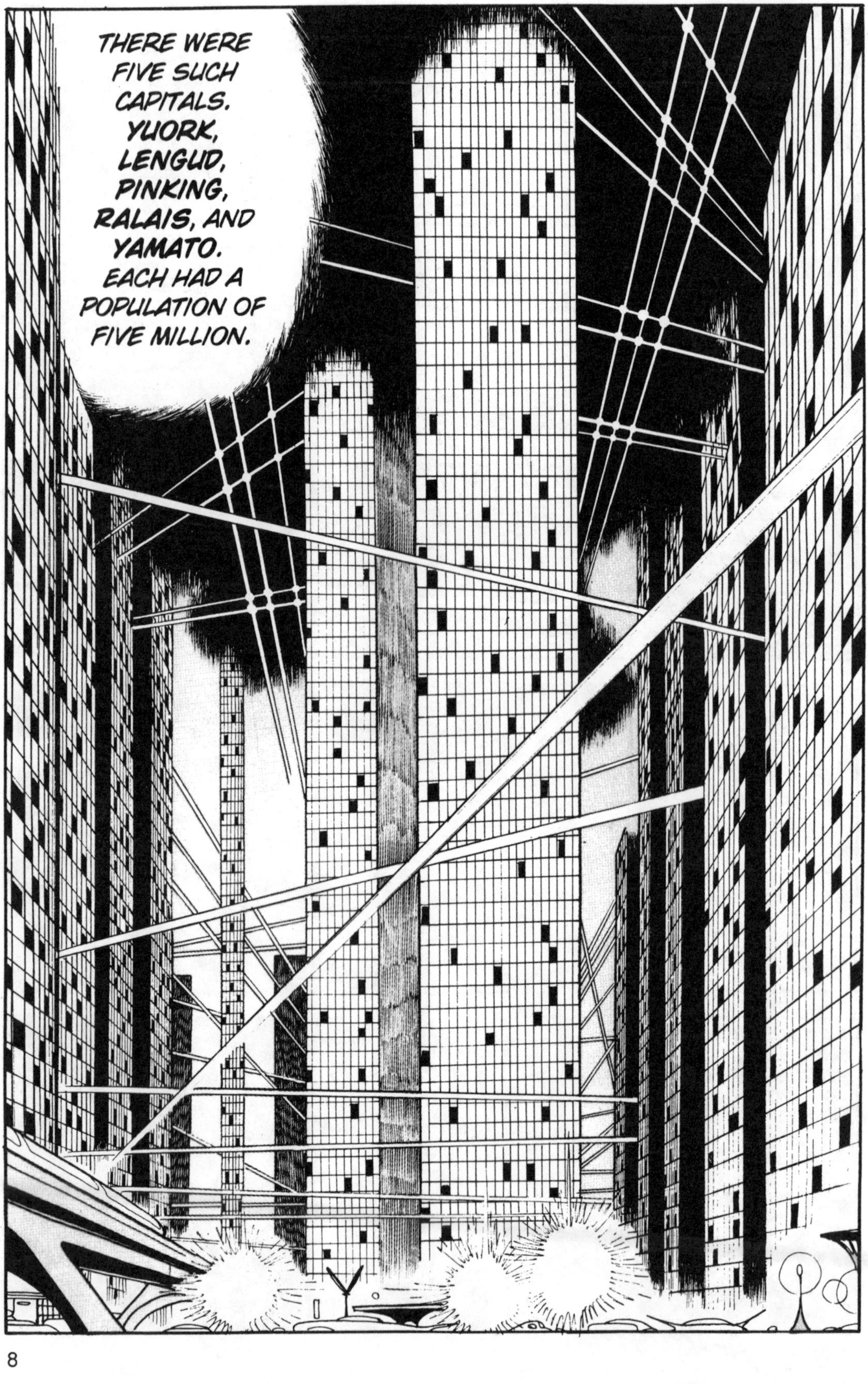
THERE WERE FIVE SUCH CAPITALS. YUORK, LENGUD, PINKING, RALAIS, AND YAMATO. EACH HAD A POPULATION OF FIVE MILLION.

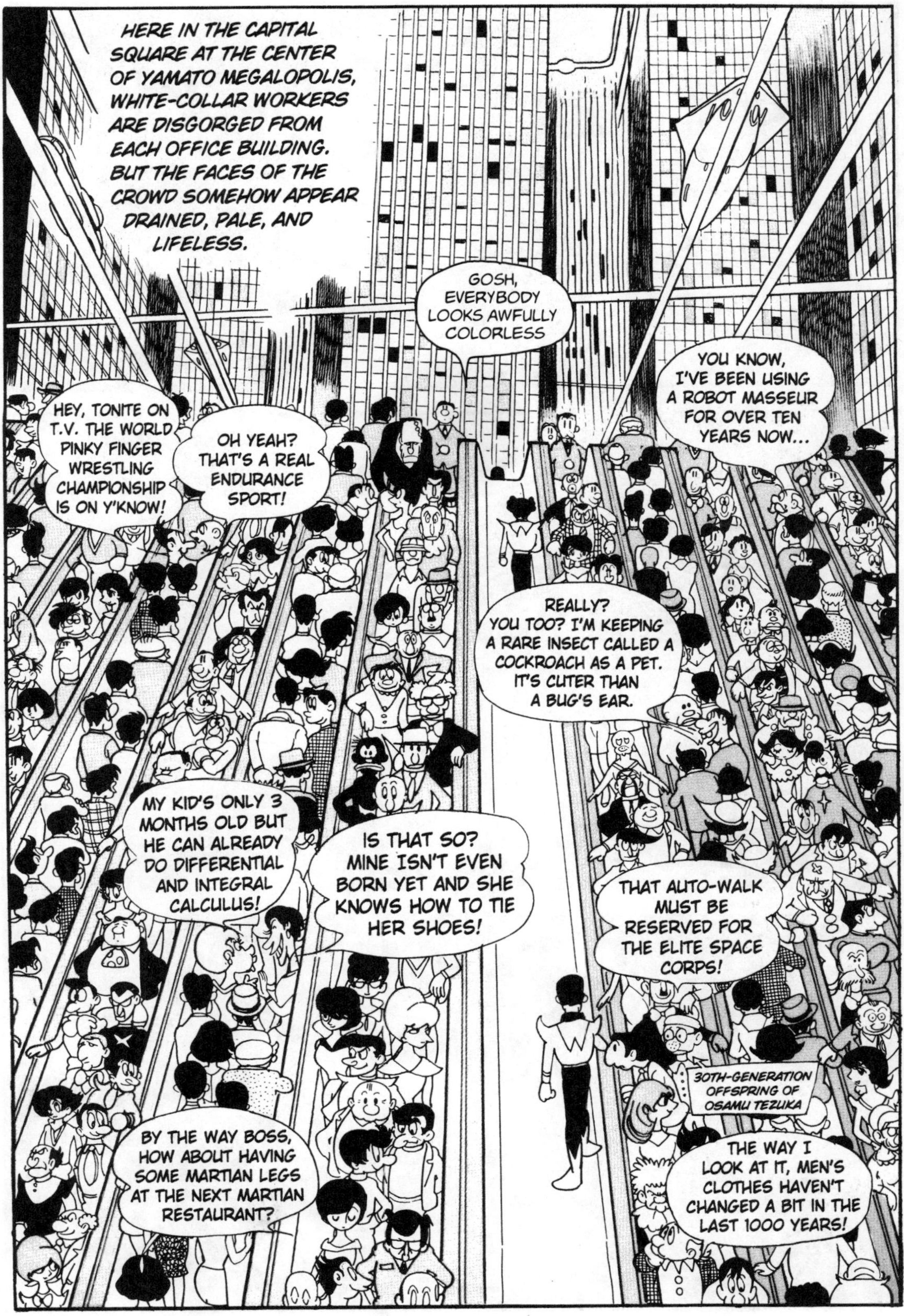
HERE IN THE CAPITAL SQUARE AT THE CENTER OF YAMATO MEGALOPOLIS, WHITE-COLLAR WORKERS ARE DISGORGED FROM EACH OFFICE BUILDING. BUT THE FACES OF THE CROWD SOMEHOW APPEAR DRAINED, PALE, AND LIFELESS.
GOSH, EVERYBODY LOOKS AWFULLY COLORLESS
YOU KNOW, I'VE BEEN USING A ROBOT MASSEUR FOR OVER TEN YEARS NOW...
REALLY? YOU TOO? I'M KEEPING A RARE INSECT CALLED A COCKROACH AS A PET. IT'S CUTER THAN A BUG'S EAR.
HEY, TONITE ON T.V. THE WORLD PINKY FINGER WRESTLING CHAMPIONSHIP IS ON Y'KNOW!
OH YEAH? THAT'S A REAL ENDURANCE SPORT!
MY KID'S ONLY 3 MONTHS OLD BUT HE CAN ALREADY DO DIFFERENTIAL AND INTEGRAL CALCULUS!
IS THAT SO? MINE ISN'T EVEN BORN YET AND SHE KNOWS HOW TO TIE HER SHOES!
THAT AUTO-WALK MUST BE RESERVED FOR THE ELITE SPACE CORPS!
30TH-GENERATION OFFSPRING OF OSAMU TEZUKA
THE WAY I LOOK AT IT, MEN'S CLOTHES HAVEN'T CHANGED A BIT IN THE LAST 1000 YEARS!
BY THE WAY BOSS, HOW ABOUT HAVING SOME MARTIAN LEGS AT THE NEXT MARTIAN RESTAURANT?

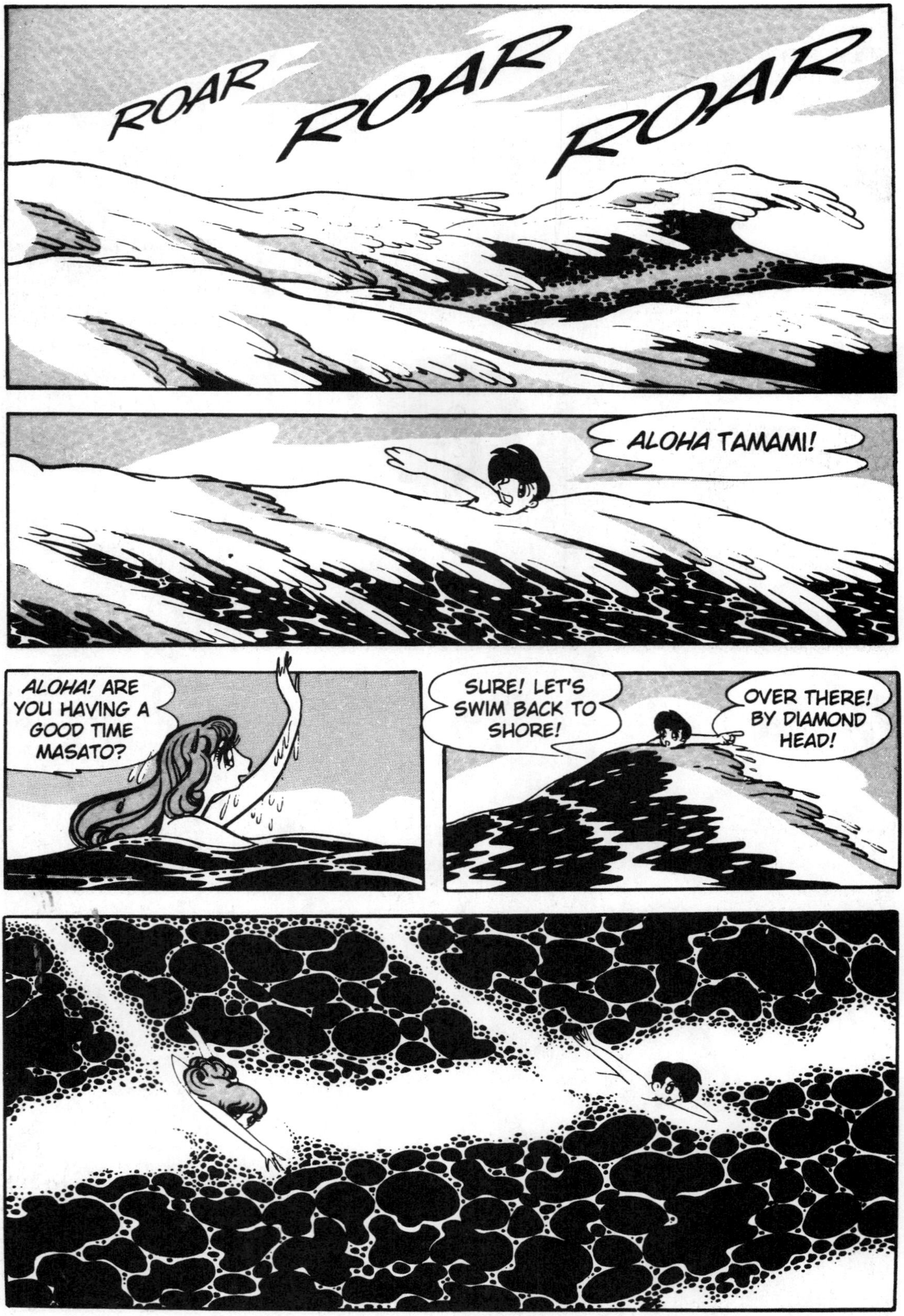
ROAR
ROAR
ROAR
ALOHA TAMAMI!
ALOHA! ARE YOU HAVING A GOOD TIME MASATO?
SURE! LET'S SWIM BACK TO SHORE!
OVER THERE! BY DIAMOND HEAD!

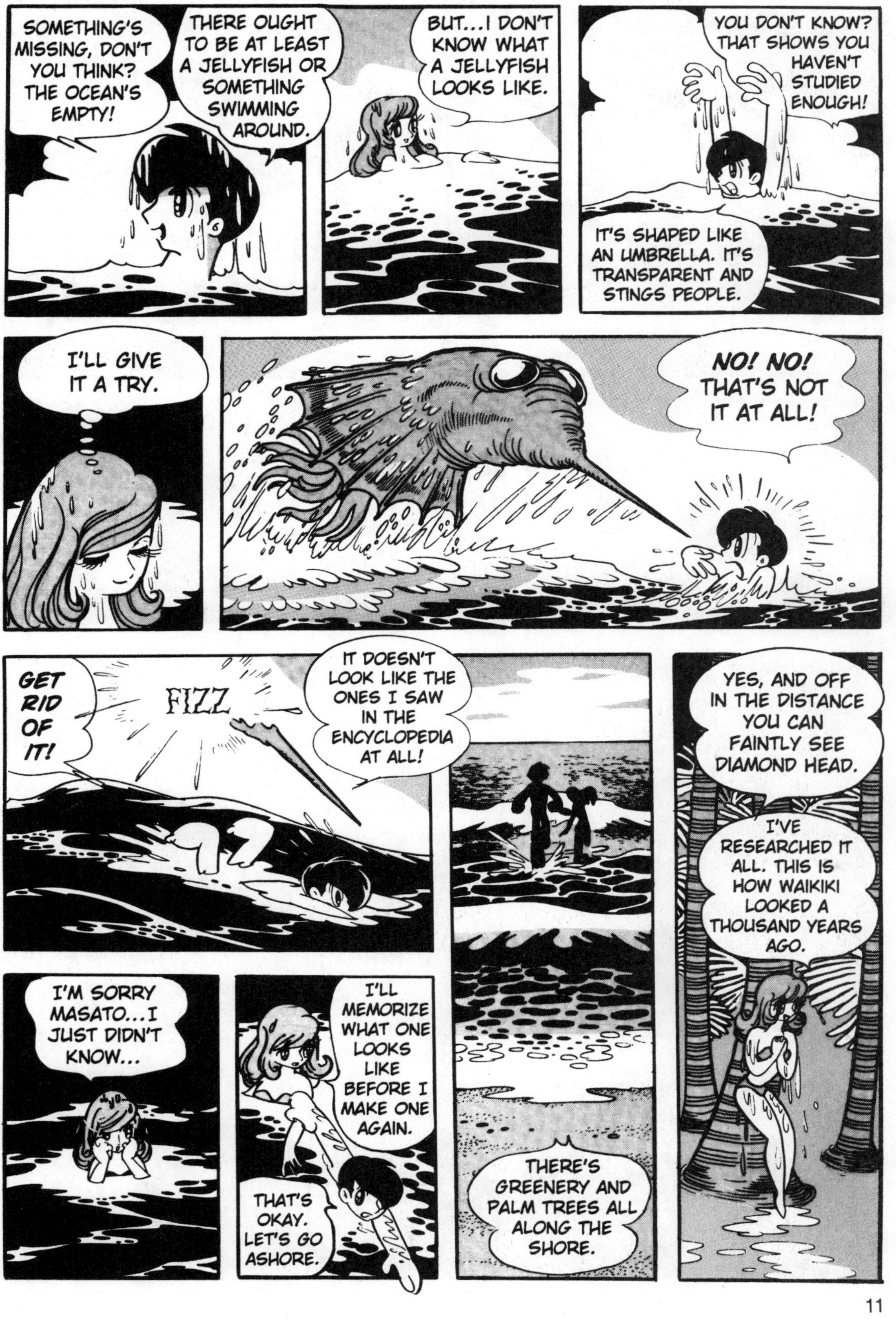
SOMETHING'S MISSING, DON'T YOU THINK? THE OCEAN'S EMPTY!
THERE OUGHT TO BE AT LEAST A JELLYFISH OR SOMETHING SWIMMING AROUND.
BUT...I DON'T KNOW WHAT A JELLYFISH LOOKS LIKE.
YOU DON'T KNOW? THAT SHOWS YOU HAVEN'T STUDIED ENOUGH!
IT'S SHAPED LIKE AN UMBRELLA. IT'S TRANSPARENT AND STINGS PEOPLE.
I'LL GIVE IT A TRY.
NO! NO! THAT'S NOT IT AT ALL!
GET RID OF IT!
FIZZ
IT DOESN'T LOOK LIKE THE ONES I SAW IN THE ENCYCLOPEDIA AT ALL!
I'M SORRY MASATO...I JUST DIDN'T KNOW...
I'LL MEMORIZE WHAT ONE LOOKS LIKE BEFORE I MAKE ONE AGAIN.
THAT'S OKAY. LET'S GO ASHORE.
THERE'S GREENERY AND PALM TREES ALL ALONG THE SHORE.
YES, AND OFF IN THE DISTANCE YOU CAN FAINTLY SEE DIAMOND HEAD.
I'VE RESEARCHED IT ALL. THIS IS HOW WAIKIKI LOOKED A THOUSAND YEARS AGO.

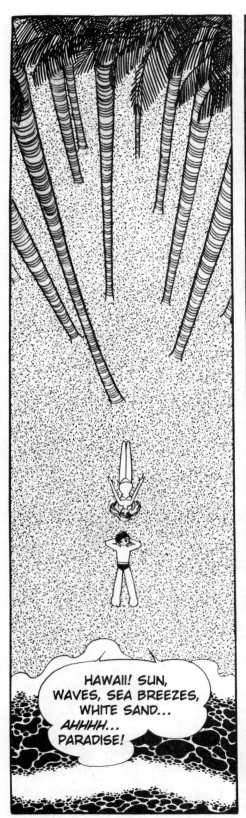

HAWAII! SUN, WAVES, SEA BREEZES, WHITE SAND... AHHHH... PARADISE!

NOT ONLY THAT, BUT YOU'RE HERE WITH ME TOO TAMAMI. I'VE GOT EVERYTHING... EVERYTHING!

I'M HAPPY.

ME TOO.

AS LONG AS YOU KEEP ME NEAR YOU.

WOULD I EVER LET GO OF YOU? NOT AS LONG AS I HAVE HANDS!

BZZZZZ

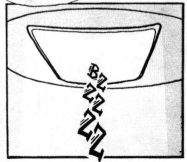

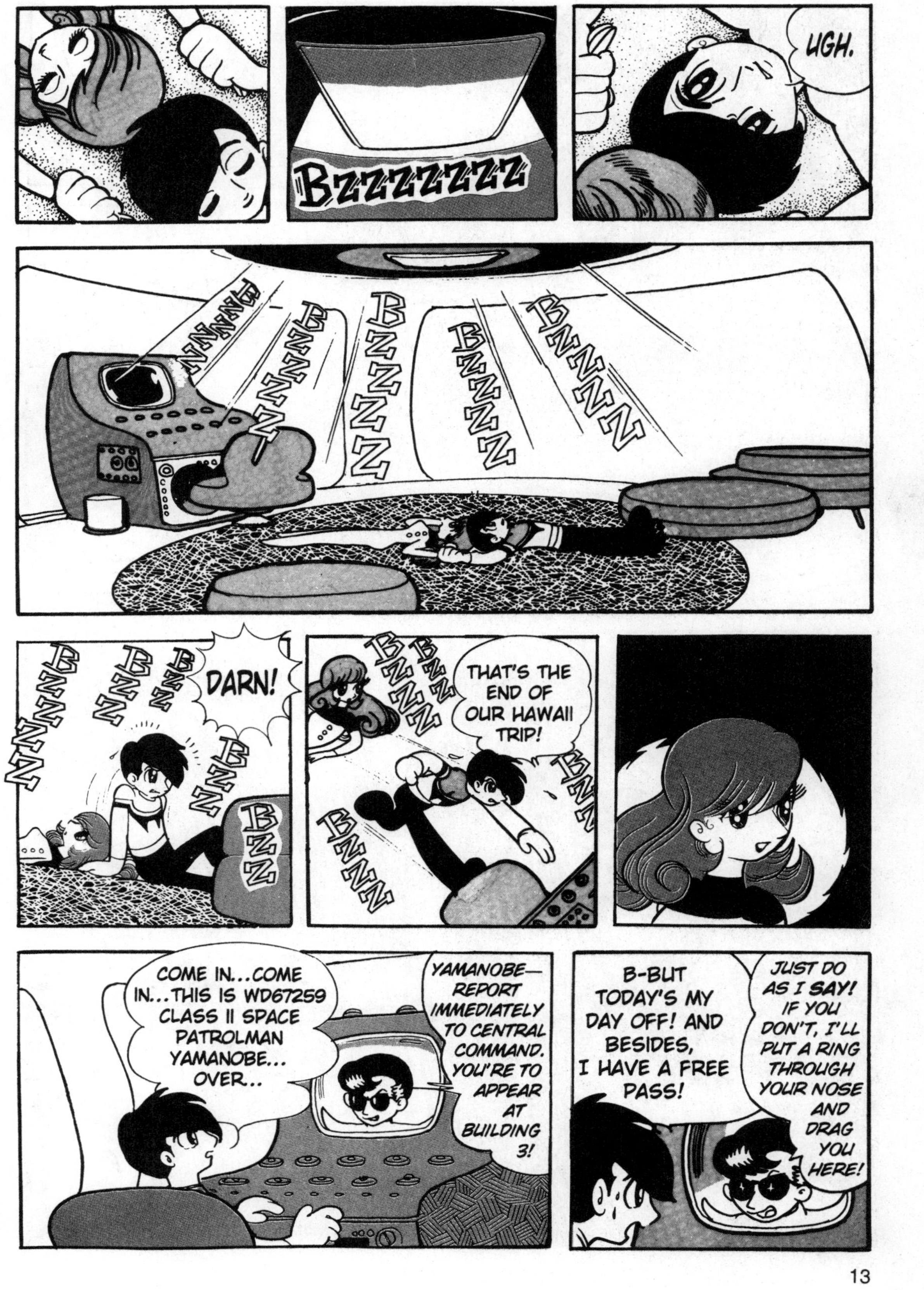

BZZZZZZZZ
UGH.
DARN!
THAT'S THE END OF OUR HAWAII TRIP!
COME IN...COME IN...THIS IS WD67259 CLASS II SPACE PATROLMAN YAMANOBE... OVER...
YAMANOBE— REPORT IMMEDIATELY TO CENTRAL COMMAND. YOU'RE TO APPEAR AT BUILDING 3!
B-BUT TODAY'S MY DAY OFF! AND BESIDES, I HAVE A FREE PASS!
JUST DO AS I *SAY!* IF YOU DON'T, I'LL PUT A RING THROUGH YOUR NOSE AND DRAG YOU HERE!

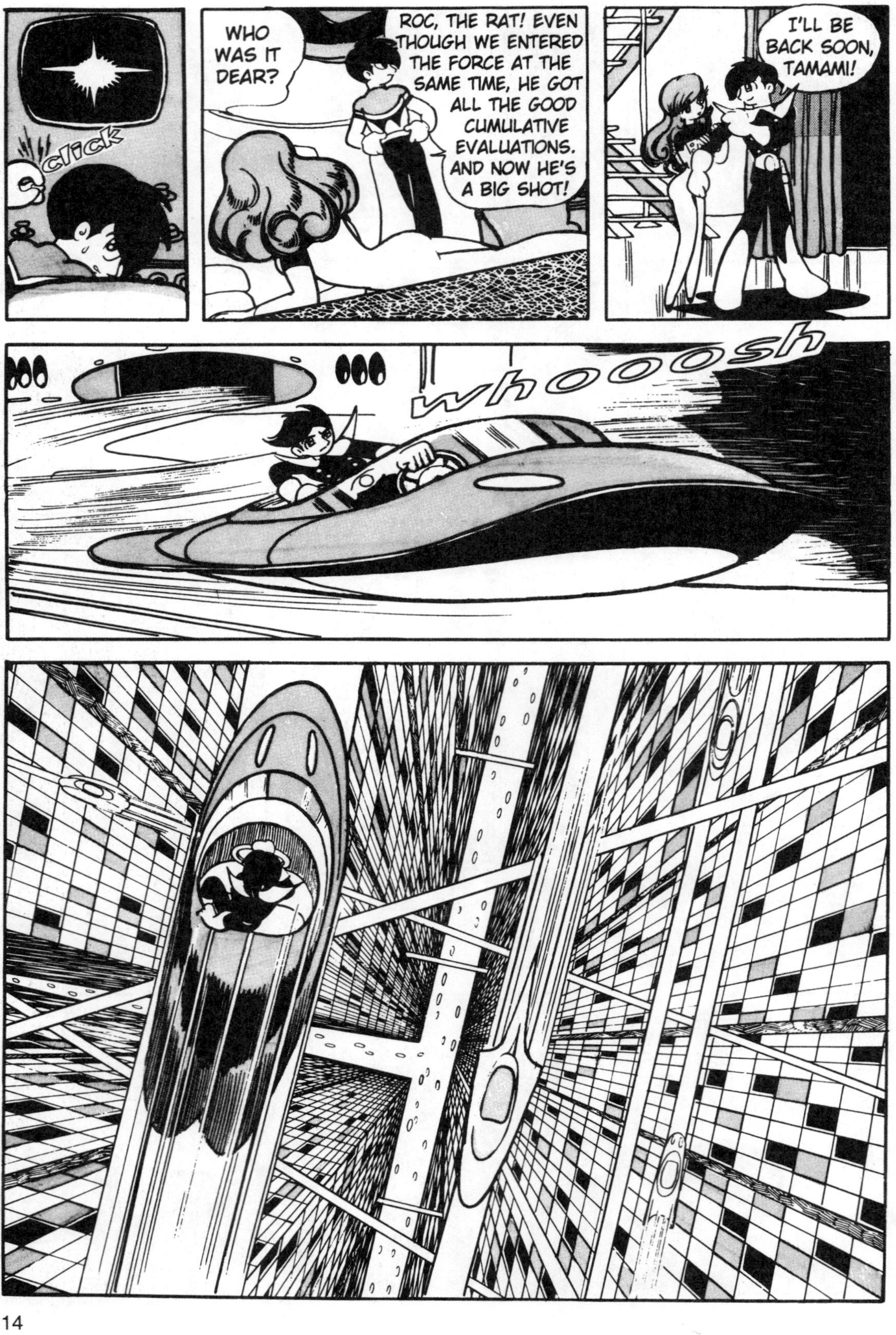
click
WHO WAS IT DEAR?
ROC, THE RAT! EVEN THOUGH WE ENTERED THE FORCE AT THE SAME TIME, HE GOT ALL THE GOOD CUMULATIVE EVALUATIONS. AND NOW HE'S A BIG SHOT!
I'LL BE BACK SOON, TAMAMI!
whoooosh

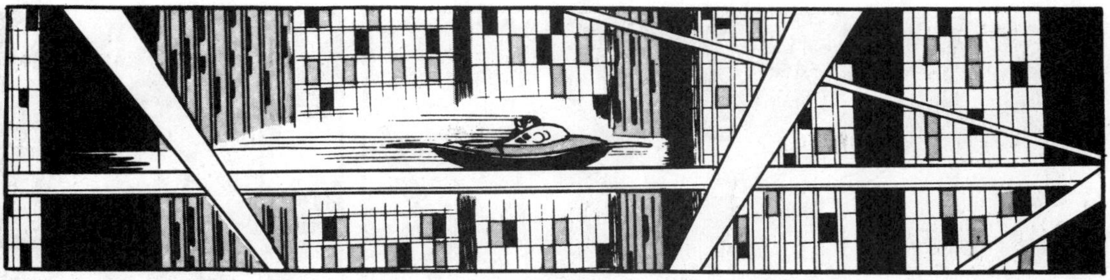
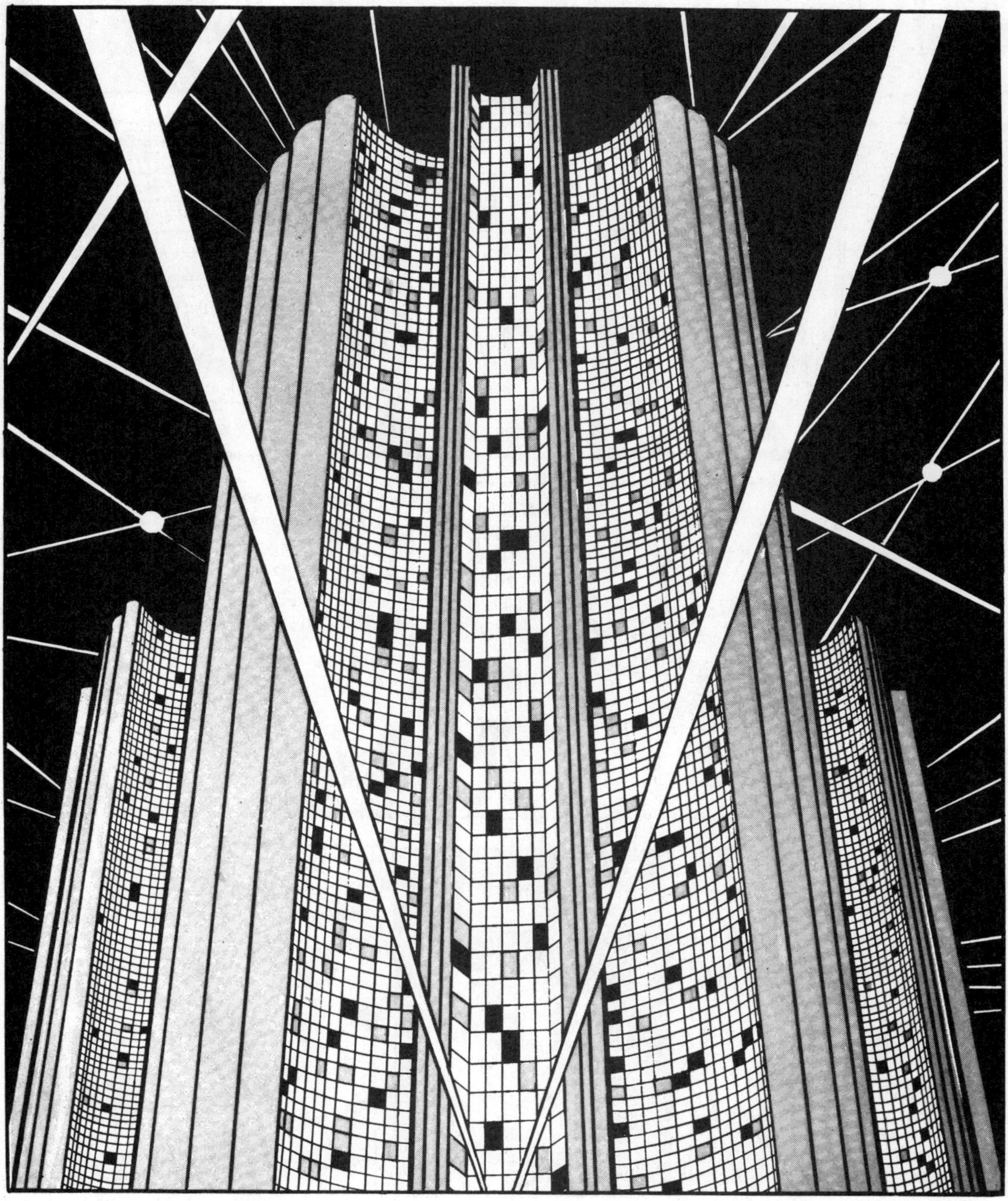

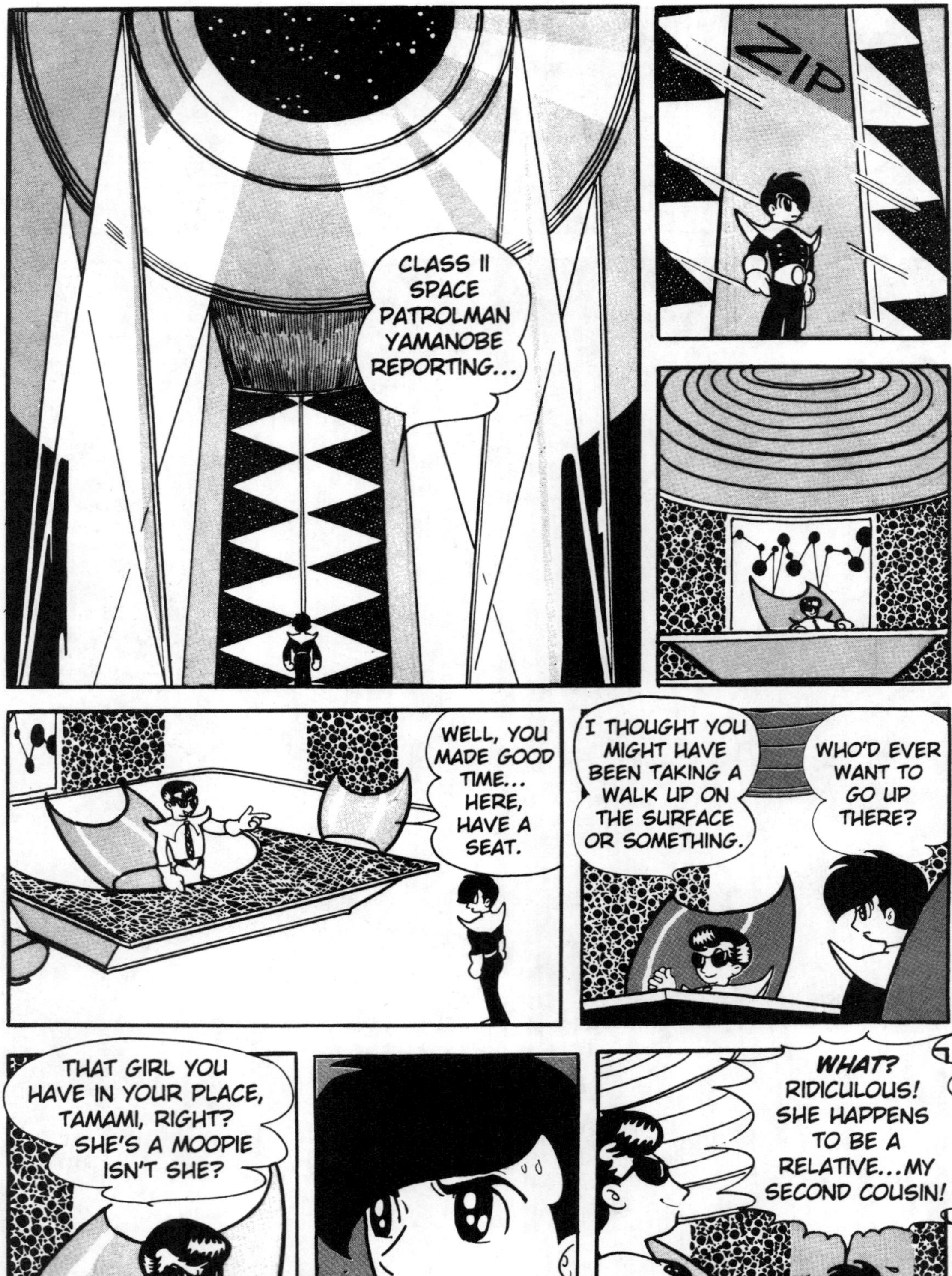
CLASS II SPACE PATROLMAN YAMANOBE REPORTING...
ZIP
WELL, YOU MADE GOOD TIME... HERE, HAVE A SEAT.
I THOUGHT YOU MIGHT HAVE BEEN TAKING A WALK UP ON THE SURFACE OR SOMETHING.
WHO'D EVER WANT TO GO UP THERE?
THAT GIRL YOU HAVE IN YOUR PLACE, TAMAMI, RIGHT? SHE'S A MOOPIE ISN'T SHE?
WHAT? RIDICULOUS! SHE HAPPENS TO BE A RELATIVE...MY SECOND COUSIN!

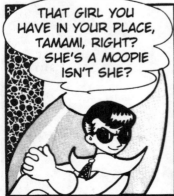

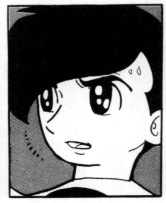

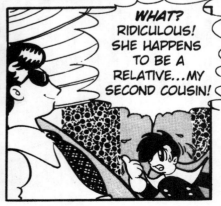

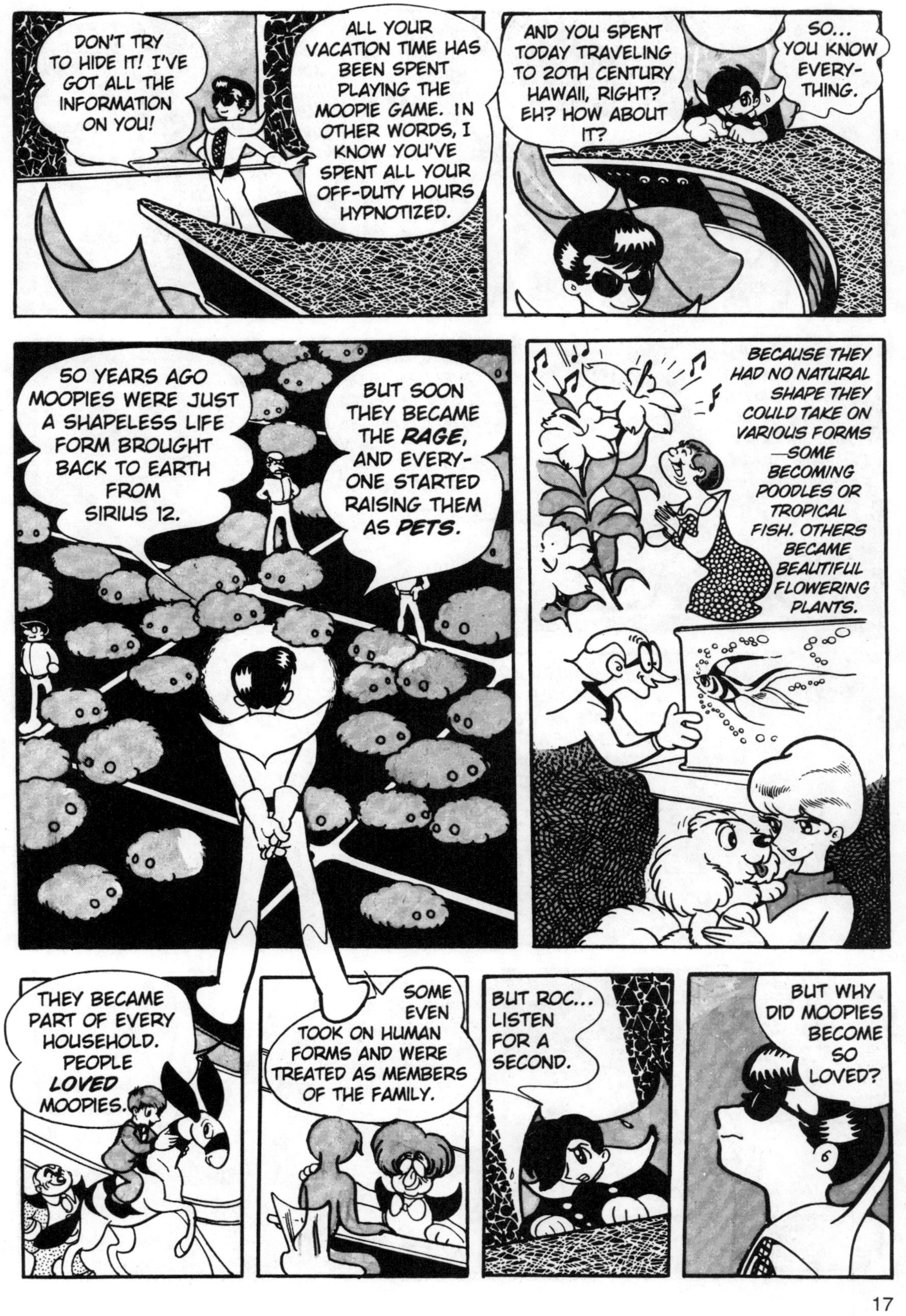
DON'T TRY TO HIDE IT! I'VE GOT ALL THE INFORMATION ON YOU!
ALL YOUR VACATION TIME HAS BEEN SPENT PLAYING THE MOOPIE GAME. IN OTHER WORDS, I KNOW YOU'VE SPENT ALL YOUR OFF-DUTY HOURS HYPNOTIZED.
AND YOU SPENT TODAY TRAVELING TO 20TH CENTURY HAWAII, RIGHT? EH? HOW ABOUT IT?
SO... YOU KNOW EVERY-THING.
50 YEARS AGO MOOPIES WERE JUST A SHAPELESS LIFE FORM BROUGHT BACK TO EARTH FROM SIRIUS 12.
BUT SOON THEY BECAME THE RAGE, AND EVERY-ONE STARTED RAISING THEM AS PETS.
BECAUSE THEY HAD NO NATURAL SHAPE THEY COULD TAKE ON VARIOUS FORMS —SOME BECOMING POODLES OR TROPICAL FISH. OTHERS BECAME BEAUTIFUL FLOWERING PLANTS.
THEY BECAME PART OF EVERY HOUSEHOLD. PEOPLE LOVED MOOPIES.
SOME EVEN TOOK ON HUMAN FORMS AND WERE TREATED AS MEMBERS OF THE FAMILY.
BUT ROC... LISTEN FOR A SECOND.
BUT WHY DID MOOPIES BECOME SO LOVED?

 IT WAS BECAUSE THEY POSSESS A MYSTERIOUS POWER.

 THEY COULD STIMULATE MAN'S BRAIN WITH *SUPER-SONIC SOUND WAVES* AND INDUCE A DREAM-LIKE STATE IN HIM.

AND THIS WAS CALLED THE *MOOPIE GAME.*

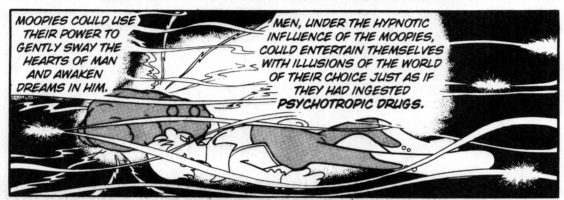 MOOPIES COULD USE THEIR POWER TO GENTLY SWAY THE HEARTS OF MAN AND AWAKEN DREAMS IN HIM.

MEN, UNDER THE HYPNOTIC INFLUENCE OF THE MOOPIES, COULD ENTERTAIN THEMSELVES WITH ILLUSIONS OF THE WORLD OF THEIR CHOICE JUST AS IF THEY HAD INGESTED *PSYCHOTROPIC DRUGS.*

 ROC, I...

 WITHOUT MOVING AN INCH, PEOPLE COULD BE IN CLEOPATRA'S PALACE, PARIS IN THE AGE OF NAPOLEON, OR THAT MOVIE MECCA, HOLLYWOOD.

 ROC! WILL YOU LISTEN TO WHAT I HAVE TO SAY?!

 MOOPIE GAMES ARE DANGEROUS... *EXTREMELY DANGEROUS...*

 AS YOU KNOW, THE SOLAR SYSTEM HAS BEEN IN A STATE OF *DECLINE* FOR THE LAST 500 YEARS.

BUT IN SPITE OF THIS CRISIS MEN HAVE BECOME INEXCUSABLY LETHARGIC.

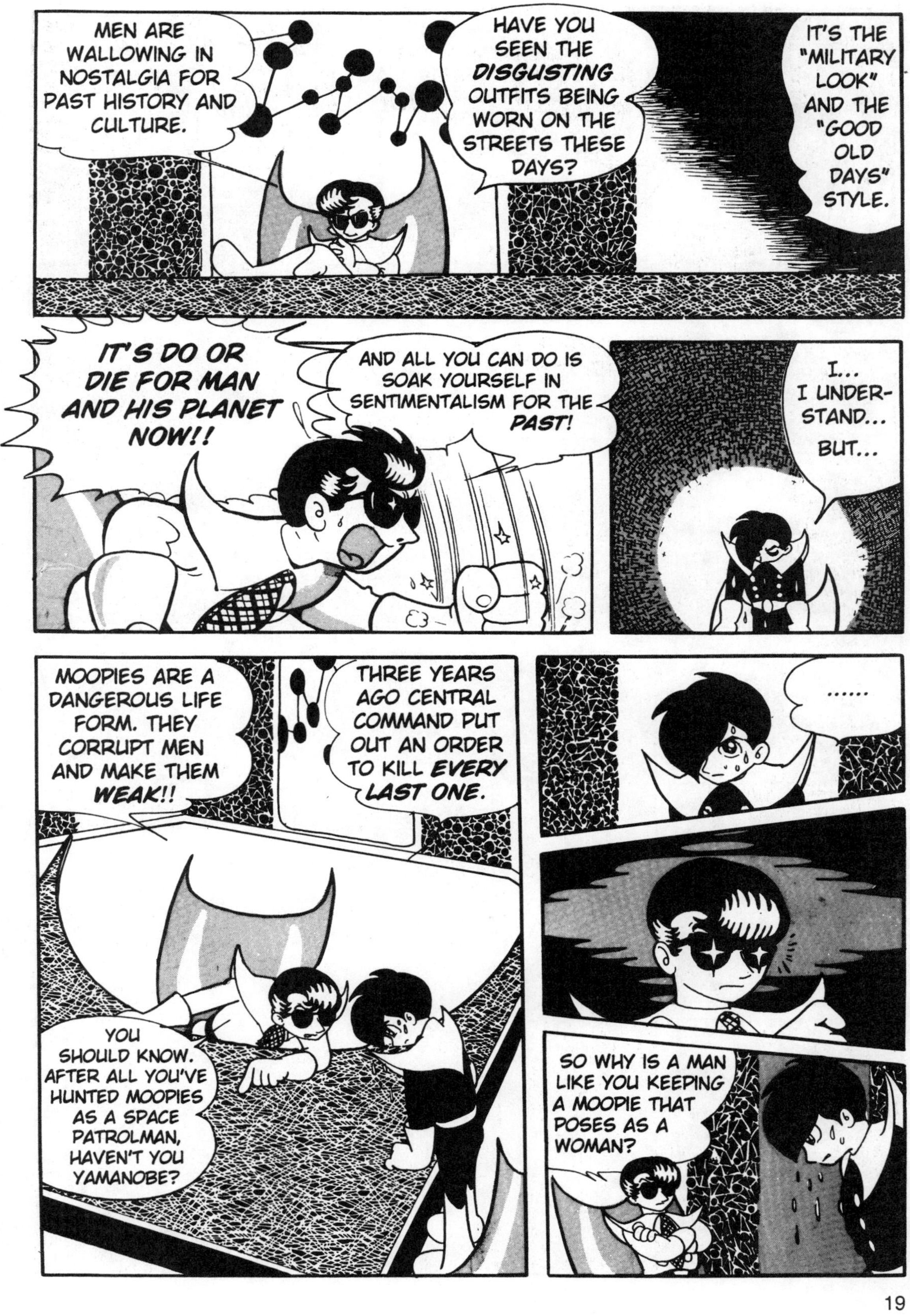
MEN ARE WALLOWING IN NOSTALGIA FOR PAST HISTORY AND CULTURE.
HAVE YOU SEEN THE *DISGUSTING* OUTFITS BEING WORN ON THE STREETS THESE DAYS?
IT'S THE "MILITARY LOOK" AND THE "GOOD OLD DAYS" STYLE.
IT'S DO OR DIE FOR MAN AND HIS PLANET NOW!!
AND ALL YOU CAN DO IS SOAK YOURSELF IN SENTIMENTALISM FOR THE *PAST*!
I... I UNDERSTAND... BUT...
MOOPIES ARE A DANGEROUS LIFE FORM. THEY CORRUPT MEN AND MAKE THEM *WEAK*!!
THREE YEARS AGO CENTRAL COMMAND PUT OUT AN ORDER TO KILL *EVERY LAST ONE*.
YOU SHOULD KNOW. AFTER ALL YOU'VE HUNTED MOOPIES AS A SPACE PATROLMAN, HAVEN'T YOU YAMANOBE?
......
SO WHY IS A MAN LIKE YOU KEEPING A MOOPIE THAT POSES AS A WOMAN?

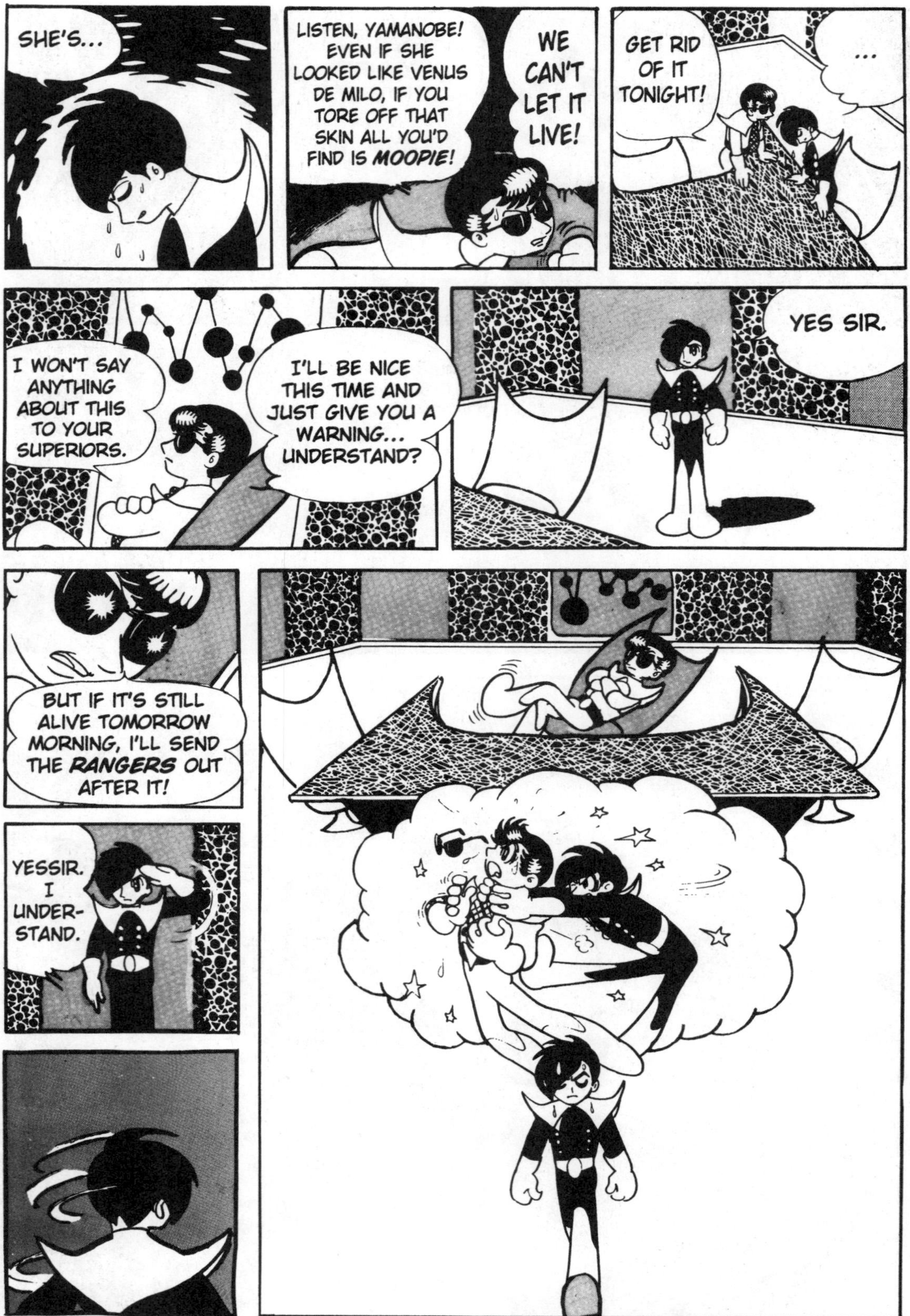
SHE'S...
LISTEN, YAMANOBE! EVEN IF SHE LOOKED LIKE VENUS DE MILO, IF YOU TORE OFF THAT SKIN ALL YOU'D FIND IS MOOPIE!
WE CAN'T LET IT LIVE!
GET RID OF IT TONIGHT!
...
I WON'T SAY ANYTHING ABOUT THIS TO YOUR SUPERIORS.
I'LL BE NICE THIS TIME AND JUST GIVE YOU A WARNING... UNDERSTAND?
YES SIR.
BUT IF IT'S STILL ALIVE TOMORROW MORNING, I'LL SEND THE RANGERS OUT AFTER IT!
YESSIR. I UNDER-STAND.

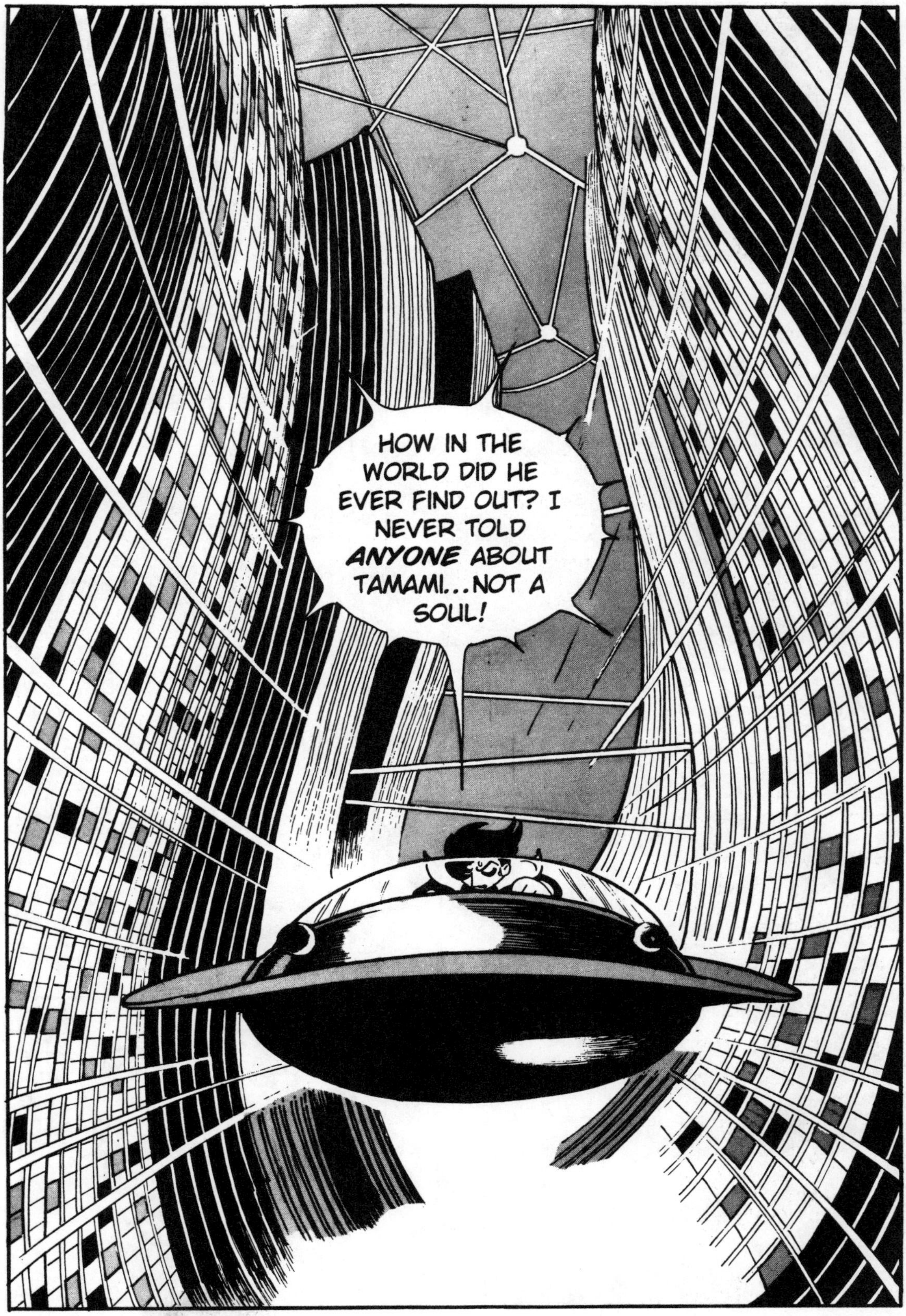
HOW IN THE WORLD DID HE EVER FIND OUT? I NEVER TOLD ANYONE ABOUT TAMAMI...NOT A SOUL!

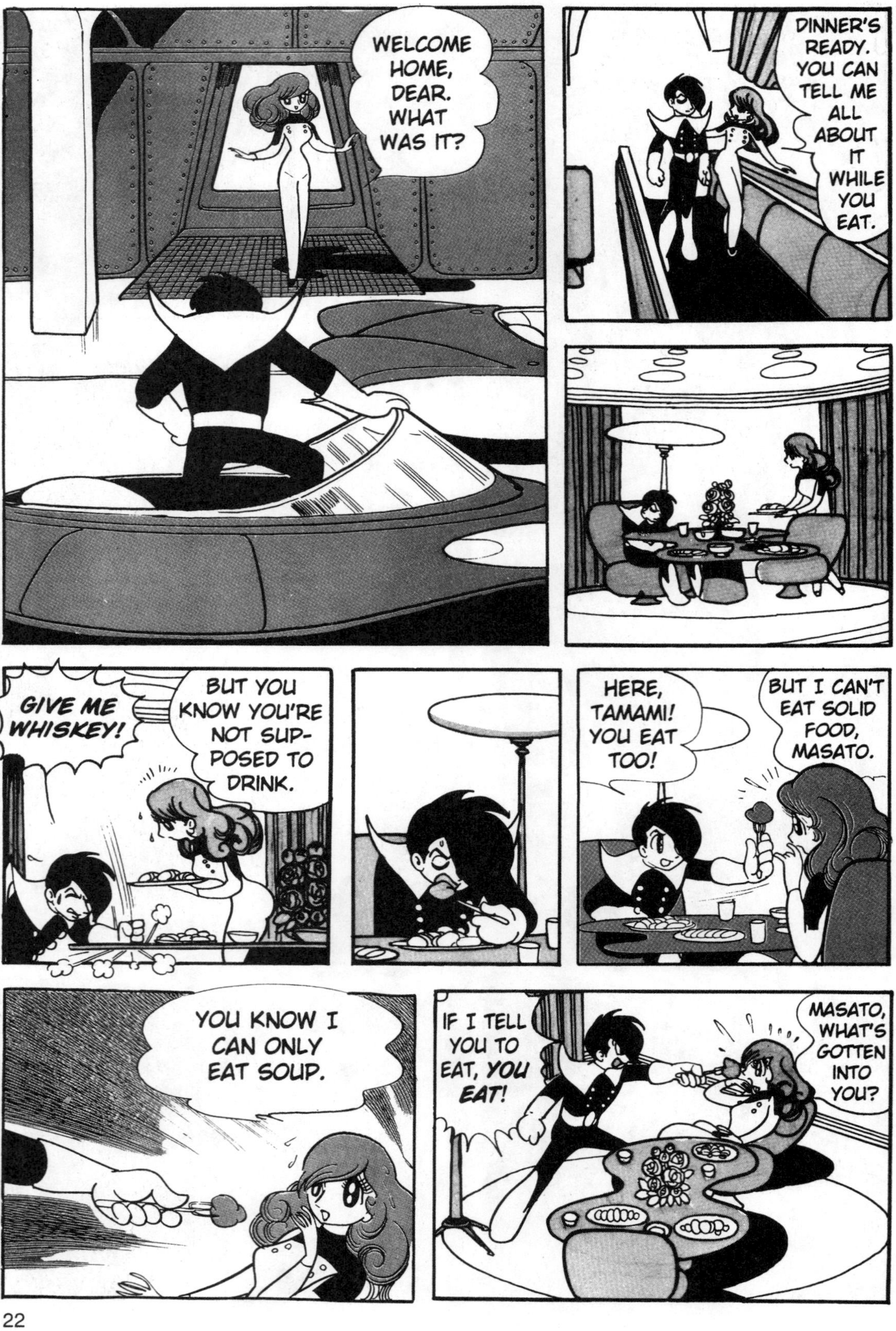
WELCOME HOME, DEAR. WHAT WAS IT?
DINNER'S READY. YOU CAN TELL ME ALL ABOUT IT WHILE YOU EAT.
GIVE ME WHISKEY!
BUT YOU KNOW YOU'RE NOT SUP-POSED TO DRINK.
HERE, TAMAMI! YOU EAT TOO!
BUT I CAN'T EAT SOLID FOOD, MASATO.
YOU KNOW I CAN ONLY EAT SOUP.
IF I TELL YOU TO EAT, YOU EAT!
MASATO, WHAT'S GOTTEN INTO YOU?

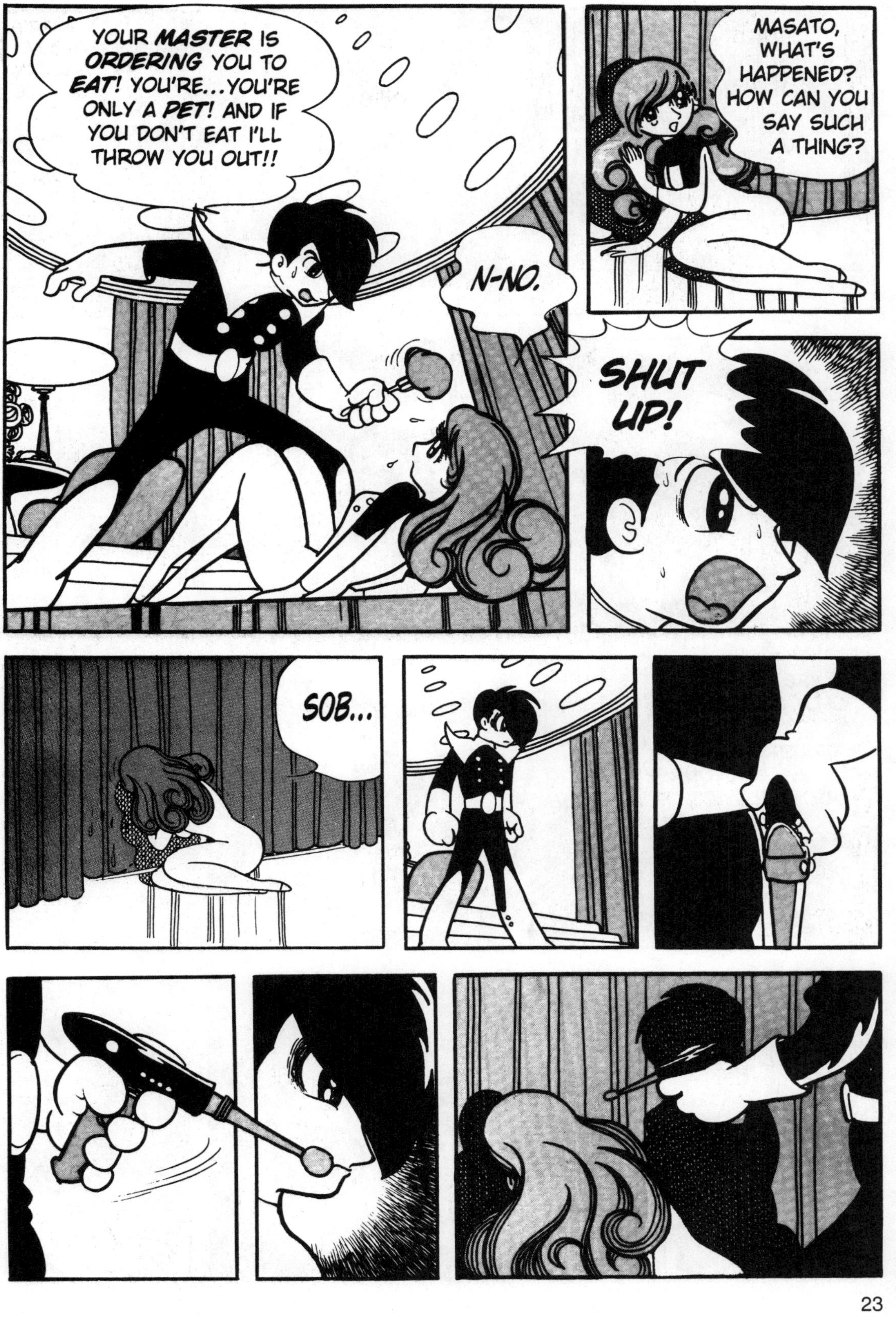
YOUR MASTER IS ORDERING YOU TO EAT! YOU'RE...YOU'RE ONLY A PET! AND IF YOU DON'T EAT I'LL THROW YOU OUT!!
N-NO.
MASATO, WHAT'S HAPPENED? HOW CAN YOU SAY SUCH A THING?
SHUT UP!
SOB...

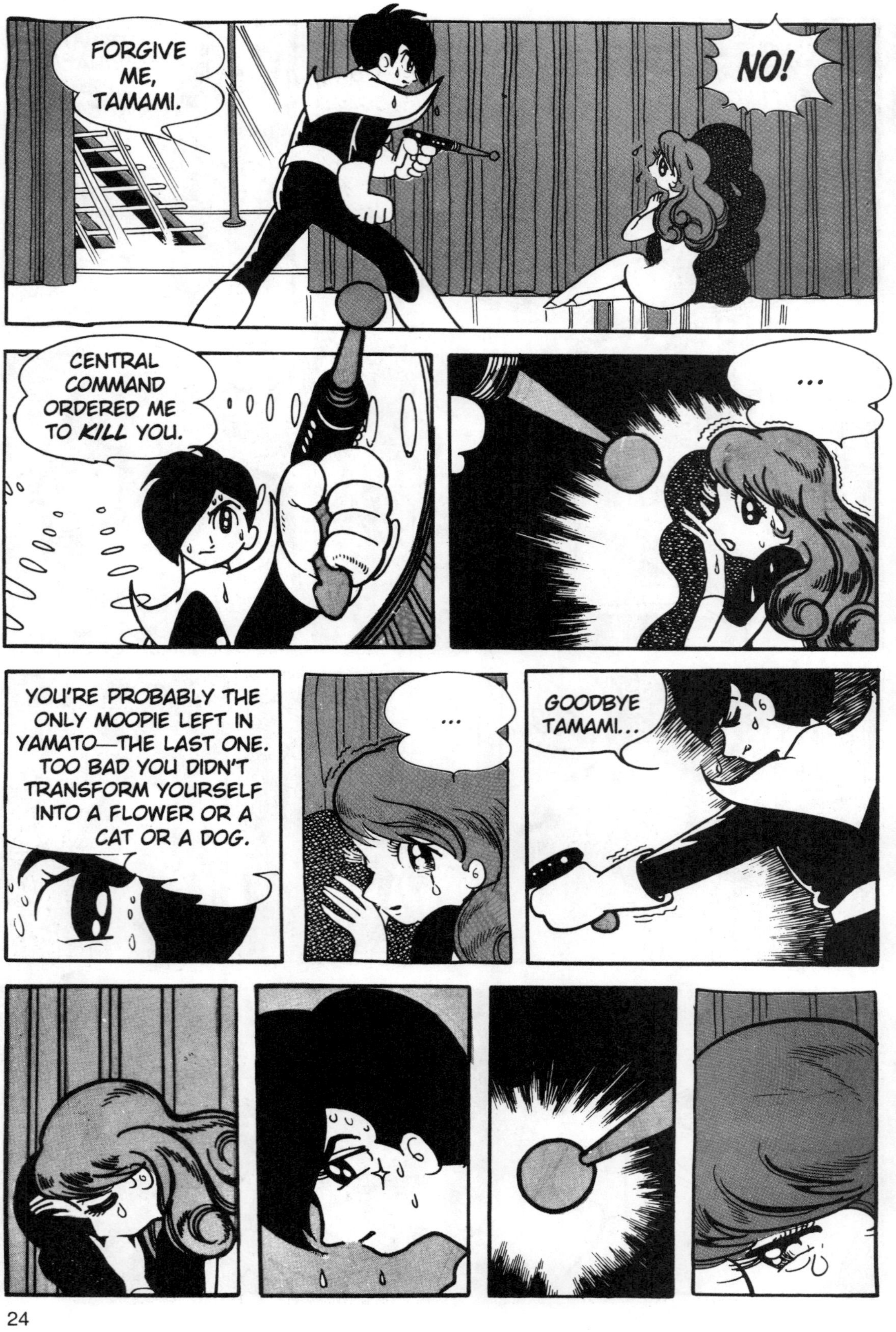
FORGIVE ME, TAMAMI.
NO!
CENTRAL COMMAND ORDERED ME TO KILL YOU.
...
YOU'RE PROBABLY THE ONLY MOOPIE LEFT IN YAMATO—THE LAST ONE. TOO BAD YOU DIDN'T TRANSFORM YOURSELF INTO A FLOWER OR A CAT OR A DOG.
...
GOODBYE TAMAMI...

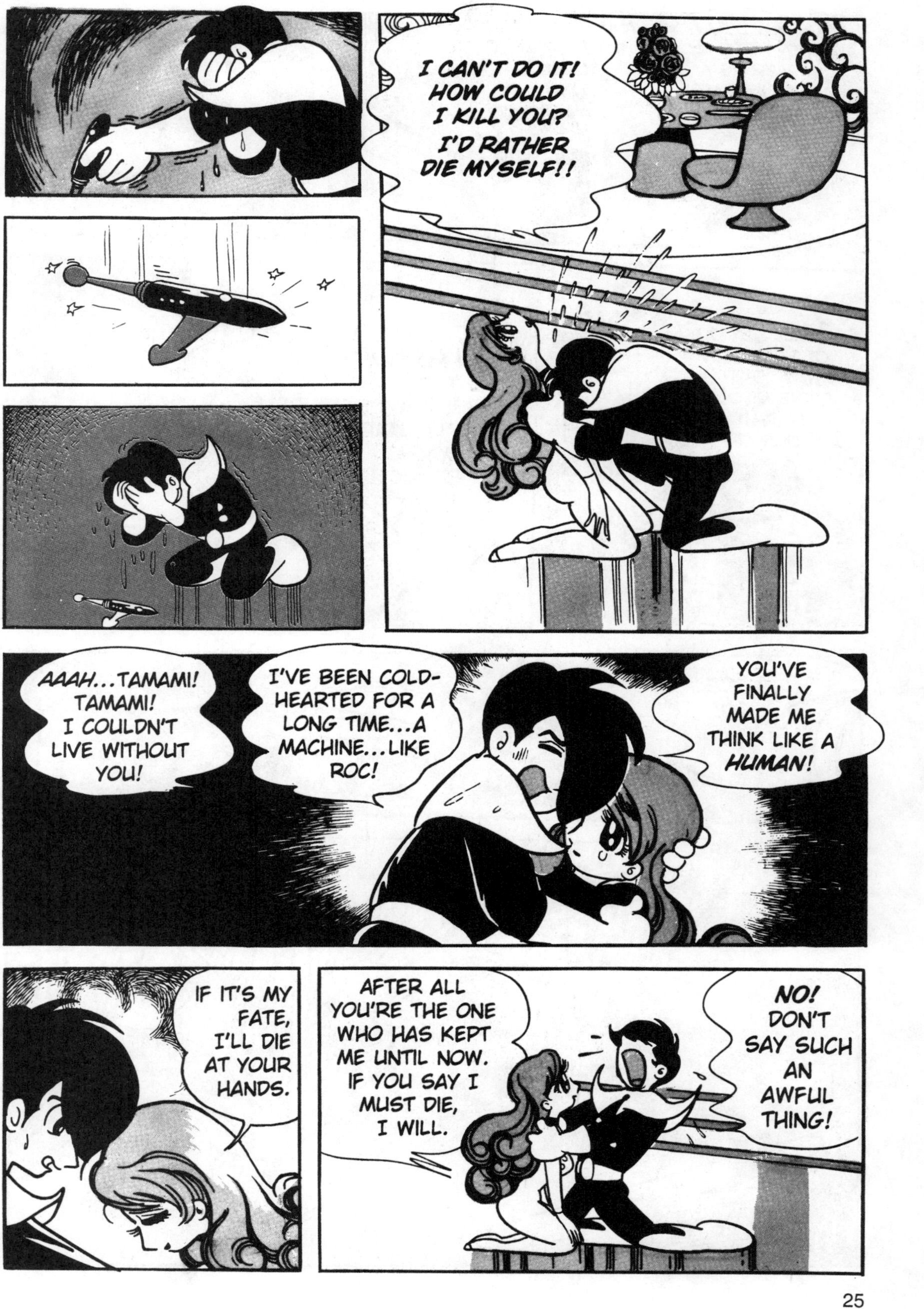
I CAN'T DO IT! HOW COULD I KILL YOU? I'D RATHER DIE MYSELF!!
AAAH...TAMAMI! TAMAMI! I COULDN'T LIVE WITHOUT YOU!
I'VE BEEN COLD-HEARTED FOR A LONG TIME...A MACHINE...LIKE ROC!
YOU'VE FINALLY MADE ME THINK LIKE A *HUMAN*!
IF IT'S MY FATE, I'LL DIE AT YOUR HANDS.
AFTER ALL YOU'RE THE ONE WHO HAS KEPT ME UNTIL NOW. IF YOU SAY I MUST DIE, I WILL.
NO! DON'T SAY SUCH AN AWFUL THING!

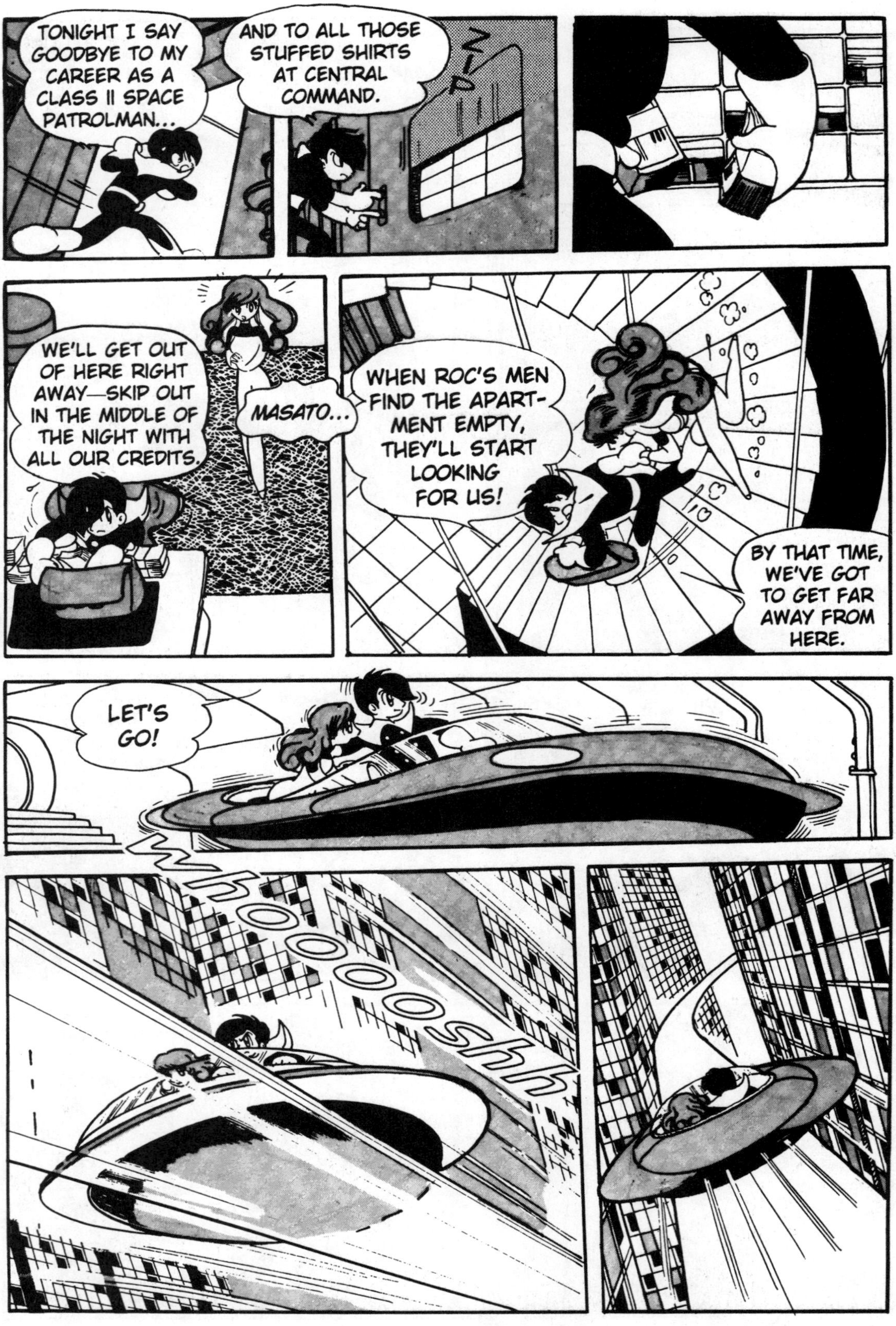
TONIGHT I SAY GOODBYE TO MY CAREER AS A CLASS II SPACE PATROLMAN...
AND TO ALL THOSE STUFFED SHIRTS AT CENTRAL COMMAND.
ZIP
WE'LL GET OUT OF HERE RIGHT AWAY—SKIP OUT IN THE MIDDLE OF THE NIGHT WITH ALL OUR CREDITS.
MASATO...
WHEN ROC'S MEN FIND THE APARTMENT EMPTY, THEY'LL START LOOKING FOR US!
BY THAT TIME, WE'VE GOT TO GET FAR AWAY FROM HERE.
LET'S GO!
Whooooshh

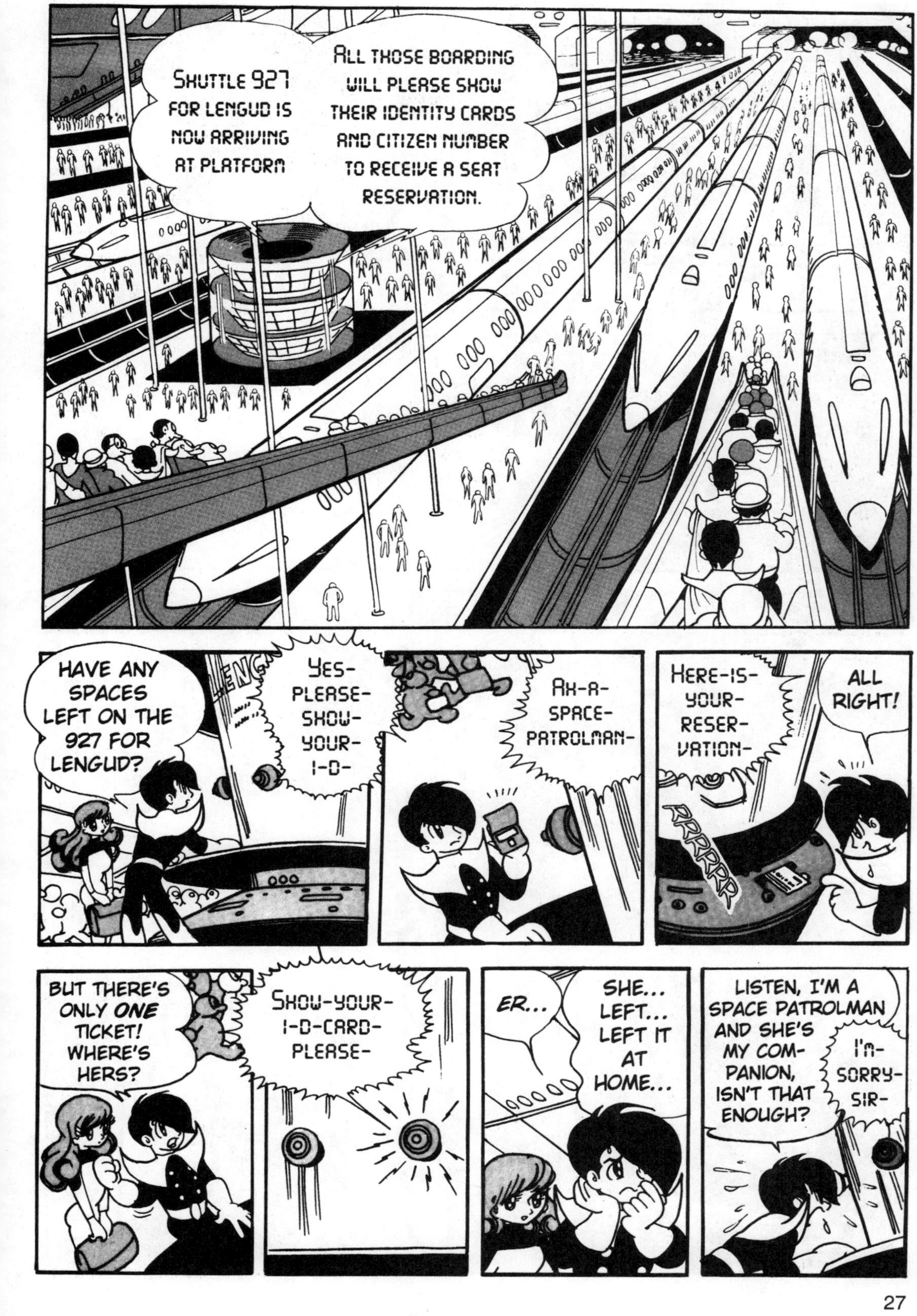
Shuttle 927 for Lengud is now arriving at platform
All those boarding will please show their identity cards and citizen number to receive a seat reservation.
HAVE ANY SPACES LEFT ON THE 927 FOR LENGUD?
Yes-please-show-your-I-D-
Ah-a-space-patrolman-
Here-is-your-reser-vation-
ALL RIGHT!
BUT THERE'S ONLY *ONE* TICKET! WHERE'S HERS?
Show-your-I-D-card-please-
ER...
SHE... LEFT... LEFT IT AT HOME...
LISTEN, I'M A SPACE PATROLMAN AND SHE'S MY COM-PANION, ISN'T THAT ENOUGH?
I'm-sorry-sir-

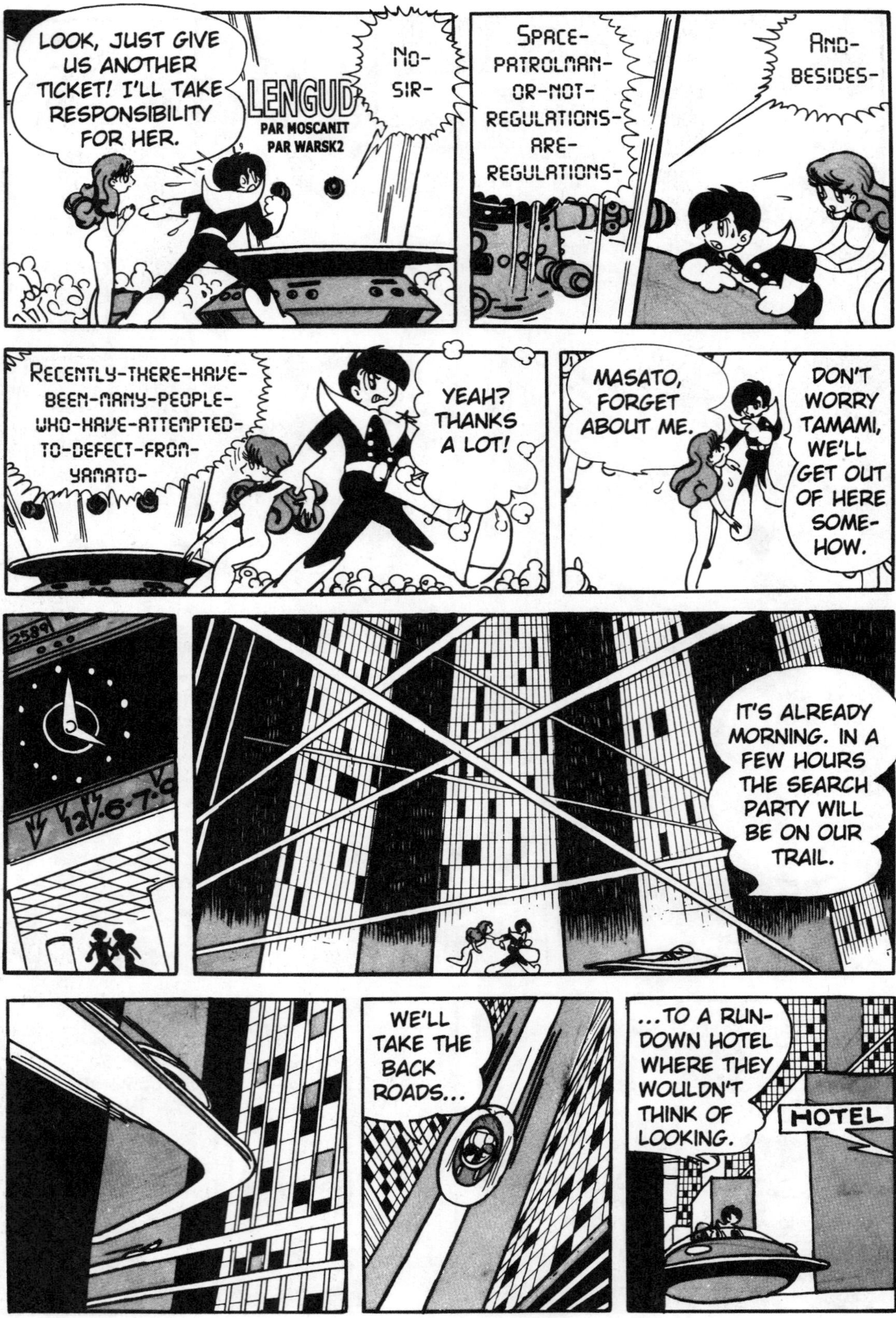
LOOK, JUST GIVE US ANOTHER TICKET! I'LL TAKE RESPONSIBILITY FOR HER.
NO-SIR-
SPACE-PATROLMAN-OR-NOT-REGULATIONS-ARE-REGULATIONS-
AND-BESIDES-
RECENTLY-THERE-HAVE-BEEN-MANY-PEOPLE-WHO-HAVE-ATTEMPTED-TO-DEFECT-FROM-YAMATO-
YEAH? THANKS A LOT!
MASATO, FORGET ABOUT ME.
DON'T WORRY TAMAMI, WE'LL GET OUT OF HERE SOMEHOW.
IT'S ALREADY MORNING. IN A FEW HOURS THE SEARCH PARTY WILL BE ON OUR TRAIL.
WE'LL TAKE THE BACK ROADS...
...TO A RUN-DOWN HOTEL WHERE THEY WOULDN'T THINK OF LOOKING.
HOTEL

WELL... EARLY CUSTOMERS!

WE NEED A ROOM.

YOUR NAME AND I.D., PLEASE...

LOOK, DO ME A FAVOR.

OH... I SEE... WELL, IN THAT CASE, YOUR PAPERS ARE *ALL IN ORDER.*

GOOD MORNING CITIZENS. WE NOW HAVE A BULLETIN FROM CENTRAL COMMAND. AUTHORITIES ARE LOOKING FOR CLASS II SPACE PATROLMAN MASATO YAMANOBE.

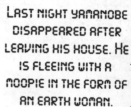

LAST NIGHT YAMANOBE DISAPPEARED AFTER LEAVING HIS HOUSE. HE IS FLEEING WITH A NOOPIE IN THE FORM OF AN EARTH WOMAN.

IF ANY CITIZEN HAS ANY INFORMATION PERTAINING TO THE COUPLE...

.....

TAK

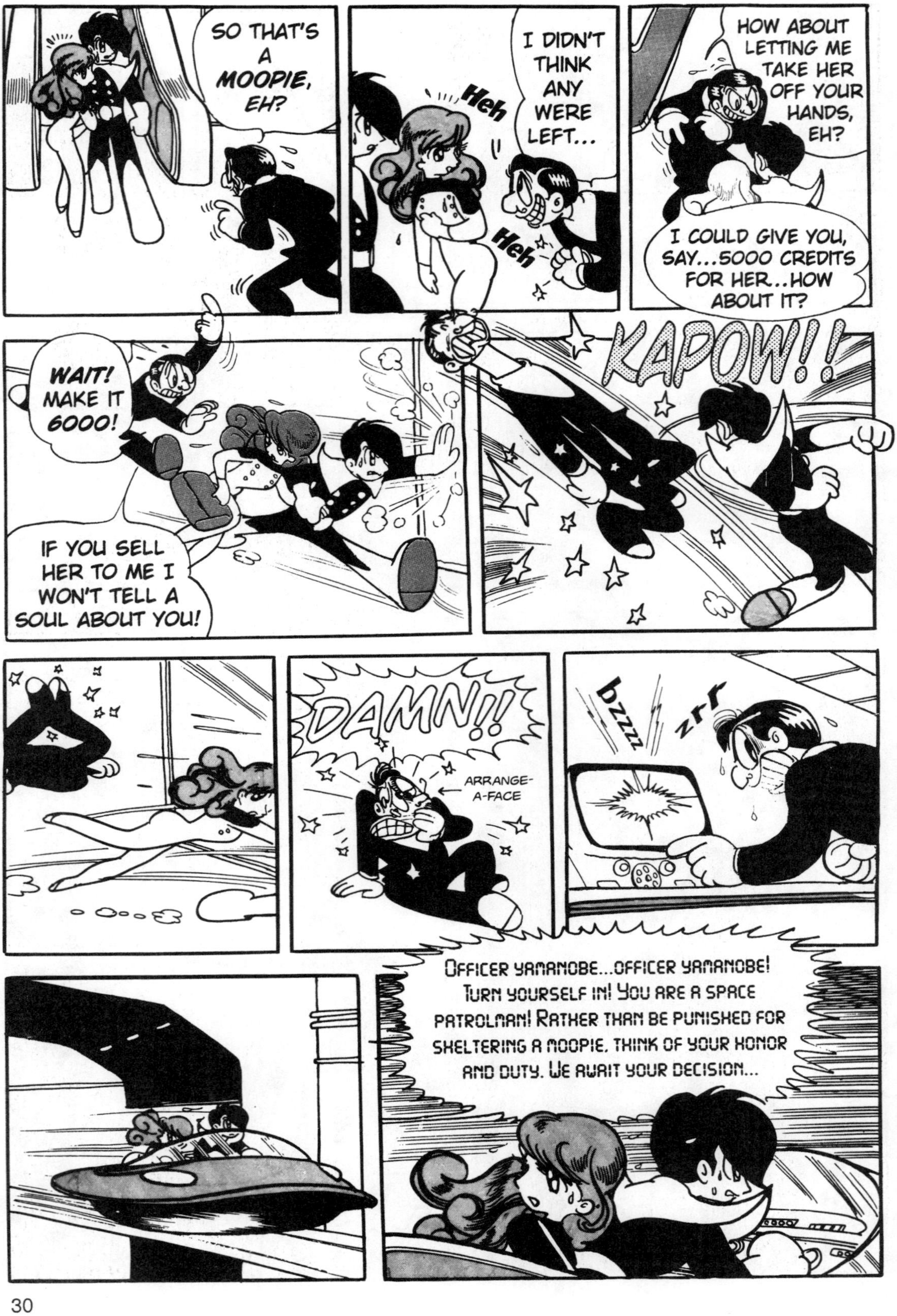
SO THAT'S A MOOPIE, EH?
Heh
I DIDN'T THINK ANY WERE LEFT...
Heh
HOW ABOUT LETTING ME TAKE HER OFF YOUR HANDS, EH?
I COULD GIVE YOU, SAY...5000 CREDITS FOR HER..HOW ABOUT IT?
WAIT! MAKE IT 6000!
IF YOU SELL HER TO ME I WON'T TELL A SOUL ABOUT YOU!
KAPOW!!
DAMN!!
ARRANGE-A-FACE
bzzzz
zrr
OFFICER YAMANOBE...OFFICER YAMANOBE! TURN YOURSELF IN! YOU ARE A SPACE PATROLMAN! RATHER THAN BE PUNISHED FOR SHELTERING A MOOPIE, THINK OF YOUR HONOR AND DUTY. WE AWAIT YOUR DECISION...

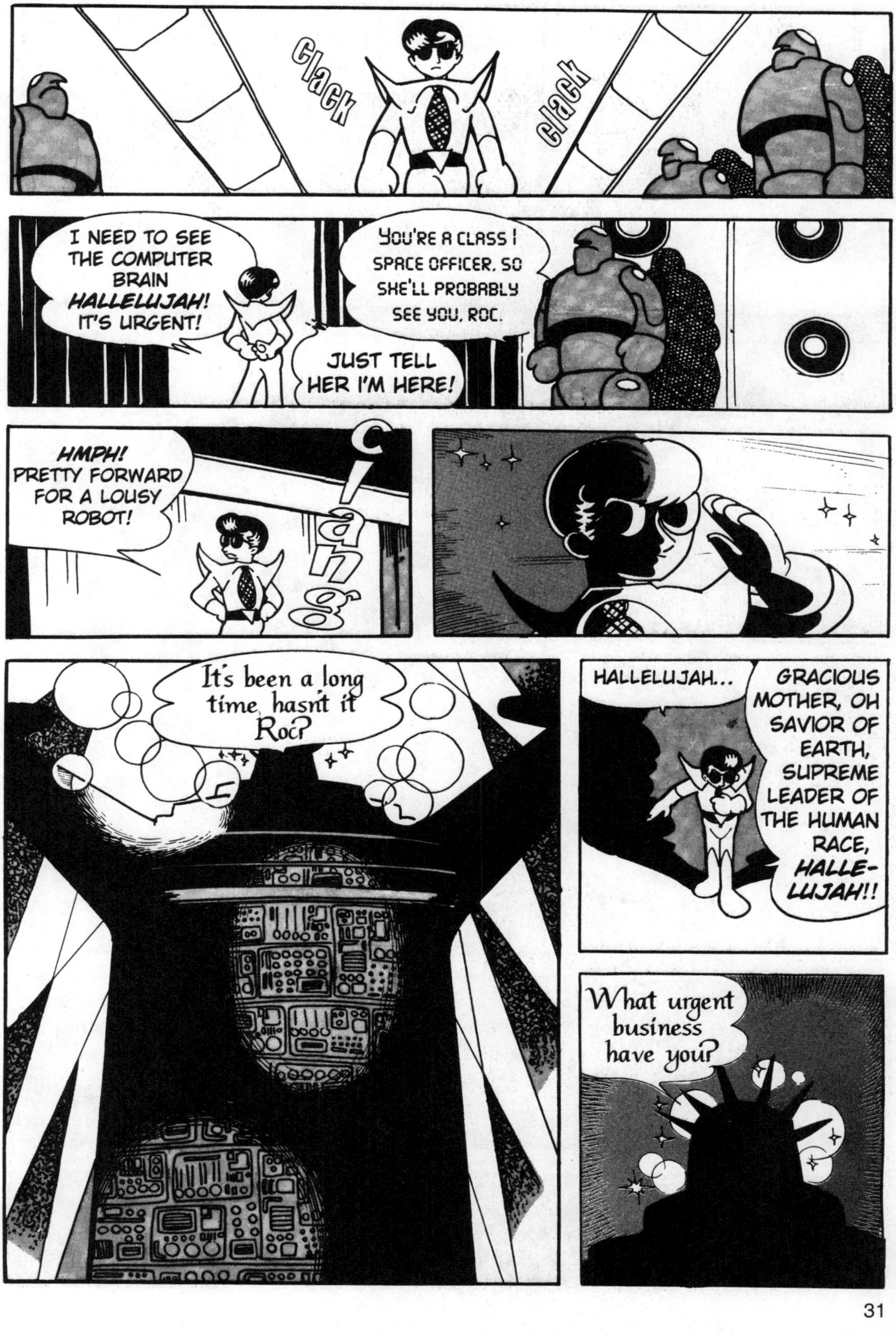
clack
clack
I NEED TO SEE THE COMPUTER BRAIN HALLELUJAH! IT'S URGENT!
YOU'RE A CLASS I SPACE OFFICER, SO SHE'LL PROBABLY SEE YOU, ROC.
JUST TELL HER I'M HERE!
HMPH! PRETTY FORWARD FOR A LOUSY ROBOT!
clang
It's been a long time, hasn't it Roc?
HALLELUJAH...
GRACIOUS MOTHER, OH SAVIOR OF EARTH, SUPREME LEADER OF THE HUMAN RACE, HALLE-LUJAH!!
What urgent business have you?

YOUR CAL-CULATIONS ARE INFALLIBLE.

WE AT CENTRAL COMMAND FOLLOW YOUR ORDERS TO THE LETTER.

Good.

BUT I'VE MADE ONE SLIGHT MISTAKE.

Mistake?

YOU ORDERED ME TO KILL ALL THE MOOPIES BUT...

ONE MOOPIE REMAINED, AND IT HAS FLED WITH ITS OWNER.

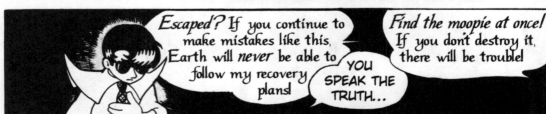

Escaped? If you continue to make mistakes like this, Earth will *never* be able to follow my recovery plans!

YOU SPEAK THE TRUTH...

Find the moopie at once! If you don't destroy it, there will be trouble!

Kill it!

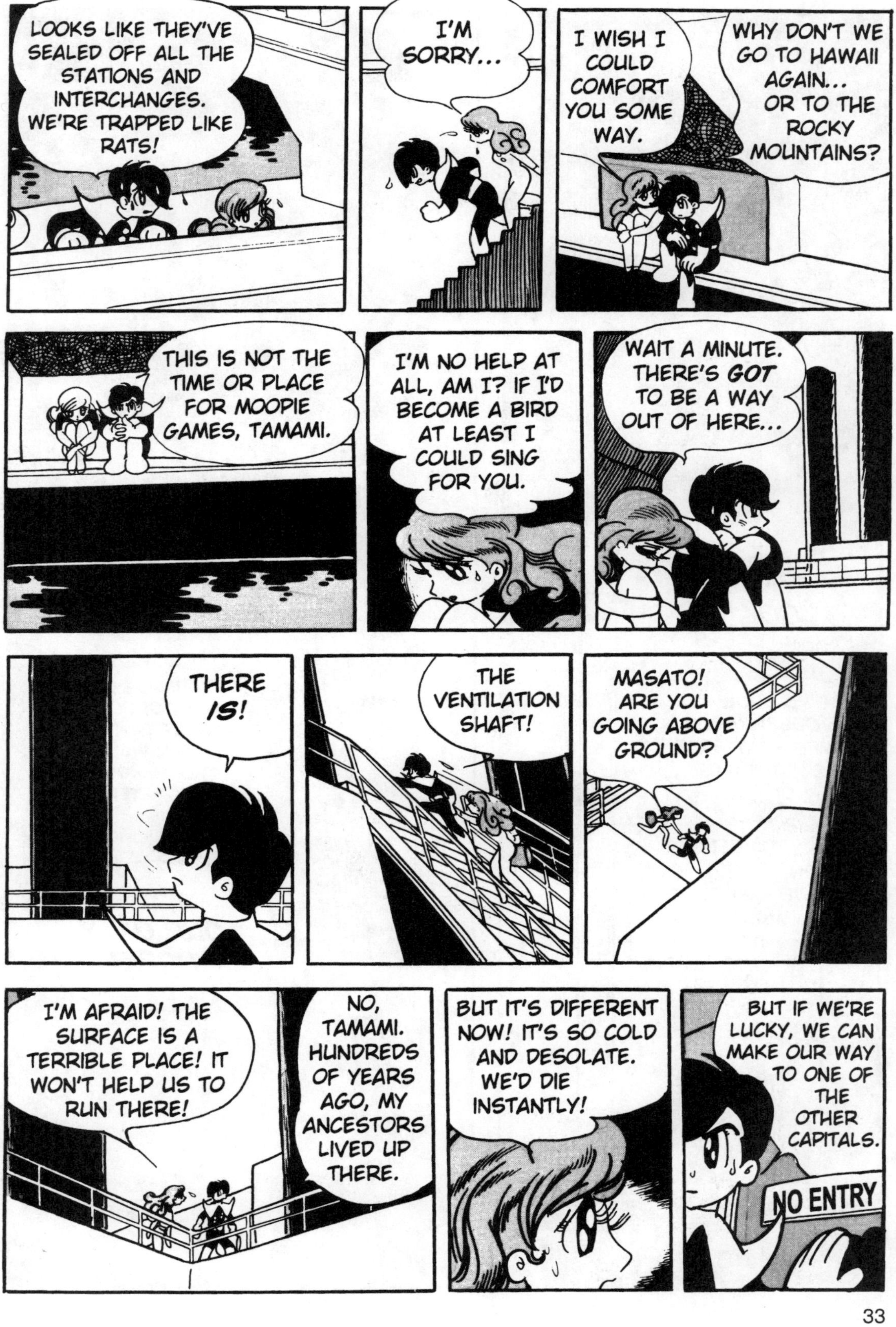
LOOKS LIKE THEY'VE SEALED OFF ALL THE STATIONS AND INTERCHANGES. WE'RE TRAPPED LIKE RATS!
I'M SORRY...
I WISH I COULD COMFORT YOU SOME WAY.
WHY DON'T WE GO TO HAWAII AGAIN... OR TO THE ROCKY MOUNTAINS?
THIS IS NOT THE TIME OR PLACE FOR MOOPIE GAMES, TAMAMI.
I'M NO HELP AT ALL, AM I? IF I'D BECOME A BIRD AT LEAST I COULD SING FOR YOU.
WAIT A MINUTE. THERE'S *GOT* TO BE A WAY OUT OF HERE...
THERE *IS*!
THE VENTILATION SHAFT!
MASATO! ARE YOU GOING ABOVE GROUND?
I'M AFRAID! THE SURFACE IS A TERRIBLE PLACE! IT WON'T HELP US TO RUN THERE!
NO, TAMAMI. HUNDREDS OF YEARS AGO, MY ANCESTORS LIVED UP THERE.
BUT IT'S DIFFERENT NOW! IT'S SO COLD AND DESOLATE. WE'D DIE INSTANTLY!
BUT IF WE'RE LUCKY, WE CAN MAKE OUR WAY TO ONE OF THE OTHER CAPITALS.
NO ENTRY

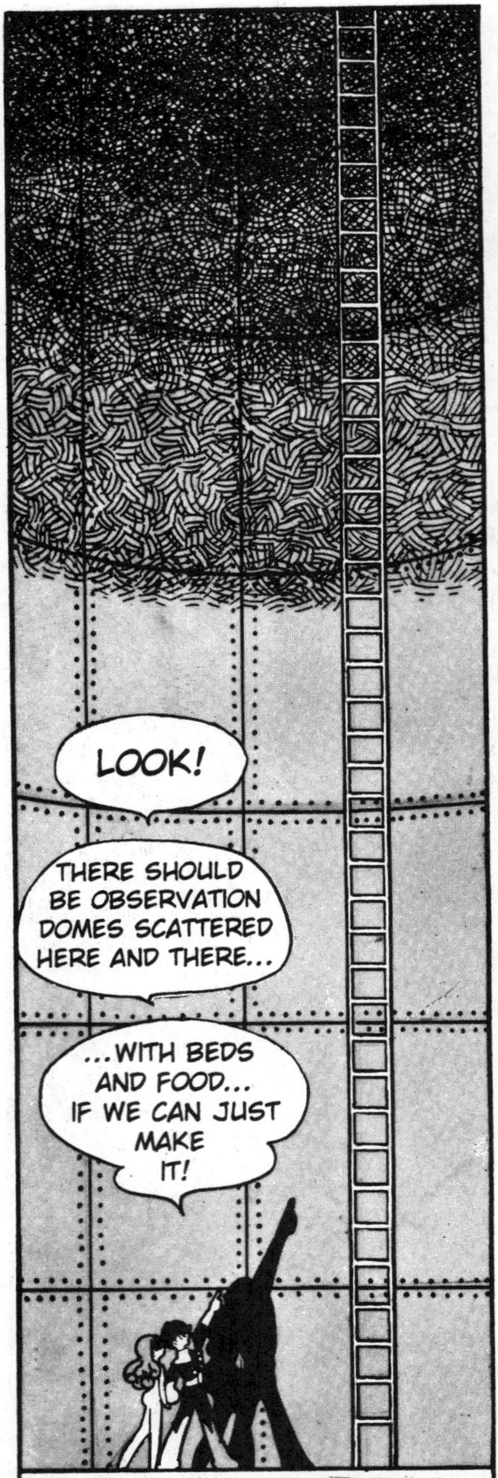
LOOK!
THERE SHOULD BE OBSERVATION DOMES SCATTERED HERE AND THERE...
...WITH BEDS AND FOOD... IF WE CAN JUST MAKE IT!
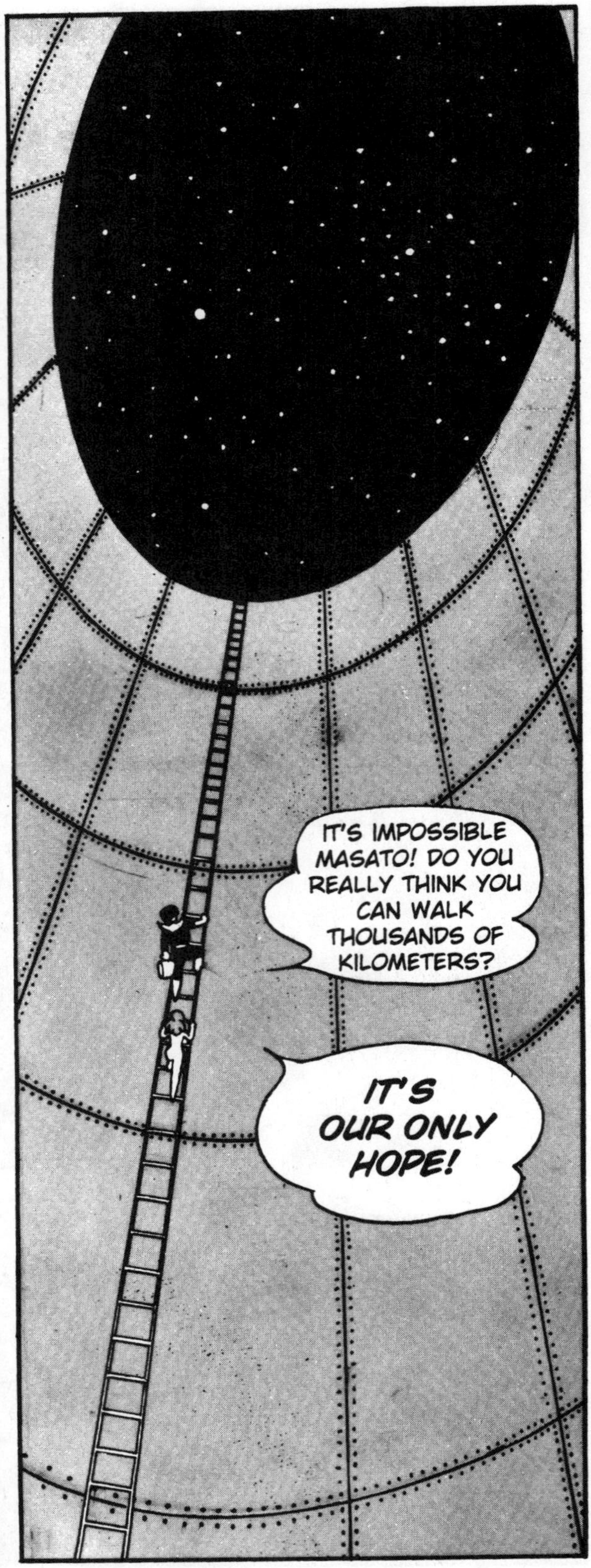
IT'S IMPOSSIBLE MASATO! DO YOU REALLY THINK YOU CAN WALK THOUSANDS OF KILOMETERS?
IT'S OUR ONLY HOPE!

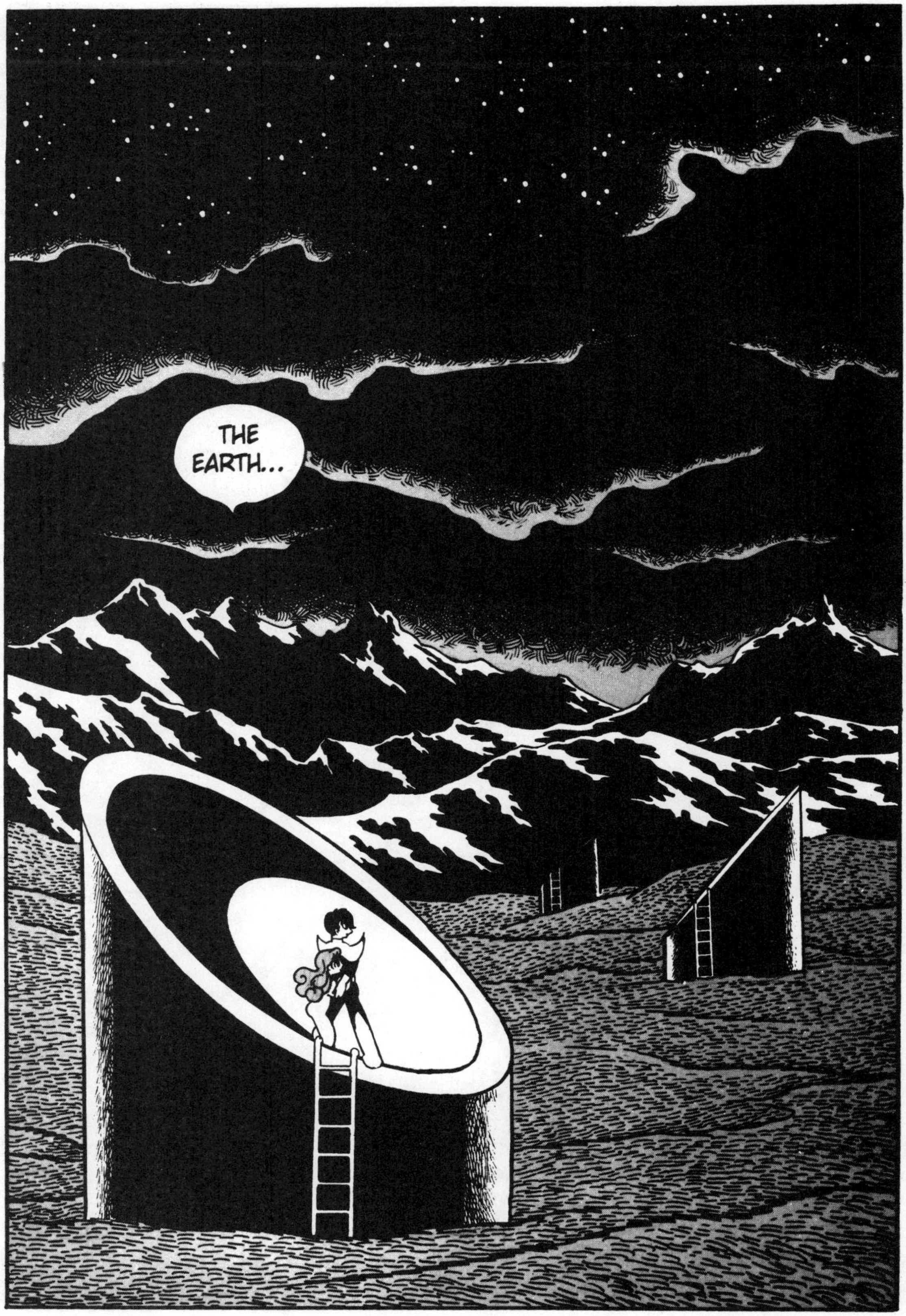
THE EARTH...

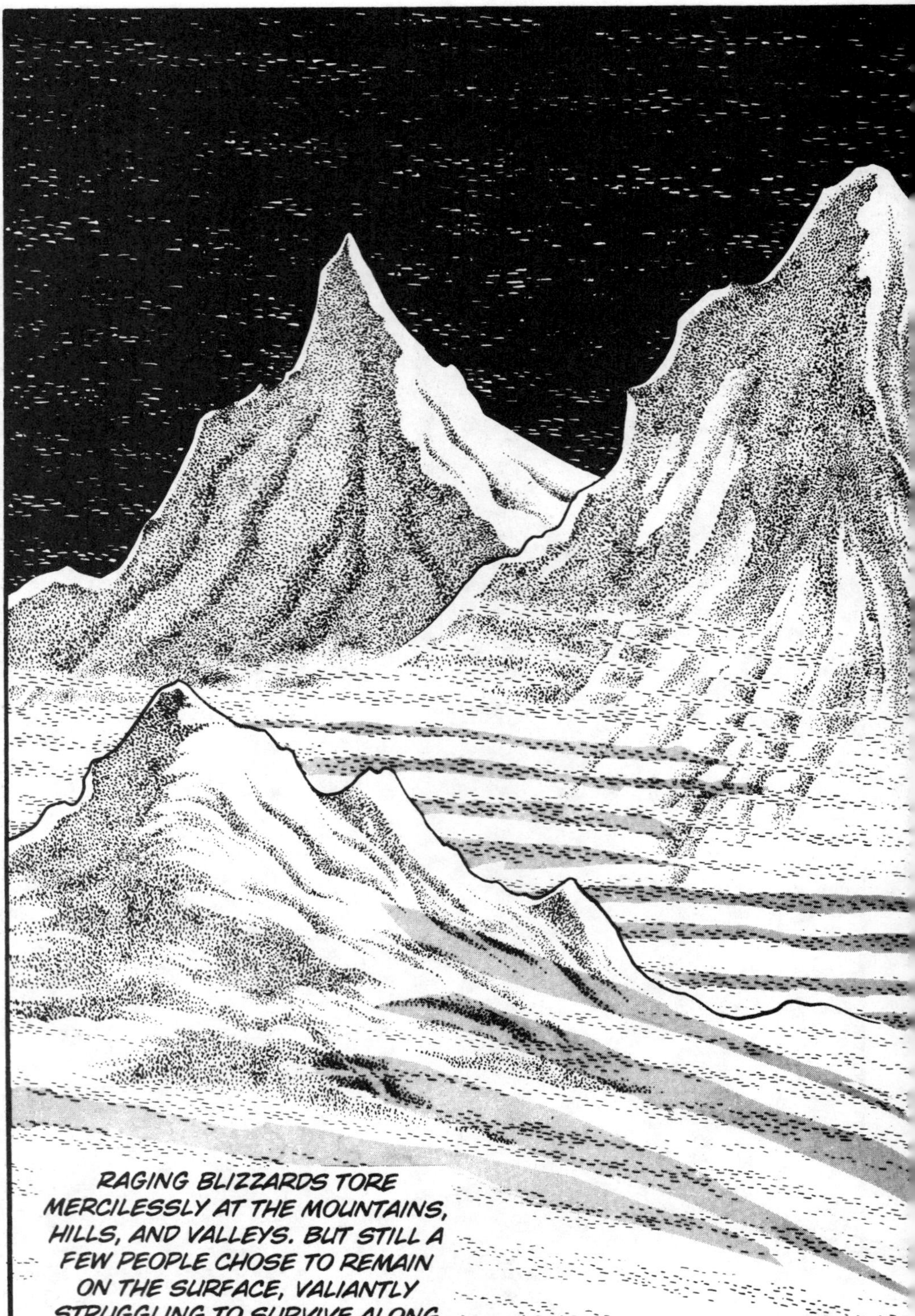
RAGING BLIZZARDS TORE MERCILESSLY AT THE MOUNTAINS, HILLS, AND VALLEYS. BUT STILL A FEW PEOPLE CHOSE TO REMAIN ON THE SURFACE, VALIANTLY STRUGGLING TO SURVIVE ALONG WITH THE REST OF DOOMED CREATION.

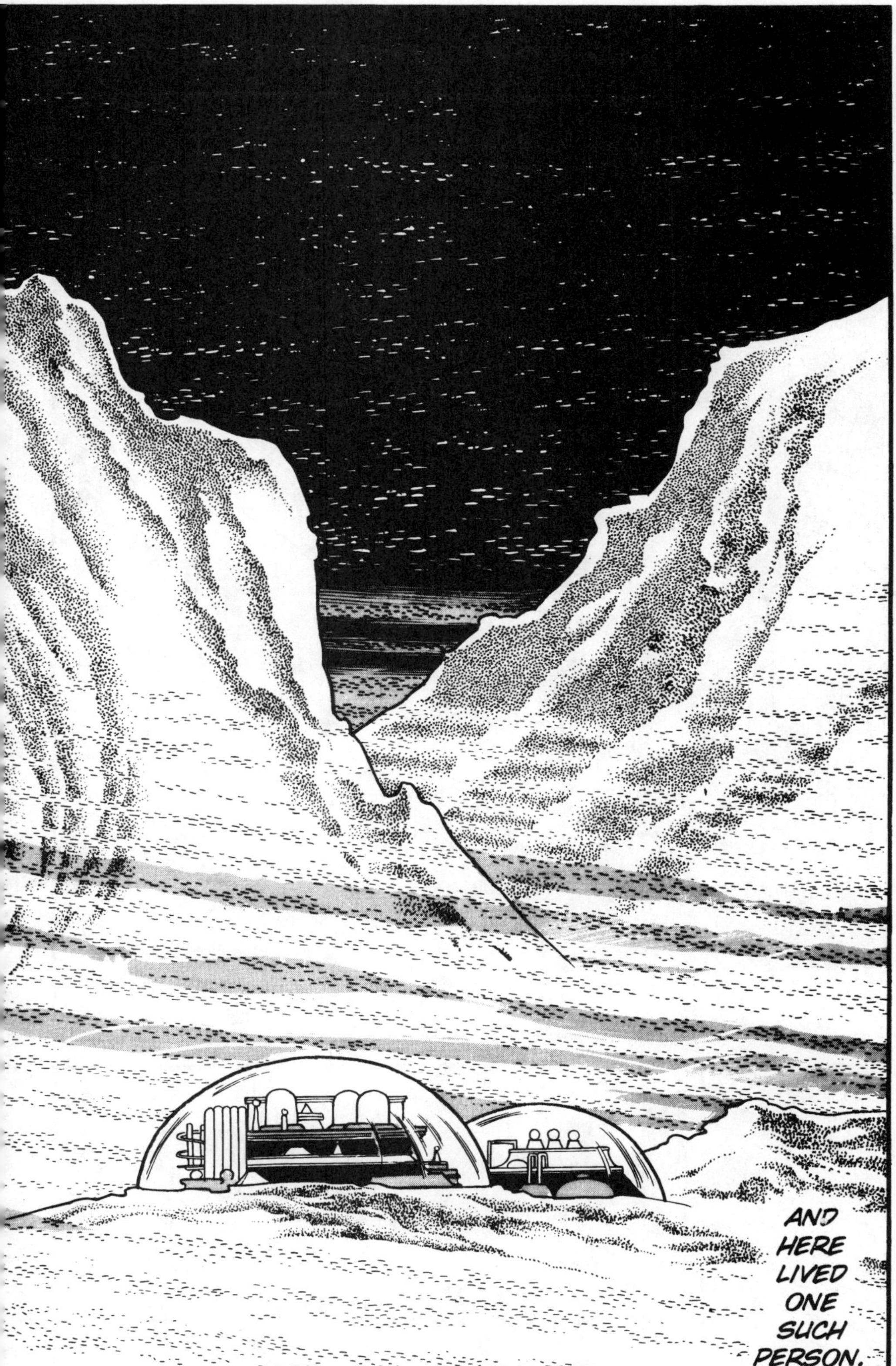
AND HERE LIVED ONE SUCH PERSON.

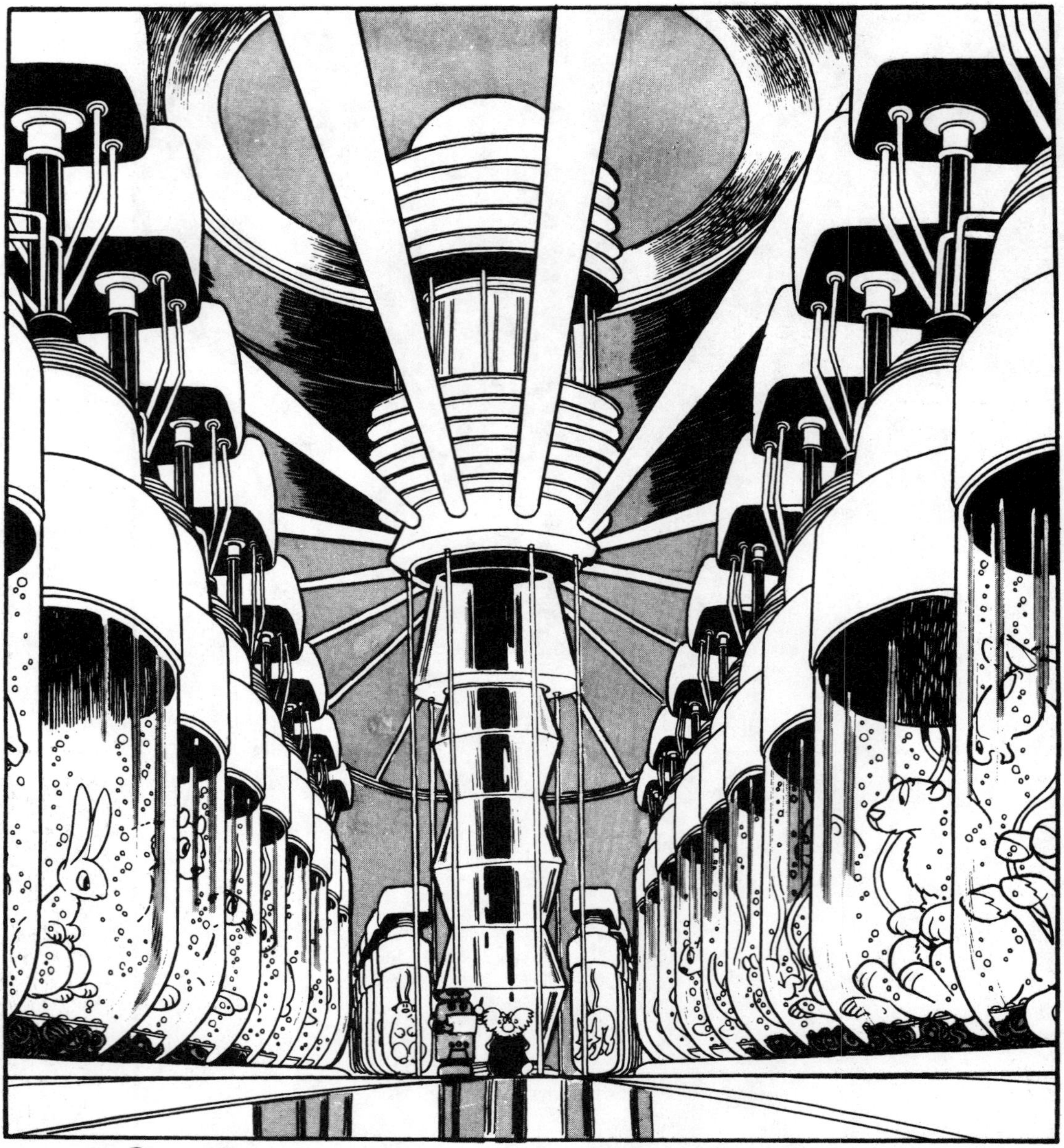
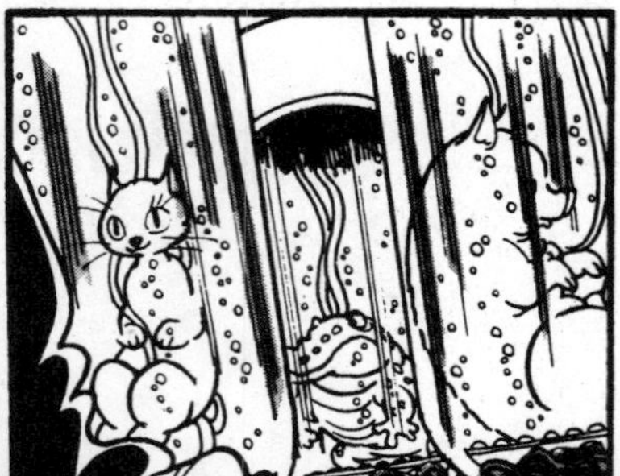
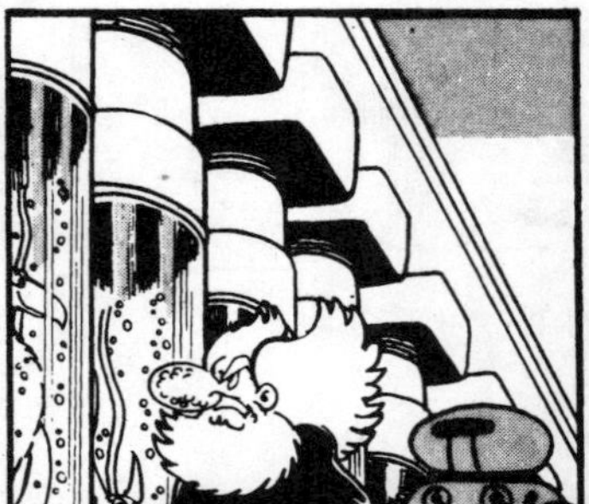
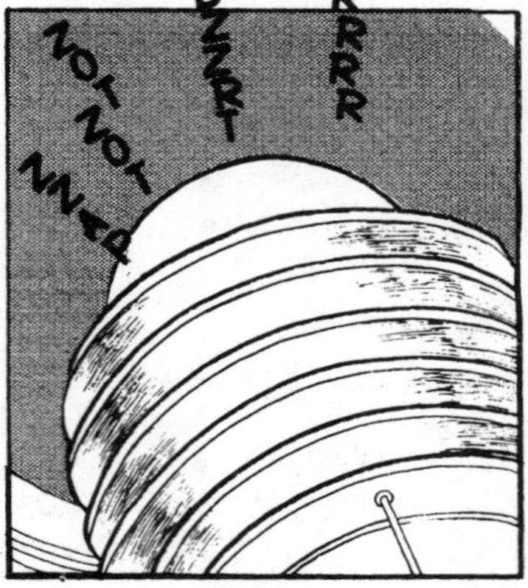
BZZRT
RRRR

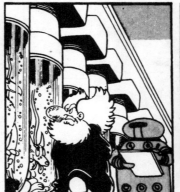

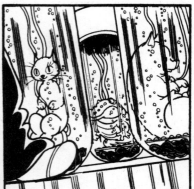

GOOD MORNING, *OLIVER!*

HOW ARE YOU TODAY, *LEM?*

AND YOU, *WYND-HAM?*

MY BEAUTIFUL CHILDREN...

GOOD MORNING, PAPA!

OH, *BRADBURY...* WHAT ARE YOU READING TODAY?

GOETHE'S *THE SORROWS OF YOUNG WERTHER.*

YOU READ *THAT* ALREADY?

DR. SARUTA...

YES?

THE REAL WORLD MUST BE WONDERFUL, IS IT NOT?

I'M TIRED OF LIVING IN THIS TUBE. I WANT TO GO AND SEE WHAT IS OUTSIDE.

NO! THE SECOND YOU SET FOOT OUTSIDE THAT ARTIFICIAL AMNIOTIC FLUID, YOU'D DIE!

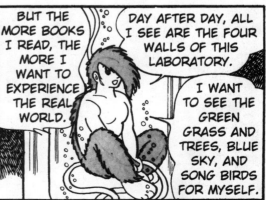
BUT THE MORE BOOKS I READ, THE MORE I WANT TO EXPERIENCE THE REAL WORLD.

DAY AFTER DAY, ALL I SEE ARE THE FOUR WALLS OF THIS LABORATORY.

I WANT TO SEE THE GREEN GRASS AND TREES, BLUE SKY, AND SONG BIRDS FOR MYSELF.

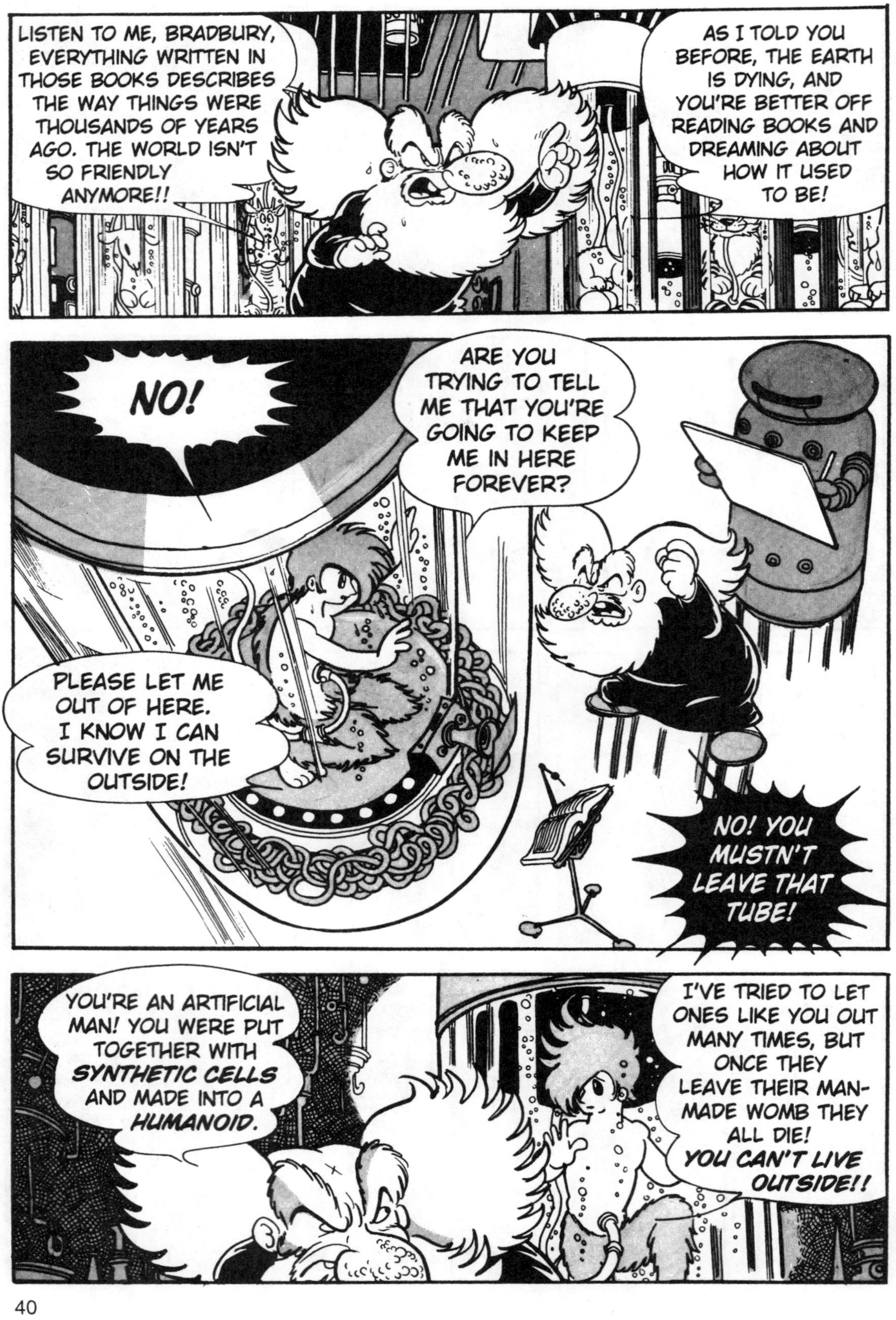
LISTEN TO ME, BRADBURY, EVERYTHING WRITTEN IN THOSE BOOKS DESCRIBES THE WAY THINGS WERE THOUSANDS OF YEARS AGO. THE WORLD ISN'T SO FRIENDLY ANYMORE!!
AS I TOLD YOU BEFORE, THE EARTH IS DYING, AND YOU'RE BETTER OFF READING BOOKS AND DREAMING ABOUT HOW IT USED TO BE!
NO!
ARE YOU TRYING TO TELL ME THAT YOU'RE GOING TO KEEP ME IN HERE FOREVER?
PLEASE LET ME OUT OF HERE. I KNOW I CAN SURVIVE ON THE OUTSIDE!
NO! YOU MUSTN'T LEAVE THAT TUBE!
YOU'RE AN ARTIFICIAL MAN! YOU WERE PUT TOGETHER WITH SYNTHETIC CELLS AND MADE INTO A HUMANOID.
I'VE TRIED TO LET ONES LIKE YOU OUT MANY TIMES, BUT ONCE THEY LEAVE THEIR MAN-MADE WOMB THEY ALL DIE! YOU CAN'T LIVE OUTSIDE!!

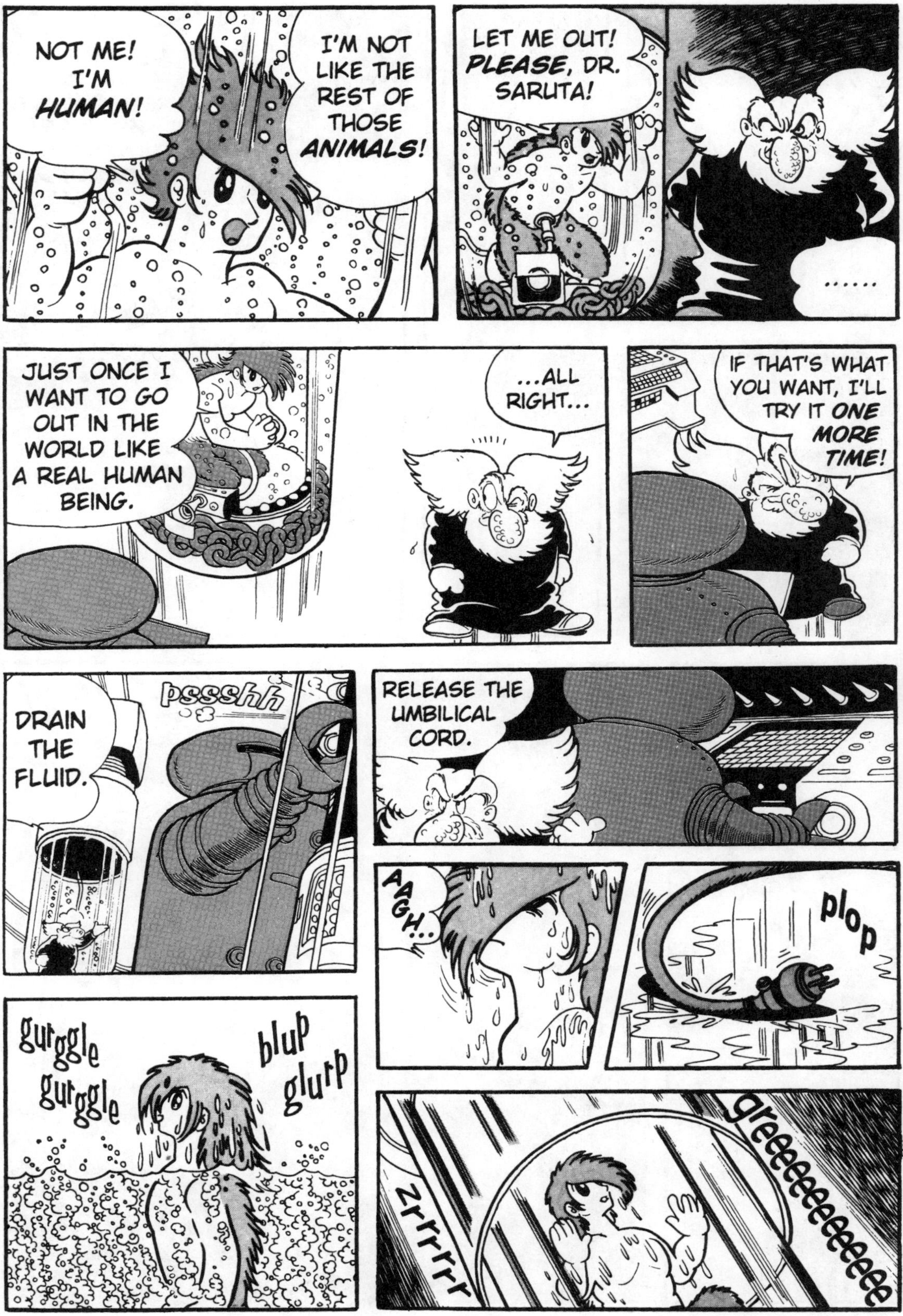
NOT ME! I'M HUMAN!
I'M NOT LIKE THE REST OF THOSE ANIMALS!
LET ME OUT! PLEASE, DR. SARUTA!
......
JUST ONCE I WANT TO GO OUT IN THE WORLD LIKE A REAL HUMAN BEING.
...ALL RIGHT...
IF THAT'S WHAT YOU WANT, I'LL TRY IT ONE MORE TIME!
DRAIN THE FLUID.
pssshh
RELEASE THE UMBILICAL CORD.
AAGH...
plop
gurggle gurggle
blup glurp
zrrrrr
greeeeeeeeeeee

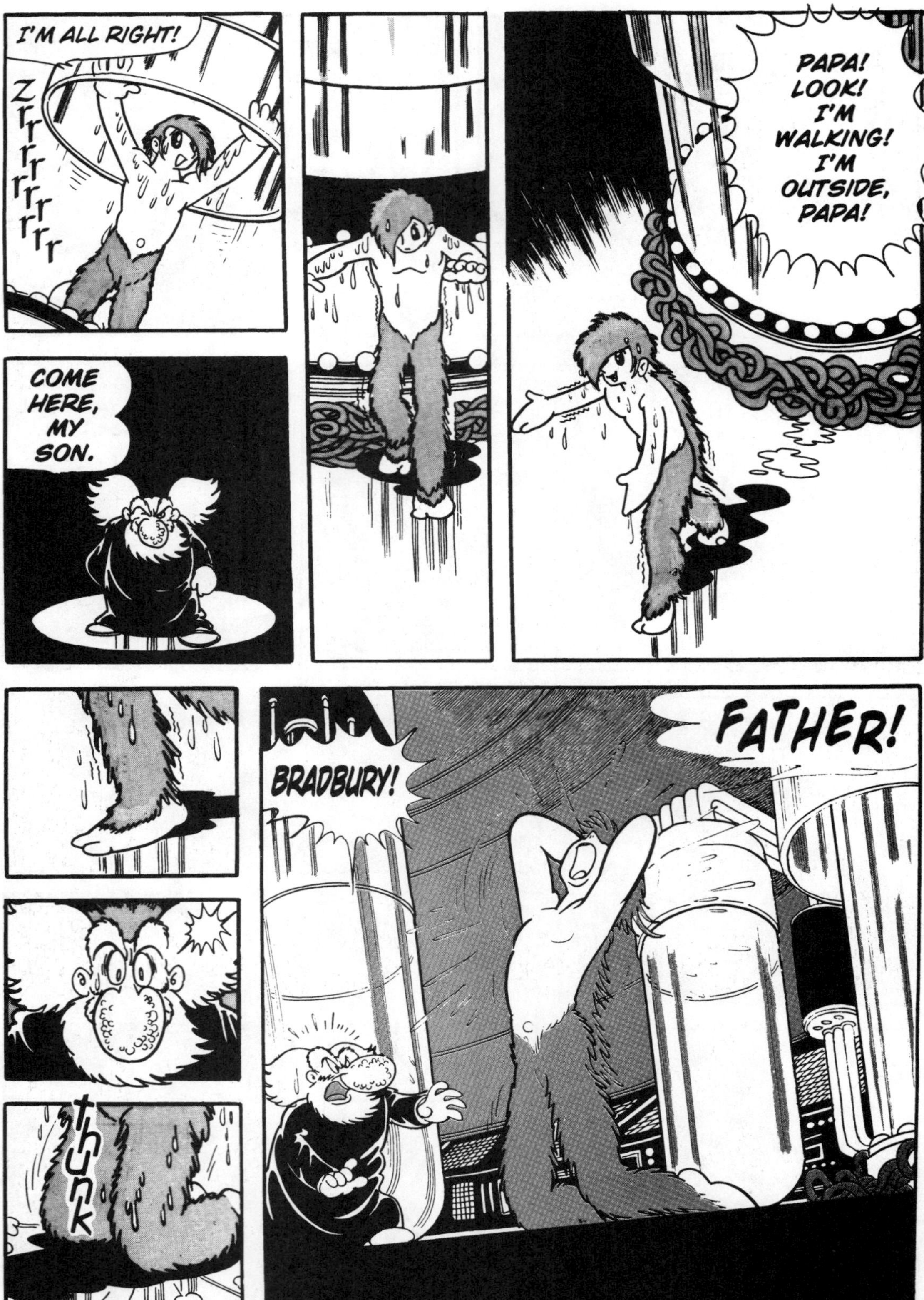
I'M ALL RIGHT!
Zrrrrrrrrrrr
COME HERE, MY SON.
PAPA! LOOK! I'M WALKING! I'M OUTSIDE, PAPA!
thunk
FATHER!
BRADBURY!

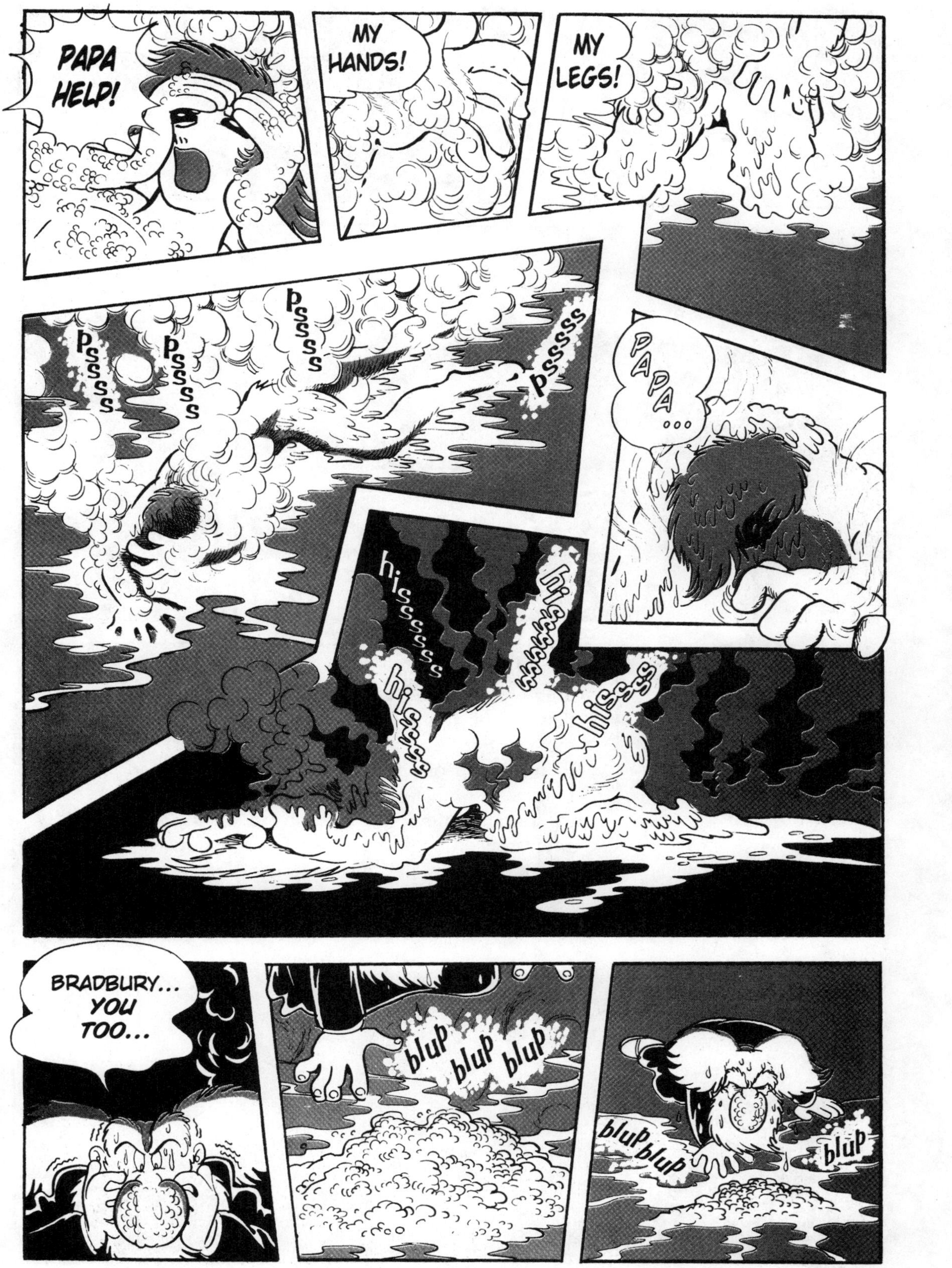
PAPA HELP!
MY HANDS!
MY LEGS!
pssss
pssss
pssss
psssss
PAPA...
hissssss
hissss
hisssssss
hissss
BRADBURY... YOU TOO...
blup blup blup
blup blup
blup

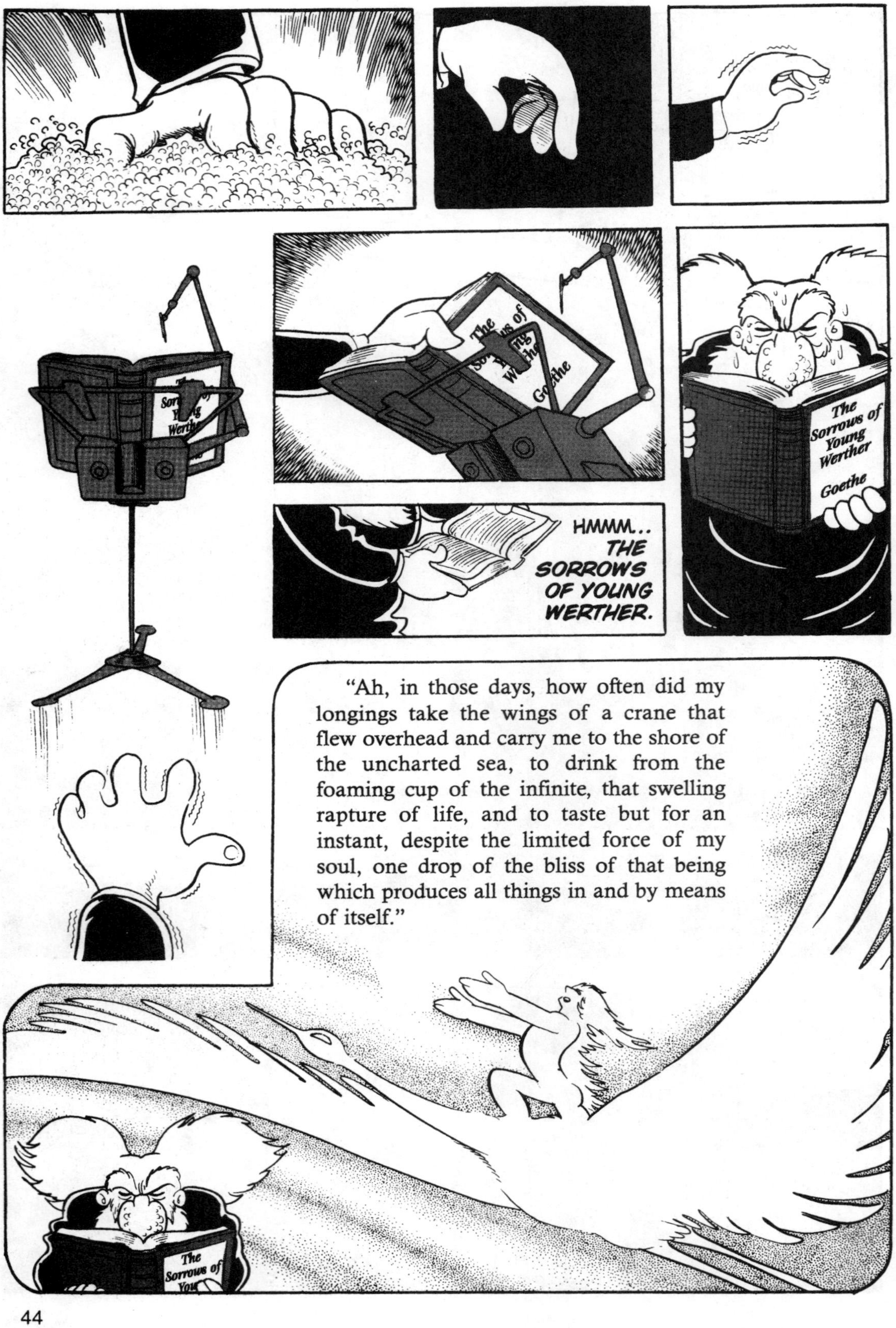
The Sorrows of Young Werther Goethe
HMMM... THE SORROWS OF YOUNG WERTHER.
"Ah, in those days, how often did my longings take the wings of a crane that flew overhead and carry me to the shore of the uncharted sea, to drink from the foaming cup of the infinite, that swelling rapture of life, and to taste but for an instant, despite the limited force of my soul, one drop of the bliss of that being which produces all things in and by means of itself."

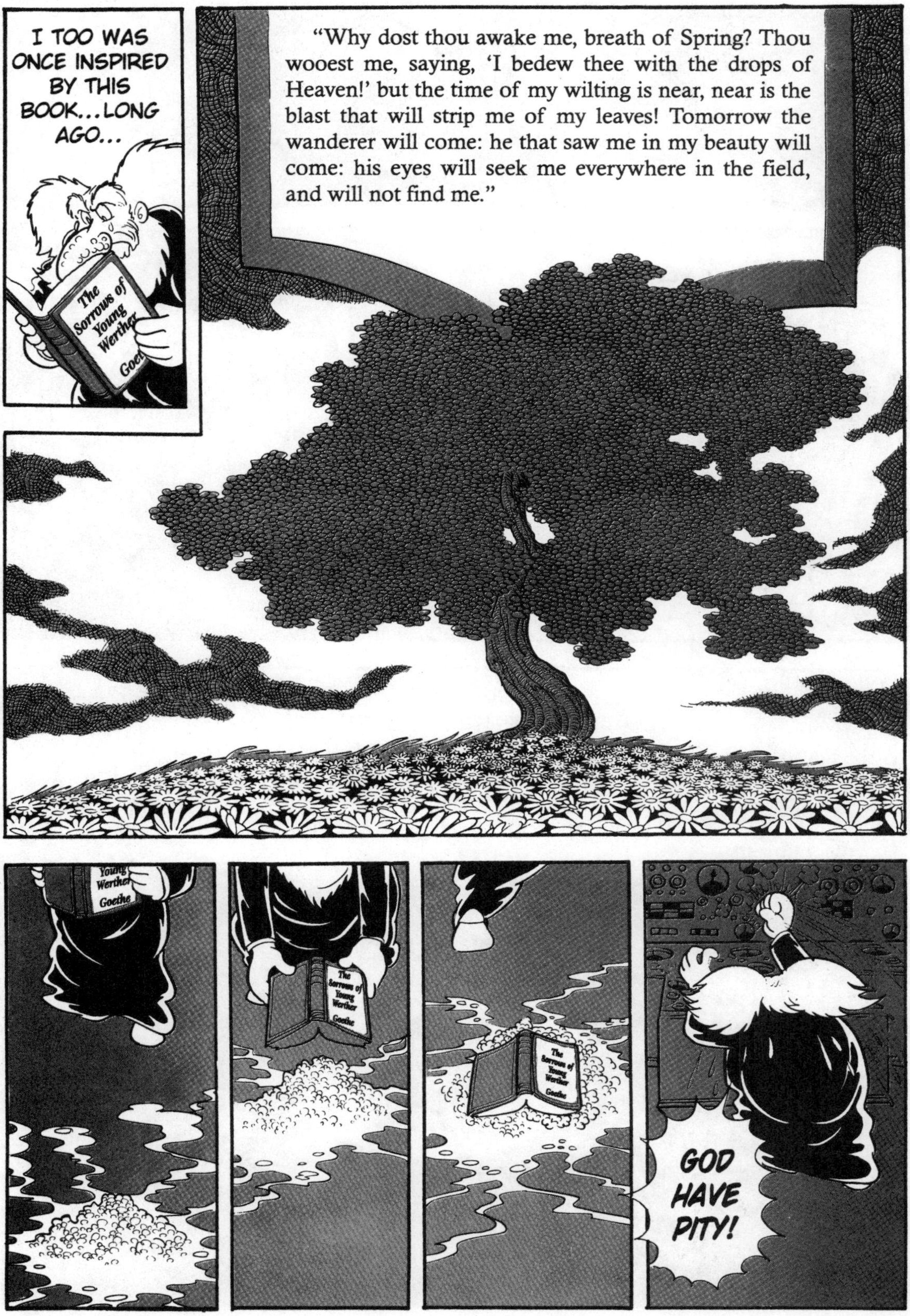
I TOO WAS ONCE INSPIRED BY THIS BOOK...LONG AGO...
The Sorrows of Young Werther
Goethe
"Why dost thou awake me, breath of Spring? Thou wooest me, saying, 'I bedew thee with the drops of Heaven!' but the time of my wilting is near, near is the blast that will strip me of my leaves! Tomorrow the wanderer will come: he that saw me in my beauty will come: his eyes will seek me everywhere in the field, and will not find me."
GOD HAVE PITY!

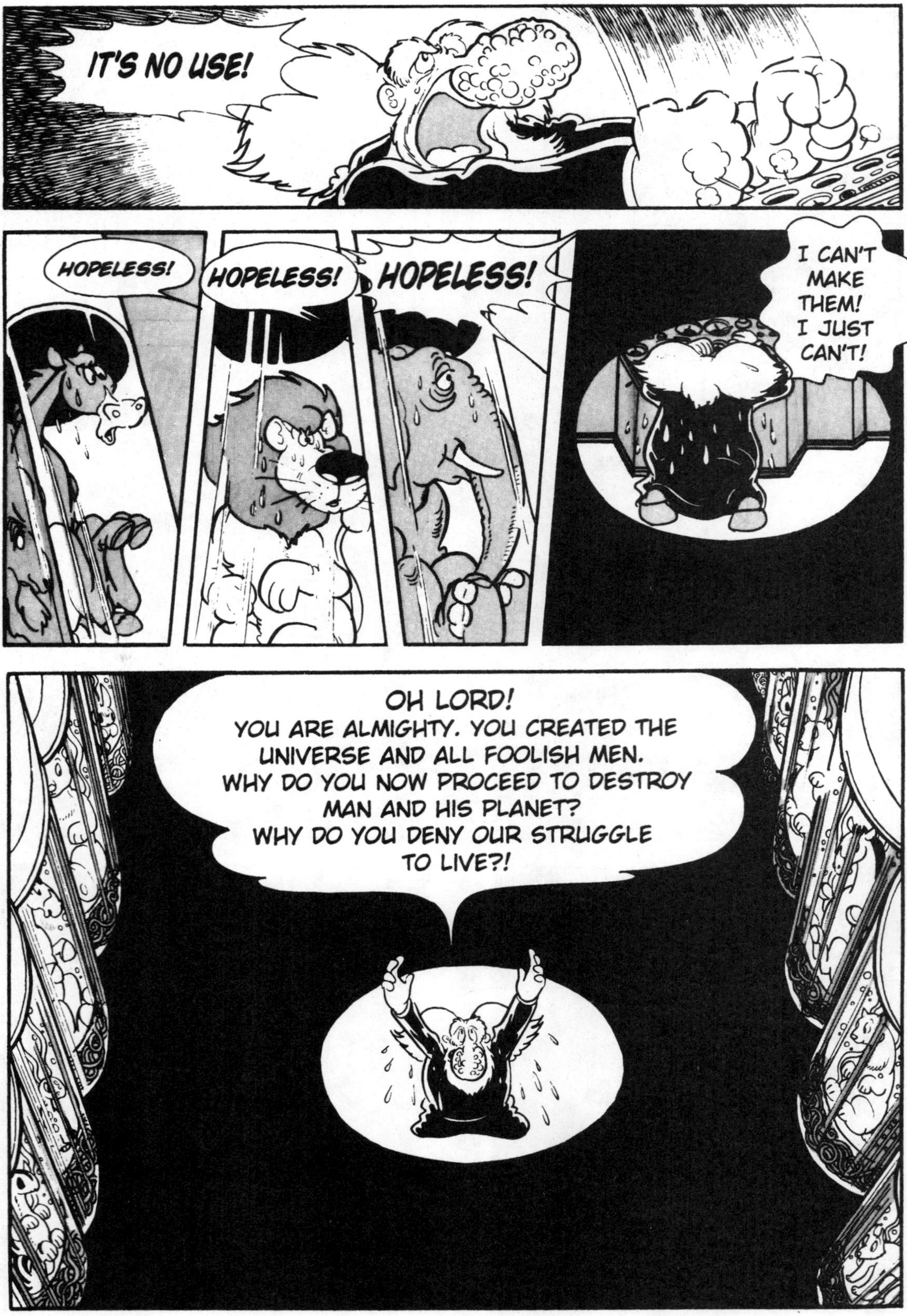
IT'S NO USE!
HOPELESS!
HOPELESS!
HOPELESS!
I CAN'T MAKE THEM! I JUST CAN'T!
OH LORD! YOU ARE ALMIGHTY. YOU CREATED THE UNIVERSE AND ALL FOOLISH MEN. WHY DO YOU NOW PROCEED TO DESTROY MAN AND HIS PLANET? WHY DO YOU DENY OUR STRUGGLE TO LIVE?!

I'M 166 YEARS OLD, YET I'M NOTHING MORE THAN A SPECK OF DUST TO YOU.

I ONCE HAD A DREAM THOUGH...

THERE ARE NO HORSES, DOGS, CATS, OR MONKEYS IN THIS WORLD ANY LONGER. LIONS, TIGERS, AND BEARS ALL VANISHED AGES AGO. ONLY A FEW FISH, INSECTS, AND RODENTS REMAIN. SO I CREATED REPLICAS...

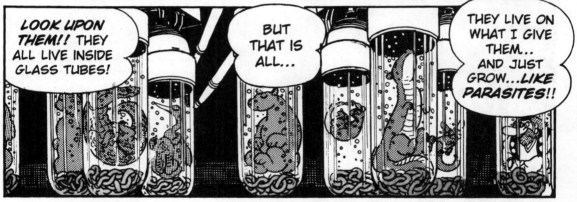

LOOK UPON THEM!! THEY ALL LIVE INSIDE GLASS TUBES!

BUT THAT IS ALL...

THEY LIVE ON WHAT I GIVE THEM... AND JUST GROW...LIKE PARASITES!!

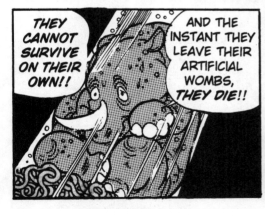

THEY CANNOT SURVIVE ON THEIR OWN!!

AND THE INSTANT THEY LEAVE THEIR ARTIFICIAL WOMBS, THEY DIE!!

CAN THIS BE CALLED LIFE?

GOD!

I DO NOT HAVE LONG TO LIVE!

TEACH ME THE SECRET OF LIFE.

JUST GIVE ME THE KEY TO THE PUZZLE, THAT'S ALL I ASK!

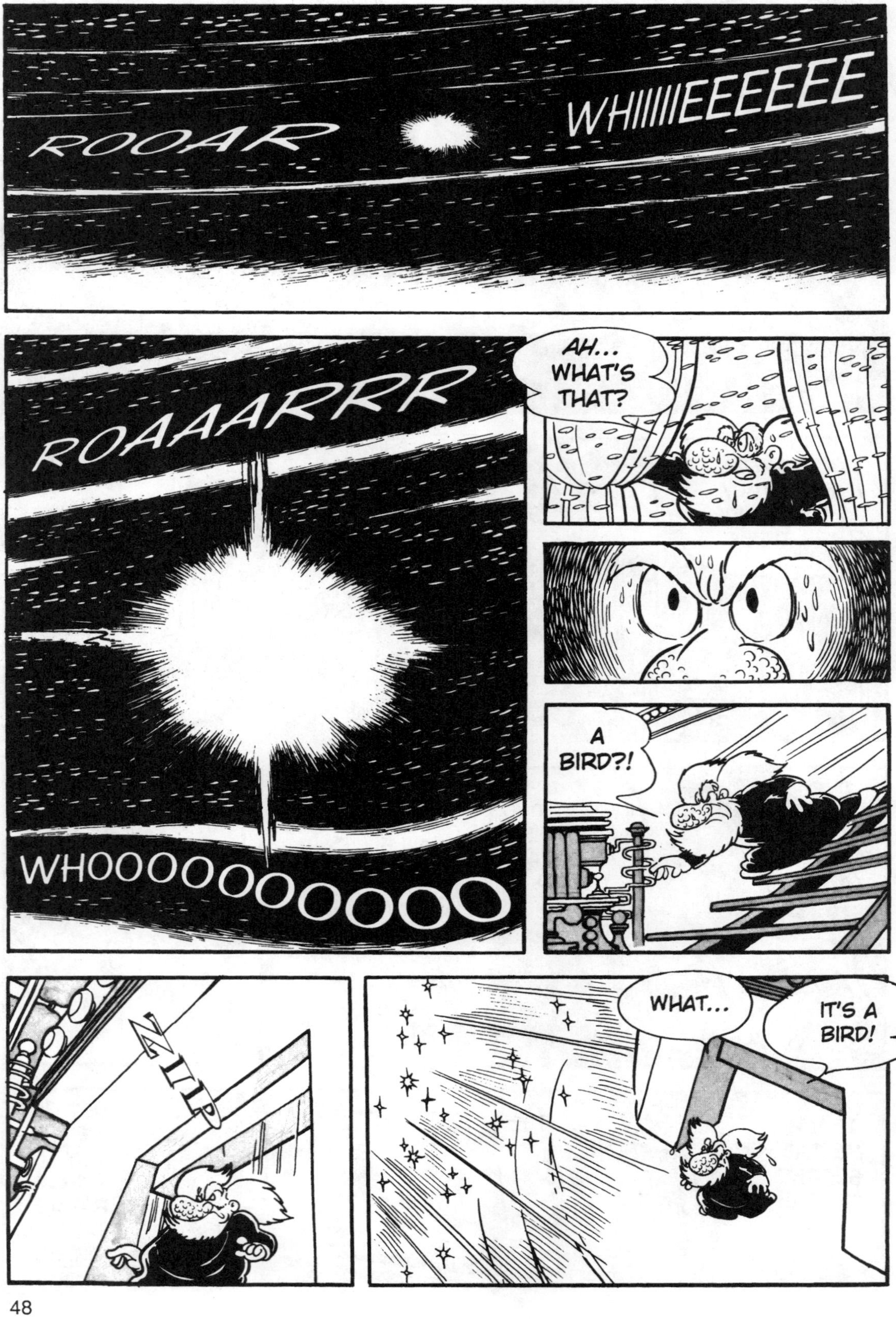
ROOAR
WHIIIIIIEEEEEE
ROAAARRR
WHOOOOOOOOOOO
AH... WHAT'S THAT?
A BIRD?!
ZIIP
WHAT...
IT'S A BIRD!

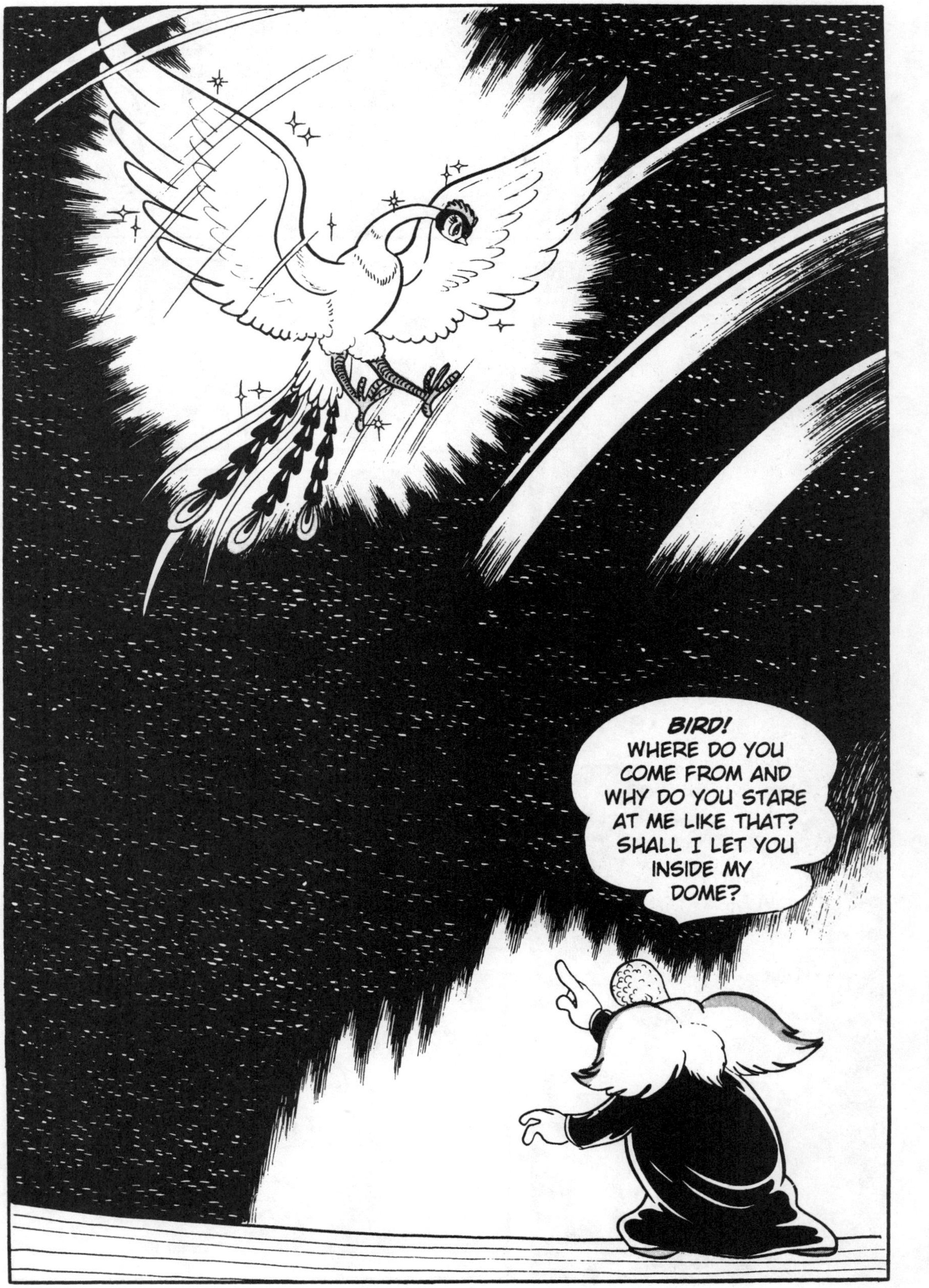
BIRD! WHERE DO YOU COME FROM AND WHY DO YOU STARE AT ME LIKE THAT? SHALL I LET YOU INSIDE MY DOME?

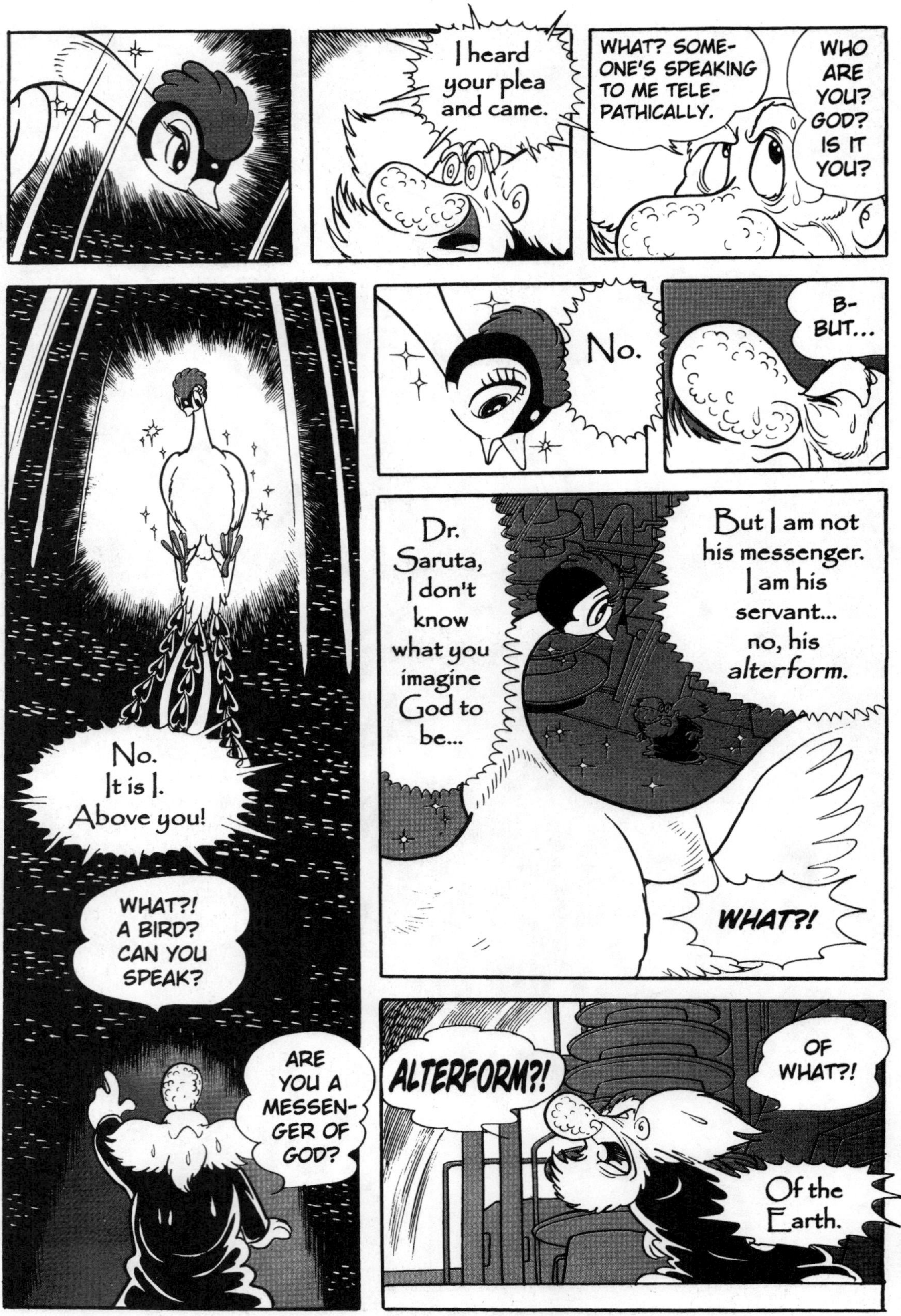
I heard your plea and came.
WHAT? SOME-ONE'S SPEAKING TO ME TELE-PATHICALLY.
WHO ARE YOU? GOD? IS IT YOU?
No. It is I. Above you!
WHAT?! A BIRD? CAN YOU SPEAK?
ARE YOU A MESSEN-GER OF GOD?
No.
B-BUT...
Dr. Saruta, I don't know what you imagine God to be...
But I am not his messenger. I am his servant... no, his *alterform*.
WHAT?!
ALTERFORM?!
OF WHAT?!
Of the Earth.

THE EARTH'S ALTERFORM? WHAT DO YOU MEAN?

I DON'T UNDERSTAND ANYTHING YOU ARE SAYING!!

The Earth is alive. It is a living entity.

But it is dying now...like a sick man...

BIRD! WHAT DO YOU MEAN, THE EARTH IS ALIVE? DON'T BE RIDICULOUS!

Of course you can't understand. To you, the Earth seems huge.

It's like bacteria having no idea that the body they inhabit is also a living being...

BUT WHAT ARE YOU, FOR HEAVEN'S SAKE?

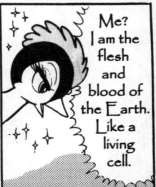

Me? I am the flesh and blood of the Earth. Like a living cell.

AUGH... I MUST BE GOING CRAZY.

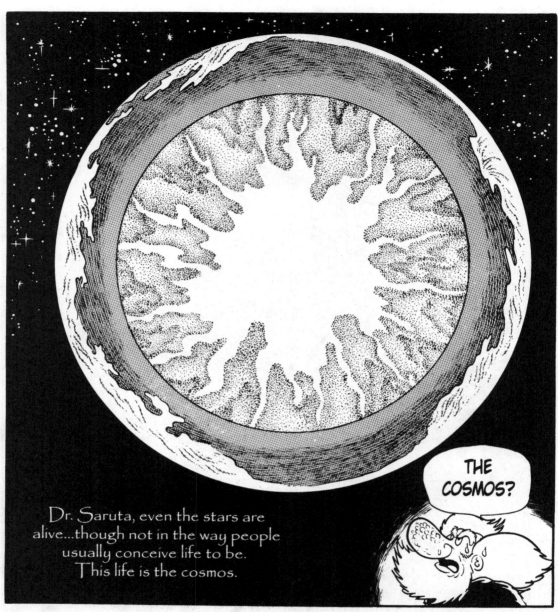

Dr. Saruta, even the stars are alive...though not in the way people usually conceive life to be. This life is the cosmos.

THE COSMOS?

Your sun is also alive.

As are all the stars in the milky way.

All active stars are alive. They are the cosmos.

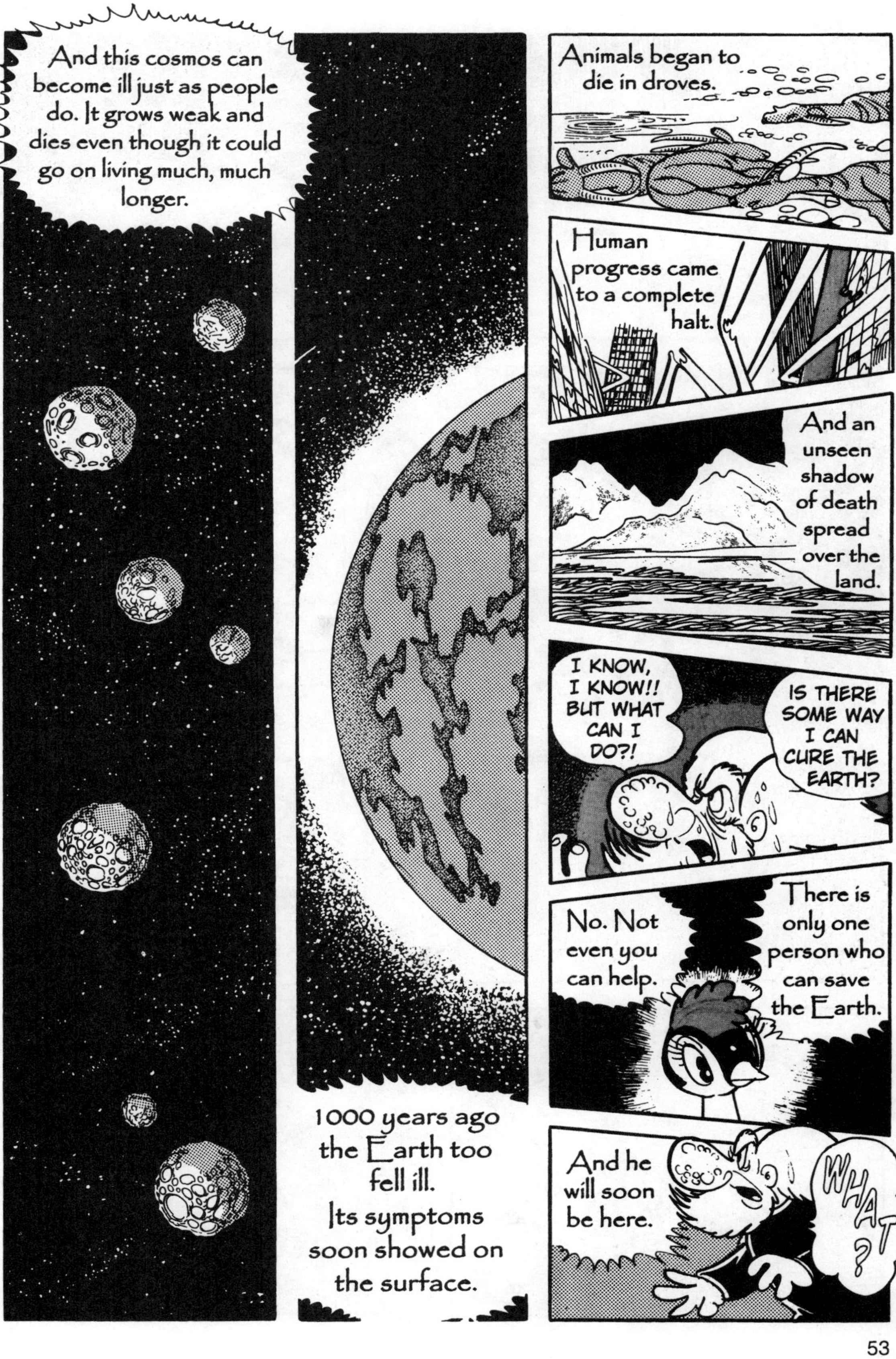
And this cosmos can become ill just as people do. It grows weak and dies even though it could go on living much, much longer.
1000 years ago the Earth too fell ill.
Its symptoms soon showed on the surface.
Animals began to die in droves.
Human progress came to a complete halt.
And an unseen shadow of death spread over the land.
I KNOW, I KNOW!! BUT WHAT CAN I DO?!
IS THERE SOME WAY I CAN CURE THE EARTH?
No. Not even you can help.
There is only one person who can save the Earth.
And he will soon be here.
WHAT?

I have shown him the way and he is now approaching.

AH! I CAN SEE SOMEONE COMING!!

Roo ooaaaaarr

Whoooooiiiiiee

ROBITA! BRING THEM IN!!

YES-SIR-

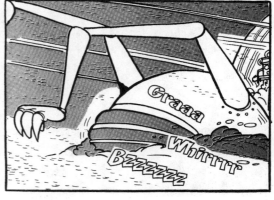

Graaa

Whirrrr

Bzzzzzz

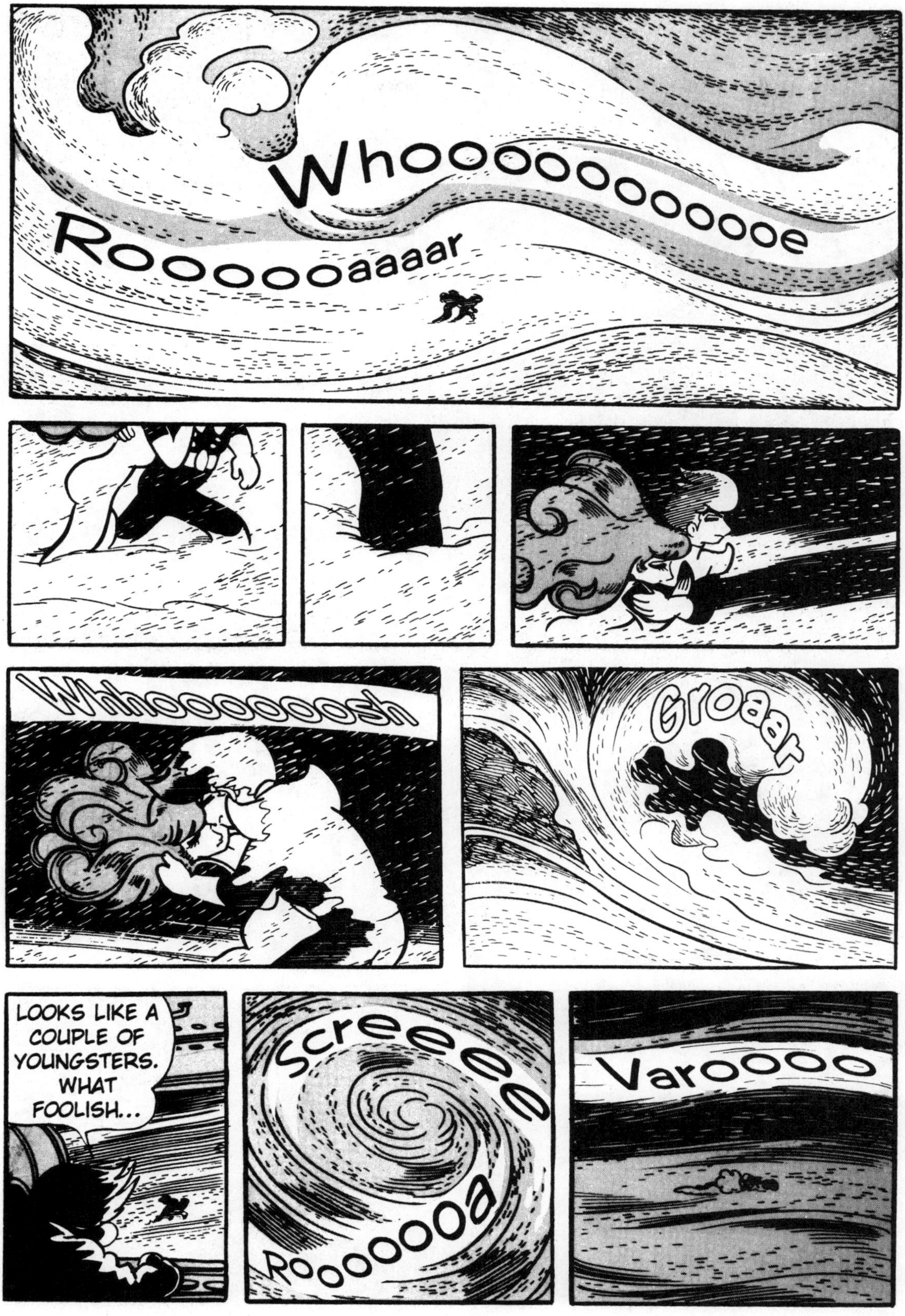
Whooooooooooe
Rooooooaaaar
Whoooooooosh
Groaar
LOOKS LIKE A COUPLE OF YOUNGSTERS. WHAT FOOLISH...
Screeee
Roooooa
Varoooo

BZZZZZZZZZZ

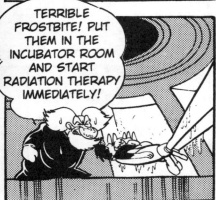

TERRIBLE FROSTBITE! PUT THEM IN THE INCUBATOR ROOM AND START RADIATION THERAPY IMMEDIATELY!

RECK-LESS FOOLS!

Whiee!

Whieee Snort!

THIS IS NO TIME FOR AN ARTIFICIAL CREATURE TO BE MAKING A FUSS! THESE ARE TWO REAL LIVE PEOPLE I'M TRYING TO SAVE! SO QUIT *HORSING* AROUND!

TAMAMI!

TAMAMI!

DON'T WORRY, MY BOY. TAMAMI IS RESTING IN THE NEXT ROOM.

WHA?

GET SOME SLEEP. TOMORROW THE BLIZZARD WILL STOP AND I'LL MEET YOU IN THE DINING ROOM.

GOOD NIGHT!

Grooooaaaarrrr

Whoooooeeeee

Varooooooooooooo

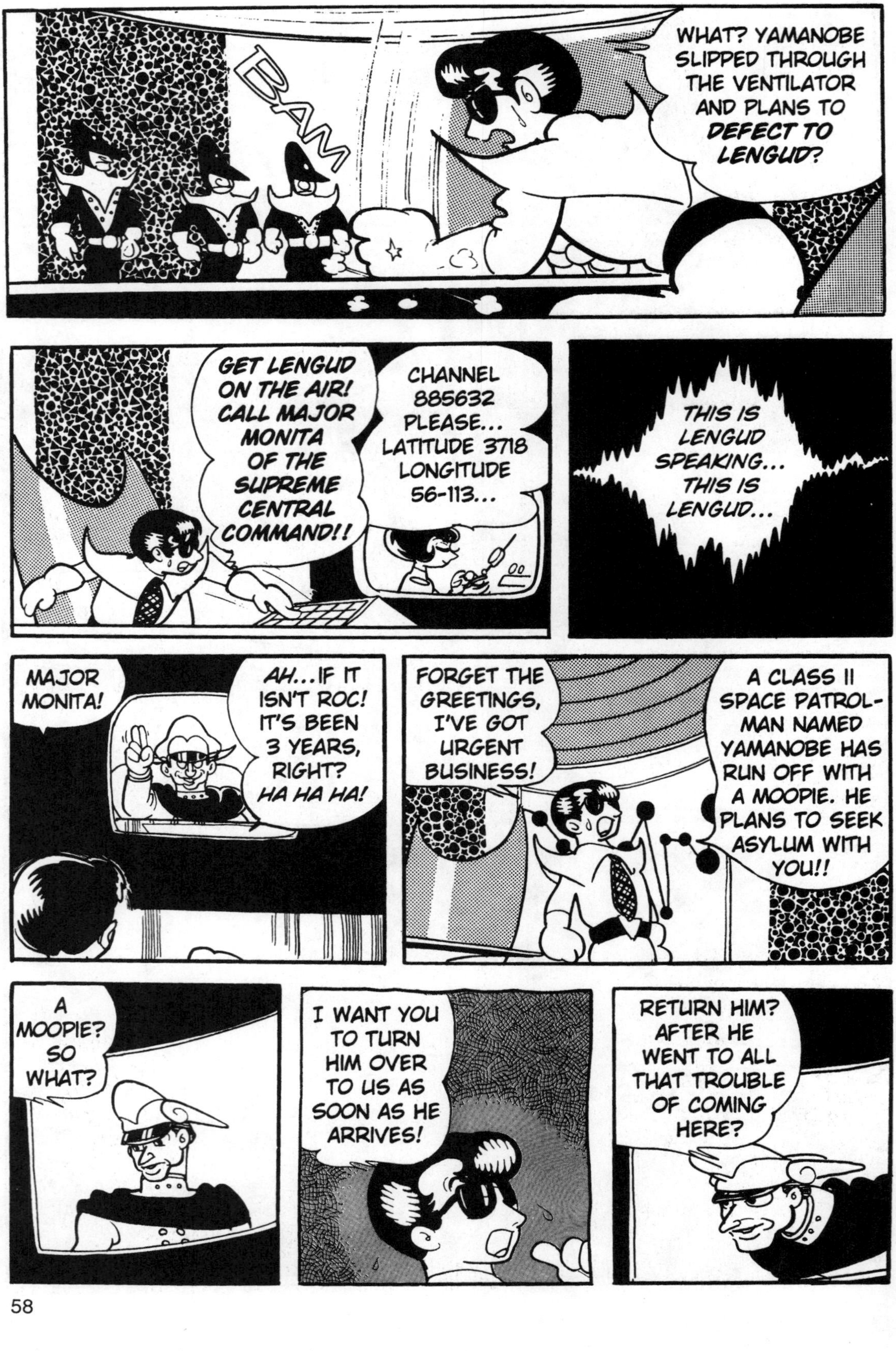
BAM
WHAT? YAMANOBE SLIPPED THROUGH THE VENTILATOR AND PLANS TO DEFECT TO LENGUD?
GET LENGUD ON THE AIR! CALL MAJOR MONITA OF THE SUPREME CENTRAL COMMAND!!
CHANNEL 885632 PLEASE... LATITUDE 3718 LONGITUDE 56-113...
THIS IS LENGUD SPEAKING... THIS IS LENGUD...
MAJOR MONITA!
AH...IF IT ISN'T ROC! IT'S BEEN 3 YEARS, RIGHT? HA HA HA!
FORGET THE GREETINGS, I'VE GOT URGENT BUSINESS!
A CLASS II SPACE PATROL-MAN NAMED YAMANOBE HAS RUN OFF WITH A MOOPIE. HE PLANS TO SEEK ASYLUM WITH YOU!!
A MOOPIE? SO WHAT?
I WANT YOU TO TURN HIM OVER TO US AS SOON AS HE ARRIVES!
RETURN HIM? AFTER HE WENT TO ALL THAT TROUBLE OF COMING HERE?

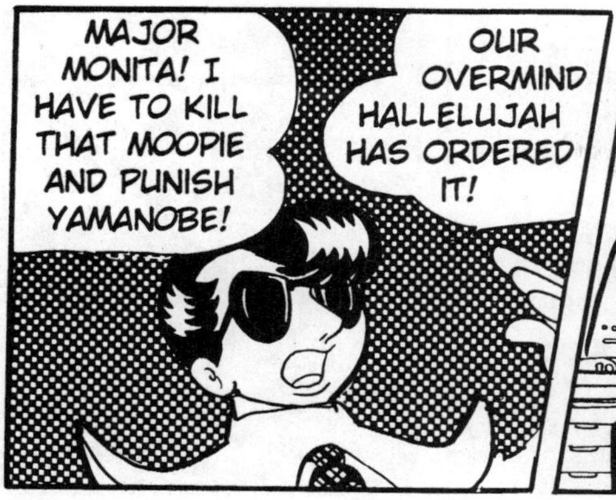
MAJOR MONITA! I HAVE TO KILL THAT MOOPIE AND PUNISH YAMANOBE!
OUR OVERMIND HALLELUJAH HAS ORDERED IT!
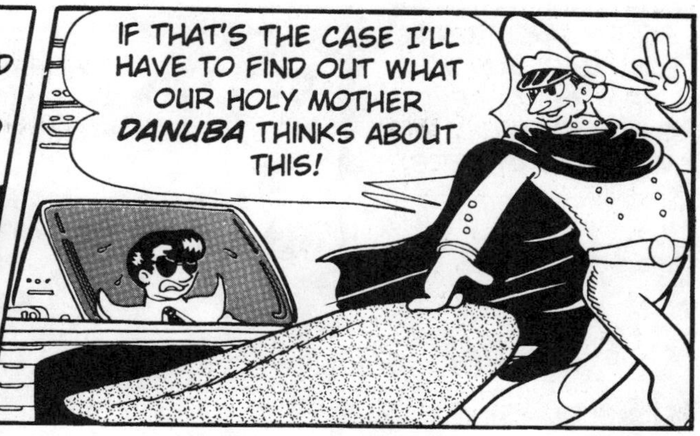
IF THAT'S THE CASE I'LL HAVE TO FIND OUT WHAT OUR HOLY MOTHER DANUBA THINKS ABOUT THIS!
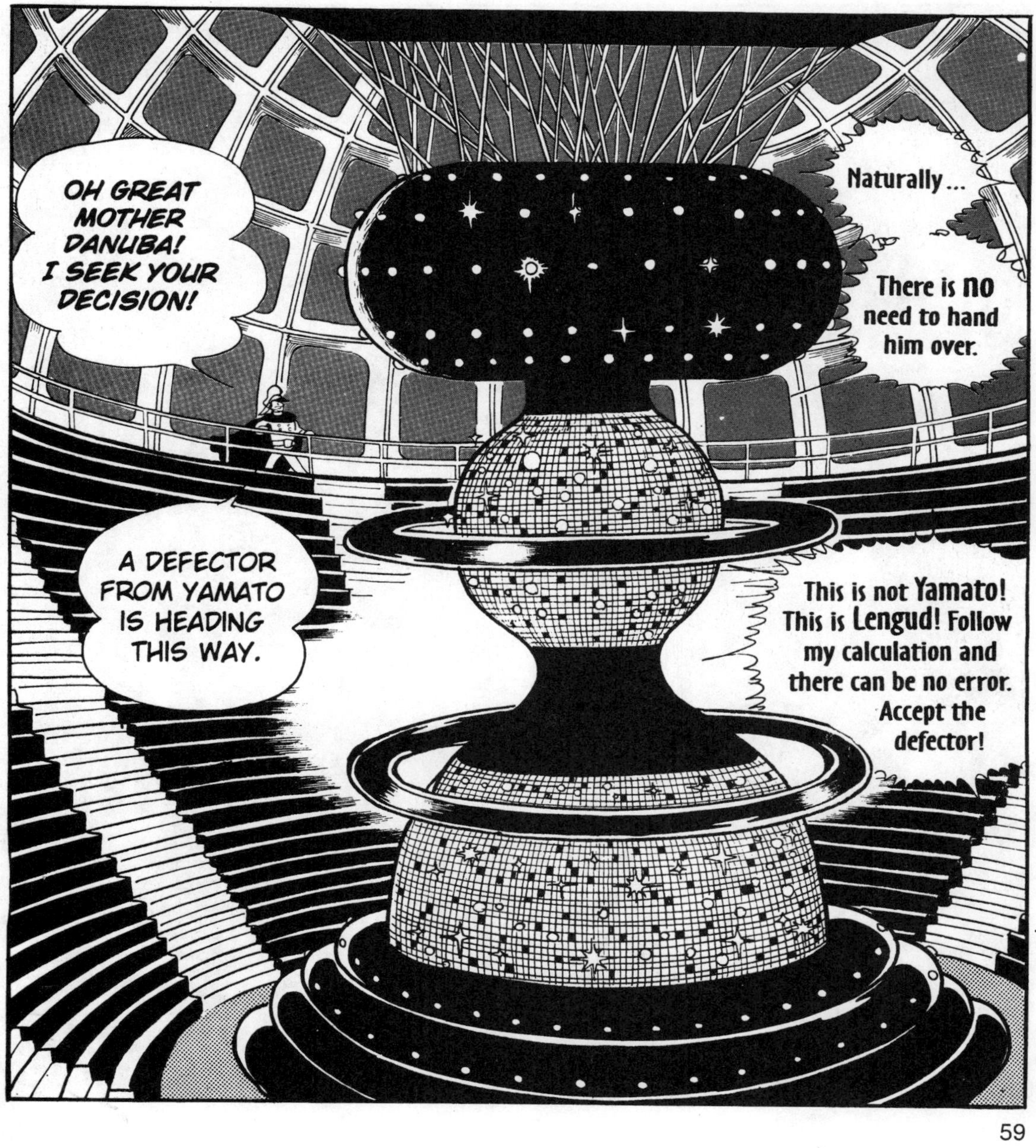
OH GREAT MOTHER DANUBA! I SEEK YOUR DECISION!
A DEFECTOR FROM YAMATO IS HEADING THIS WAY.
Naturally...
There is NO need to hand him over.
This is not Yamato! This is Lengud! Follow my calculation and there can be no error. Accept the defector!

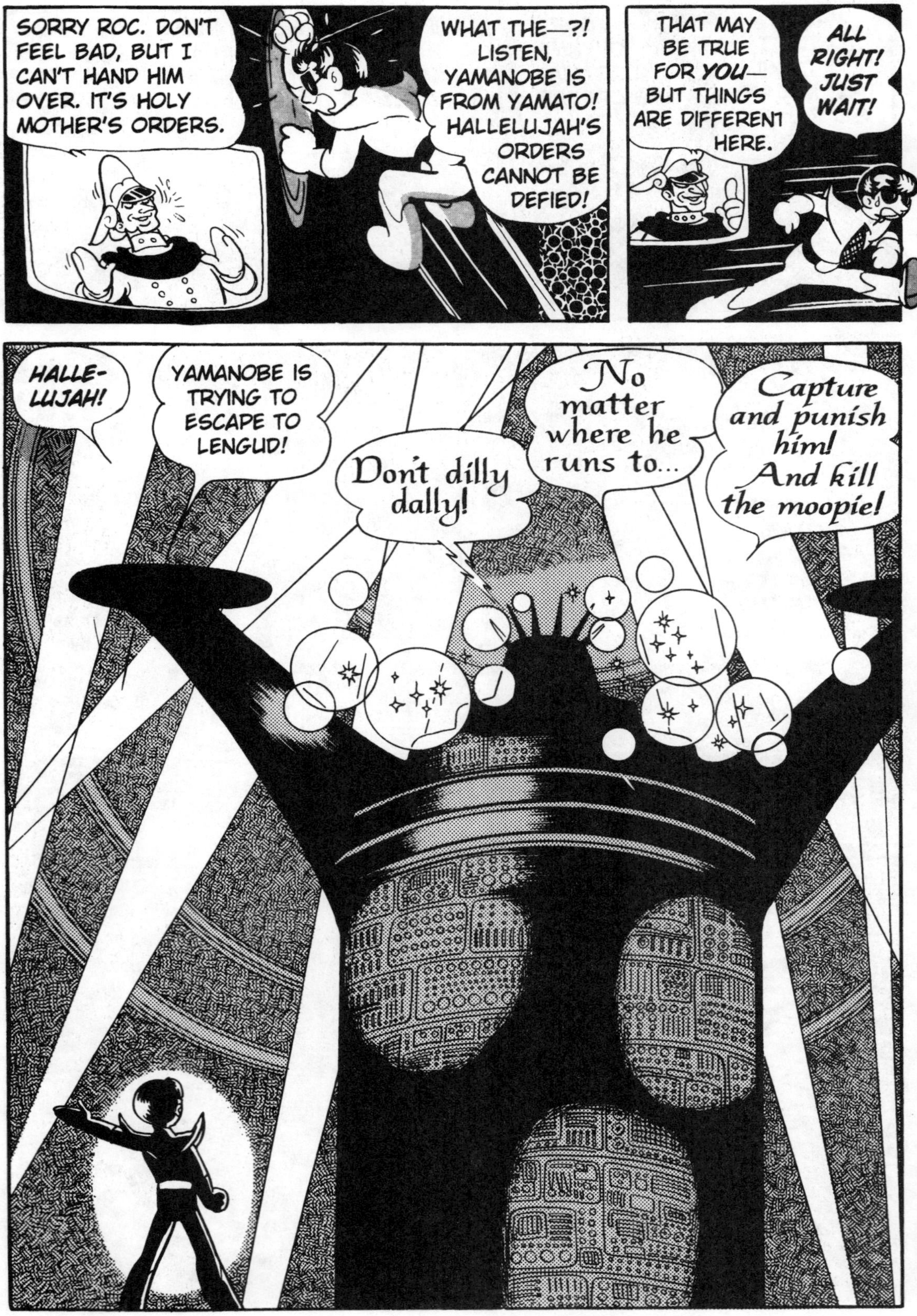
SORRY ROC. DON'T FEEL BAD, BUT I CAN'T HAND HIM OVER. IT'S HOLY MOTHER'S ORDERS.
WHAT THE—?! LISTEN, YAMANOBE IS FROM YAMATO! HALLELUJAH'S ORDERS CANNOT BE DEFIED!
THAT MAY BE TRUE FOR *YOU*— BUT THINGS ARE DIFFERENT HERE.
ALL RIGHT! JUST WAIT!
HALLE-LUJAH!
YAMANOBE IS TRYING TO ESCAPE TO LENGUD!
No matter where he runs to...
Capture and punish him! And kill the moopie!
Don't dilly dally!

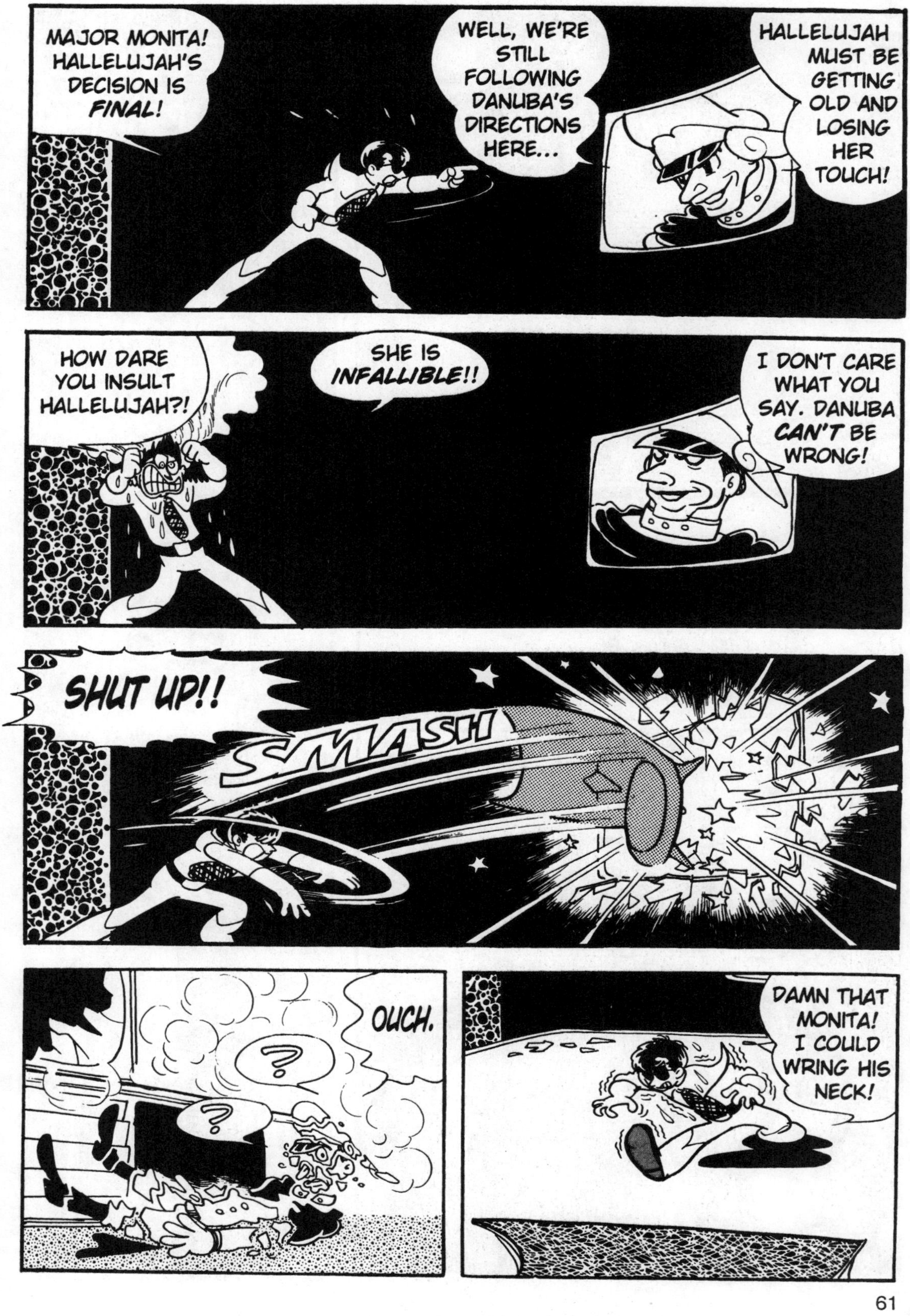
MAJOR MONITA! HALLELUJAH'S DECISION IS FINAL!
WELL, WE'RE STILL FOLLOWING DANUBA'S DIRECTIONS HERE...
HALLELUJAH MUST BE GETTING OLD AND LOSING HER TOUCH!
HOW DARE YOU INSULT HALLELUJAH?!
SHE IS INFALLIBLE!!
I DON'T CARE WHAT YOU SAY. DANUBA CAN'T BE WRONG!
SHUT UP!!
SMASH
OUCH.
?
?
DAMN THAT MONITA! I COULD WRING HIS NECK!

ORDER ONE COMPANY OF SURFACE RANGERS TOPSIDE IMMEDIATELY TO SEARCH FOR YAMANOBE. DESTROY HIM AND THE MOOPIE ON CONTACT!

TAKE 100 RADAR DOGS. THEY'LL SPOT HIM IN NO TIME.

MAKE SURE YOU KILL HIM. DON'T ALLOW ANYTHING TO GET IN YOUR WAY!

YESSIR!

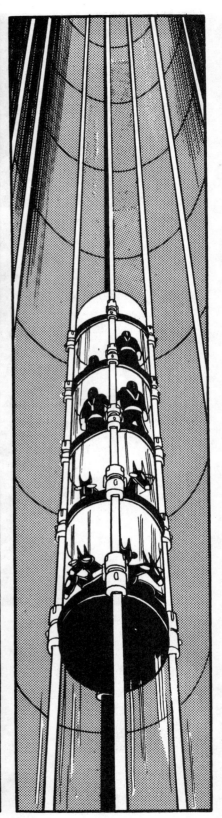

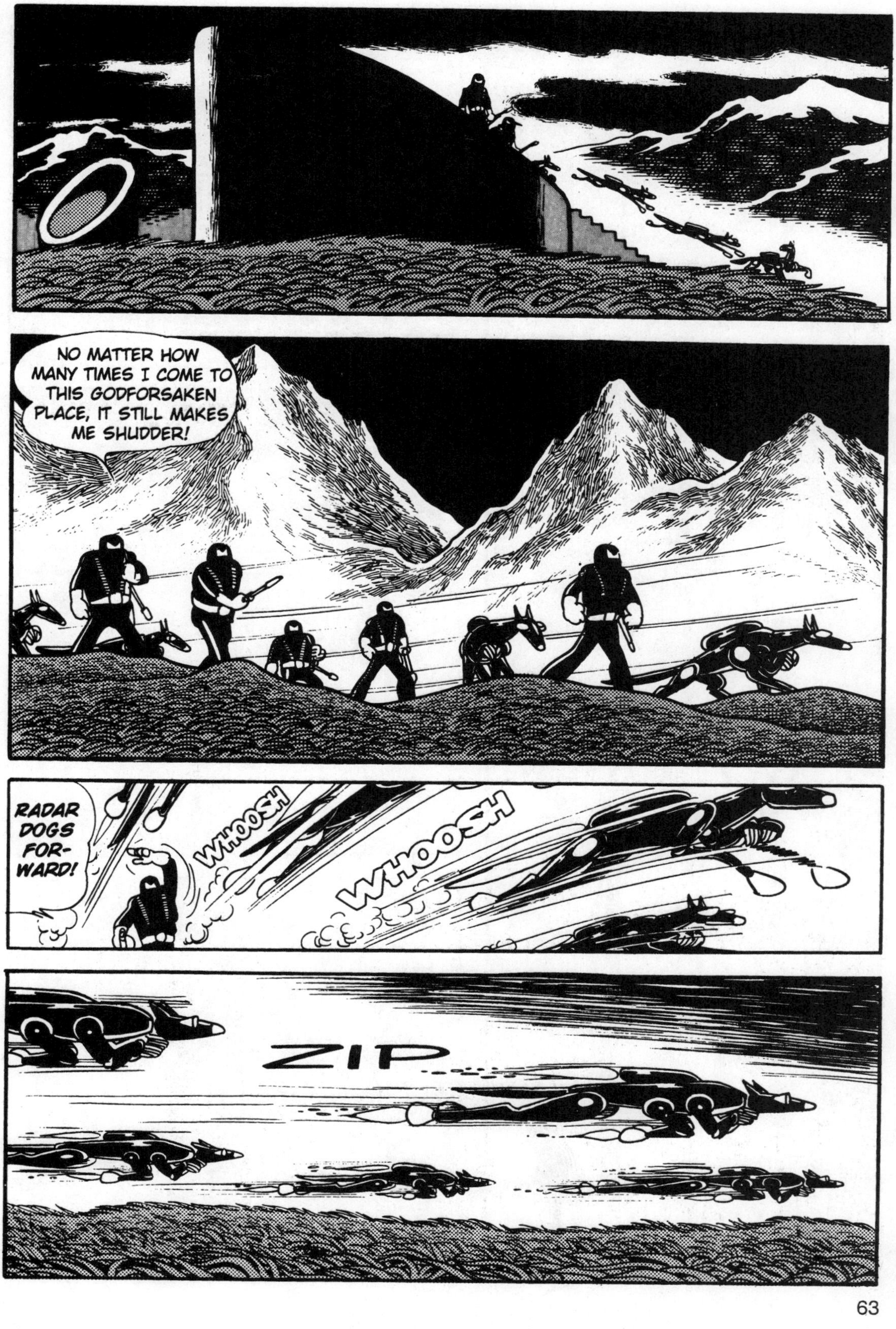
NO MATTER HOW MANY TIMES I COME TO THIS GODFORSAKEN PLACE, IT STILL MAKES ME SHUDDER!
WHOOSH
WHOOSH
RADAR DOGS FOR-WARD!
ZIP

Beep Beep

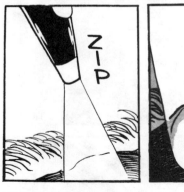

ZIP

ONE HAS LOCKED ONTO YAMANOBE'S TRAIL! HE'S HEADING WEST!

OKAY. GOOD WORK!

THIS IS THE BEST SUNRISE I'VE SEEN IN TEN YEARS.

GOOD MORNING, SON.

HAVE A GOOD SLEEP?

WHERE'S TAMAMI!!?

WHO ARE YOU AND WHAT HAVE YOU DONE WITH HER?!

RELAX, MY BOY!

RADIATION THERAPY IS A LITTLE ROUGH ON MOOPIES. I'M TREATING HER IN A DIFFERENT ROOM SO SHE CAN KEEP HER HUMAN FORM.

SO YOU KNOW SHE'S A MOOPIE... WHO ARE YOU?!

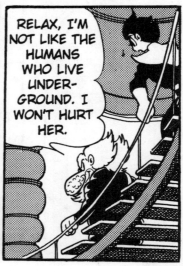

RELAX, I'M NOT LIKE THE HUMANS WHO LIVE UNDER-GROUND. I WON'T HURT HER.

WHAT HAVE YOU DONE TO HER?

WHY HAVE YOU LOCKED HER UP IN THAT TUBE?

TAKE YOUR HANDS OFF ME! LET ME EXPLAIN!

MY NAME IS DR. SARUTA.

I'VE LIVED ALONE HERE FOR 50 YEARS NOW.

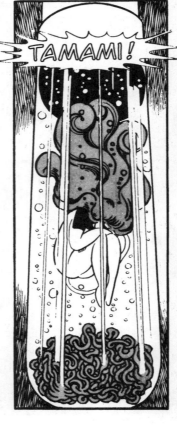

TAMAMI!

DR. SARUTA? I'VE HEARD YOUR NAME BEFORE... ARE YOU REALLY HIM?

I'M YAMA-NOBE— A SPACE PATROL-MAN.
I'VE OFTEN HEARD OF YOU FROM SPACE PATROLMEN AT CENTRAL COMMAND.
A DEFECTOR.
HOW DID YOU KNOW?
IT'S OBVIOUS. ONLY SOMEONE CRAZY OR RUNNING AWAY WOULD BE FOOLISH ENOUGH TO WALK ON THE SURFACE IN A BLIZZARD LIKE THAT WITHOUT AN ANTI-COLD SUIT.

DR. SARUTA!!

HIS NAME WAS ALREADY A LEGEND.
IN HIS YOUTH HE TRAVELED THE FOUR CORNERS OF THE UNIVERSE, WANDERING FROM STAR TO STAR, DOING PROLIFIC RESEARCH ON THE COSMOS.
AFTER RETURNING TO EARTH, HE GREW TO DETEST THE SUBTERRANEAN WORLD AND WITHDREW INTO A HERMIT'S EXISTENCE IN HIS SURFACE DOME, BUT HIS HEART STILL HELD AN ENORMOUS LOVE FOR MANKIND AND THE EARTH UPON WHICH HE LIVED.

SFX: CLANG CLANG CLANG

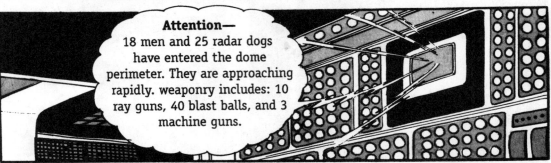

Attention—
18 men and 25 radar dogs have entered the dome perimeter. They are approaching rapidly. weaponry includes: 10 ray guns, 40 blast balls, and 3 machine guns.

DAMN! ROC'S SENT HIS MEN OUT TO KILL ME!

DR. SARUTA, IF I STAY HERE, YOU'LL BE ENDANGERED TOO. I'M GOING TO TRY TO GET AWAY.

RELEASE TAMAMI PLEASE... *NOW.*

WAIT A MINUTE THERE...HER BODY IS WEAK. IF WE TAKE HER OUT, SHE WON'T BE ABLE TO RETAIN HER HUMAN FORM.

THIS CAPSULE IS MAINTAINED AT THE CORRECT TEMPERATURE, PRESSURE, AND CHEMICAL COMPOSITION FOR A MOOPIE. SHE SHOULD REMAIN IN IT TO RECUPERATE FOR AT LEAST ANOTHER MONTH.

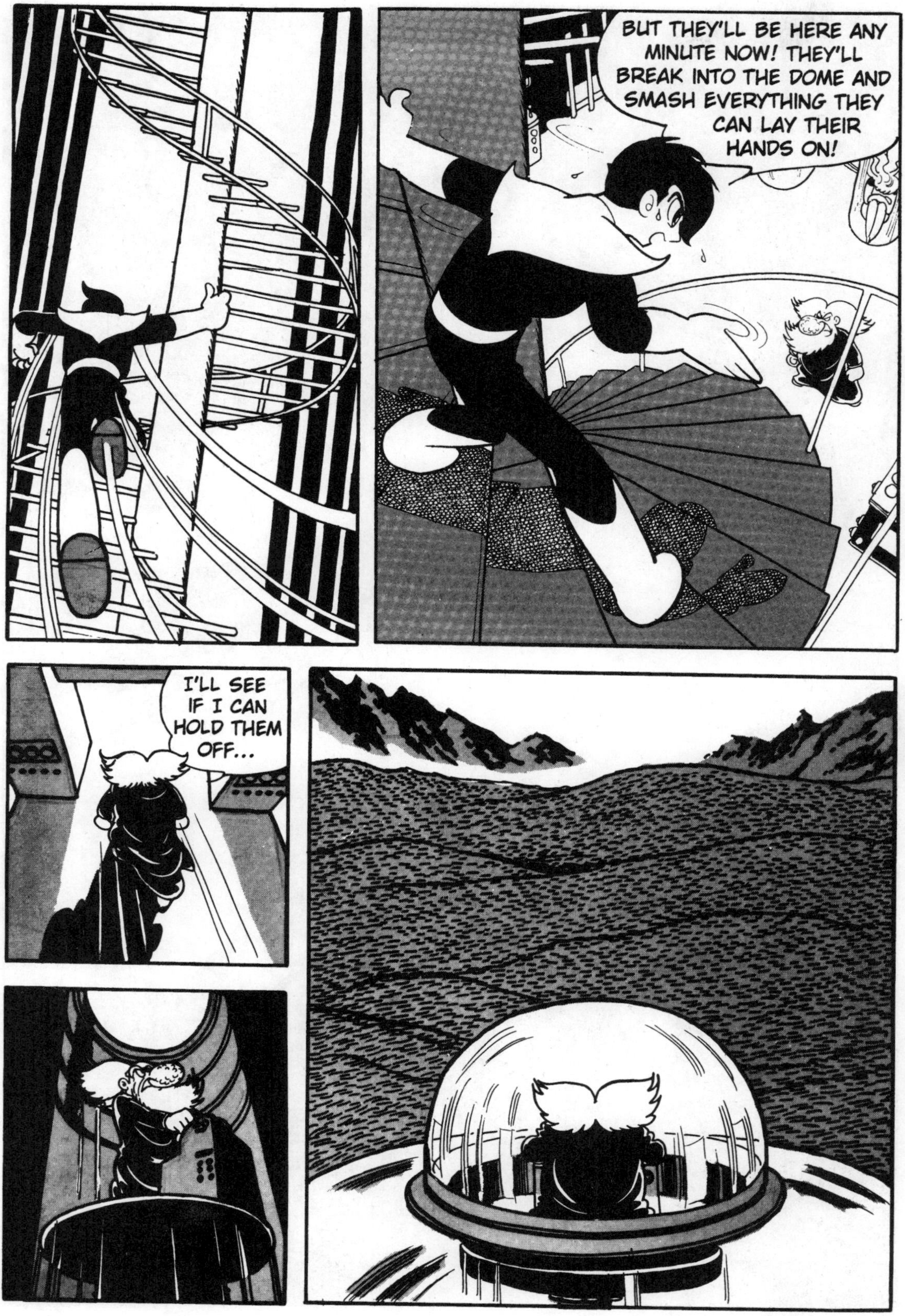
BUT THEY'LL BE HERE ANY MINUTE NOW! THEY'LL BREAK INTO THE DOME AND SMASH EVERYTHING THEY CAN LAY THEIR HANDS ON!
I'LL SEE IF I CAN HOLD THEM OFF...

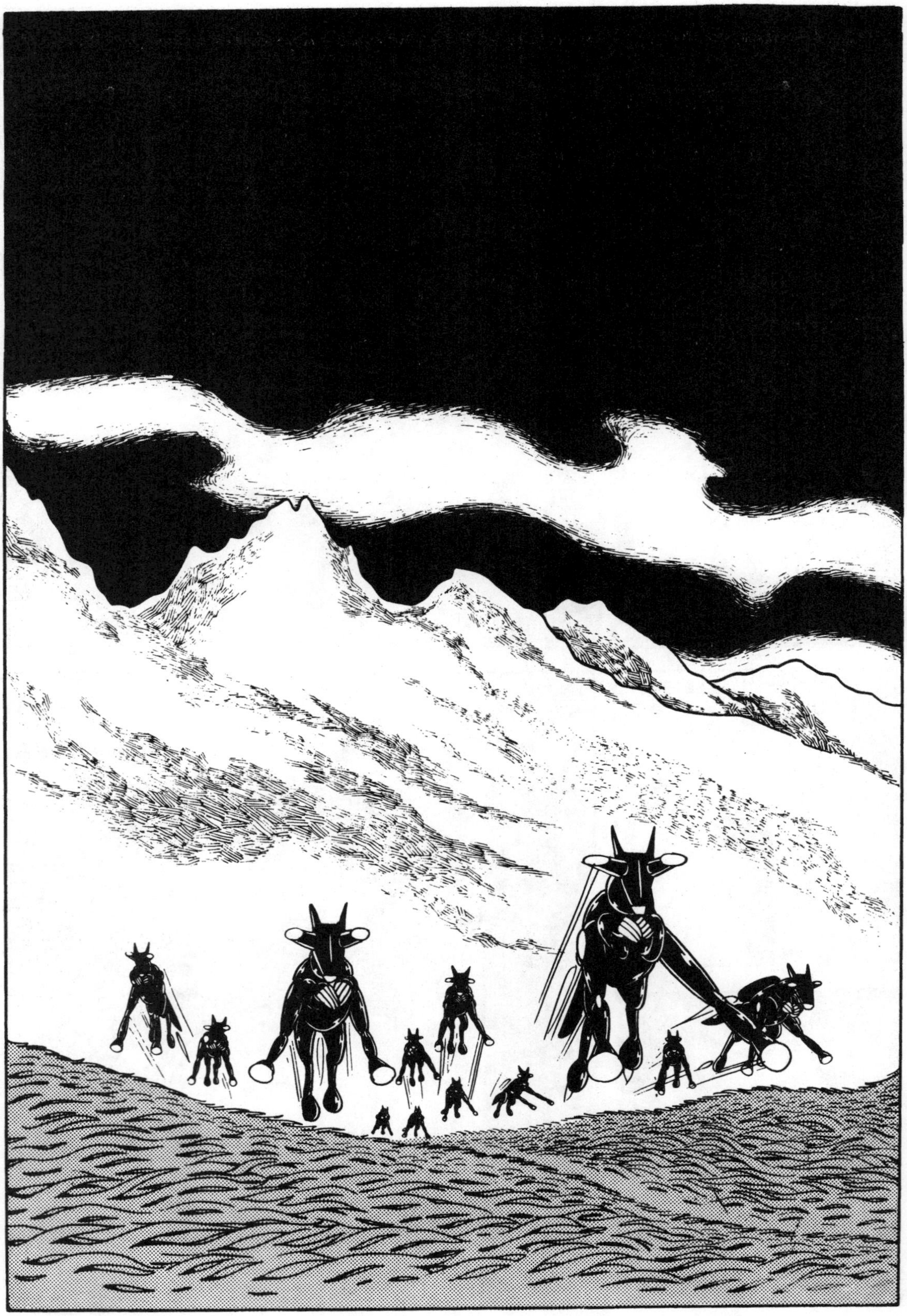

ZIP

ATTENTION WHOEVER RESIDES IN THIS DOME! YOU ARE HARBORING A YOUNG MAN AND WOMAN.

YAMATO CENTRAL COMMAND ORDERS YOU TO HAND THEM OVER. THEY ARE CRIMINAL DEFECTORS.

THERE'S NO ONE HERE LIKE THAT!!

REFUSE AND YOU WILL BE SEARCHED FORCIBLY!

HUMPH!

IMPRESSIVE TALK FOR A MERE RADAR DOG...

71

DR. SARUTA, WHY DID YOU COVER FOR US?

I HEARD ABOUT YOU FROM THE PHOENIX.

PHOENIX? YOU MEAN THAT STRANGE BIRD THAT WE FOLLOWED HERE?

YES! THAT SAME BIRD TOLD ME THAT IT IS YOUR DESTINY TO CARRY OUT AN IMPORTANT MISSION!

WHA?

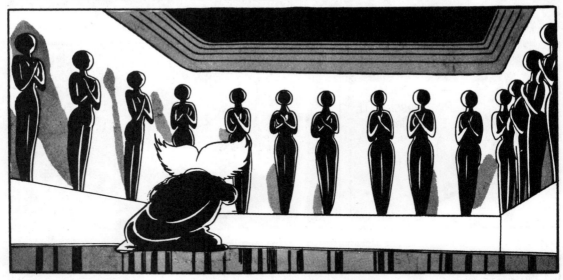

MY DAUGHTERS!!

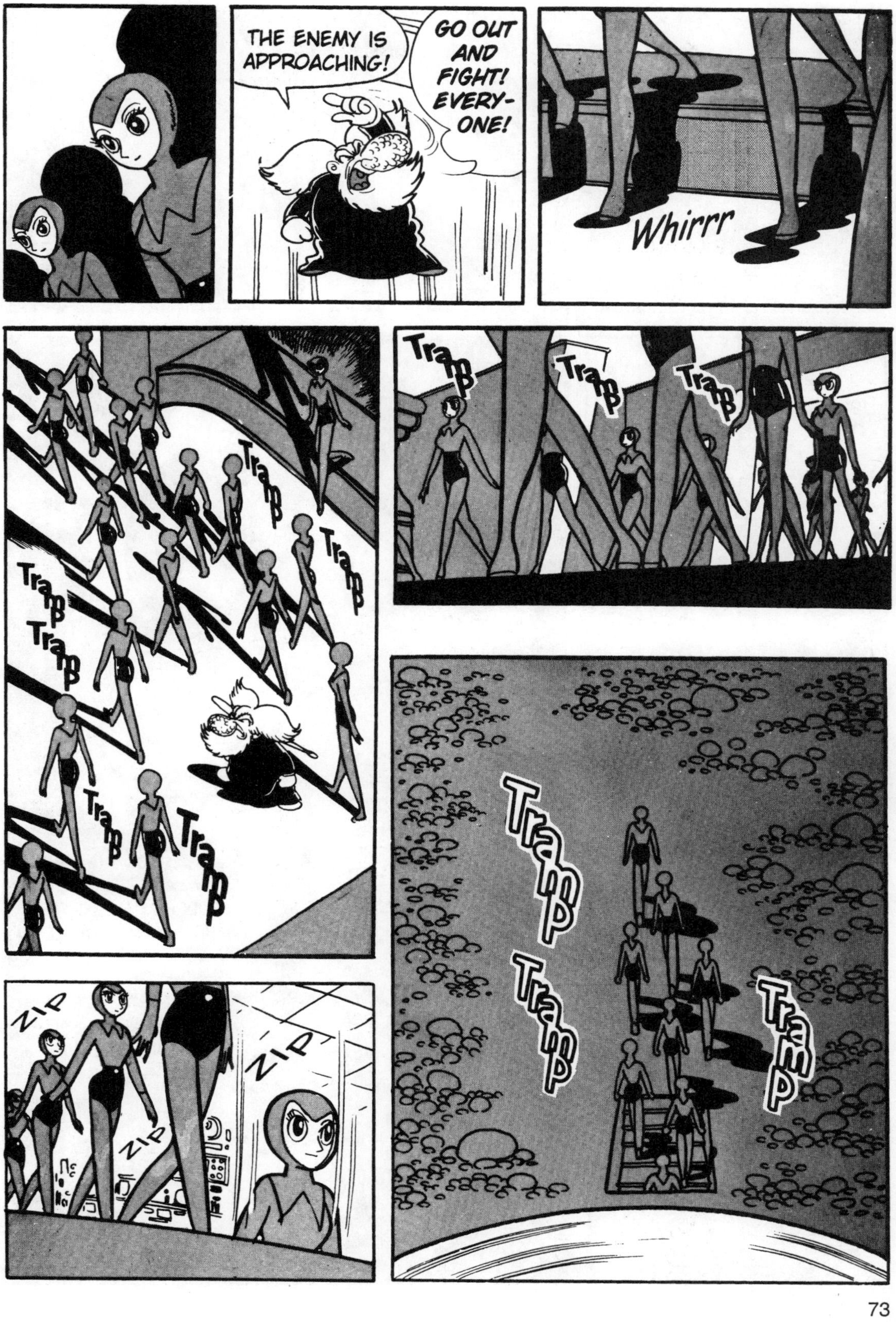
THE ENEMY IS APPROACHING!
GO OUT AND FIGHT! EVERY-ONE!
Whirrr
Tramp
Tramp
Tramp
Tramp
Tramp
Tramp
Tramp
Tramp
Tramp
ZIP
ZIP
ZIP
Tramp
Tramp
Tramp

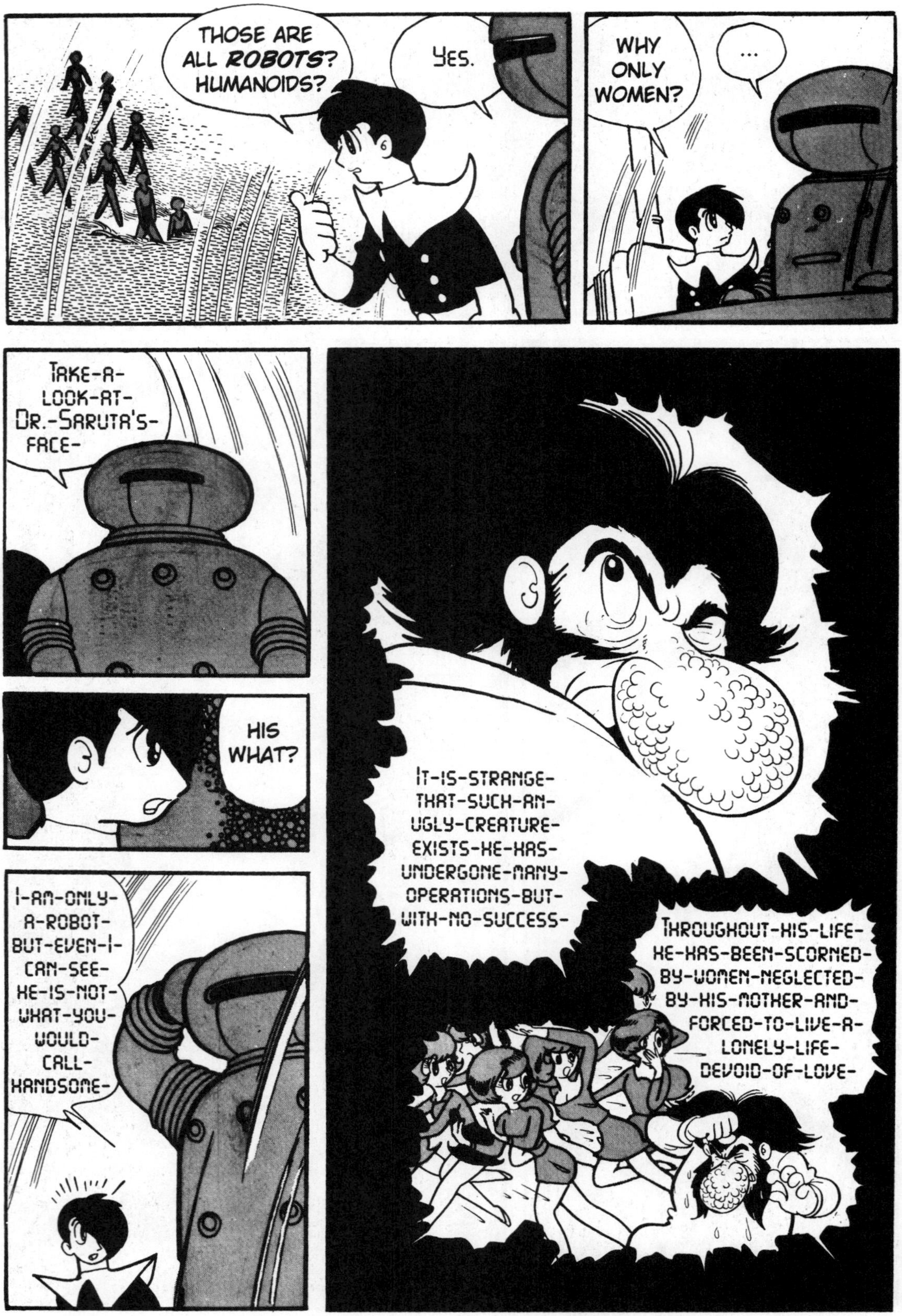
THOSE ARE ALL ROBOTS? HUMANOIDS?
YES.
WHY ONLY WOMEN?
...
TAKE-A-LOOK-AT-DR.-SARUTA'S-FACE-
HIS WHAT?
I-AM-ONLY-A-ROBOT-BUT-EVEN-I-CAN-SEE-HE-IS-NOT-WHAT-YOU-WOULD-CALL-HANDSOME-
IT-IS-STRANGE-THAT-SUCH-AN-UGLY-CREATURE-EXISTS-HE-HAS-UNDERGONE-MANY-OPERATIONS-BUT-WITH-NO-SUCCESS-
THROUGHOUT-HIS-LIFE-HE-HAS-BEEN-SCORNED-BY-WOMEN-NEGLECTED-BY-HIS-MOTHER-AND-FORCED-TO-LIVE-A-LONELY-LIFE-DEVOID-OF-LOVE-

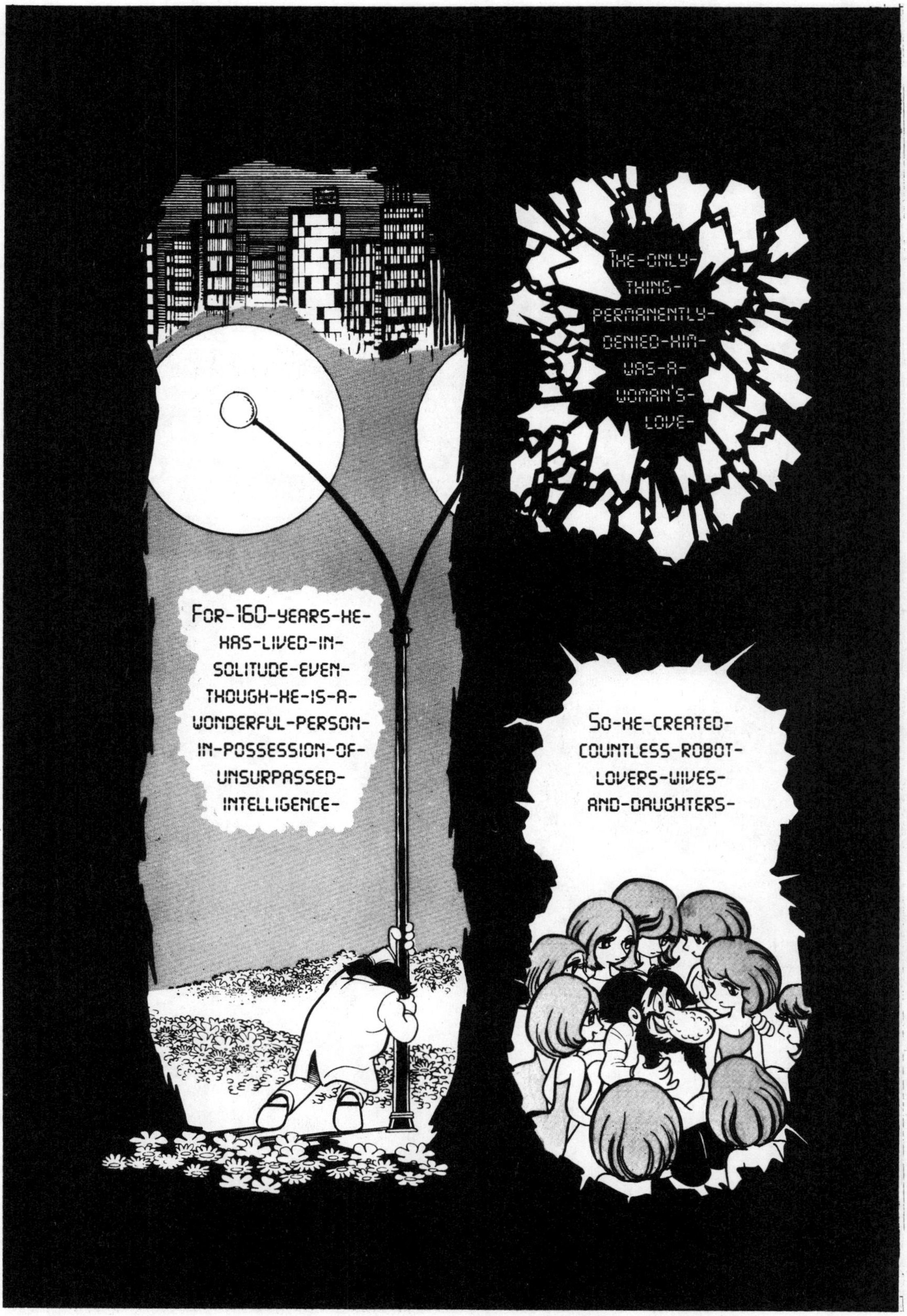
For-160-years-he-has-lived-in-solitude-even-though-he-is-a-wonderful-person-in-possession-of-unsurpassed-intelligence-
The-only-thing-permanently-denied-him-was-a-woman's-love-
So-he-created-countless-robot-lovers-wives-and-daughters-

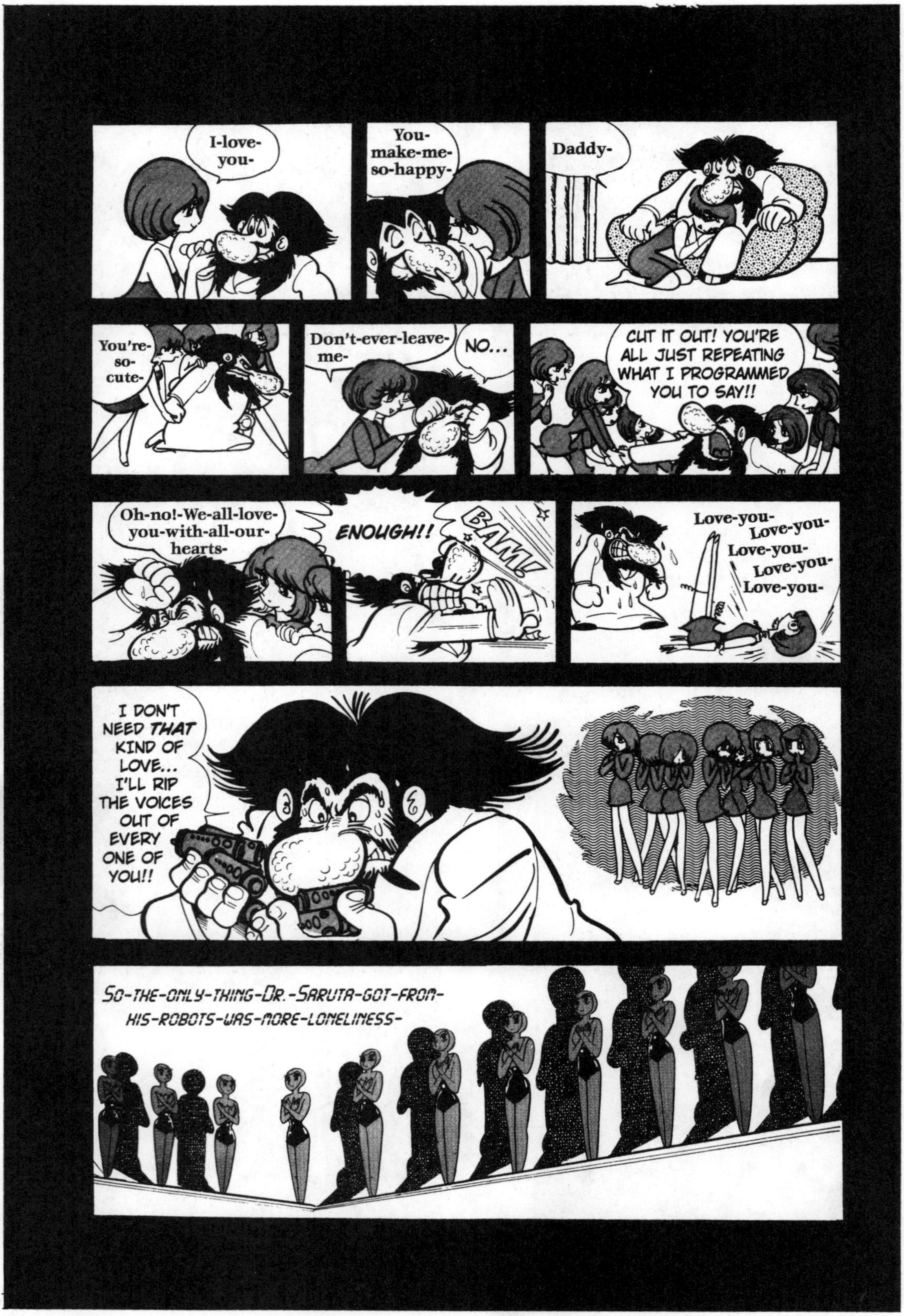
I-love-you-
You-make-me-so-happy-
Daddy-
You're-so-cute-
Don't-ever-leave-me-
NO...
CUT IT OUT! YOU'RE ALL JUST REPEATING WHAT I PROGRAMMED YOU TO SAY!!
Oh-no!-We-all-love-you-with-all-our-hearts-
ENOUGH!!
BAM!
Love-you-
Love-you-
Love-you-
Love-you-
Love-you-
I DON'T NEED THAT KIND OF LOVE... I'LL RIP THE VOICES OUT OF EVERY ONE OF YOU!!
So-the-only-thing-Dr.-Saruta-got-from-his-robots-was-more-loneliness-

THOSE-VOICELESS-REDESIGNED-ROBOT-WOMEN-HAVE-BEEN-IN-STORAGE-FOR-YEARS-WAITING-TO-SERVE-HIM-

AND-NOW-THEY-HAVE-GONE-TO-DO-BATTLE-ALL-FOR-DR.-SARUTA-

BUT DON'T THEY HATE THE DOCTOR?

HATE-HIM?-WHY?-THEY-LOVE-HIM-

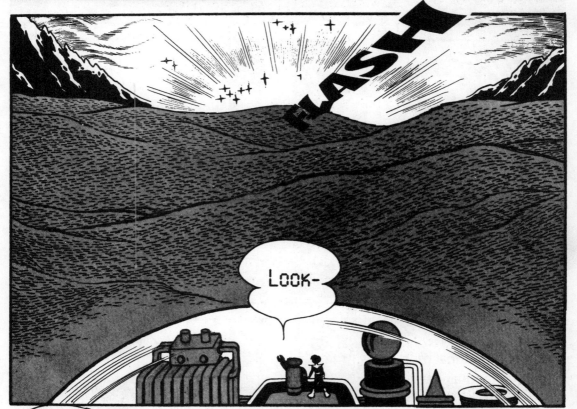

FLASH

LOOK-

WHAT'S THAT LIGHT?

THEY-HAVE-ENGAGED-THE-ENEMY-AND-SELF-DESTRUCTED-

LOOK-AGAIN-

FLASH

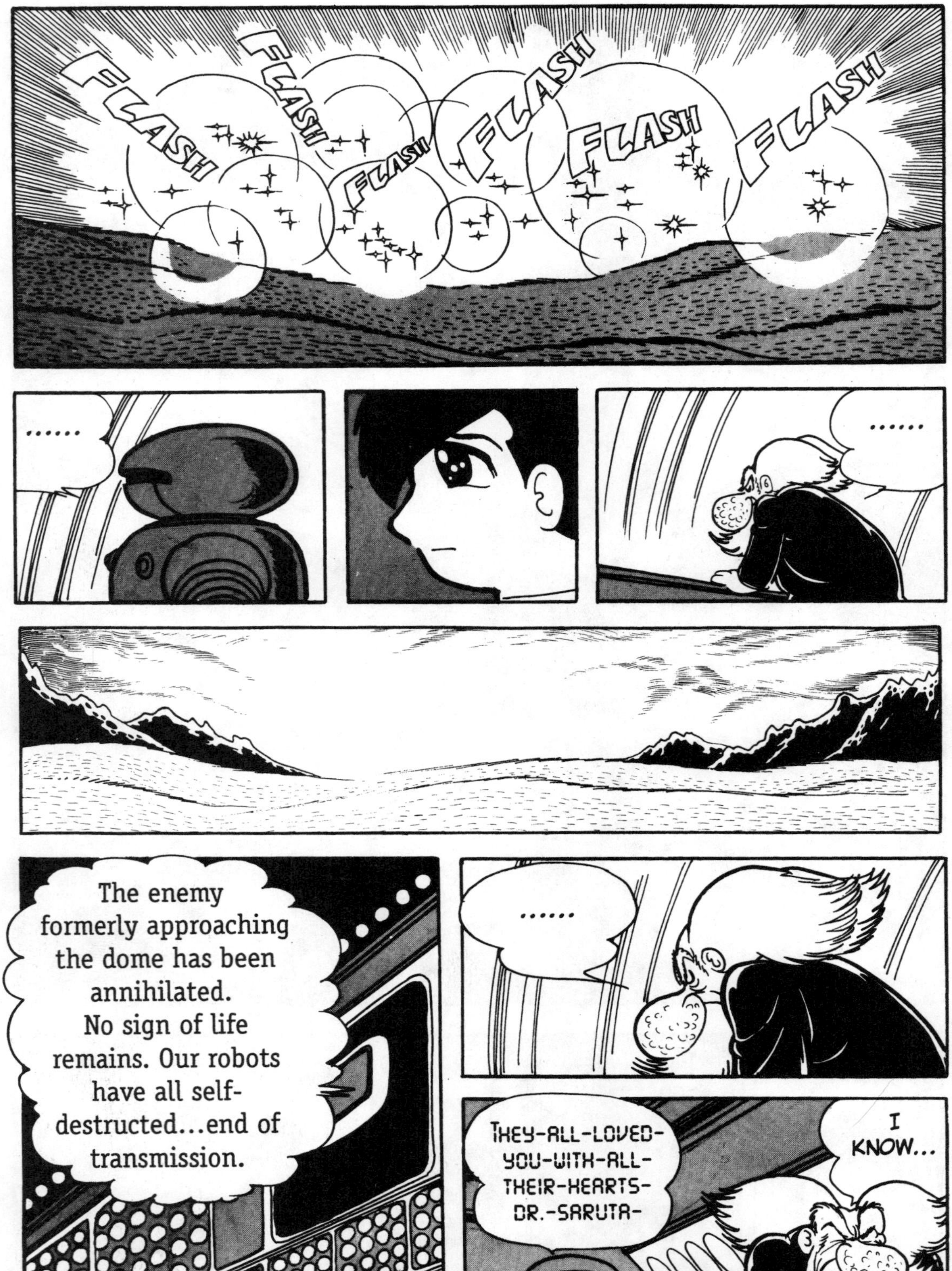
FLASH
FLASH
FLASH
FLASH
FLASH
FLASH
......
......
The enemy formerly approaching the dome has been annihilated. No sign of life remains. Our robots have all self-destructed...end of transmission.
......
THEY-ALL-LOVED-YOU-WITH-ALL-THEIR-HEARTS-DR.-SARUTA-
I KNOW...

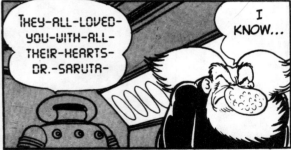

YOUR PURSUERS HAVE ALL BEEN DESTROYED. IT SEEMS YOU CAN RELAX NOW, YAMANOBE.

YES, I KNOW.

DOCTOR!

I'LL STAY HERE AFTER ALL.

THAT'S THE RIGHT DECISION FOR BOTH YOU AND THE MOOPIE!

IN RETURN, I ASK THAT YOU TELL ME... WHAT IS THIS MISSION I AM TO FULFILL?

I'LL TELL YOU SOON ENOUGH. FIRST GIVE ME TIME TO THINK.

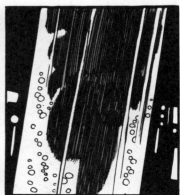

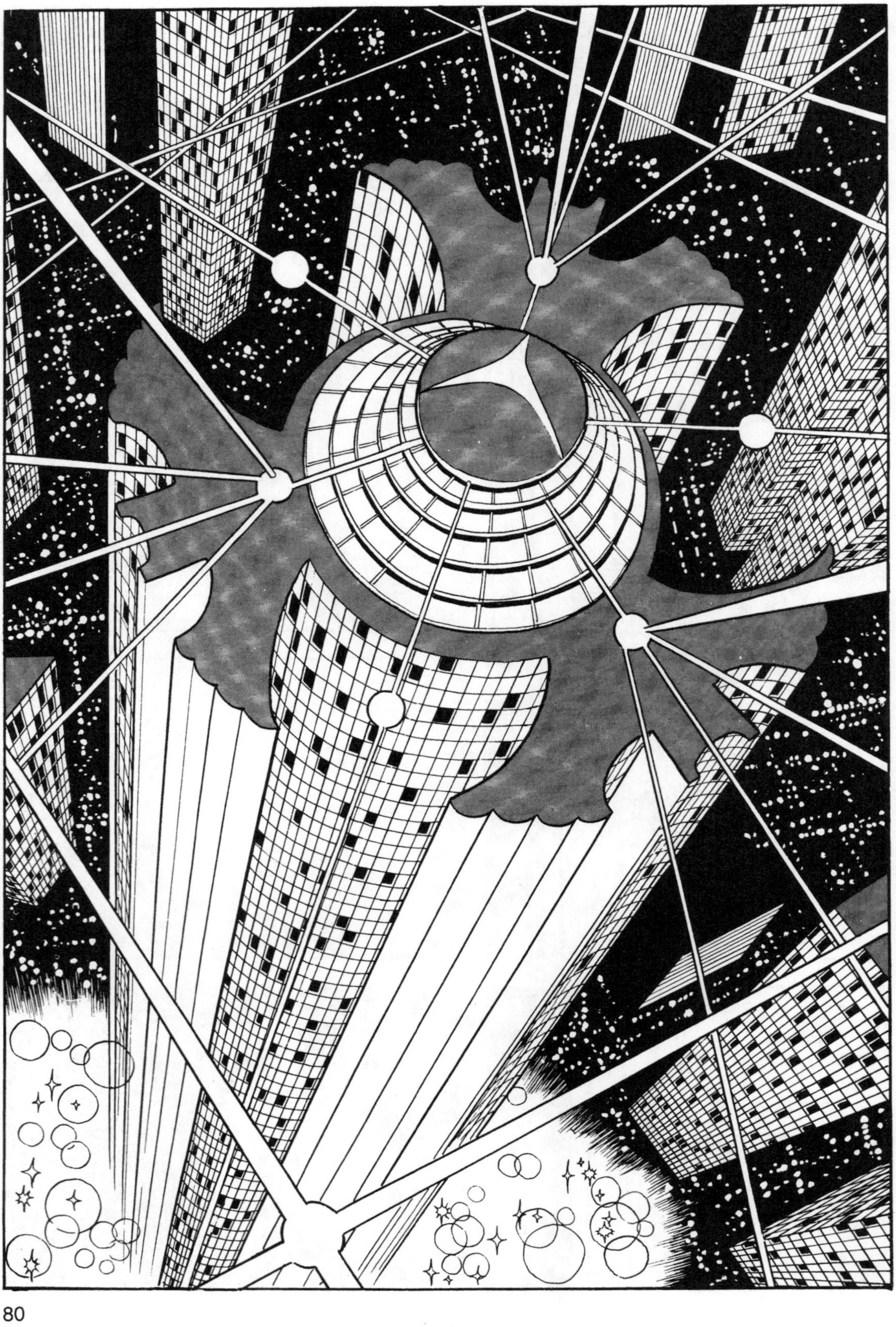

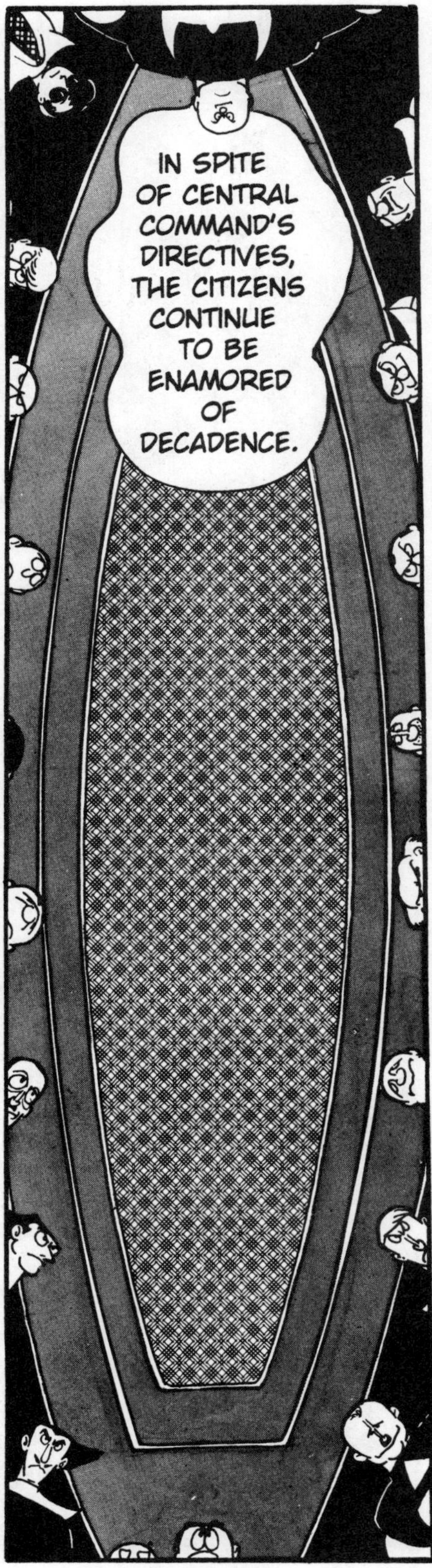
IN SPITE OF CENTRAL COMMAND'S DIRECTIVES, THE CITIZENS CONTINUE TO BE ENAMORED OF DECADENCE.

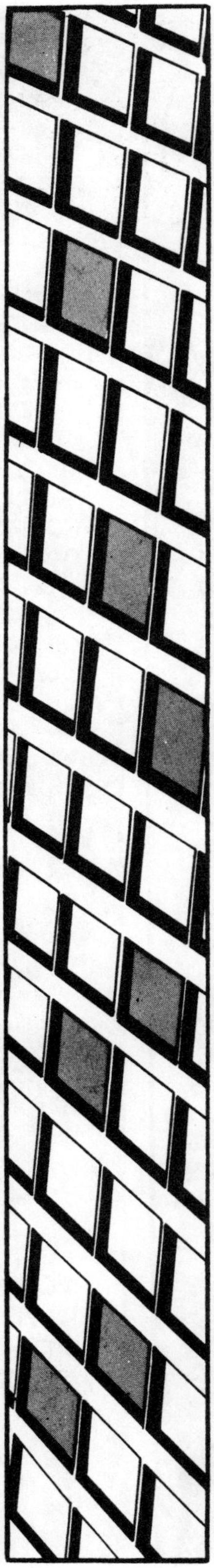

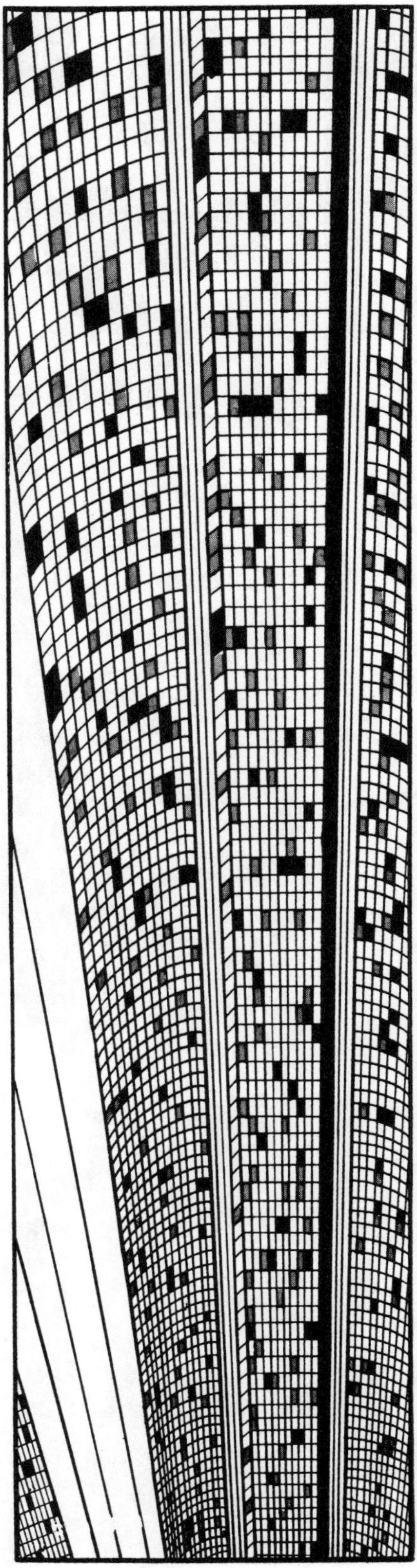

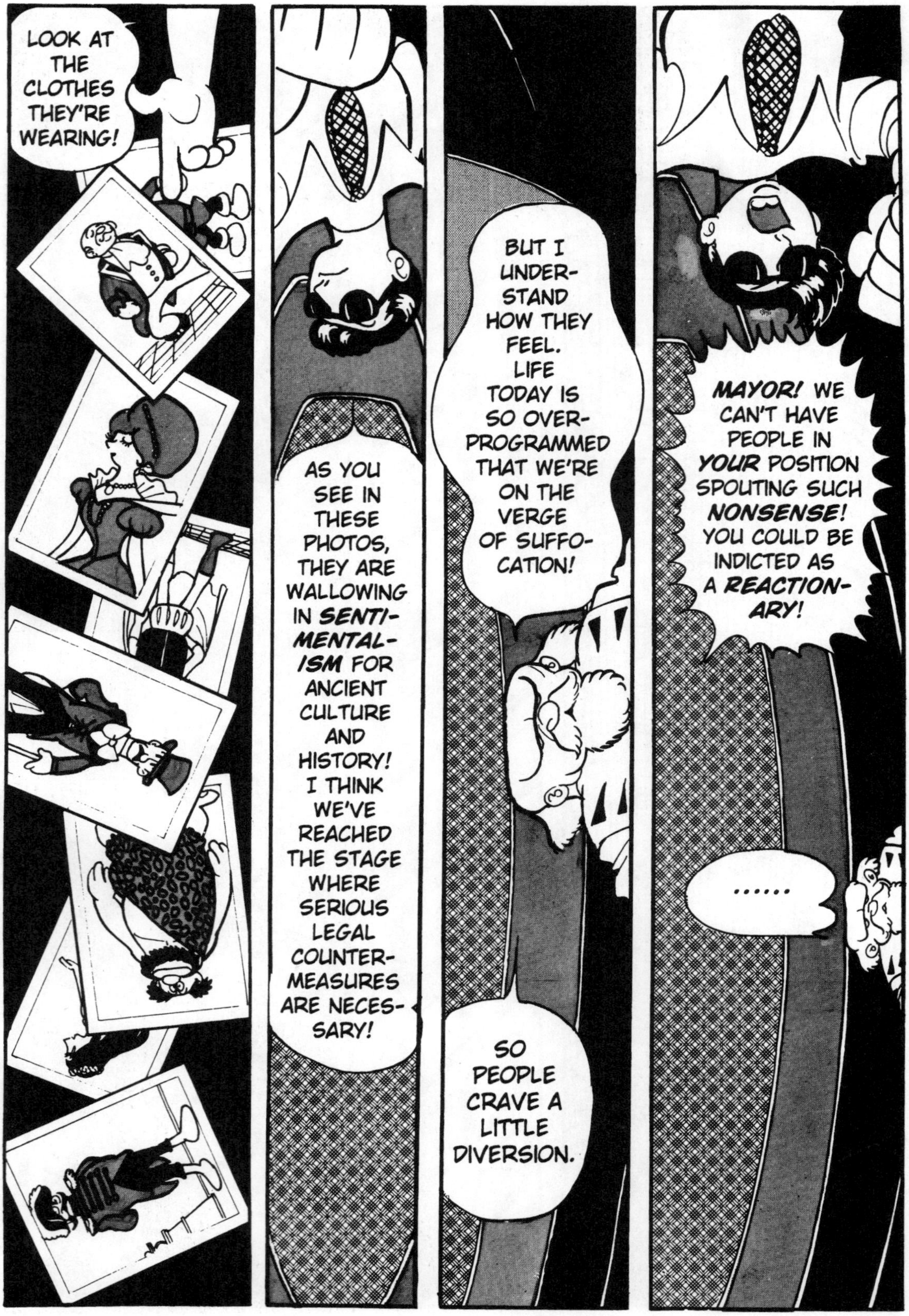
LOOK AT THE CLOTHES THEY'RE WEARING!
AS YOU SEE IN THESE PHOTOS, THEY ARE WALLOWING IN SENTIMENTALISM FOR ANCIENT CULTURE AND HISTORY! I THINK WE'VE REACHED THE STAGE WHERE SERIOUS LEGAL COUNTERMEASURES ARE NECESSARY!
BUT I UNDERSTAND HOW THEY FEEL. LIFE TODAY IS SO OVERPROGRAMMED THAT WE'RE ON THE VERGE OF SUFFOCATION!
SO PEOPLE CRAVE A LITTLE DIVERSION.
MAYOR! WE CAN'T HAVE PEOPLE IN YOUR POSITION SPOUTING SUCH NONSENSE! YOU COULD BE INDICTED AS A REACTIONARY!
......

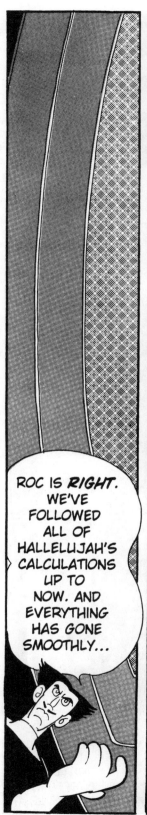

ROC IS *RIGHT*. WE'VE FOLLOWED ALL OF HALLELUJAH'S CALCULATIONS UP TO NOW. AND EVERYTHING HAS GONE SMOOTHLY...

AT A TIME LIKE THIS, WHEN MANKIND IS FACED WITH A *CRISIS*, WE WOULD BE BETTER OFF FOLLOWING HALLELUJAH'S CALCULATIONS RATHER THAN SOME SENTIMENTAL HUMAN POLITICIAN... WOULDN'T WE, MR. MAYOR?

YES BUT...

THAT'S WHY WE CAN'T ALLOW ANY ACTIONS WHICH ARE INDEPENDENT OF HALLELU-JAH'S DICTATES! NOT EVEN THE STYLE OF DRESS!

BUT WHAT, FOR INSTANCE, IF I ONLY WANTED TO EAT SOME *OATMEAL* FOR BREAKFAST?

IS THAT IN THE DIRECTIVES FROM HALLE-LUJAH?

NO.

IF NOT, THEN EVEN OATMEAL IS OUT. IT'S *SYN-THETIC BREAD* FOR EVERY-ONE!

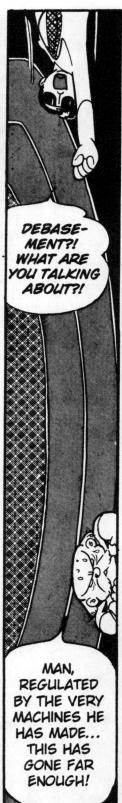

MAYOR, LET'S FOLLOW HALLELUJAH'S COMMANDS AND PASS THE *DRESS CONTROL LAW!!*

......

I SAY NO. IT WOULD BE A DEBASEMENT OF BASIC HUMAN RIGHTS!

DEBASE-MENT?! WHAT ARE YOU TALKING ABOUT?!

MAN, REGULATED BY THE VERY MACHINES HE HAS MADE... THIS HAS GONE FAR ENOUGH!

MR. CHAIRMAN! I MAKE A NO CONFIDENCE MOTION IN REGARDS TO THE MAYOR. HE IS NO LONGER QUALIFIED FOR THIS POST!!

RELAX, RELAX.

MAYOR! YOU ARE OF COURSE AWARE THOSE WHO DEFY HALLELUJAH FORFEIT THEIR CITIZENSHIP!

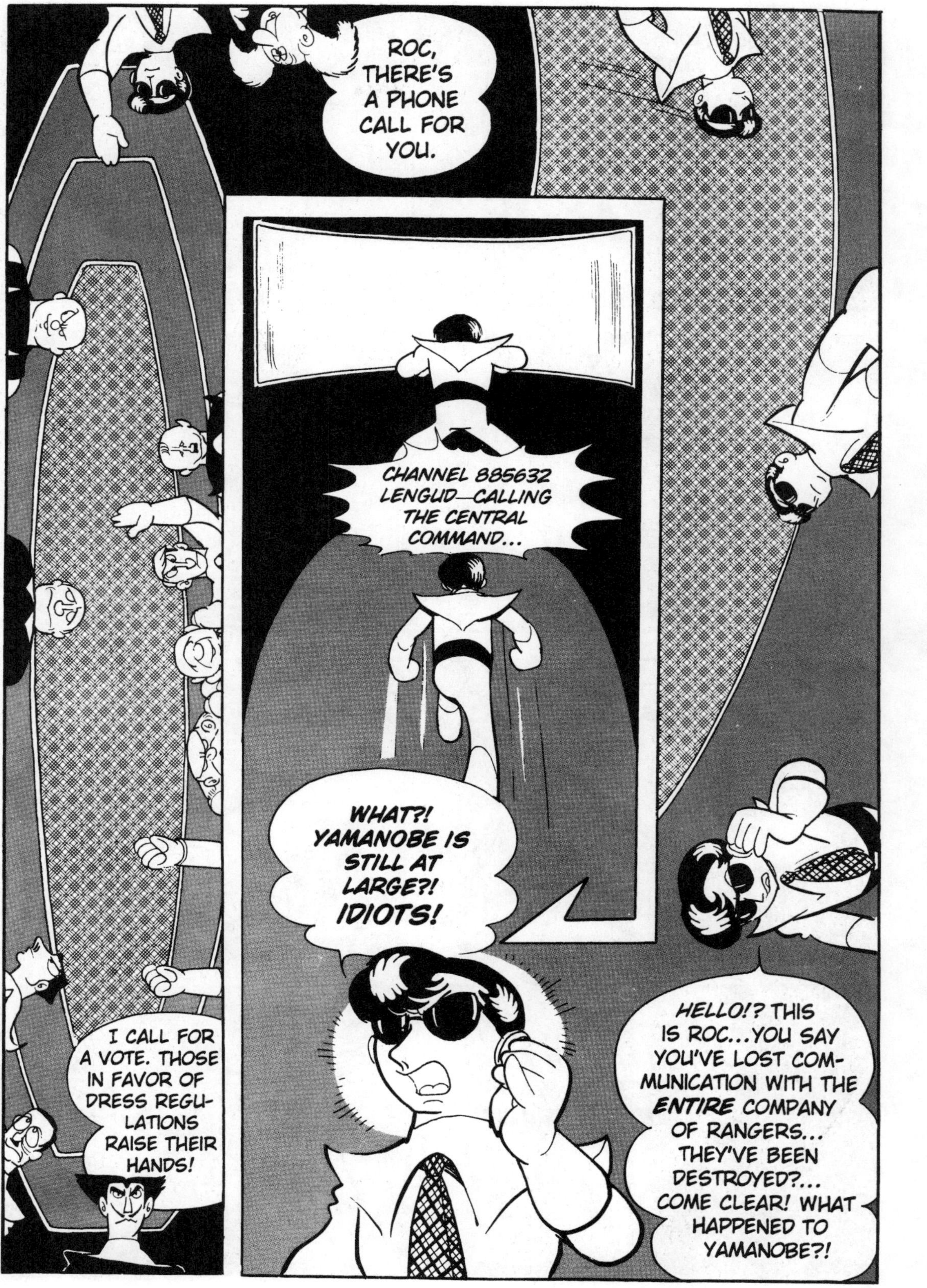
ROC, THERE'S A PHONE CALL FOR YOU.
CHANNEL 885632 LENGUD—CALLING THE CENTRAL COMMAND...
HELLO!? THIS IS ROC...YOU SAY YOU'VE LOST COM-MUNICATION WITH THE ENTIRE COMPANY OF RANGERS... THEY'VE BEEN DESTROYED?... COME CLEAR! WHAT HAPPENED TO YAMANOBE?!
WHAT?! YAMANOBE IS STILL AT LARGE?! IDIOTS!
I CALL FOR A VOTE. THOSE IN FAVOR OF DRESS REGU-LATIONS RAISE THEIR HANDS!

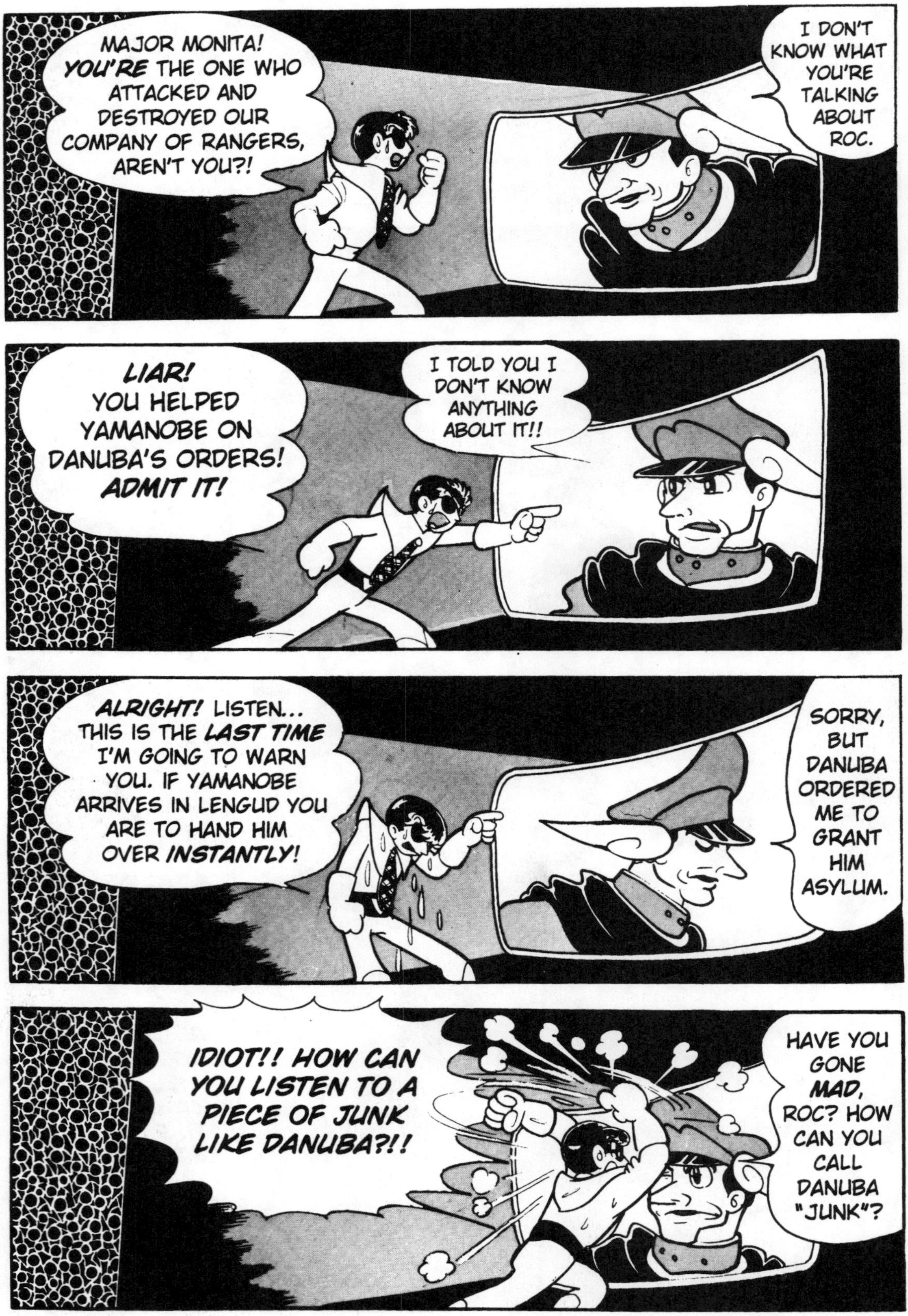
MAJOR MONITA! YOU'RE THE ONE WHO ATTACKED AND DESTROYED OUR COMPANY OF RANGERS, AREN'T YOU?!
I DON'T KNOW WHAT YOU'RE TALKING ABOUT ROC.
LIAR! YOU HELPED YAMANOBE ON DANUBA'S ORDERS! ADMIT IT!
I TOLD YOU I DON'T KNOW ANYTHING ABOUT IT!!
ALRIGHT! LISTEN... THIS IS THE LAST TIME I'M GOING TO WARN YOU. IF YAMANOBE ARRIVES IN LENGUD YOU ARE TO HAND HIM OVER INSTANTLY!
SORRY, BUT DANUBA ORDERED ME TO GRANT HIM ASYLUM.
IDIOT!! HOW CAN YOU LISTEN TO A PIECE OF JUNK LIKE DANUBA?!!
HAVE YOU GONE MAD, ROC? HOW CAN YOU CALL DANUBA "JUNK"?

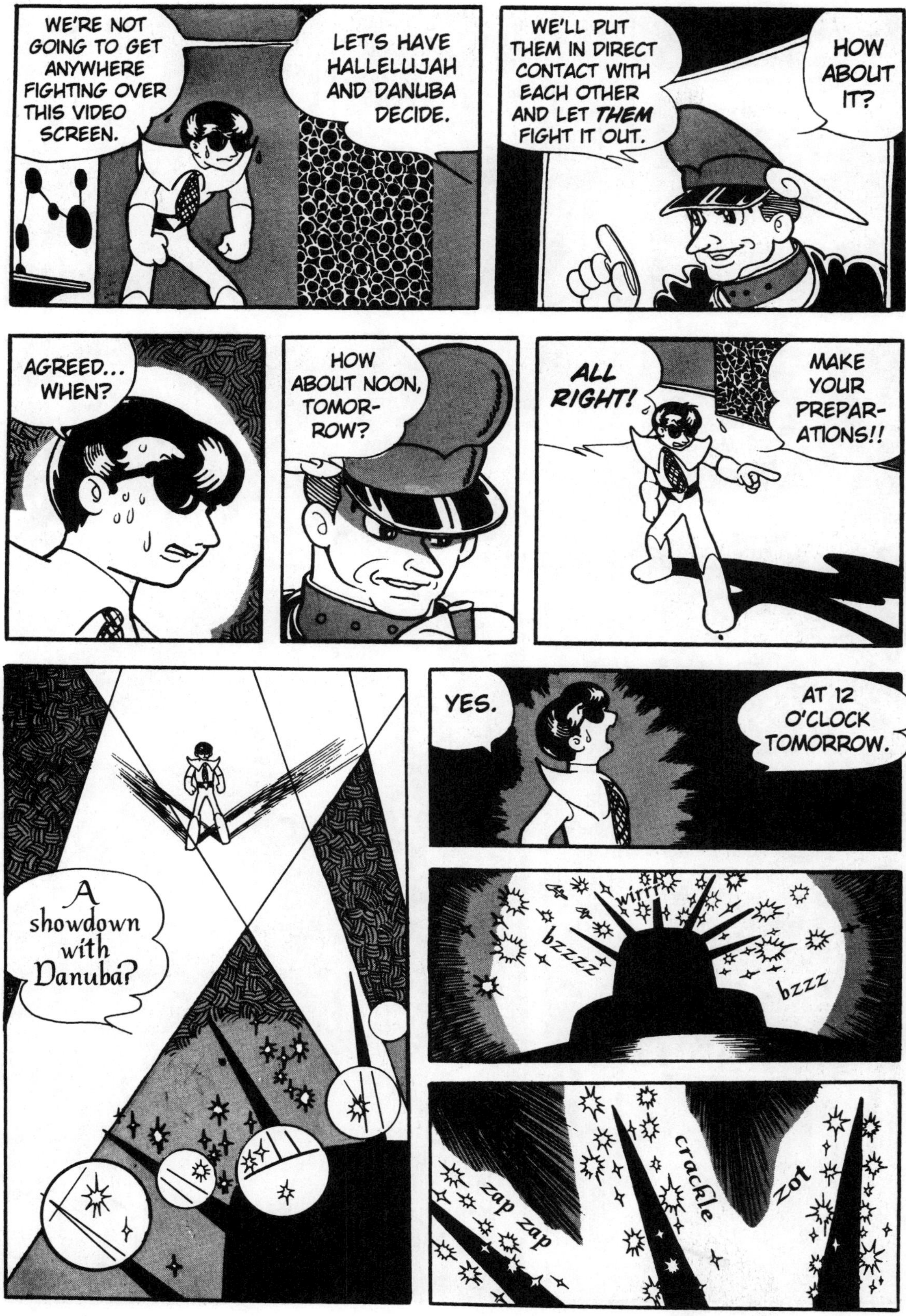
WE'RE NOT GOING TO GET ANYWHERE FIGHTING OVER THIS VIDEO SCREEN.
LET'S HAVE HALLELUJAH AND DANUBA DECIDE.
WE'LL PUT THEM IN DIRECT CONTACT WITH EACH OTHER AND LET *THEM* FIGHT IT OUT.
HOW ABOUT IT?
AGREED... WHEN?
HOW ABOUT NOON, TOMOR-ROW?
ALL RIGHT!
MAKE YOUR PREPAR-ATIONS!!
YES.
AT 12 O'CLOCK TOMORROW.
A showdown with Danuba?
wirrr
bzzzz
bzzz
zap zap
crackle
zot

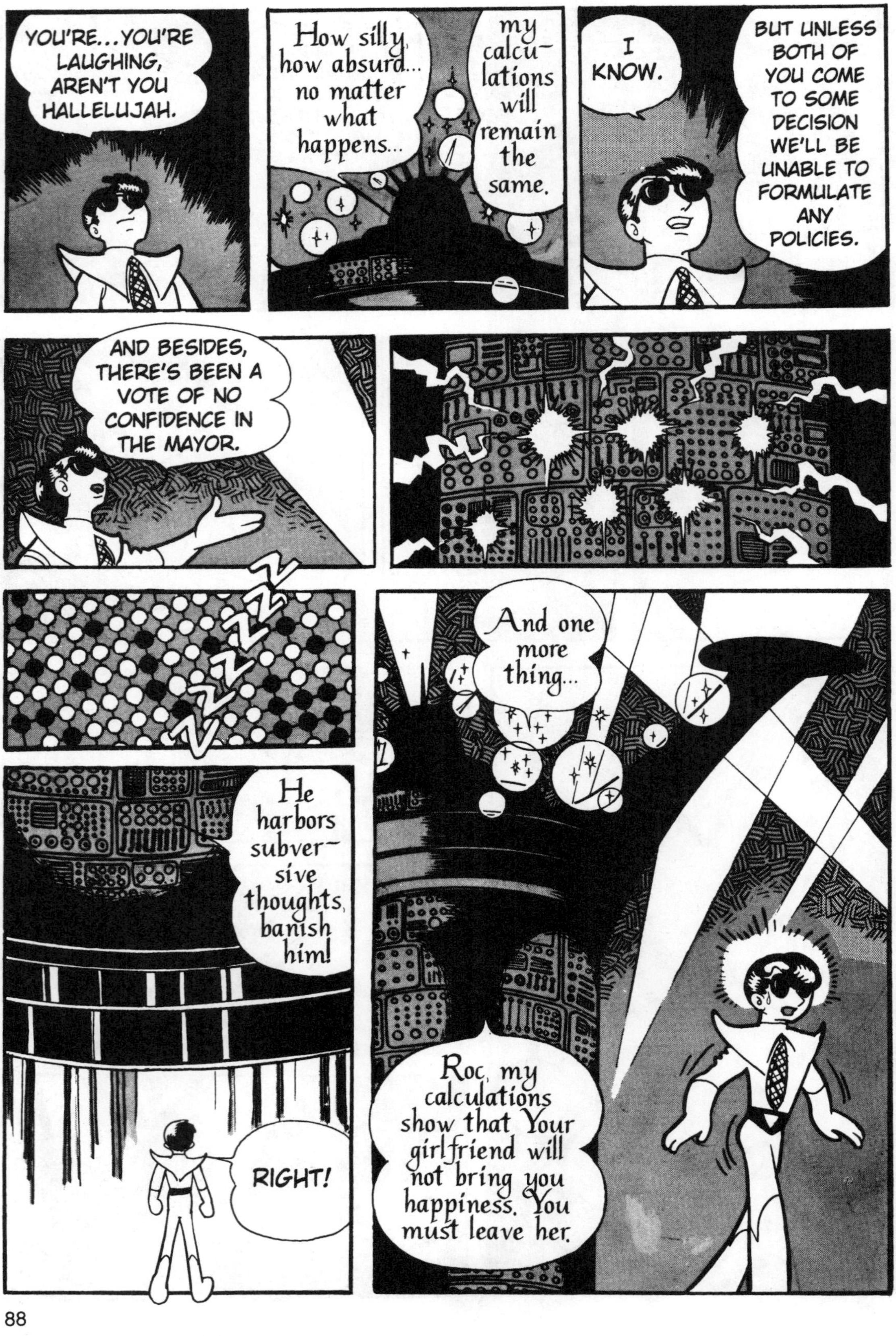
YOU'RE...YOU'RE LAUGHING, AREN'T YOU HALLELUJAH.
How silly, how absurd... no matter what happens...
my calcu-lations will remain the same.
I KNOW.
BUT UNLESS BOTH OF YOU COME TO SOME DECISION WE'LL BE UNABLE TO FORMULATE ANY POLICIES.
AND BESIDES, THERE'S BEEN A VOTE OF NO CONFIDENCE IN THE MAYOR.
ZZZZZZZ
He harbors subver-sive thoughts, banish him!
RIGHT!
And one more thing...
Roc, my calculations show that Your girlfriend will not bring you happiness. You must leave her.

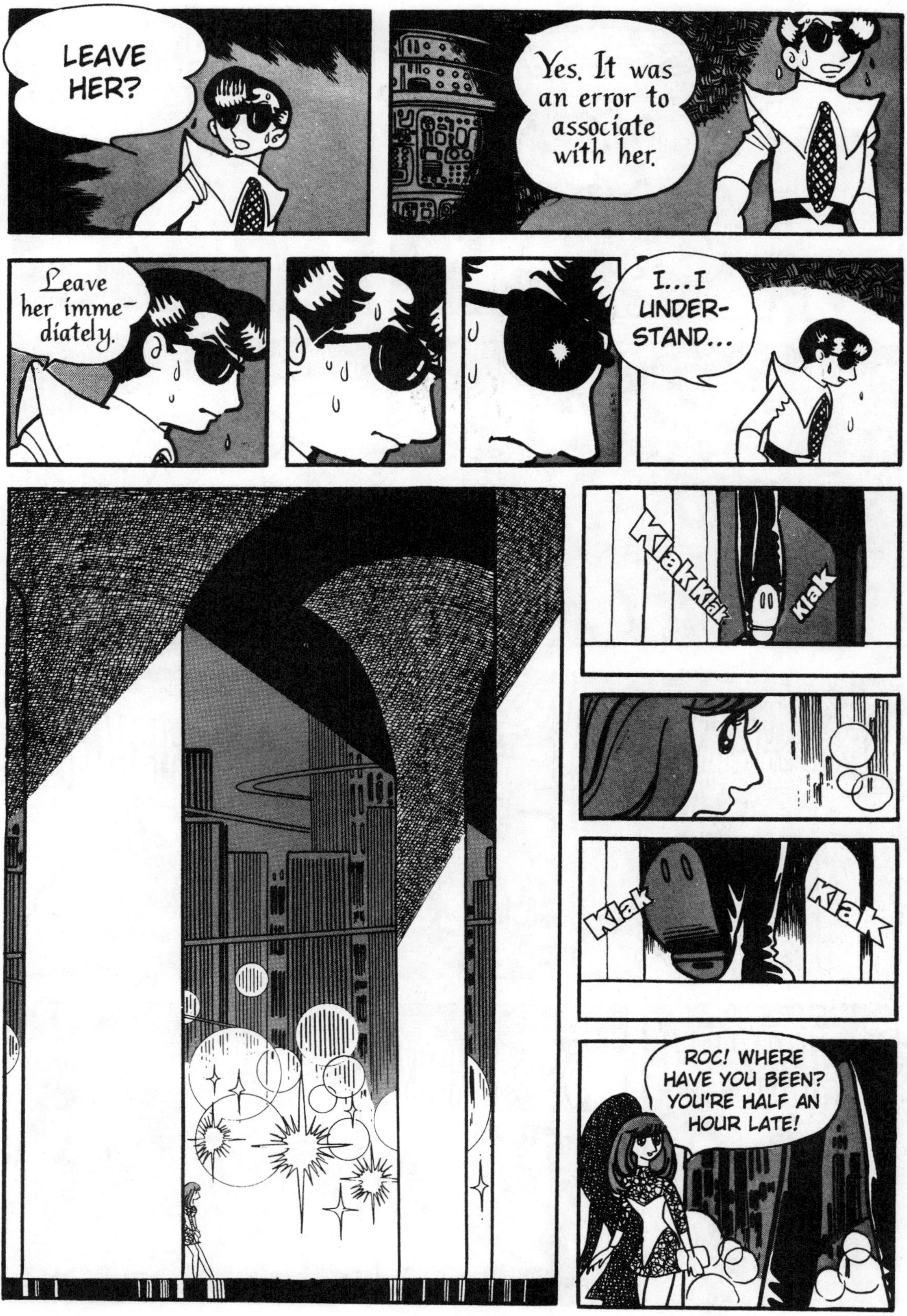
LEAVE HER?
Yes. It was an error to associate with her.
Leave her immediately.
I...I UNDERSTAND...
Klak Klak
Klak
Klak
Klak
ROC! WHERE HAVE YOU BEEN? YOU'RE HALF AN HOUR LATE!

SSSSSHHHHHHH
SSSSSHHHHHHH
VROOOOM
NO!!
SSSSHHHHHHH
SSSSHHHH
N-NO!
SSSSSHHHHHHH
SSSSSHHHHHHH
SSSSHHHH
SSSHHHHH

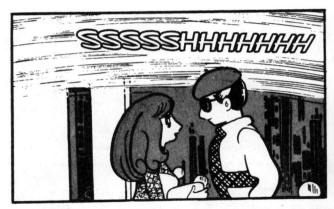

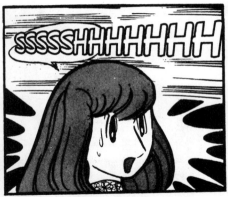

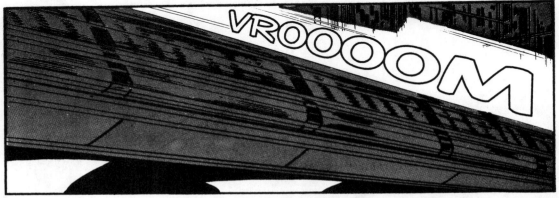

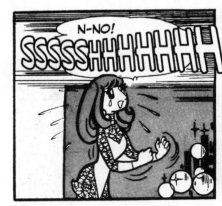

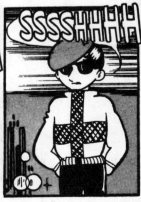

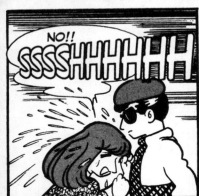

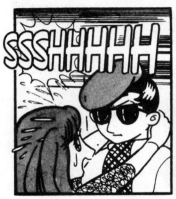

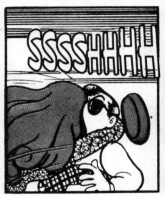

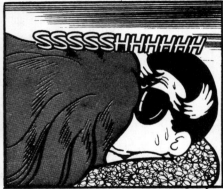

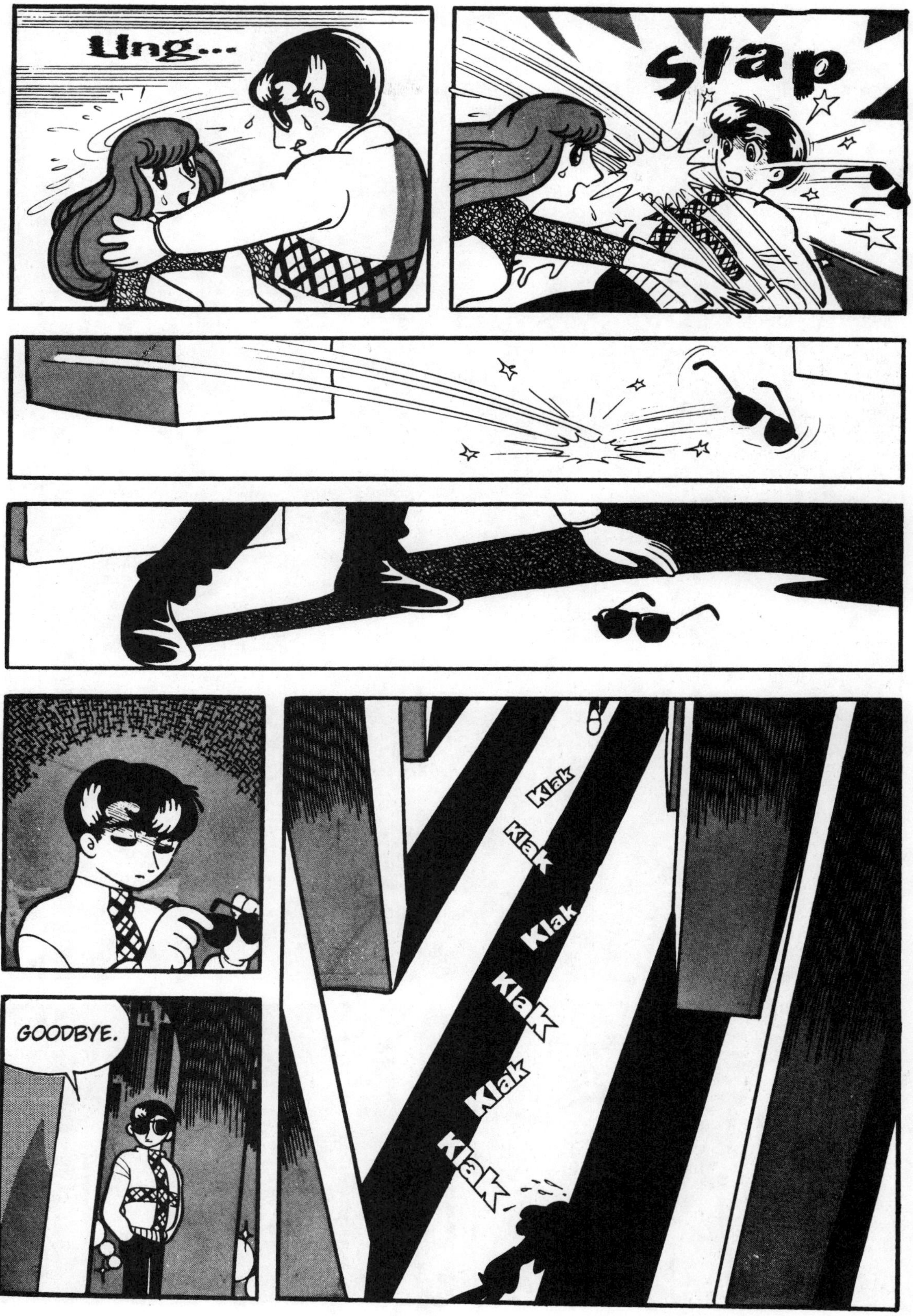
Ung...
Slap
GOODBYE.
Klak
Klak
Klak
Klak
Klak
Klak

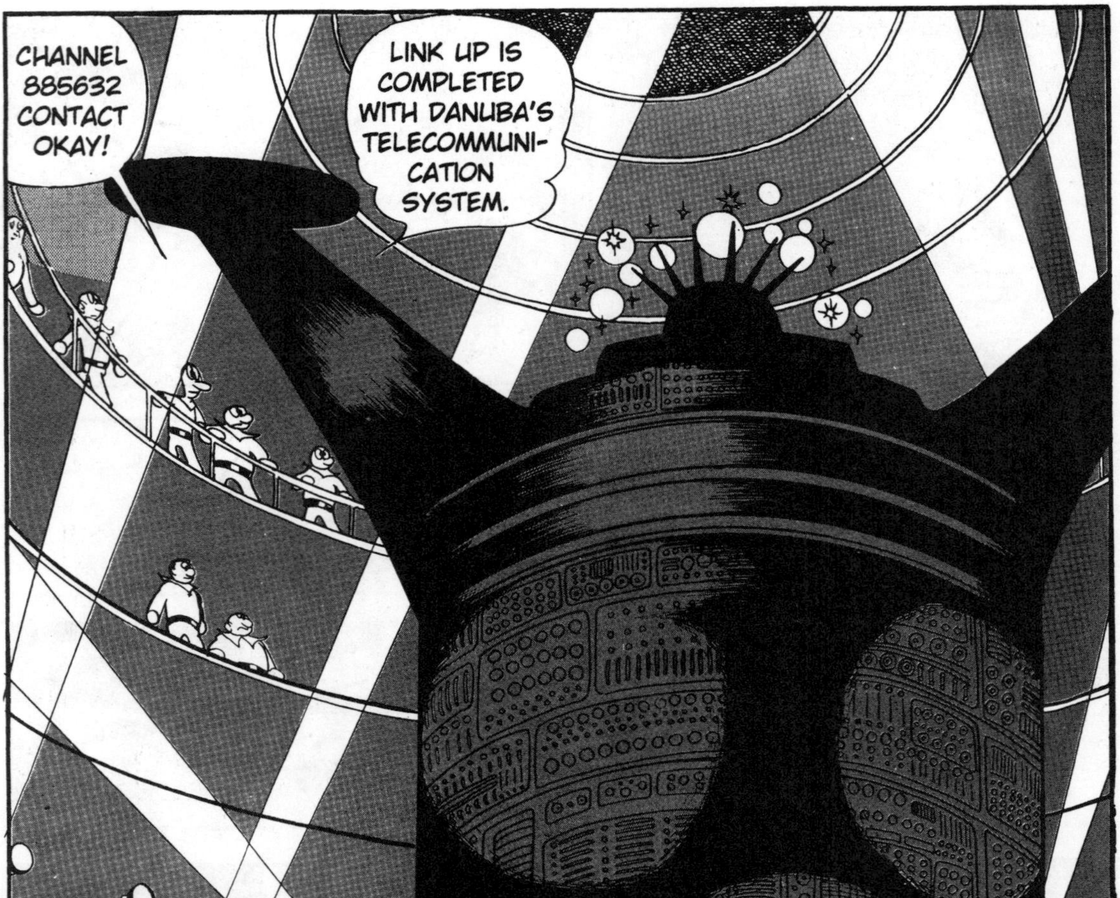
CHANNEL 885632 CONTACT OKAY!
LINK UP IS COMPLETED WITH DANUBA'S TELECOMMUNI-CATION SYSTEM.
WHAT TIME IS IT?
IT'LL BE TWELVE O'CLOCK IN FIVE MINUTES.
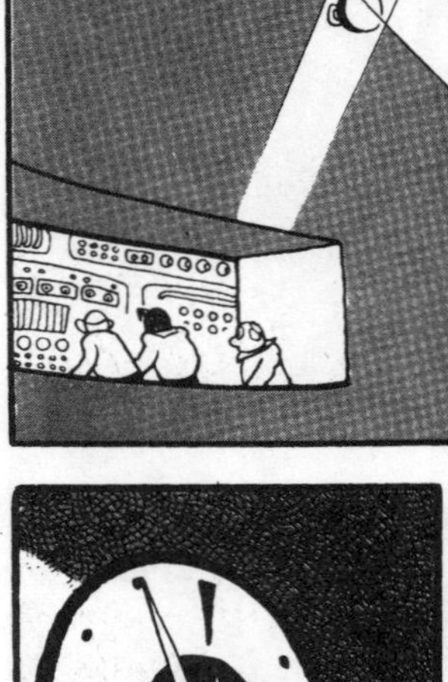
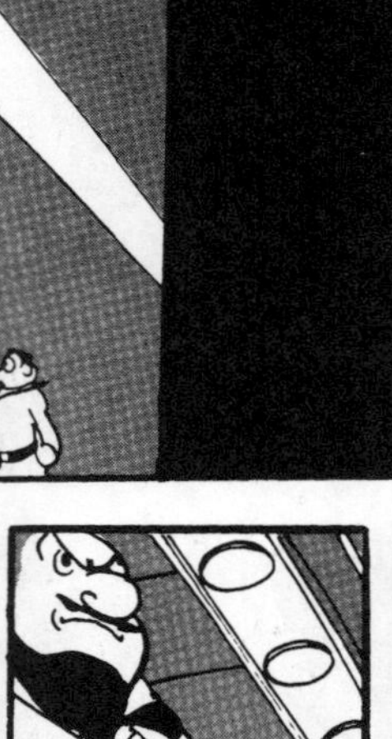
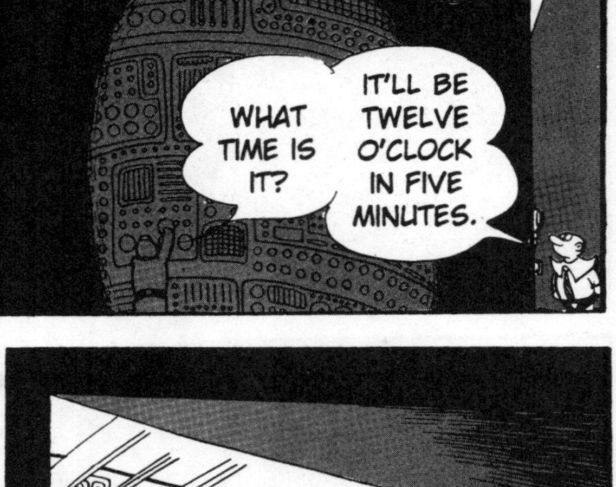

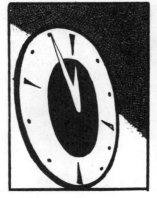

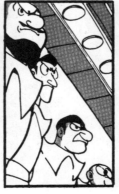

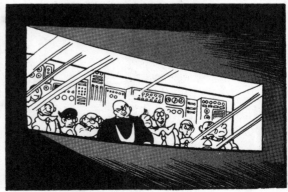

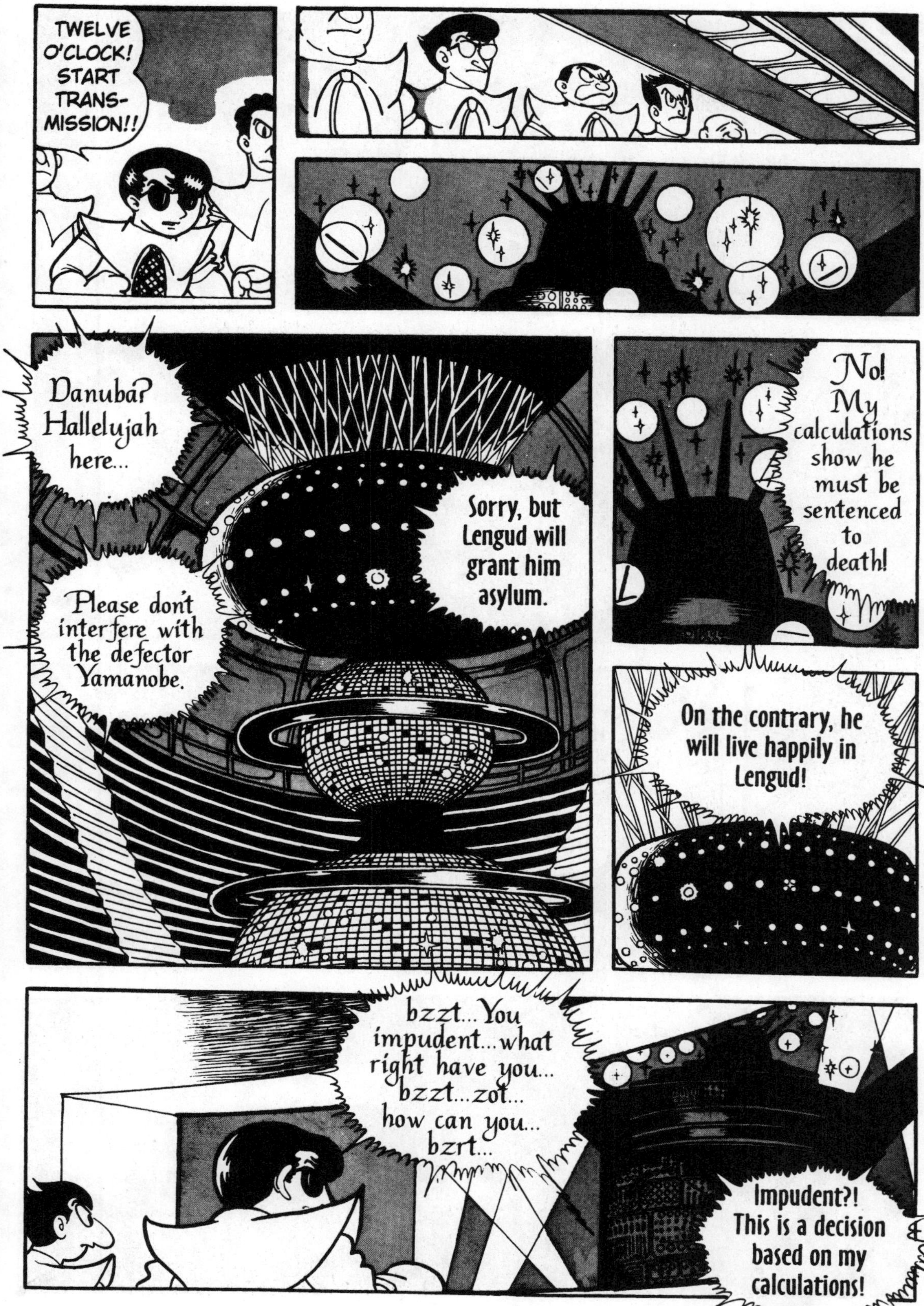
TWELVE O'CLOCK! START TRANS-MISSION!!
Danuba? Hallelujah here...
Please don't interfere with the defector Yamanobe.
Sorry, but Lengud will grant him asylum.
No! My calculations show he must be sentenced to death!
On the contrary, he will live happily in Lengud!
bzzt... You impudent...what right have you... bzzt...zot... how can you... bzrt...
Impudent?! This is a decision based on my calculations!

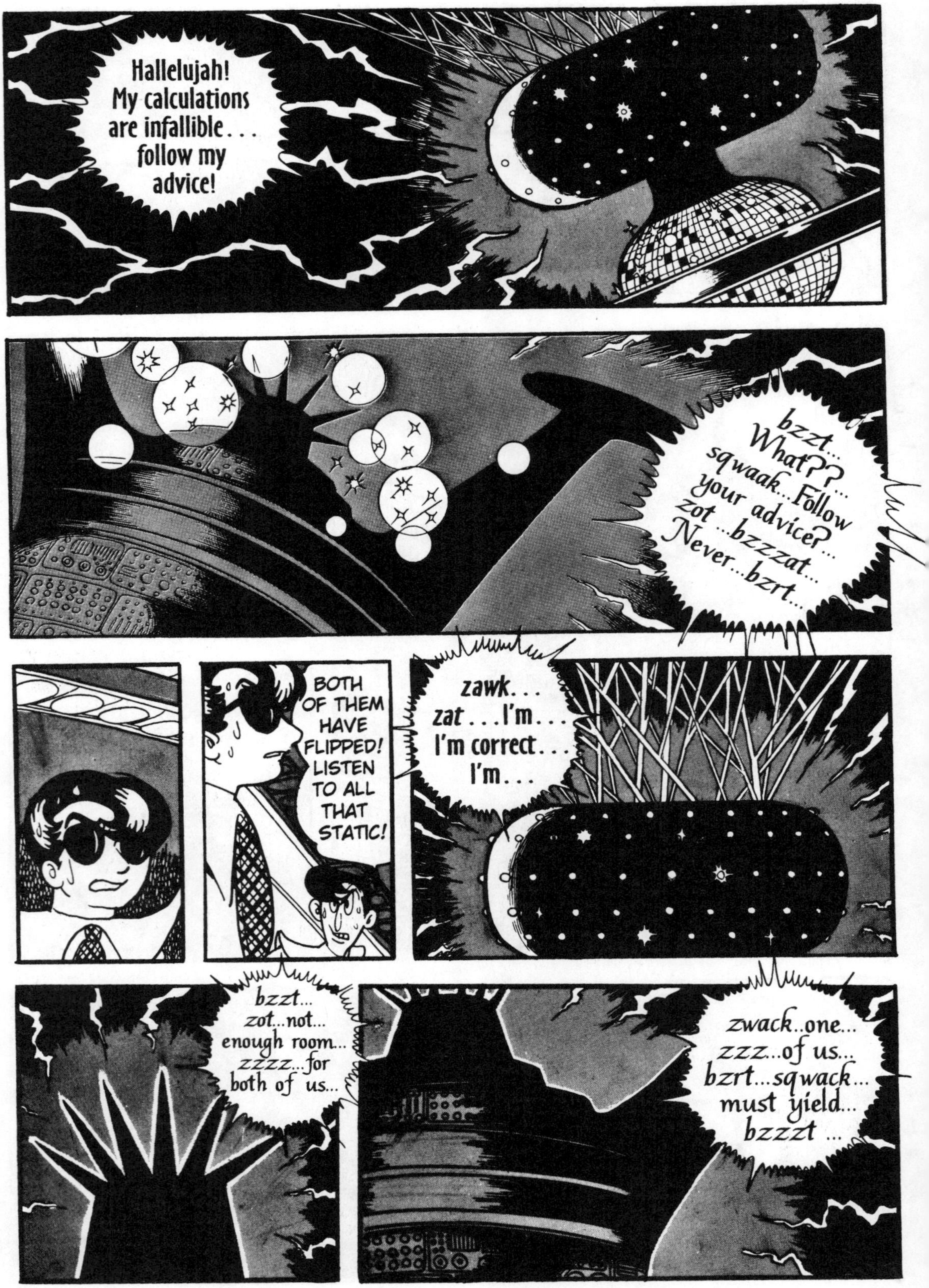
Hallelujah! My calculations are infallible... follow my advice!
bzzt... What??... sqwaak...Follow your advice?... zot...bzzzat... Never...bzrt...
BOTH OF THEM HAVE FLIPPED! LISTEN TO ALL THAT STATIC!
zawk... zat...I'm... I'm correct... I'm...
bzzt... zot...not... enough room... zzzz...for both of us...
zwack..one... zzz...of us... bzrt...sqwack... must yield... bzzzt ...

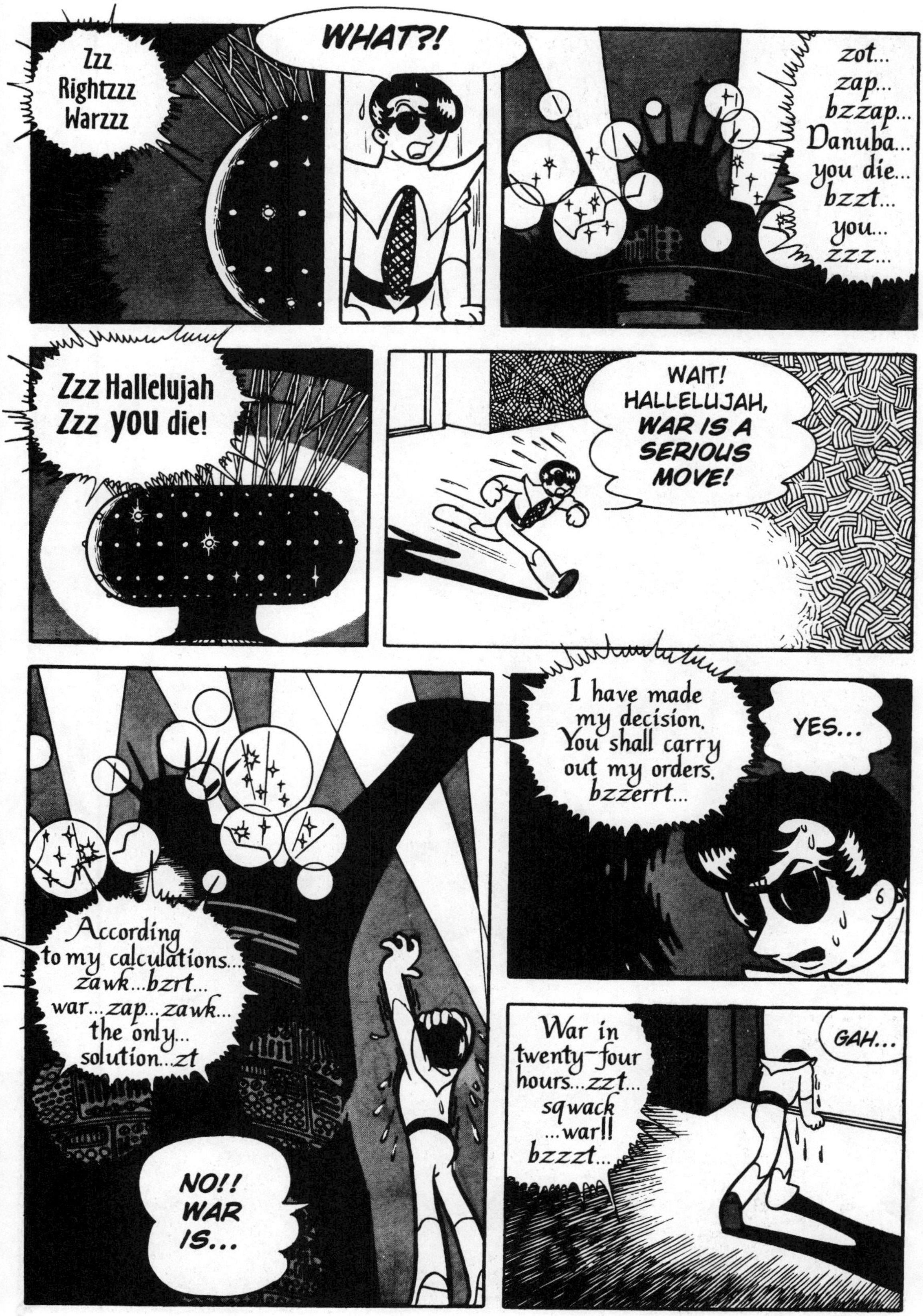
Zzz Rightzzz Warzzz
WHAT?!
zot... zap... bzzap... Danuba... you die... bzzt... you... zzz...
Zzz Hallelujah Zzz you die!
WAIT! HALLELUJAH, WAR IS A SERIOUS MOVE!
According to my calculations... zawk...bzrt... war...zap...zawk... the only... solution...zt
NO!! WAR IS...
I have made my decision. You shall carry out my orders. bzzerrt...
YES...
War in twenty-four hours...zzt... sqwack ...war!! bzzzt...
GAH...

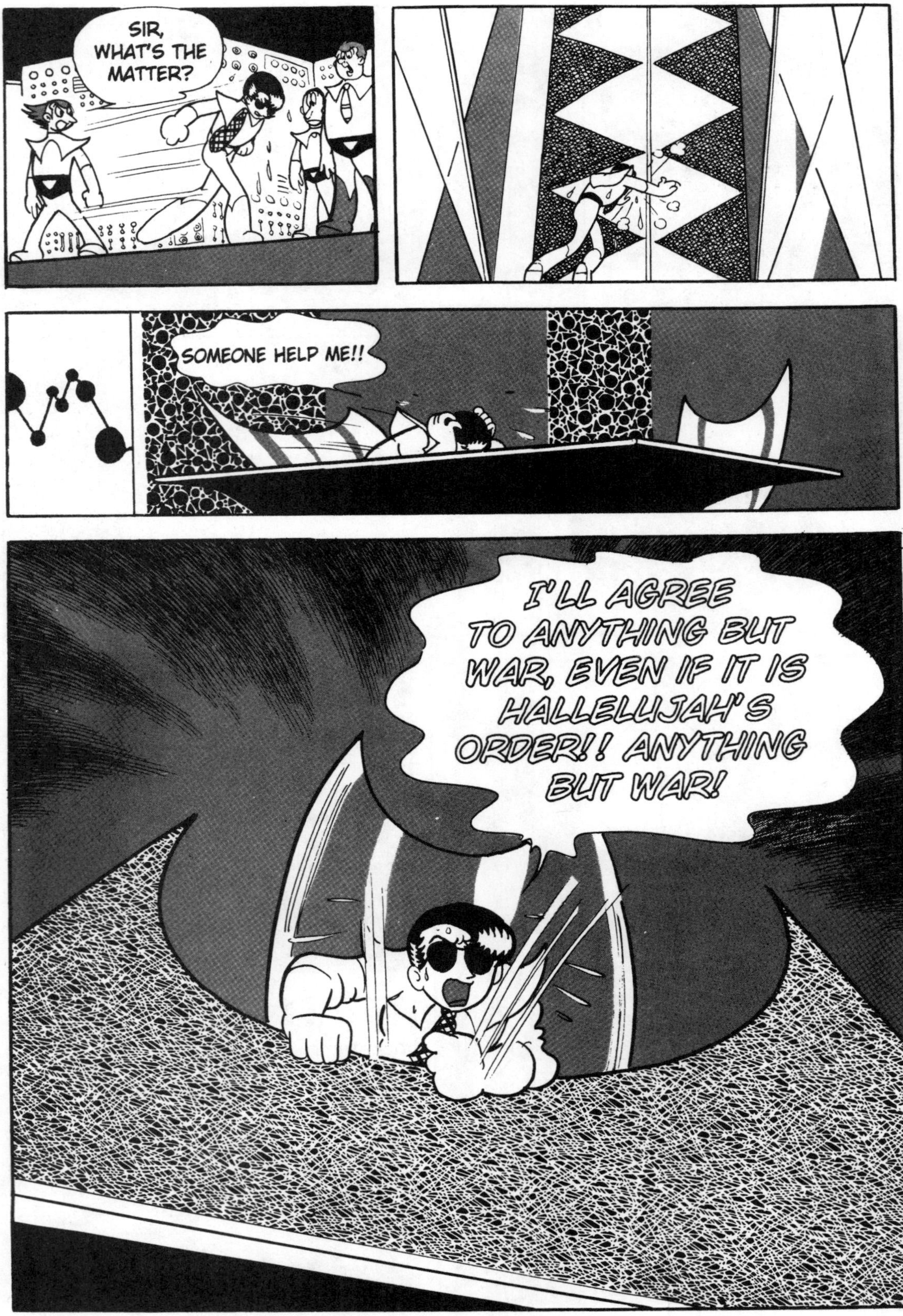
SIR, WHAT'S THE MATTER?
SOMEONE HELP ME!!
I'LL AGREE TO ANYTHING BUT WAR, EVEN IF IT IS HALLELUJAH'S ORDER!! ANYTHING BUT WAR!

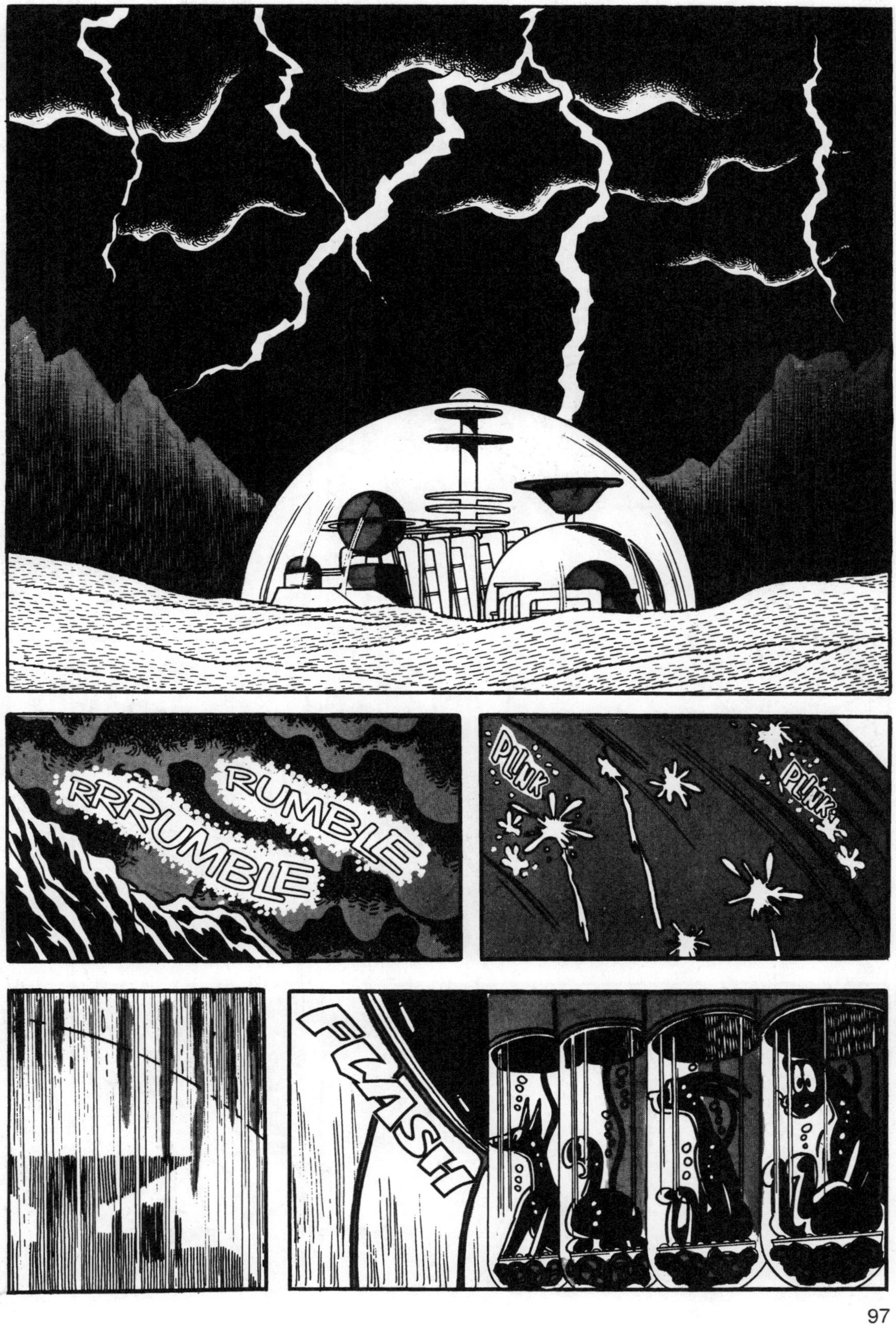
PLINK
PLINK
RUMBLE
RRRUMBLE
FLASH

YOU'VE GIVEN THE WRONG NUTRIENT SOLUTIONS TO THE ANIMALS AGAIN!!

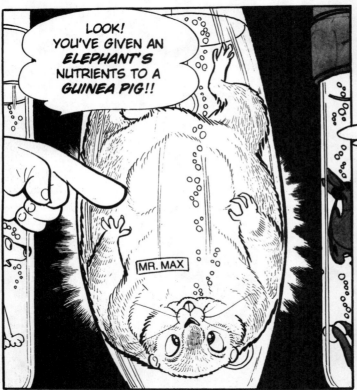
LOOK! YOU'VE GIVEN AN *ELEPHANT'S* NUTRIENTS TO A *GUINEA PIG*!!

MR. MAX

THE OVERDOSE WILL KILL HIM! WE MUST HELP HIM FAST!!

ERP

NOW LISTEN TO ME, YAMANOBE.

THESE ANIMALS ARE NOT NATURAL. THEY'RE LIKE EMBRYOS IN A WOMB, AND THEY DEPEND ON AN OUTSIDE SUPPLY OF FOOD TO LIVE!!

BUT CAN'T YOU LET THEM OUTSIDE OF THE TUBES?

NO!

THE MOMENT THEY'RE EXPOSED TO OUTSIDE AIR THEY DIE. THEY LIVE ONLY IN THE TUBES.

BUT I FEEL SORRY FOR THEM.

SORRY!

HUMPH!

WHAT ABOUT THE MILLIONS OF HUMANS CRAMMED INTO UNDERGROUND CITIES AND CONTROLLED BY SOME FIENDISH ELECTRONIC COMPUTER?

WHERE THOSE WHO TRY TO ESCAPE ARE KILLED!

DON'T YOU THINK THEY'RE WORSE OFF?

WELL, IF YOU PUT IT THAT WAY.

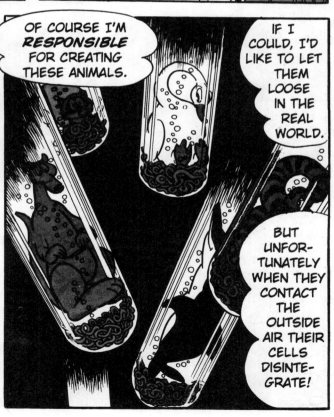

OF COURSE I'M *RESPONSIBLE* FOR CREATING THESE ANIMALS.

IF I COULD, I'D LIKE TO LET THEM LOOSE IN THE REAL WORLD.

BUT UNFORTUNATELY WHEN THEY CONTACT THE OUTSIDE AIR THEIR CELLS DISINTEGRATE!

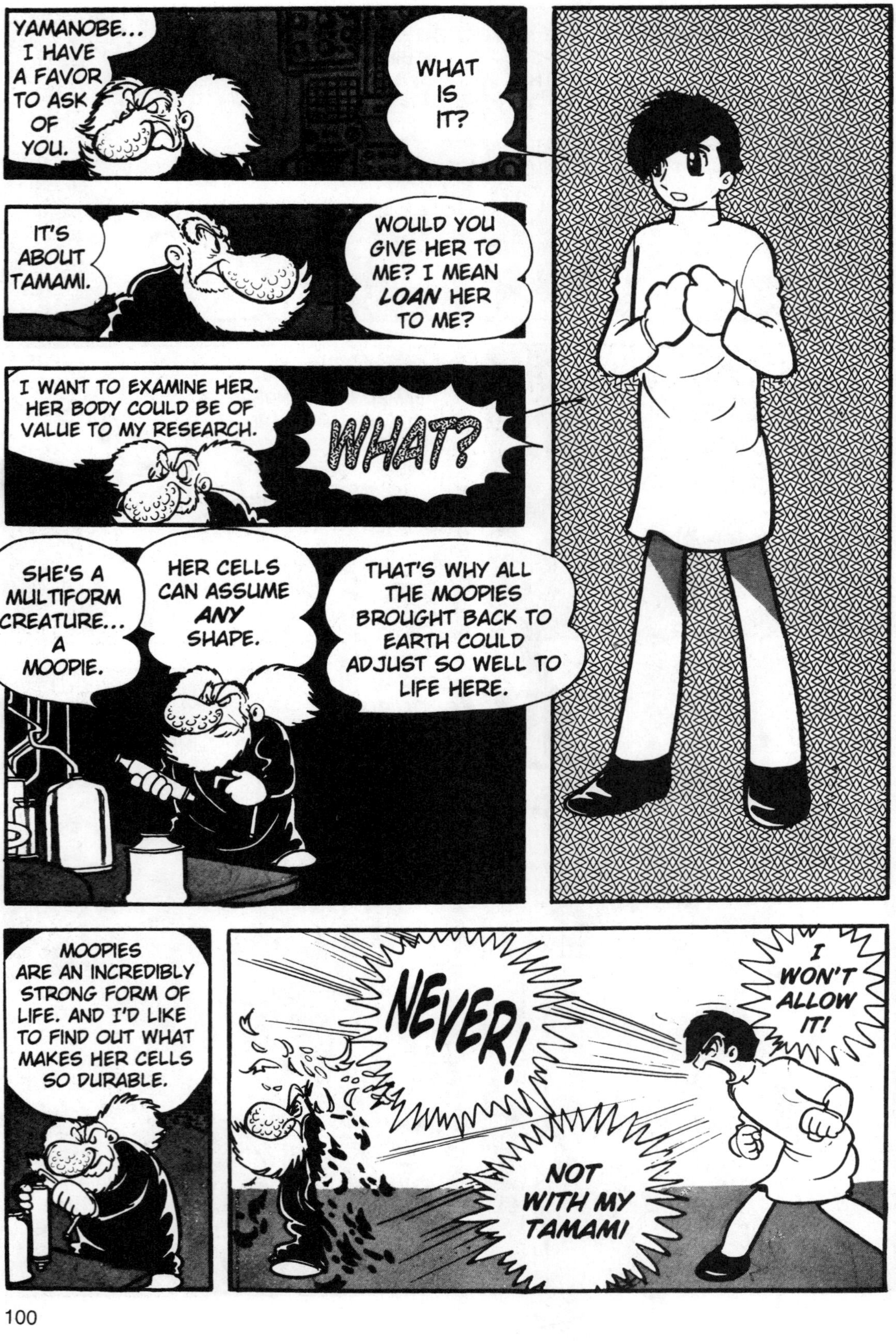
YAMANOBE... I HAVE A FAVOR TO ASK OF YOU.
WHAT IS IT?
IT'S ABOUT TAMAMI.
WOULD YOU GIVE HER TO ME? I MEAN LOAN HER TO ME?
I WANT TO EXAMINE HER. HER BODY COULD BE OF VALUE TO MY RESEARCH.
WHAT?
SHE'S A MULTIFORM CREATURE... A MOOPIE.
HER CELLS CAN ASSUME ANY SHAPE.
THAT'S WHY ALL THE MOOPIES BROUGHT BACK TO EARTH COULD ADJUST SO WELL TO LIFE HERE.
MOOPIES ARE AN INCREDIBLY STRONG FORM OF LIFE. AND I'D LIKE TO FIND OUT WHAT MAKES HER CELLS SO DURABLE.
NEVER!
I WON'T ALLOW IT!
NOT WITH MY TAMAMI

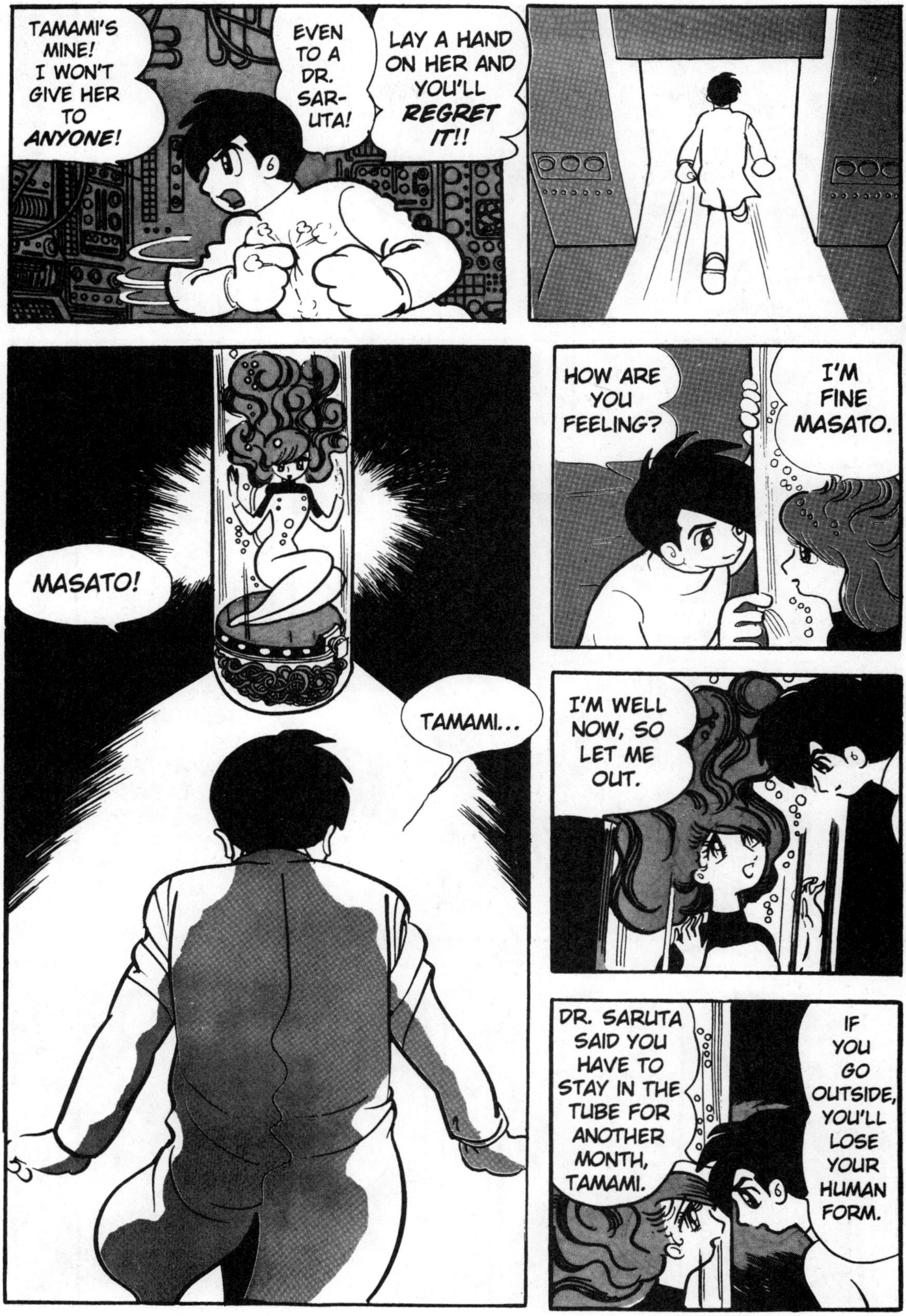
TAMAMI'S MINE! I WON'T GIVE HER TO *ANYONE*!
EVEN TO A DR. SARUTA!
LAY A HAND ON HER AND YOU'LL *REGRET IT*!!
MASATO!
TAMAMI...
HOW ARE YOU FEELING?
I'M FINE MASATO.
I'M WELL NOW, SO LET ME OUT.
DR. SARUTA SAID YOU HAVE TO STAY IN THE TUBE FOR ANOTHER MONTH, TAMAMI.
IF YOU GO OUTSIDE, YOU'LL LOSE YOUR HUMAN FORM.

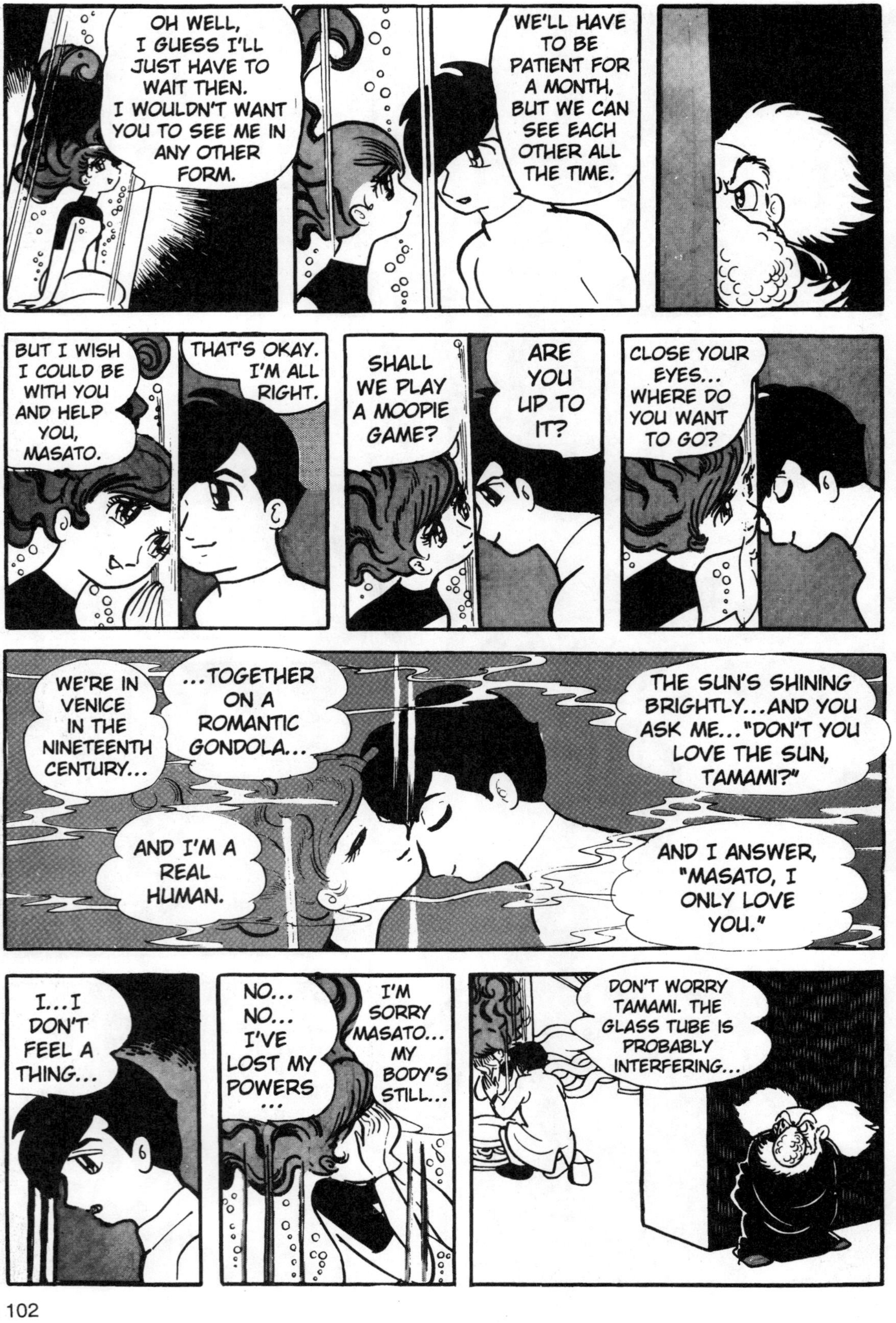

OH WELL, I GUESS I'LL JUST HAVE TO WAIT THEN. I WOULDN'T WANT YOU TO SEE ME IN ANY OTHER FORM.
WE'LL HAVE TO BE PATIENT FOR A MONTH, BUT WE CAN SEE EACH OTHER ALL THE TIME.
BUT I WISH I COULD BE WITH YOU AND HELP YOU, MASATO.
THAT'S OKAY. I'M ALL RIGHT.
SHALL WE PLAY A MOOPIE GAME?
ARE YOU UP TO IT?
CLOSE YOUR EYES... WHERE DO YOU WANT TO GO?
WE'RE IN VENICE IN THE NINETEENTH CENTURY...
...TOGETHER ON A ROMANTIC GONDOLA...
AND I'M A REAL HUMAN.
THE SUN'S SHINING BRIGHTLY...AND YOU ASK ME..."DON'T YOU LOVE THE SUN, TAMAMI?"
AND I ANSWER, "MASATO, I ONLY LOVE YOU."
I...I DON'T FEEL A THING...
NO... NO... I'VE LOST MY POWERS ...
I'M SORRY MASATO... MY BODY'S STILL...
DON'T WORRY TAMAMI. THE GLASS TUBE IS PROBABLY INTERFERING...

I HAVE TO FEED FIFTY-FIVE ARTIFICIAL ANIMALS BY TEN O'CLOCK. I'LL BE BACK LATER.

SEE YOU LATER TAMAMI!

I'LL BE WAITING MASATO...

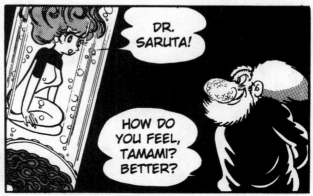

DR. SARUTA!

HOW DO YOU FEEL, TAMAMI? BETTER?

YAMANOBE'S BEEN A REAL HELP. I'M GRATEFUL TO HIM.

TAMAMI, I'VE BEEN WAITING UNTIL YOU'RE WELL TO TALK TO YOU.

AS A MOOPIE, YOU'RE THE ONLY ANIMAL OF YOUR KIND LEFT ON EARTH, AND...

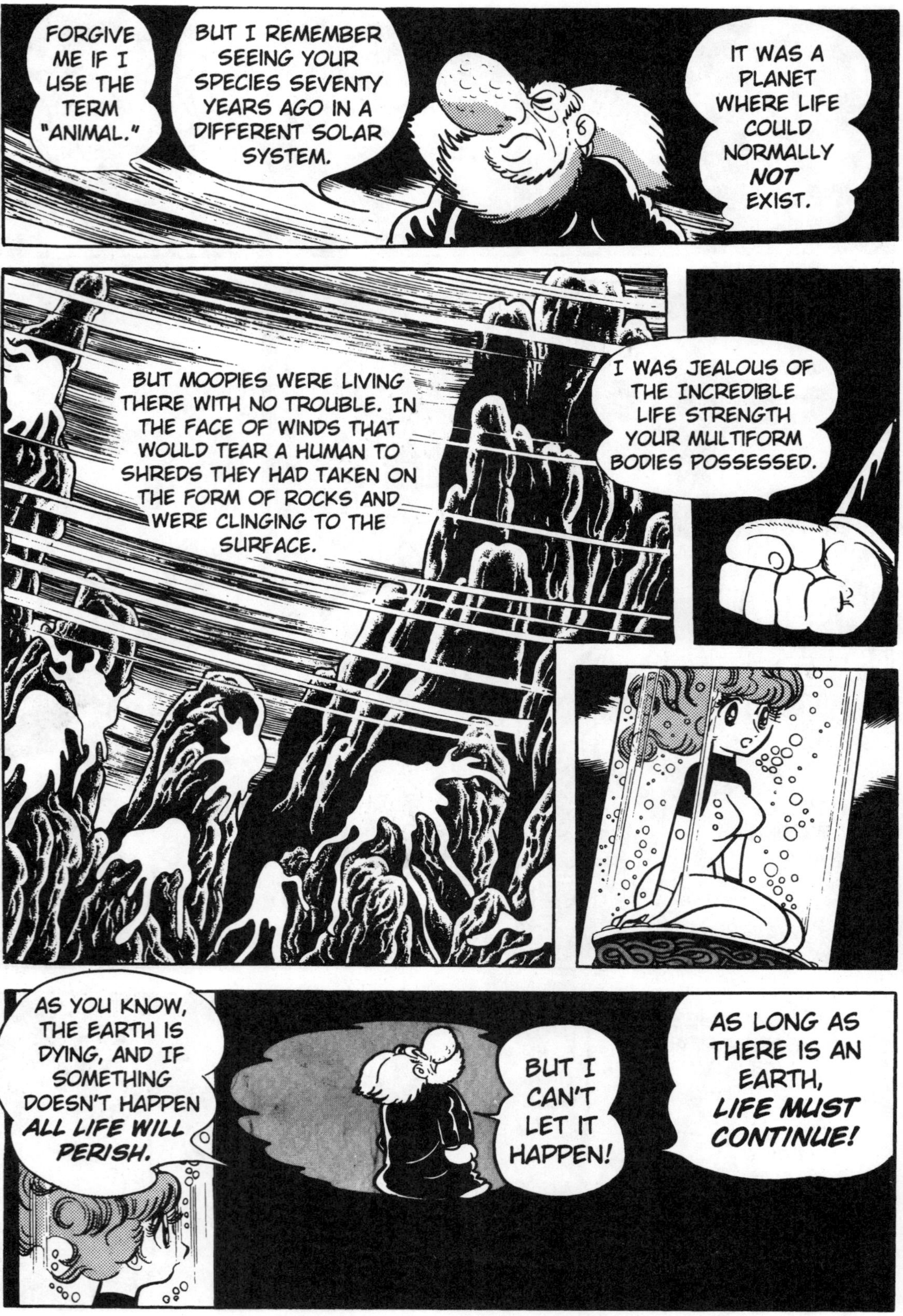

FORGIVE ME IF I USE THE TERM "ANIMAL."
BUT I REMEMBER SEEING YOUR SPECIES SEVENTY YEARS AGO IN A DIFFERENT SOLAR SYSTEM.
IT WAS A PLANET WHERE LIFE COULD NORMALLY ***NOT*** EXIST.
BUT MOOPIES WERE LIVING THERE WITH NO TROUBLE. IN THE FACE OF WINDS THAT WOULD TEAR A HUMAN TO SHREDS THEY HAD TAKEN ON THE FORM OF ROCKS AND WERE CLINGING TO THE SURFACE.
I WAS JEALOUS OF THE INCREDIBLE LIFE STRENGTH YOUR MULTIFORM BODIES POSSESSED.
AS YOU KNOW, THE EARTH IS DYING, AND IF SOMETHING DOESN'T HAPPEN ***ALL LIFE WILL PERISH.***
BUT I CAN'T LET IT HAPPEN!
AS LONG AS THERE IS AN EARTH, ***LIFE MUST CONTINUE!***

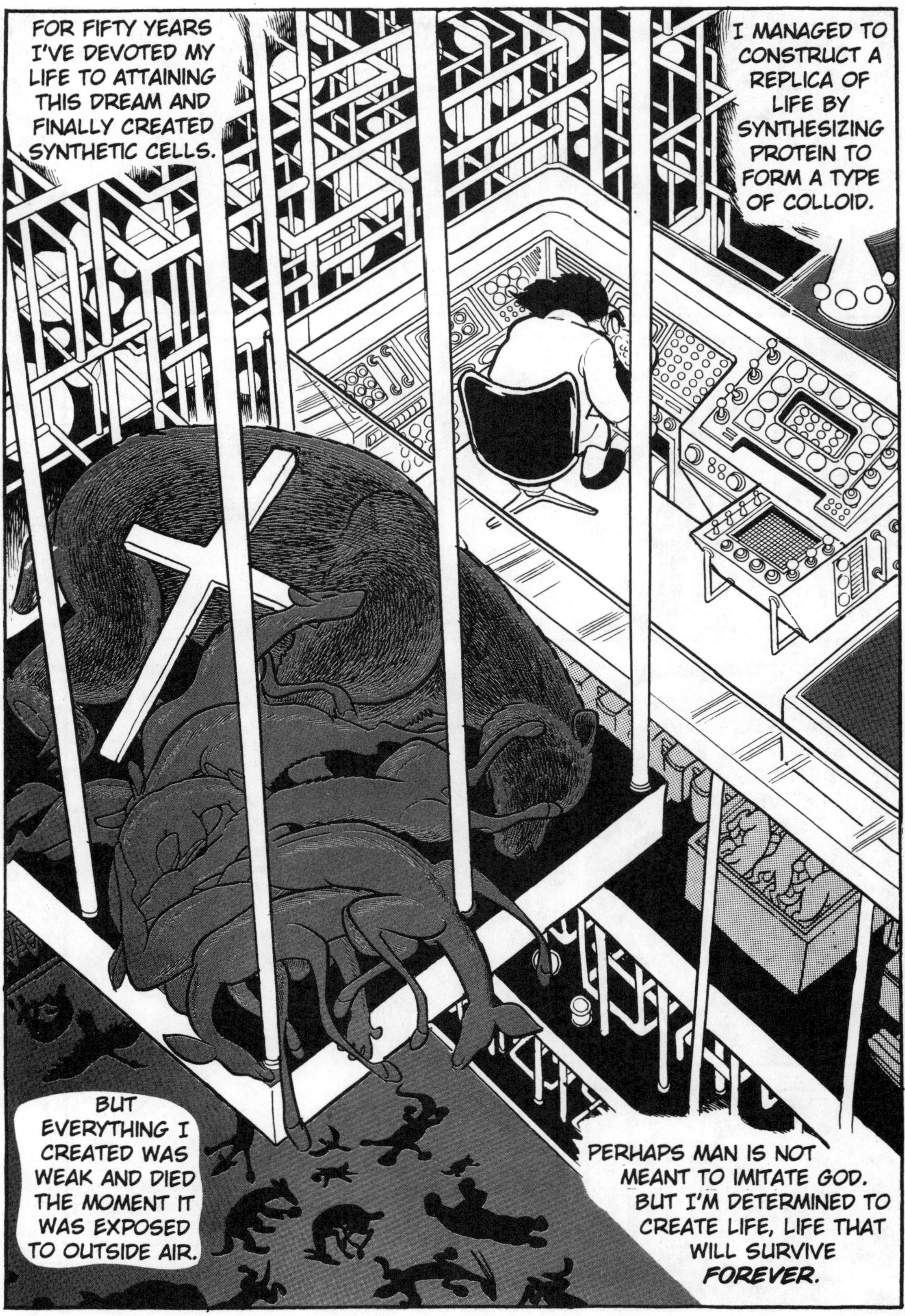
FOR FIFTY YEARS I'VE DEVOTED MY LIFE TO ATTAINING THIS DREAM AND FINALLY CREATED SYNTHETIC CELLS.
I MANAGED TO CONSTRUCT A REPLICA OF LIFE BY SYNTHESIZING PROTEIN TO FORM A TYPE OF COLLOID.
BUT EVERYTHING I CREATED WAS WEAK AND DIED THE MOMENT IT WAS EXPOSED TO OUTSIDE AIR.
PERHAPS MAN IS NOT MEANT TO IMITATE GOD. BUT I'M DETERMINED TO CREATE LIFE, LIFE THAT WILL SURVIVE *FOREVER*.

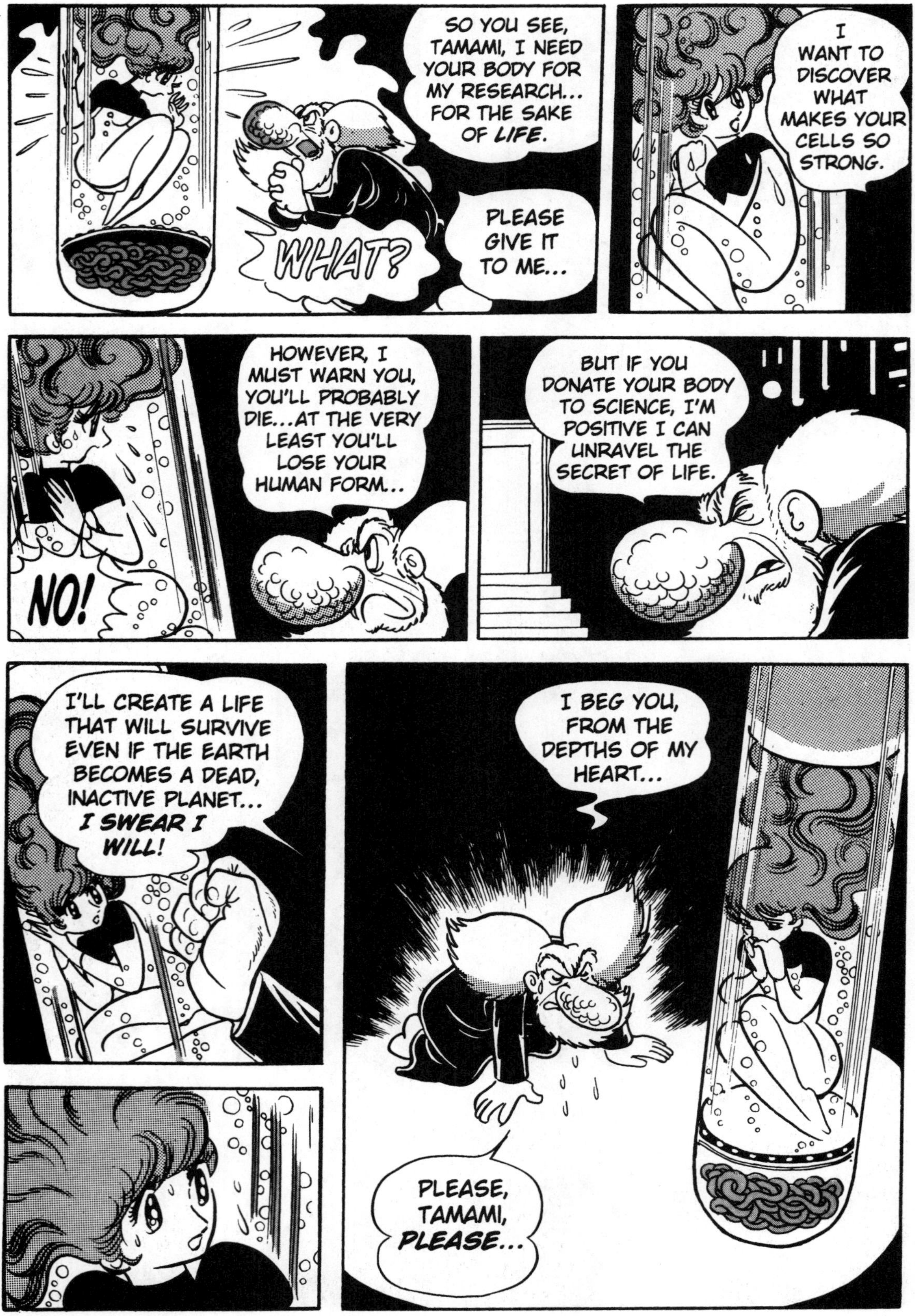
SO YOU SEE, TAMAMI, I NEED YOUR BODY FOR MY RESEARCH... FOR THE SAKE OF LIFE.
WHAT?
PLEASE GIVE IT TO ME...
I WANT TO DISCOVER WHAT MAKES YOUR CELLS SO STRONG.
HOWEVER, I MUST WARN YOU, YOU'LL PROBABLY DIE...AT THE VERY LEAST YOU'LL LOSE YOUR HUMAN FORM...
NO!
BUT IF YOU DONATE YOUR BODY TO SCIENCE, I'M POSITIVE I CAN UNRAVEL THE SECRET OF LIFE.
I'LL CREATE A LIFE THAT WILL SURVIVE EVEN IF THE EARTH BECOMES A DEAD, INACTIVE PLANET... I SWEAR I WILL!
I BEG YOU, FROM THE DEPTHS OF MY HEART...
PLEASE, TAMAMI, PLEASE...

AND YOU'LL BE ABLE TO SAVE MANKIND?
WHAT?
MANKIND?! DID YOU SAY MAN-KIND?!!
THIS IS NOT THE TIME TO DIFFERENTIATE BETWEEN HUMANS, ANIMALS, INSECTS, OR PLANTS!! WE'RE ALL IN THE SAME BOAT!
ALL ONE FAMILY!
IT DOESN'T MATTER IF HUMANITY PERISHES AS LONG AS LIFE CONTINUES!!
CAN YOU WAIT UNTIL TOMORROW FOR MY ANSWER?
AAAH... TAKE AS LONG AS YOU PLEASE.
KLAK KLAK
MASATO...!!

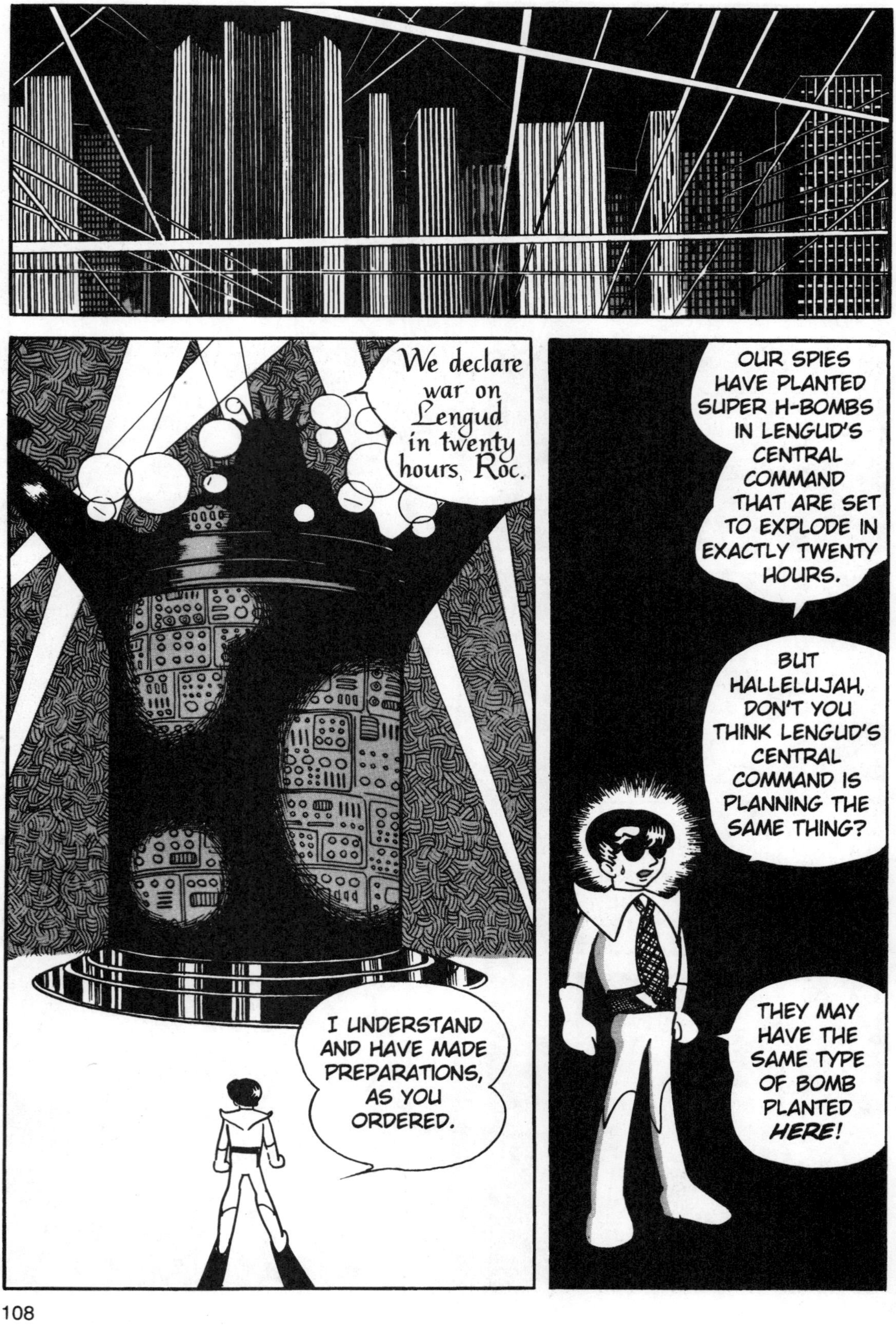
We declare war on Lengud in twenty hours, Roc.
I UNDERSTAND AND HAVE MADE PREPARATIONS, AS YOU ORDERED.
OUR SPIES HAVE PLANTED SUPER H-BOMBS IN LENGUD'S CENTRAL COMMAND THAT ARE SET TO EXPLODE IN EXACTLY TWENTY HOURS.
BUT HALLELUJAH, DON'T YOU THINK LENGUD'S CENTRAL COMMAND IS PLANNING THE SAME THING?
THEY MAY HAVE THE SAME TYPE OF BOMB PLANTED HERE!

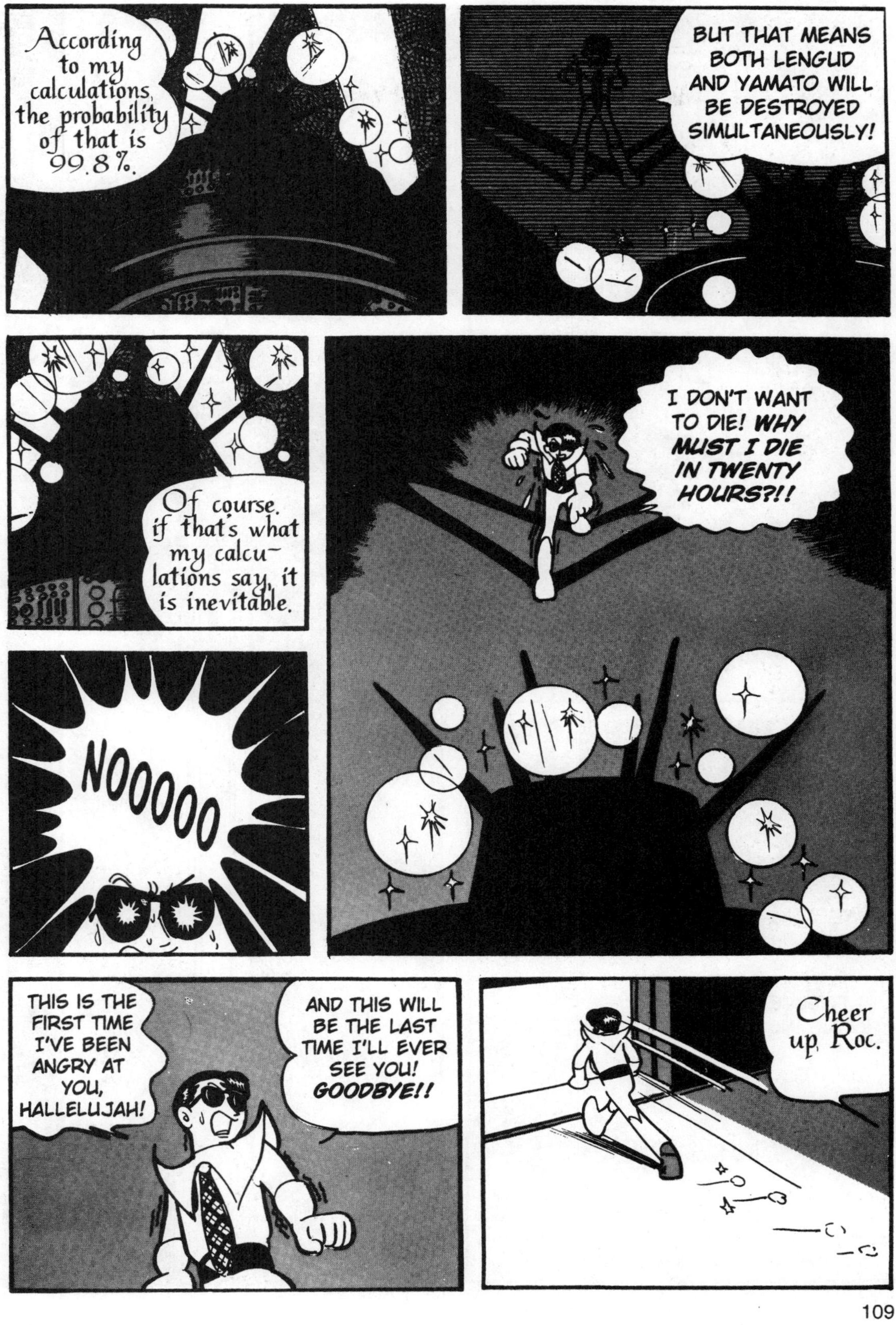
According to my calculations, the probability of that is 99.8%.
BUT THAT MEANS BOTH LENGUD AND YAMATO WILL BE DESTROYED SIMULTANEOUSLY!
Of course. if that's what my calculations say, it is inevitable.
NOOOOO
I DON'T WANT TO DIE! WHY MUST I DIE IN TWENTY HOURS?!!
THIS IS THE FIRST TIME I'VE BEEN ANGRY AT YOU, HALLELUJAH!
AND THIS WILL BE THE LAST TIME I'LL EVER SEE YOU! GOODBYE!!
Cheer up, Roc.

BRING ALL MY CREDITS. NO, WAIT, I WON'T NEED THEM ANYMORE.

A-TRIP-MASTER?-

IN TWELVE HOURS, NO MORE YAMATO...

SEE YOU AROUND...

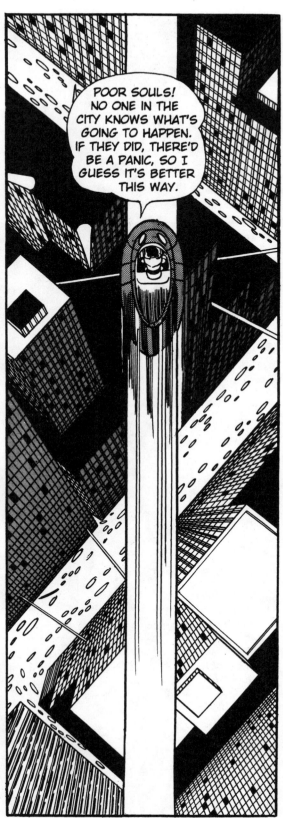

POOR SOULS! NO ONE IN THE CITY KNOWS WHAT'S GOING TO HAPPEN. IF THEY DID, THERE'D BE A PANIC, SO I GUESS IT'S BETTER THIS WAY.

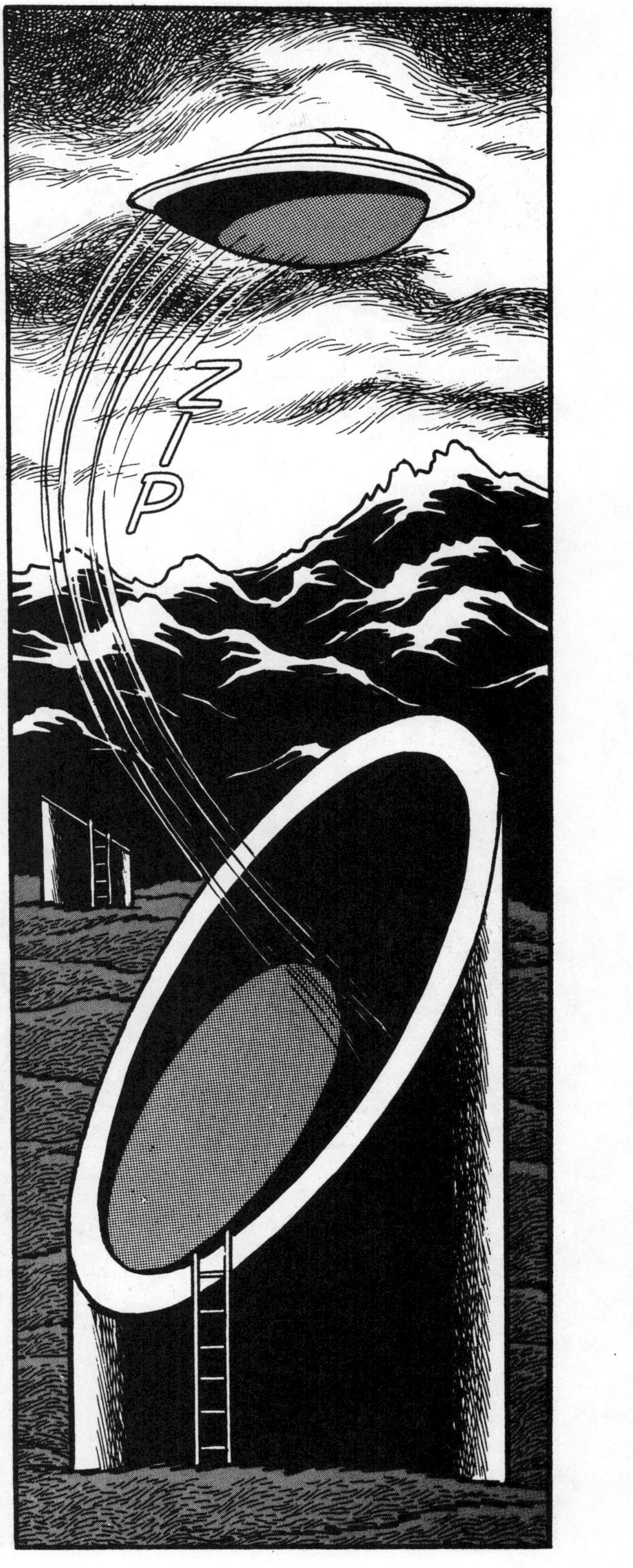
ZIP
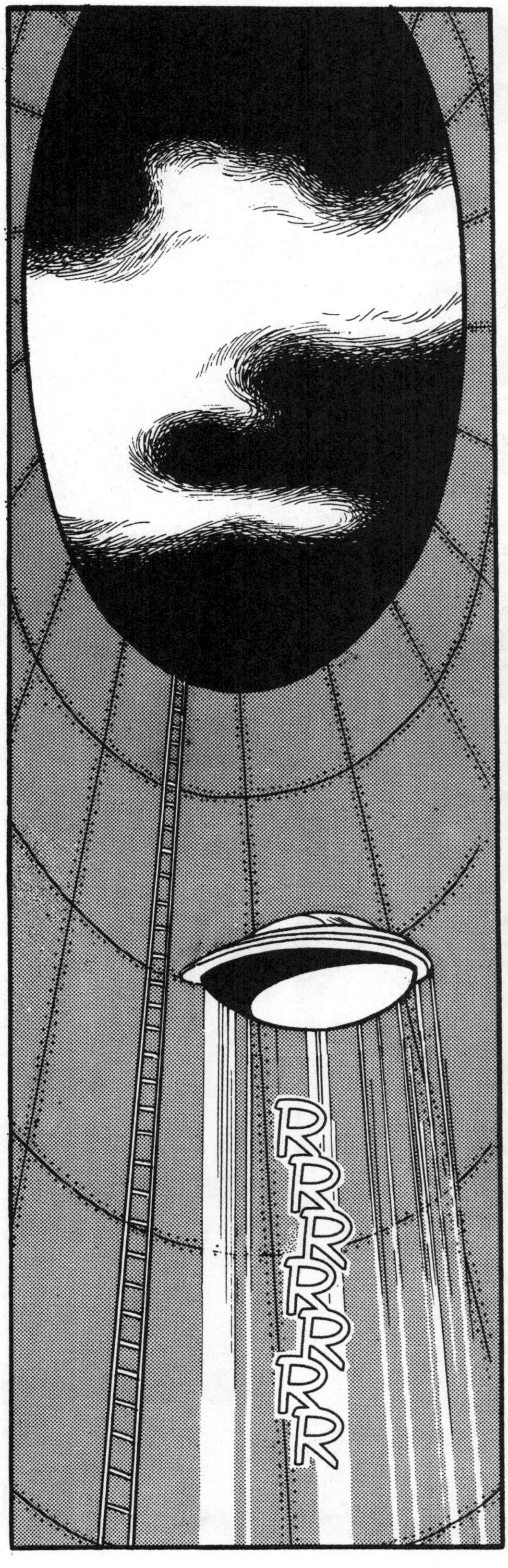
RRRRRRR

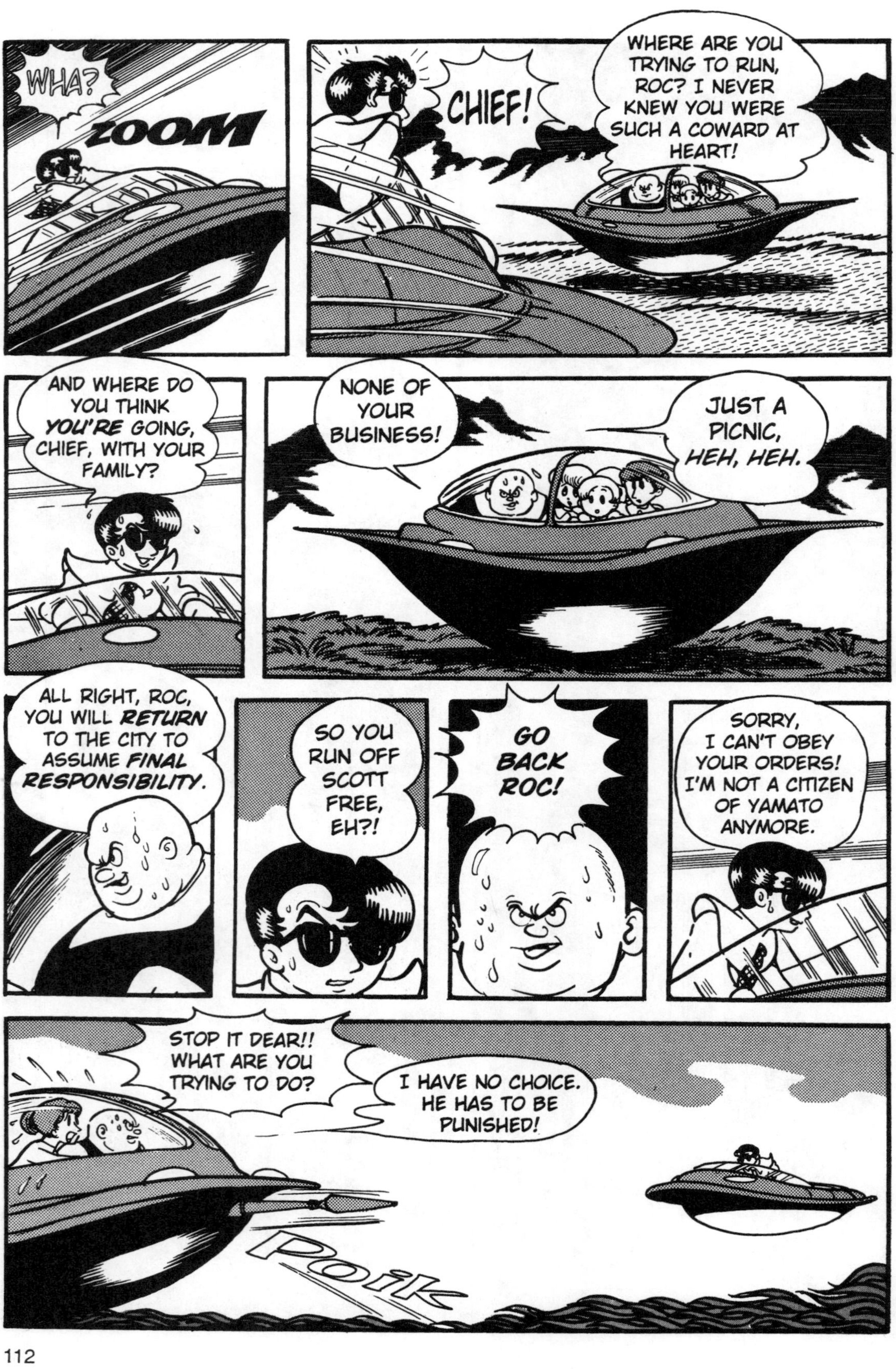
WHA?
ZOOM
CHIEF!
WHERE ARE YOU TRYING TO RUN, ROC? I NEVER KNEW YOU WERE SUCH A COWARD AT HEART!
AND WHERE DO YOU THINK *YOU'RE* GOING, CHIEF, WITH YOUR FAMILY?
NONE OF YOUR BUSINESS!
JUST A PICNIC, *HEH, HEH.*
ALL RIGHT, ROC, YOU WILL ***RETURN*** TO THE CITY TO ASSUME ***FINAL RESPONSIBILITY***.
SO YOU RUN OFF SCOTT FREE, EH?!
GO BACK ROC!
SORRY, I CAN'T OBEY YOUR ORDERS! I'M NOT A CITIZEN OF YAMATO ANYMORE.
STOP IT DEAR!! WHAT ARE YOU TRYING TO DO?
I HAVE NO CHOICE. HE HAS TO BE PUNISHED!
Poik

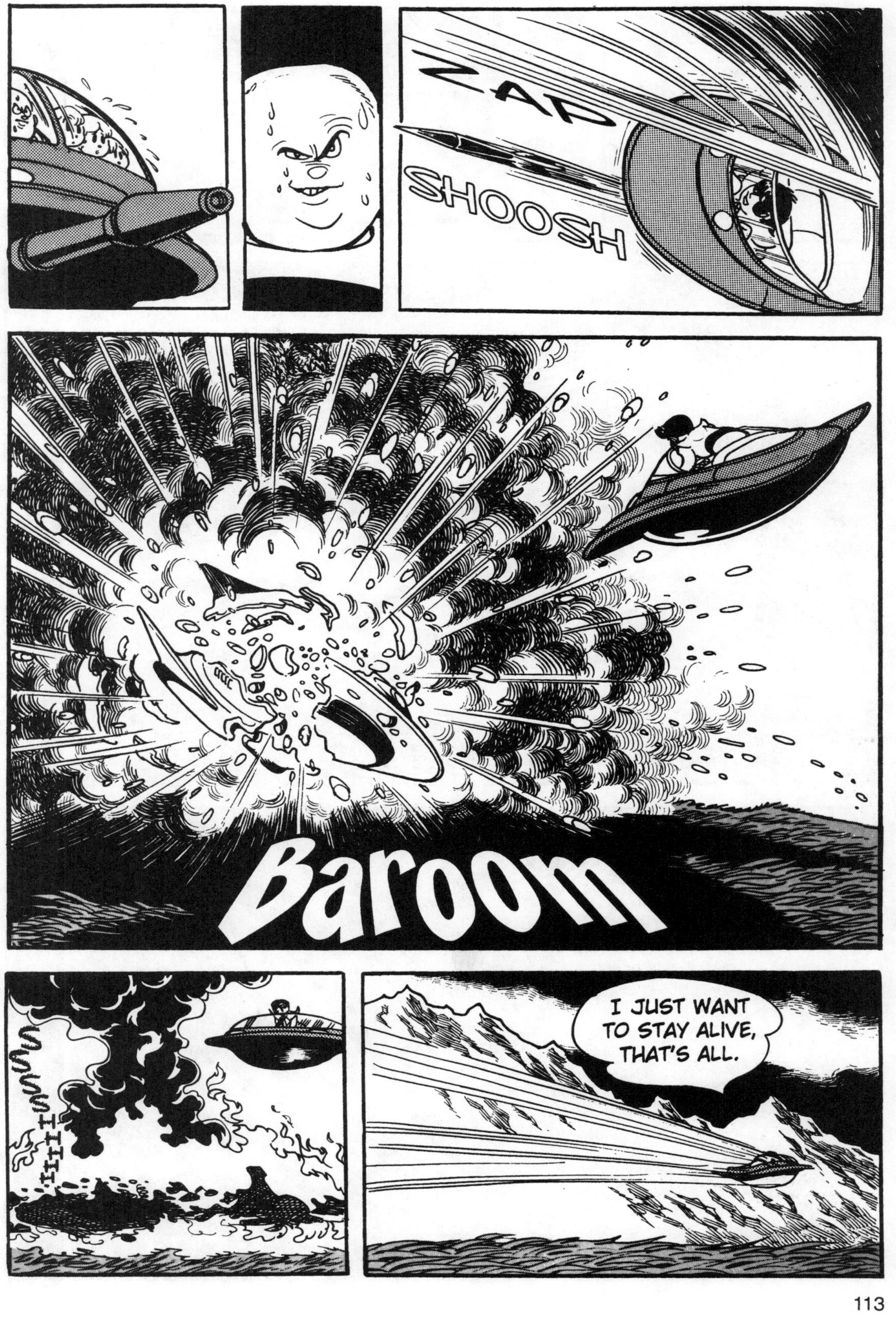
ZAP
SHOOSH
Baroom
I JUST WANT TO STAY ALIVE, THAT'S ALL.

FARE-WELL FAIR YAMATO!

NOW THEN, WHERE CAN I RUN TO?

THE OTHER THREE CAPITALS ARE A LITTLE TOO FAR...

ALL RIGHT THEN! I'LL JUST CRUISE UNTIL THE SPACE SLED'S ENERGY RUNS OUT, AND THEN I'LL WORRY ABOUT WHAT TO DO.

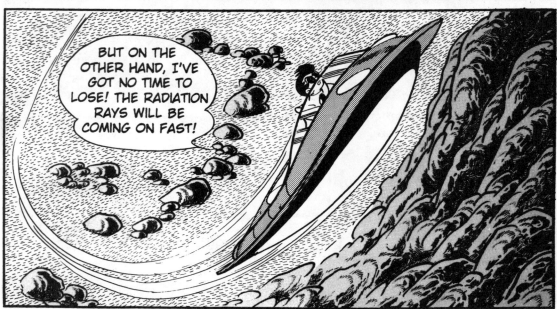

BUT ON THE OTHER HAND, I'VE GOT NO TIME TO LOSE! THE RADIATION RAYS WILL BE COMING ON FAST!

114

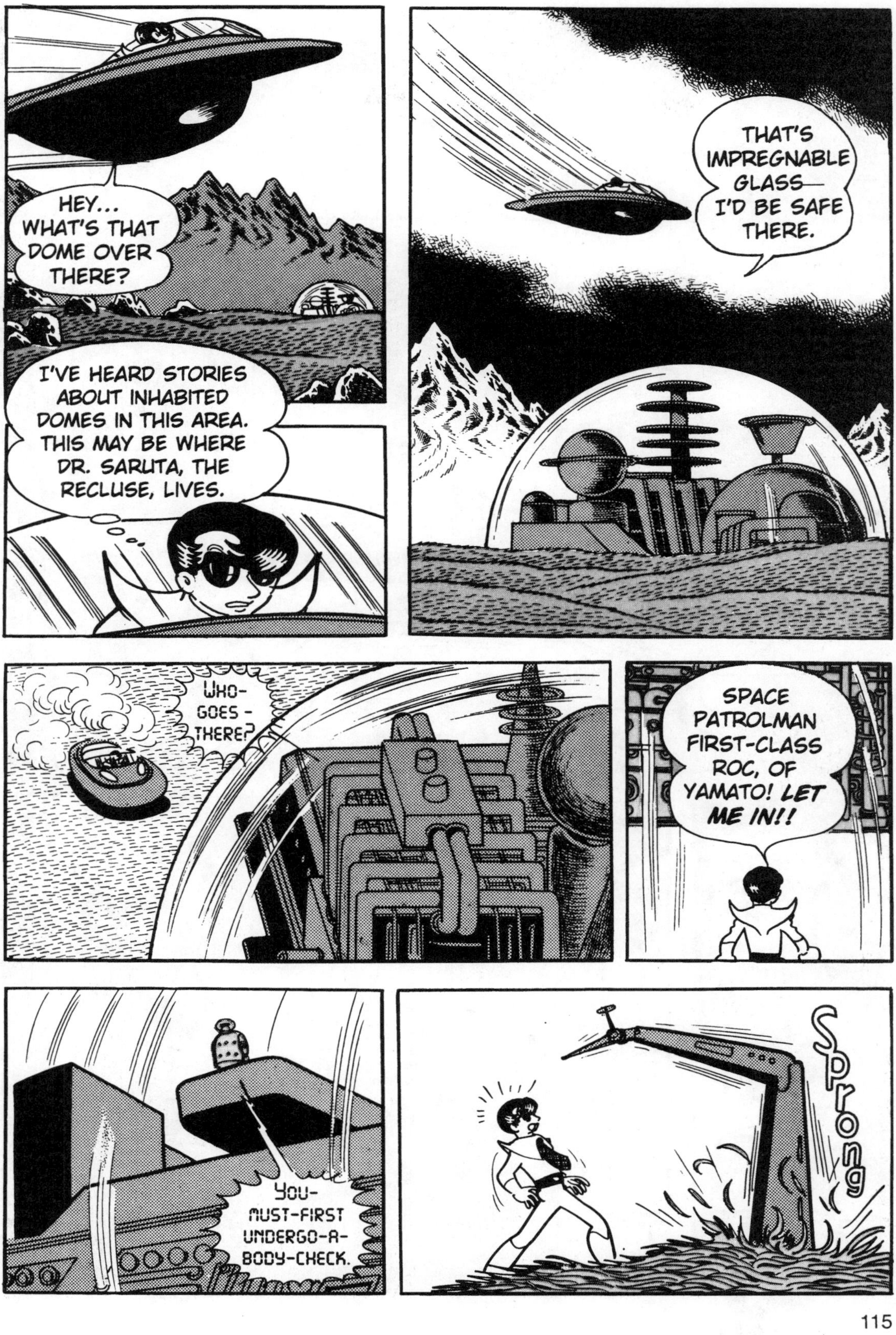
HEY... WHAT'S THAT DOME OVER THERE?
I'VE HEARD STORIES ABOUT INHABITED DOMES IN THIS AREA. THIS MAY BE WHERE DR. SARUTA, THE RECLUSE, LIVES.
THAT'S IMPREGNABLE GLASS— I'D BE SAFE THERE.
WHO-GOES-THERE?
SPACE PATROLMAN FIRST-CLASS ROC, OF YAMATO! LET ME IN!!
YOU-MUST-FIRST UNDERGO-A-BODY-CHECK.
Sprong

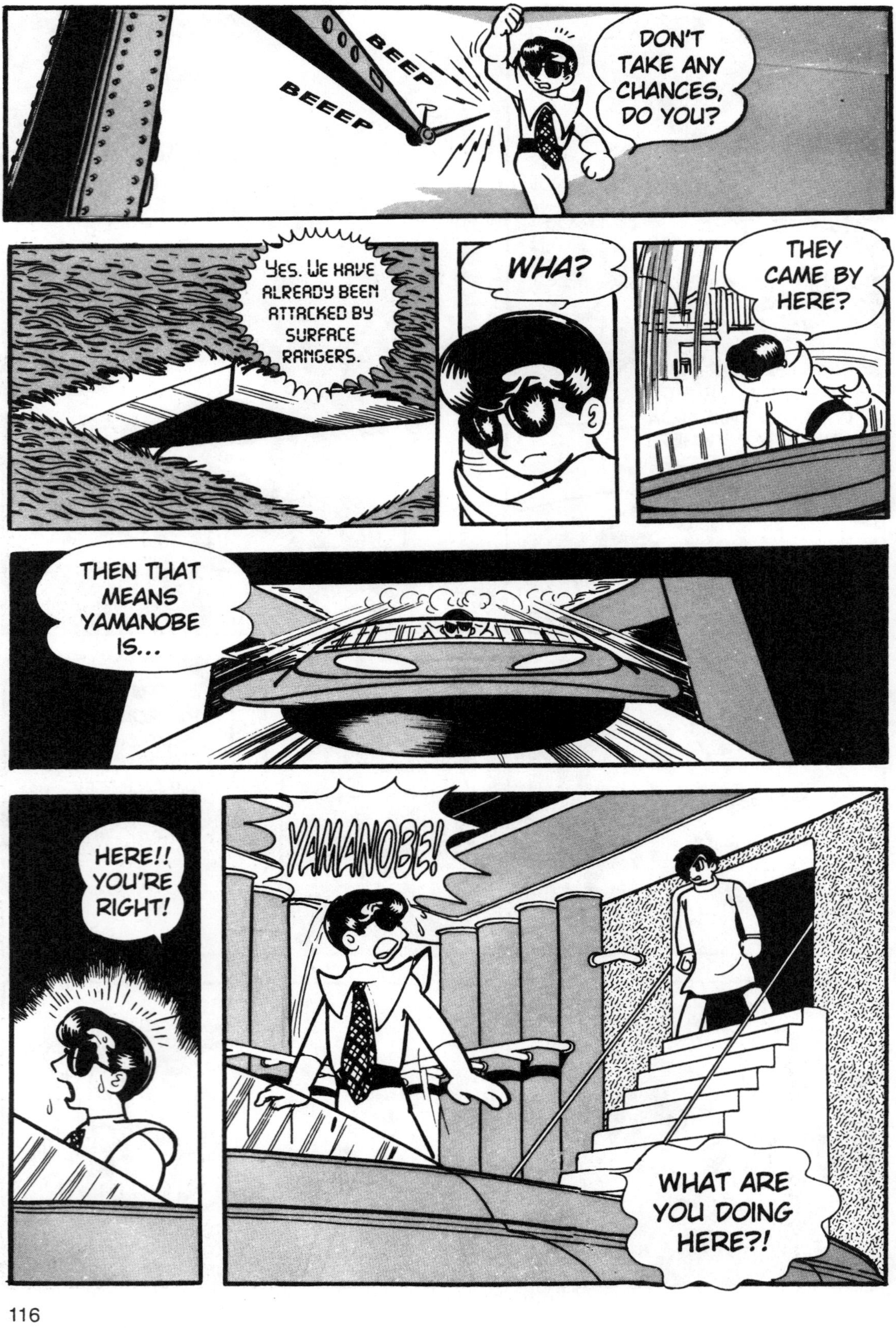
BEEP
BEEEP
DON'T TAKE ANY CHANCES, DO YOU?
YES. WE HAVE ALREADY BEEN ATTACKED BY SURFACE RANGERS.
WHA?
THEY CAME BY HERE?
THEN THAT MEANS YAMANOBE IS...
HERE!! YOU'RE RIGHT!
YAMANOBE!
WHAT ARE YOU DOING HERE?!

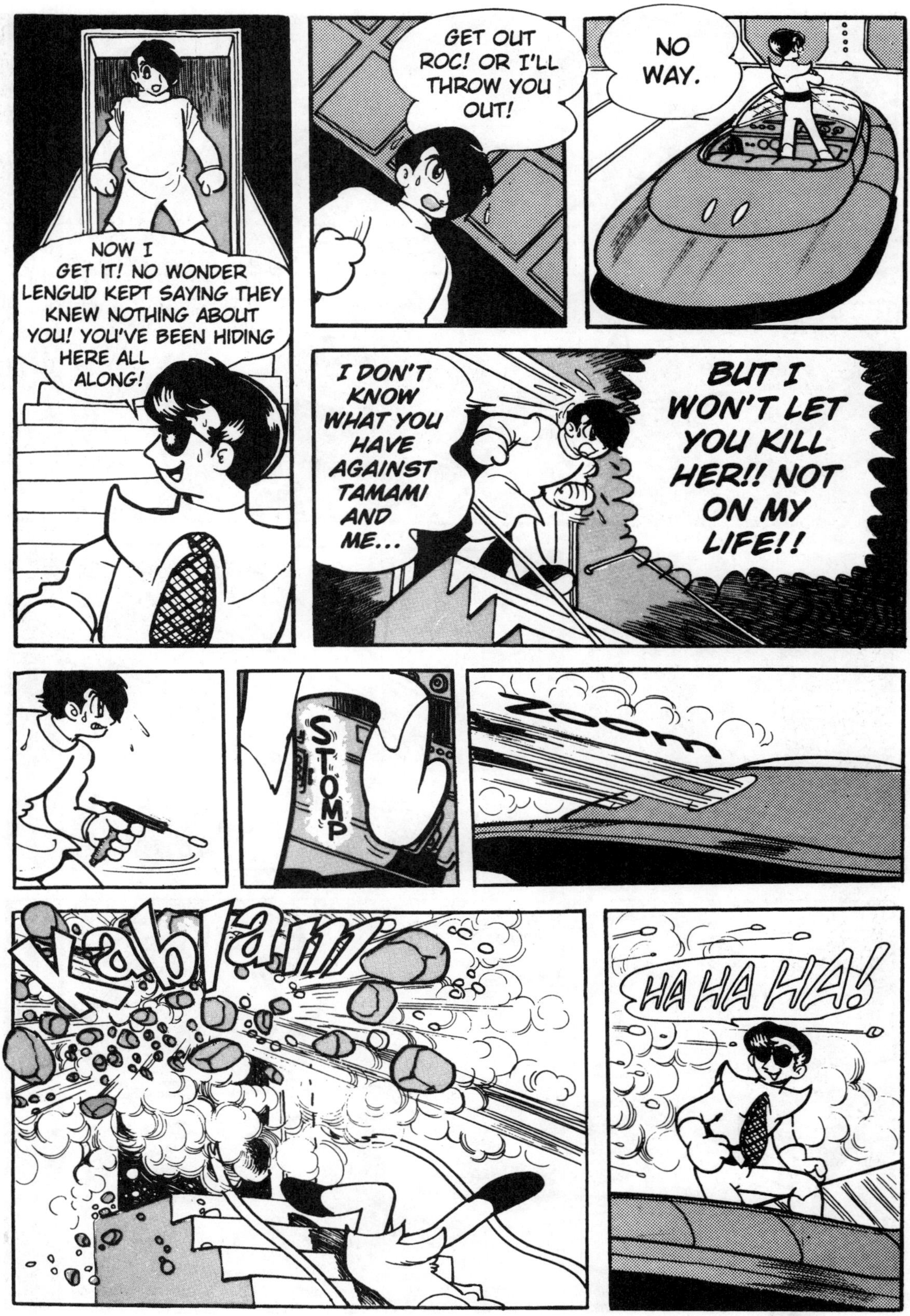
NOW I GET IT! NO WONDER LENGUD KEPT SAYING THEY KNEW NOTHING ABOUT YOU! YOU'VE BEEN HIDING HERE ALL ALONG!
GET OUT ROC! OR I'LL THROW YOU OUT!
NO WAY.
I DON'T KNOW WHAT YOU HAVE AGAINST TAMAMI AND ME...
BUT I WON'T LET YOU KILL HER!! NOT ON MY LIFE!!
STOMP
ZOOM
KABLAM
HA HA HA!

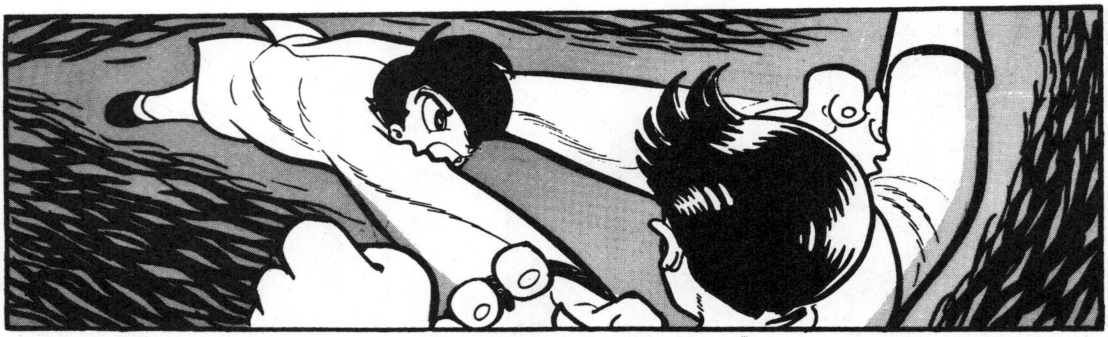

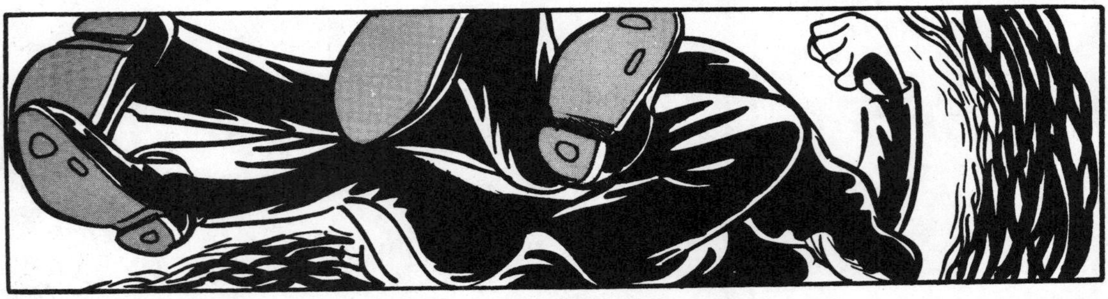

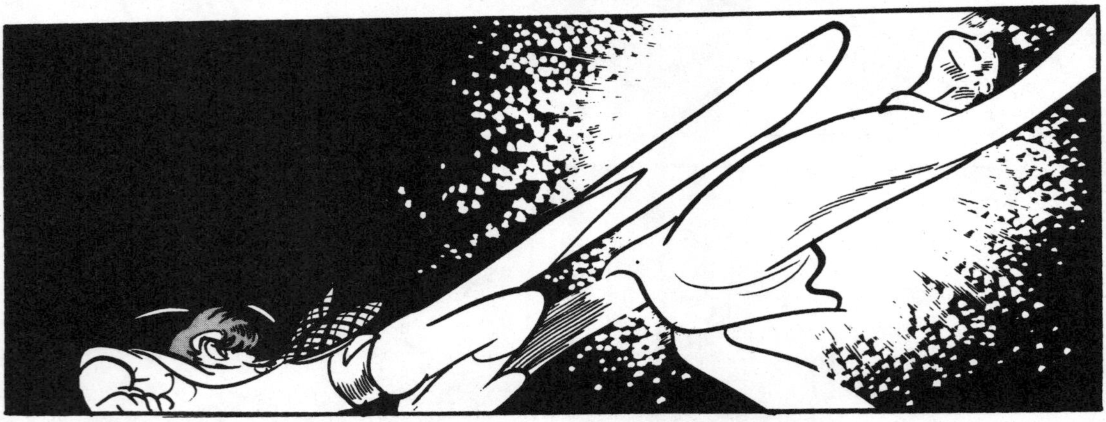

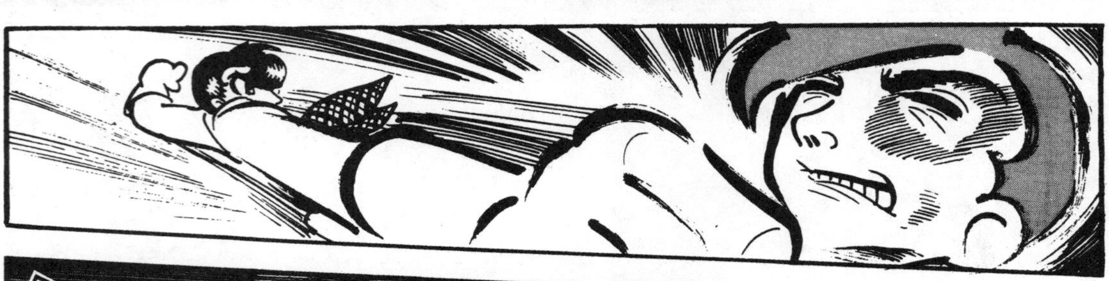

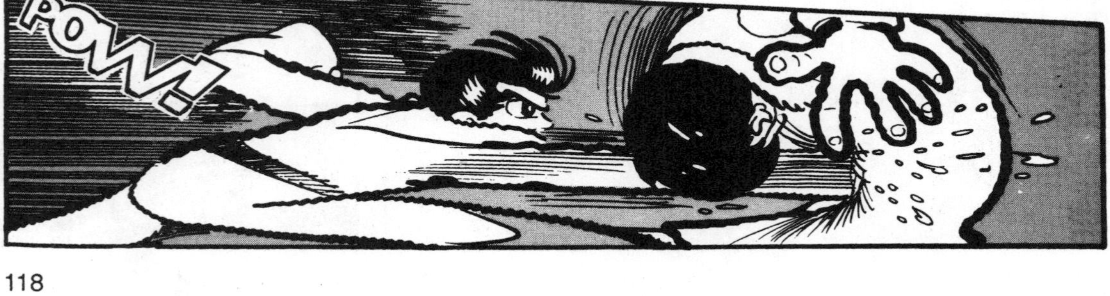
POW!

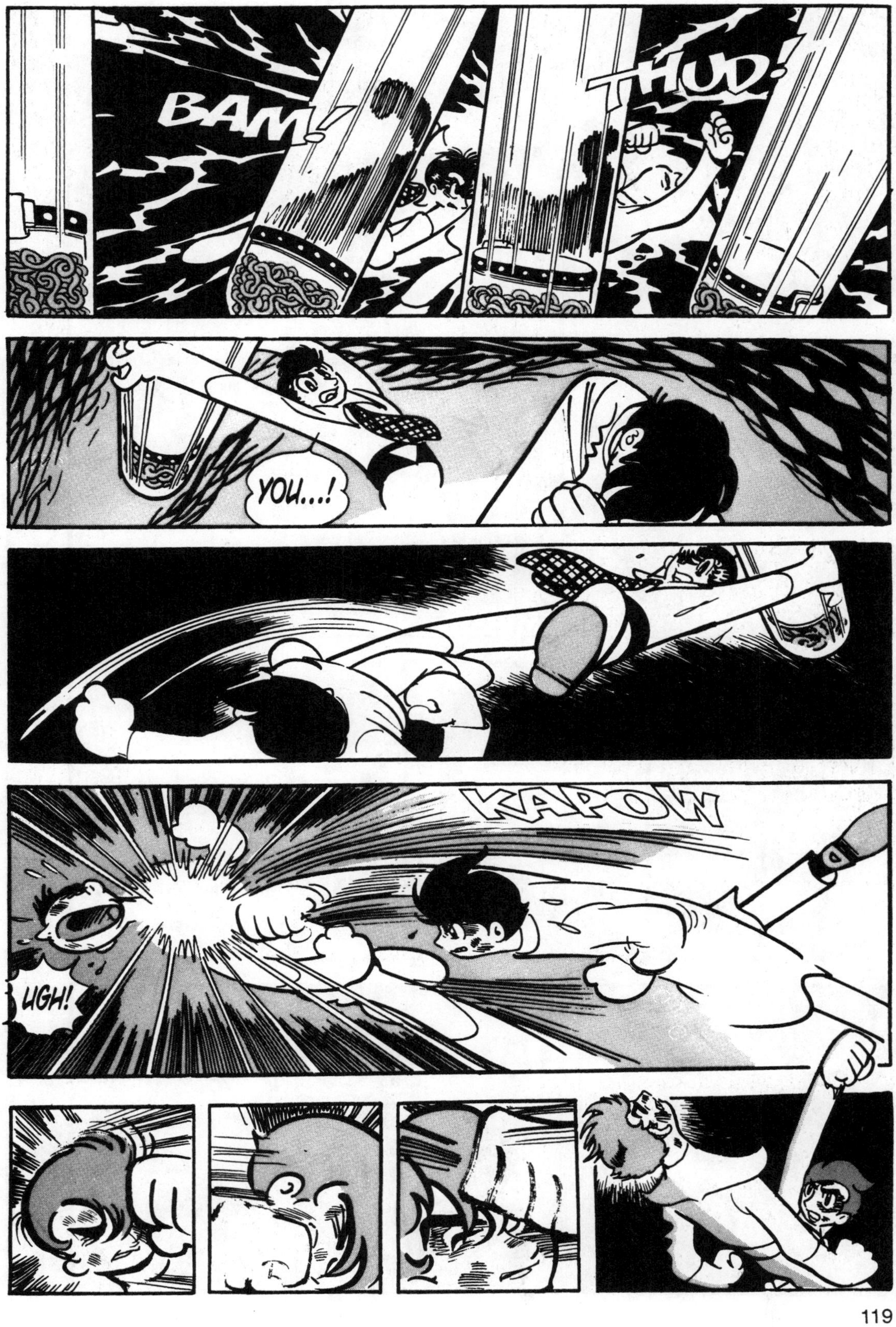
THUD!
BAM!
YOU...!
KAPOW
UGH!

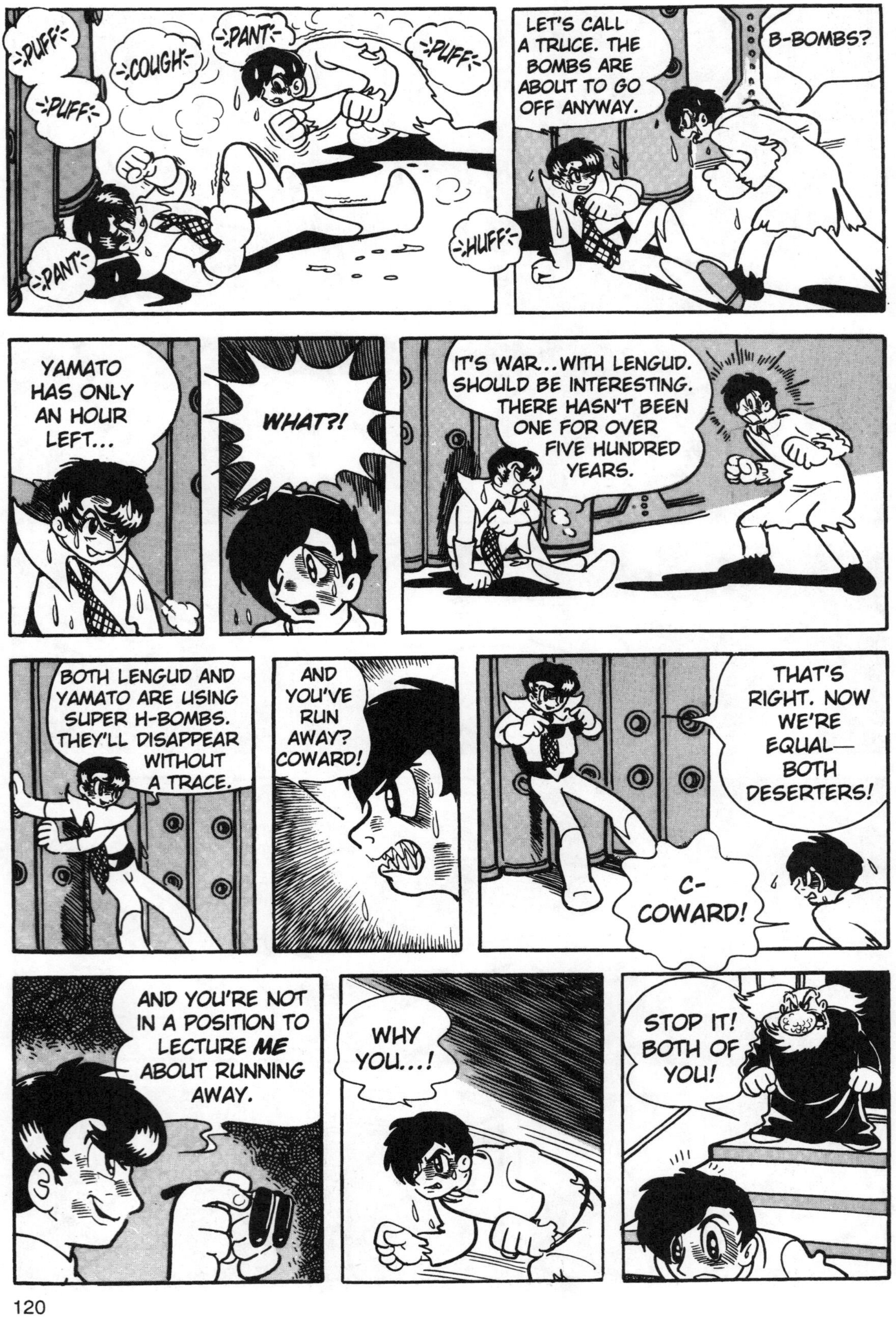
PUFF
PUFF
COUGH
PANT
PANT
PUFF
HUFF
LET'S CALL A TRUCE. THE BOMBS ARE ABOUT TO GO OFF ANYWAY.
B-BOMBS?
YAMATO HAS ONLY AN HOUR LEFT...
WHAT?!
IT'S WAR...WITH LENGUD. SHOULD BE INTERESTING. THERE HASN'T BEEN ONE FOR OVER FIVE HUNDRED YEARS.
BOTH LENGUD AND YAMATO ARE USING SUPER H-BOMBS. THEY'LL DISAPPEAR WITHOUT A TRACE.
AND YOU'VE RUN AWAY? COWARD!
THAT'S RIGHT. NOW WE'RE EQUAL—BOTH DESERTERS!
C-COWARD!
AND YOU'RE NOT IN A POSITION TO LECTURE *ME* ABOUT RUNNING AWAY.
WHY YOU...!
STOP IT! BOTH OF YOU!

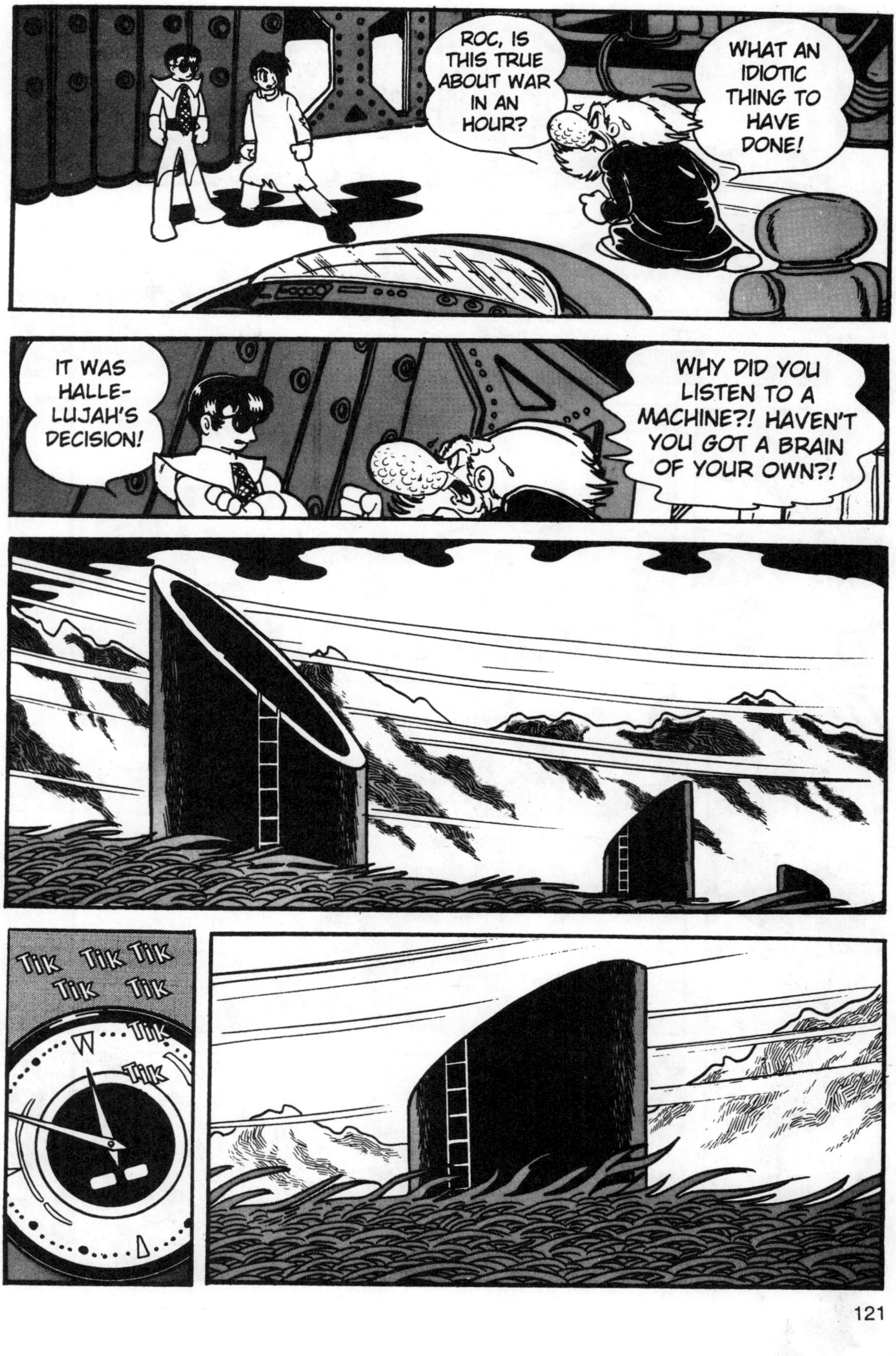
ROC, IS THIS TRUE ABOUT WAR IN AN HOUR?
WHAT AN IDIOTIC THING TO HAVE DONE!
IT WAS HALLE-LUJAH'S DECISION!
WHY DID YOU LISTEN TO A MACHINE?! HAVEN'T YOU GOT A BRAIN OF YOUR OWN?!
Tik Tik Tik Tik Tik Tik Tik

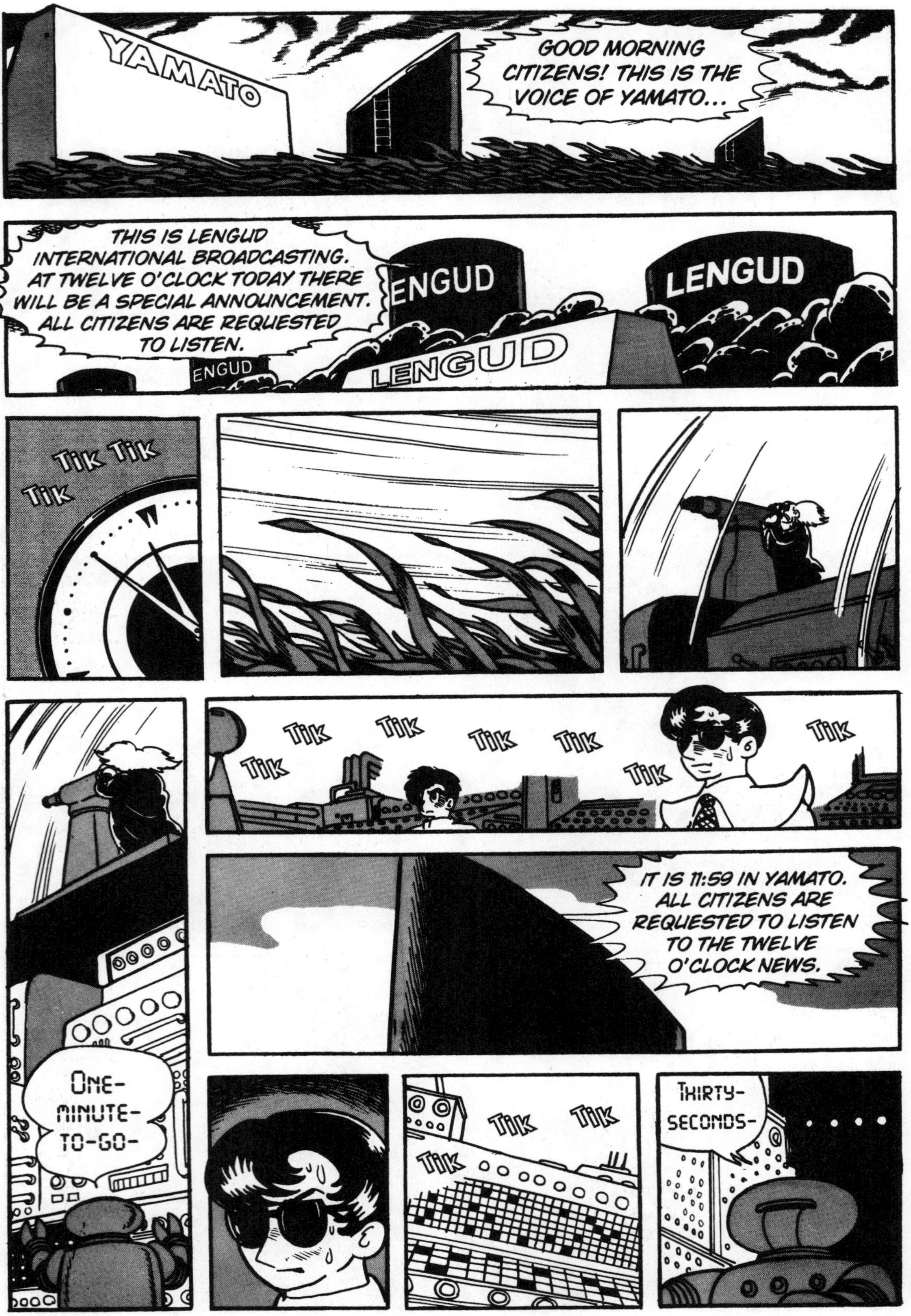
YAMATO
GOOD MORNING CITIZENS! THIS IS THE VOICE OF YAMATO...
THIS IS LENGUD INTERNATIONAL BROADCASTING. AT TWELVE O'CLOCK TODAY THERE WILL BE A SPECIAL ANNOUNCEMENT. ALL CITIZENS ARE REQUESTED TO LISTEN.
ENGUD
LENGUD
ENGUD
LENGUD
Tik Tik
Tik
Tik Tik Tik Tik Tik Tik Tik
IT IS 11:59 IN YAMATO. ALL CITIZENS ARE REQUESTED TO LISTEN TO THE TWELVE O'CLOCK NEWS.
ONE-MINUTE-TO-GO-
Tik Tik
Tik
THIRTY-SECONDS-
• • • •

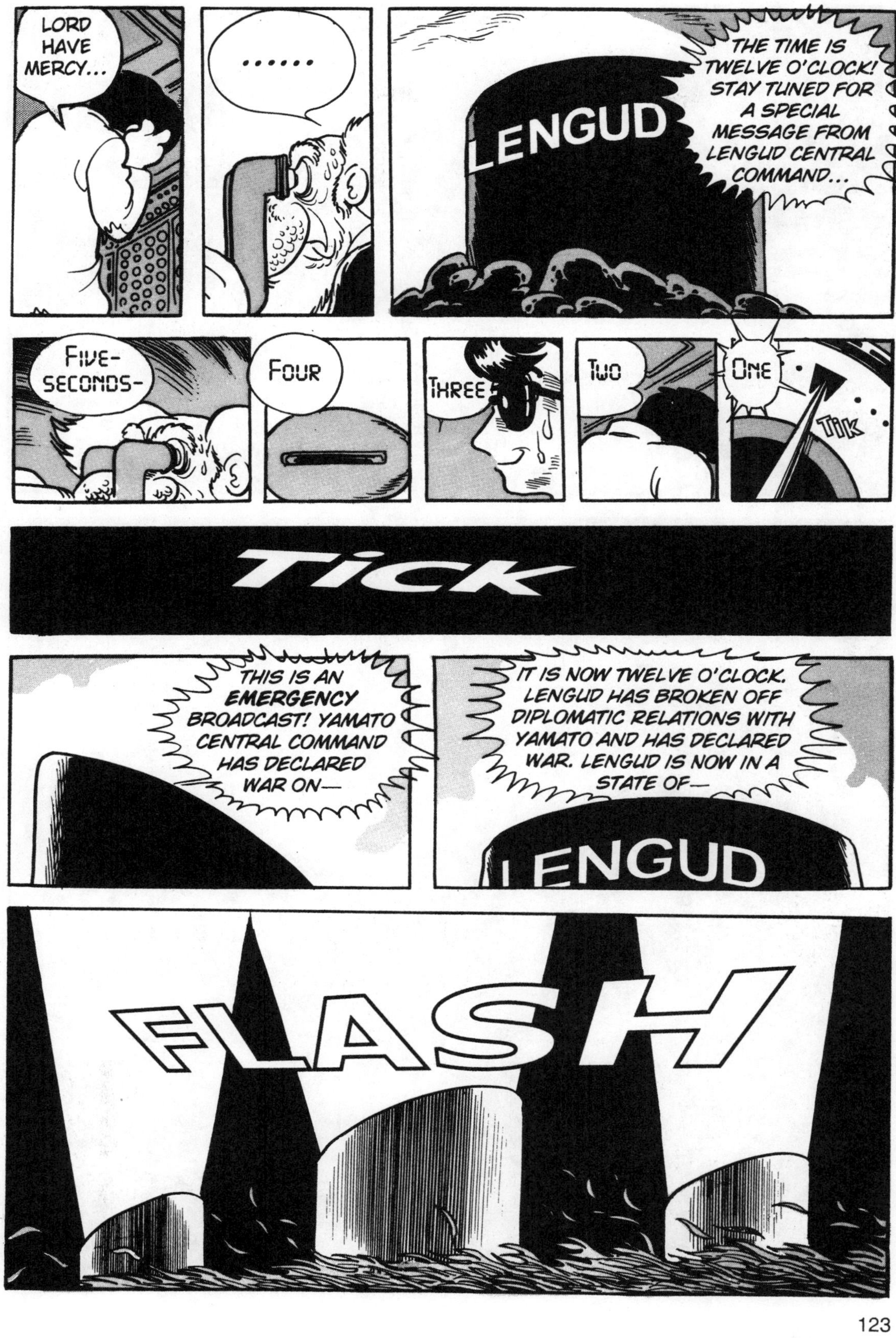
LORD HAVE MERCY...
......
LENGUD
THE TIME IS TWELVE O'CLOCK! STAY TUNED FOR A SPECIAL MESSAGE FROM LENGUD CENTRAL COMMAND...
FIVE-SECONDS-
FOUR
THREE
TWO
ONE
TIK
TICK
THIS IS AN EMERGENCY BROADCAST! YAMATO CENTRAL COMMAND HAS DECLARED WAR ON—
IT IS NOW TWELVE O'CLOCK. LENGUD HAS BROKEN OFF DIPLOMATIC RELATIONS WITH YAMATO AND HAS DECLARED WAR. LENGUD IS NOW IN A STATE OF—
LENGUD
FLASH

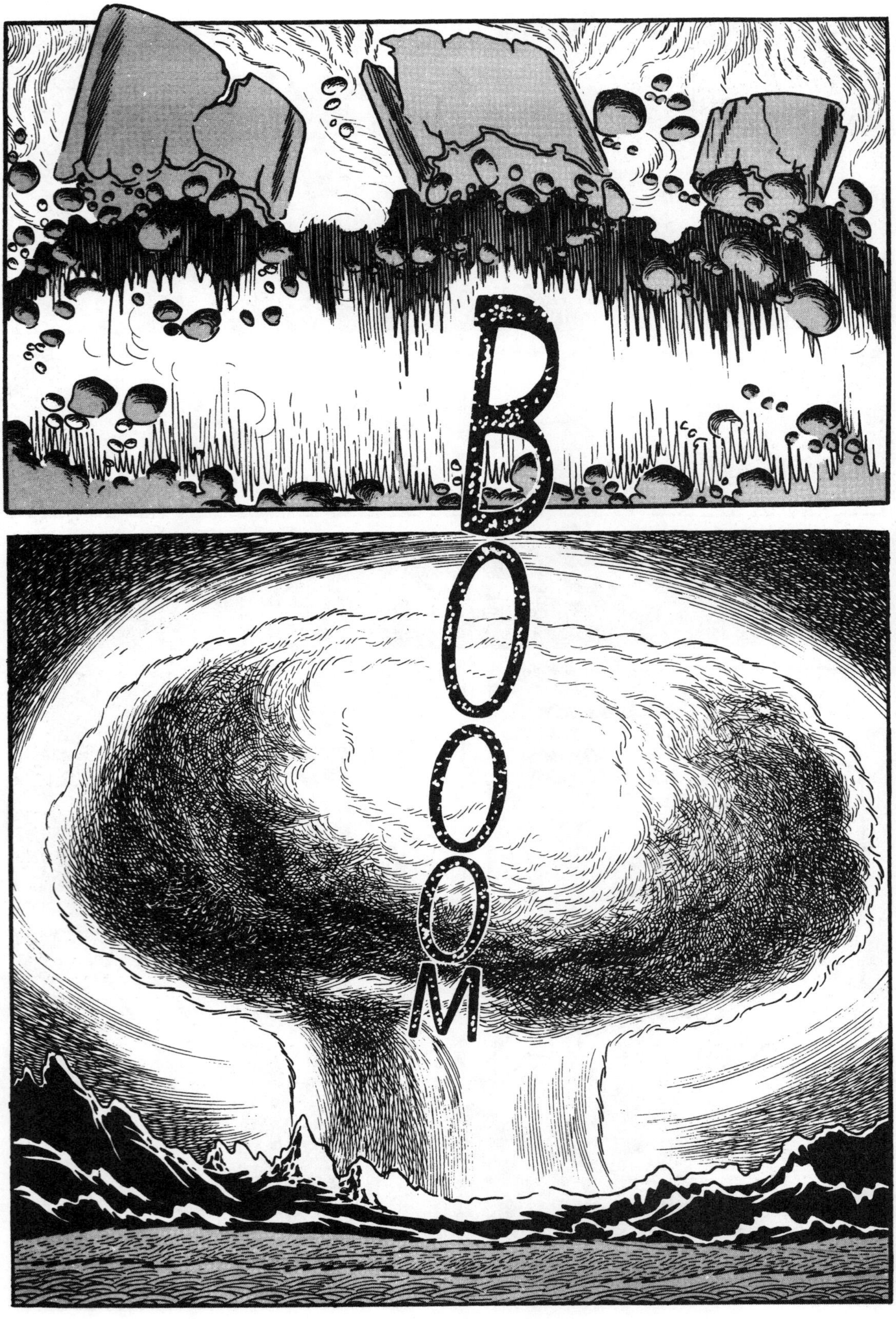
BOOOOM

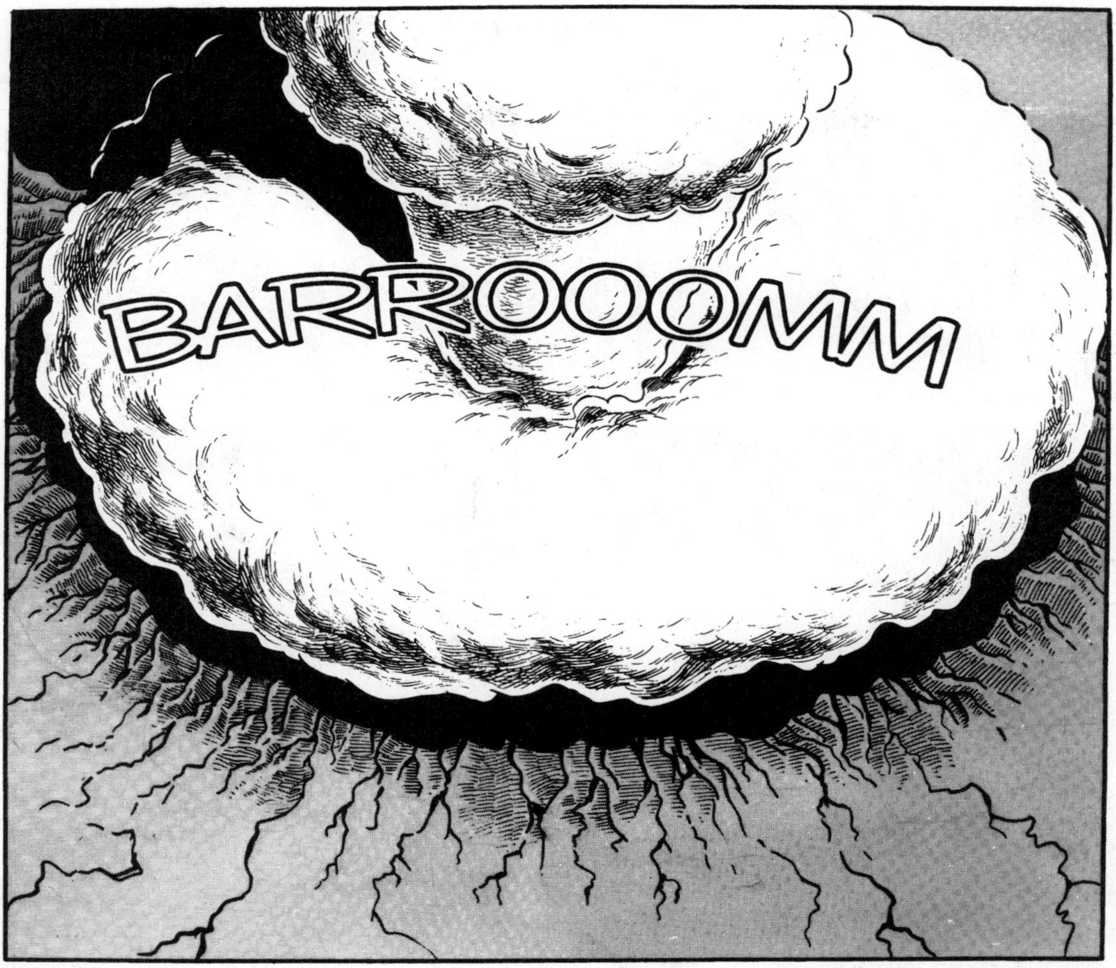
BARROOOMM

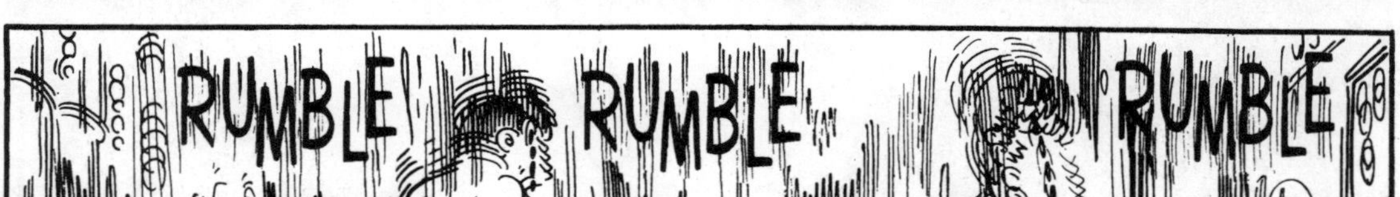
RUMBLE
RUMBLE
RUMBLE

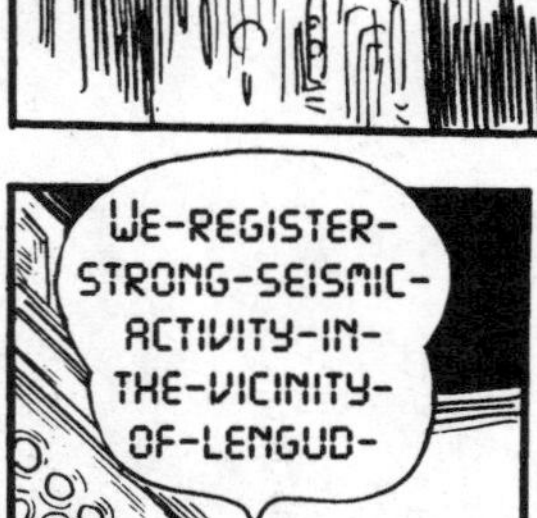
We-register-strong-seismic-activity-in-the-vicinity-of-Lengud-

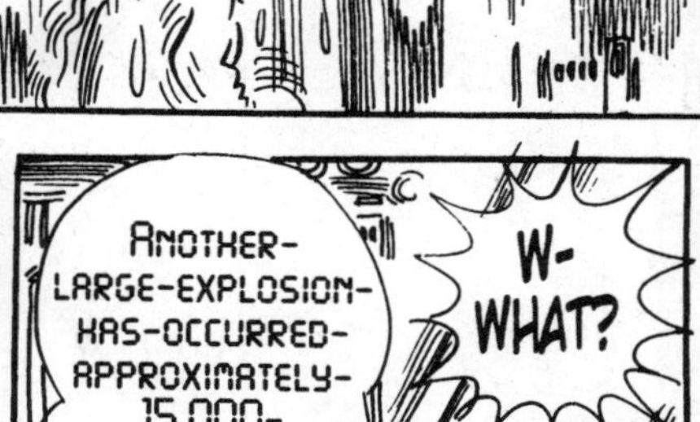
Another-large-explosion-has-occurred-approximately-15,000-kilometers-northwest-
W-WHAT?

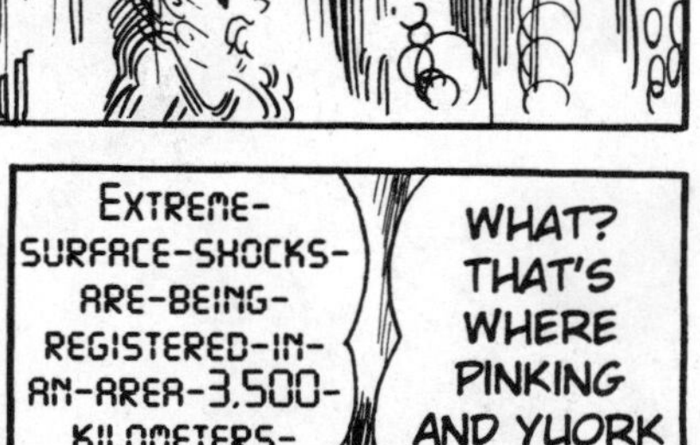
Extreme-surface-shocks-are-being-registered-in-an-area-3,500-kilometers-southeast-of-here-also-
WHAT? THAT'S WHERE PINKING AND YUORK ARE!!

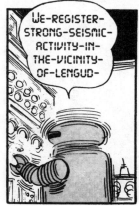

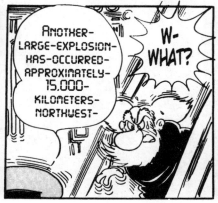

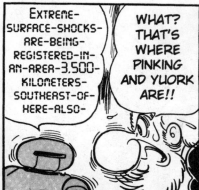

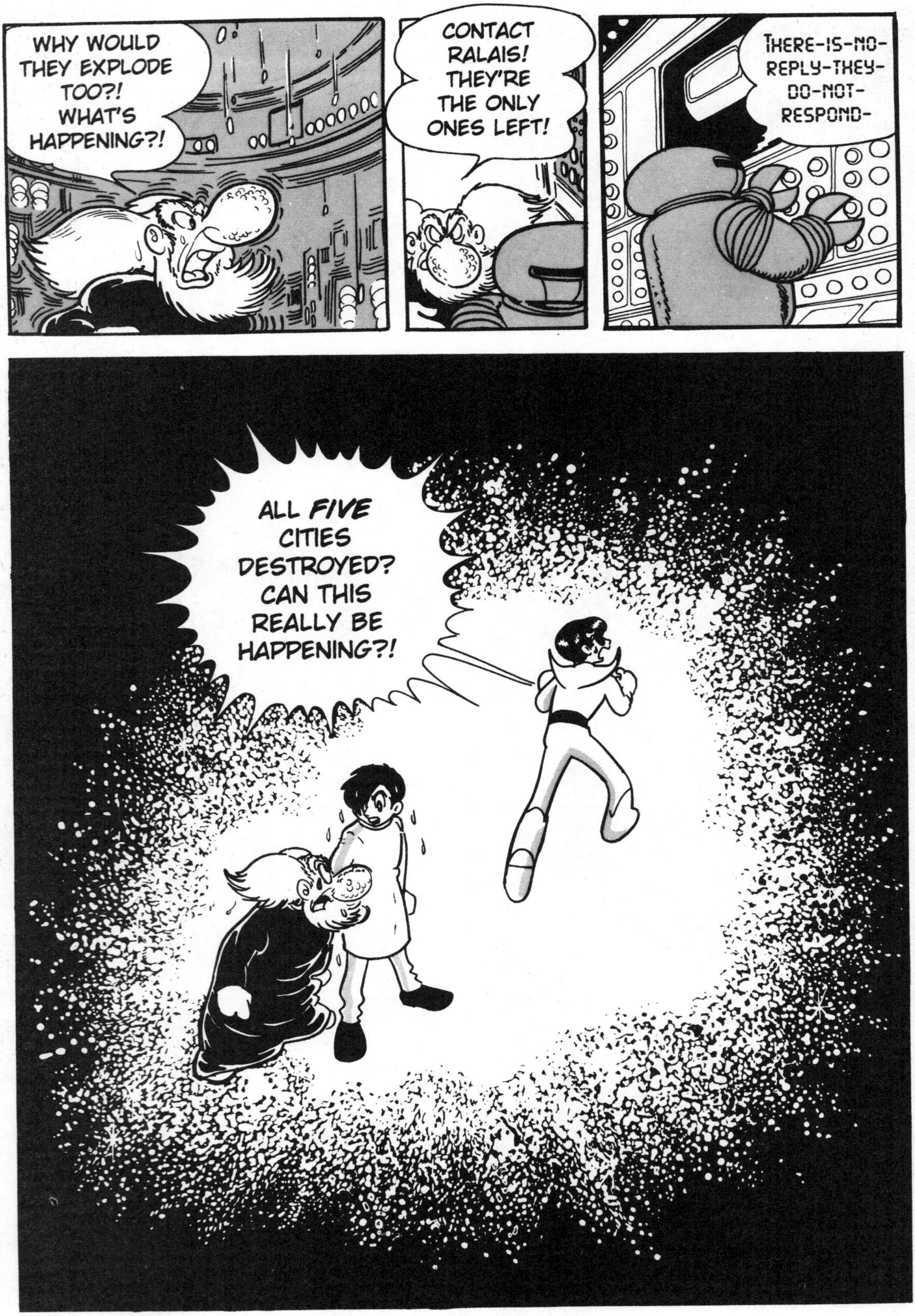
WHY WOULD THEY EXPLODE TOO?! WHAT'S HAPPENING?!
CONTACT RALAIS! THEY'RE THE ONLY ONES LEFT!
THERE-IS-NO-REPLY-THEY-DO-NOT-RESPOND-
ALL *FIVE* CITIES DESTROYED? CAN THIS REALLY BE HAPPENING?!

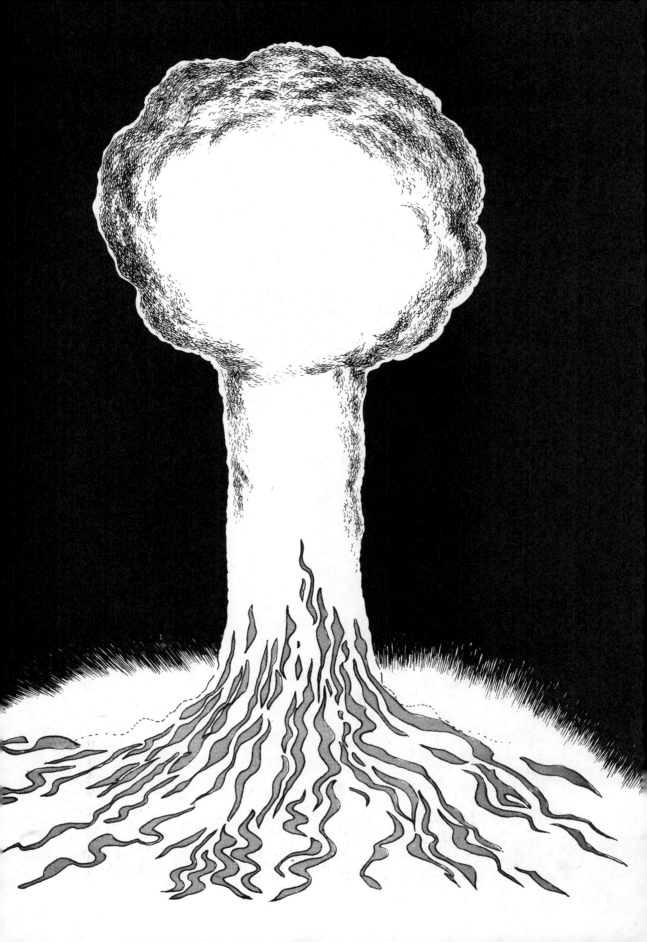

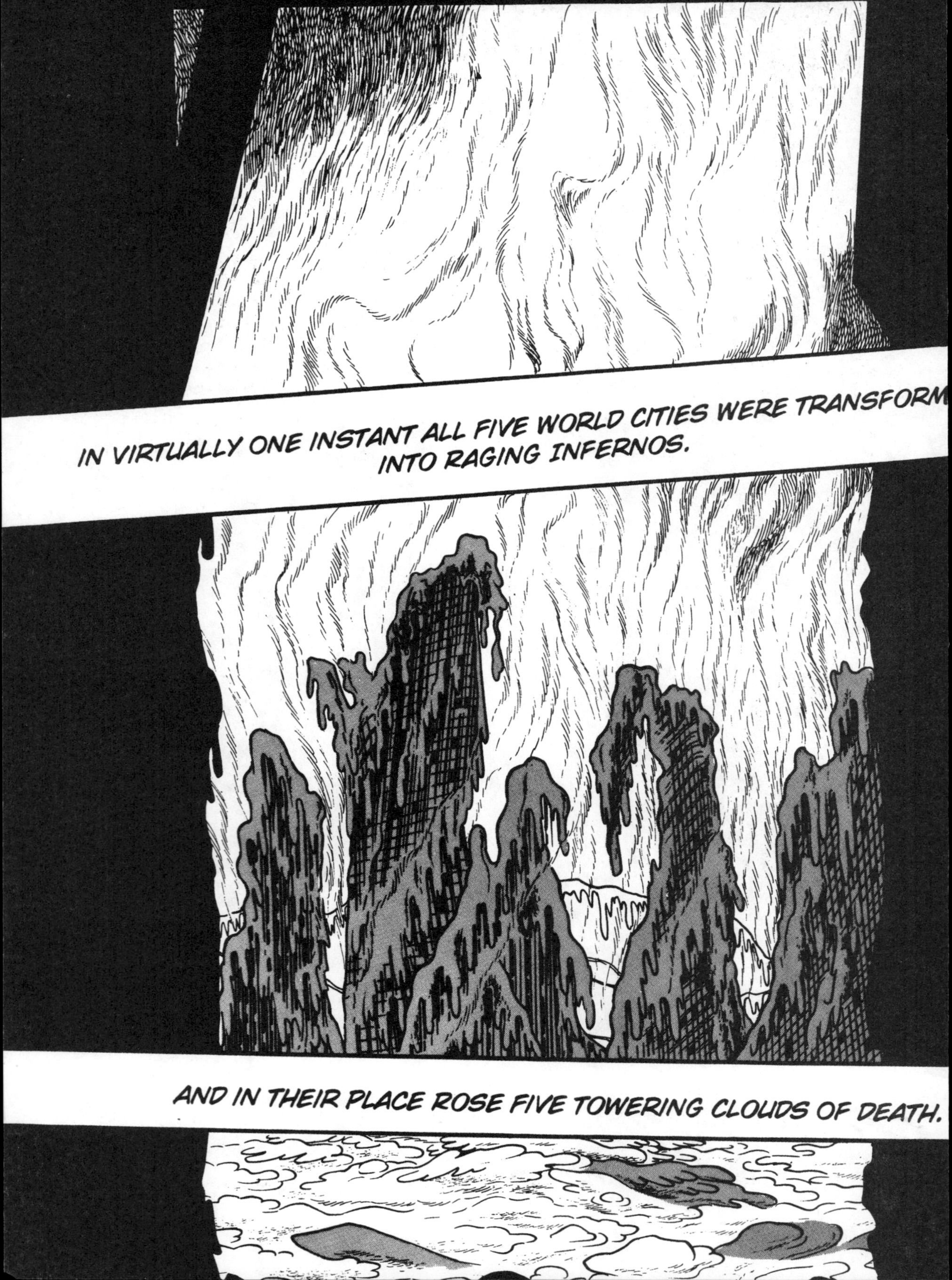
IN VIRTUALLY ONE INSTANT ALL FIVE WORLD CITIES WERE TRANSFORM
INTO RAGING INFERNOS.
AND IN THEIR PLACE ROSE FIVE TOWERING CLOUDS OF DEATH.

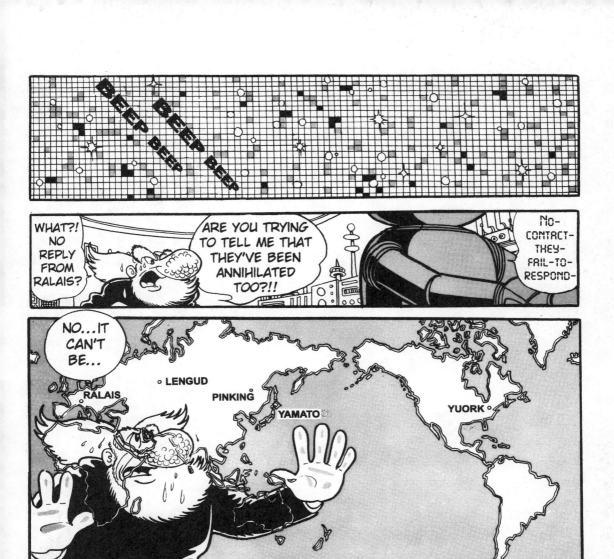

BEEP BEEP BEEP BEEP BEEP

WHAT?! NO REPLY FROM RALAIS?

ARE YOU TRYING TO TELL ME THAT THEY'VE BEEN ANNIHILATED TOO?!!

NO—CONTACT—THEY—FAIL—TO—RESPOND—

NO...IT CAN'T BE...

RALAIS

LENGUD

PINKING

YAMATO

YUORK

WITH ALL FIVE CITIES DESTROYED...

IT MEANS THE END OF MANKIND...

PROBABLY...

ISN'T THERE SOME WAY WE CAN FIND OUT IF ANYONE IS ALIVE OR NOT?

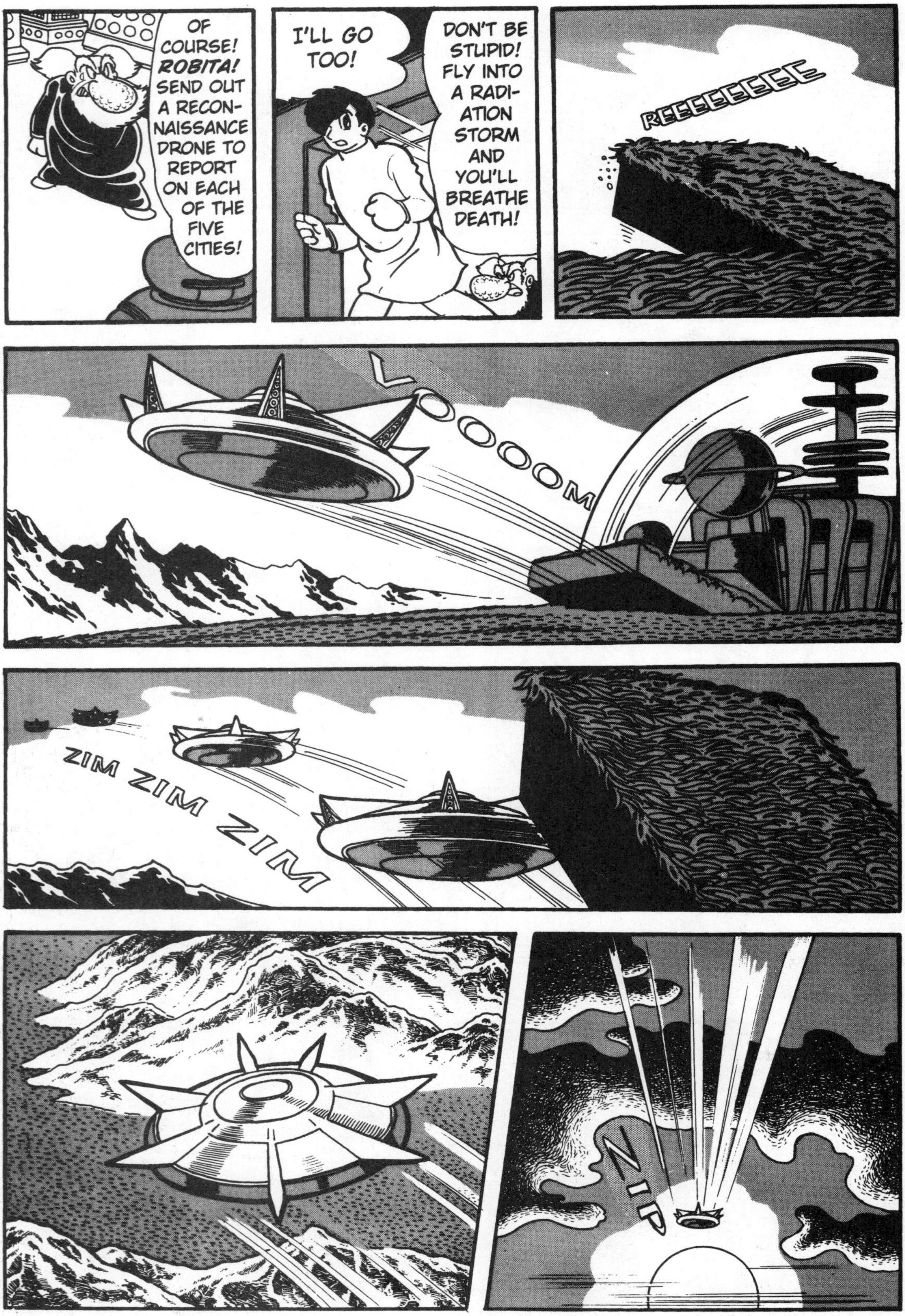
OF COURSE! ROBITA! SEND OUT A RECONNAISSANCE DRONE TO REPORT ON EACH OF THE FIVE CITIES!
I'LL GO TOO!
DON'T BE STUPID! FLY INTO A RADIATION STORM AND YOU'LL BREATHE DEATH!
REEEEEEEEE
VOOOOOM
ZIM ZIM ZIM
ZIP

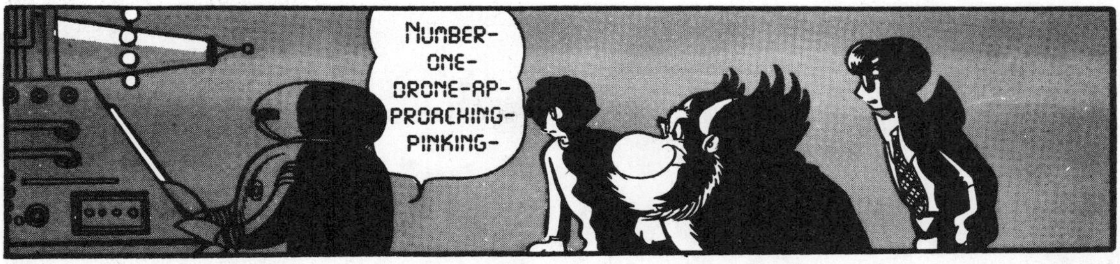
NUMBER-ONE-DRONE-APPROACHING-PINKING-
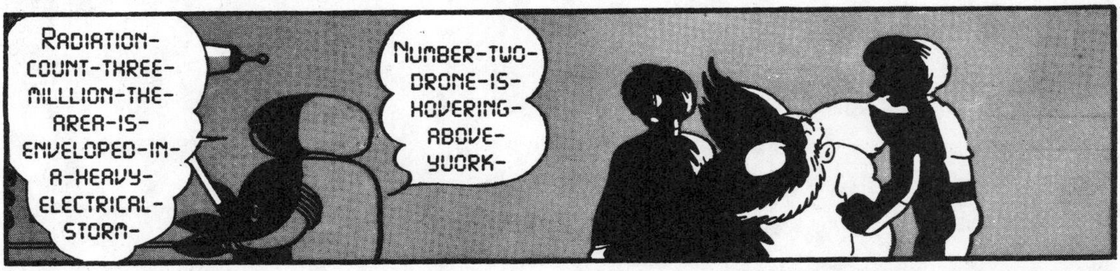
NUMBER-TWO-DRONE-IS-HOVERING-ABOVE-YUORK-
RADIATION-COUNT-THREE-MILLLION-THE-ARER-IS-ENVELOPED-IN-A-HEAVY-ELECTRICAL-STORM-
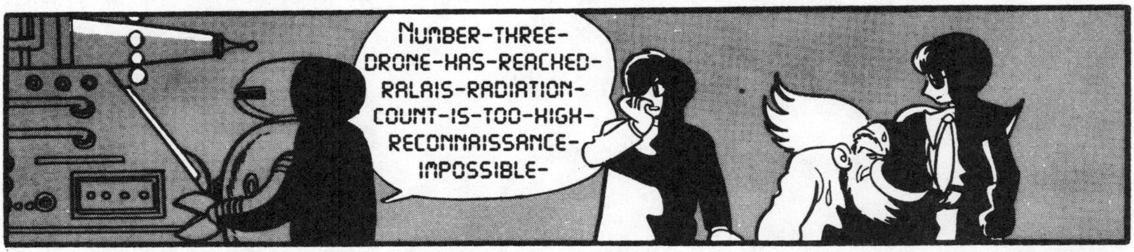
NUMBER-THREE-DRONE-HAS-REACHED-RALAIS-RADIATION-COUNT-IS-TOO-HIGH-RECONNAISSANCE-IMPOSSIBLE-
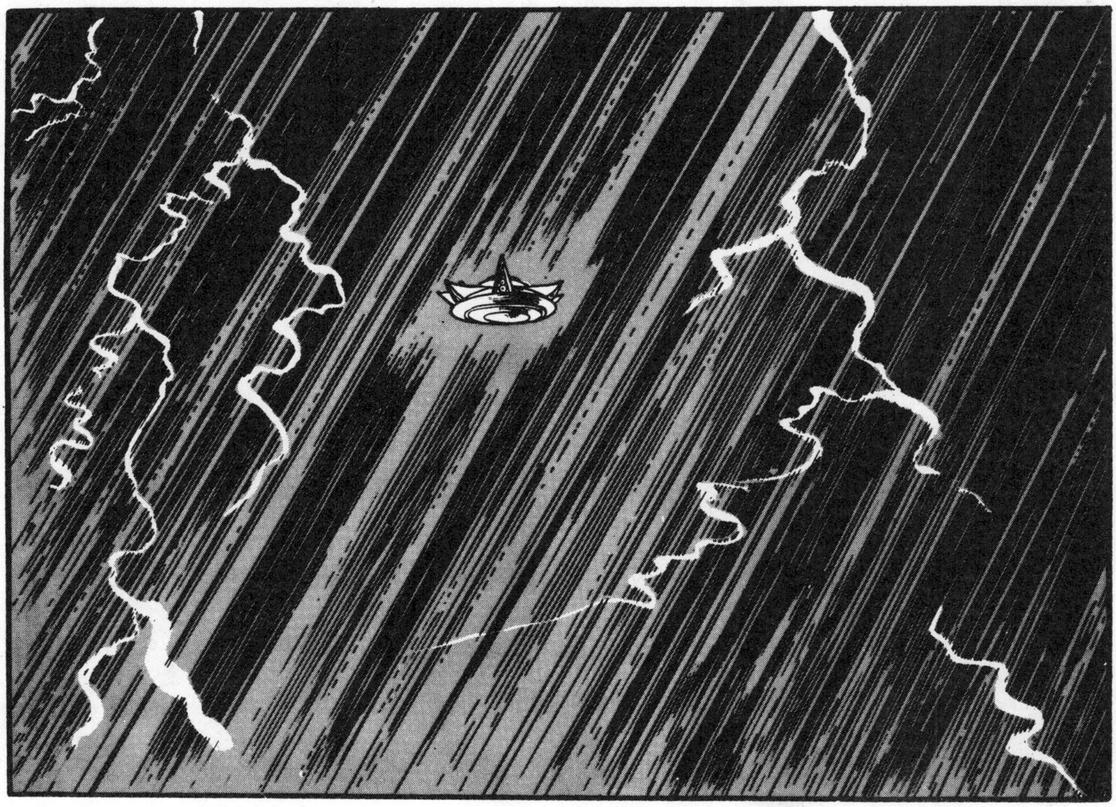

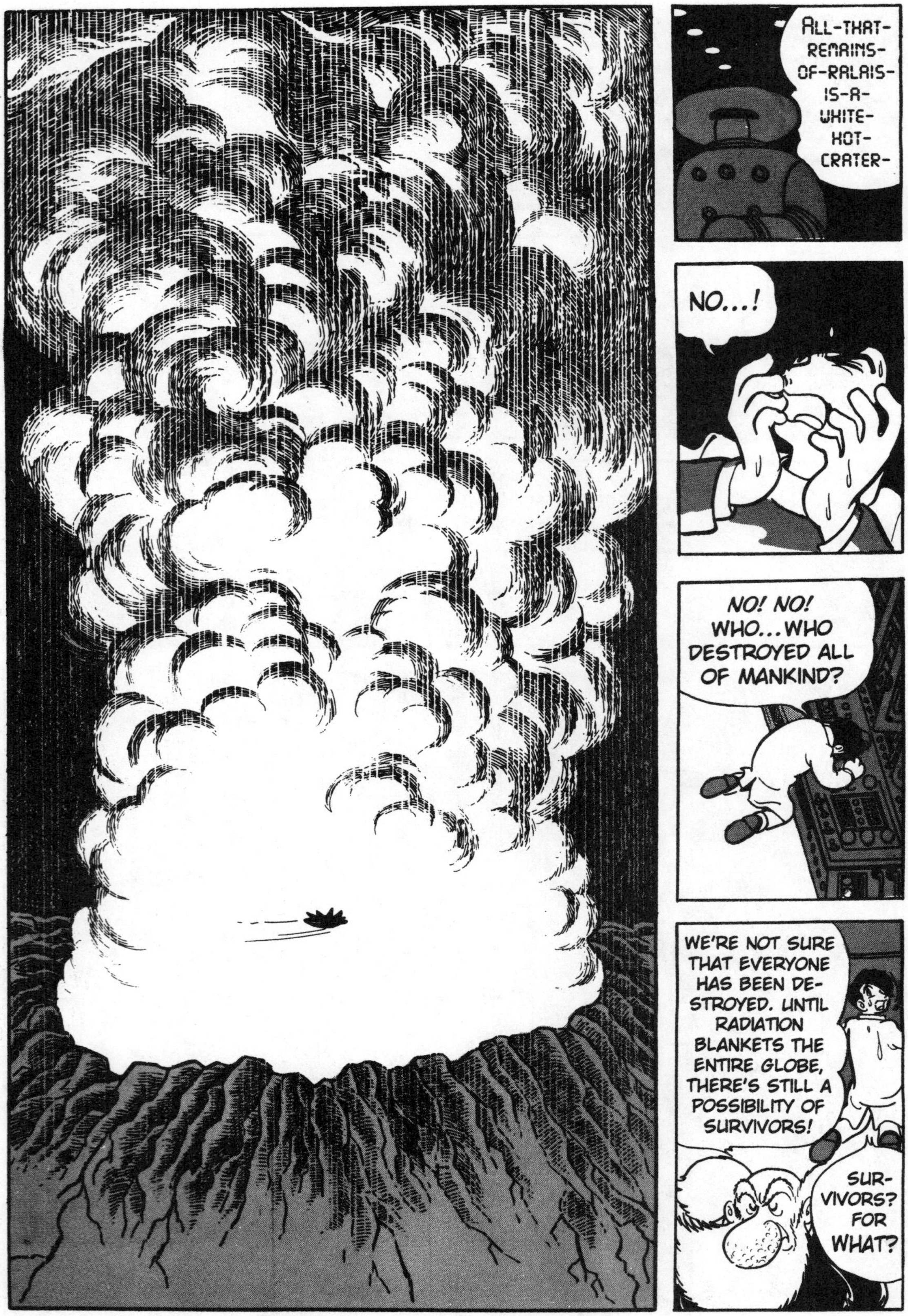
ALL-THAT-REMAINS-OF-RALAIS-IS-A-WHITE-HOT-CRATER-
NO...!
NO! NO! WHO...WHO DESTROYED ALL OF MANKIND?
WE'RE NOT SURE THAT EVERYONE HAS BEEN DE-STROYED. UNTIL RADIATION BLANKETS THE ENTIRE GLOBE, THERE'S STILL A POSSIBILITY OF SURVIVORS!
SUR-VIVORS? FOR WHAT?

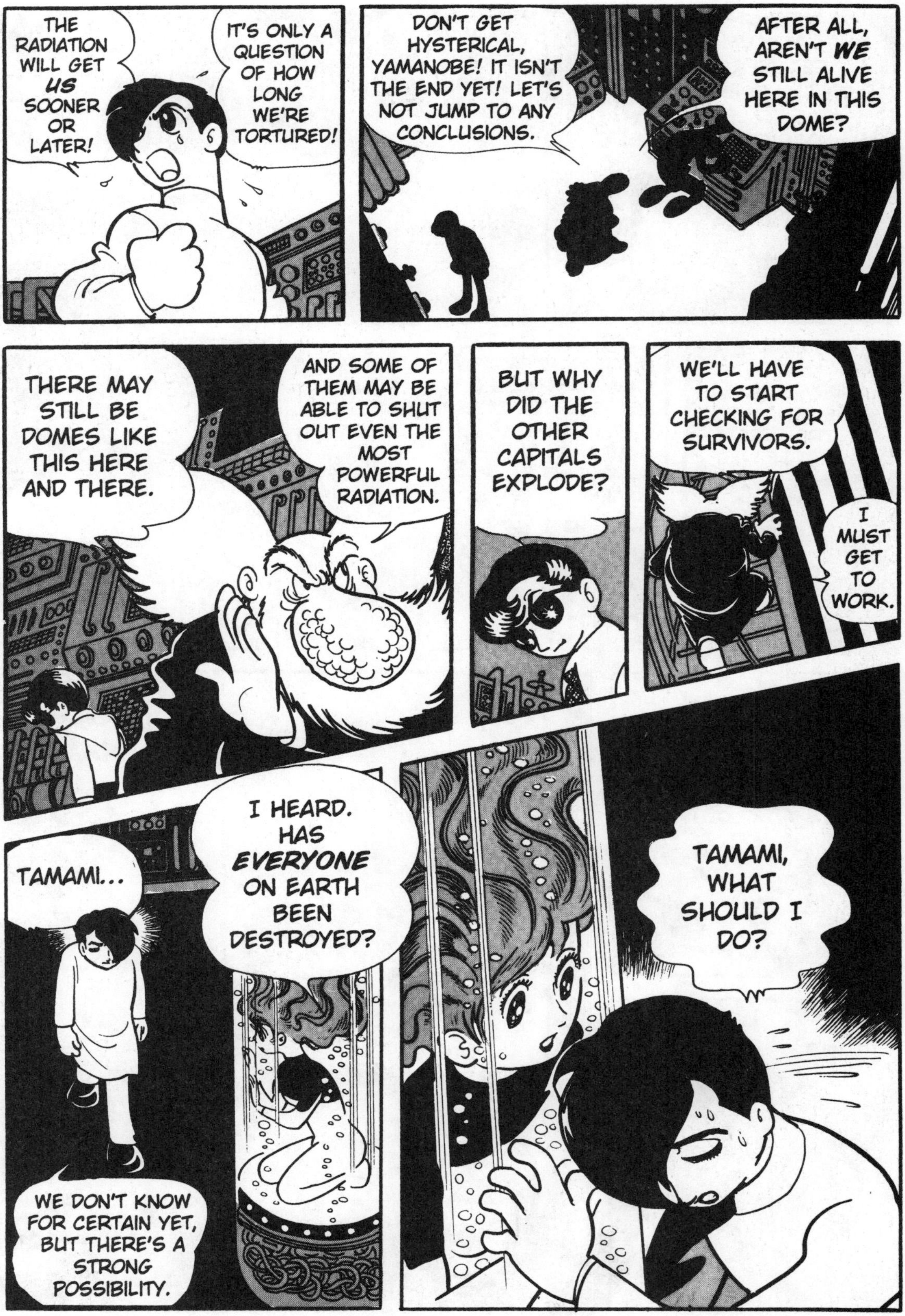
THE RADIATION WILL GET *US* SOONER OR LATER!
IT'S ONLY A QUESTION OF HOW LONG WE'RE TORTURED!
DON'T GET HYSTERICAL, YAMANOBE! IT ISN'T THE END YET! LET'S NOT JUMP TO ANY CONCLUSIONS.
AFTER ALL, AREN'T *WE* STILL ALIVE HERE IN THIS DOME?
THERE MAY STILL BE DOMES LIKE THIS HERE AND THERE.
AND SOME OF THEM MAY BE ABLE TO SHUT OUT EVEN THE MOST POWERFUL RADIATION.
BUT WHY DID THE OTHER CAPITALS EXPLODE?
WE'LL HAVE TO START CHECKING FOR SURVIVORS.
I MUST GET TO WORK.
TAMAMI...
I HEARD. HAS *EVERYONE* ON EARTH BEEN DESTROYED?
WE DON'T KNOW FOR CERTAIN YET, BUT THERE'S A STRONG POSSIBILITY.
TAMAMI, WHAT SHOULD I DO?

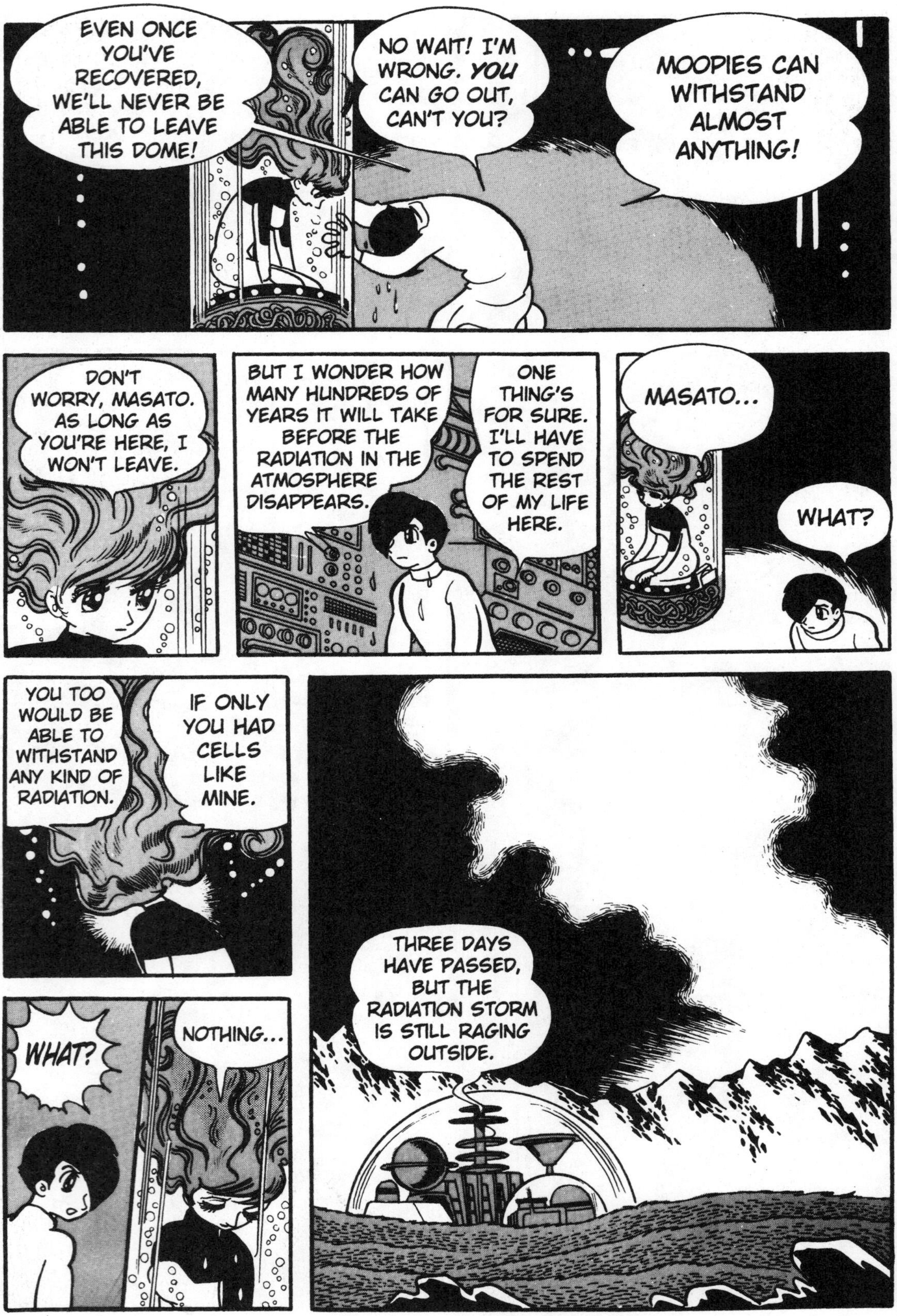
EVEN ONCE YOU'VE RECOVERED, WE'LL NEVER BE ABLE TO LEAVE THIS DOME!
NO WAIT! I'M WRONG. YOU CAN GO OUT, CAN'T YOU?
MOOPIES CAN WITHSTAND ALMOST ANYTHING!
DON'T WORRY, MASATO. AS LONG AS YOU'RE HERE, I WON'T LEAVE.
BUT I WONDER HOW MANY HUNDREDS OF YEARS IT WILL TAKE BEFORE THE RADIATION IN THE ATMOSPHERE DISAPPEARS.
ONE THING'S FOR SURE. I'LL HAVE TO SPEND THE REST OF MY LIFE HERE.
MASATO...
WHAT?
YOU TOO WOULD BE ABLE TO WITHSTAND ANY KIND OF RADIATION.
IF ONLY YOU HAD CELLS LIKE MINE.
WHAT?
NOTHING...
THREE DAYS HAVE PASSED, BUT THE RADIATION STORM IS STILL RAGING OUTSIDE.

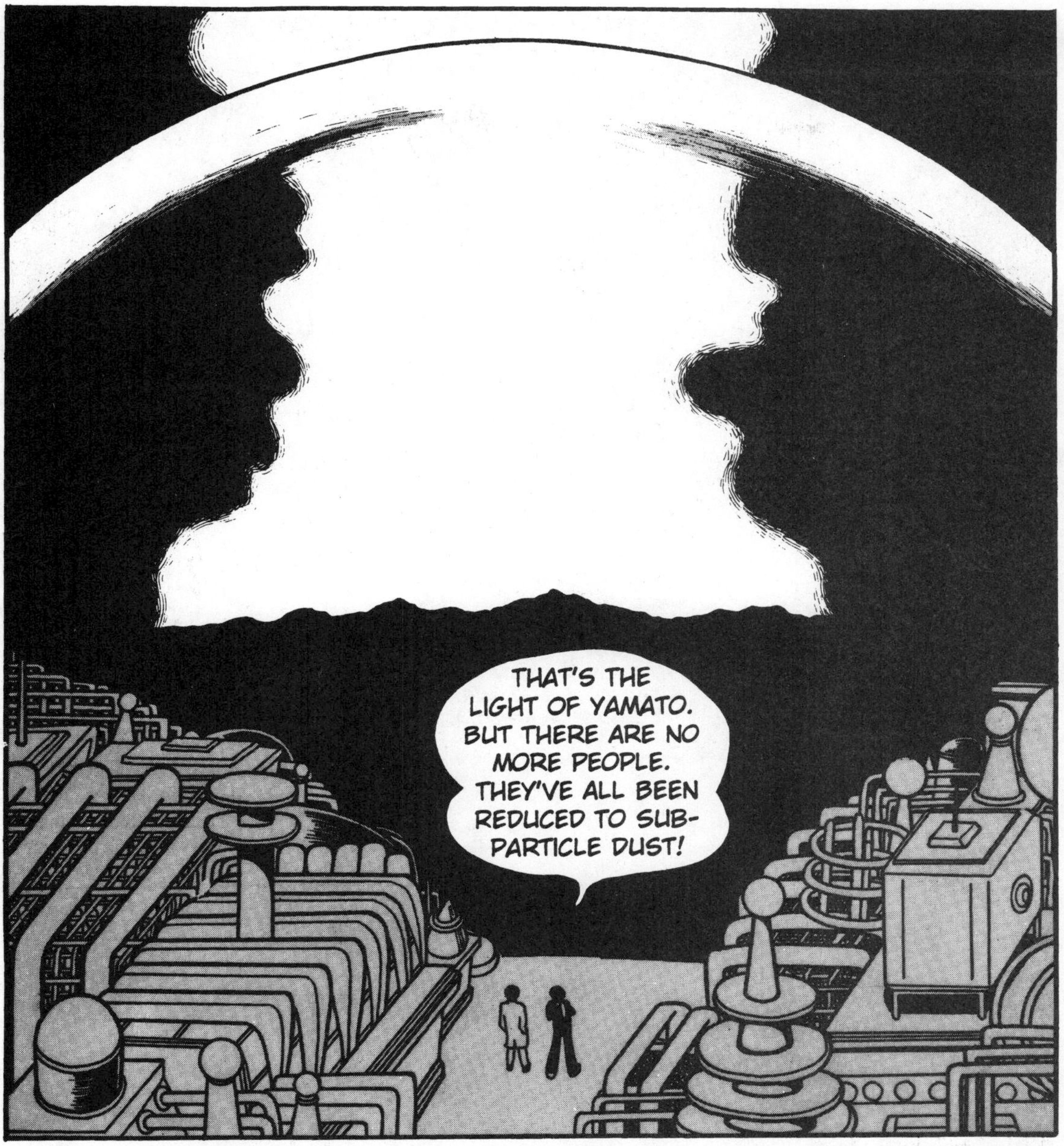
THAT'S THE LIGHT OF YAMATO. BUT THERE ARE NO MORE PEOPLE. THEY'VE ALL BEEN REDUCED TO SUB-PARTICLE DUST!

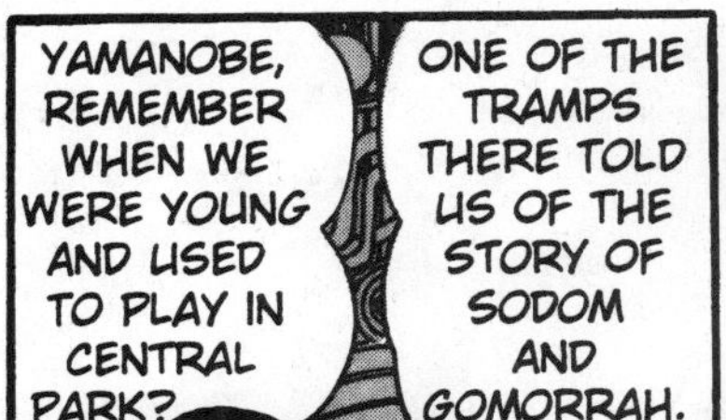
YAMANOBE, REMEMBER WHEN WE WERE YOUNG AND USED TO PLAY IN CENTRAL PARK?
ONE OF THE TRAMPS THERE TOLD US OF THE STORY OF SODOM AND GOMORRAH.

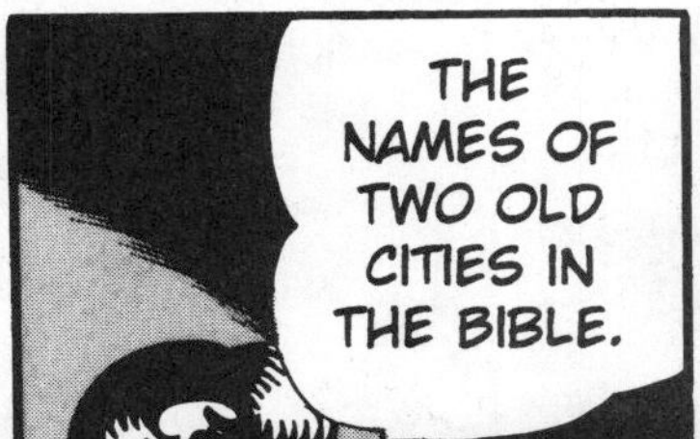
THE NAMES OF TWO OLD CITIES IN THE BIBLE.

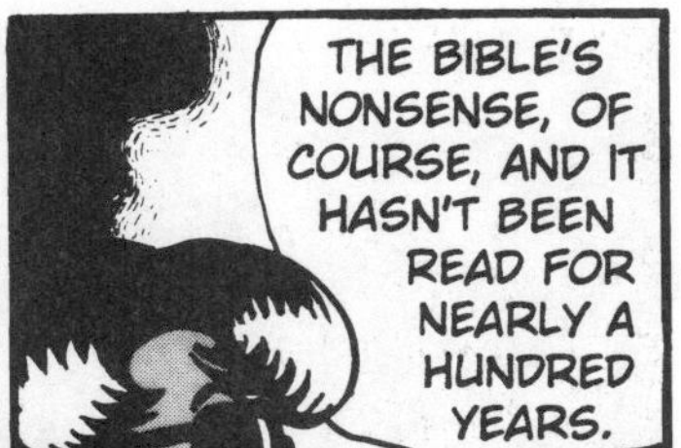
THE BIBLE'S NONSENSE, OF COURSE, AND IT HASN'T BEEN READ FOR NEARLY A HUNDRED YEARS.

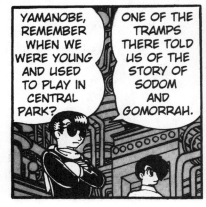

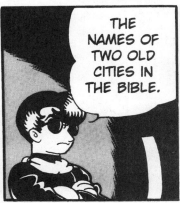

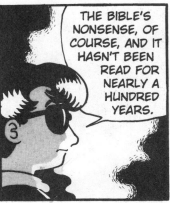

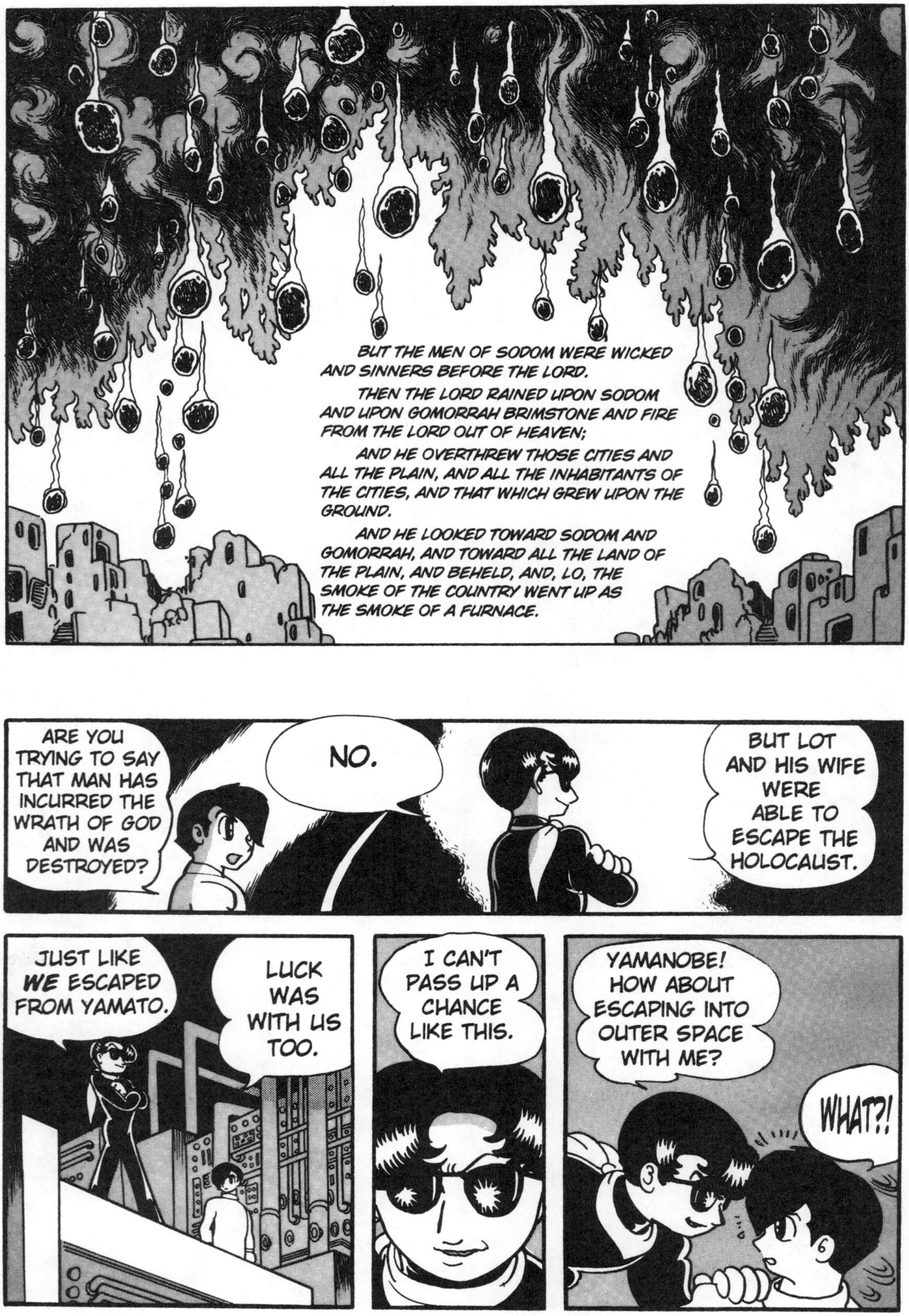
BUT THE MEN OF SODOM WERE WICKED AND SINNERS BEFORE THE LORD.
THEN THE LORD RAINED UPON SODOM AND UPON GOMORRAH BRIMSTONE AND FIRE FROM THE LORD OUT OF HEAVEN;
AND HE OVERTHREW THOSE CITIES AND ALL THE PLAIN, AND ALL THE INHABITANTS OF THE CITIES, AND THAT WHICH GREW UPON THE GROUND.
AND HE LOOKED TOWARD SODOM AND GOMORRAH, AND TOWARD ALL THE LAND OF THE PLAIN, AND BEHELD, AND, LO, THE SMOKE OF THE COUNTRY WENT UP AS THE SMOKE OF A FURNACE.
ARE YOU TRYING TO SAY THAT MAN HAS INCURRED THE WRATH OF GOD AND WAS DESTROYED?
NO.
BUT LOT AND HIS WIFE WERE ABLE TO ESCAPE THE HOLOCAUST.
JUST LIKE WE ESCAPED FROM YAMATO.
LUCK WAS WITH US TOO.
I CAN'T PASS UP A CHANCE LIKE THIS.
YAMANOBE! HOW ABOUT ESCAPING INTO OUTER SPACE WITH ME?
WHAT?!

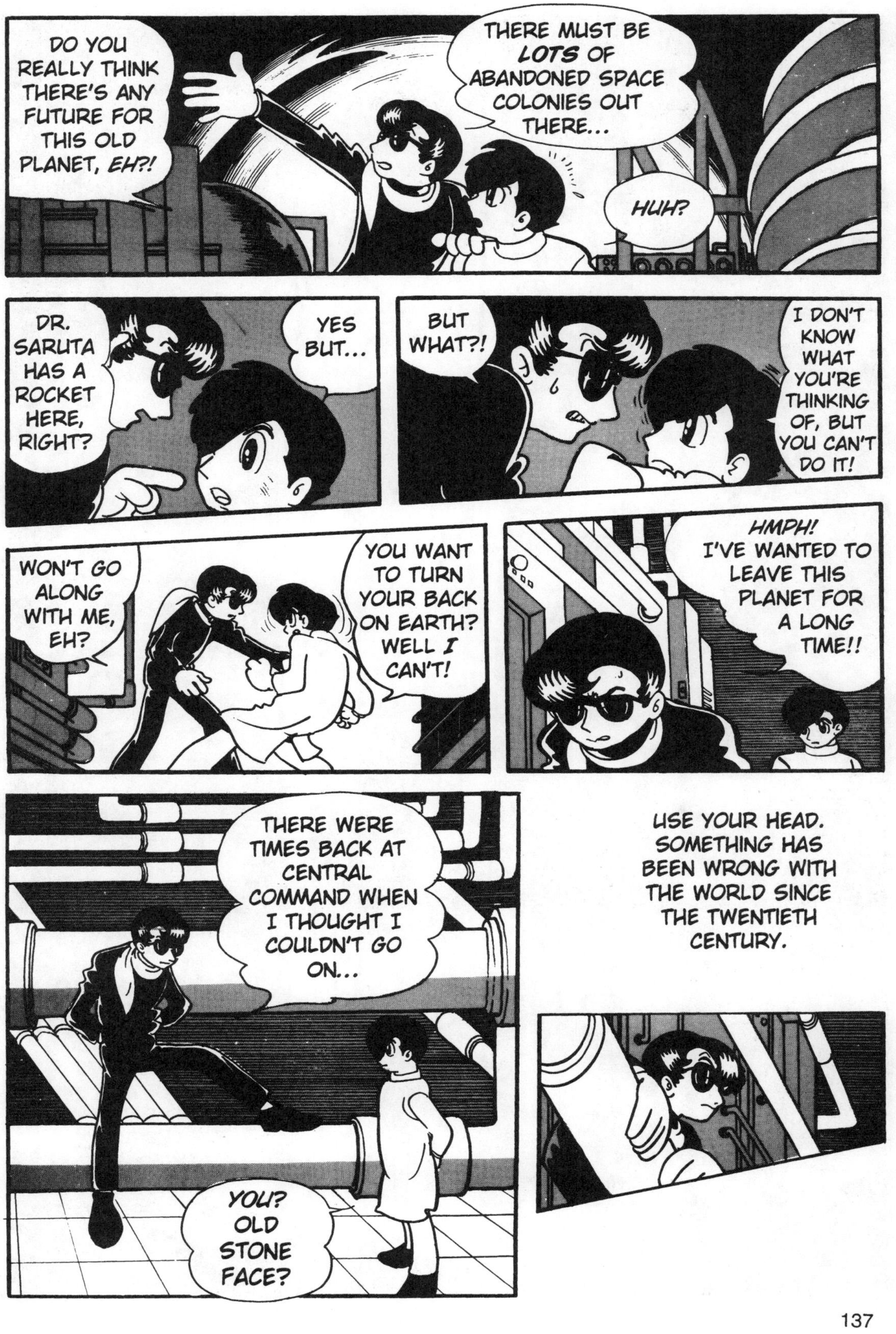
DO YOU REALLY THINK THERE'S ANY FUTURE FOR THIS OLD PLANET, EH?!
THERE MUST BE LOTS OF ABANDONED SPACE COLONIES OUT THERE...
HUH?
DR. SARUTA HAS A ROCKET HERE, RIGHT?
YES BUT...
BUT WHAT?!
I DON'T KNOW WHAT YOU'RE THINKING OF, BUT YOU CAN'T DO IT!
WON'T GO ALONG WITH ME, EH?
YOU WANT TO TURN YOUR BACK ON EARTH? WELL I CAN'T!
HMPH! I'VE WANTED TO LEAVE THIS PLANET FOR A LONG TIME!!
THERE WERE TIMES BACK AT CENTRAL COMMAND WHEN I THOUGHT I COULDN'T GO ON...
YOU? OLD STONE FACE?
USE YOUR HEAD. SOMETHING HAS BEEN WRONG WITH THE WORLD SINCE THE TWENTIETH CENTURY.

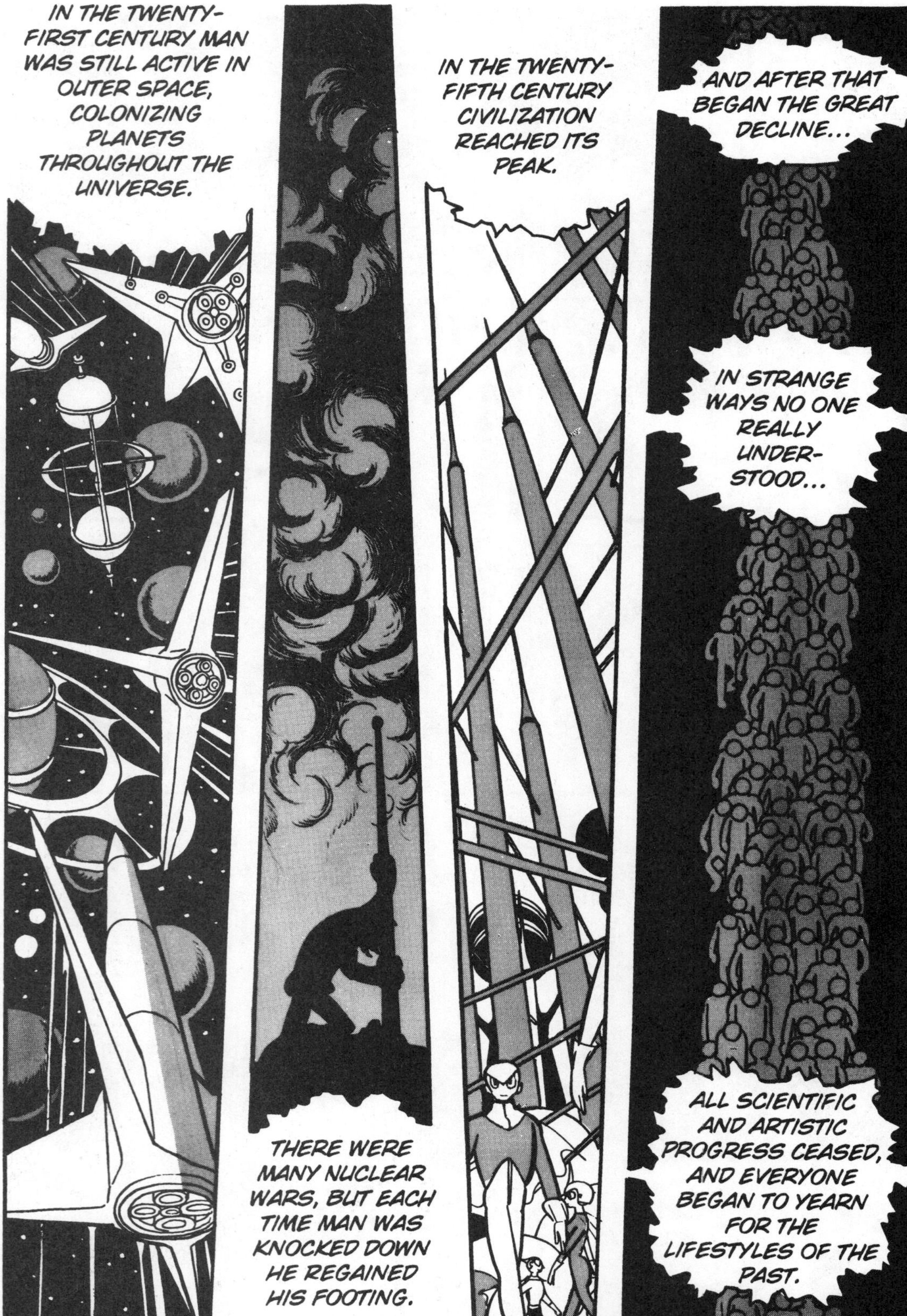
IN THE TWENTY-FIRST CENTURY MAN WAS STILL ACTIVE IN OUTER SPACE, COLONIZING PLANETS THROUGHOUT THE UNIVERSE.
THERE WERE MANY NUCLEAR WARS, BUT EACH TIME MAN WAS KNOCKED DOWN HE REGAINED HIS FOOTING.
IN THE TWENTY-FIFTH CENTURY CIVILIZATION REACHED ITS PEAK.
AND AFTER THAT BEGAN THE GREAT DECLINE...
IN STRANGE WAYS NO ONE REALLY UNDER-STOOD...
ALL SCIENTIFIC AND ARTISTIC PROGRESS CEASED, AND EVERYONE BEGAN TO YEARN FOR THE LIFESTYLES OF THE PAST.

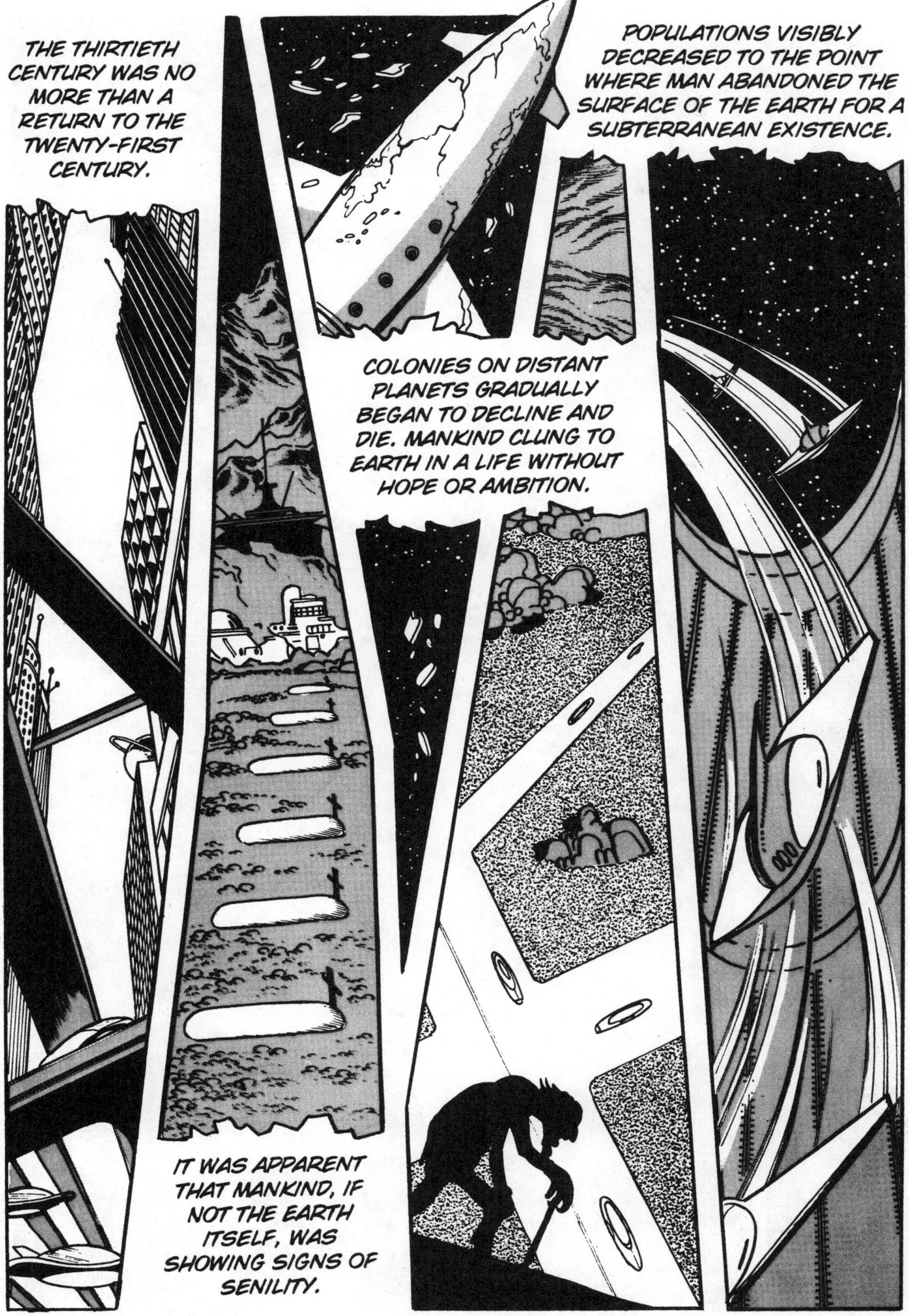
POPULATIONS VISIBLY DECREASED TO THE POINT WHERE MAN ABANDONED THE SURFACE OF THE EARTH FOR A SUBTERRANEAN EXISTENCE.
COLONIES ON DISTANT PLANETS GRADUALLY BEGAN TO DECLINE AND DIE. MANKIND CLUNG TO EARTH IN A LIFE WITHOUT HOPE OR AMBITION.
THE THIRTIETH CENTURY WAS NO MORE THAN A RETURN TO THE TWENTY-FIRST CENTURY.
IT WAS APPARENT THAT MANKIND, IF NOT THE EARTH ITSELF, WAS SHOWING SIGNS OF SENILITY.

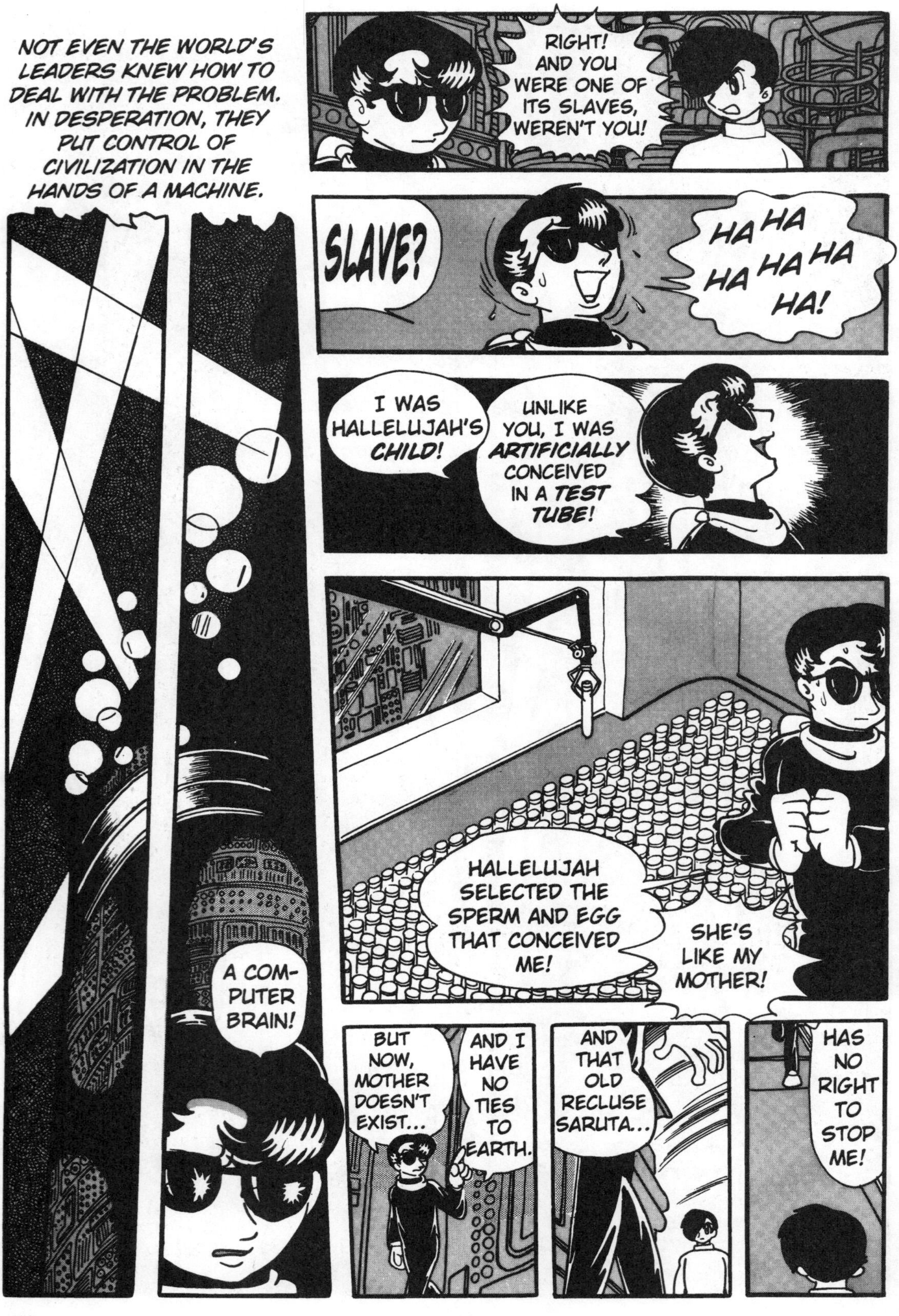
NOT EVEN THE WORLD'S LEADERS KNEW HOW TO DEAL WITH THE PROBLEM. IN DESPERATION, THEY PUT CONTROL OF CIVILIZATION IN THE HANDS OF A MACHINE.
A COM-PUTER BRAIN!
RIGHT! AND YOU WERE ONE OF ITS SLAVES, WEREN'T YOU!
SLAVE?
HA HA HA HA HA HA!
I WAS HALLELUJAH'S CHILD!
UNLIKE YOU, I WAS ARTIFICIALLY CONCEIVED IN A TEST TUBE!
HALLELUJAH SELECTED THE SPERM AND EGG THAT CONCEIVED ME!
SHE'S LIKE MY MOTHER!
BUT NOW, MOTHER DOESN'T EXIST...
AND I HAVE NO TIES TO EARTH.
AND THAT OLD RECLUSE SARUTA...
HAS NO RIGHT TO STOP ME!

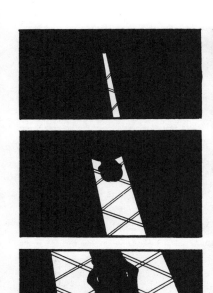

CLANG

KLAK KLAK

KLAK KLAK

THIS MUST BE THE SILO.

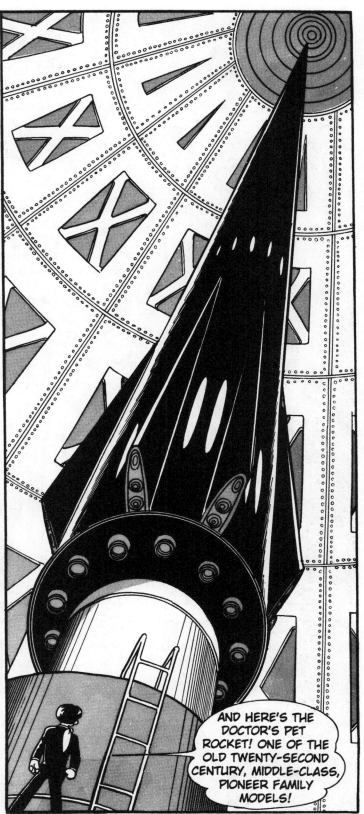

AND HERE'S THE DOCTOR'S PET ROCKET! ONE OF THE OLD TWENTY-SECOND CENTURY, MIDDLE-CLASS, PIONEER FAMILY MODELS!

I COULD FLY THIS THING WITH MY EYES CLOSED, HEH HEH.

HEH HEH... I'LL BE BACK FOR A SPIN LATER!

JUST WAIT, RUSTY OLD ROCKET!

THE MOOPIE WOMAN!

SO YOU'LL CONSENT TO MY REQUEST?

YES ...

THANK YOU! YOU... YOU'RE A GOOD PERSON... I'LL SEE THAT YOUR KINDNESS SHALL NOT BE IN VAIN... I'LL SOLVE THE MYSTERY OF YOUR CELL STRUCTURE!

DR. SARUTA, ONCE YOU'VE UNLOCKED THE SECRET ...

I WANT YOU TO GRANT ME A FAVOR.

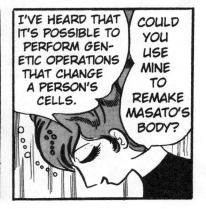

I'VE HEARD THAT IT'S POSSIBLE TO PERFORM GENETIC OPERATIONS THAT CHANGE A PERSON'S CELLS.

COULD YOU USE MINE TO REMAKE MASATO'S BODY?

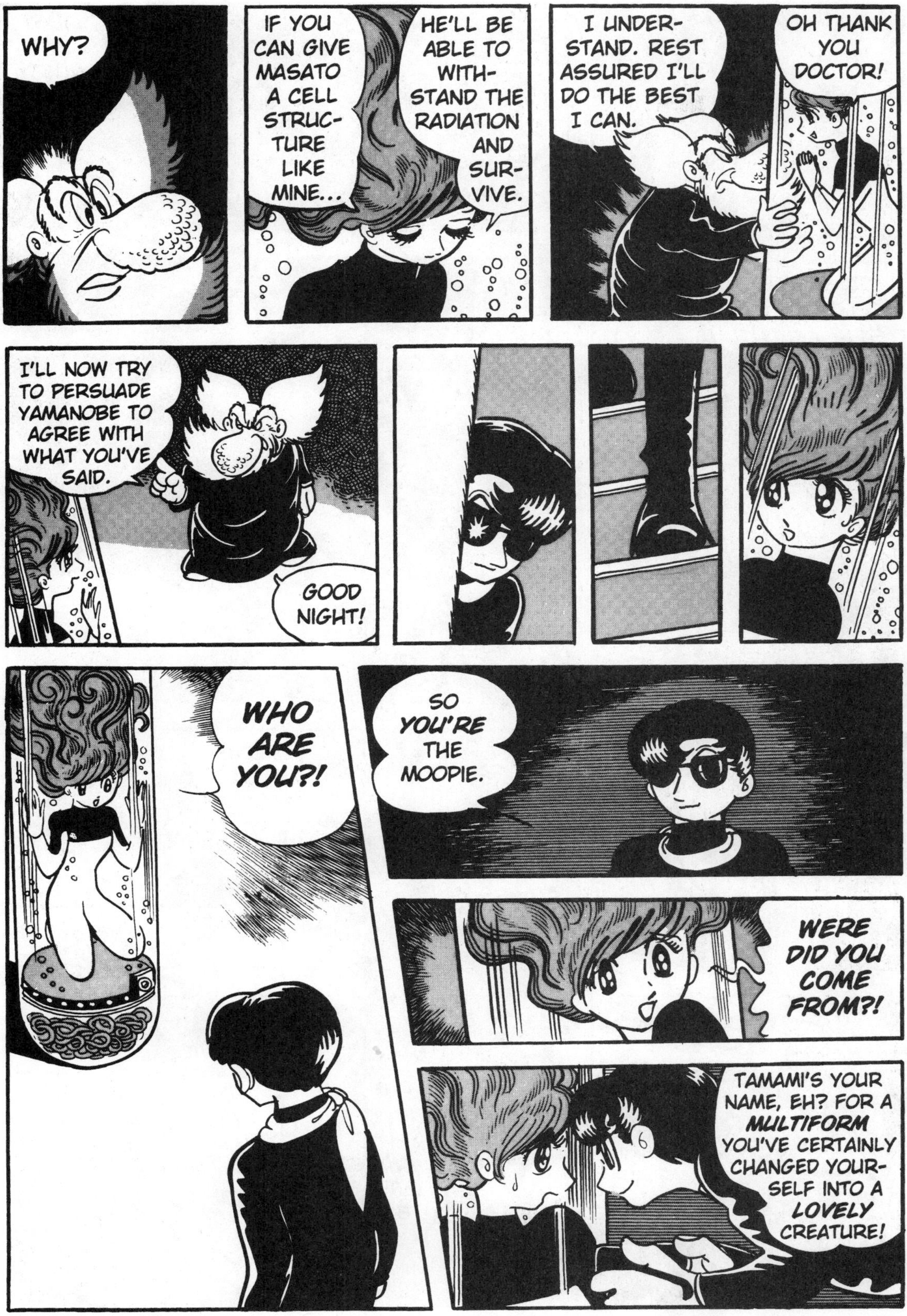
WHY?
IF YOU CAN GIVE MASATO A CELL STRUCTURE LIKE MINE...
HE'LL BE ABLE TO WITHSTAND THE RADIATION AND SURVIVE.
I UNDERSTAND. REST ASSURED I'LL DO THE BEST I CAN.
OH THANK YOU DOCTOR!
I'LL NOW TRY TO PERSUADE YAMANOBE TO AGREE WITH WHAT YOU'VE SAID.
GOOD NIGHT!
WHO ARE YOU?!
SO YOU'RE THE MOOPIE.
WERE DID YOU COME FROM?!
TAMAMI'S YOUR NAME, EH? FOR A MULTIFORM YOU'VE CERTAINLY CHANGED YOURSELF INTO A LOVELY CREATURE!

YOU MUST BE ROC...MASATO'S BOSS AT CENTRAL COMMAND.

IN THE FLESH.

SO YOU'VE FOLLOWED US! STAY AWAY!! DON'T COME NEAR ME!

GO AWAY! DON'T TOUCH ME!

DON'T BE SO HARD ON ME.

I'VE CHANGED MY MIND ABOUT MOOPIES.

YOU'RE A *REAL* WOMAN ...IN EVERY WAY.

AND I *NEED* ONE.

WITH- OUT A WOMAN ON SOME DIS- TANT PLANET, THERE'LL BE NO LITTLE ROCS RUNNING AROUND.

WHAT DO YOU SAY TO LEAVING WITH ME ON SARUTA'S ROCKET?

TO THE ENDS OF THE UNI- VERSE...

WE CAN EVEN BUZZ BY YOUR HOME PLANET, TAMAMI.

PLEASE GO AWAY!

HEH HEH...

I'LL GET YOU OUT OF THIS THING.

NO! STOP!

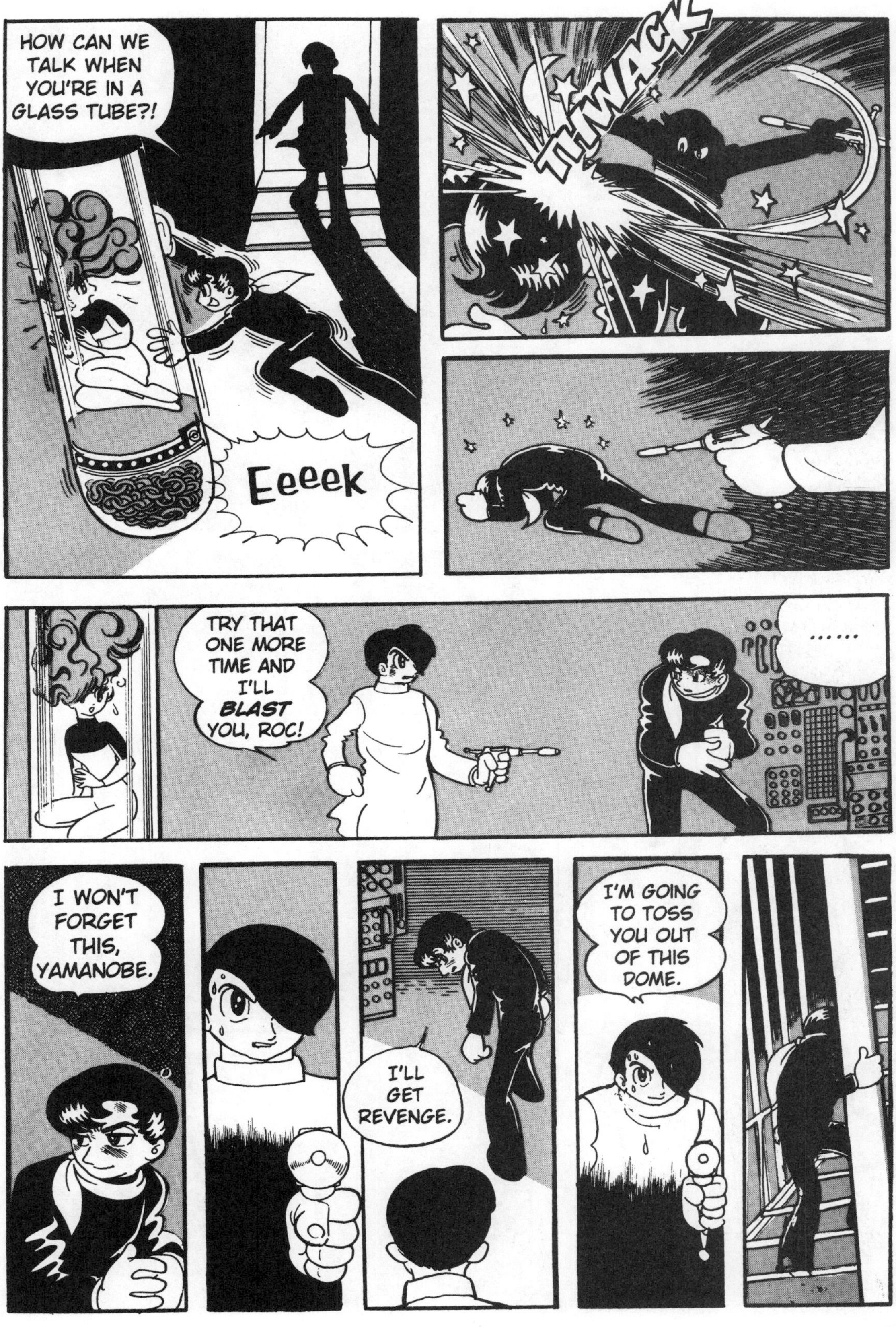
HOW CAN WE TALK WHEN YOU'RE IN A GLASS TUBE?!
Eeeek
TWACK
TRY THAT ONE MORE TIME AND I'LL *BLAST* YOU, ROC!
......
I WON'T FORGET THIS, YAMANOBE.
I'LL GET REVENGE.
I'M GOING TO TOSS YOU OUT OF THIS DOME.

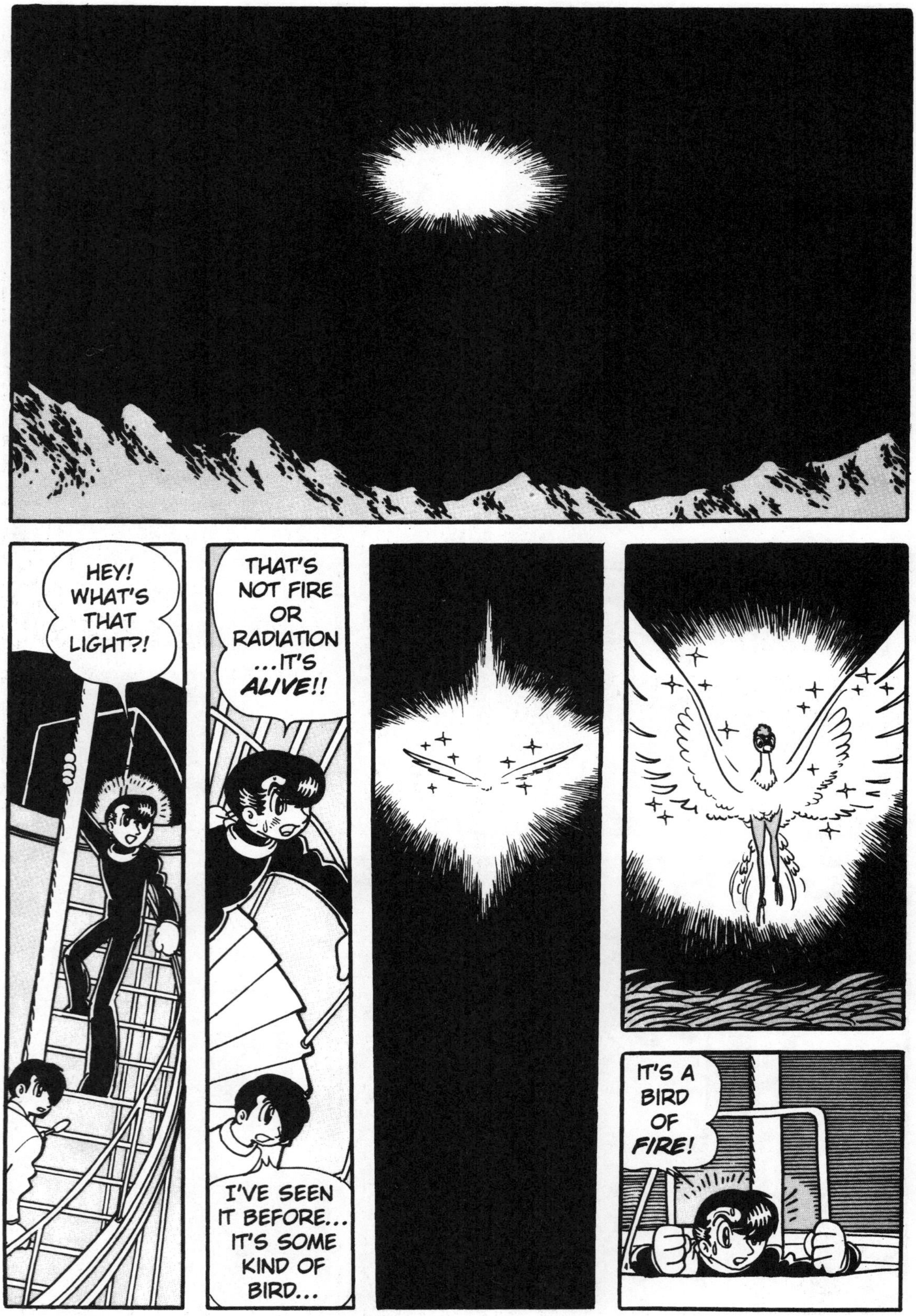
HEY! WHAT'S THAT LIGHT?!
THAT'S NOT FIRE OR RADIATION ...IT'S ALIVE!!
I'VE SEEN IT BEFORE... IT'S SOME KIND OF BIRD...
IT'S A BIRD OF FIRE!

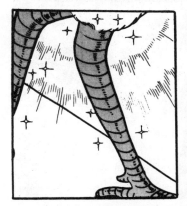

LOOK! SHE'S ACTIVATED THE ENTRANCE!

SHE'S COMING IN-SIDE!!

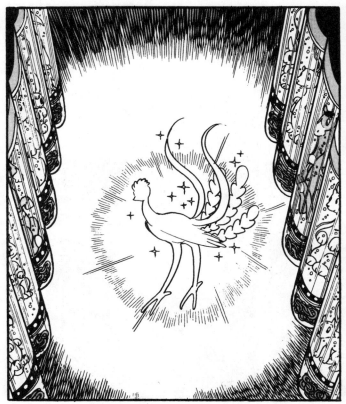

TAKE THIS, YOU MONSTER!

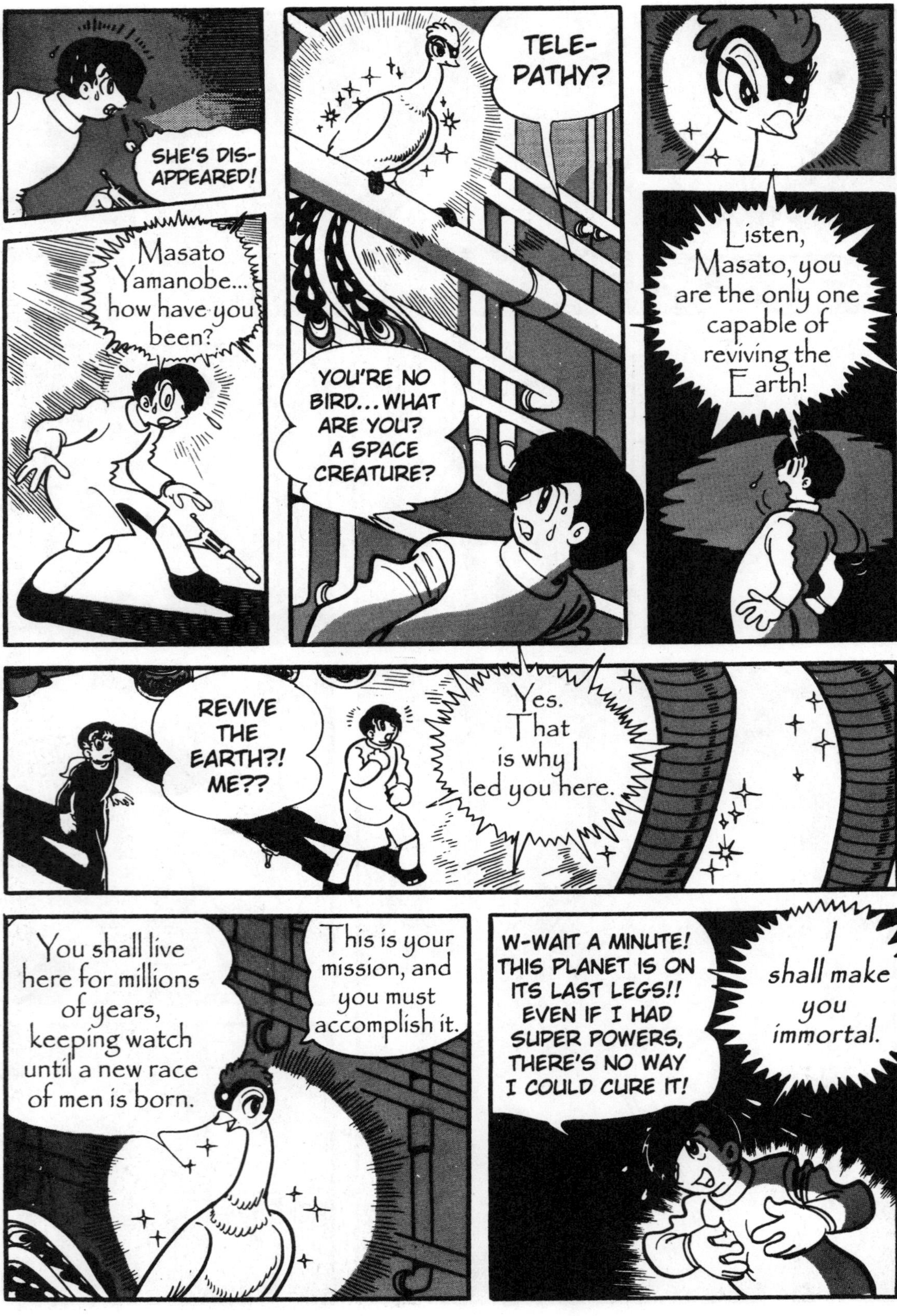
SHE'S DIS-APPEARED!
Masato Yamanobe... how have you been?
TELE-PATHY?
YOU'RE NO BIRD... WHAT ARE YOU? A SPACE CREATURE?
Listen, Masato, you are the only one capable of reviving the Earth!
REVIVE THE EARTH?! ME??
Yes. That is why I led you here.
You shall live here for millions of years, keeping watch until a new race of men is born.
This is your mission, and you must accomplish it.
W-WAIT A MINUTE! THIS PLANET IS ON ITS LAST LEGS!! EVEN IF I HAD SUPER POWERS, THERE'S NO WAY I COULD CURE IT!
I shall make you immortal.

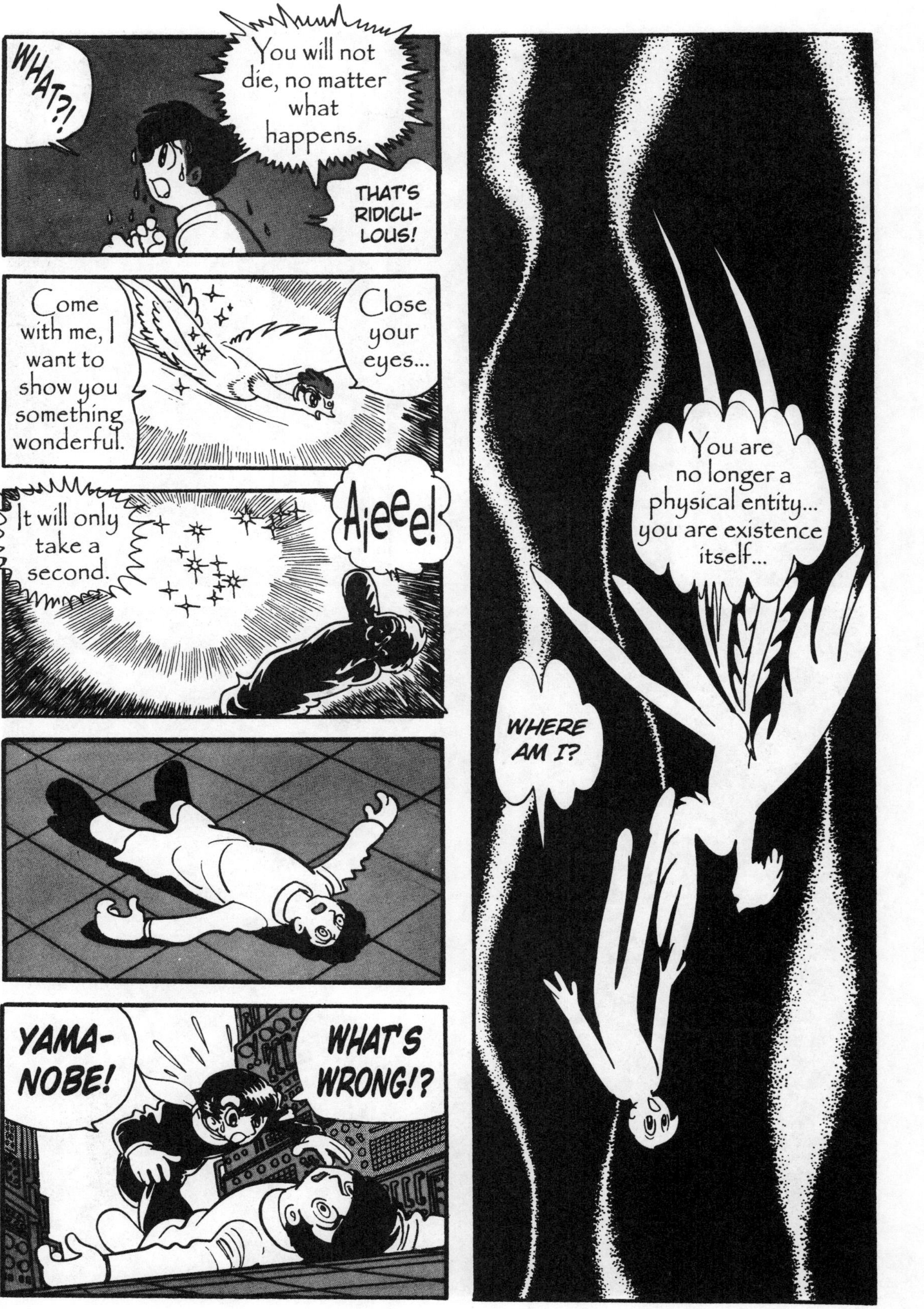
You will not die, no matter what happens.
WHAT?!
THAT'S RIDICULOUS!
Come with me, I want to show you something wonderful.
Close your eyes...
It will only take a second.
Aieeee!
YAMA-NOBE!
WHAT'S WRONG!?
WHERE AM I?
You are no longer a physical entity... you are existence itself...

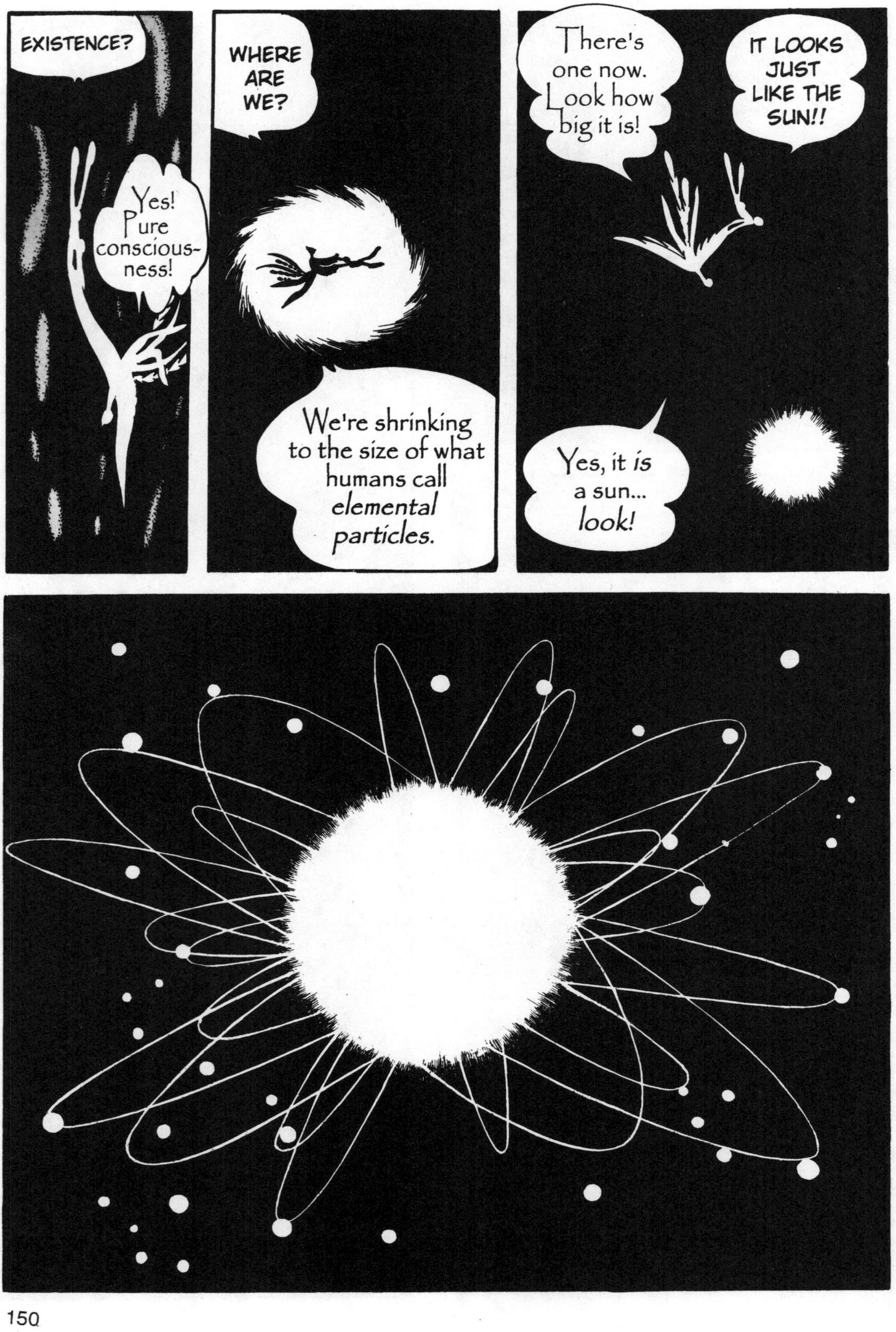
EXISTENCE?
Yes! Pure consciousness!
WHERE ARE WE?
We're shrinking to the size of what humans call *elemental particles.*
There's one now. Look how big it is!
IT LOOKS JUST LIKE THE SUN!!
Yes, it *is* a sun... *look!*

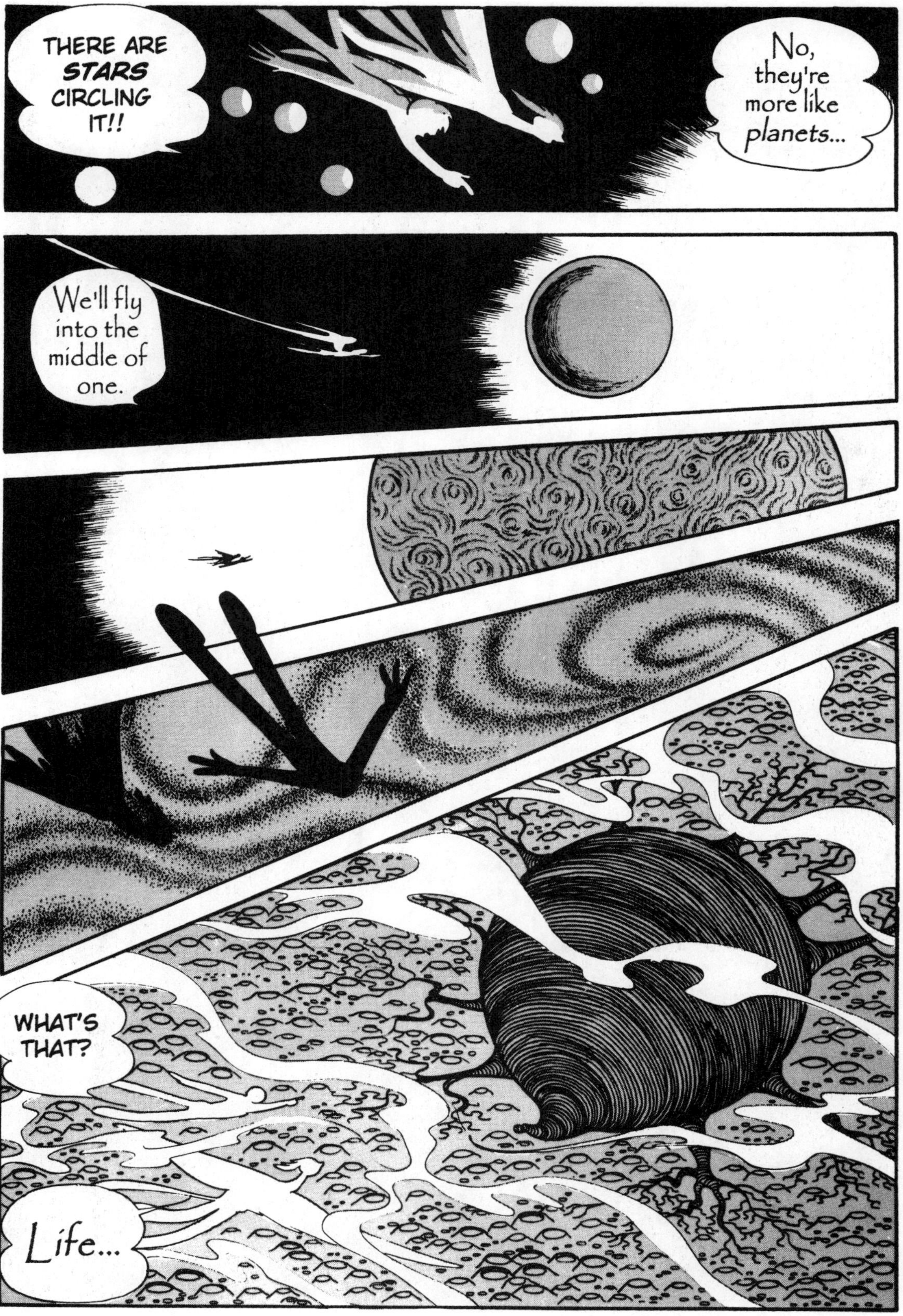
THERE ARE STARS CIRCLING IT!!
No, they're more like planets...
We'll fly into the middle of one.
WHAT'S THAT?
Life...

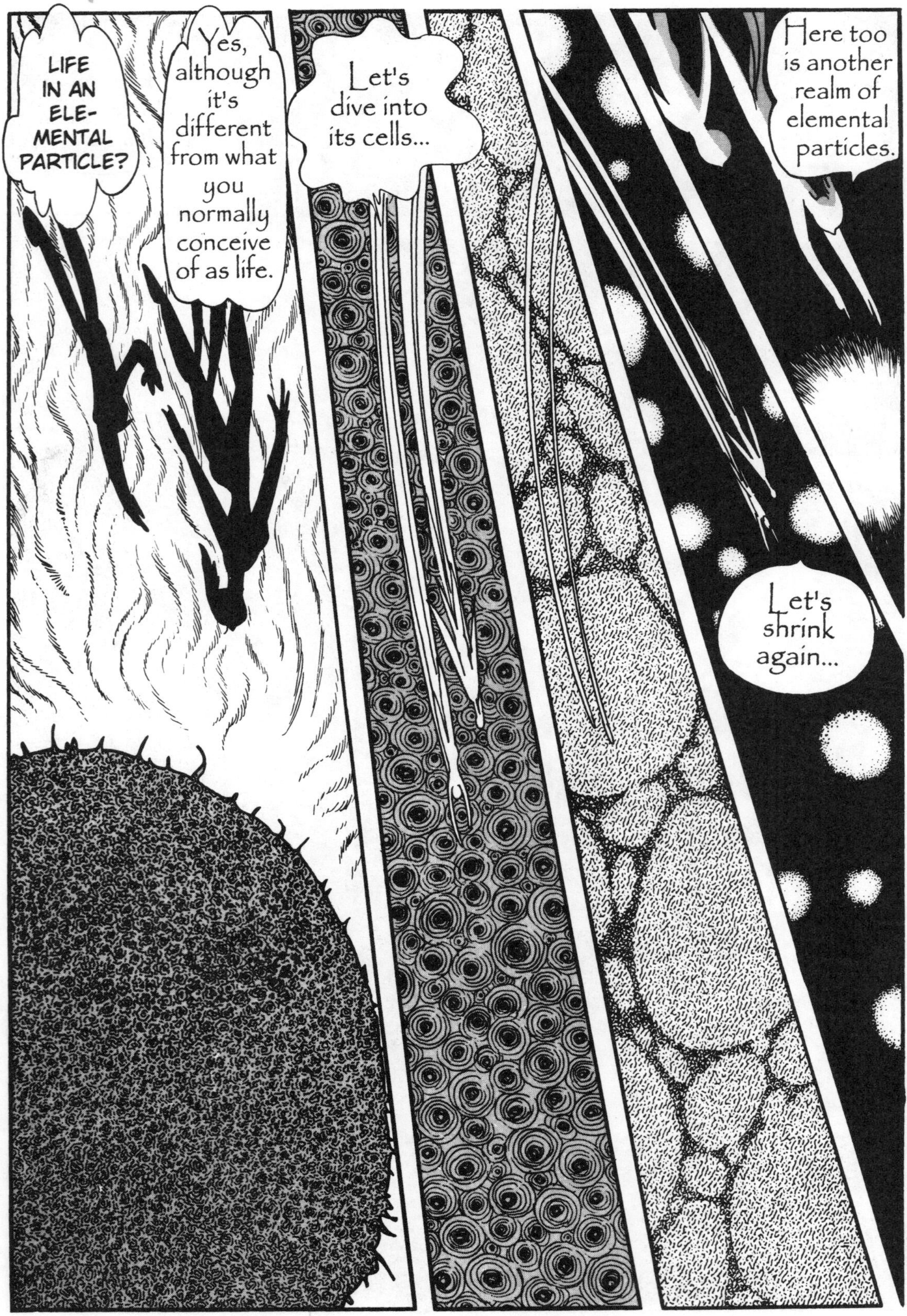
LIFE IN AN ELE-MENTAL PARTICLE?
Yes, although it's different from what you normally conceive of as life.
Let's dive into its cells...
Here too is another realm of elemental particles.
Let's shrink again...

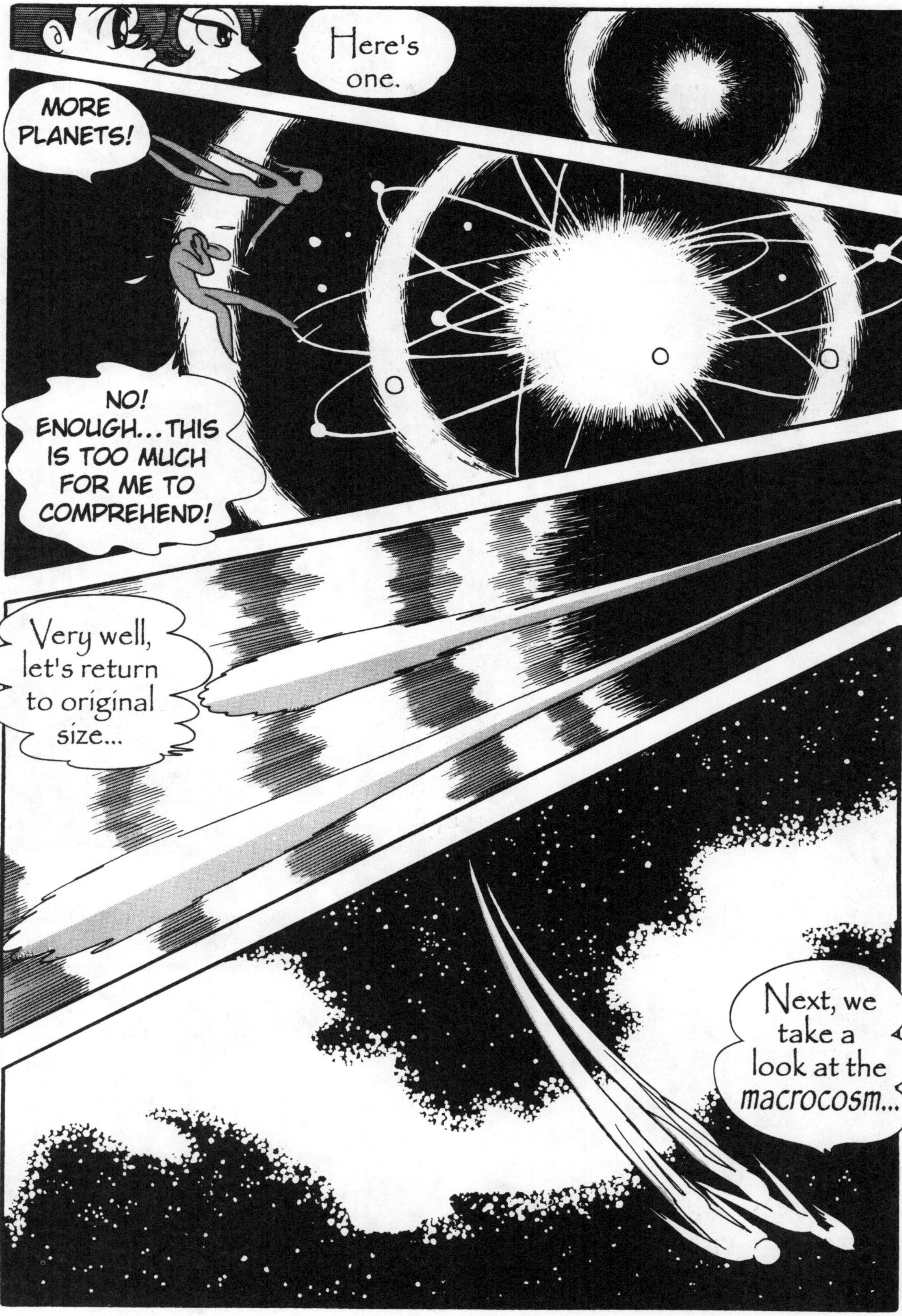
Here's one.
MORE PLANETS!
NO! ENOUGH...THIS IS TOO MUCH FOR ME TO COMPREHEND!
Very well, let's return to original size...
Next, we take a look at the *macrocosm*...

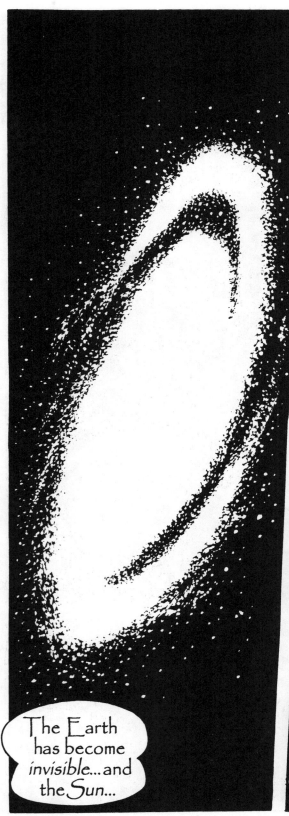

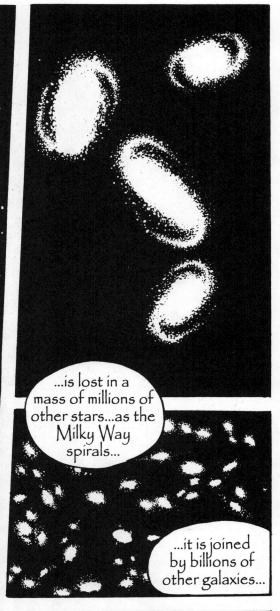

The Earth has become invisible...and the Sun...
...is lost in a mass of millions of other stars...as the Milky Way spirals...
...it is joined by billions of other galaxies...
...to form the macro-cosm...
THAT'S THE LIMIT OF THE UNI-VERSE, ISN'T IT?

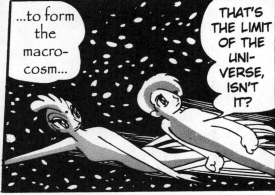

As far as a *human* conception of the Universe is concerned, it *is* the limit, Masato...

But it is enveloped in something even larger.

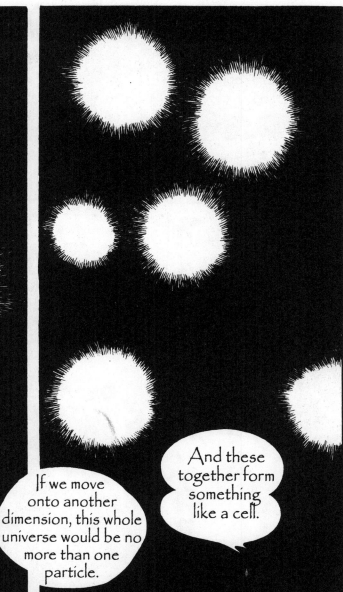

If we move onto another dimension, this whole universe would be no more than one particle.

And these together form something like a cell.

And the cells in turn form another life.

WAIT! YOU'RE TELLING ME THAT THE WHOLE UNIVERSE IS ONLY A SINGLE CELL IN A LIVING CREATURE? WHAT IS THIS CREATURE?

A Cosmos.

A COSMOS?

STOP! STOP! I NEED TO THINK!

From the microcosm to the macrocosm they're all alive...

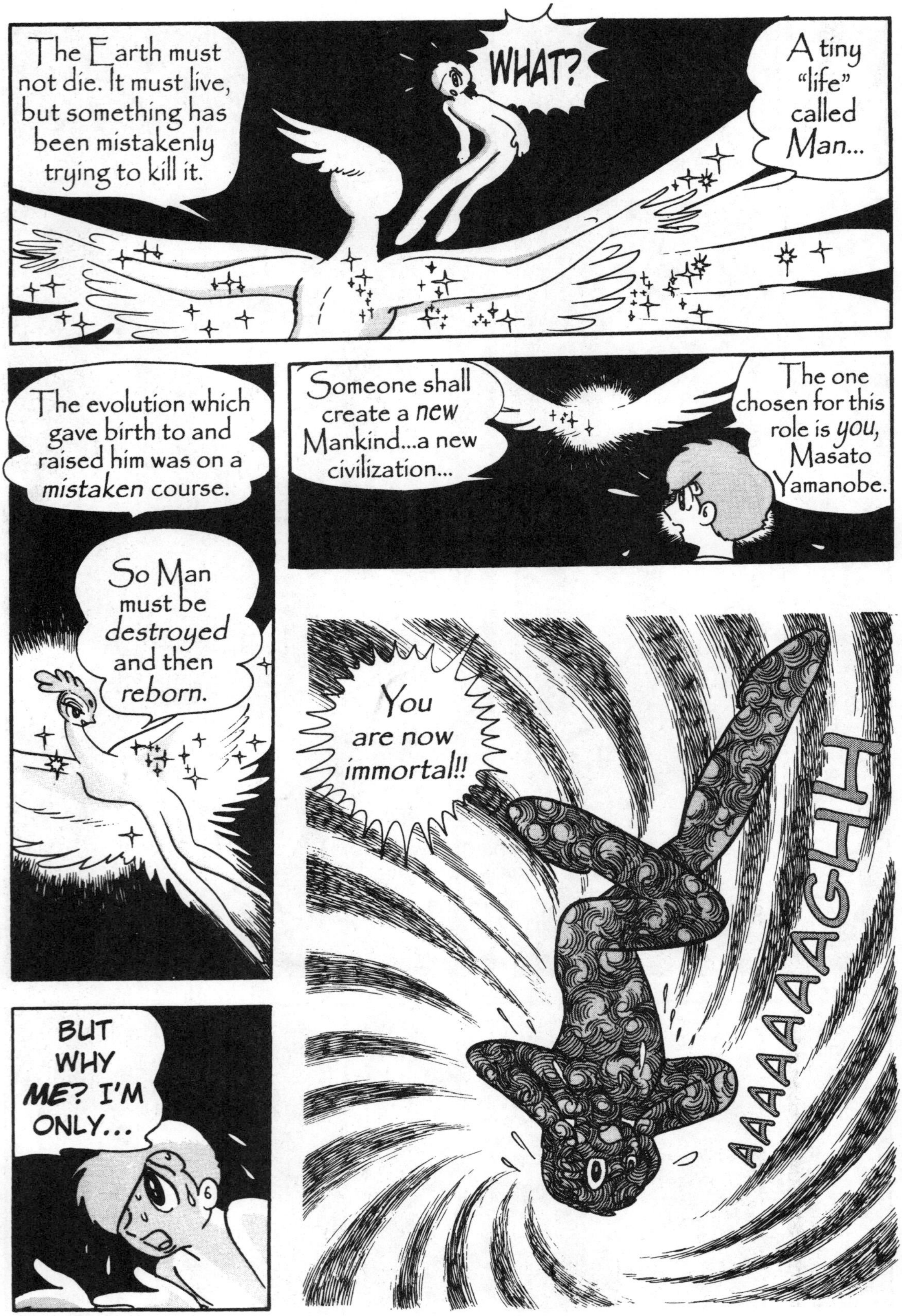
The Earth must not die. It must live, but something has been mistakenly trying to kill it.
WHAT?
A tiny "life" called Man...
The evolution which gave birth to and raised him was on a mistaken course.
So Man must be destroyed and then reborn.
Someone shall create a new Mankind...a new civilization...
The one chosen for this role is you, Masato Yamanobe.
BUT WHY ME? I'M ONLY...
You are now immortal!!
AAAAAAGHH

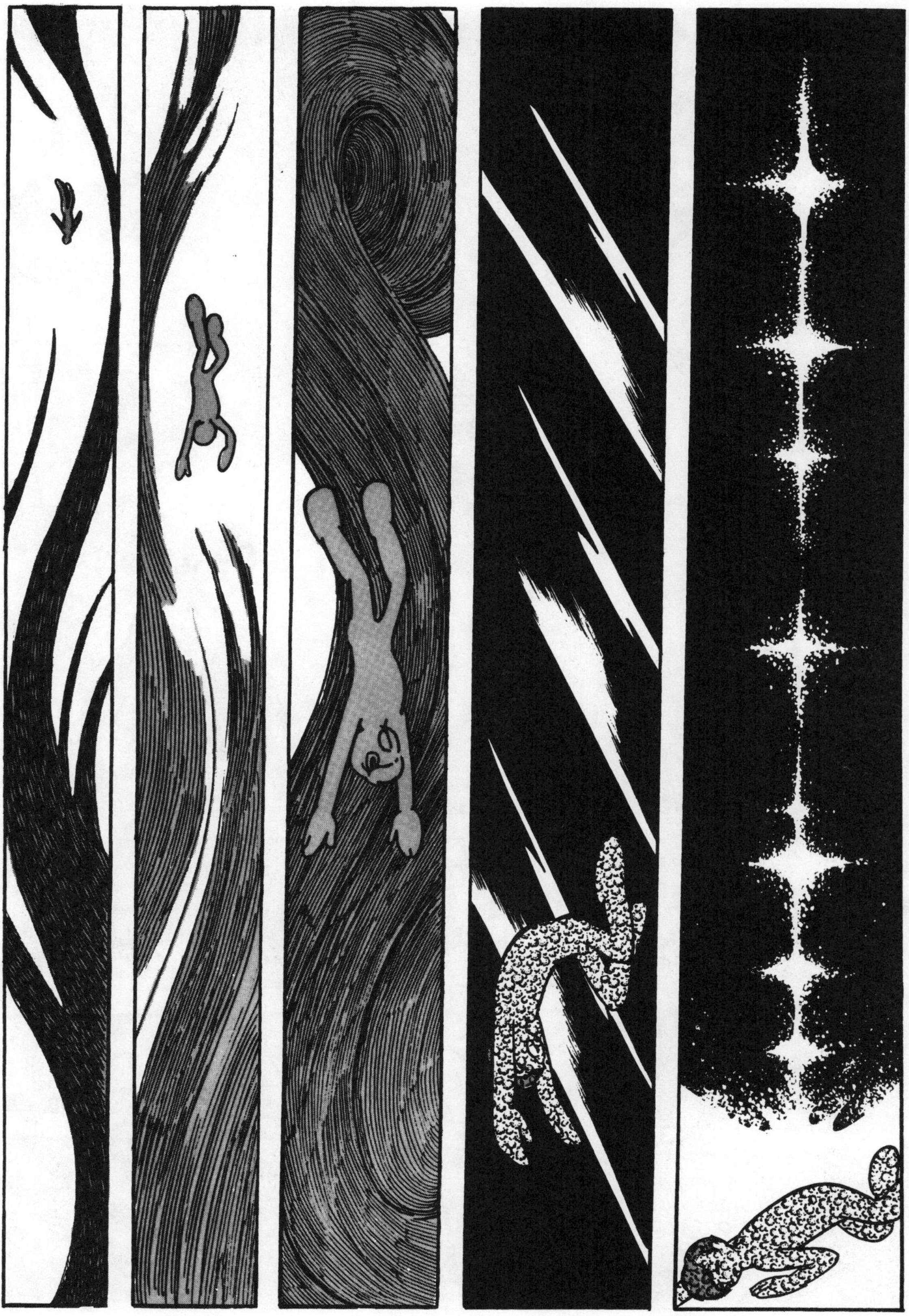

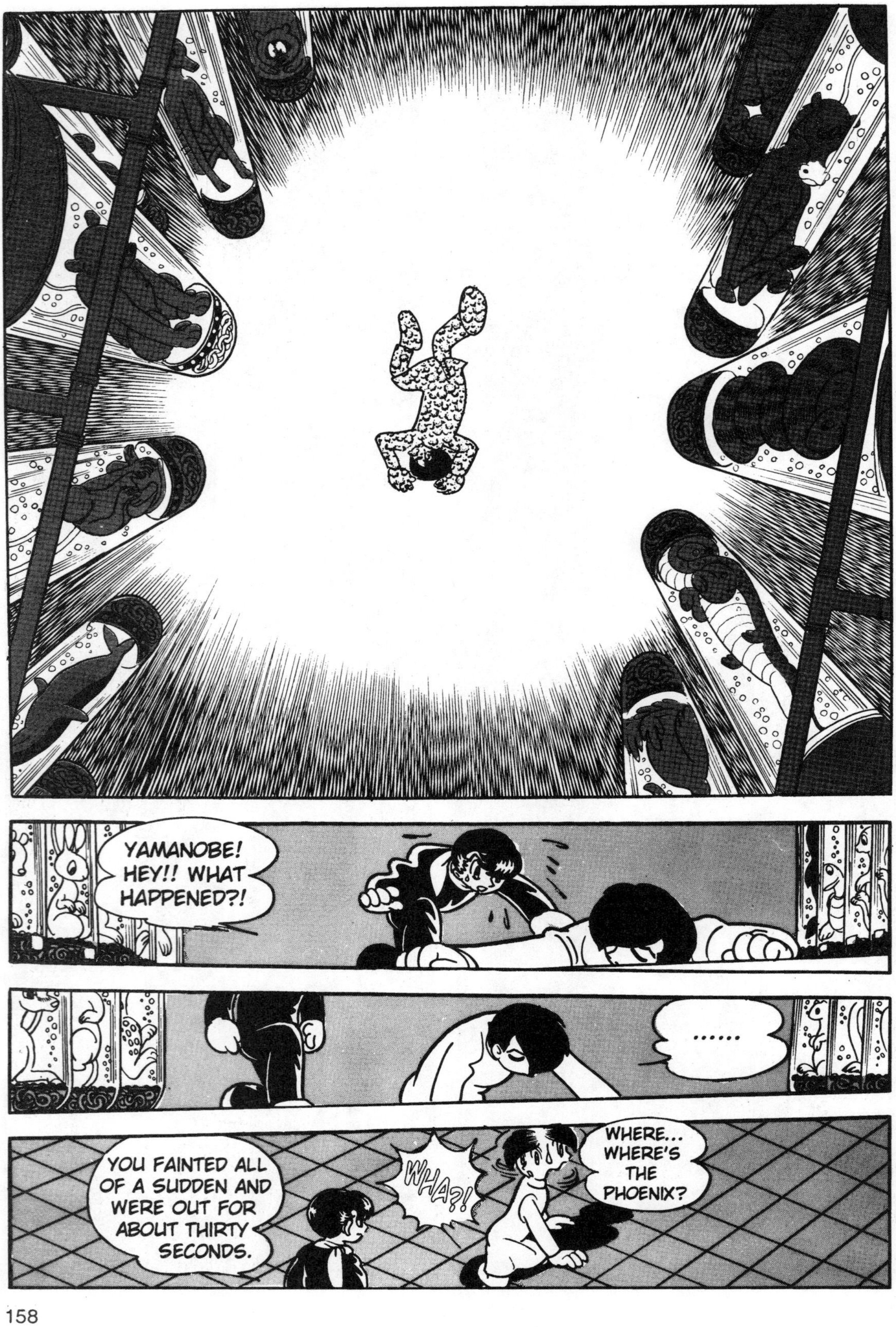
YAMANOBE! HEY!! WHAT HAPPENED?!
......
WHERE... WHERE'S THE PHOENIX?
WHA?!
YOU FAINTED ALL OF A SUDDEN AND WERE OUT FOR ABOUT THIRTY SECONDS.

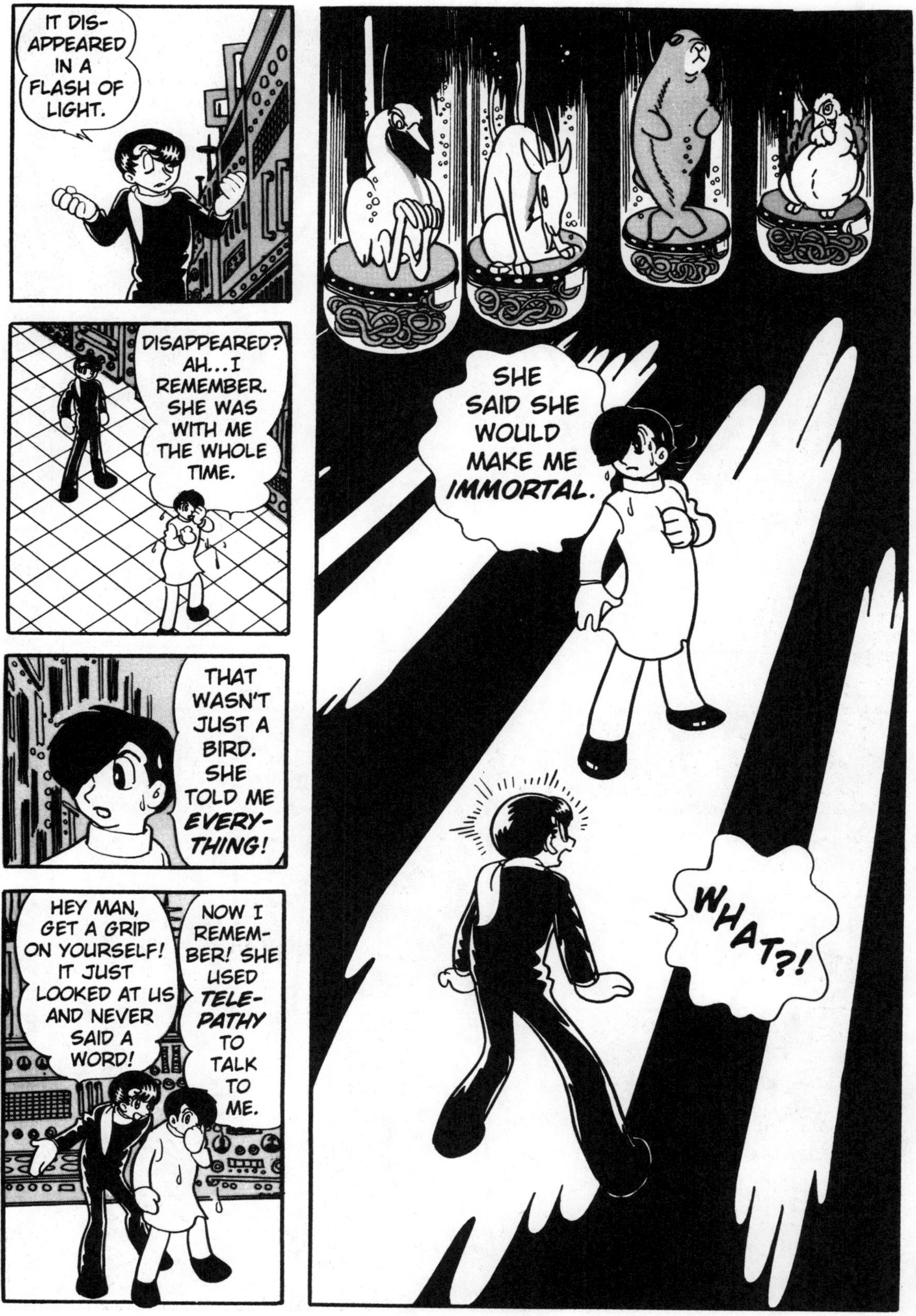
IT DIS-APPEARED IN A FLASH OF LIGHT.
DISAPPEARED? AH...I REMEMBER. SHE WAS WITH ME THE WHOLE TIME.
THAT WASN'T JUST A BIRD. SHE TOLD ME *EVERYTHING*!
HEY MAN, GET A GRIP ON YOURSELF! IT JUST LOOKED AT US AND NEVER SAID A WORD!
NOW I REMEMBER! SHE USED *TELEPATHY* TO TALK TO ME.
SHE SAID SHE WOULD MAKE ME *IMMORTAL*.
WHAT?!

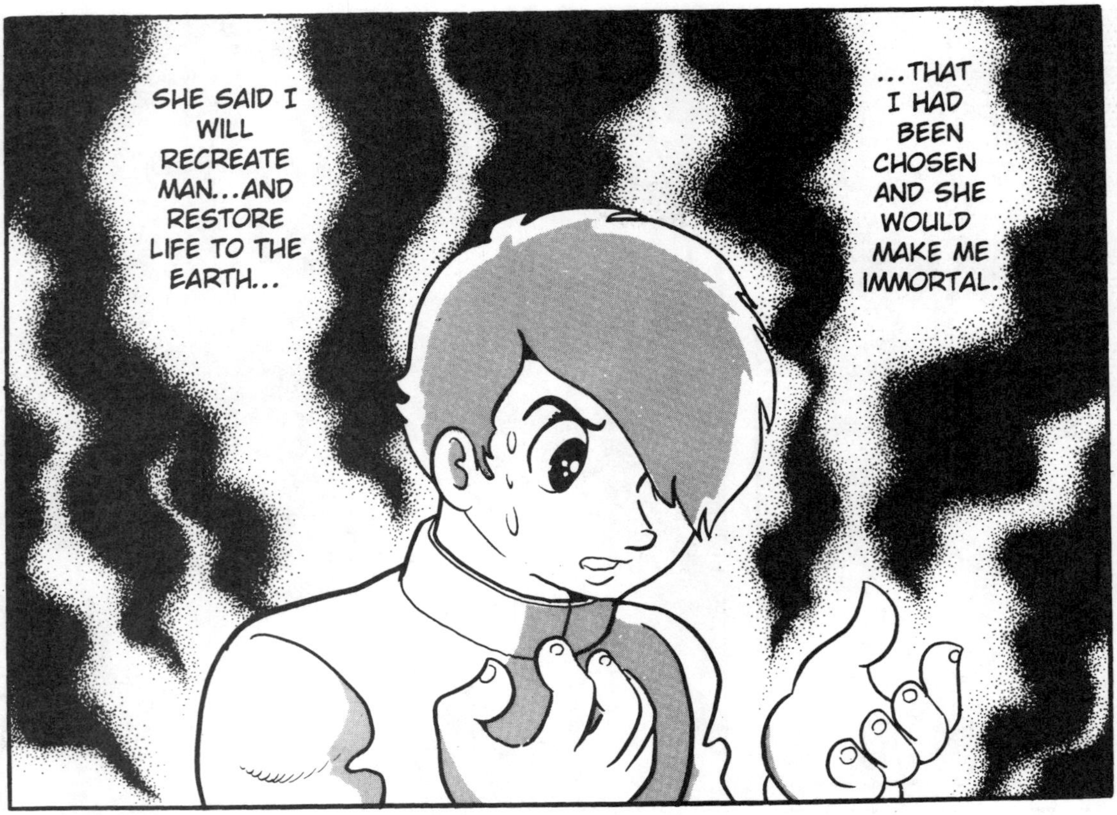
SHE SAID I WILL RECREATE MAN...AND RESTORE LIFE TO THE EARTH...
...THAT I HAD BEEN CHOSEN AND SHE WOULD MAKE ME IMMORTAL.

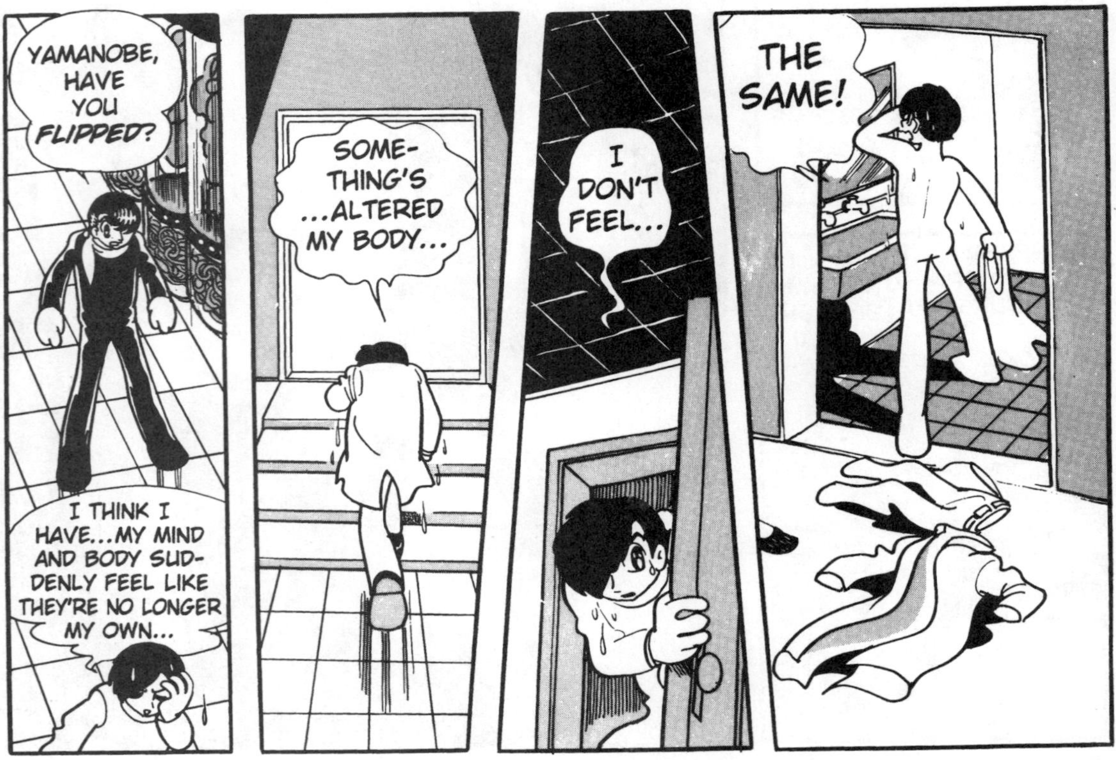
YAMANOBE, HAVE YOU FLIPPED?
I THINK I HAVE...MY MIND AND BODY SUDDENLY FEEL LIKE THEY'RE NO LONGER MY OWN...
SOMETHING'S ...ALTERED MY BODY...
I DON'T FEEL...
THE SAME!

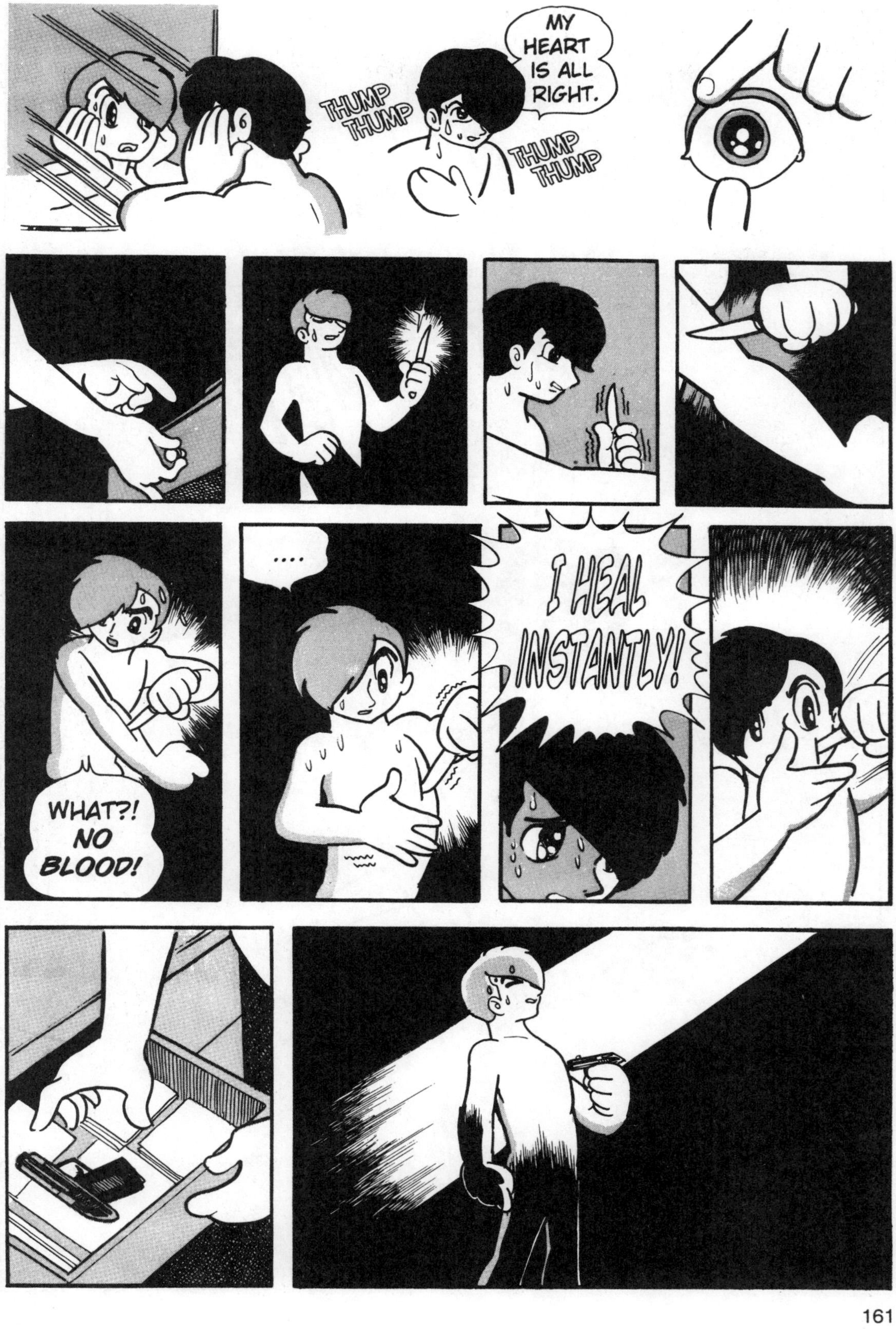
THUMP THUMP
MY HEART IS ALL RIGHT.
THUMP THUMP
WHAT?! NO BLOOD!
....
I HEAL INSTANTLY!

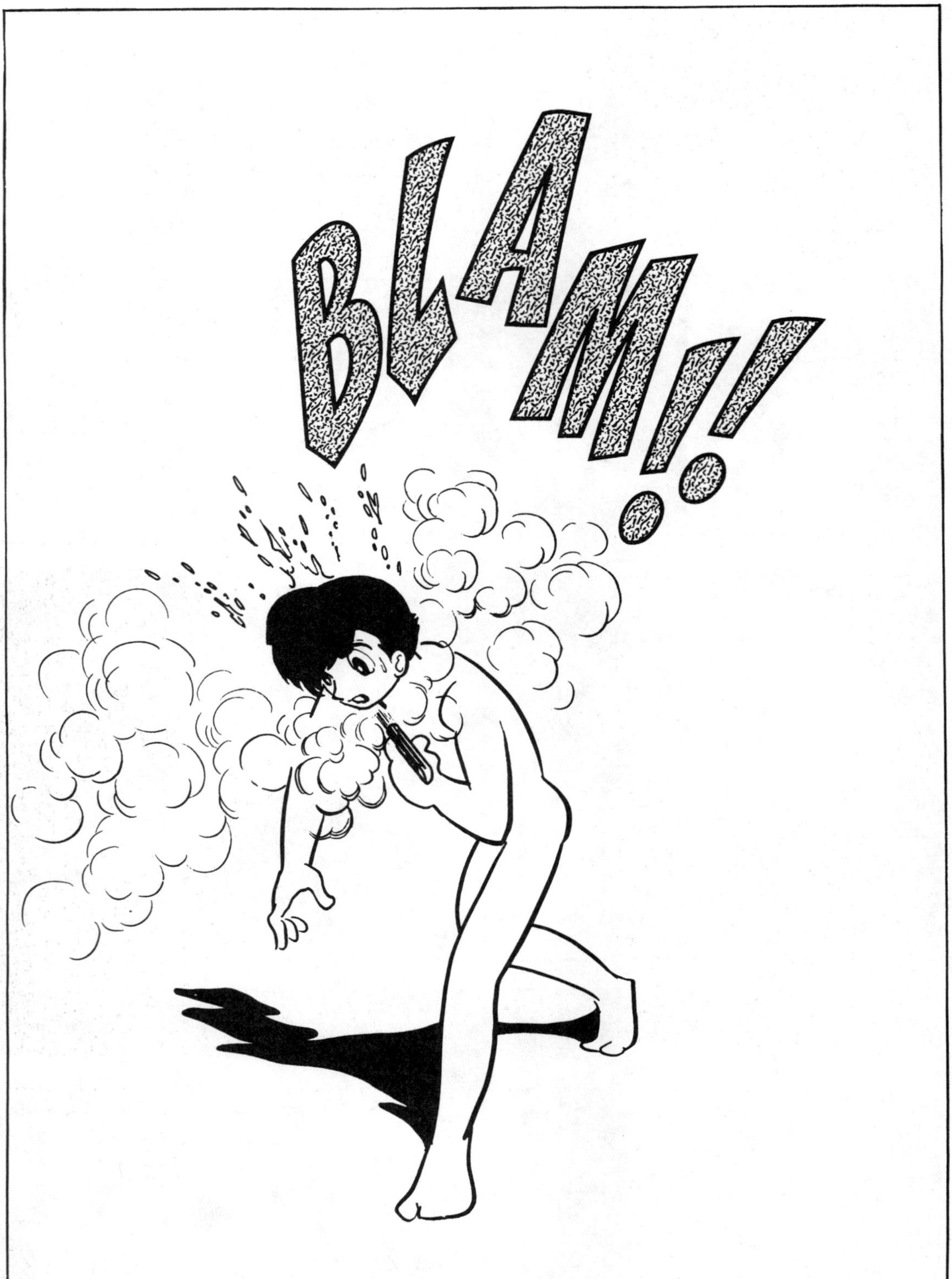
BLAM!!

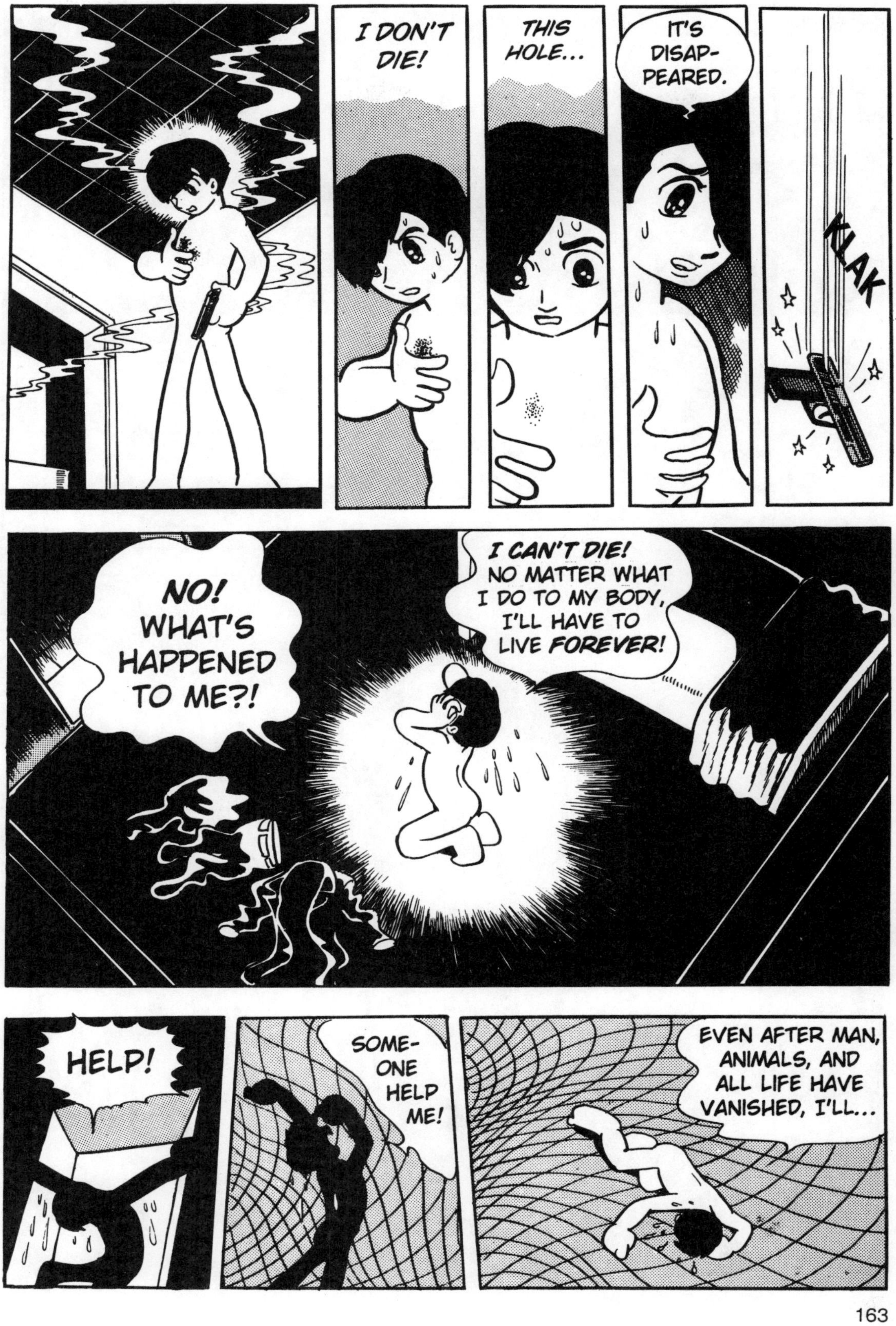
I DON'T DIE!
THIS HOLE...
IT'S DISAPPEARED.
KLAK
NO! WHAT'S HAPPENED TO ME?!
I CAN'T DIE! NO MATTER WHAT I DO TO MY BODY, I'LL HAVE TO LIVE FOREVER!
HELP!
SOMEONE HELP ME!
EVEN AFTER MAN, ANIMALS, AND ALL LIFE HAVE VANISHED, I'LL...

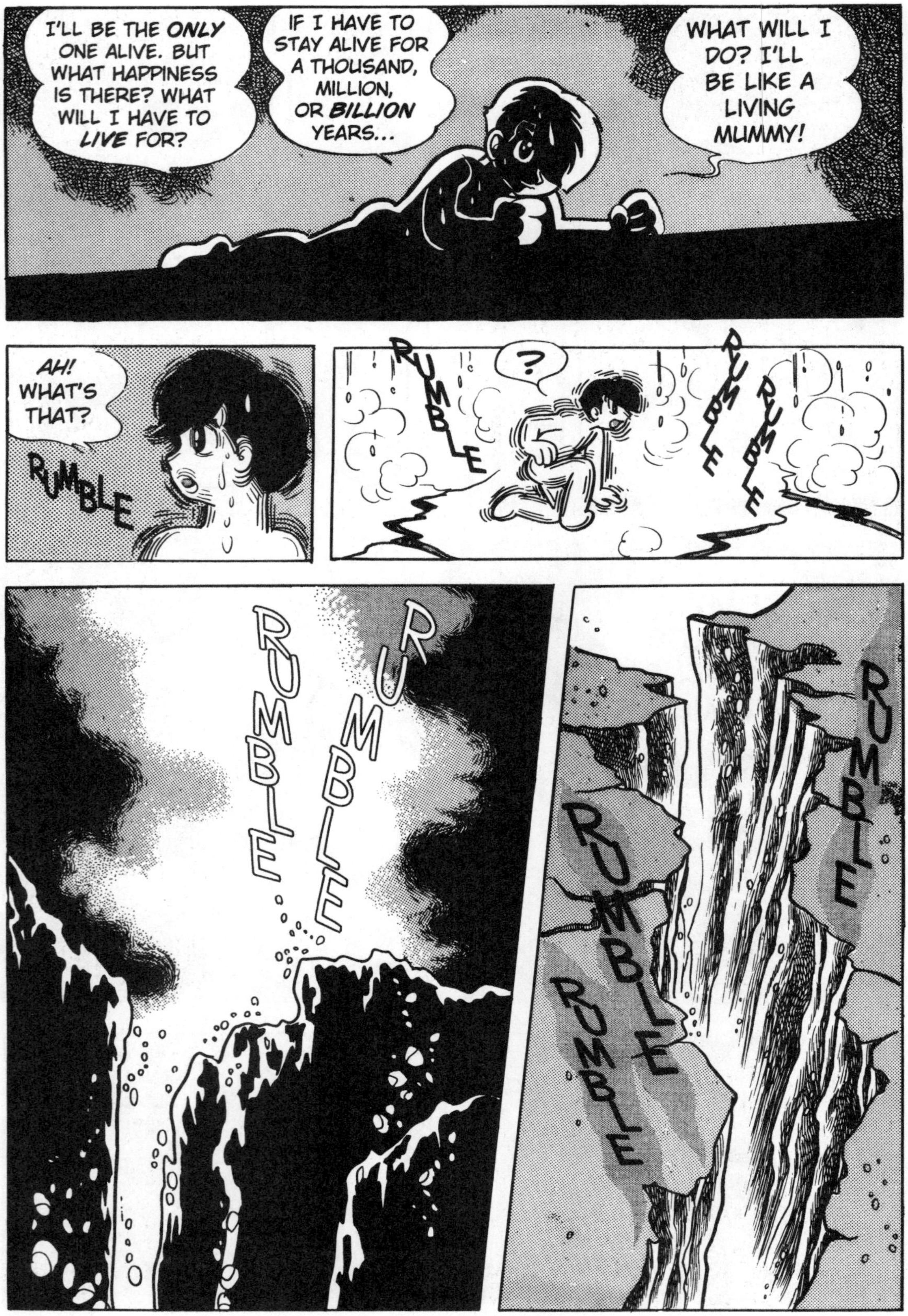
I'LL BE THE ONLY ONE ALIVE. BUT WHAT HAPPINESS IS THERE? WHAT WILL I HAVE TO LIVE FOR?
IF I HAVE TO STAY ALIVE FOR A THOUSAND, MILLION, OR BILLION YEARS...
WHAT WILL I DO? I'LL BE LIKE A LIVING MUMMY!
AH! WHAT'S THAT?
RUMBLE
RUMBLE
?
RUMBLE
RUMBLE
RUMBLE
RUMBLE
RUMBLE
RUMBLE
RUMBLE

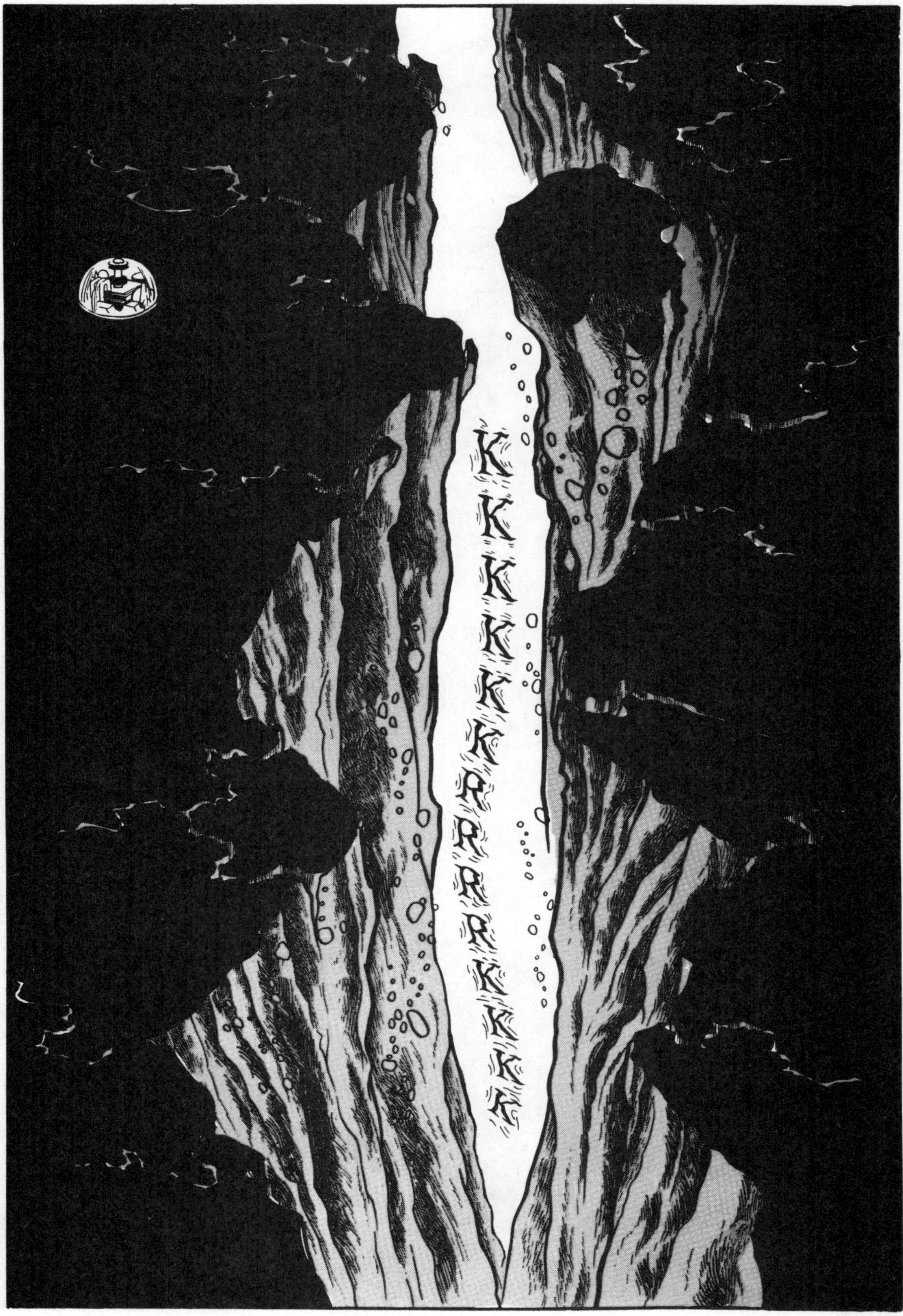
KKKKKKRRRRKKKK

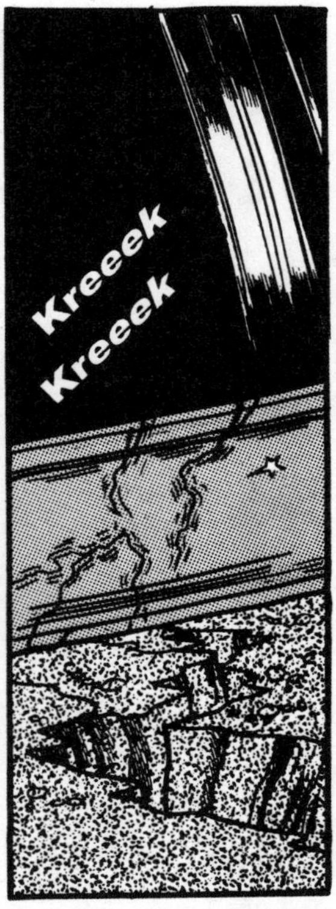
Kreeek
Kreeek
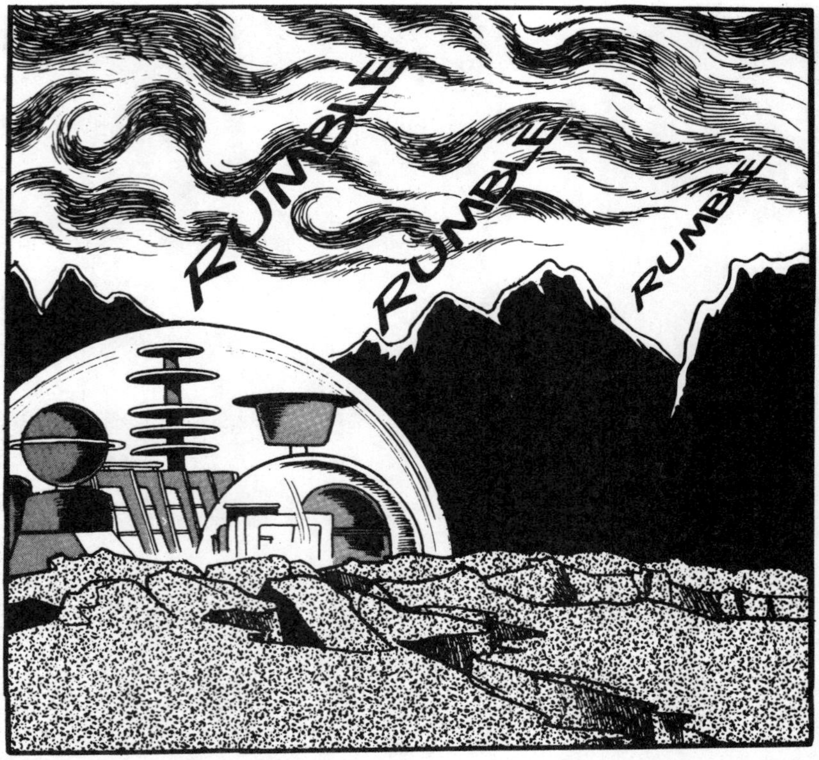
RUMBLE
RUMBLE
RUMBLE
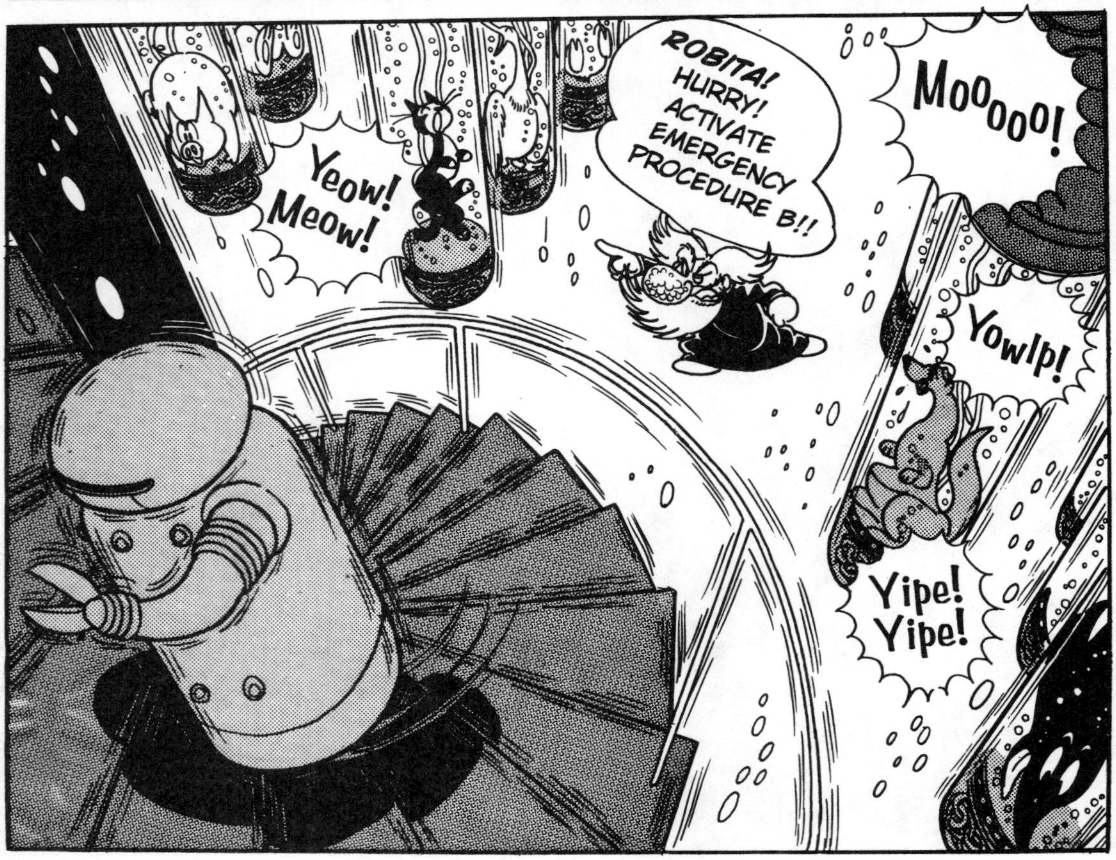
Moooooo!
ROBITA! HURRY! ACTIVATE EMERGENCY PROCEDURE B!!
Yeow! Meow!
Yowlp!
Yipe! Yipe!

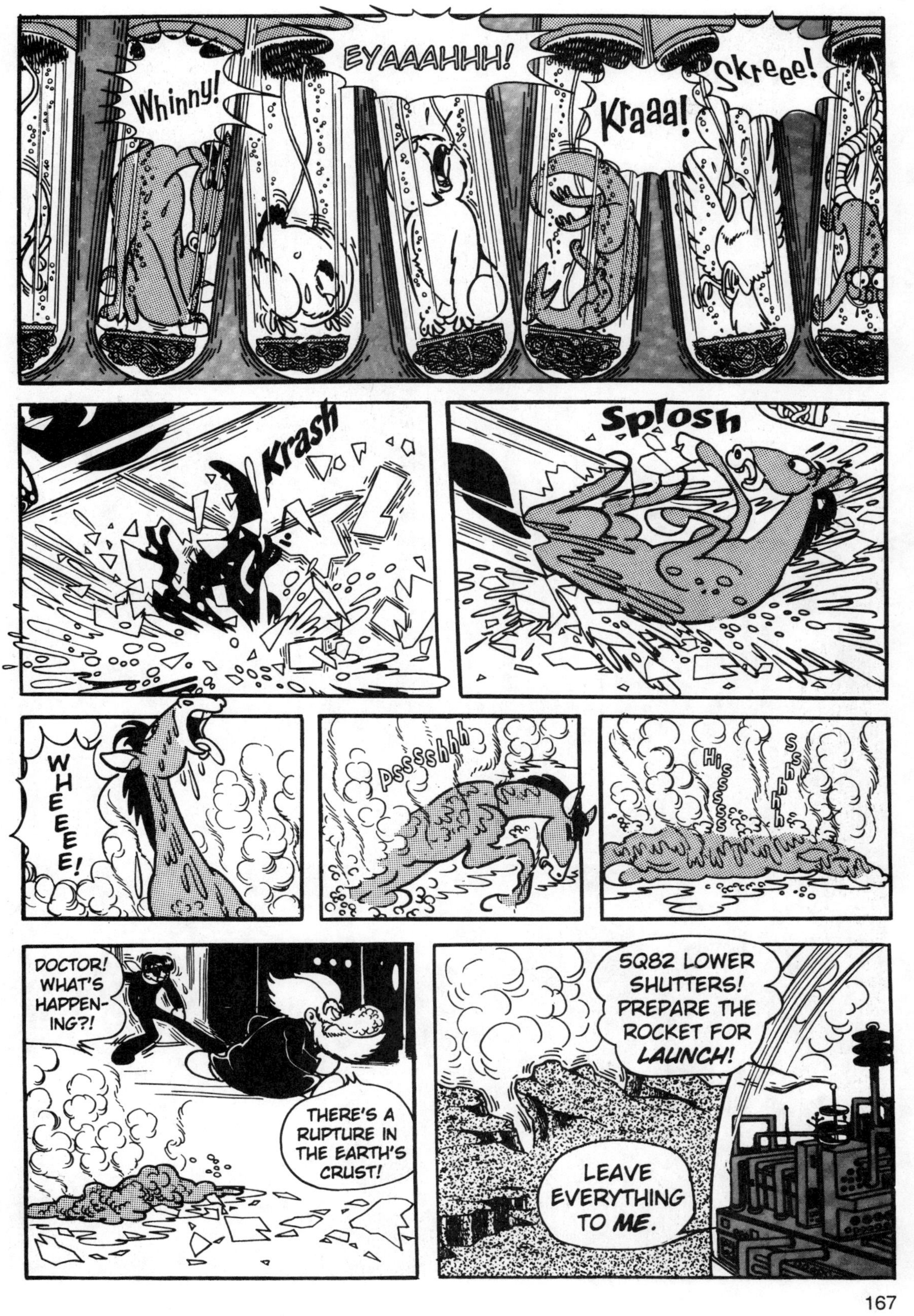
Whinny!
EYAAAHHH!
Kraaa!
Skreee!
Krash
Splosh
WHEEEEE!
Psssshhh
Hissssss
Sshhhh
DOCTOR! WHAT'S HAPPEN-ING?!
THERE'S A RUPTURE IN THE EARTH'S CRUST!
5Q82 LOWER SHUTTERS! PREPARE THE ROCKET FOR LAUNCH!
LEAVE EVERYTHING TO ME.

RRRRRRRR

WHRRRRRRRR

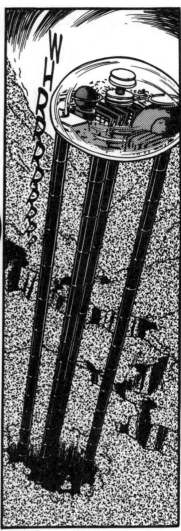

WHRRRRRR

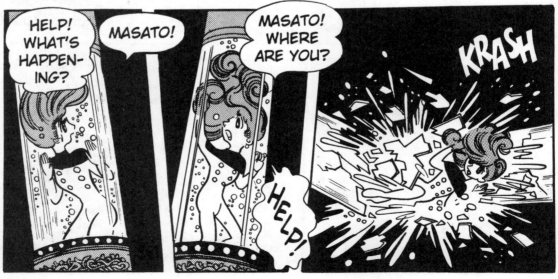

HELP! WHAT'S HAPPENING?

MASATO!

MASATO! WHERE ARE YOU?

HELP!

KRASH

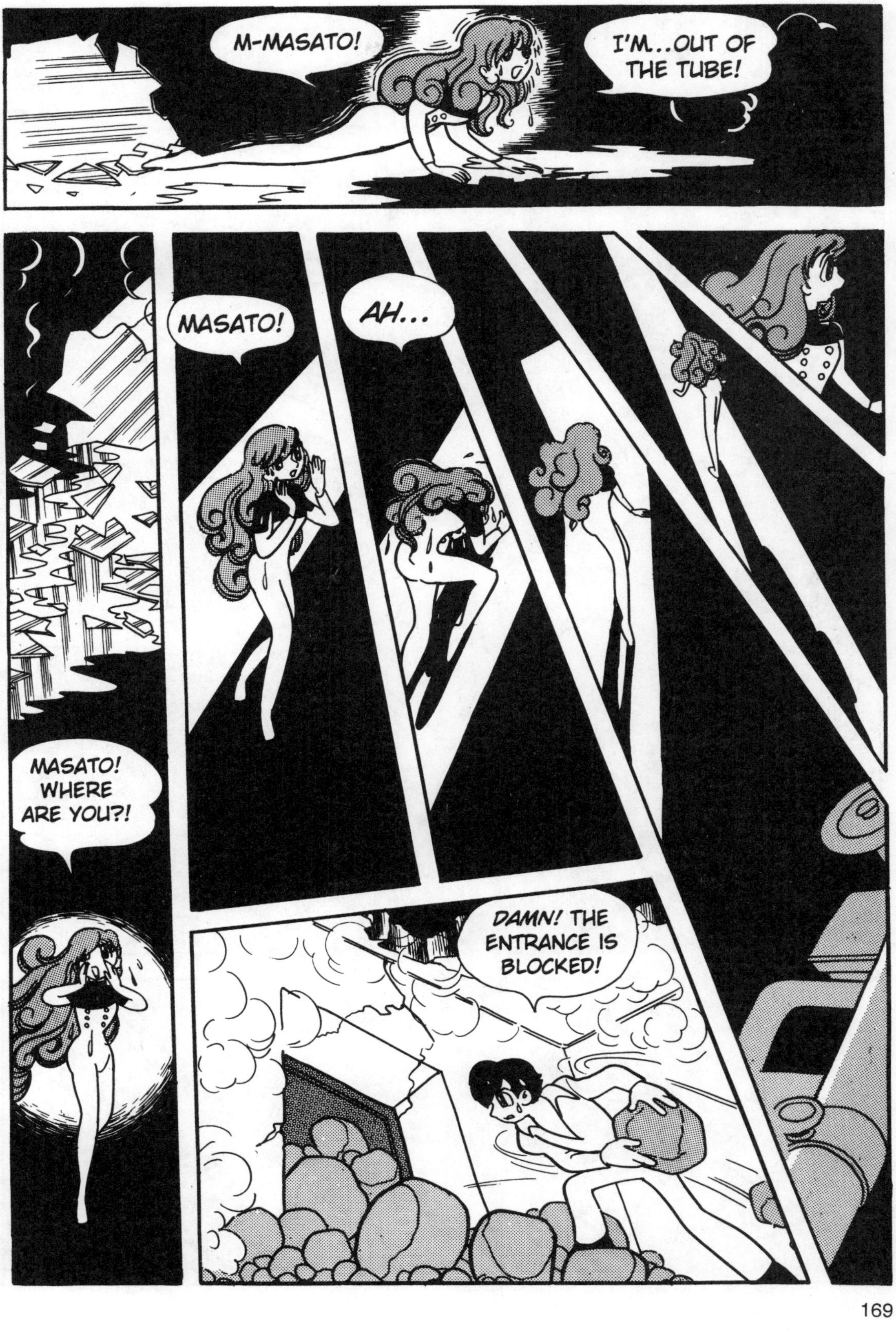
I'M...OUT OF THE TUBE!
M-MASATO!
AH...
MASATO!
DAMN! THE ENTRANCE IS BLOCKED!
MASATO! WHERE ARE YOU?!

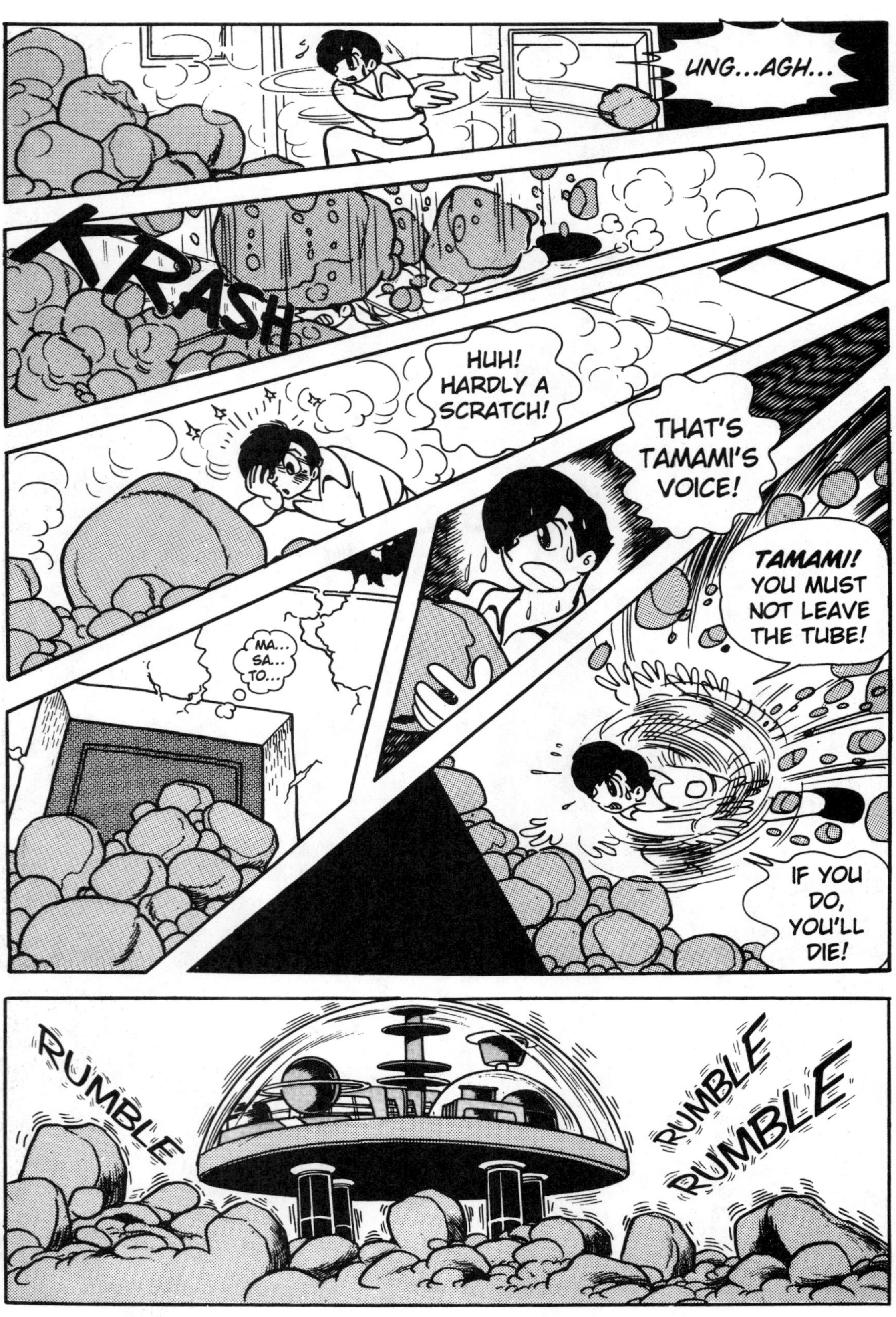
UNG...AGH...
KRASH
HUH! HARDLY A SCRATCH!
MA... SA... TO...
THAT'S TAMAMI'S VOICE!
TAMAMI! YOU MUST NOT LEAVE THE TUBE!
IF YOU DO, YOU'LL DIE!
RUMBLE
RUMBLE
RUMBLE

I PREDICTED THIS WOULD HAPPEN!

BECAUSE OF THE ATOMIC BLASTS!

DOCTOR-THE-RADIATION-COUNT-INSIDE-THE-DOME-IS-RISING—

WHAT?!

HOW HIGH HAS IT RISEN?

IT-IS-SAFE-AT-PRESENT-BUT-IT-WILL-SOON-EXCEED-TOLERANCE-LEVELS—

THERE MUST BE A CRACK SOMEWHERE THAT'S LET IN OUTSIDE AIR!

IT-SEEMS-THAT-WAY—

I SEE...

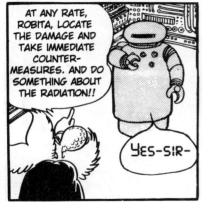

AT ANY RATE, ROBITA, LOCATE THE DAMAGE AND TAKE IMMEDIATE COUNTER-MEASURES. AND DO SOMETHING ABOUT THE RADIATION!!

YES-SIR-

AND ONE MORE THING...

PREPARE THE ROCKET...

WHY?

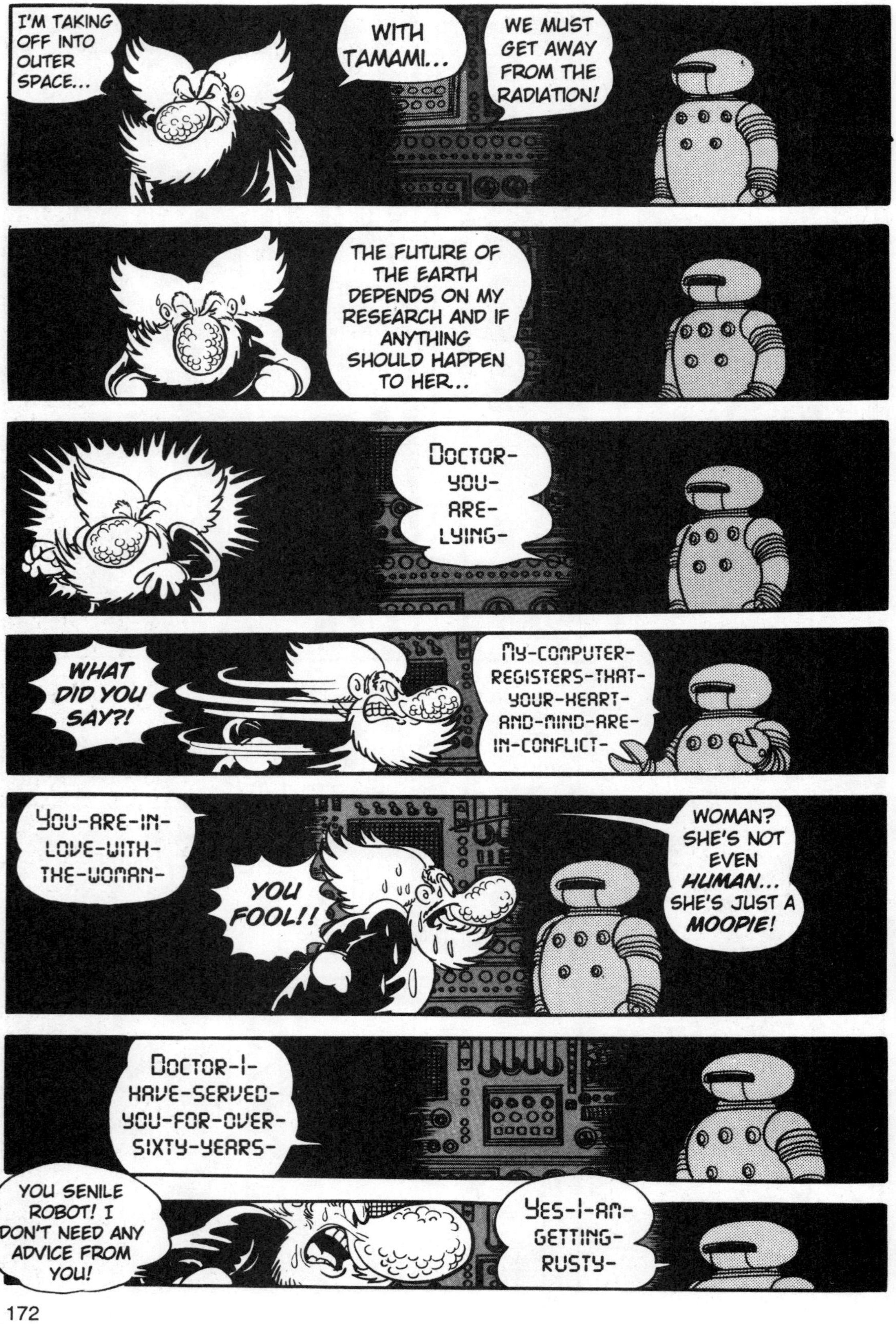

I'M TAKING OFF INTO OUTER SPACE...
WITH TAMAMI...
WE MUST GET AWAY FROM THE RADIATION!
THE FUTURE OF THE EARTH DEPENDS ON MY RESEARCH AND IF ANYTHING SHOULD HAPPEN TO HER...
DOCTOR-YOU-ARE-LYING-
WHAT DID YOU SAY?!
MY-COMPUTER-REGISTERS-THAT-YOUR-HEART-AND-MIND-ARE-IN-CONFLICT-
YOU-ARE-IN-LOVE-WITH-THE-WOMAN-
YOU FOOL!!
WOMAN? SHE'S NOT EVEN HUMAN... SHE'S JUST A MOOPIE!
DOCTOR-I-HAVE-SERVED-YOU-FOR-OVER-SIXTY-YEARS-
YOU SENILE ROBOT! I DON'T NEED ANY ADVICE FROM YOU!
YES-I-AM-GETTING-RUSTY-

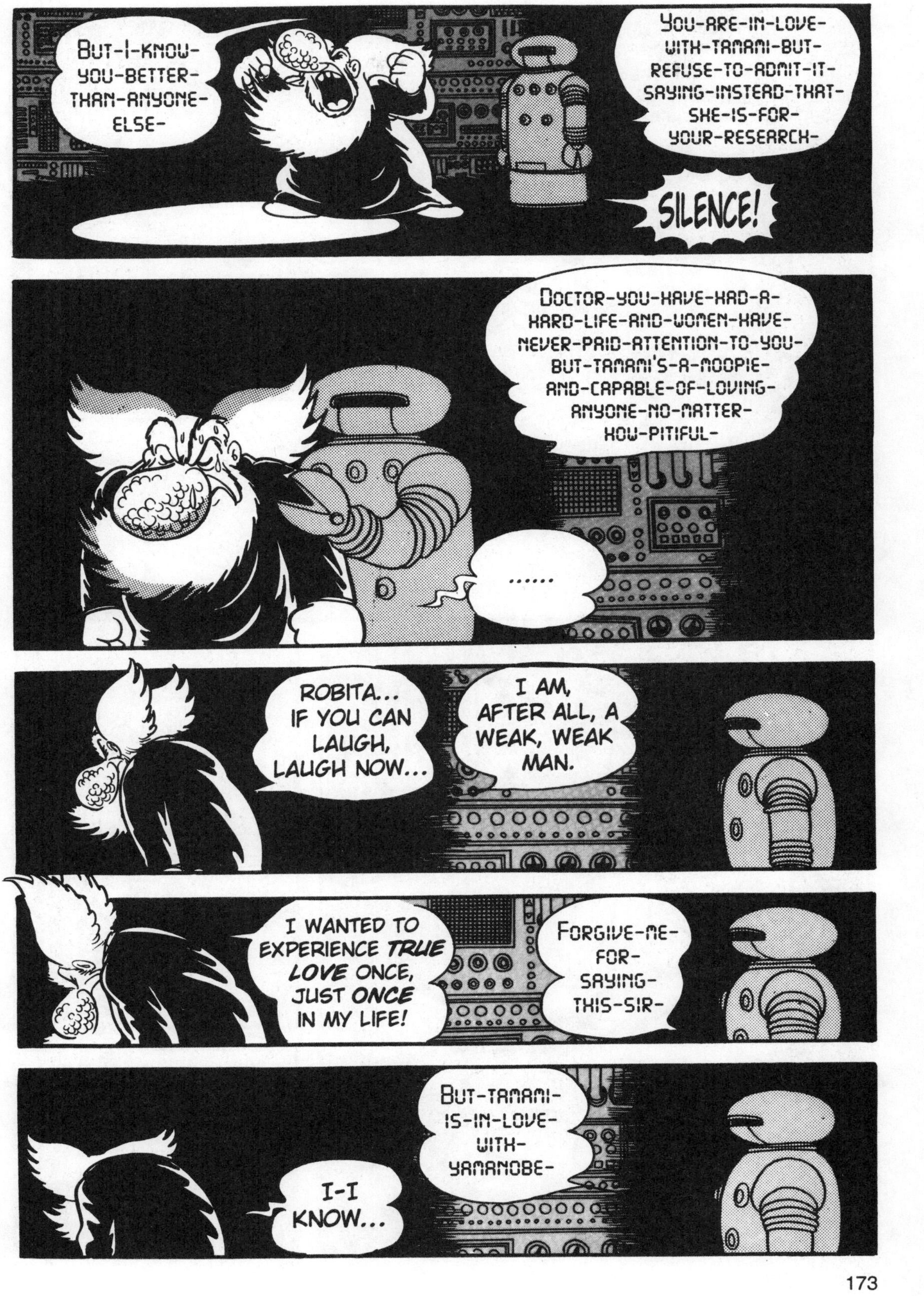
But-I-know-you-better-than-anyone-else-
You-are-in-love-with-Tamami-but-refuse-to-admit-it-saying-instead-that-she-is-for-your-research-
SILENCE!
Doctor-you-have-had-a-hard-life-and-women-have-never-paid-attention-to-you-but-Tamami's-a-moopie-and-capable-of-loving-anyone-no-matter-how-pitiful-
......
ROBITA... IF YOU CAN LAUGH, LAUGH NOW...
I AM, AFTER ALL, A WEAK, WEAK MAN.
I WANTED TO EXPERIENCE ***TRUE LOVE*** ONCE, JUST ***ONCE*** IN MY LIFE!
Forgive-me-for-saying-this-sir-
But-Tamami-is-in-love-with-Yamanobe-
I-I KNOW...

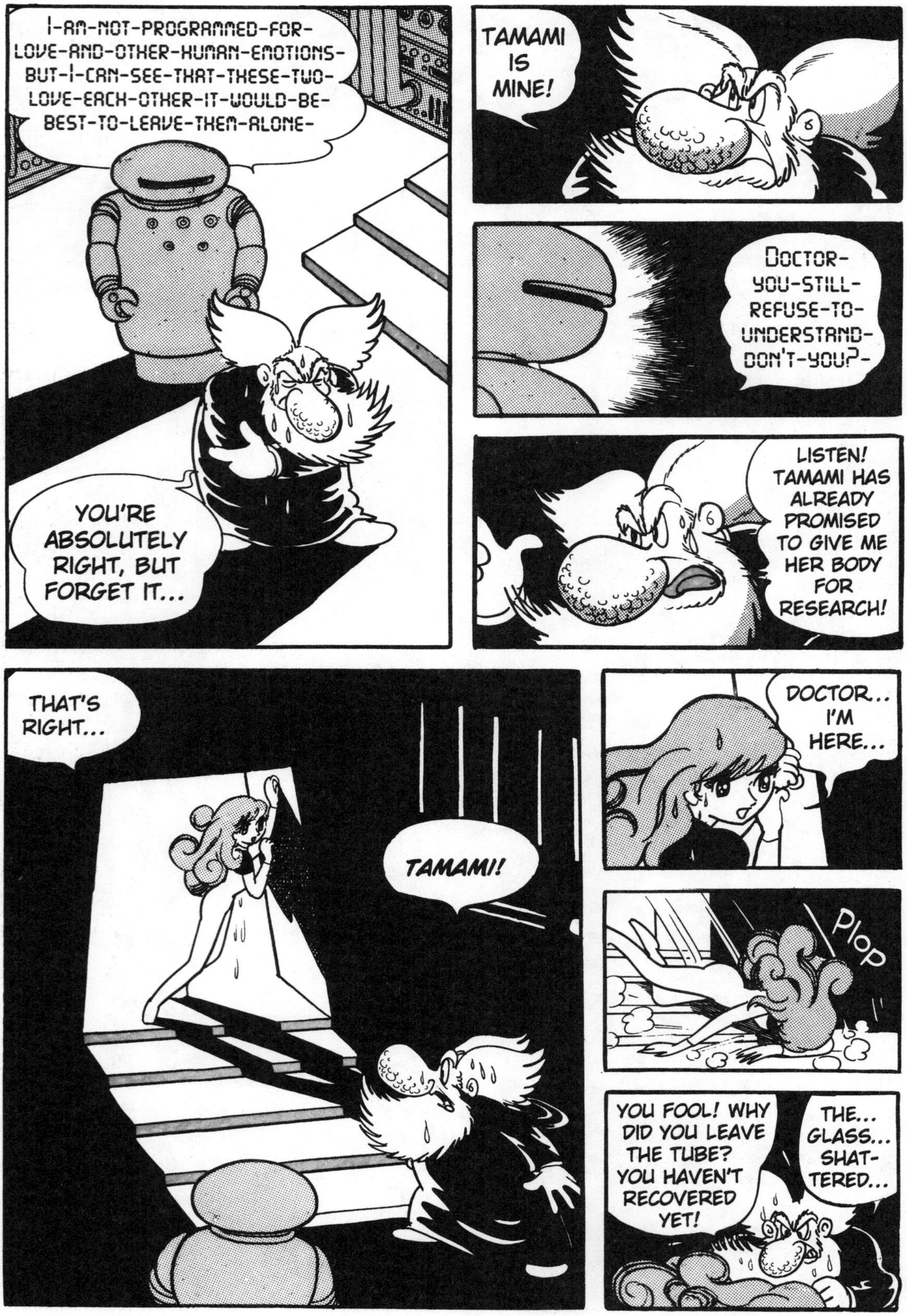
I-AM-NOT-PROGRAMMED-FOR-LOVE-AND-OTHER-HUMAN-EMOTIONS-BUT-I-CAN-SEE-THAT-THESE-TWO-LOVE-EACH-OTHER-IT-WOULD-BE-BEST-TO-LEAVE-THEM-ALONE-
YOU'RE ABSOLUTELY RIGHT, BUT FORGET IT...
TAMAMI IS MINE!
DOCTOR-YOU-STILL-REFUSE-TO-UNDERSTAND-DON'T-YOU?-
LISTEN! TAMAMI HAS ALREADY PROMISED TO GIVE ME HER BODY FOR RESEARCH!
THAT'S RIGHT...
TAMAMI!
DOCTOR... I'M HERE...
Plop
YOU FOOL! WHY DID YOU LEAVE THE TUBE? YOU HAVEN'T RECOVERED YET!
THE... GLASS... SHAT-TERED...

HAVE... HAVE YOU TALKED TO MASATO YET?

ER...NO... NOT YET...BUT WE HAVEN'T A MOMENT TO LOSE! WE'VE GOT TO GET YOU INTO THE LAB RIGHT AWAY!

WHY?

YOU REALLY WANT TO KNOW?

RADIATION IS LEAKING INTO THE DOME.

AND IT'S GETTING CLOSE TO THE DANGER LEVEL!

WHAT?

DON'T JUST STAND THERE, ROBITA! GO OUT AND MEASURE THE RADIATION LEVELS! REPORT BACK AS SOON AS YOU HAVE A READING!

DOCTOR, YOU WILL KEEP YOUR PROMISE, WON'T YOU?

TO GIVE MASATO A CELL STRUCTURE LIKE MINE...

DON'T WORRY! I'LL DO EVERYTHING I CAN TO ENSURE HIS SURVIVAL!

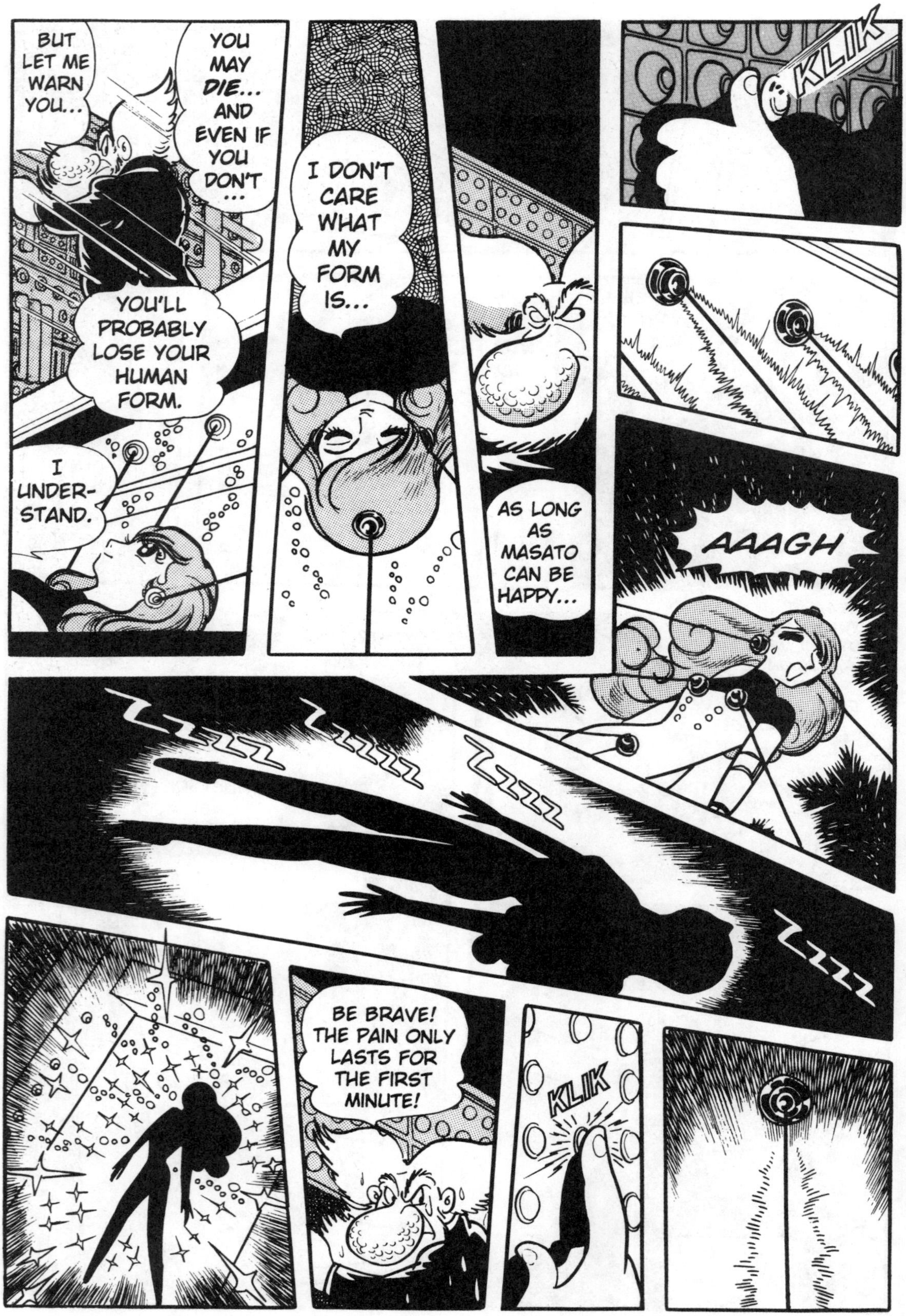
BUT LET ME WARN YOU...
YOU MAY DIE... AND EVEN IF YOU DON'T ...
YOU'LL PROBABLY LOSE YOUR HUMAN FORM.
I UNDERSTAND.
I DON'T CARE WHAT MY FORM IS...
AS LONG AS MASATO CAN BE HAPPY...
KLIK
AAAGH
ZZZZ
ZZZZZZ
ZZZZZ
ZZZZ
BE BRAVE! THE PAIN ONLY LASTS FOR THE FIRST MINUTE!
KLIK

SO BEAUTIFUL...

THIS IS GOOD-BYE...

rrring

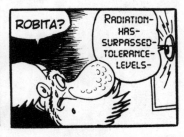

ROBITA?

RADIATION-HAS-SURPASSED-TOLERANCE-LEVELS-

HMM...

DID YOU FIND THE LEAK?

NOT-YET-SIR-

AT-THIS-RATE-RADIATION-SICK-NESS-SYMPTOMS-WILL-OCCUR-IN-HUMANS-IN-TWELVE-HOURS-

I MUST HURRY...

I'VE GOT TO FINISH MY RESEARCH BEFORE I COLLAPSE!

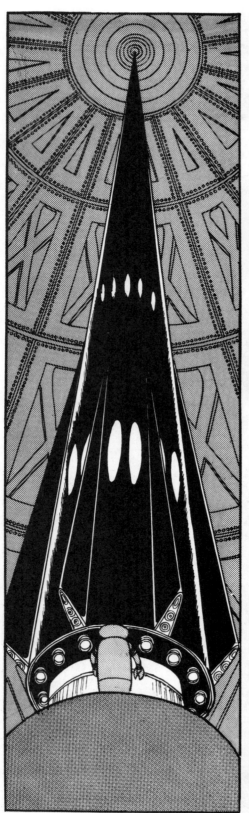

HEY TIN MAN ...

WHAT ARE YOU DOING UP THERE?

PRELAUNCH-PROCEDURE-

PRELAUNCH PROCEDURE? FOR WHOM?

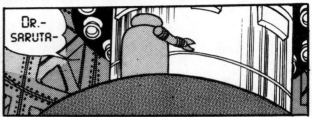

DR.-SARUTA-

SO THE OLD MAN'S RUNNING AWAY, EH?

INCORRECT-THIS-IS-ONLY-A-CONTINGENCY-MEASURE-

GET OUT OF MY WAY, TIN CAN, THIS ROCKET'S FOR ME!

AND NO ONE ELSE!!

NO-

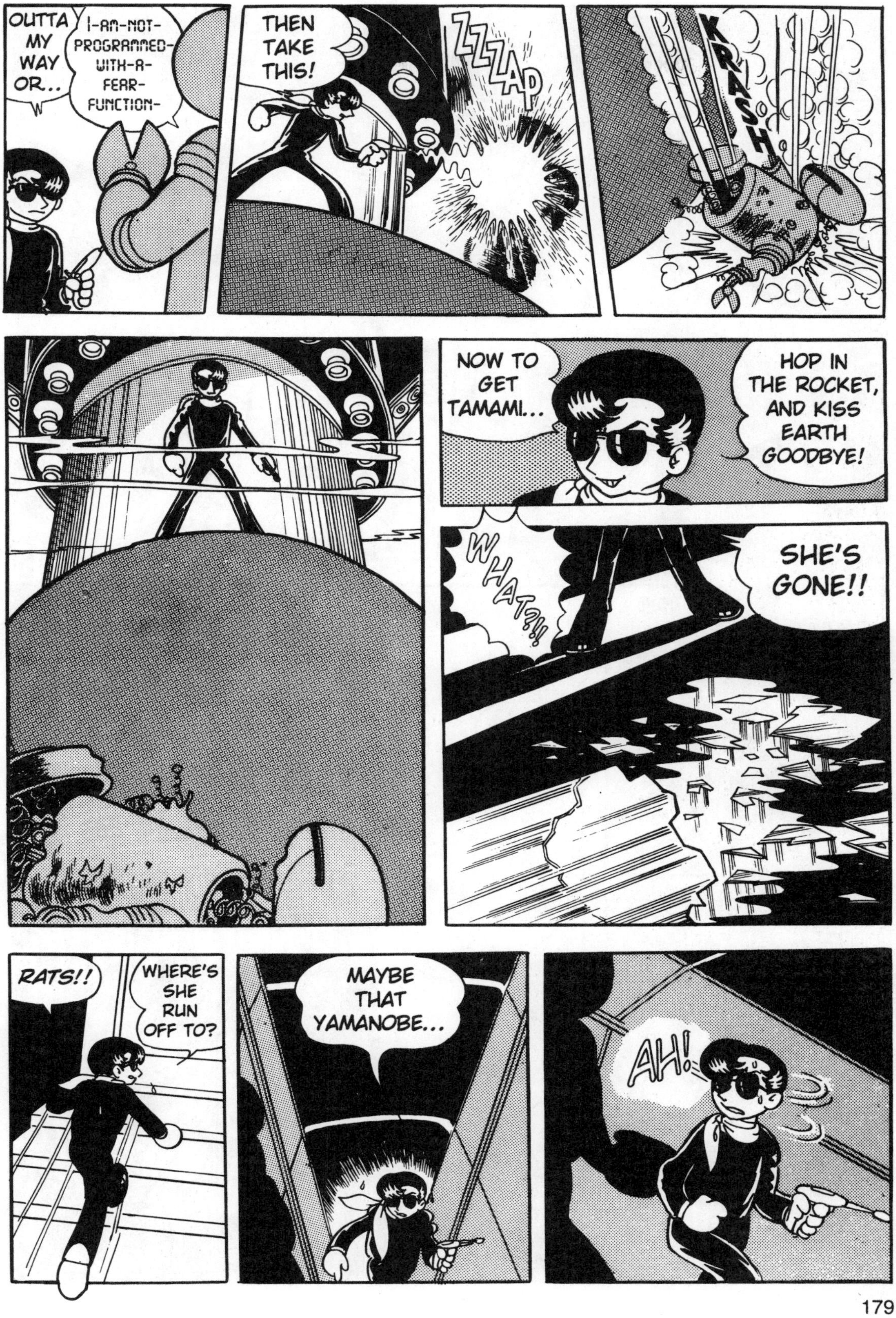
OUTTA MY WAY OR...
I-AM-NOT-PROGRAMMED-WITH-A-FEAR-FUNCTION-
THEN TAKE THIS!
ZZZZAP
KRASH
NOW TO GET TAMAMI...
HOP IN THE ROCKET, AND KISS EARTH GOODBYE!
WHAT?!!
SHE'S GONE!!
RATS!!
WHERE'S SHE RUN OFF TO?
MAYBE THAT YAMANOBE...
AH!

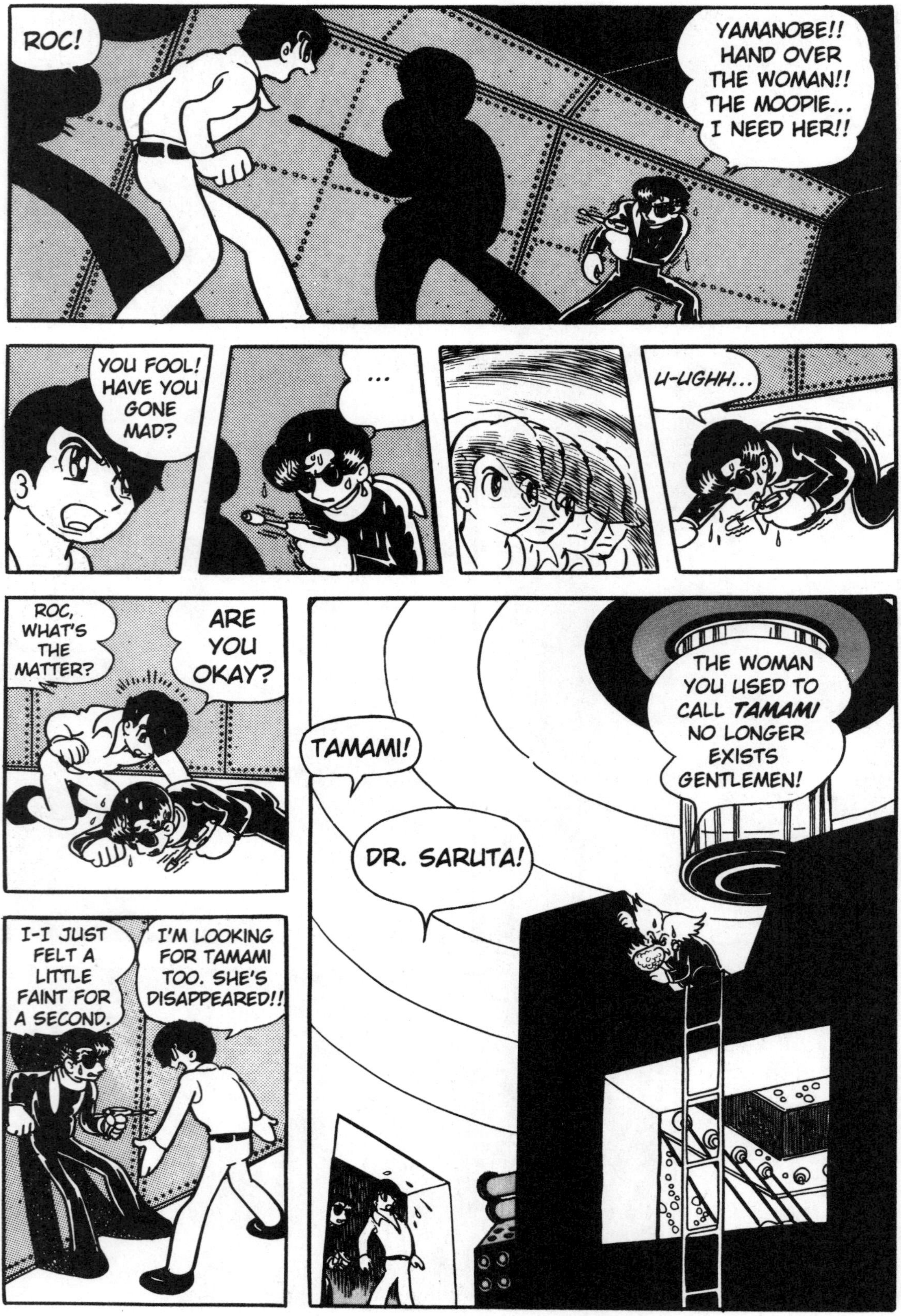
ROC!
YAMANOBE!! HAND OVER THE WOMAN!! THE MOOPIE... I NEED HER!!
YOU FOOL! HAVE YOU GONE MAD?
...
U-UGHH...
ROC, WHAT'S THE MATTER?
ARE YOU OKAY?
I-I JUST FELT A LITTLE FAINT FOR A SECOND.
I'M LOOKING FOR TAMAMI TOO. SHE'S DISAPPEARED!!
TAMAMI!
DR. SARUTA!
THE WOMAN YOU USED TO CALL *TAMAMI* NO LONGER EXISTS GENTLEMEN!

TAMAMI HAS REVERTED BACK TO HER MOOPIE FORM!

OH NO!!

TAMAMI!!

H-HOW COULD HE...

TAMAMI...

SARUTA!

OF ALL THE INHUMAN...

I'LL KILL YOU!

HEH...I'M AFRAID YOU'RE A LITTLE LATE, MY BOY. BOTH OF US ARE AS GOOD AS FINISHED ANYWAY!

WHAT?

TAKE A LOOK AT THE *GEIGER COUNTER!* THIS DOME IS SATURATED WITH RADIATION!

AIR LEAKED IN FROM THE OUTSIDE, AND WHEN I FOUND OUT IT WAS TOO LATE. THE LEAST I COULD DO IN THE TIME REMAINING WAS TO SOLVE THE SECRET OF TAMAMI'S CELL STRUCTURE WITH COMPUTER ANALYSIS.

AH!

SHE DONATED HER BODY TO ME. I HAVE COMPLETED MY EXPERIMENT.

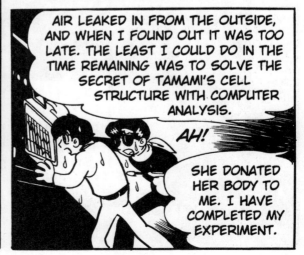

I HAVE THE INFORMATION RIGHT HERE, YAMANOBE!

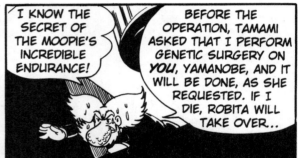

I KNOW THE SECRET OF THE MOOPIE'S INCREDIBLE ENDURANCE!

BEFORE THE OPERATION, TAMAMI ASKED THAT I PERFORM GENETIC SURGERY ON *YOU*, YAMANOBE, AND IT WILL BE DONE, AS SHE REQUESTED. IF I DIE, ROBITA WILL TAKE OVER...

DOCTOR! ROBITA IS NO MORE!!

WHAT?

I DESTROYED HIM...

DESTROYED ROBITA?!

I WAS PLANNING TO ESCAPE TO OUTER SPACE WITH TAMAMI IN THE ROCKET!

ROBITA GOT IN THE WAY!!

GOING INTO SPACE WOULDN'T HAVE HELPED YOU ANYWAY.

IT'S TOO LATE! YOUR BODY IS BEING SATURATED WITH RADIATION! THE SYMPTOMS SHOULD ALREADY BE APPEARING AND YOU'LL SOON DIE!!

HEH HEH... WELL IF THAT'S THE CASE...

IT EXPLAINS WHY I WAS DIZZY A MINUTE AGO...

HA! HA! HA!

ALL MY PLANS...

WHAT A JOKE!! HA HA!

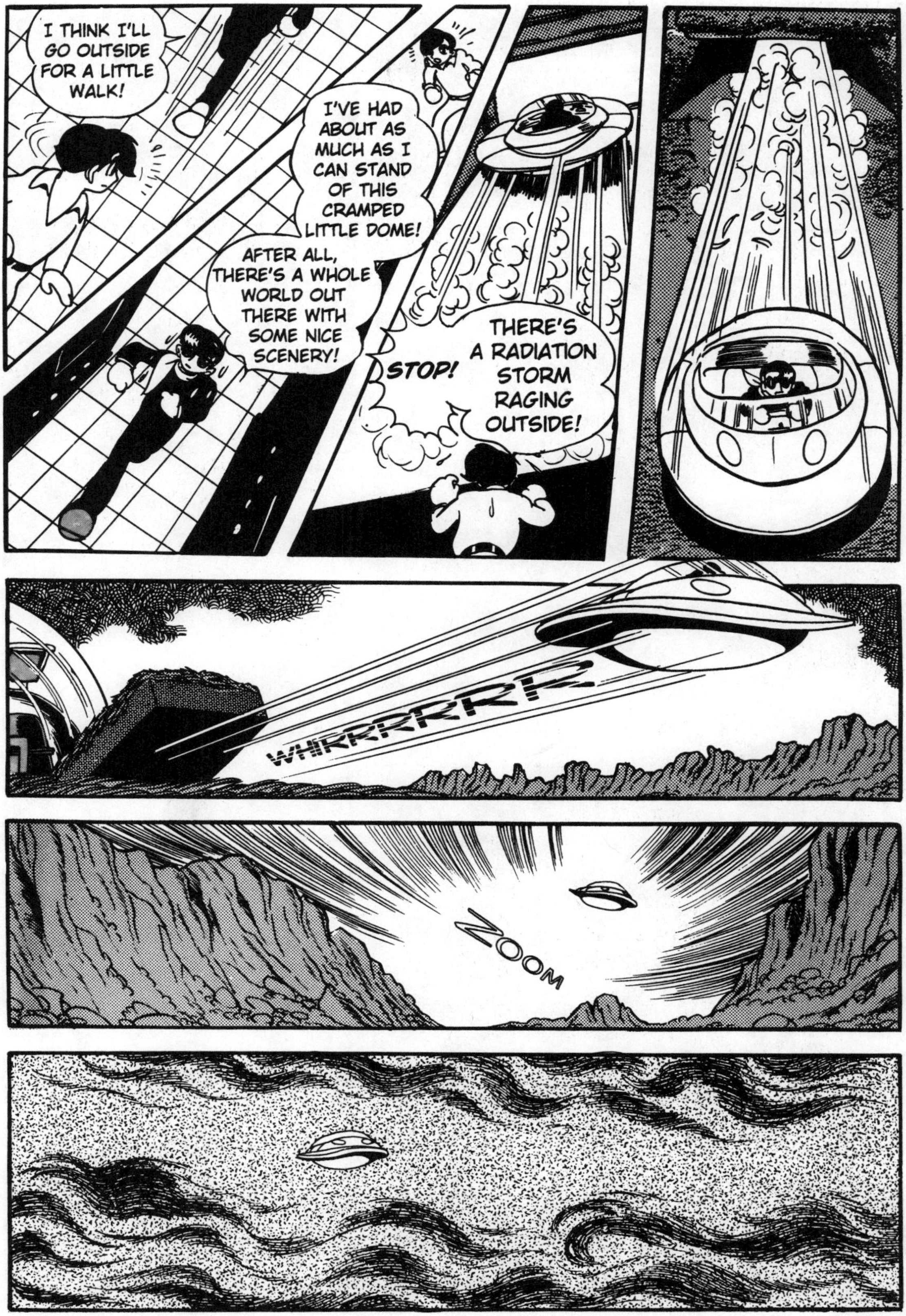
I THINK I'LL GO OUTSIDE FOR A LITTLE WALK!
I'VE HAD ABOUT AS MUCH AS I CAN STAND OF THIS CRAMPED LITTLE DOME!
AFTER ALL, THERE'S A WHOLE WORLD OUT THERE WITH SOME NICE SCENERY!
STOP!
THERE'S A RADIATION STORM RAGING OUTSIDE!
WHIRRRRRRR
ZOOM

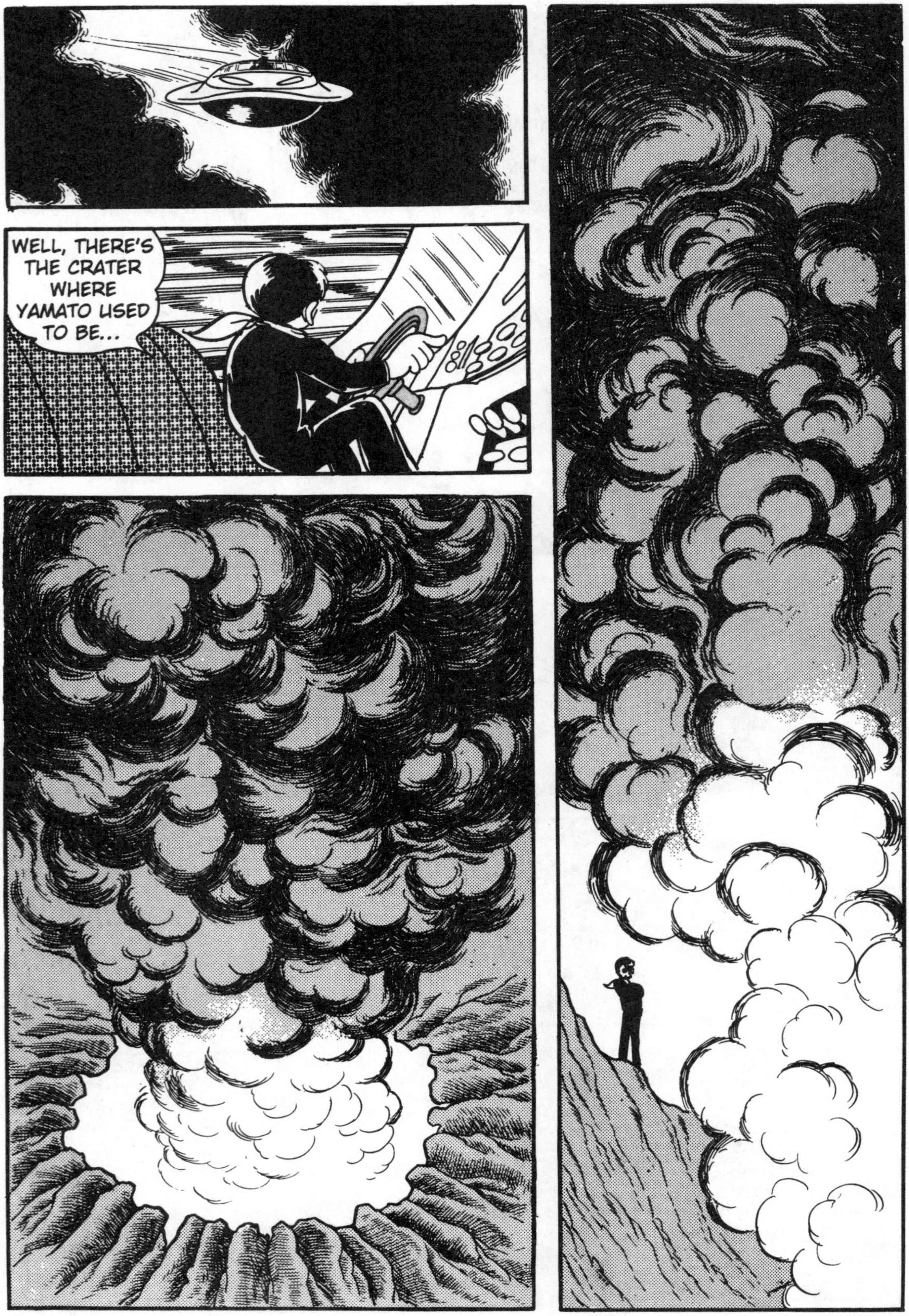
WELL, THERE'S THE CRATER WHERE YAMATO USED TO BE...

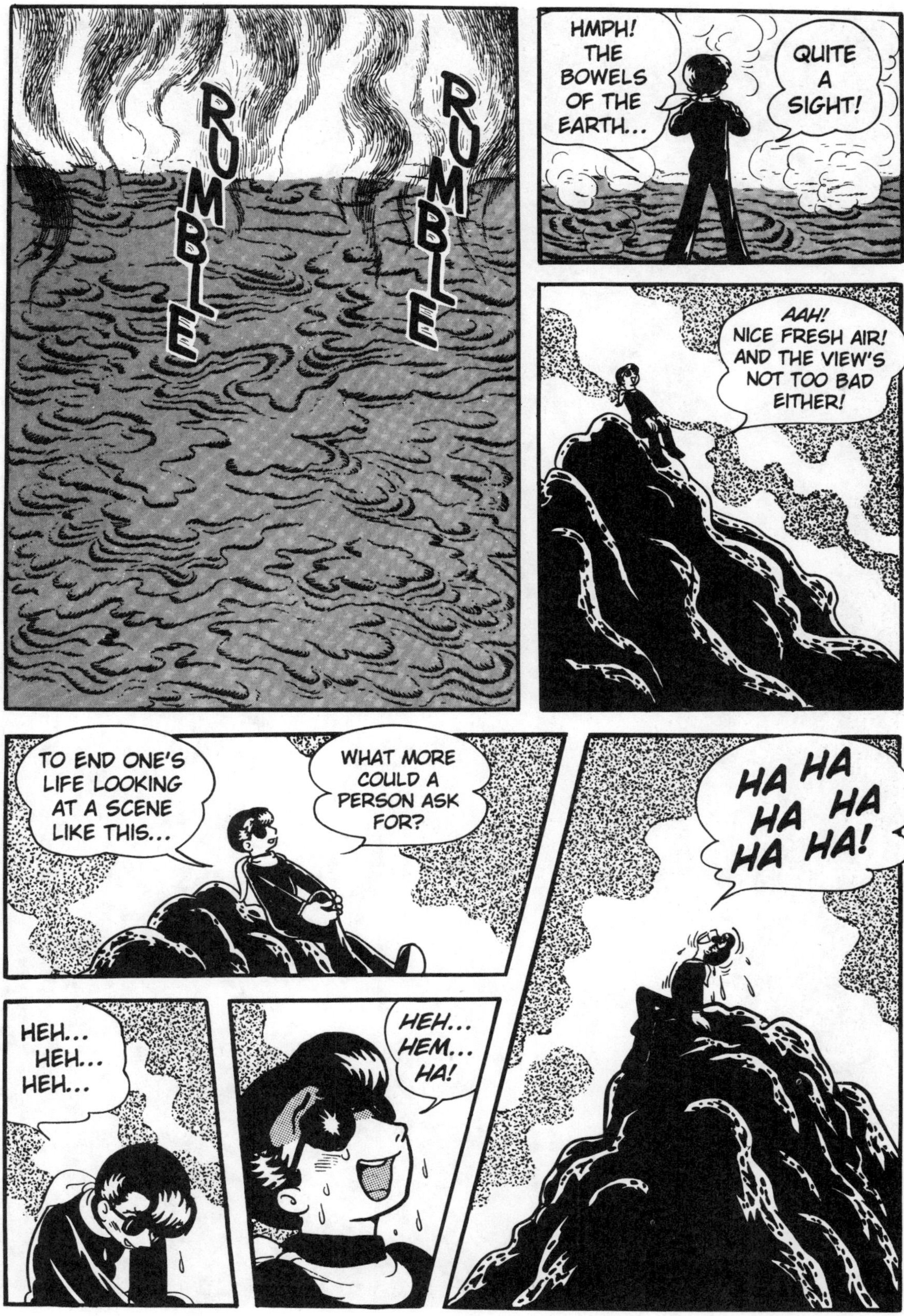
RUMBLE
RUMBLE
HMPH! THE BOWELS OF THE EARTH...
QUITE A SIGHT!
AAH! NICE FRESH AIR! AND THE VIEW'S NOT TOO BAD EITHER!
TO END ONE'S LIFE LOOKING AT A SCENE LIKE THIS...
WHAT MORE COULD A PERSON ASK FOR?
HEH... HEH... HEH...
HEH... HEM... HA!
HA HA HA HA HA HA!

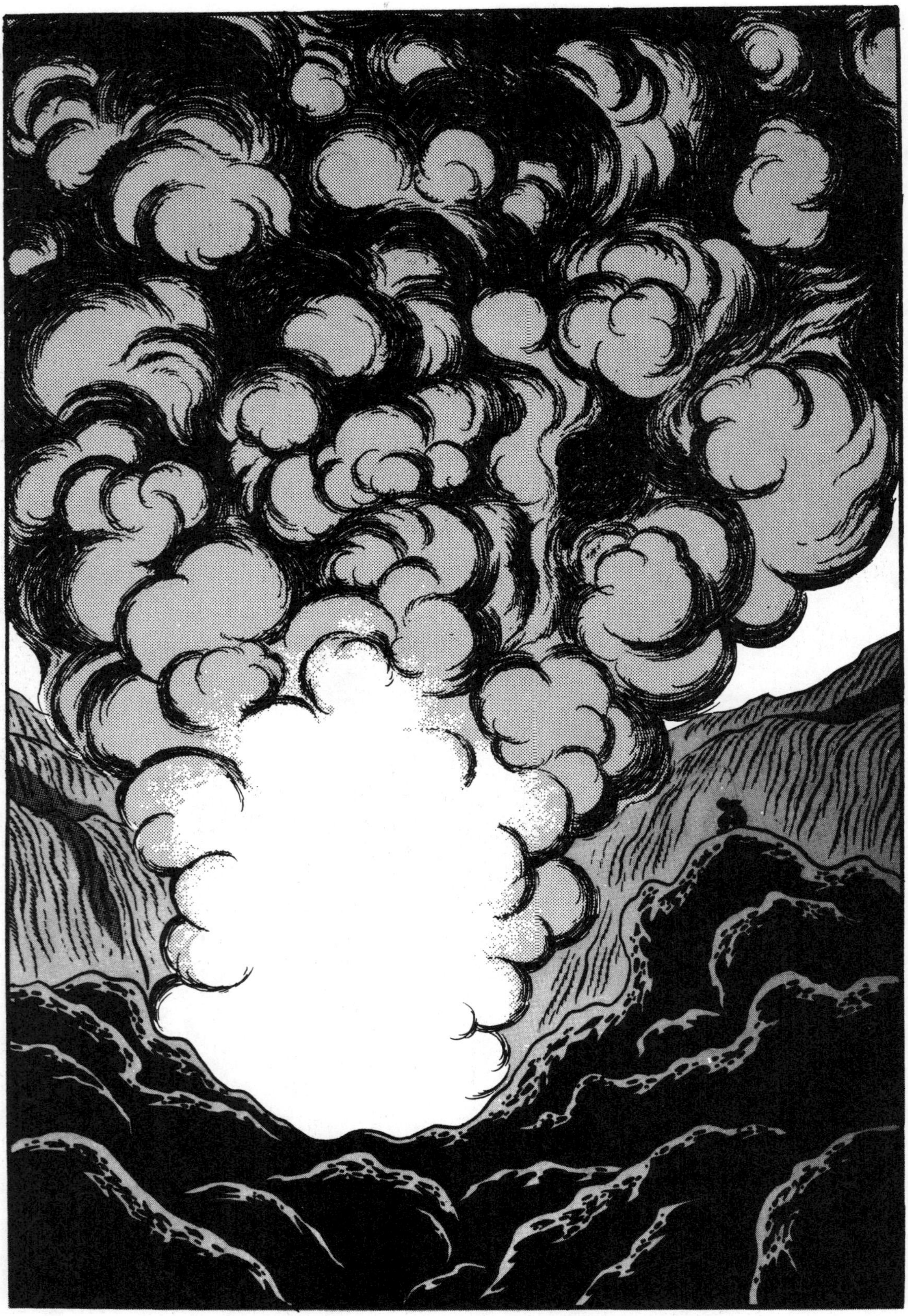

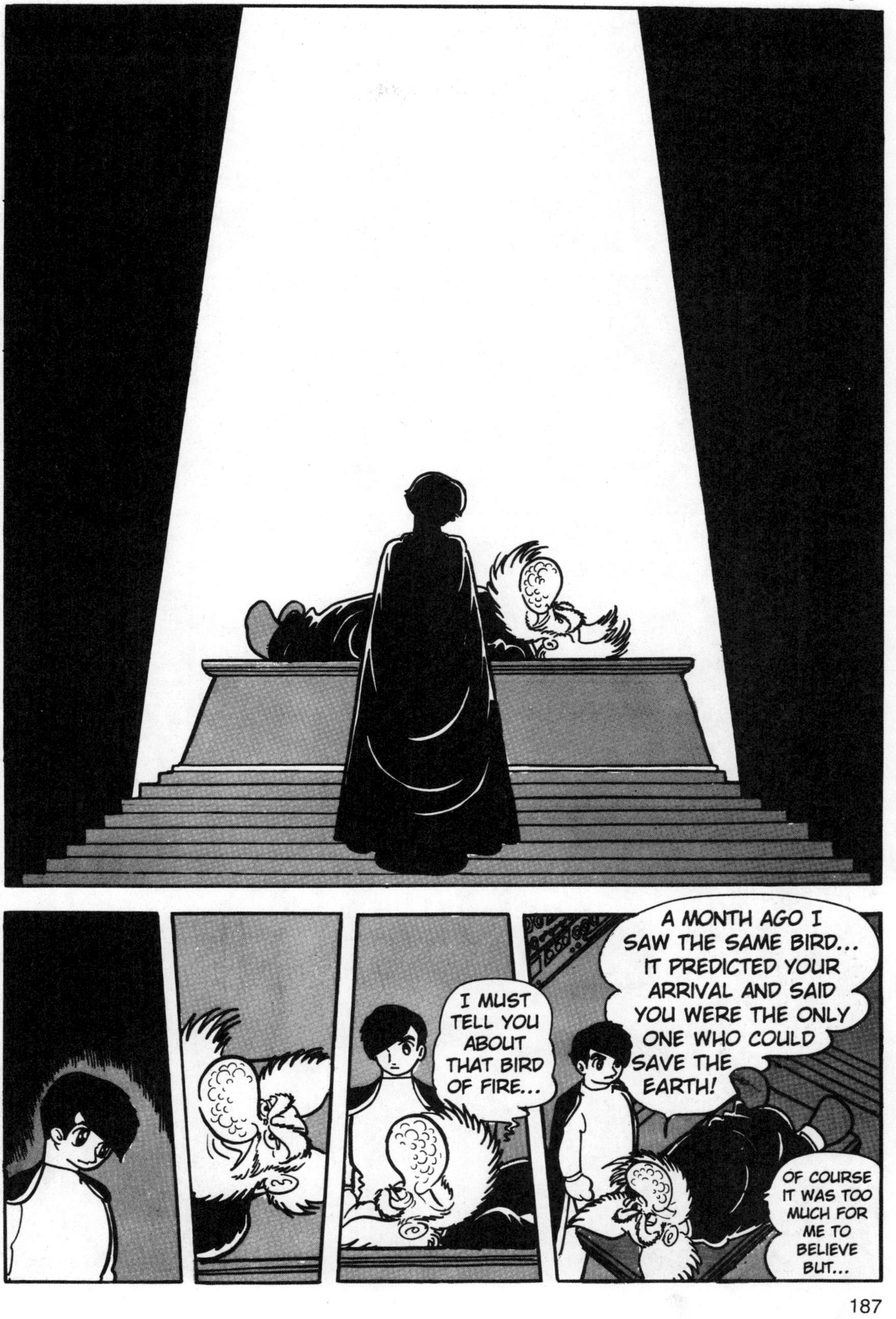
I MUST TELL YOU ABOUT THAT BIRD OF FIRE...
A MONTH AGO I SAW THE SAME BIRD... IT PREDICTED YOUR ARRIVAL AND SAID YOU WERE THE ONLY ONE WHO COULD SAVE THE EARTH!
OF COURSE IT WAS TOO MUCH FOR ME TO BELIEVE BUT...

IF IT'S TRUE THAT THE BIRD HAS MADE YOU IMMORTAL...

I GUESS I'LL HAVE TO ACKNOWLEDGE THAT SOME OMNISCIENT POWER DOES EXIST IN THE UNIVERSE.

IT MAY BE WHAT MEN HAVE ALWAYS CALLED GOD.

OR PERHAPS IT'S A *SUPER LIFE-FORM* WHICH TRANSCENDS OUR IMAGINATION!

...

YAMANOBE, I'M DEPENDING ON YOU TO NOT LET THE EARTH DOWN! CONTINUE MY RESEARCH! KEEP TRYING TO CREATE NEW LIFE!

TAMAMI SACRIFICED HERSELF SO I COULD LEARN THE SECRET OF HER CELL STRUCTURE.

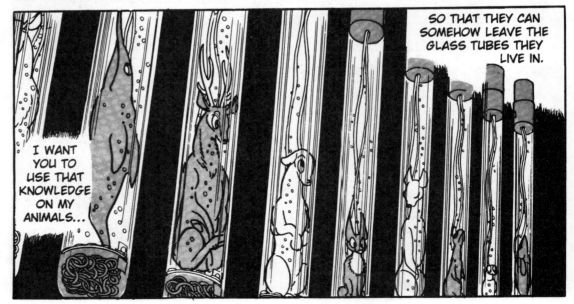

I WANT YOU TO USE THAT KNOWLEDGE ON MY ANIMALS...

SO THAT THEY CAN SOMEHOW LEAVE THE GLASS TUBES THEY LIVE IN.

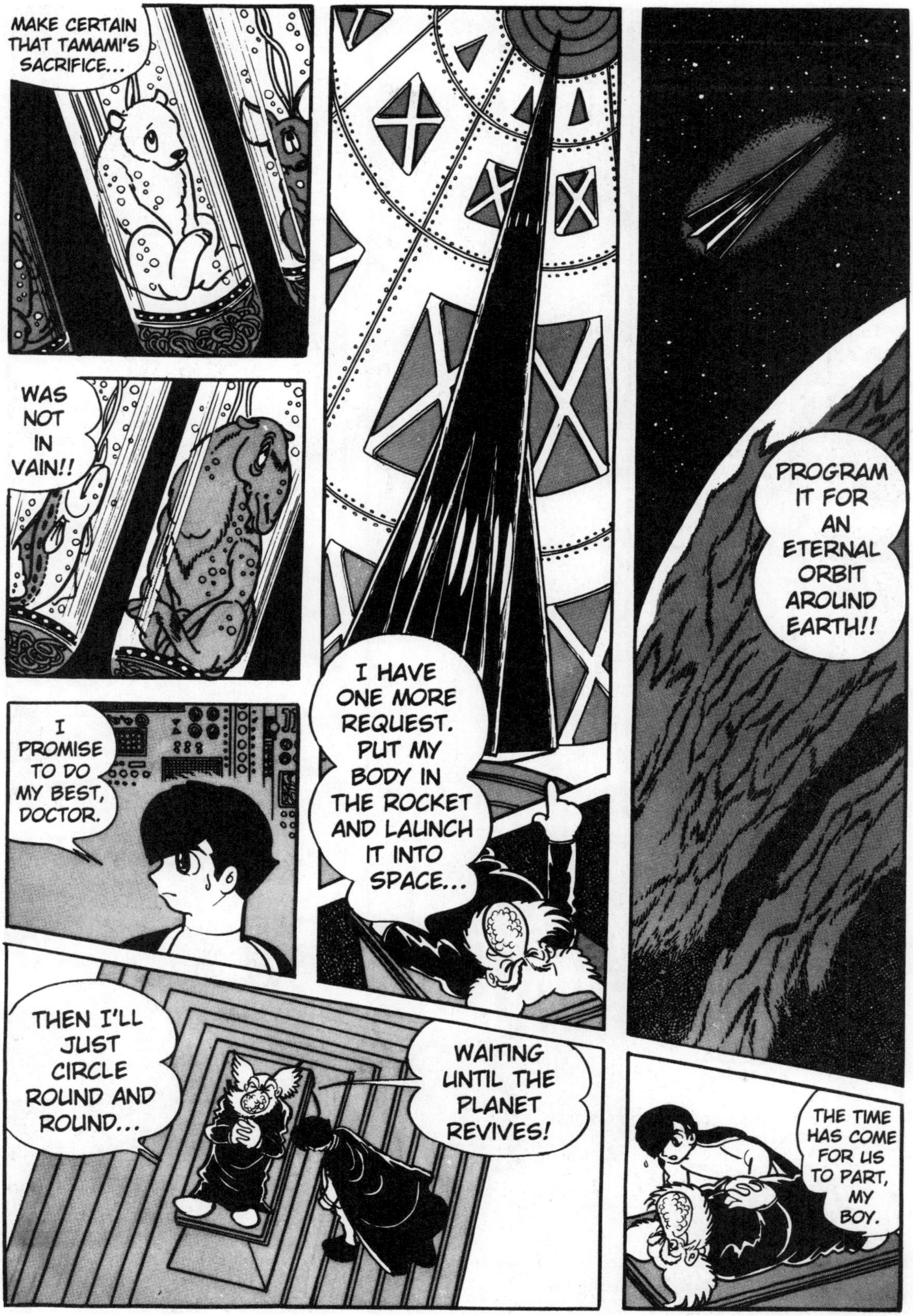
MAKE CERTAIN THAT TAMAMI'S SACRIFICE...
WAS NOT IN VAIN!!
I PROMISE TO DO MY BEST, DOCTOR.
I HAVE ONE MORE REQUEST. PUT MY BODY IN THE ROCKET AND LAUNCH IT INTO SPACE...
PROGRAM IT FOR AN ETERNAL ORBIT AROUND EARTH!!
THEN I'LL JUST CIRCLE ROUND AND ROUND...
WAITING UNTIL THE PLANET REVIVES!
THE TIME HAS COME FOR US TO PART, MY BOY.

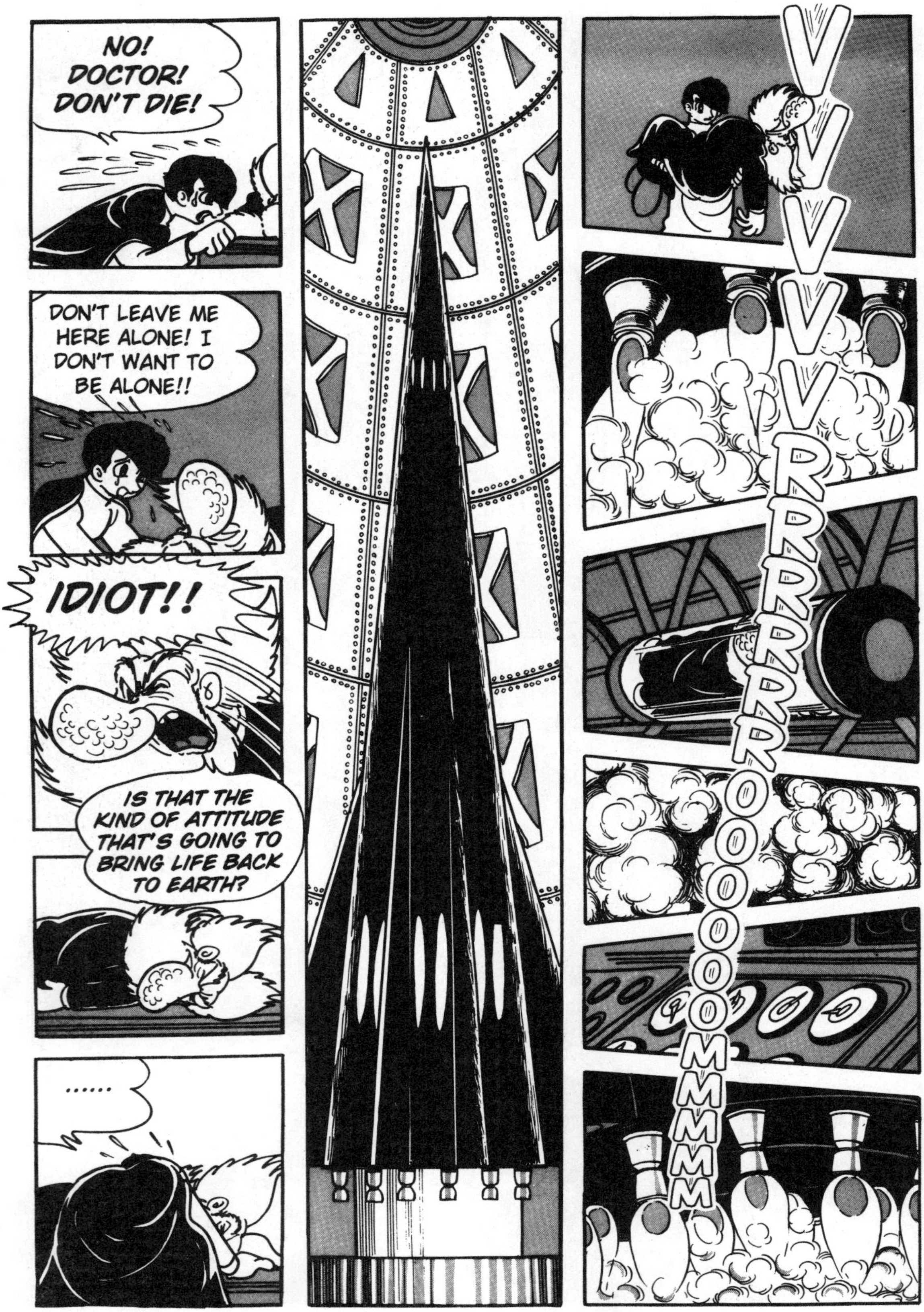
NO! DOCTOR! DON'T DIE!
DON'T LEAVE ME HERE ALONE! I DON'T WANT TO BE ALONE!!
IDIOT!!
IS THAT THE KIND OF ATTITUDE THAT'S GOING TO BRING LIFE BACK TO EARTH?
......
VVVVVVRRRRRROOOOOOOMMMMM

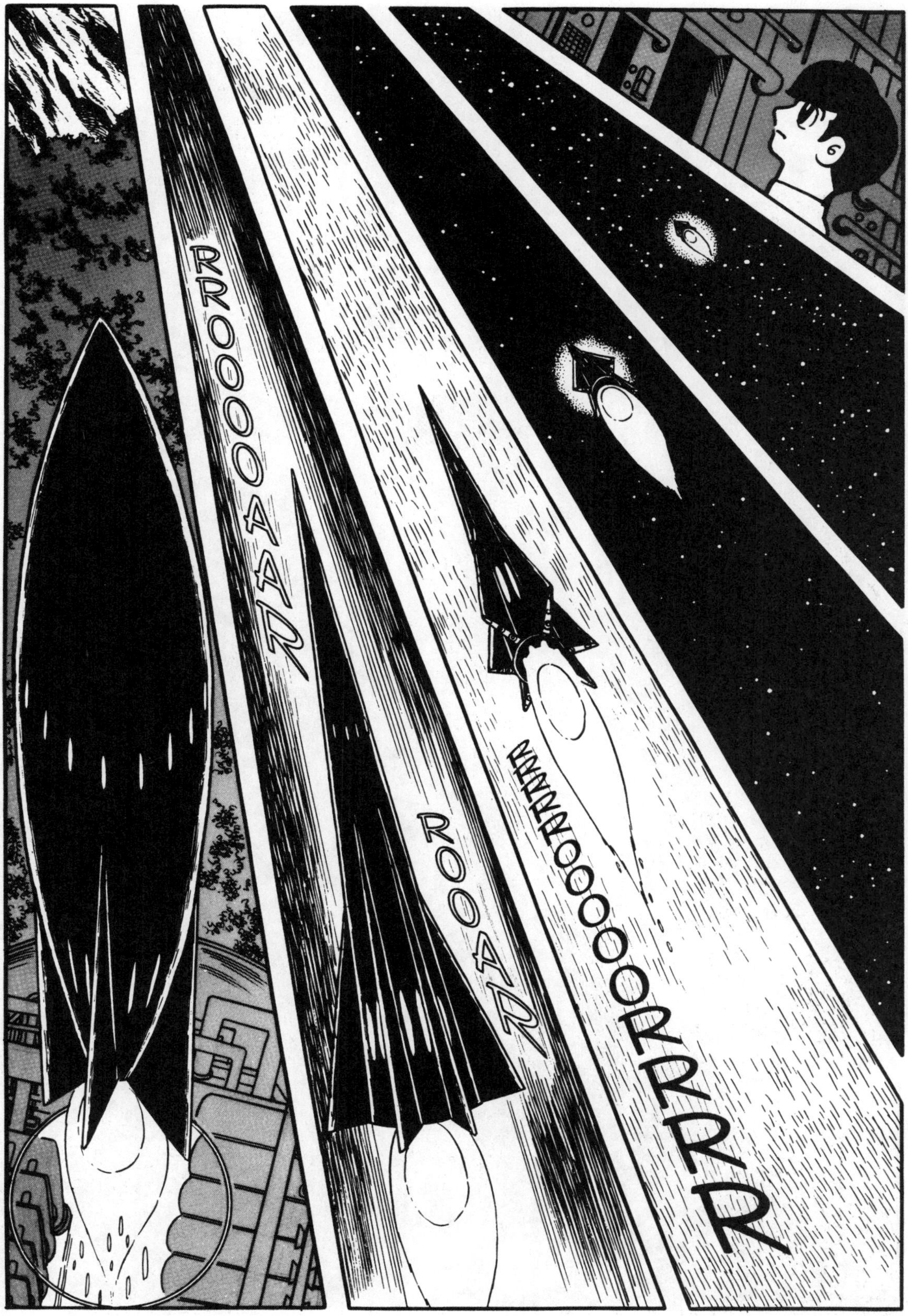
RRRROOOOOOORRRR
ROOOAR
RROOOOAAAR

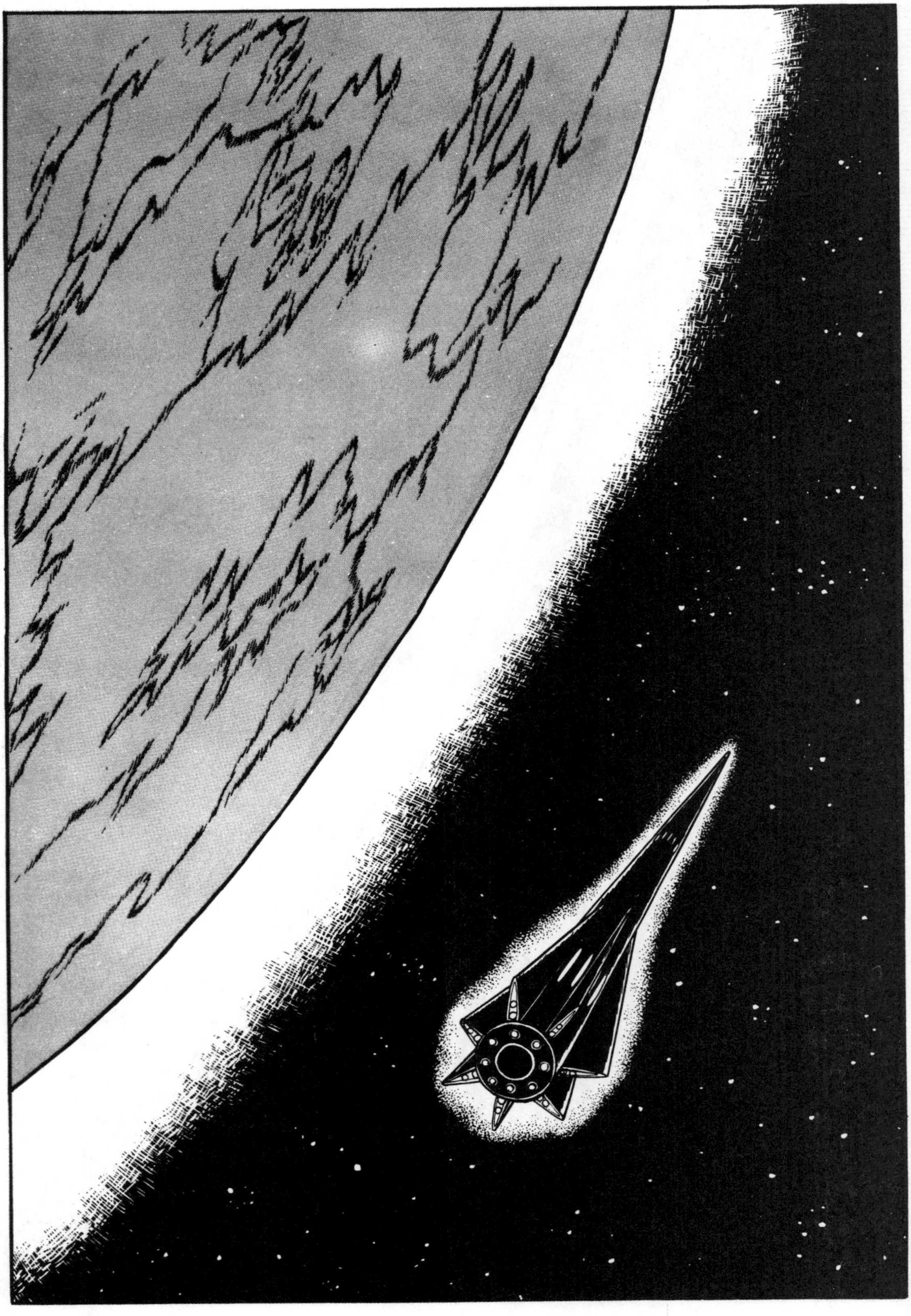

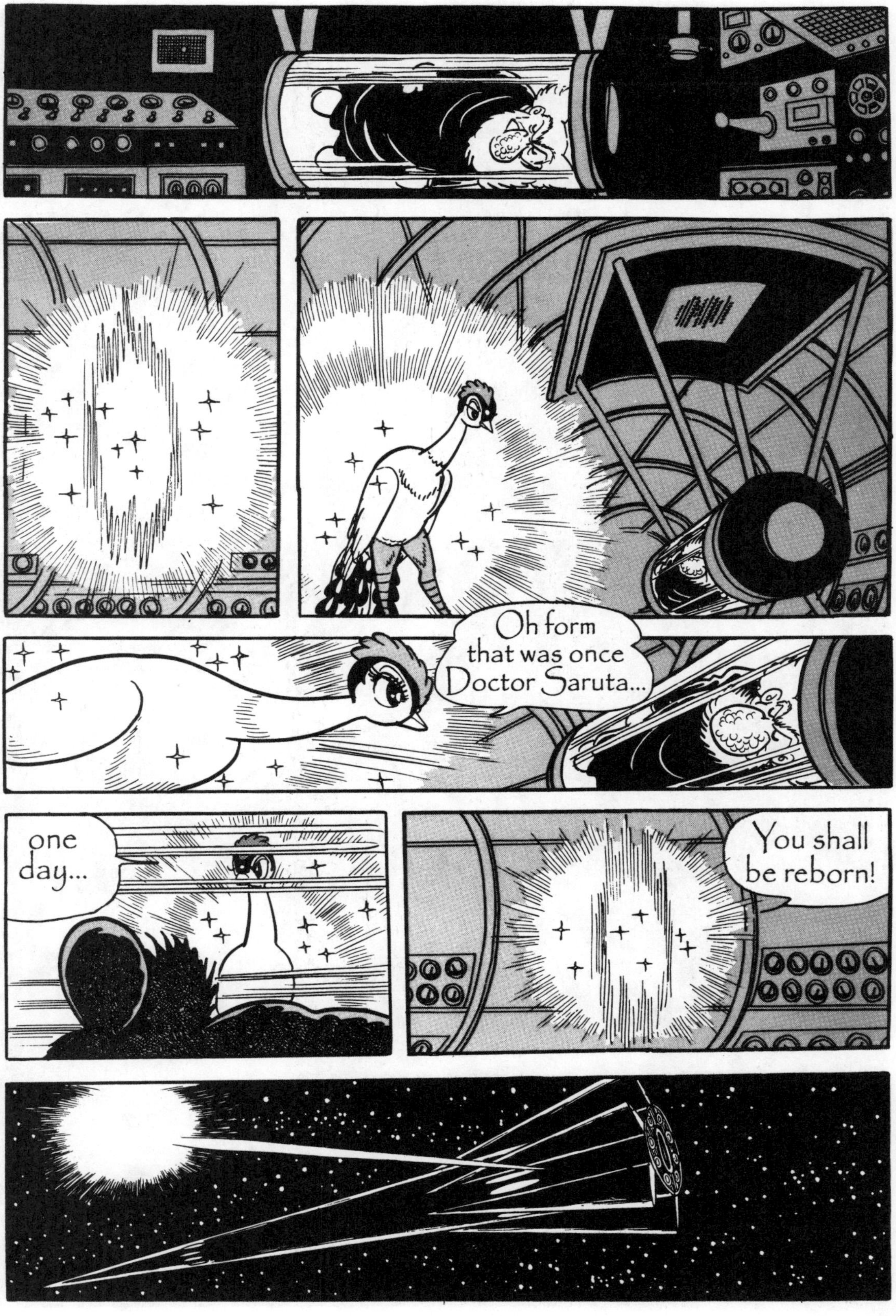
Oh form that was once Doctor Saruta...
one day...
You shall be reborn!

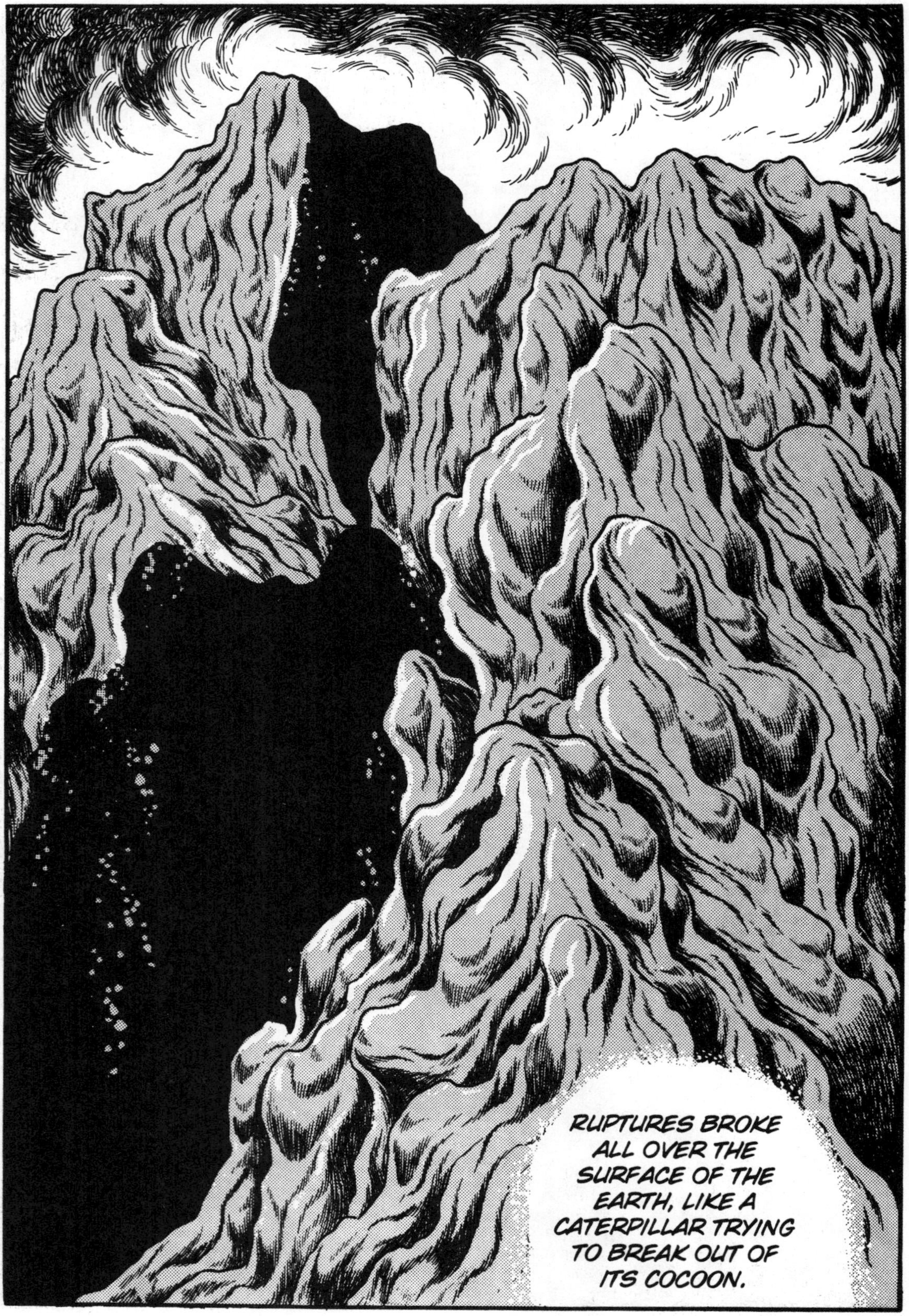
RUPTURES BROKE ALL OVER THE SURFACE OF THE EARTH, LIKE A CATERPILLAR TRYING TO BREAK OUT OF ITS COCOON.

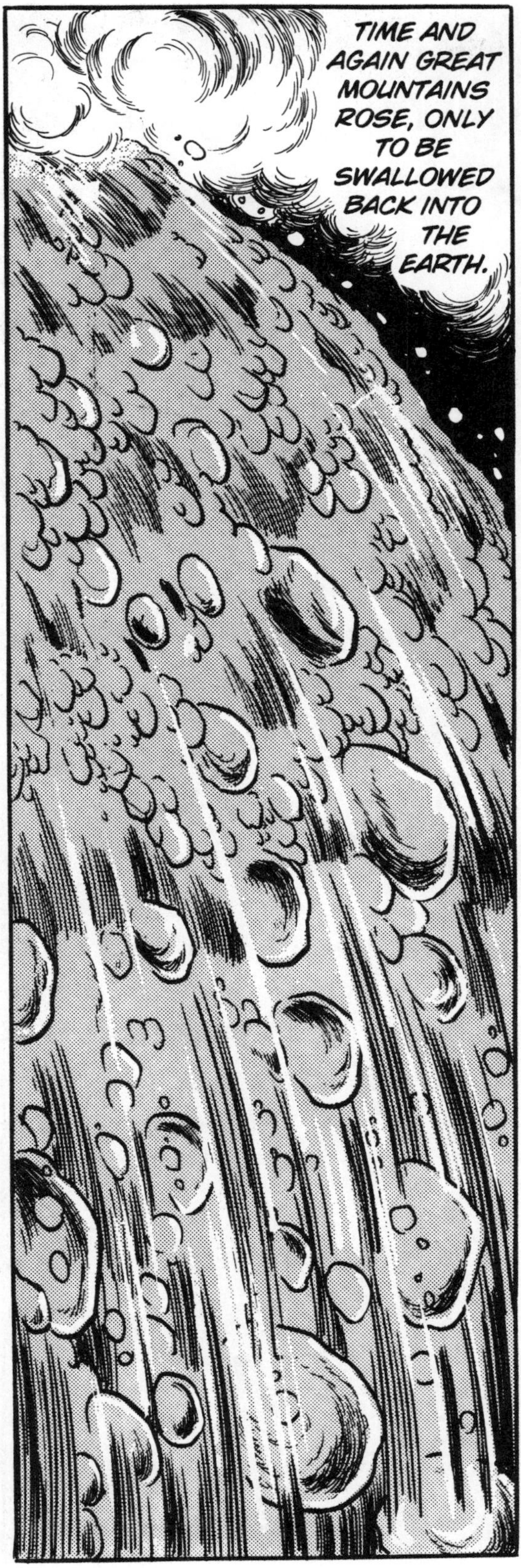
TIME AND AGAIN GREAT MOUNTAINS ROSE, ONLY TO BE SWALLOWED BACK INTO THE EARTH.

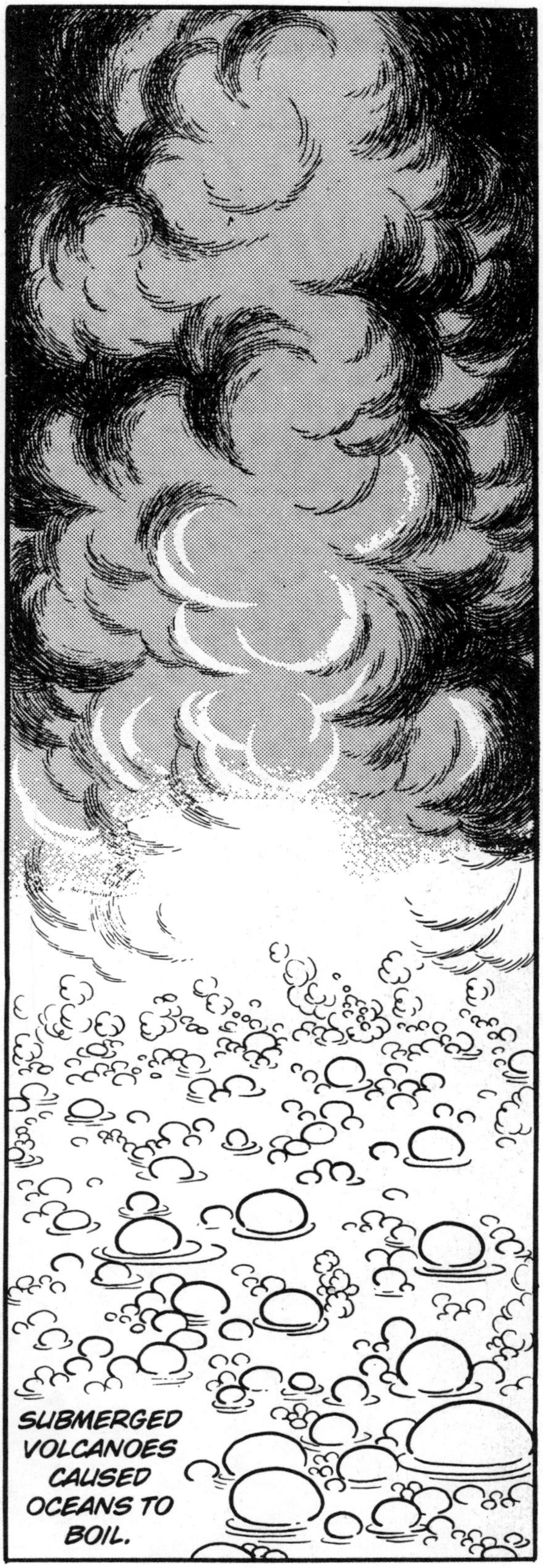
SUBMERGED VOLCANOES CAUSED OCEANS TO BOIL.

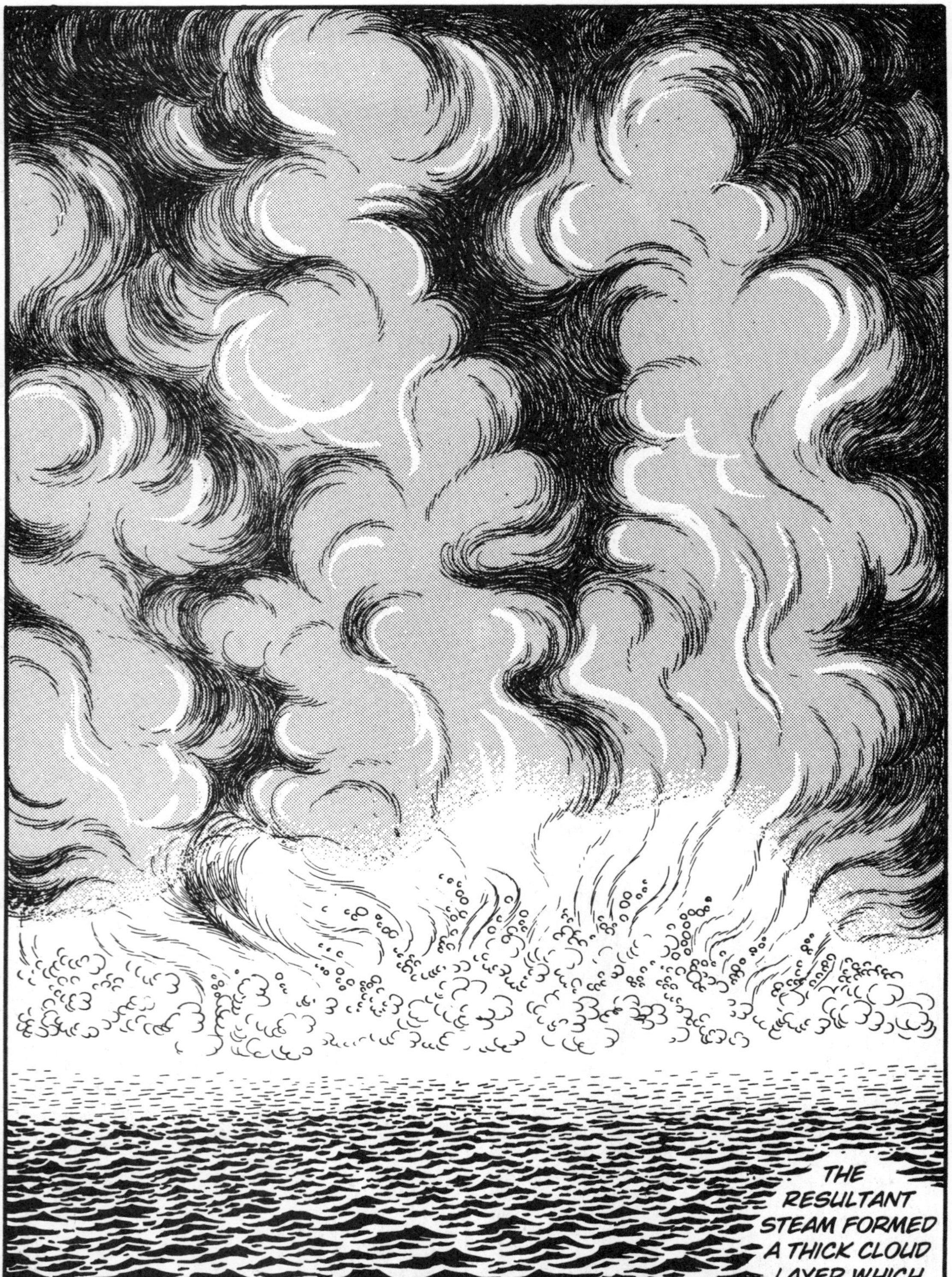
THE RESULTANT STEAM FORMED A THICK CLOUD LAYER WHICH HUNG OVER THE FIVE CONTINENTS.

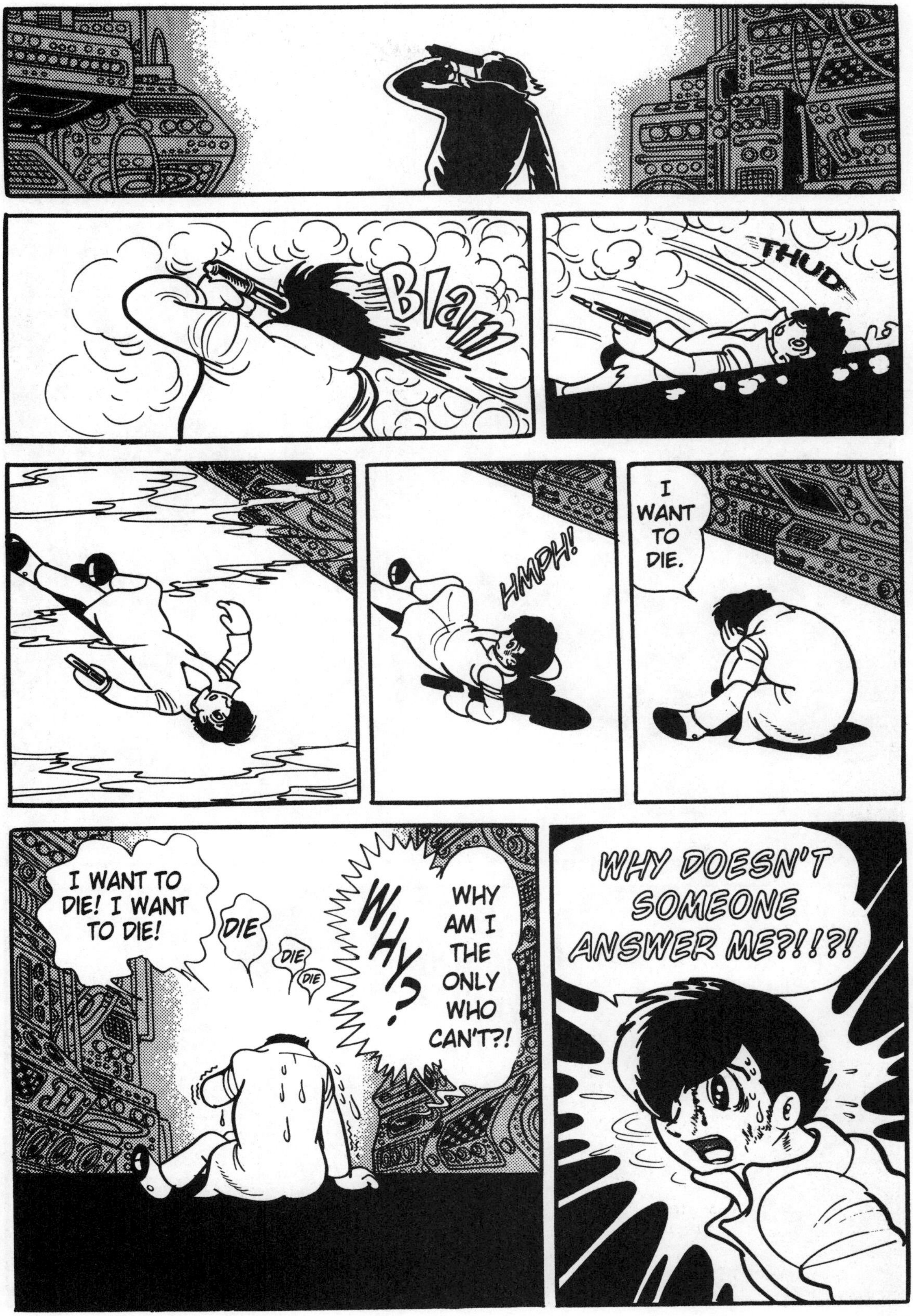
THUD
Blam
I WANT TO DIE.
HMPH!
WHY DOESN'T SOMEONE ANSWER ME?!!?!
WHY AM I THE ONLY WHO CAN'T?!
WHY?
I WANT TO DIE! I WANT TO DIE!
DIE
DIE
DIE

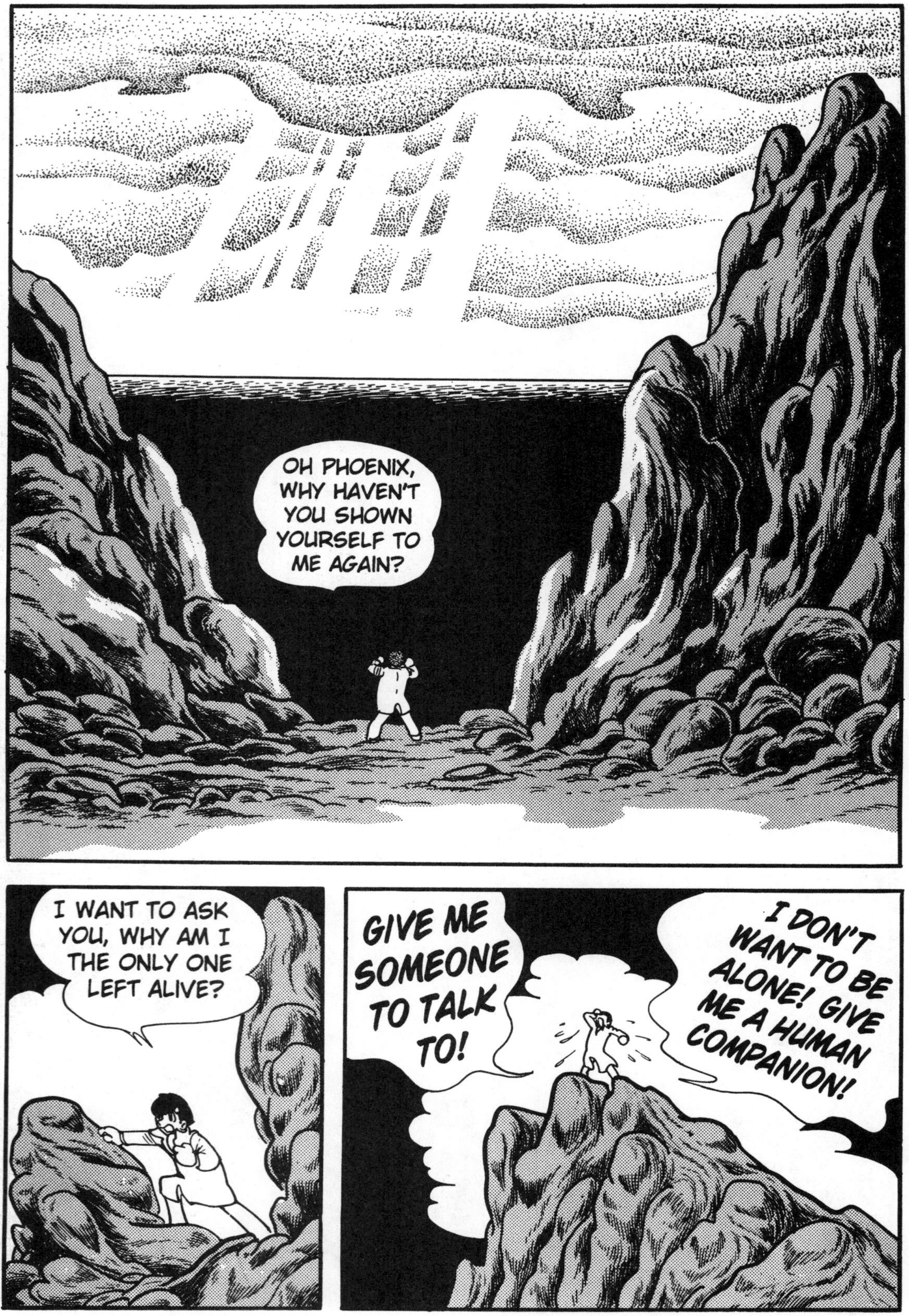
OH PHOENIX, WHY HAVEN'T YOU SHOWN YOURSELF TO ME AGAIN?
I WANT TO ASK YOU, WHY AM I THE ONLY ONE LEFT ALIVE?
GIVE ME SOMEONE TO TALK TO!
I DON'T WANT TO BE ALONE! GIVE ME A HUMAN COMPANION!

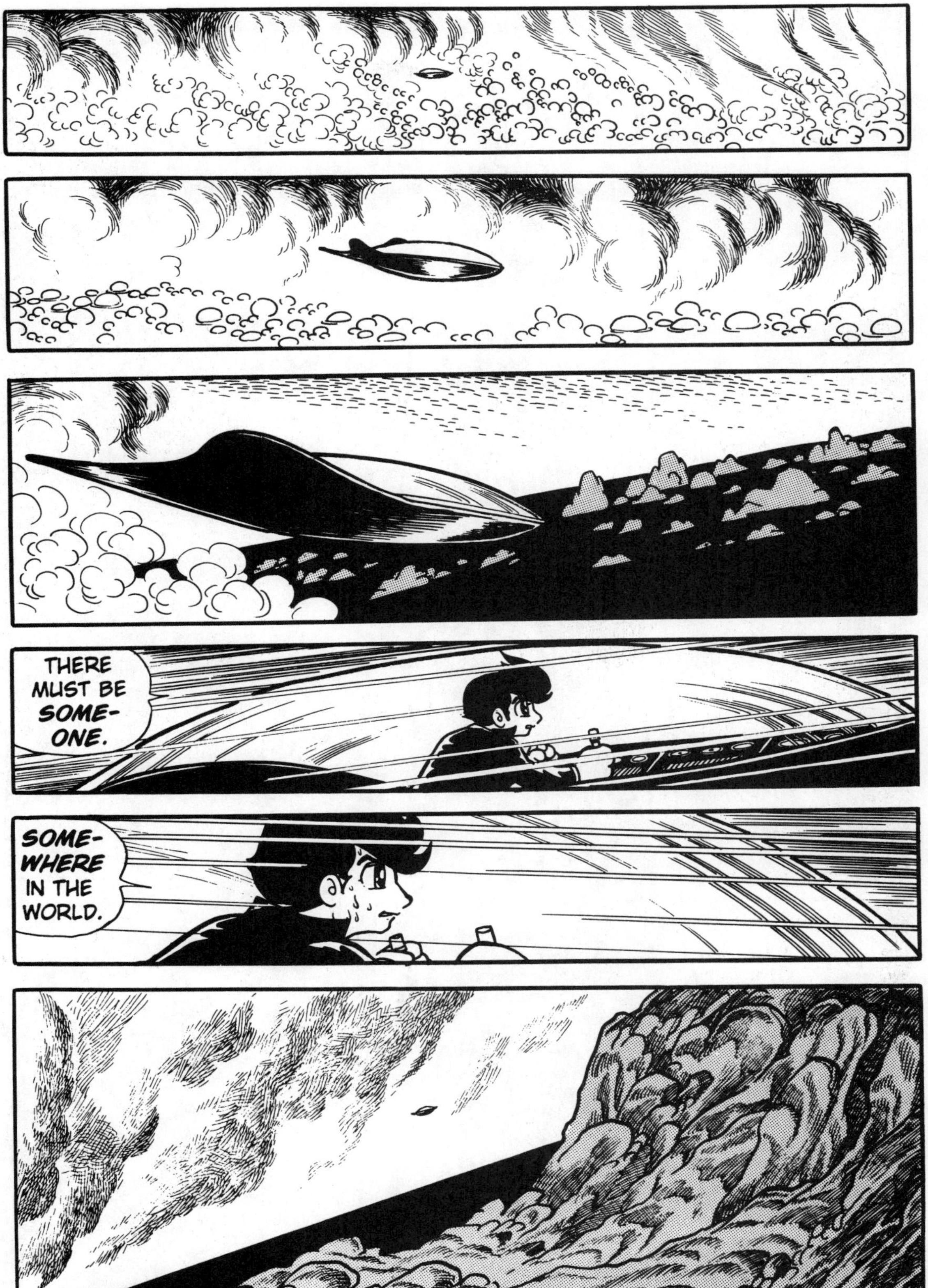
THERE MUST BE SOME-ONE.
SOME-WHERE IN THE WORLD.

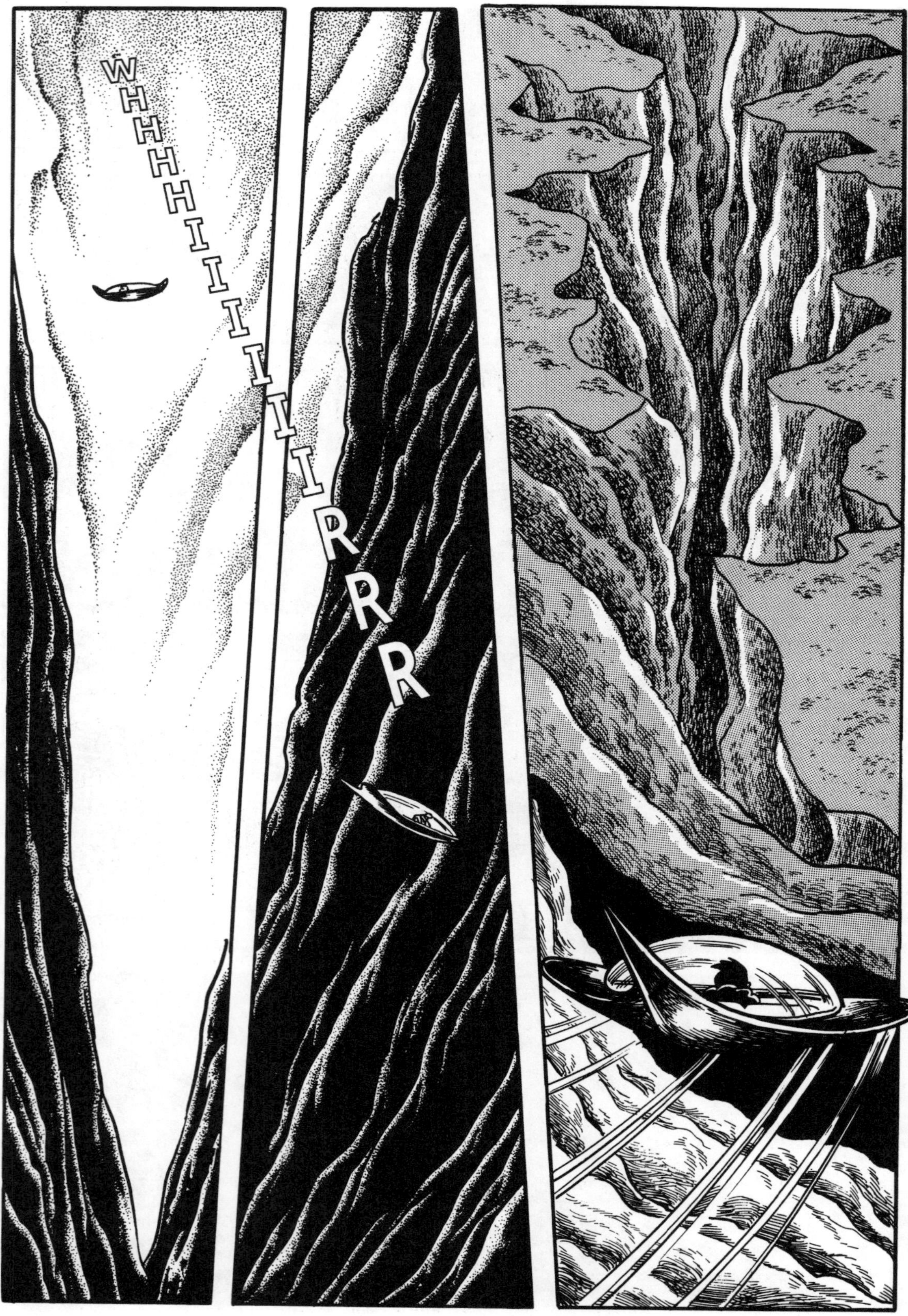
WHHHHIIIIIIRRR

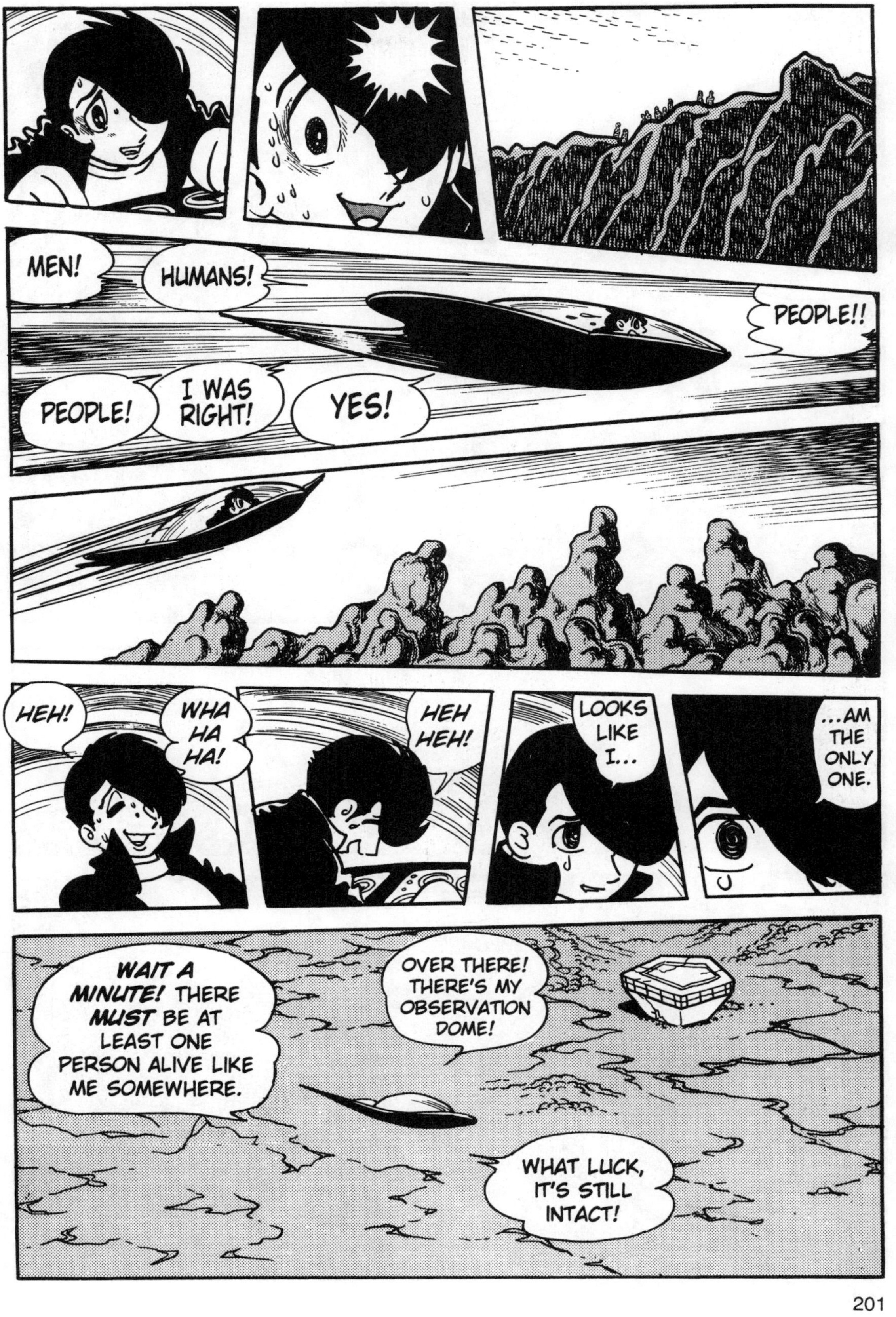
MEN!
HUMANS!
PEOPLE!!
PEOPLE!
I WAS RIGHT!
YES!
HEH!
WHA HA HA!
HEH HEH!
LOOKS LIKE I...
...AM THE ONLY ONE.
WAIT A MINUTE! THERE MUST BE AT LEAST ONE PERSON ALIVE LIKE ME SOMEWHERE.
OVER THERE! THERE'S MY OBSERVATION DOME!
WHAT LUCK, IT'S STILL INTACT!

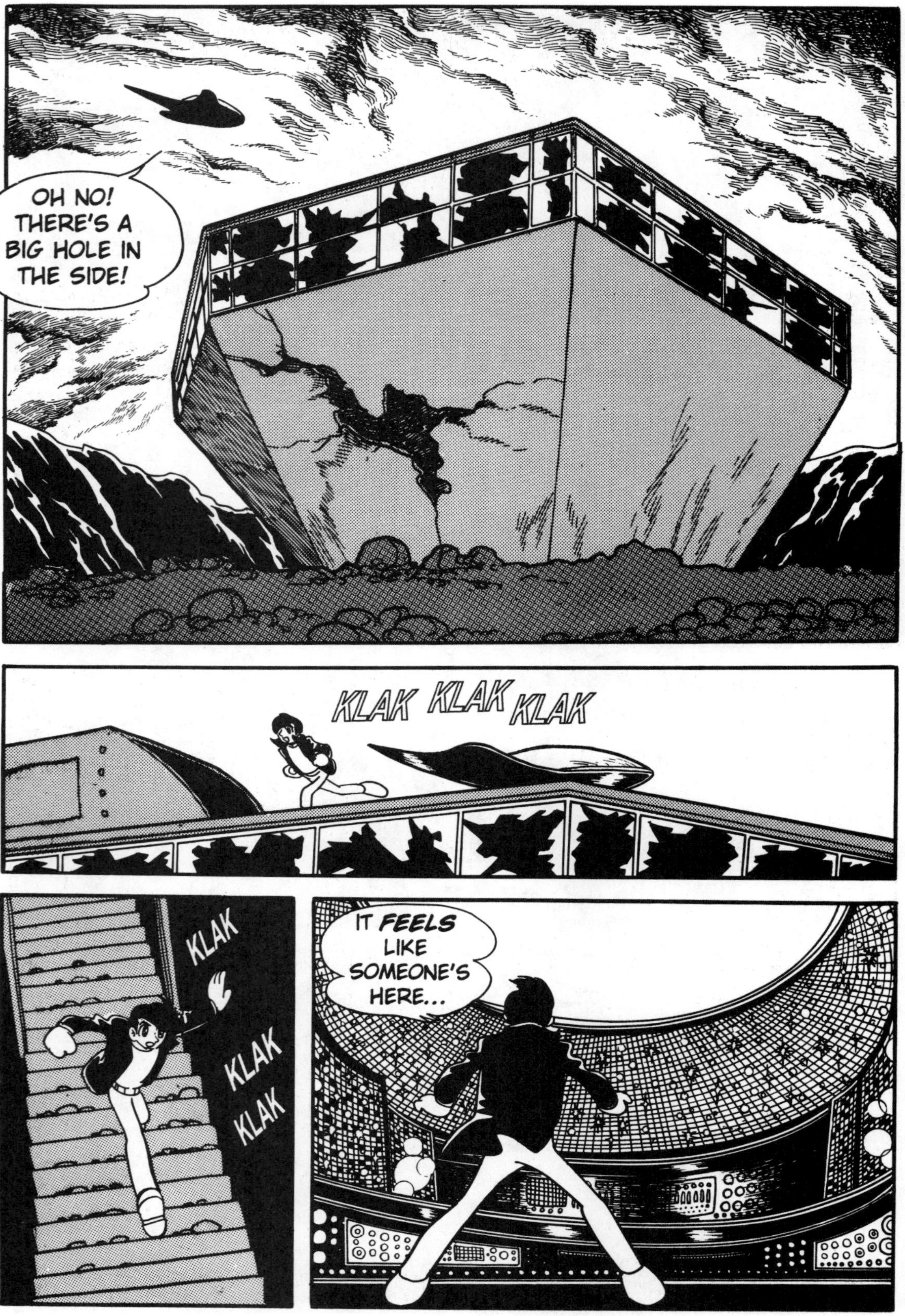
OH NO! THERE'S A BIG HOLE IN THE SIDE!
KLAK KLAK KLAK
KLAK
KLAK
KLAK
IT FEELS LIKE SOMEONE'S HERE...

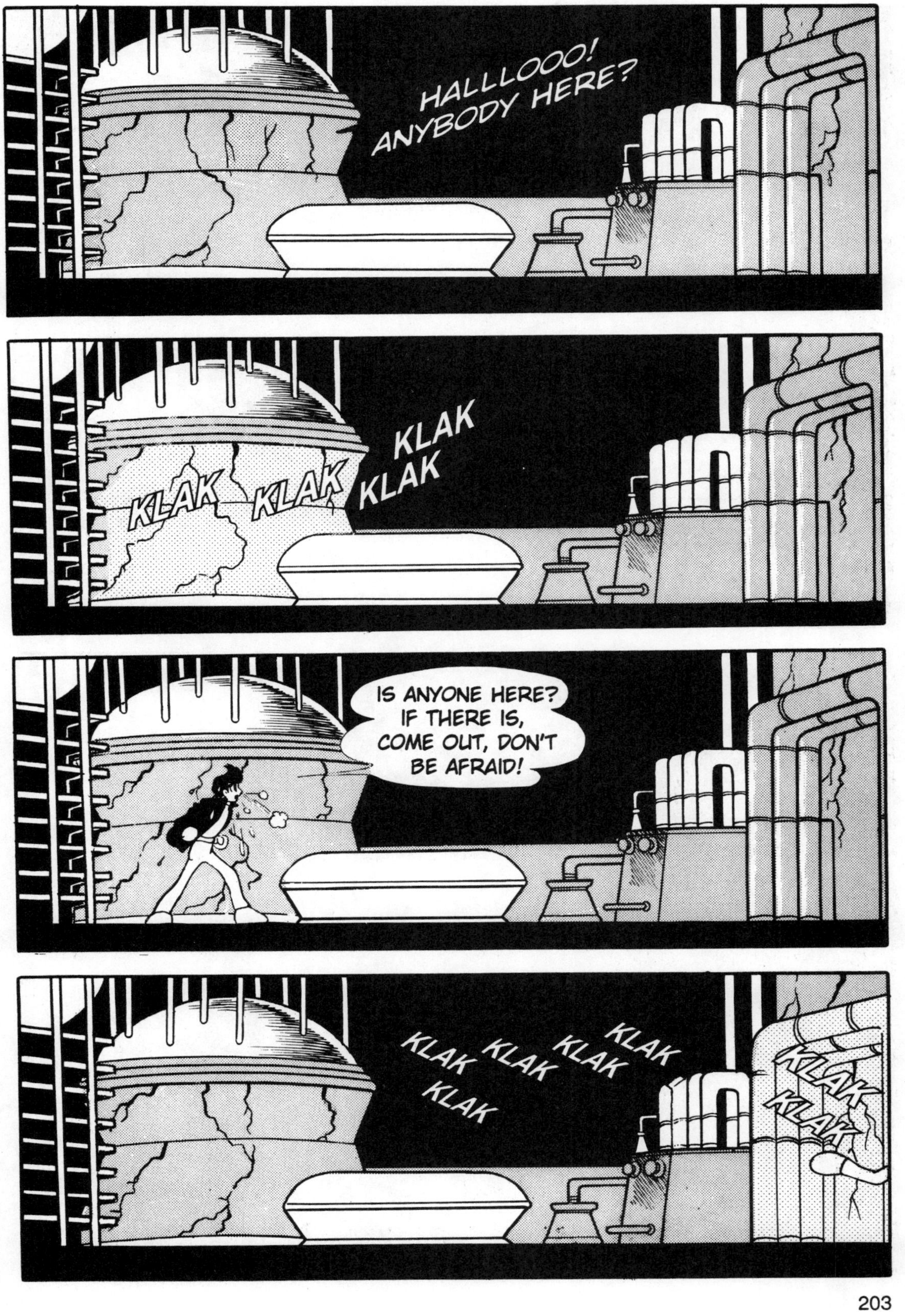
HALLLOOO! ANYBODY HERE?
KLAK KLAK
KLAK KLAK
IS ANYONE HERE? IF THERE IS, COME OUT, DON'T BE AFRAID!
KLAK KLAK
KLAK
KLAK
KLAK
KLAK
KLAK

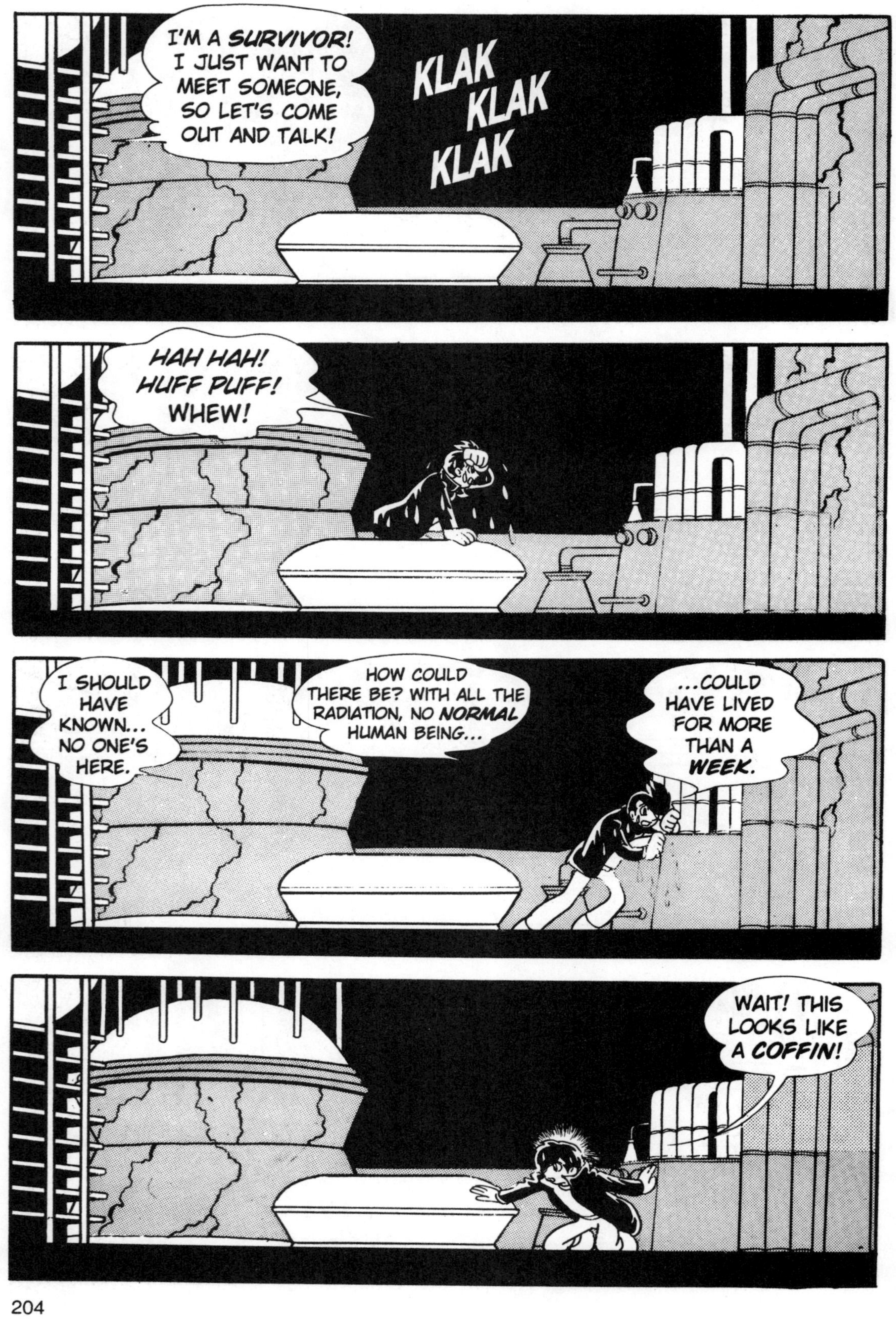
I'M A SURVIVOR! I JUST WANT TO MEET SOMEONE, SO LET'S COME OUT AND TALK!
KLAK KLAK KLAK
HAH HAH! HUFF PUFF! WHEW!
I SHOULD HAVE KNOWN... NO ONE'S HERE.
HOW COULD THERE BE? WITH ALL THE RADIATION, NO NORMAL HUMAN BEING...
...COULD HAVE LIVED FOR MORE THAN A WEEK.
WAIT! THIS LOOKS LIKE A COFFIN!

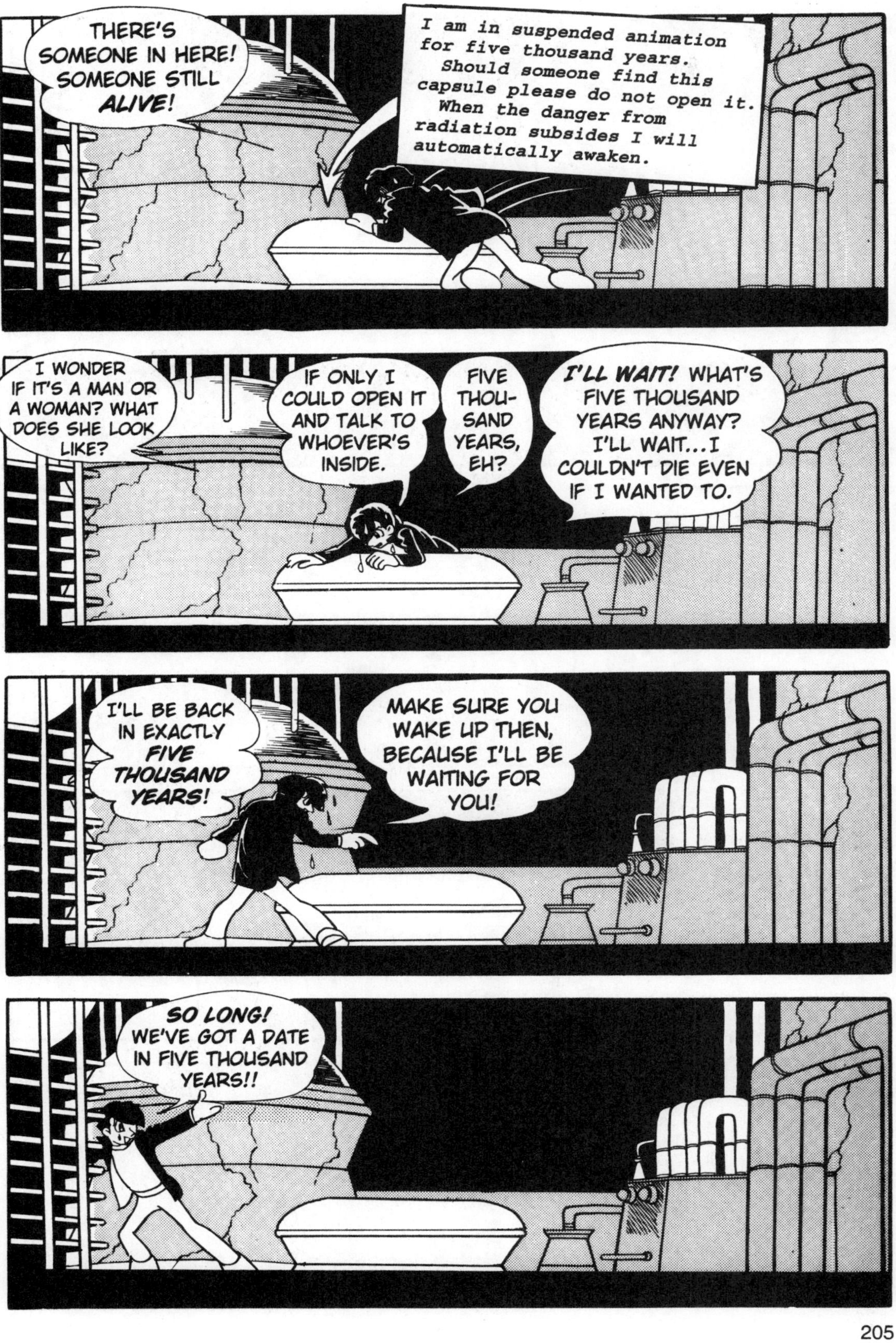
THERE'S SOMEONE IN HERE! SOMEONE STILL ***ALIVE!***
I am in suspended animation for five thousand years. Should someone find this capsule please do not open it. When the danger from radiation subsides I will automatically awaken.
I WONDER IF IT'S A MAN OR A WOMAN? WHAT DOES SHE LOOK LIKE?
IF ONLY I COULD OPEN IT AND TALK TO WHOEVER'S INSIDE.
FIVE THOUSAND YEARS, EH?
I'LL WAIT! WHAT'S FIVE THOUSAND YEARS ANYWAY? I'LL WAIT...I COULDN'T DIE EVEN IF I WANTED TO.
I'LL BE BACK IN EXACTLY ***FIVE THOUSAND YEARS!***
MAKE SURE YOU WAKE UP THEN, BECAUSE I'LL BE WAITING FOR YOU!
SO LONG! WE'VE GOT A DATE IN FIVE THOUSAND YEARS!!

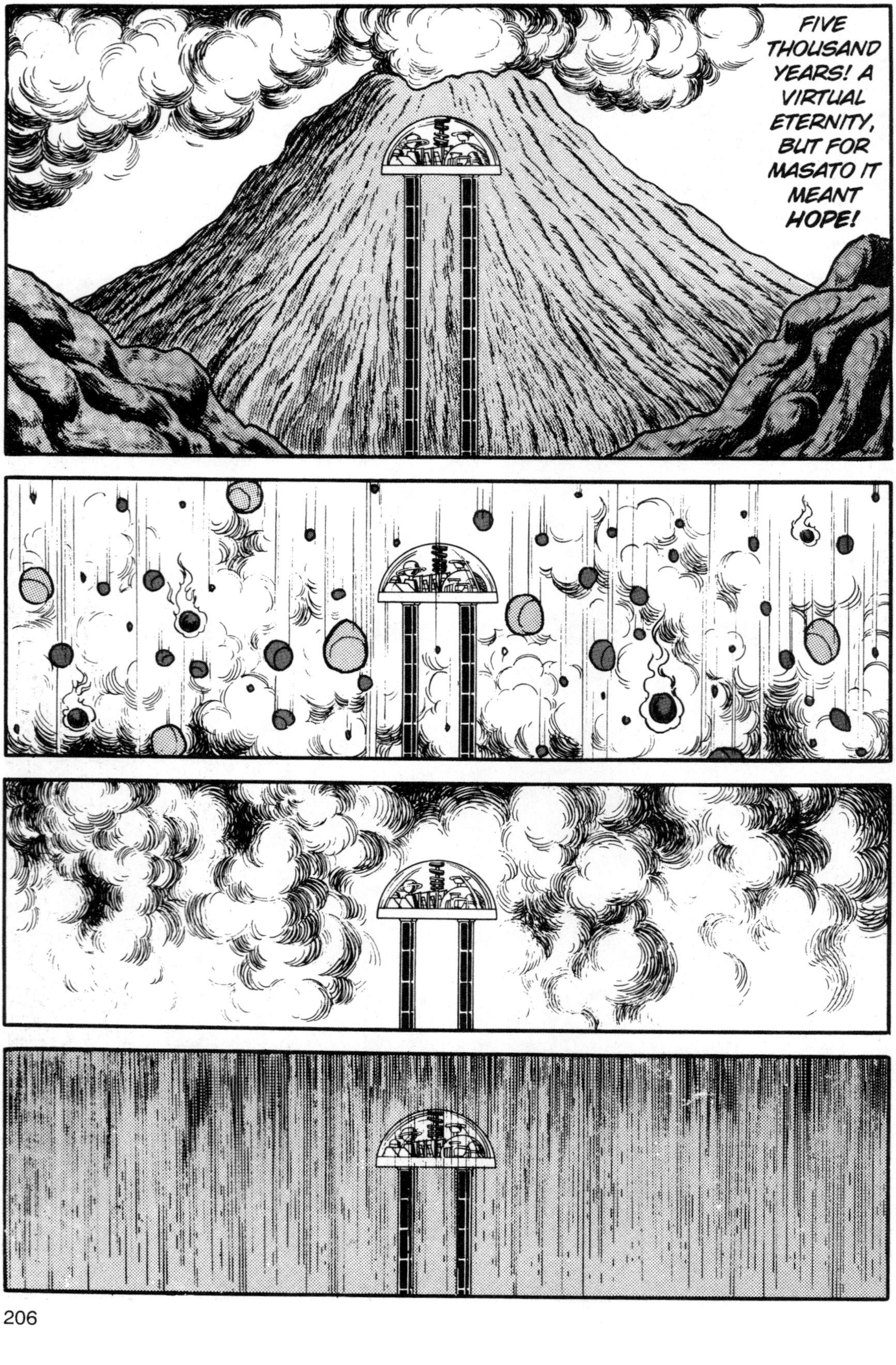
FIVE THOUSAND YEARS! A VIRTUAL ETERNITY, BUT FOR MASATO IT MEANT HOPE!

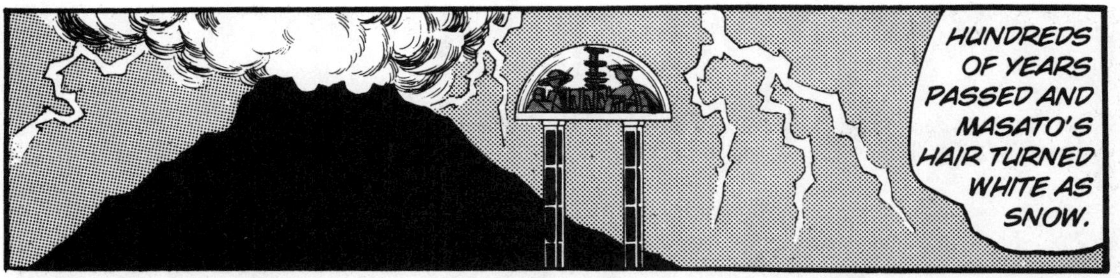
HUNDREDS OF YEARS PASSED AND MASATO'S HAIR TURNED WHITE AS SNOW.
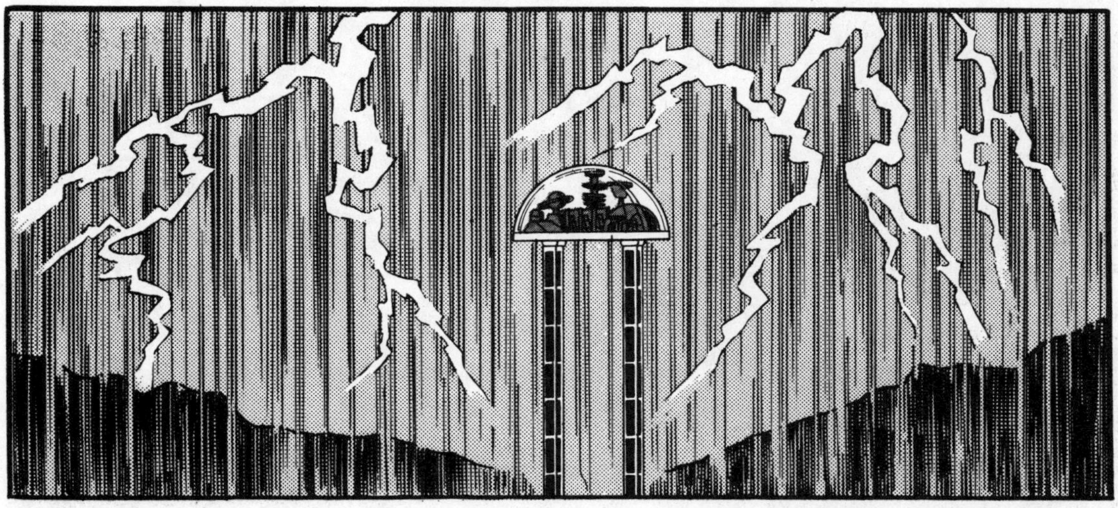
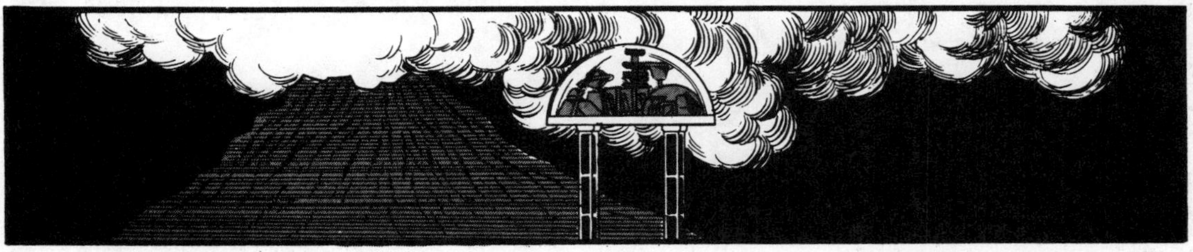
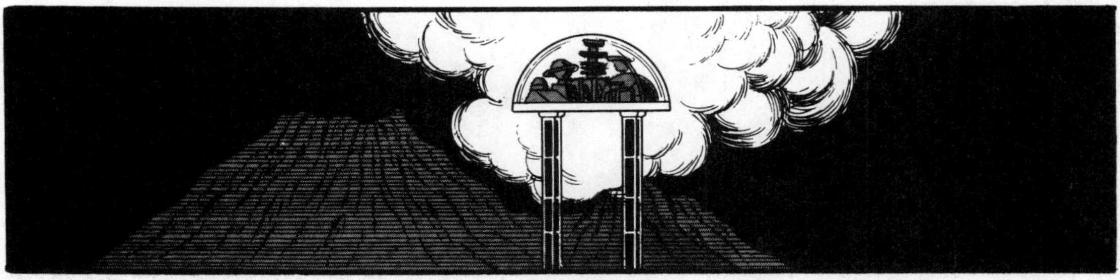
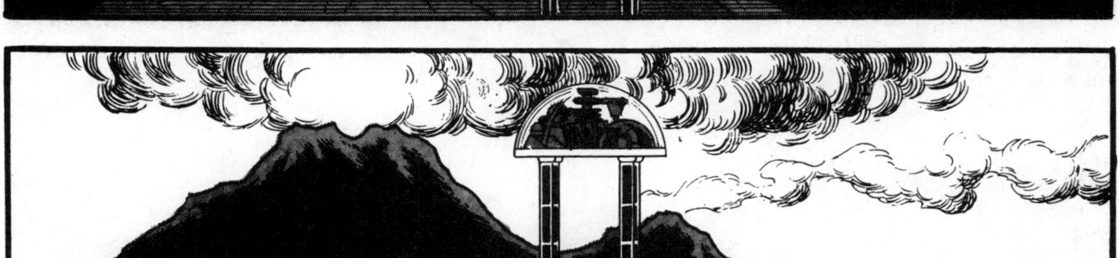

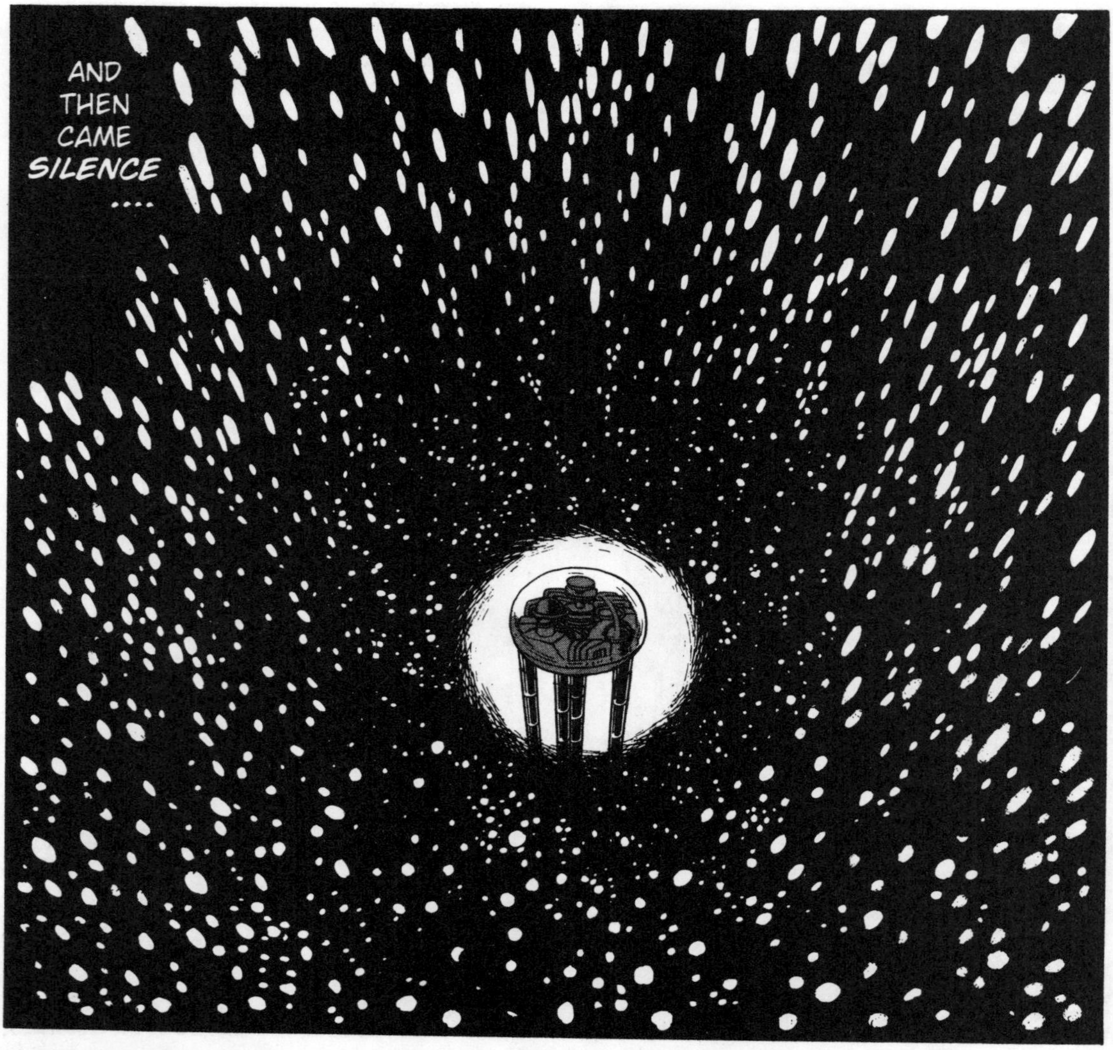
AND THEN CAME SILENCE ....

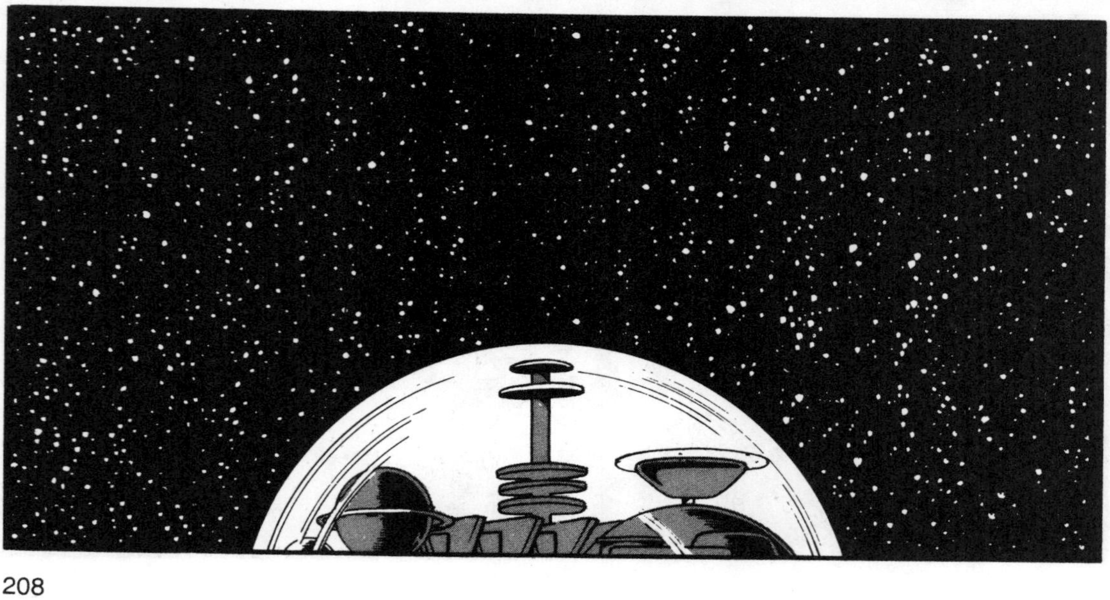

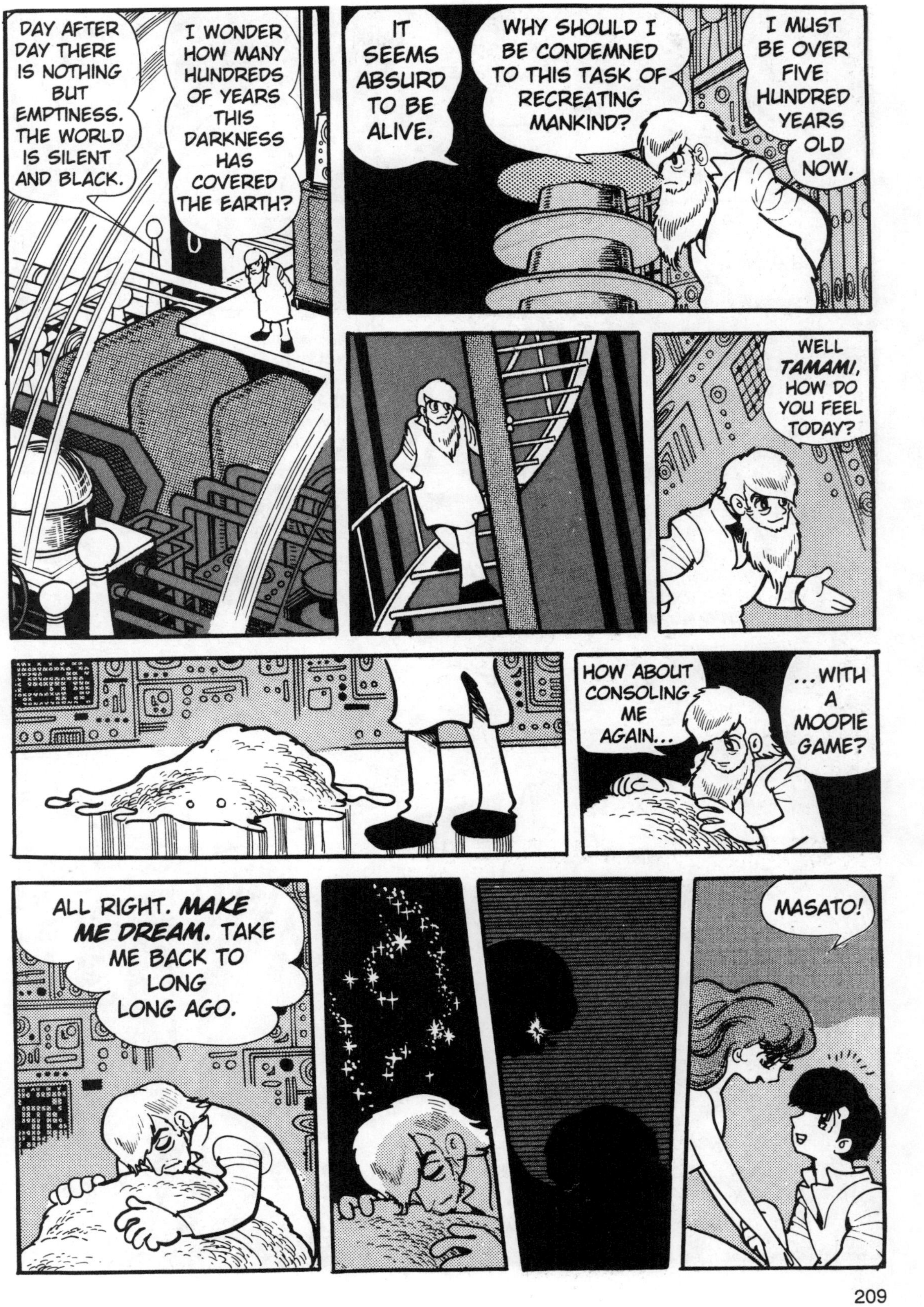
DAY AFTER DAY THERE IS NOTHING BUT EMPTINESS. THE WORLD IS SILENT AND BLACK.
I WONDER HOW MANY HUNDREDS OF YEARS THIS DARKNESS HAS COVERED THE EARTH?
IT SEEMS ABSURD TO BE ALIVE.
WHY SHOULD I BE CONDEMNED TO THIS TASK OF RECREATING MANKIND?
I MUST BE OVER FIVE HUNDRED YEARS OLD NOW.
WELL *TAMAMI*, HOW DO YOU FEEL TODAY?
HOW ABOUT CONSOLING ME AGAIN...
...WITH A MOOPIE GAME?
ALL RIGHT. ***MAKE ME DREAM.*** TAKE ME BACK TO LONG LONG AGO.
MASATO!

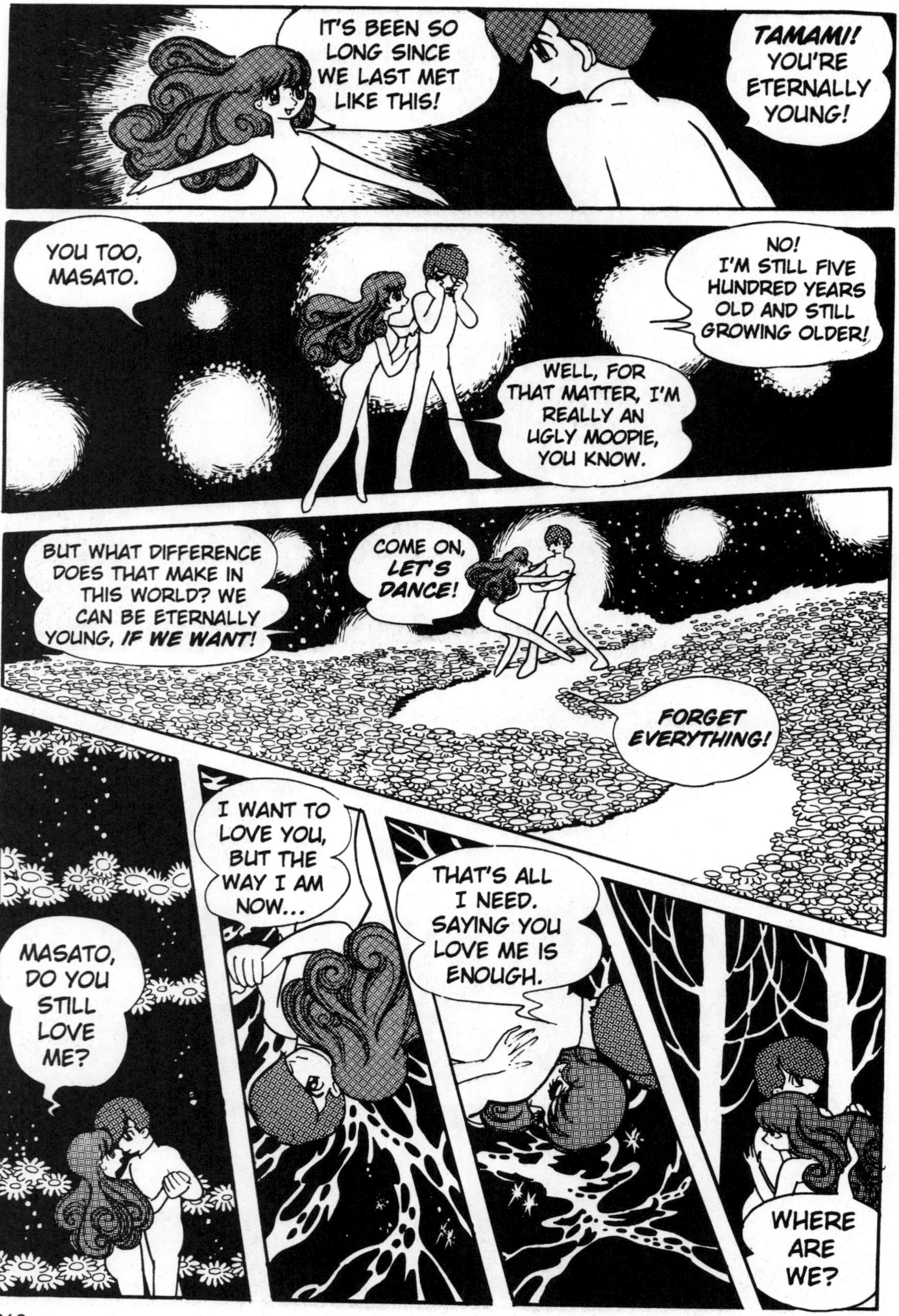
IT'S BEEN SO LONG SINCE WE LAST MET LIKE THIS!
TAMAMI! YOU'RE ETERNALLY YOUNG!
YOU TOO, MASATO.
NO! I'M STILL FIVE HUNDRED YEARS OLD AND STILL GROWING OLDER!
WELL, FOR THAT MATTER, I'M REALLY AN UGLY MOOPIE, YOU KNOW.
BUT WHAT DIFFERENCE DOES THAT MAKE IN THIS WORLD? WE CAN BE ETERNALLY YOUNG, IF WE WANT!
COME ON, LET'S DANCE!
FORGET EVERYTHING!
MASATO, DO YOU STILL LOVE ME?
I WANT TO LOVE YOU, BUT THE WAY I AM NOW...
THAT'S ALL I NEED. SAYING YOU LOVE ME IS ENOUGH.
WHERE ARE WE?

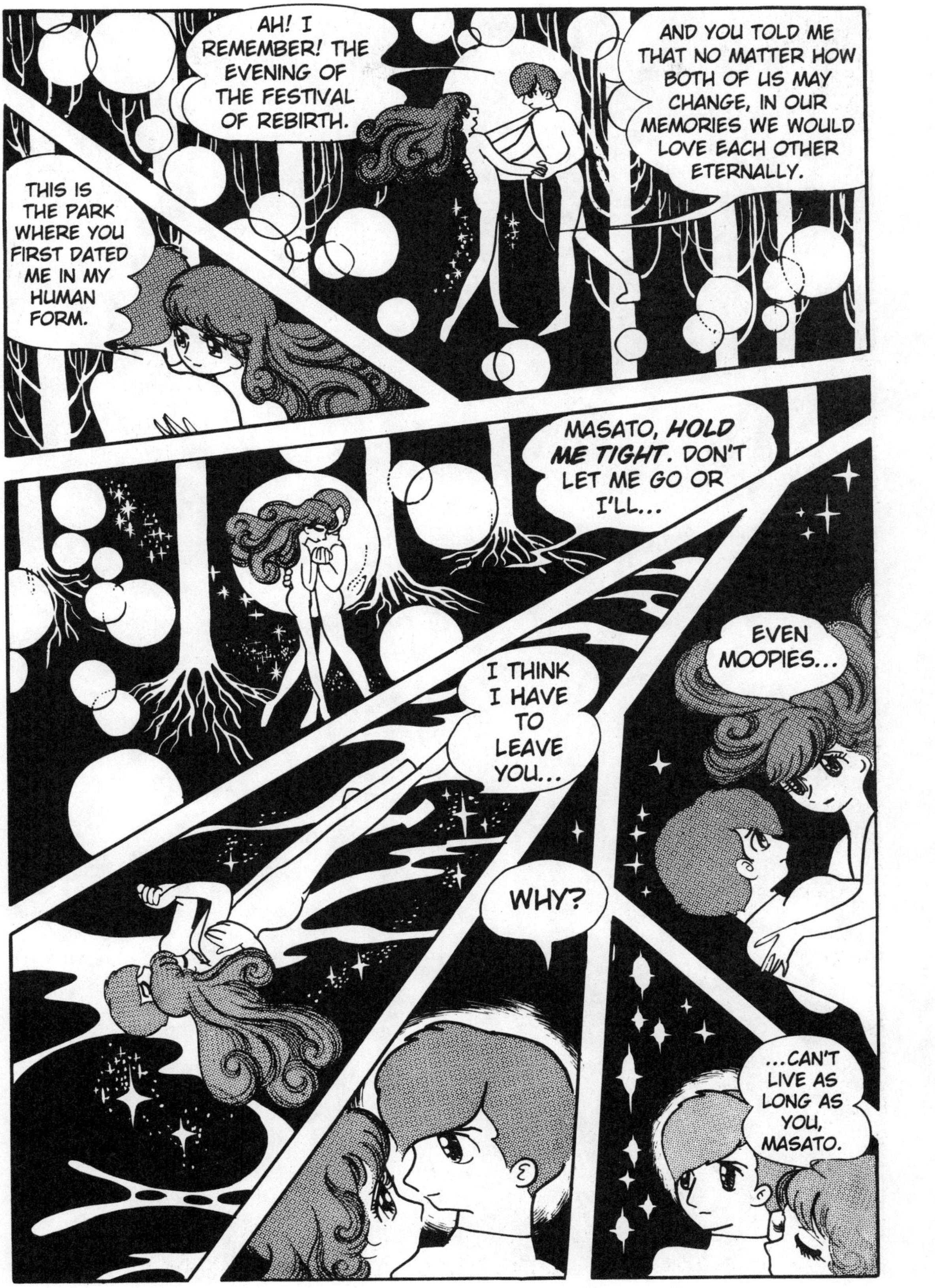
THIS IS THE PARK WHERE YOU FIRST DATED ME IN MY HUMAN FORM.
AH! I REMEMBER! THE EVENING OF THE FESTIVAL OF REBIRTH.
AND YOU TOLD ME THAT NO MATTER HOW BOTH OF US MAY CHANGE, IN OUR MEMORIES WE WOULD LOVE EACH OTHER ETERNALLY.
MASATO, **HOLD ME TIGHT**. DON'T LET ME GO OR I'LL...
I THINK I HAVE TO LEAVE YOU...
WHY?
EVEN MOOPIES...
...CAN'T LIVE AS LONG AS YOU, MASATO.

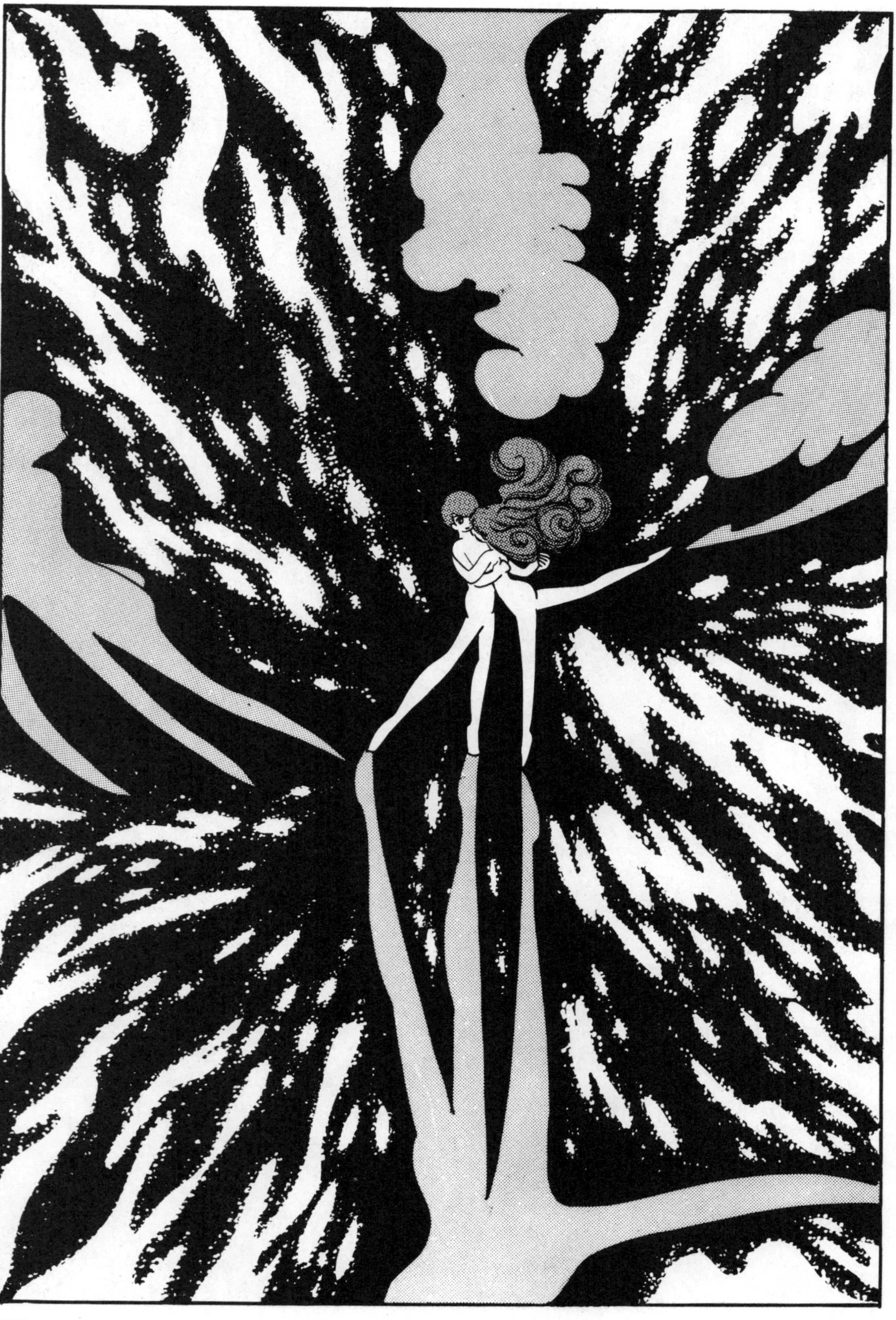

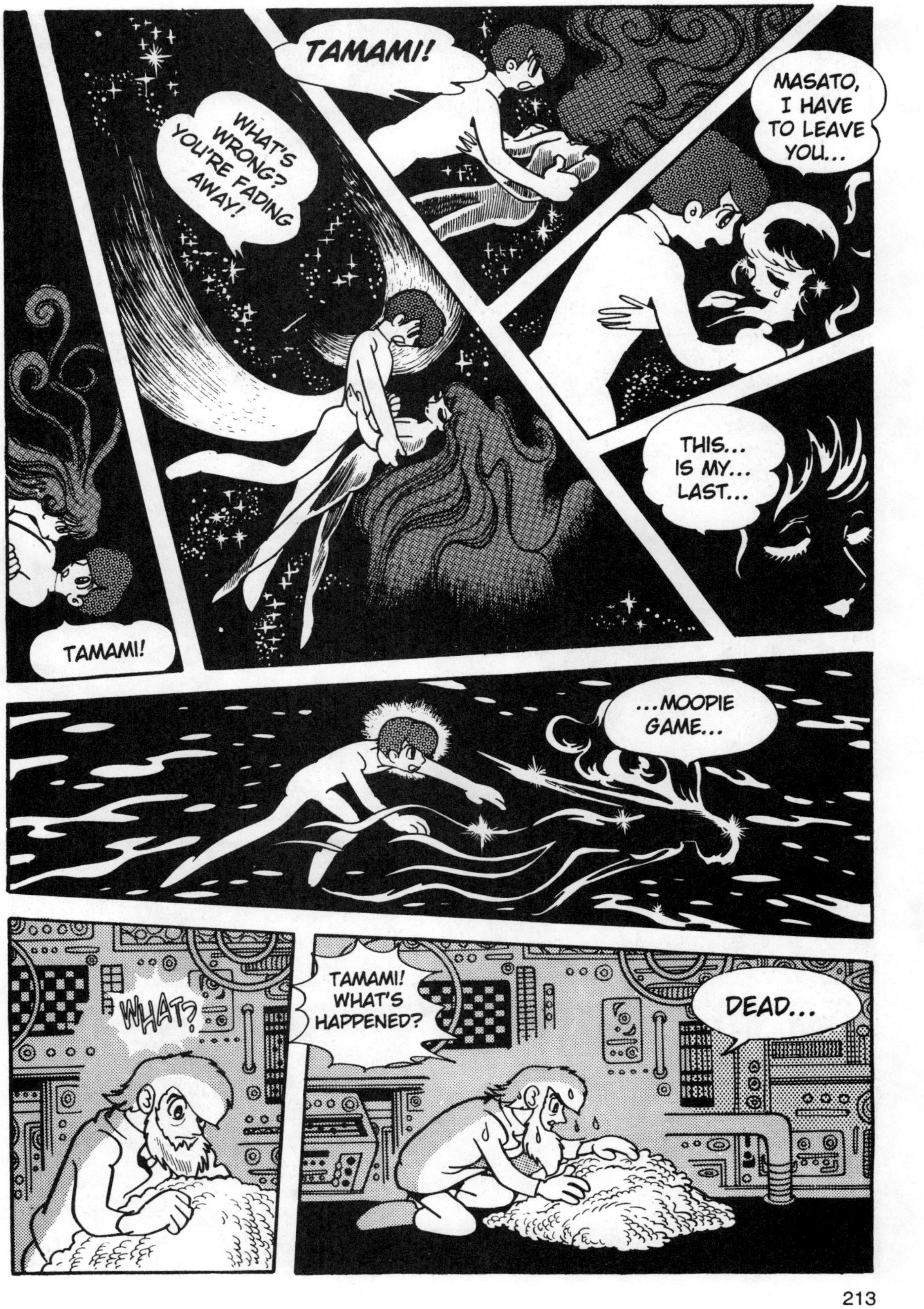
MASATO, I HAVE TO LEAVE YOU...
THIS... IS MY... LAST...
TAMAMI!
WHAT'S WRONG? YOU'RE FADING AWAY!
TAMAMI!
...MOOPIE GAME...
DEAD...
TAMAMI! WHAT'S HAPPENED?
WHAT?

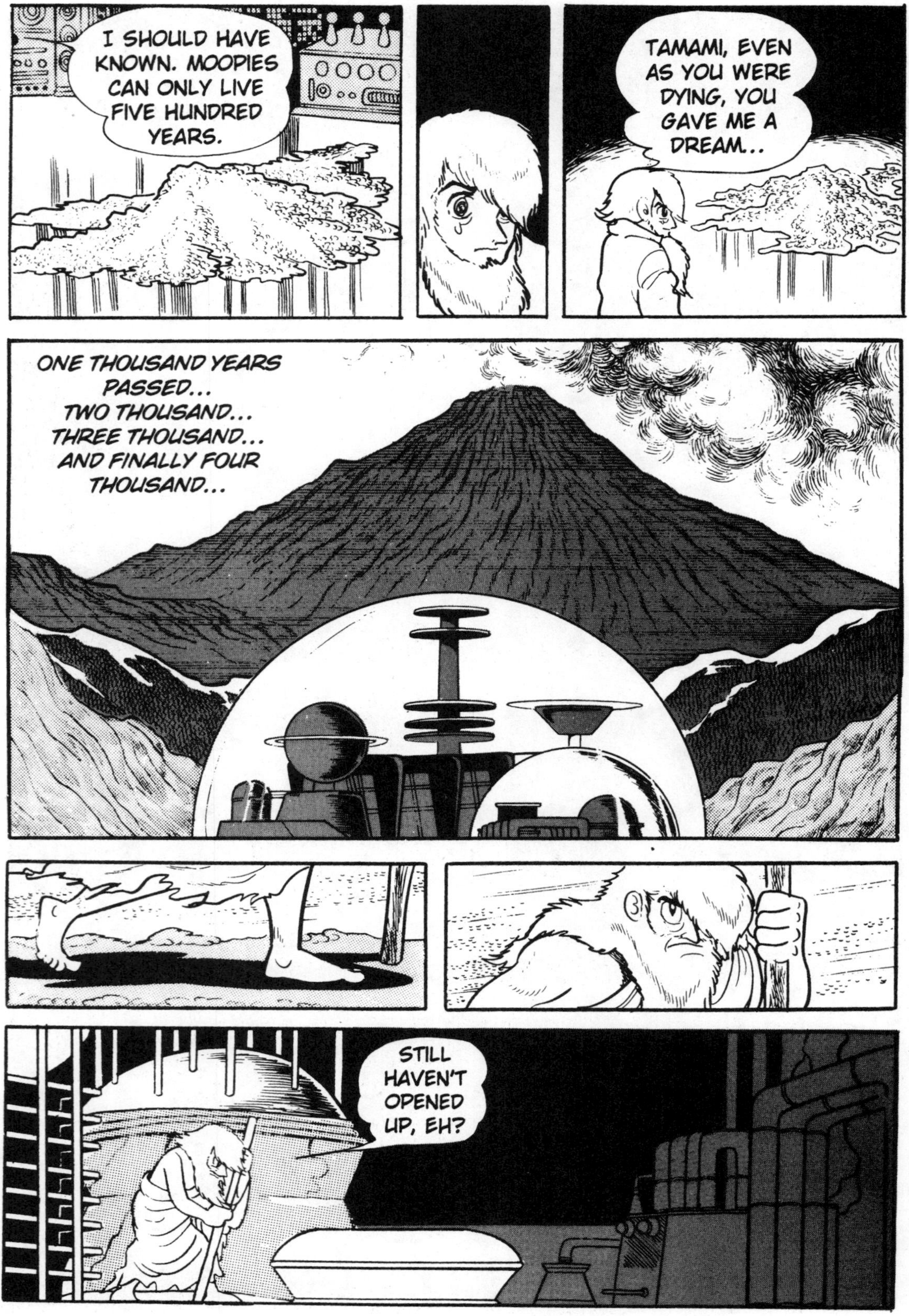
I SHOULD HAVE KNOWN. MOOPIES CAN ONLY LIVE FIVE HUNDRED YEARS.
TAMAMI, EVEN AS YOU WERE DYING, YOU GAVE ME A DREAM...
ONE THOUSAND YEARS PASSED... TWO THOUSAND... THREE THOUSAND... AND FINALLY FOUR THOUSAND...
STILL HAVEN'T OPENED UP, EH?

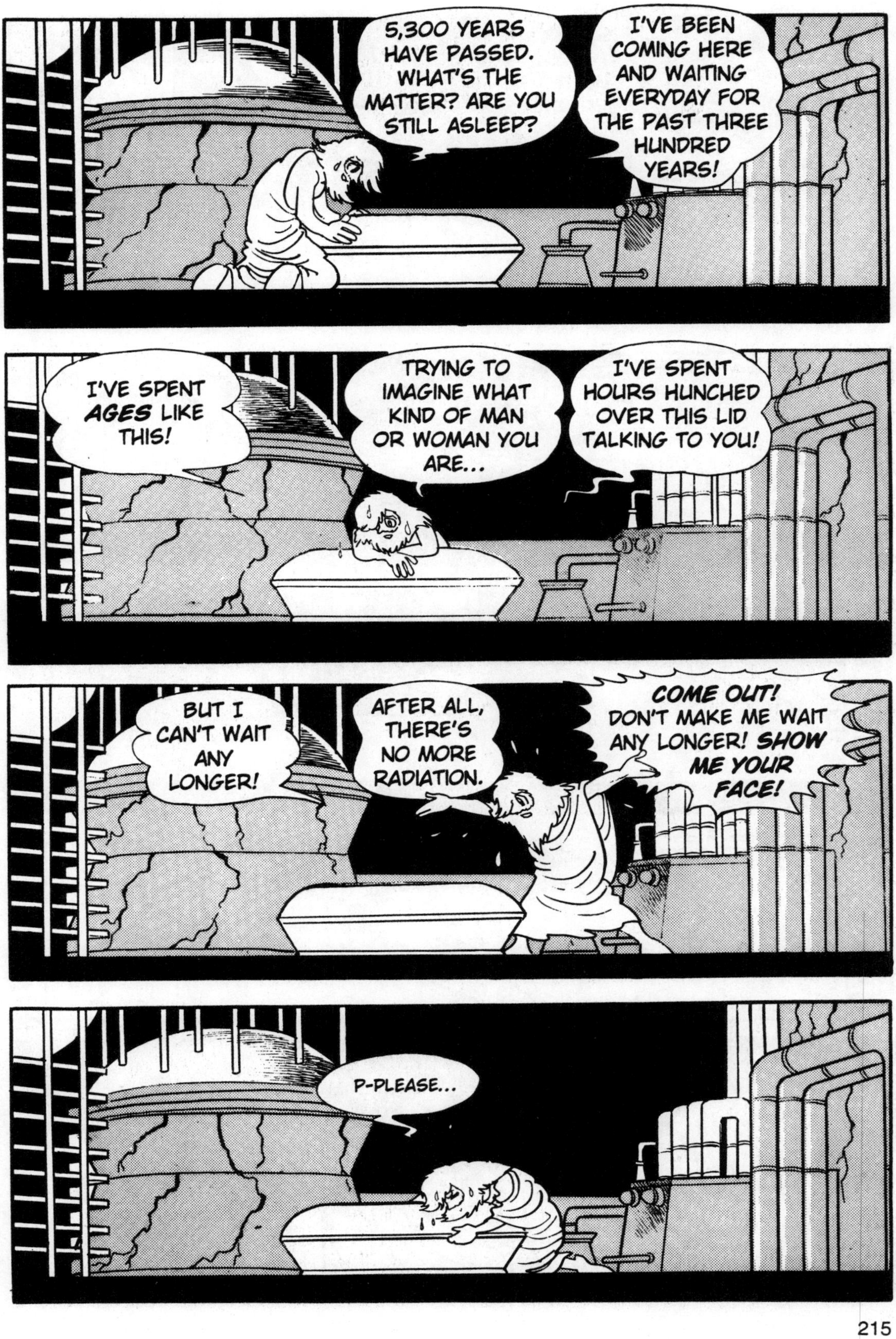
5,300 YEARS HAVE PASSED. WHAT'S THE MATTER? ARE YOU STILL ASLEEP?
I'VE BEEN COMING HERE AND WAITING EVERYDAY FOR THE PAST THREE HUNDRED YEARS!
I'VE SPENT AGES LIKE THIS!
TRYING TO IMAGINE WHAT KIND OF MAN OR WOMAN YOU ARE...
I'VE SPENT HOURS HUNCHED OVER THIS LID TALKING TO YOU!
BUT I CAN'T WAIT ANY LONGER!
AFTER ALL, THERE'S NO MORE RADIATION.
COME OUT! DON'T MAKE ME WAIT ANY LONGER! SHOW ME YOUR FACE!
P-PLEASE...

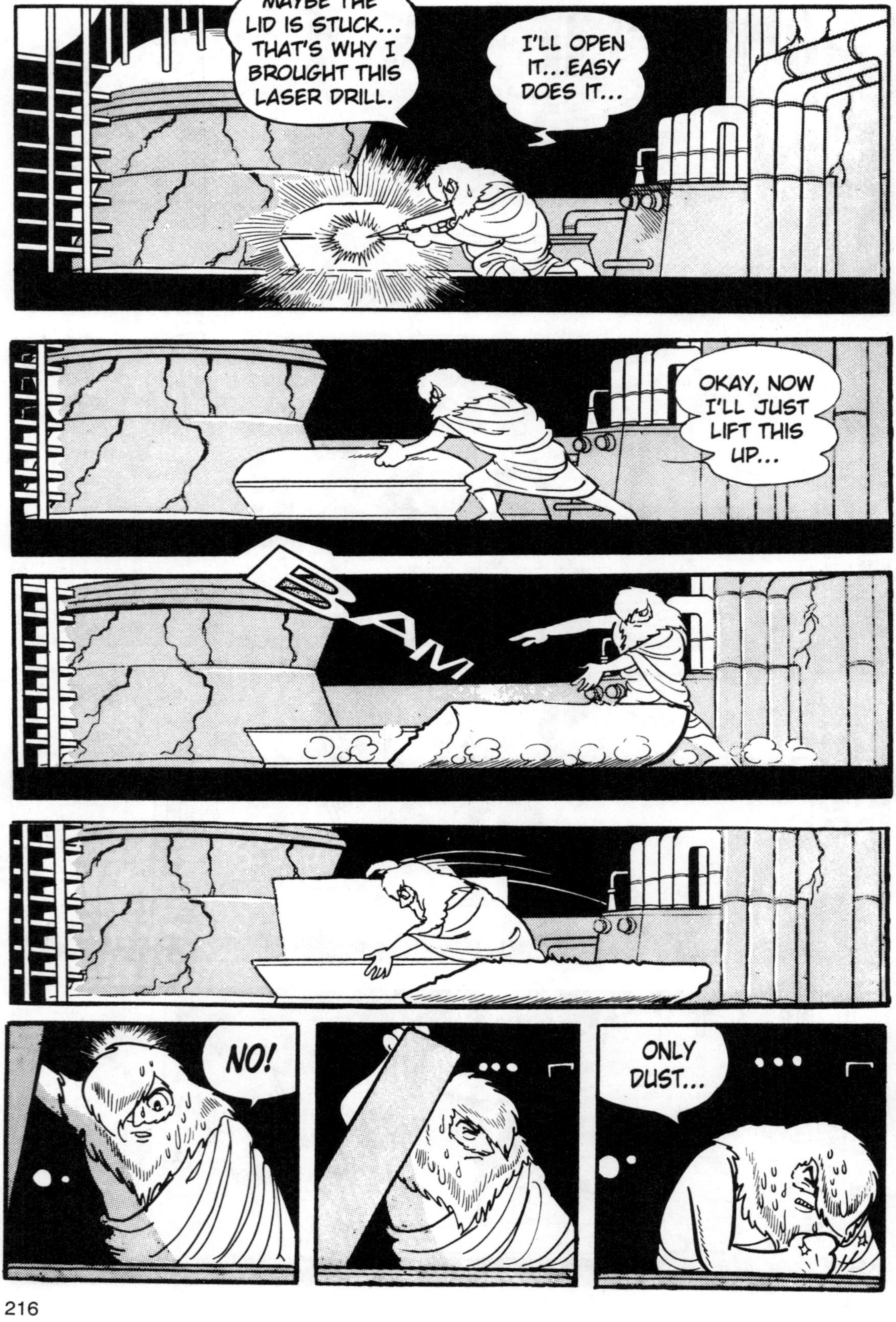
MAYBE THE LID IS STUCK... THAT'S WHY I BROUGHT THIS LASER DRILL.
I'LL OPEN IT...EASY DOES IT...
OKAY, NOW I'LL JUST LIFT THIS UP...
BAM
NO!
...
ONLY DUST...
...

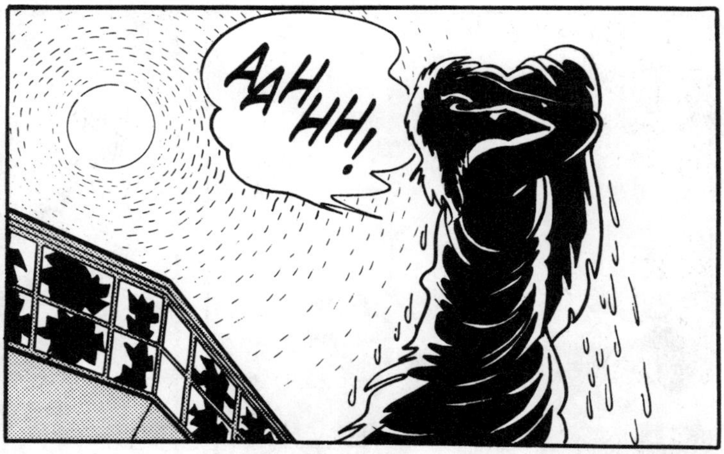
AAHHH!
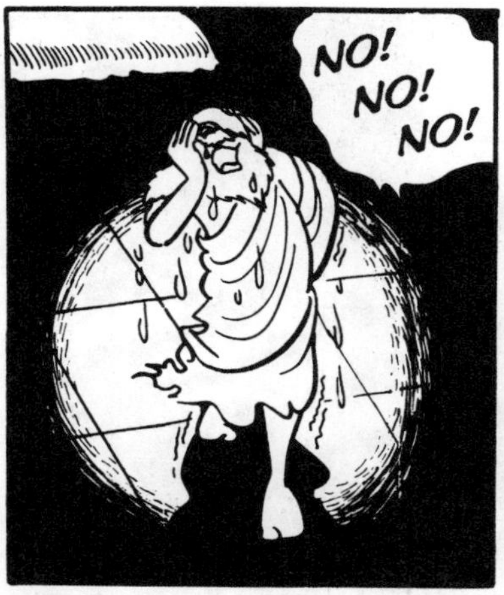
NO! NO! NO!
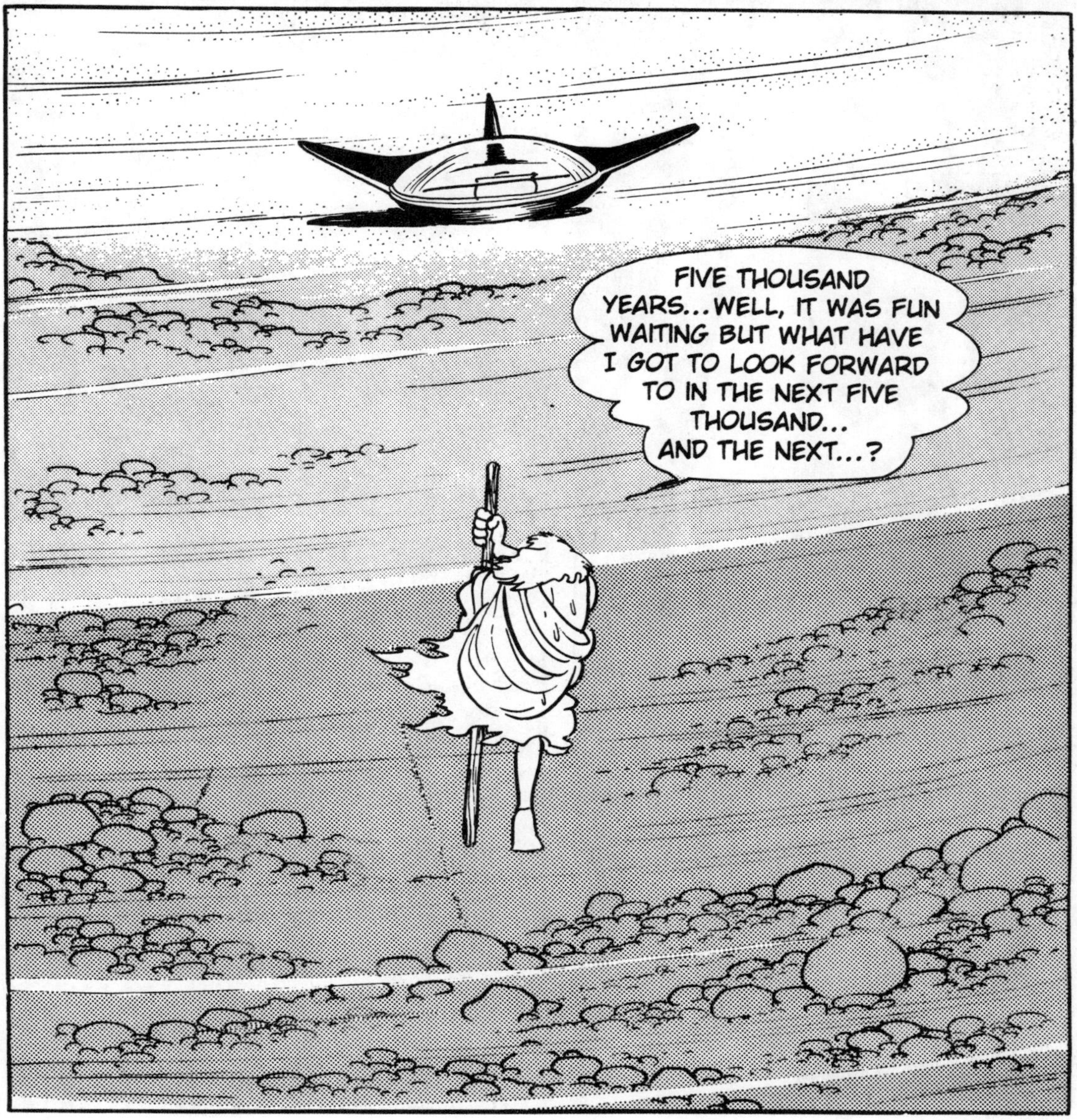
FIVE THOUSAND YEARS...WELL, IT WAS FUN WAITING BUT WHAT HAVE I GOT TO LOOK FORWARD TO IN THE NEXT FIVE THOUSAND... AND THE NEXT...?

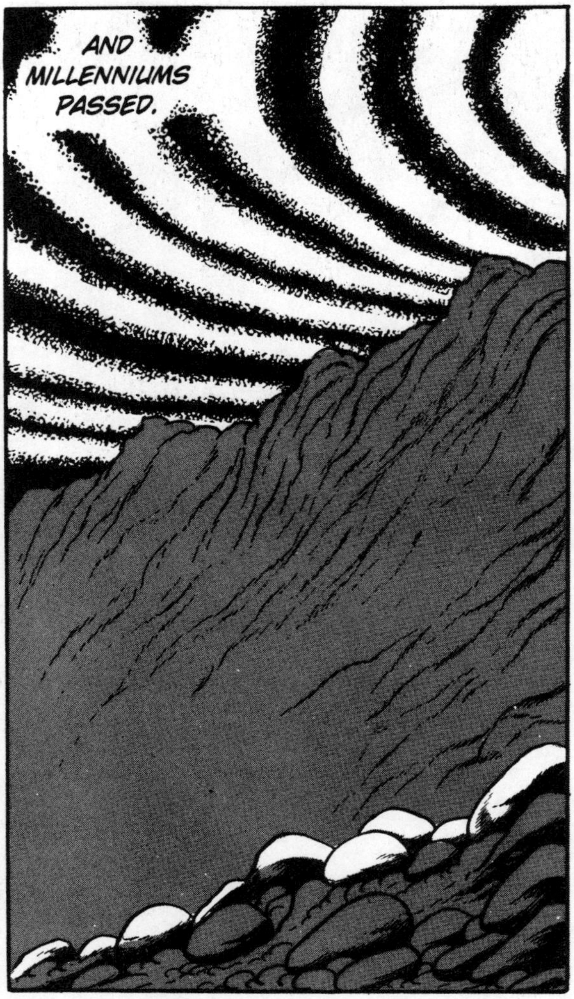
AND MILLENNIUMS PASSED.
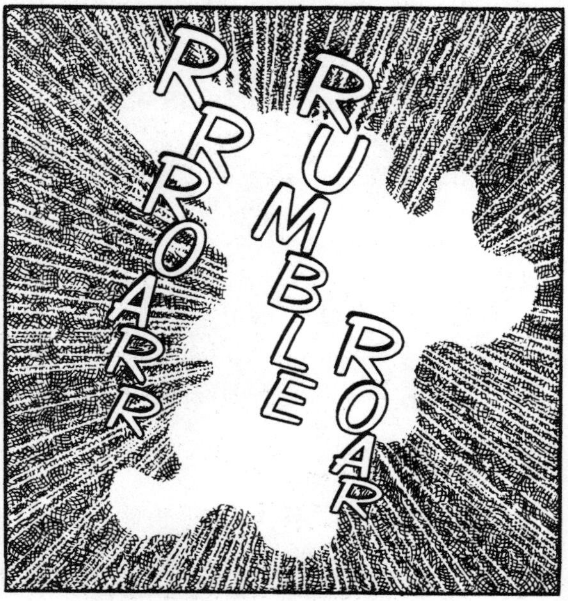
RUMBLE
ROAR
RRROARR
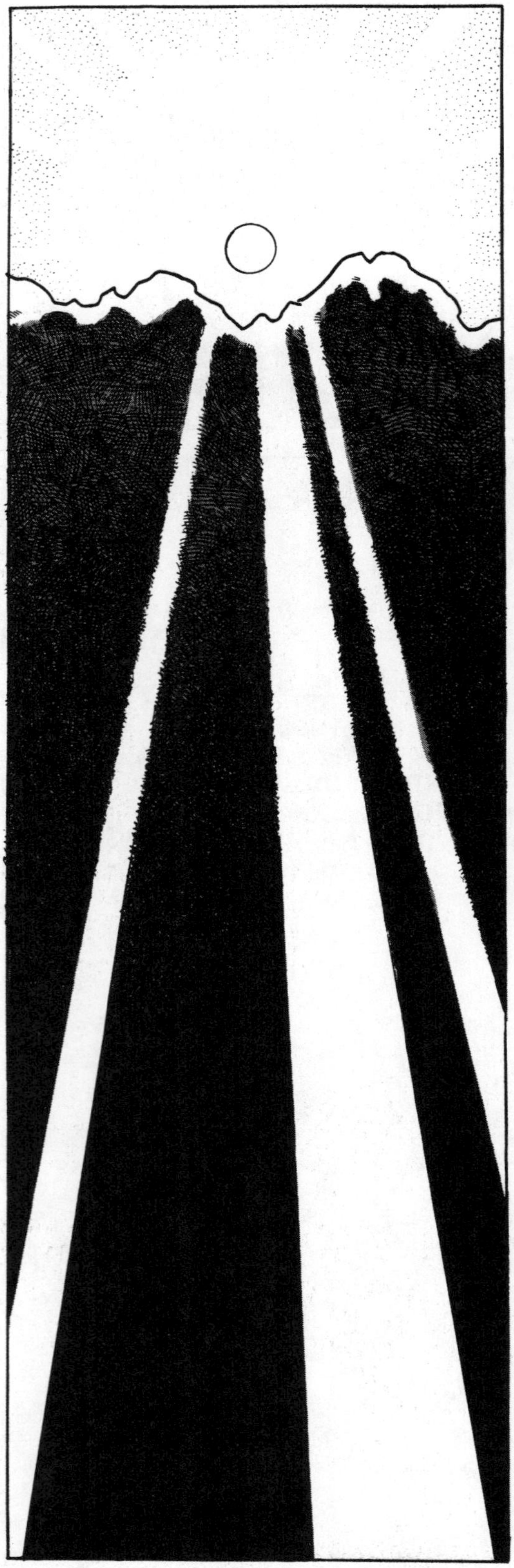

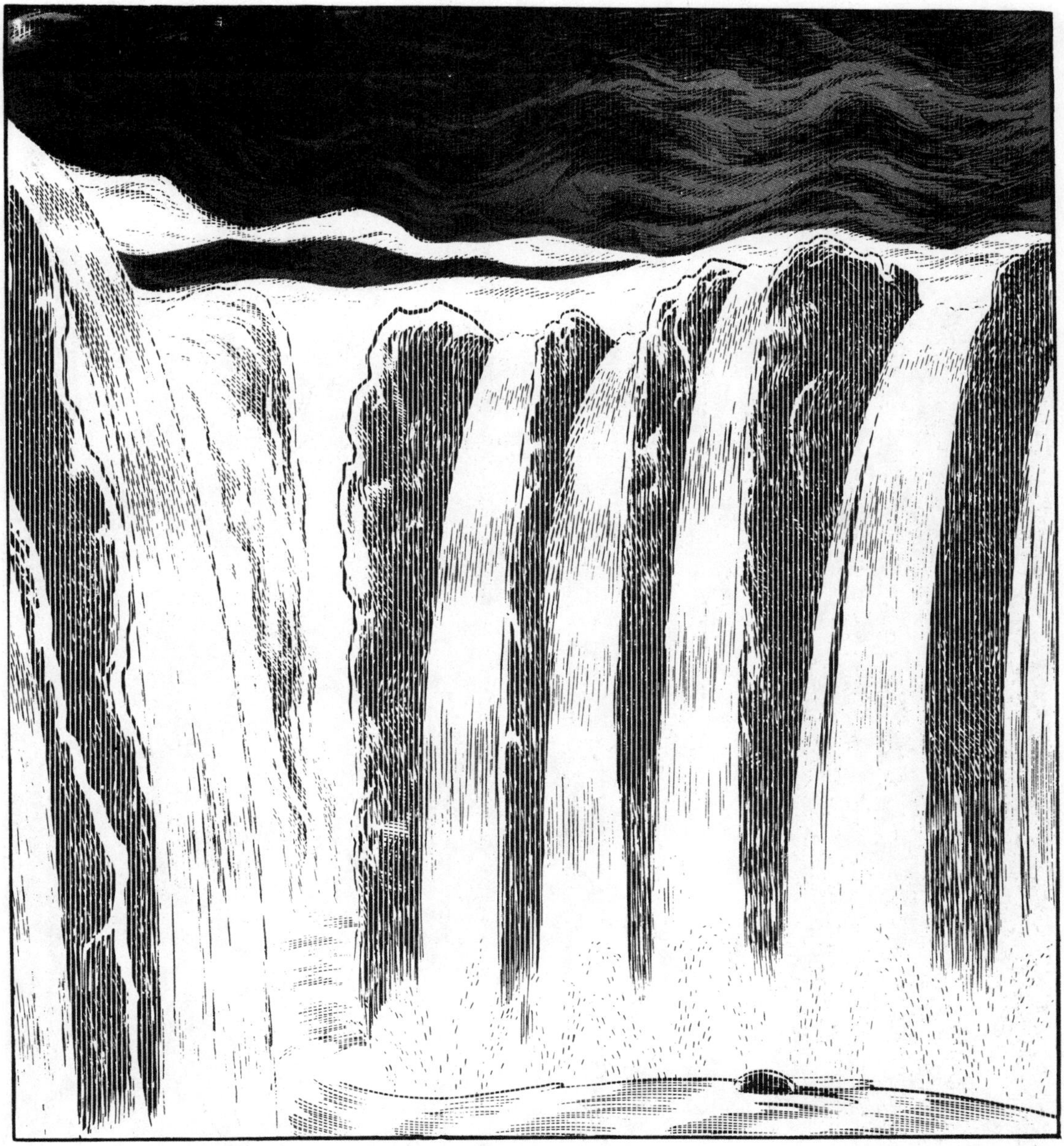

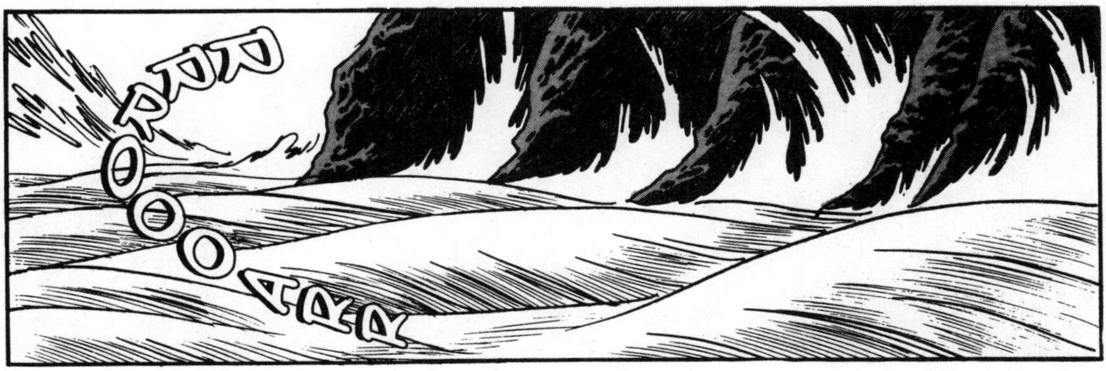
RRROOOARR

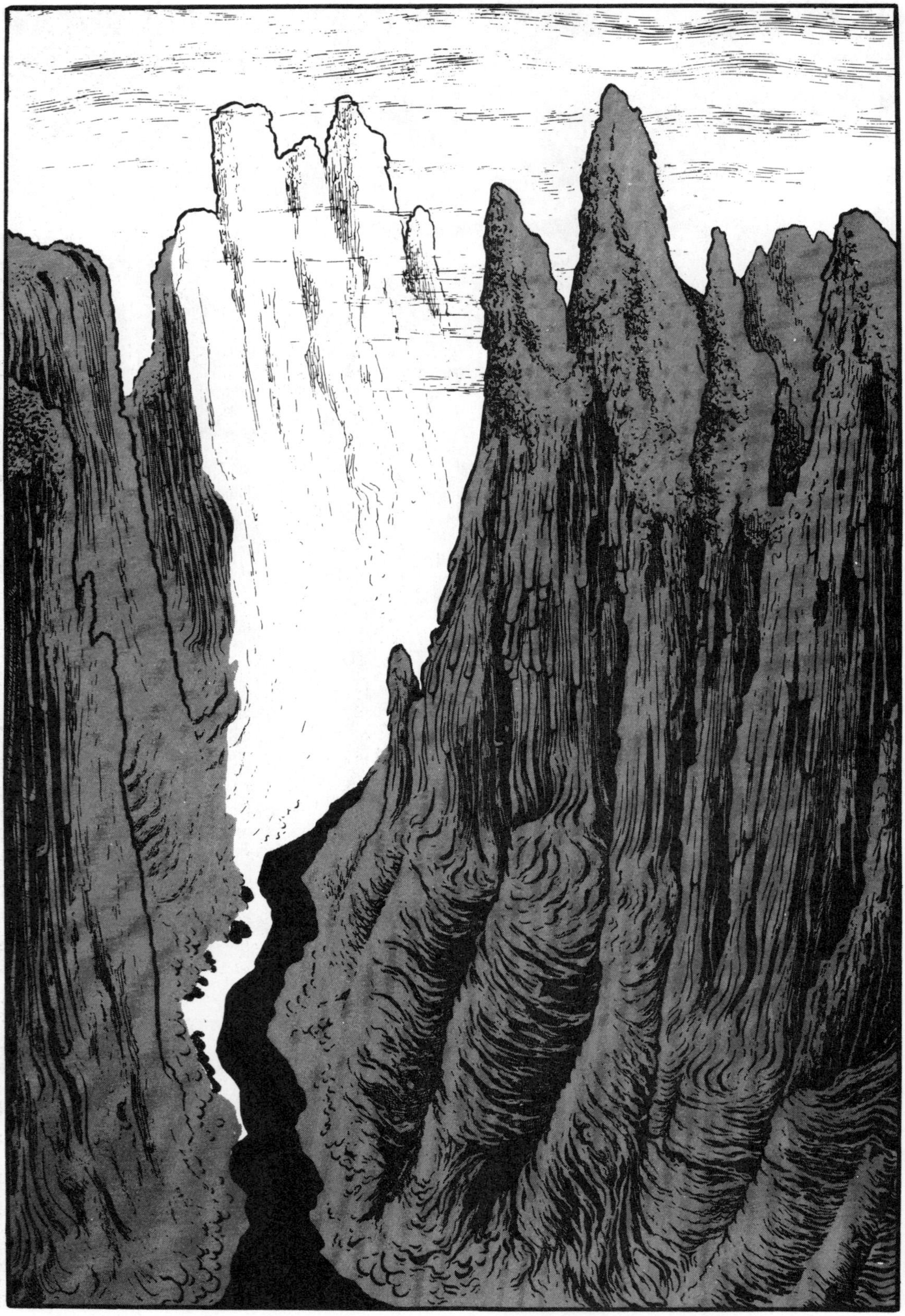

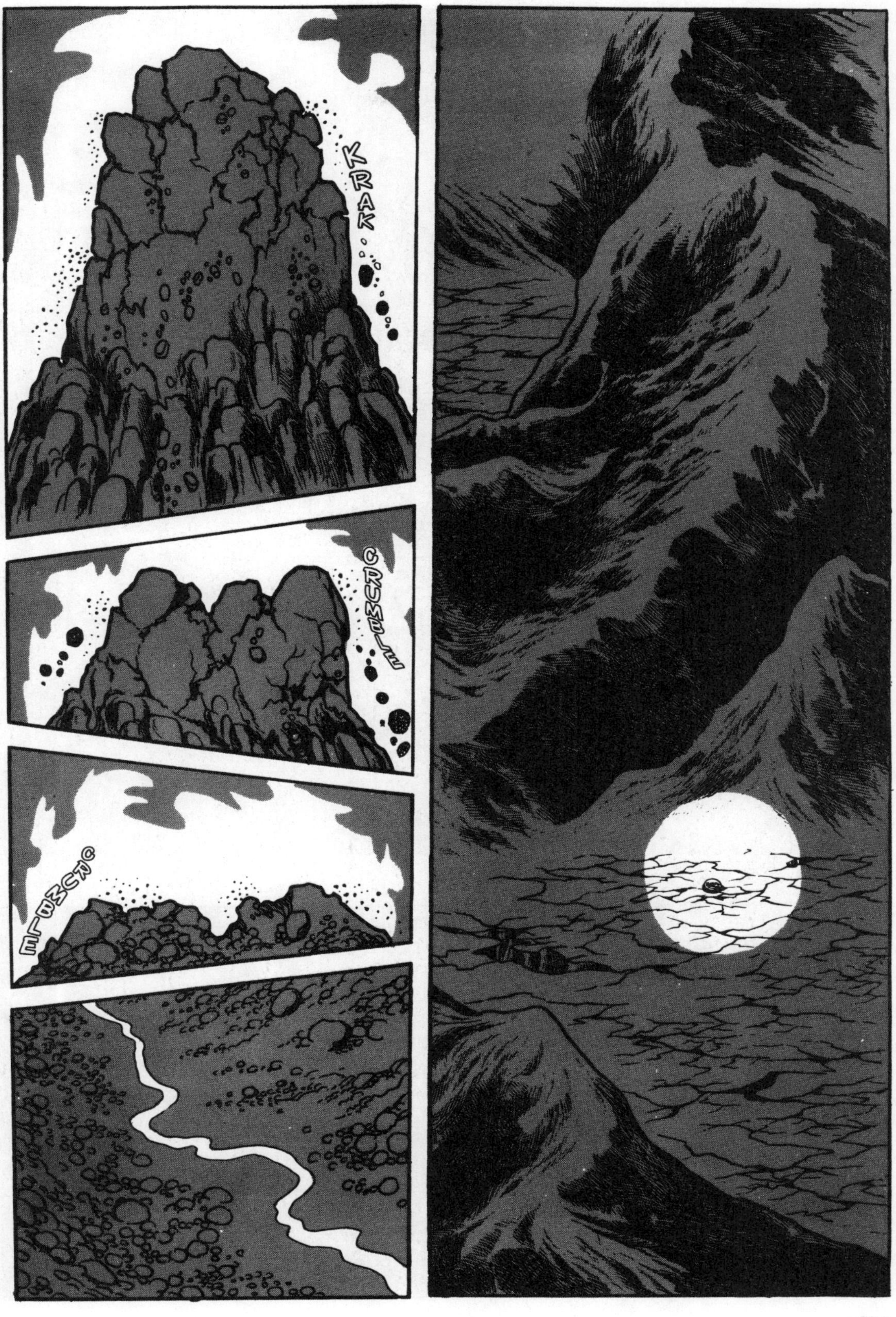
KRAK
CRUMBLE
CRUMBLE

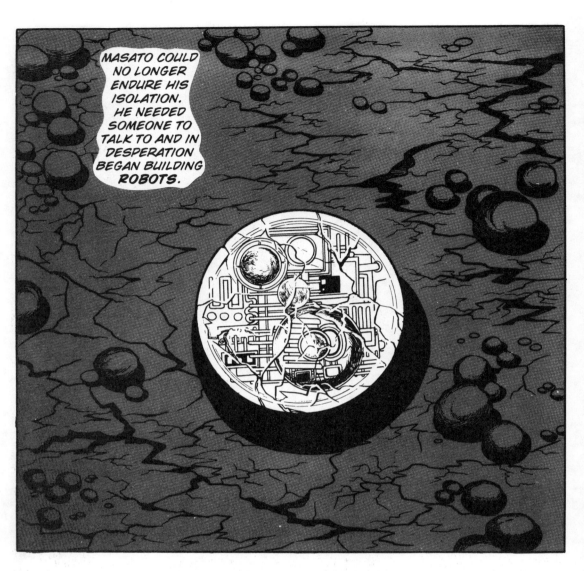

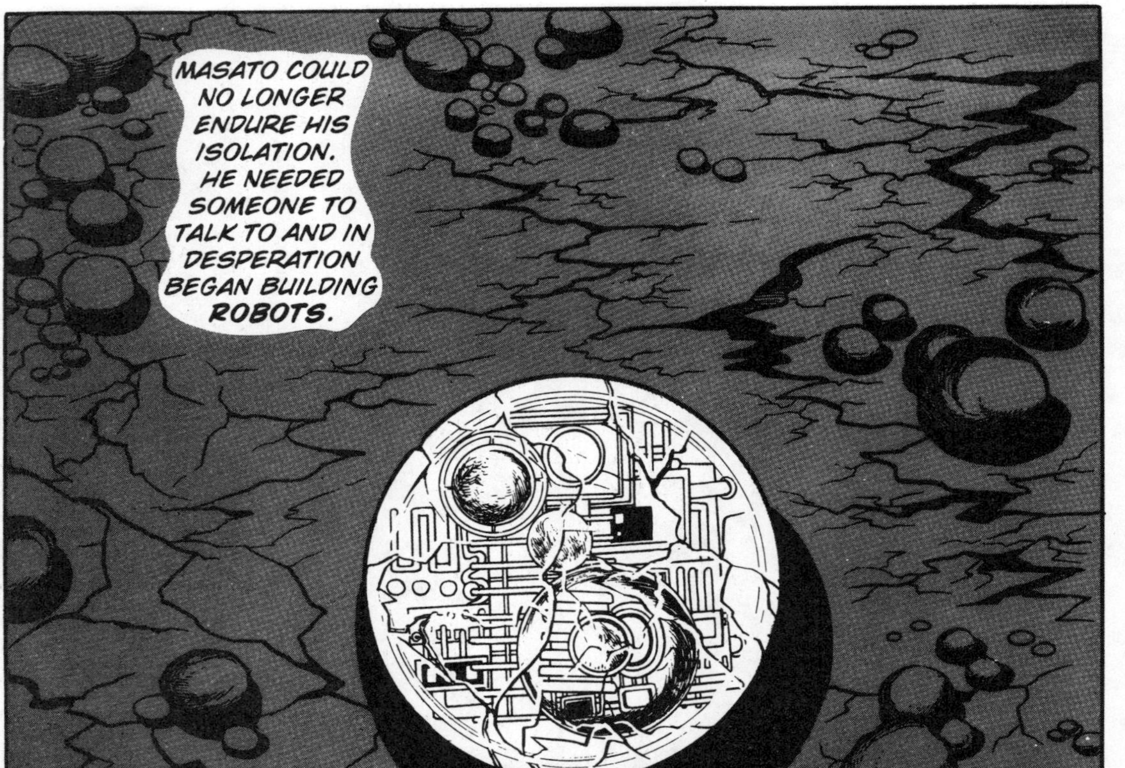
MASATO COULD NO LONGER ENDURE HIS ISOLATION. HE NEEDED SOMEONE TO TALK TO AND IN DESPERATION BEGAN BUILDING **ROBOTS**.

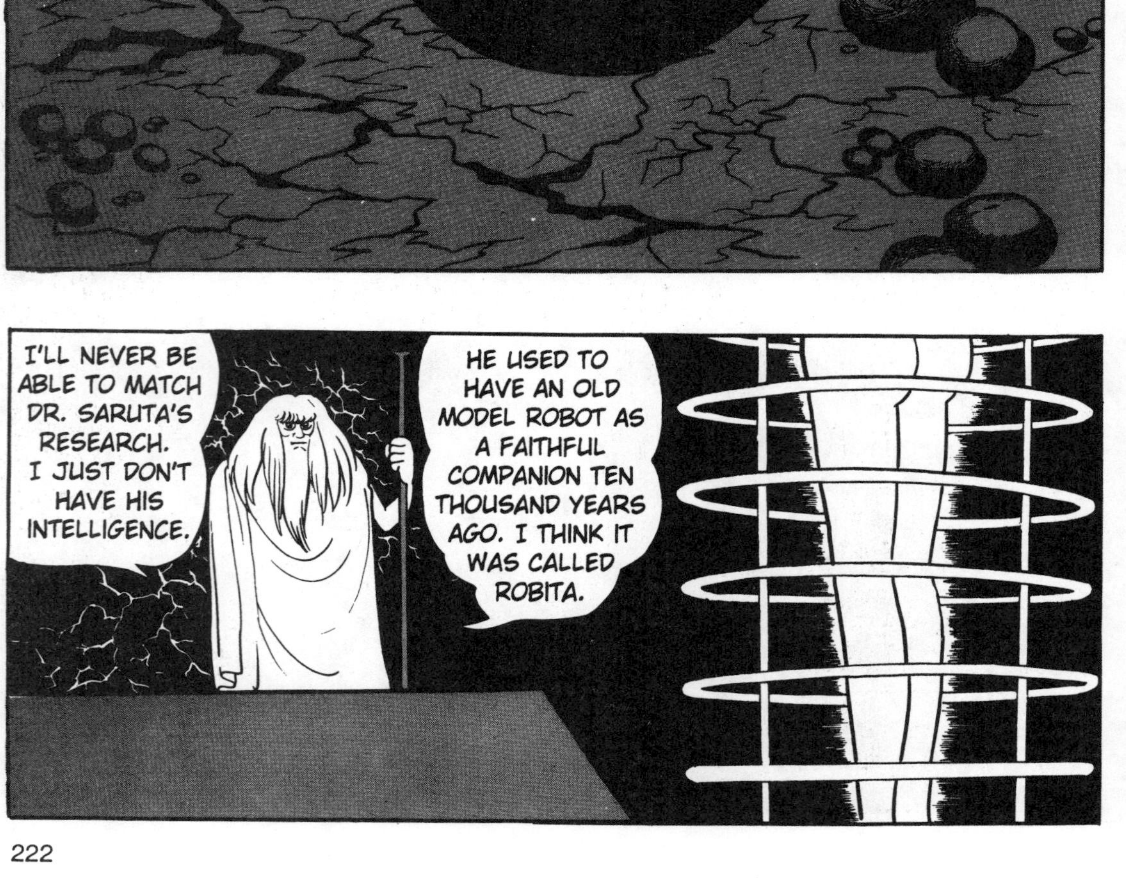
HE USED TO HAVE AN OLD MODEL ROBOT AS A FAITHFUL COMPANION TEN THOUSAND YEARS AGO. I THINK IT WAS CALLED ROBITA.
I'LL NEVER BE ABLE TO MATCH DR. SARUTA'S RESEARCH. I JUST DON'T HAVE HIS INTELLIGENCE.

IT WAS ALMOST ALIVE.
BUT MINE IS NOT LIKE ROBITA...
...BUT YOU, TAMAMI.
EVEN AFTER TEN THOUSAND YEARS, YOUR IMAGE STILL BURNS IN MY MEMORY.
THIS IS YOUR FACE.
NOW! I GIVE YOU LIFE!
WHIRRRRRRR
ZZZZZZZZZAAAAP

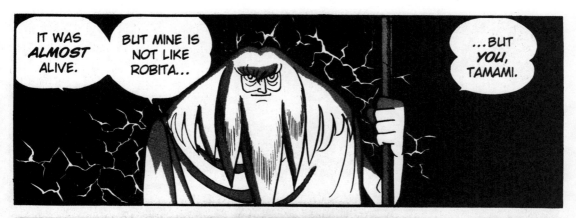

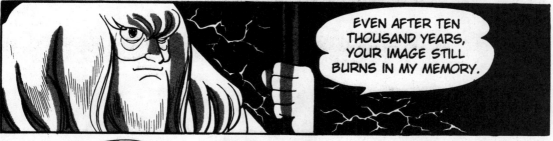

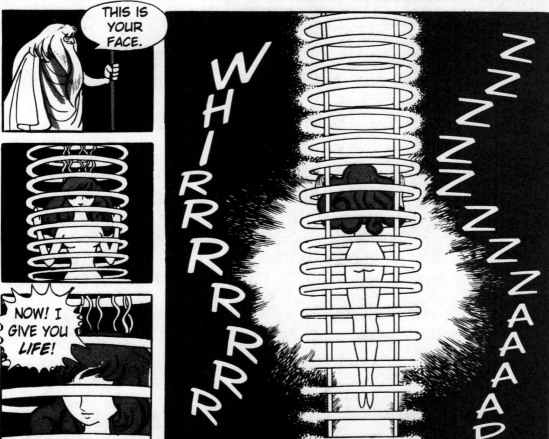

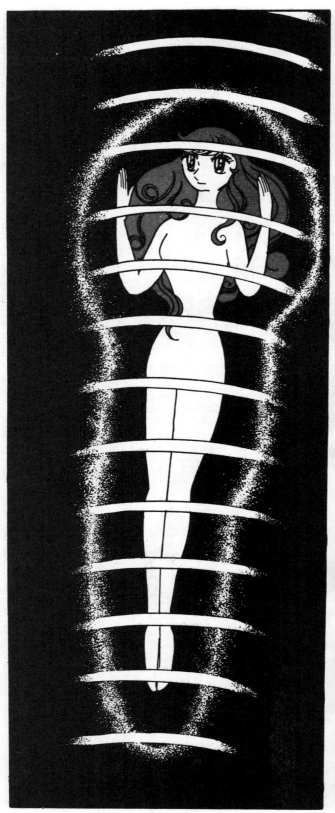

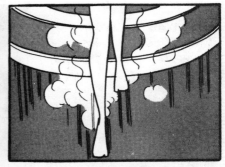

Grandfather!

MY NAME IS *MASATO*.

Masato Masato
Masatoomasadod
Dodadodadada
Daddy Papa
Ha Ha
Ha Ha

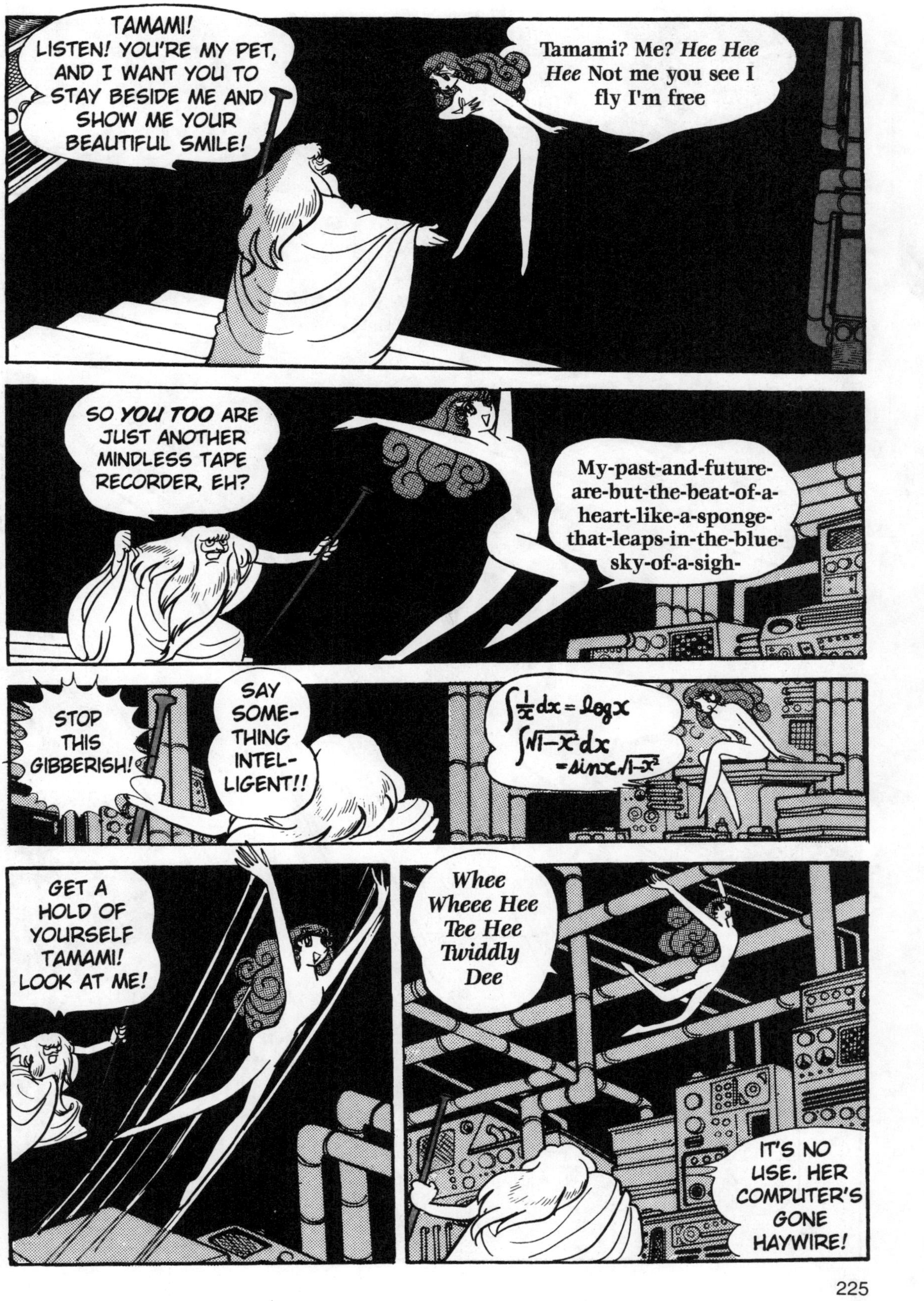
TAMAMI! LISTEN! YOU'RE MY PET, AND I WANT YOU TO STAY BESIDE ME AND SHOW ME YOUR BEAUTIFUL SMILE!
Tamami? Me? *Hee Hee Hee* Not me you see I fly I'm free
SO *YOU TOO* ARE JUST ANOTHER MINDLESS TAPE RECORDER, EH?
My-past-and-future-are-but-the-beat-of-a-heart-like-a-sponge-that-leaps-in-the-blue-sky-of-a-sigh-
STOP THIS GIBBERISH!
SAY SOMETHING INTELLIGENT!!
$\int \frac{1}{x} dx = \log x$
$\int \sqrt{1-x^2} dx = \sin x \sqrt{1-x^2}$
GET A HOLD OF YOURSELF TAMAMI! LOOK AT ME!
Whee Wheee Hee Tee Hee Twiddly Dee
IT'S NO USE. HER COMPUTER'S GONE HAYWIRE!

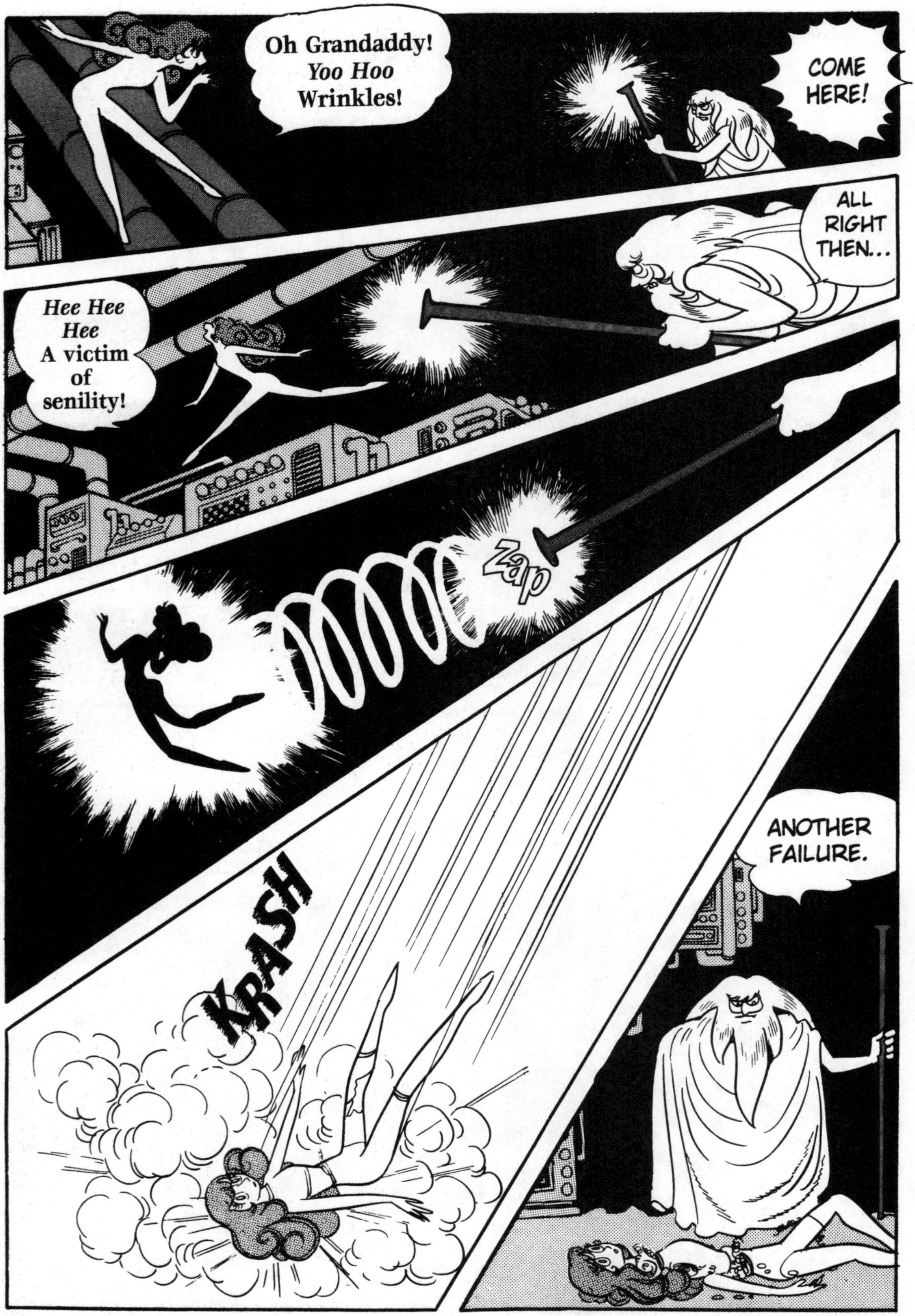
Oh Grandaddy! *Yoo Hoo* Wrinkles!
COME HERE!
Hee Hee Hee A victim of senility!
ALL RIGHT THEN...
Zap
KRASH
ANOTHER FAILURE.

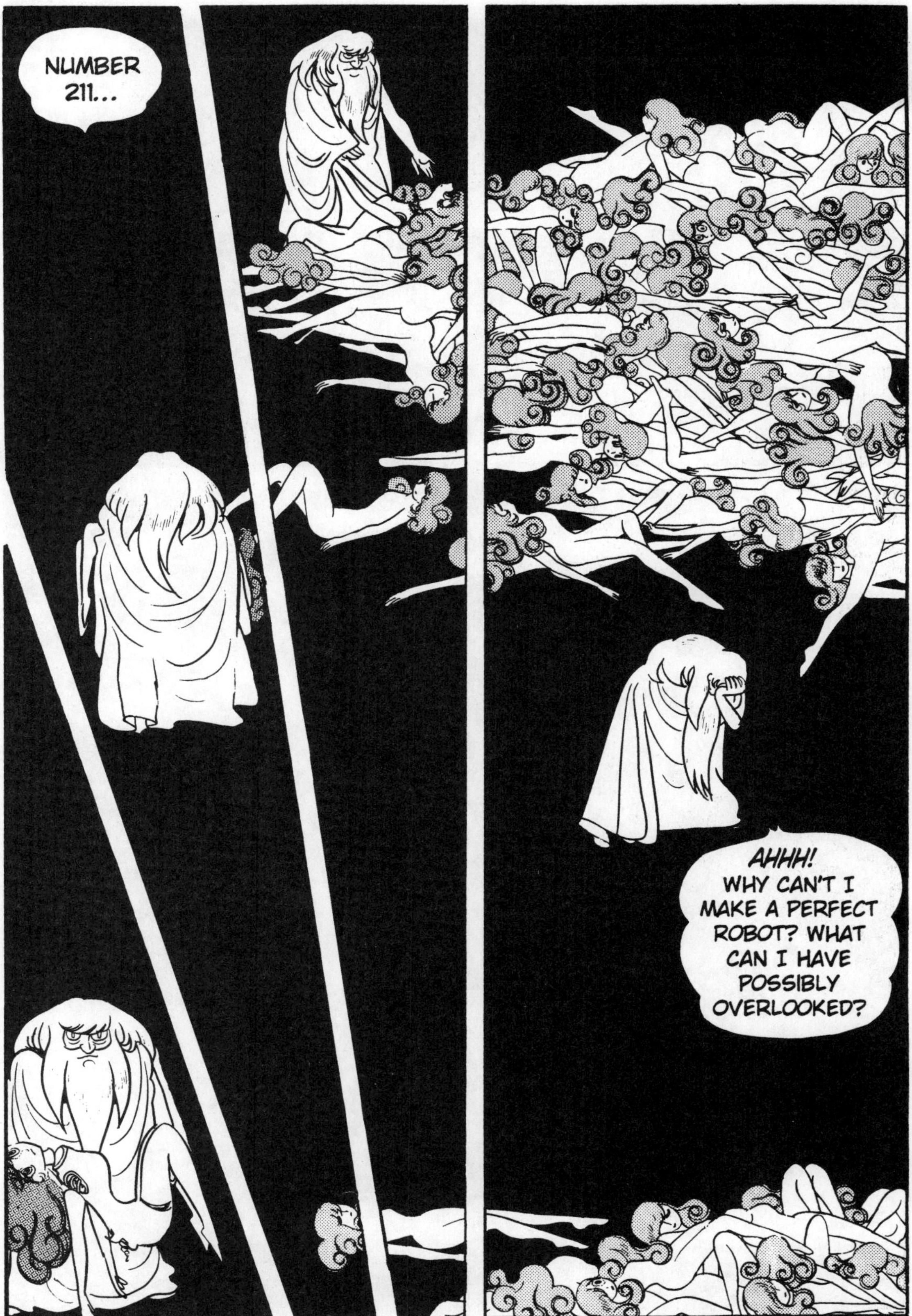
NUMBER 211...
AHHH! WHY CAN'T I MAKE A PERFECT ROBOT? WHAT CAN I HAVE POSSIBLY OVERLOOKED?

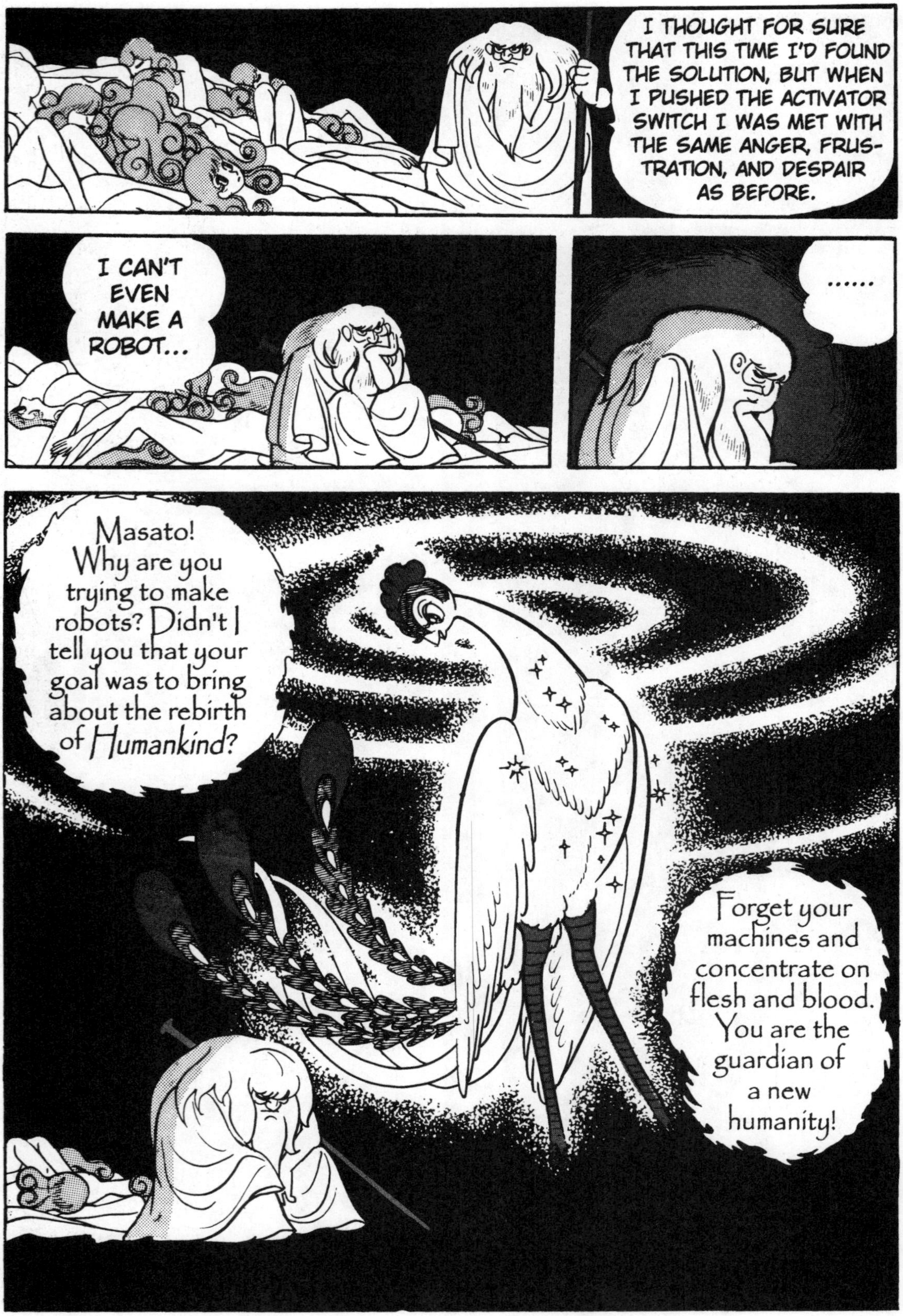
I THOUGHT FOR SURE THAT THIS TIME I'D FOUND THE SOLUTION, BUT WHEN I PUSHED THE ACTIVATOR SWITCH I WAS MET WITH THE SAME ANGER, FRUS- TRATION, AND DESPAIR AS BEFORE.
I CAN'T EVEN MAKE A ROBOT...
......
Masato! Why are you trying to make robots? Didn't I tell you that your goal was to bring about the rebirth of *Humankind*?
Forget your machines and concentrate on flesh and blood. You are the guardian of a new humanity!

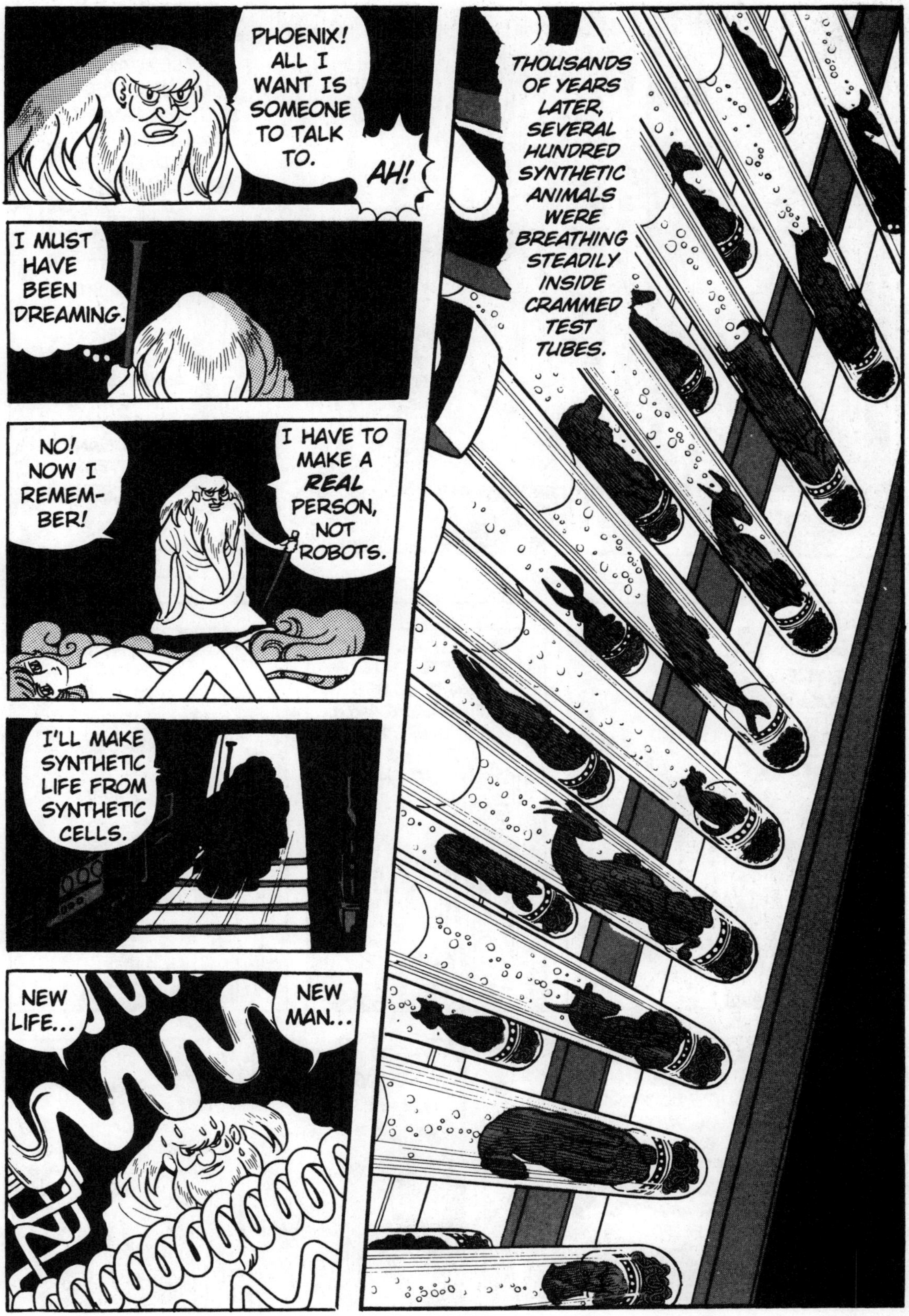
PHOENIX! ALL I WANT IS SOMEONE TO TALK TO.
AH!
I MUST HAVE BEEN DREAMING.
NO! NOW I REMEMBER!
I HAVE TO MAKE A *REAL* PERSON, NOT ROBOTS.
I'LL MAKE SYNTHETIC LIFE FROM SYNTHETIC CELLS.
NEW LIFE...
NEW MAN...
THOUSANDS OF YEARS LATER, SEVERAL HUNDRED SYNTHETIC ANIMALS WERE BREATHING STEADILY INSIDE CRAMMED TEST TUBES.

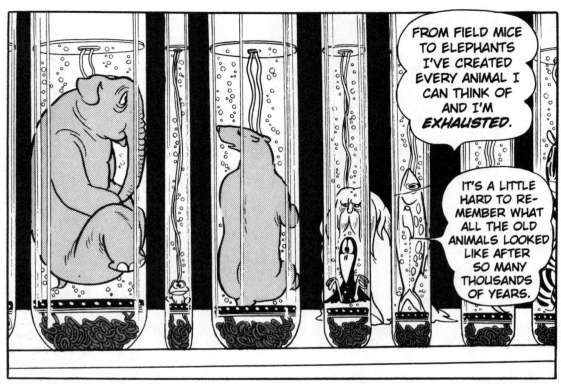

FROM FIELD MICE TO ELEPHANTS I'VE CREATED EVERY ANIMAL I CAN THINK OF AND I'M *EXHAUSTED.*

IT'S A LITTLE HARD TO RE-MEMBER WHAT ALL THE OLD ANIMALS LOOKED LIKE AFTER SO MANY THOUSANDS OF YEARS.

I THINK I GOT THE *MONKEY* RIGHT.

BUT MY MEMORY'S A LITTLE FUZZY WHEN IT COMES TO THE *KANGAROO.* JUST WHERE DID THE POUCH GO ANYWAY?

BY TRIAL AND ERROR I'VE EVEN MADE A LIKENESS OF A *HUMAN.*

SEEMS ALMOST AS THOUGH SHE'S LOOKING AT ME WITH THE EYES OF WISDOM ITSELF FROM INSIDE HER AMNIOTIC FLUID.

GOOD MORNING TAMAMI.

AR... AAH...

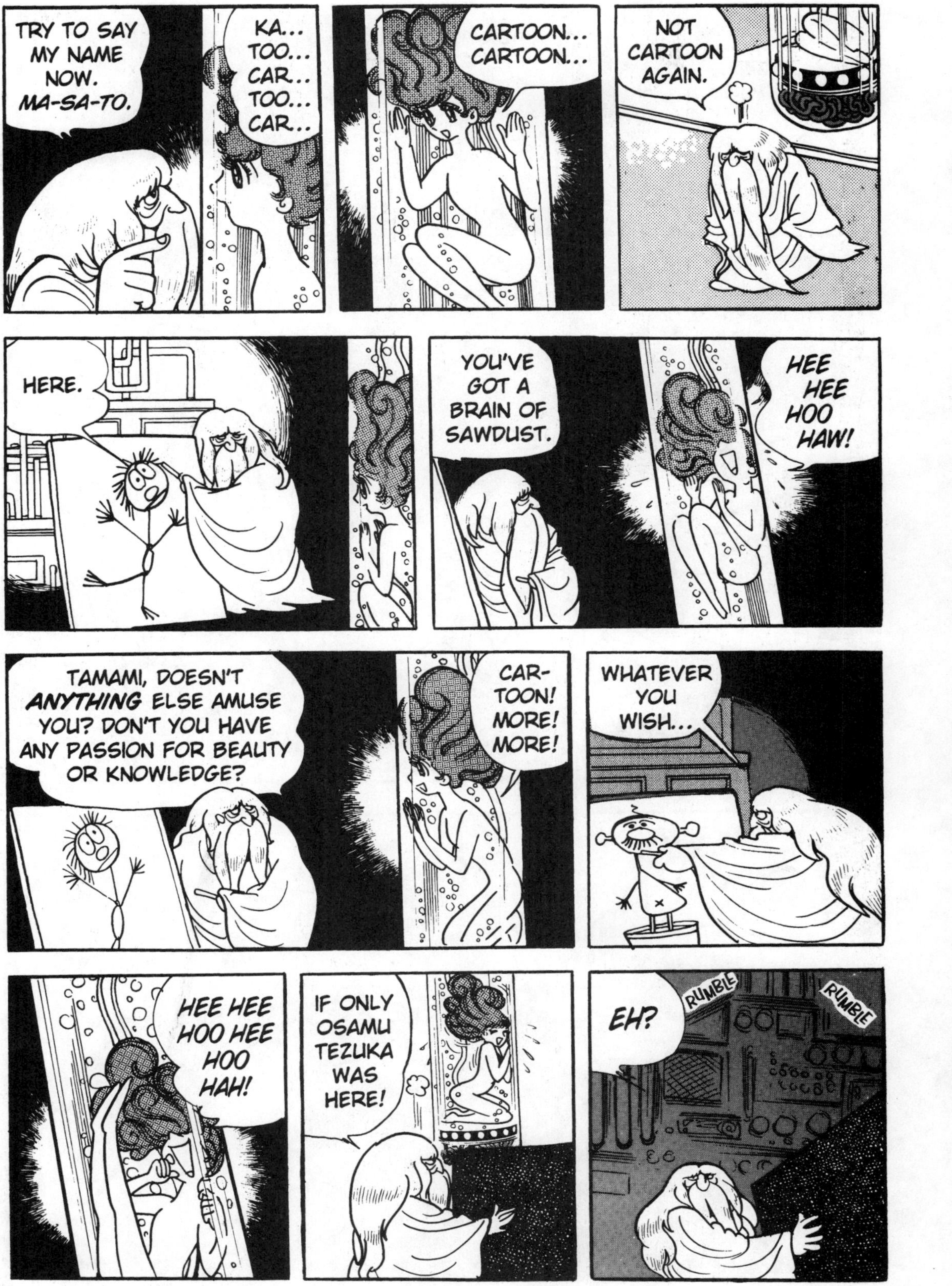
TRY TO SAY MY NAME NOW. MA-SA-TO.
KA... TOO... CAR... TOO... CAR...
CARTOON... CARTOON...
NOT CARTOON AGAIN.
HERE.
YOU'VE GOT A BRAIN OF SAWDUST.
HEE HEE HOO HAW!
TAMAMI, DOESN'T ANYTHING ELSE AMUSE YOU? DON'T YOU HAVE ANY PASSION FOR BEAUTY OR KNOWLEDGE?
CAR-TOON! MORE! MORE!
WHATEVER YOU WISH...
HEE HEE HOO HEE HOO HAH!
IF ONLY OSAMU TEZUKA WAS HERE!
EH?
RUMBLE
RUMBLE

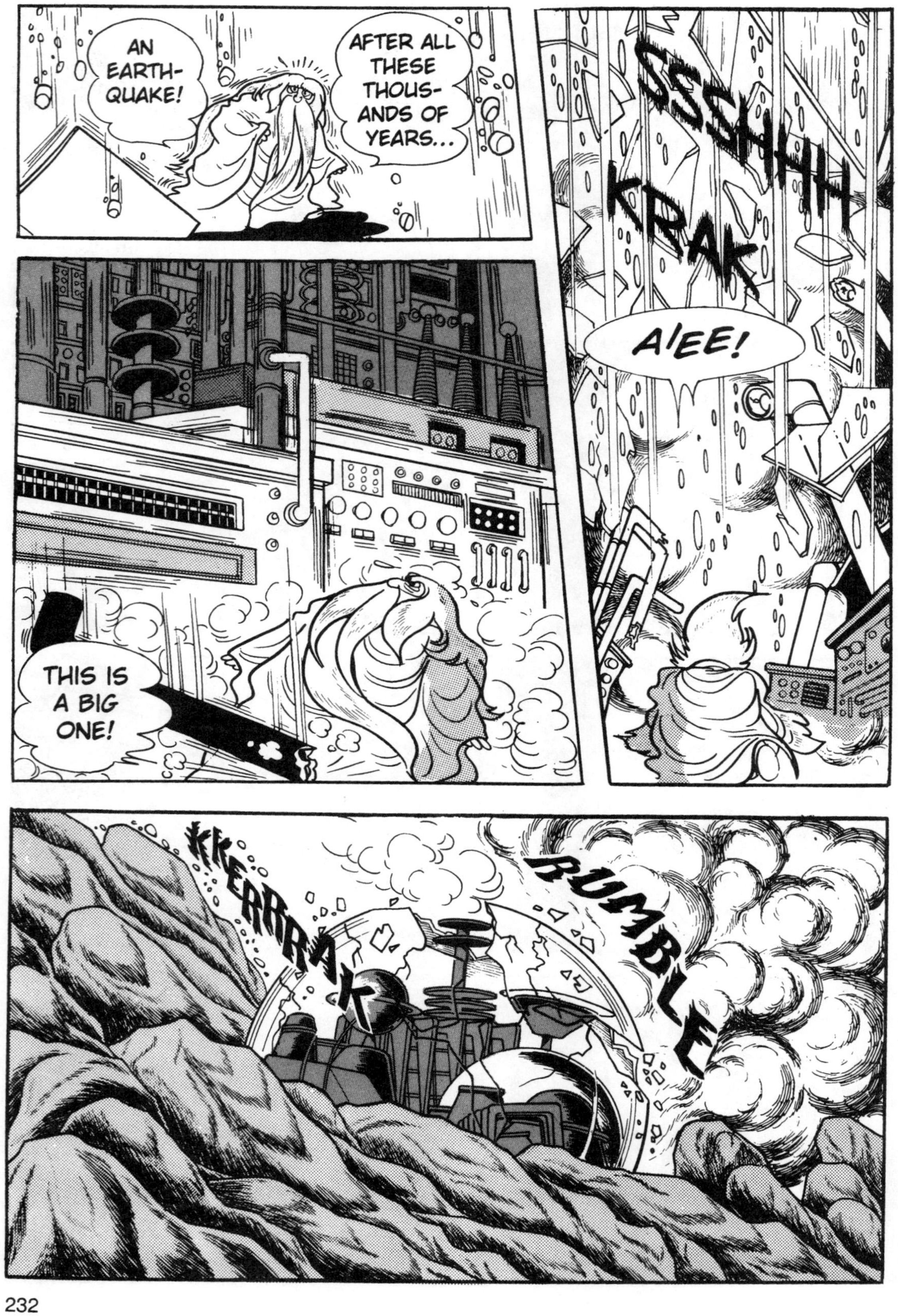
AN EARTH-QUAKE!
AFTER ALL THESE THOUS-ANDS OF YEARS...
THIS IS A BIG ONE!
SSSHHH
KRAK
AIEE!
KKERRRAK
RUMBLE

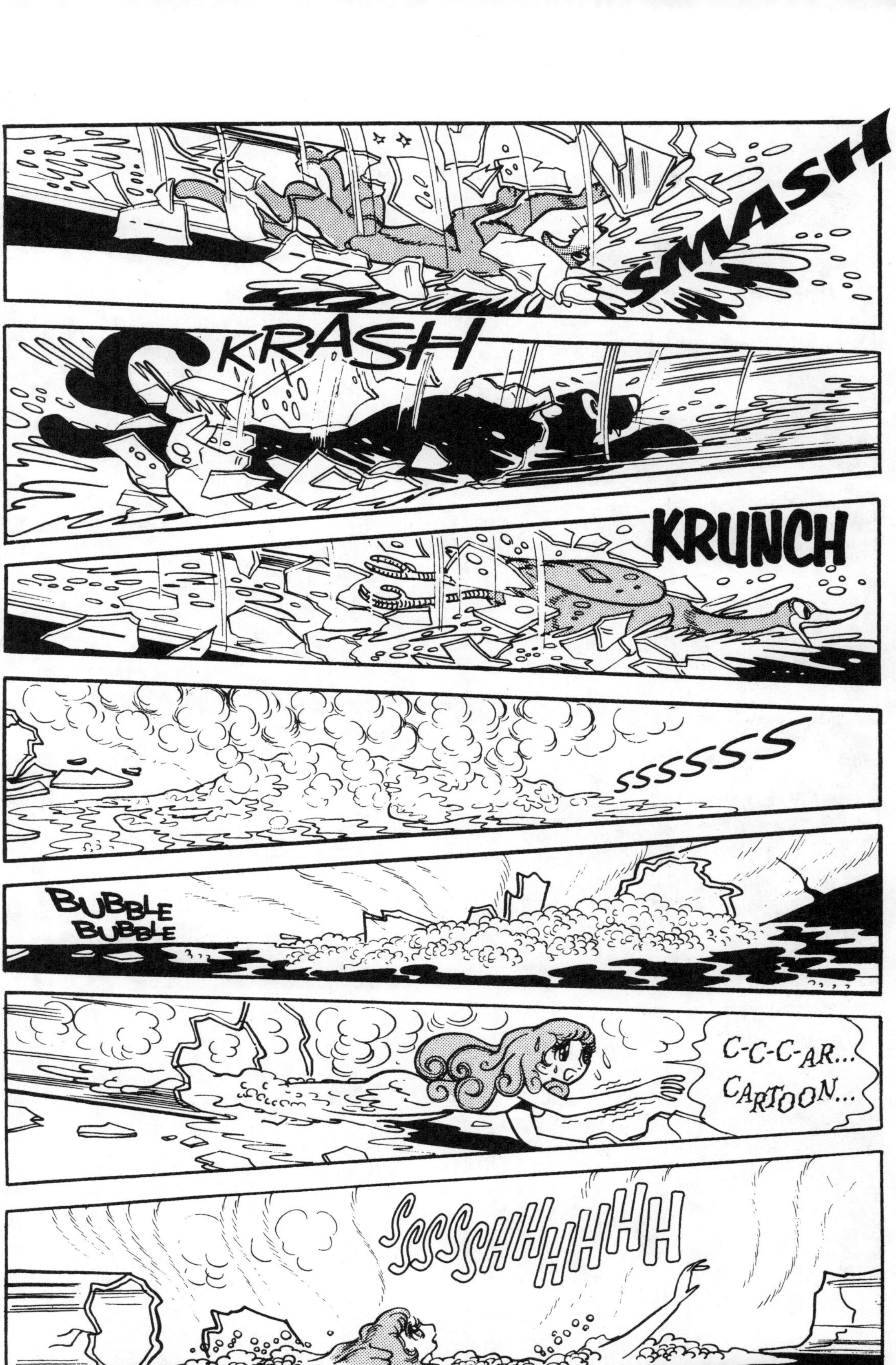
SMASH
KRASH
KRUNCH
SSSSSS
BUBBLE BUBBLE
C-C-C-AR... CARTOON...
SSSSHHHHHHH

->SNIFFLE<-...

TAMAMI...

YOU POOR DEMENTED CREATURE... TO DISSOLVE INTO FOAM WAS PROBABLY BEST FOR YOU...

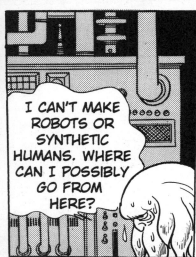

I CAN'T MAKE ROBOTS OR SYNTHETIC HUMANS. WHERE CAN I POSSIBLY GO FROM HERE?

THERE'S ONLY ONE THING LEFT FOR ME TO DO, AND THAT'S TO LET NATURE TAKE ITS COURSE AND WAIT HERE FOR THE REAPPEARANCE OF LIFE.

WAIT! IT CAN'T BE THAT I'M TO REPEAT THE WHOLE EVOLUTIONARY PROCESS?

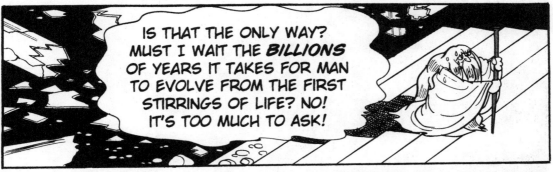

IS THAT THE ONLY WAY? MUST I WAIT THE *BILLIONS* OF YEARS IT TAKES FOR MAN TO EVOLVE FROM THE FIRST STIRRINGS OF LIFE? NO! IT'S TOO MUCH TO ASK!

TOO MUCH...

I AM SO OLD...

BUT... THIS MUST BE MY MISSION...

OH OCEAN...

ACCEPT MY GIFT— A SIMPLE MIXTURE OF CARBON, OXYGEN, AND HYDROGEN.

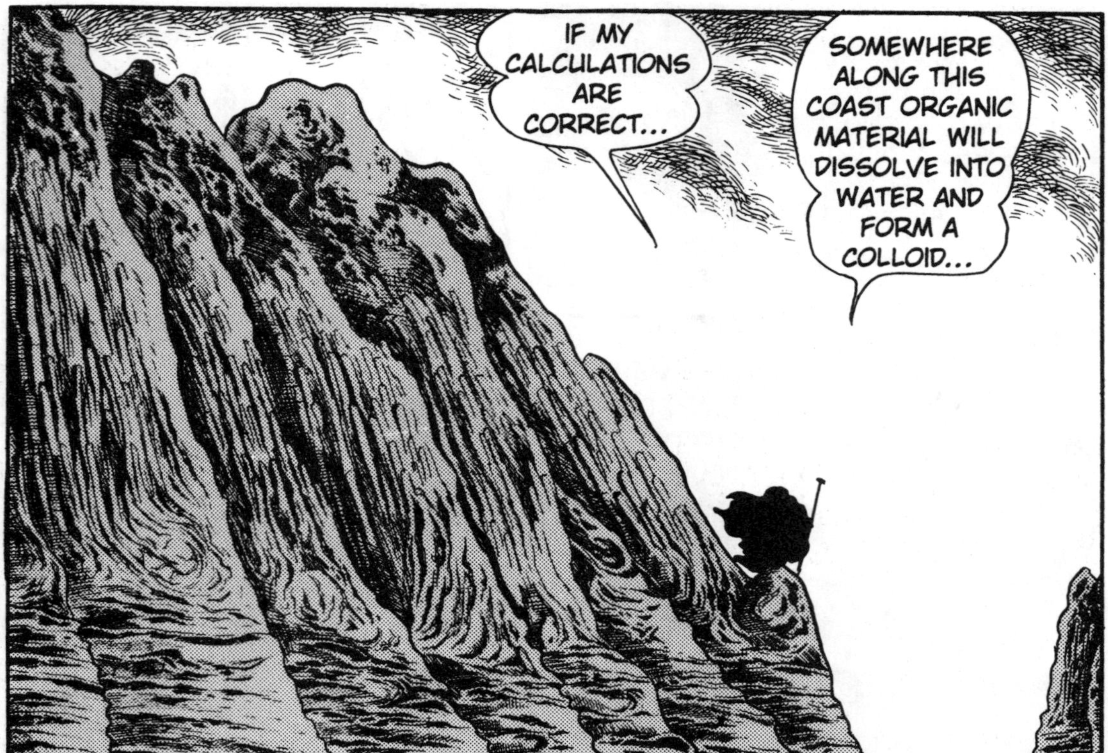
IF MY CALCULATIONS ARE CORRECT...
SOMEWHERE ALONG THIS COAST ORGANIC MATERIAL WILL DISSOLVE INTO WATER AND FORM A COLLOID...
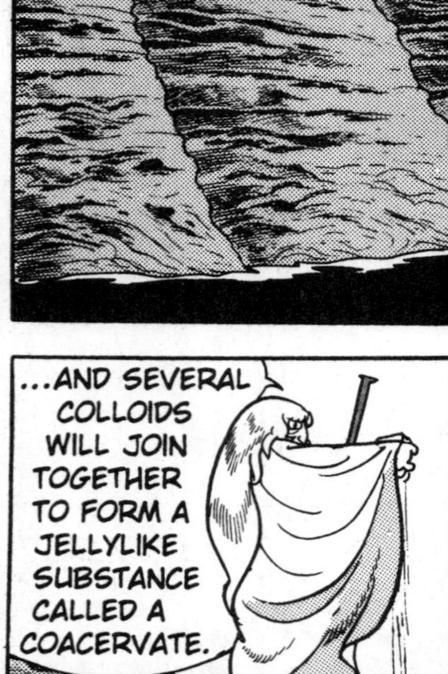
...AND SEVERAL COLLOIDS WILL JOIN TOGETHER TO FORM A JELLYLIKE SUBSTANCE CALLED A COACERVATE.
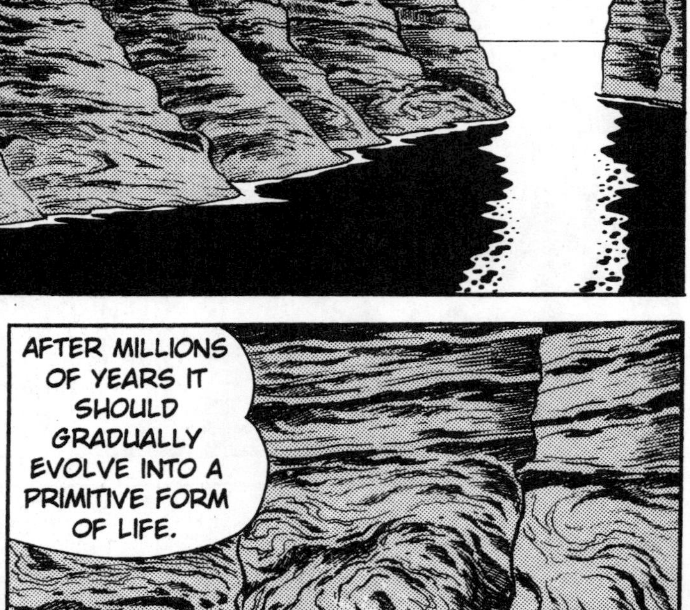
AFTER MILLIONS OF YEARS IT SHOULD GRADUALLY EVOLVE INTO A PRIMITIVE FORM OF LIFE.

I'LL WAIT.
NO MATTER HOW MANY BILLIONS OF YEARS IT TAKES.
THE OCEAN WAS SILENT SAVE FOR THE SOUND OF WAVES AND SURF BREAKING AGAINST THE SHORE. AN OCEAN BREEZE CARRIED THESE TIDINGS TO THE DOME BUT NO SIGN OF LIFE APPEARED ANYWHERE.
MASATO'S FLESH HAD LONG SINCE VANISHED IN DECAY. BUT HE REMAINED ALIVE.

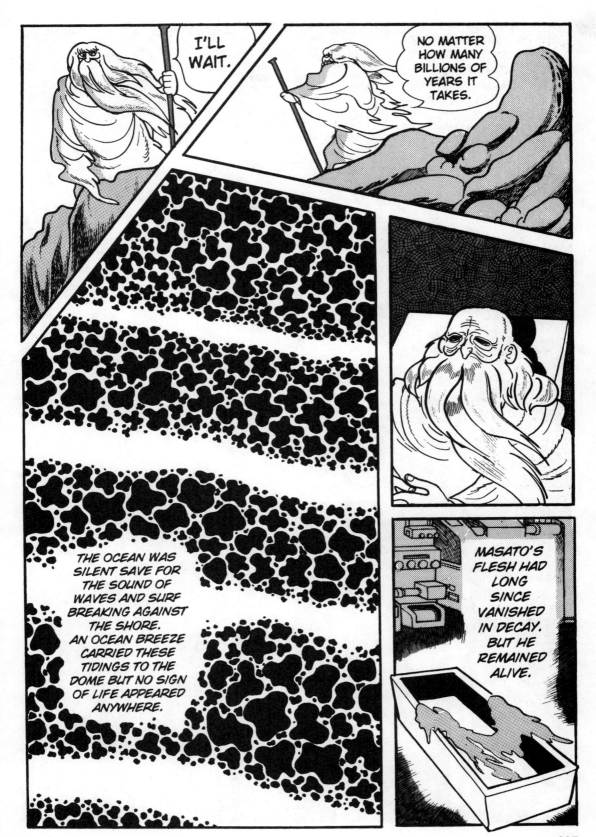

MASATO BECAME PURE EXISTENCE—A FORCE WHICH CEASELESSLY KEPT WATCH OVER THE SLOWLY EVOLVING STRAINS OF LIFE. HE TRANSCENDED TIME AND SPACE...

THE ORGANIC MATERIAL THAT HAD BECOME COACERVATES BEGAN TO ENLARGE BY ABSORBING SURROUNDING MATERIAL.

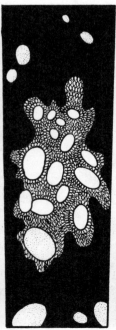

AND WHEN IT REACHED A SPECIFIC SIZE...

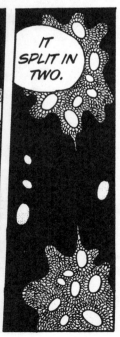

IT SPLIT IN TWO.

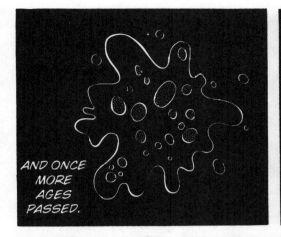

AND ONCE MORE AGES PASSED.

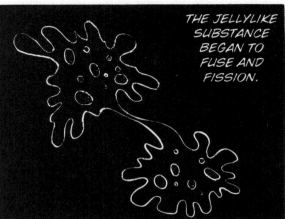

THE JELLYLIKE SUBSTANCE BEGAN TO FUSE AND FISSION.

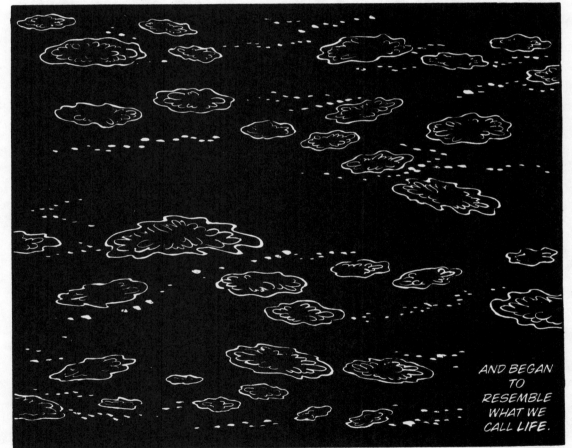

AND BEGAN TO RESEMBLE WHAT WE CALL *LIFE*.

AND FINALLY...

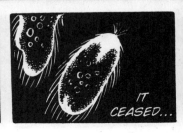

IT CEASED...

TO BE INANIMATE.

IT POSSESSED WHIPLIKE TAILS...

CILIA...

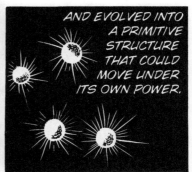

AND EVOLVED INTO A PRIMITIVE STRUCTURE THAT COULD MOVE UNDER ITS OWN POWER.

CELLS COMBINED...

...CREATING LARGER ORGANISMS, AND SMALLER UNITS OF LIFE MASSED TO FORM MORE COMPLEX ONES.

EVENTUALLY TWO DISTINCT FORMS OF LIFE EVOLVED— PLANT AND ANIMAL.

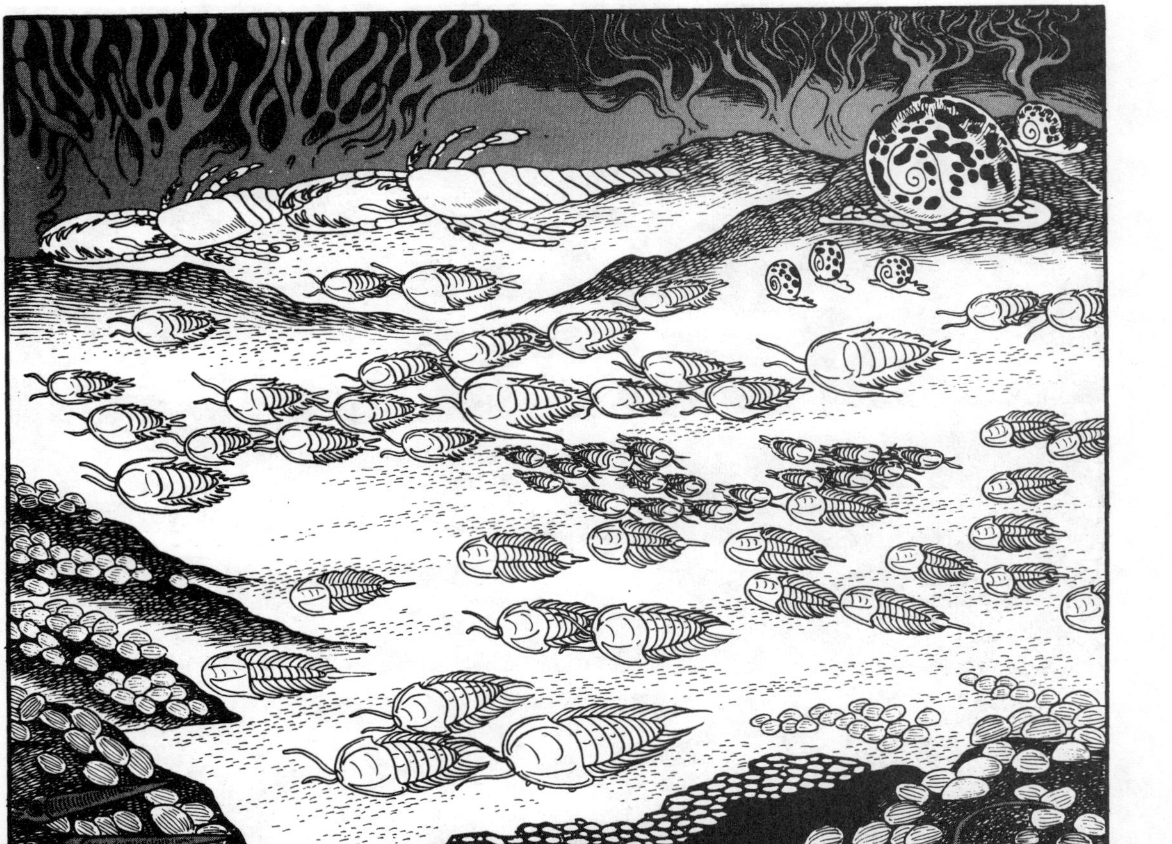

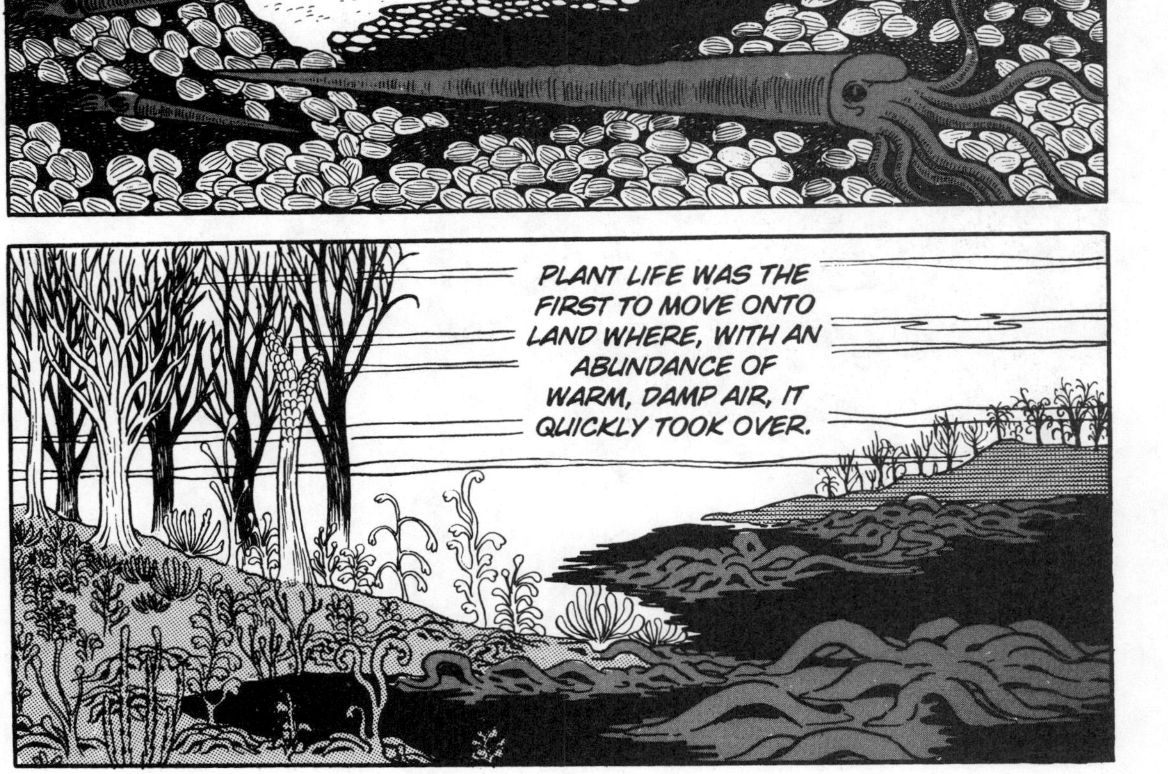
PLANT LIFE WAS THE FIRST TO MOVE ONTO LAND WHERE, WITH AN ABUNDANCE OF WARM, DAMP AIR, IT QUICKLY TOOK OVER.

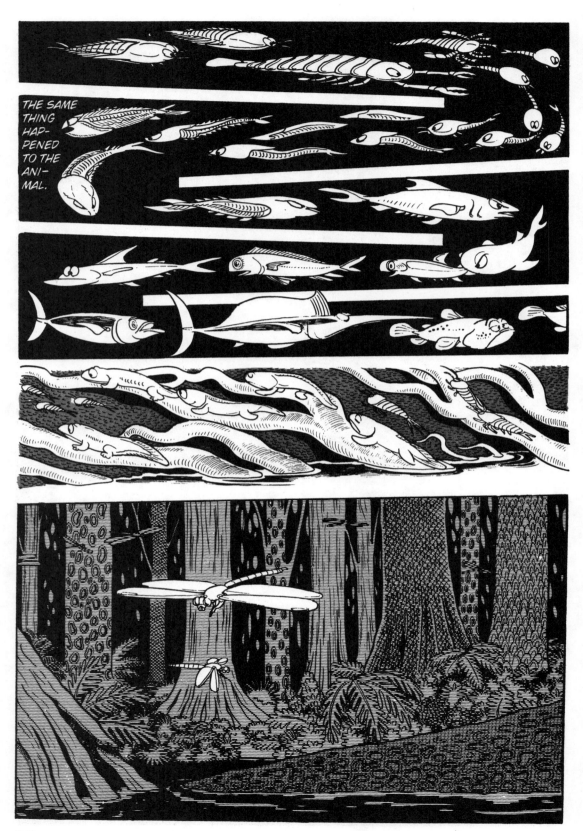

THE SAME THING HAP-PENED TO THE ANI-MAL.

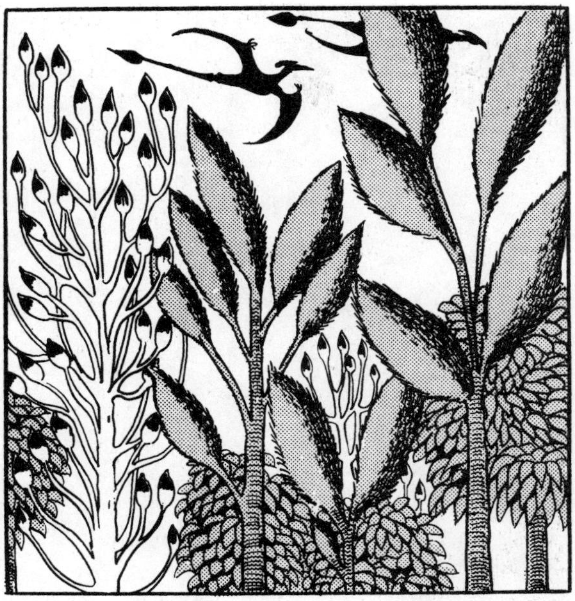

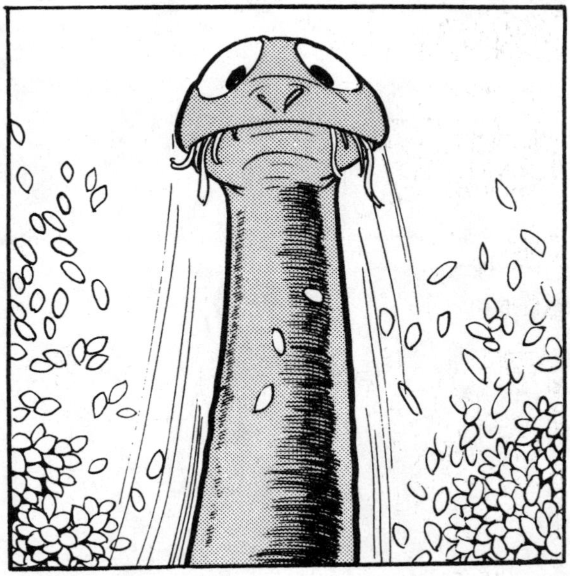

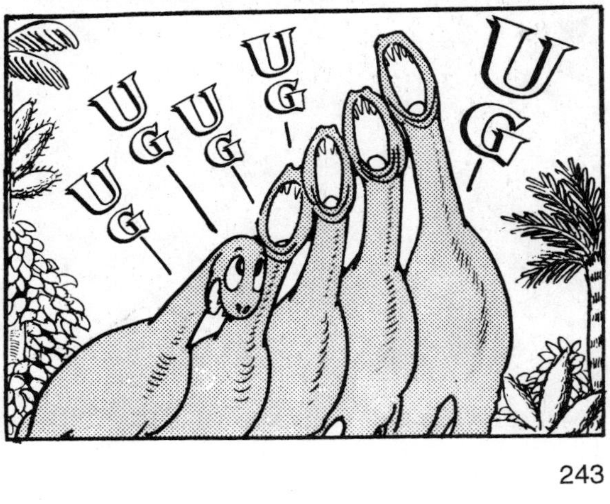
UG
UG
UG
UG
UG

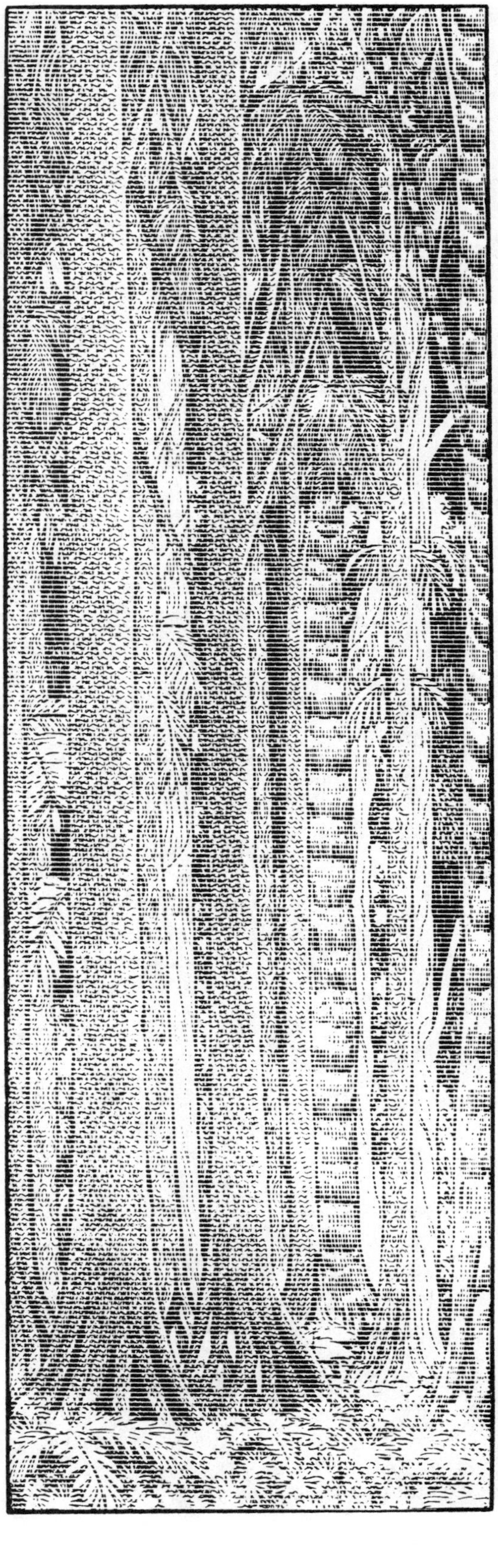

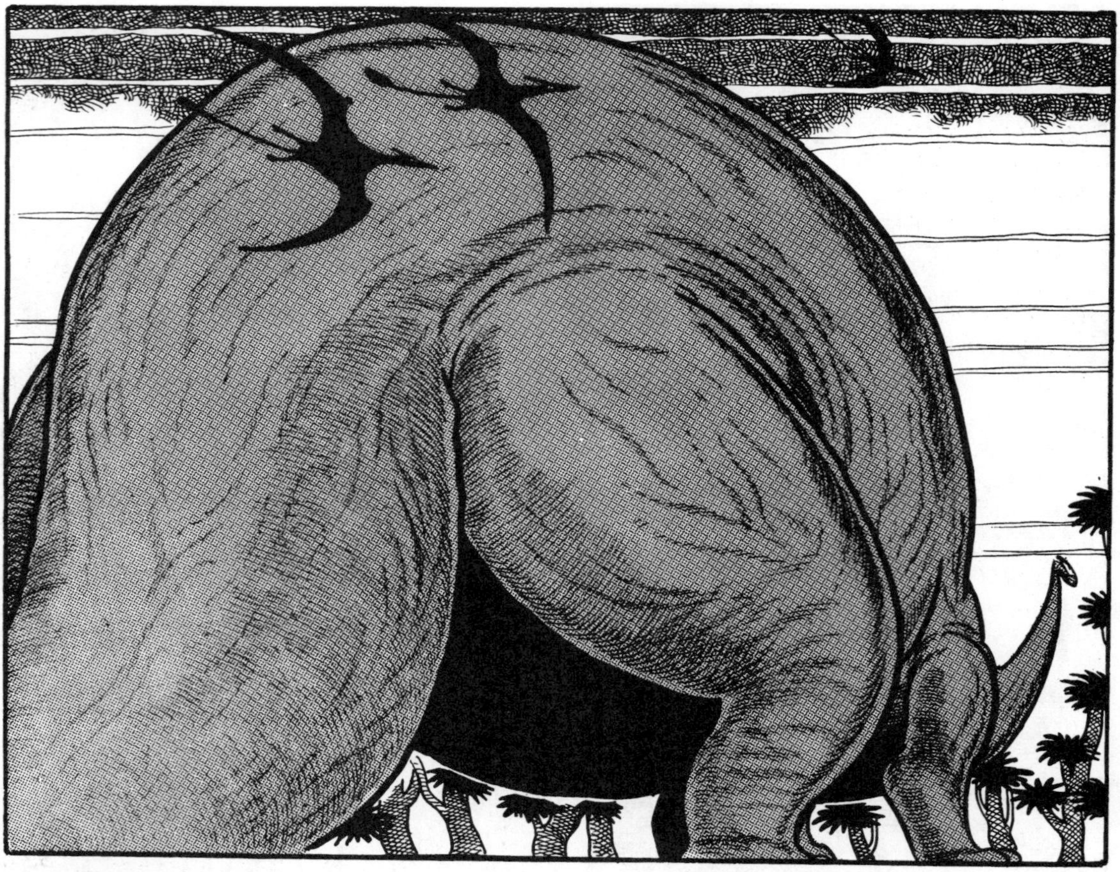

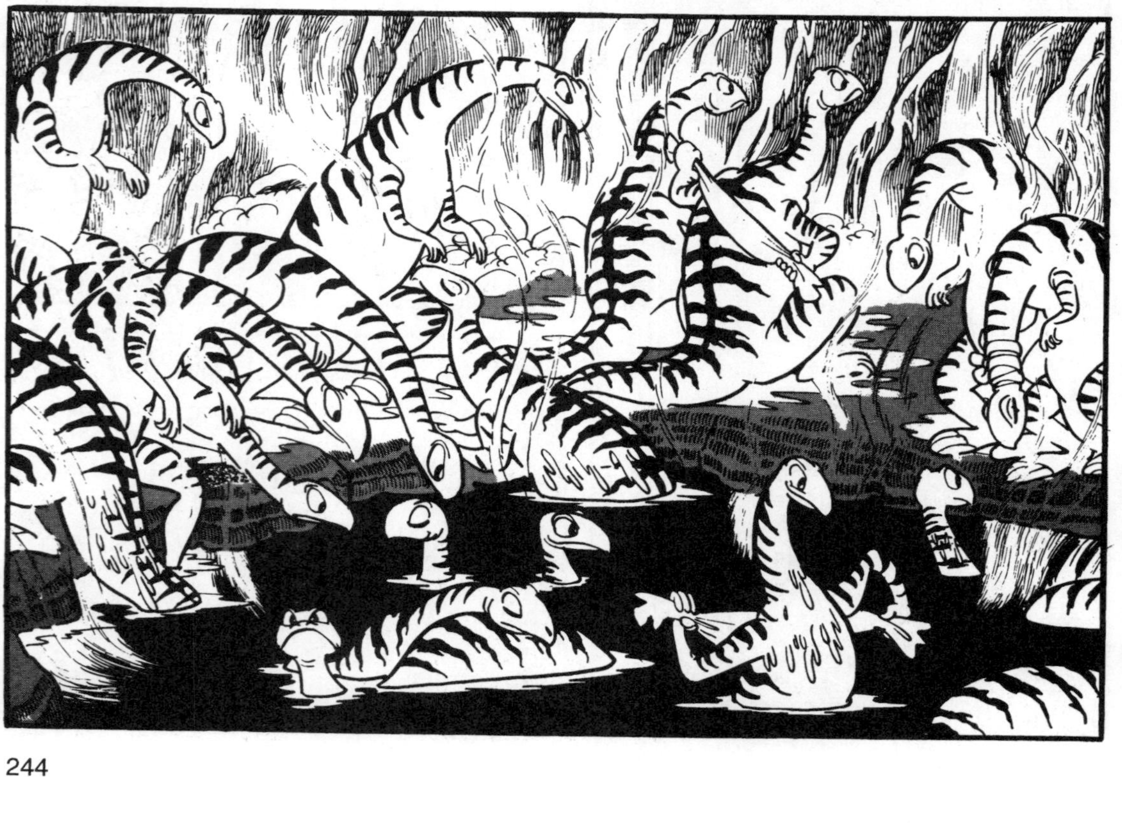

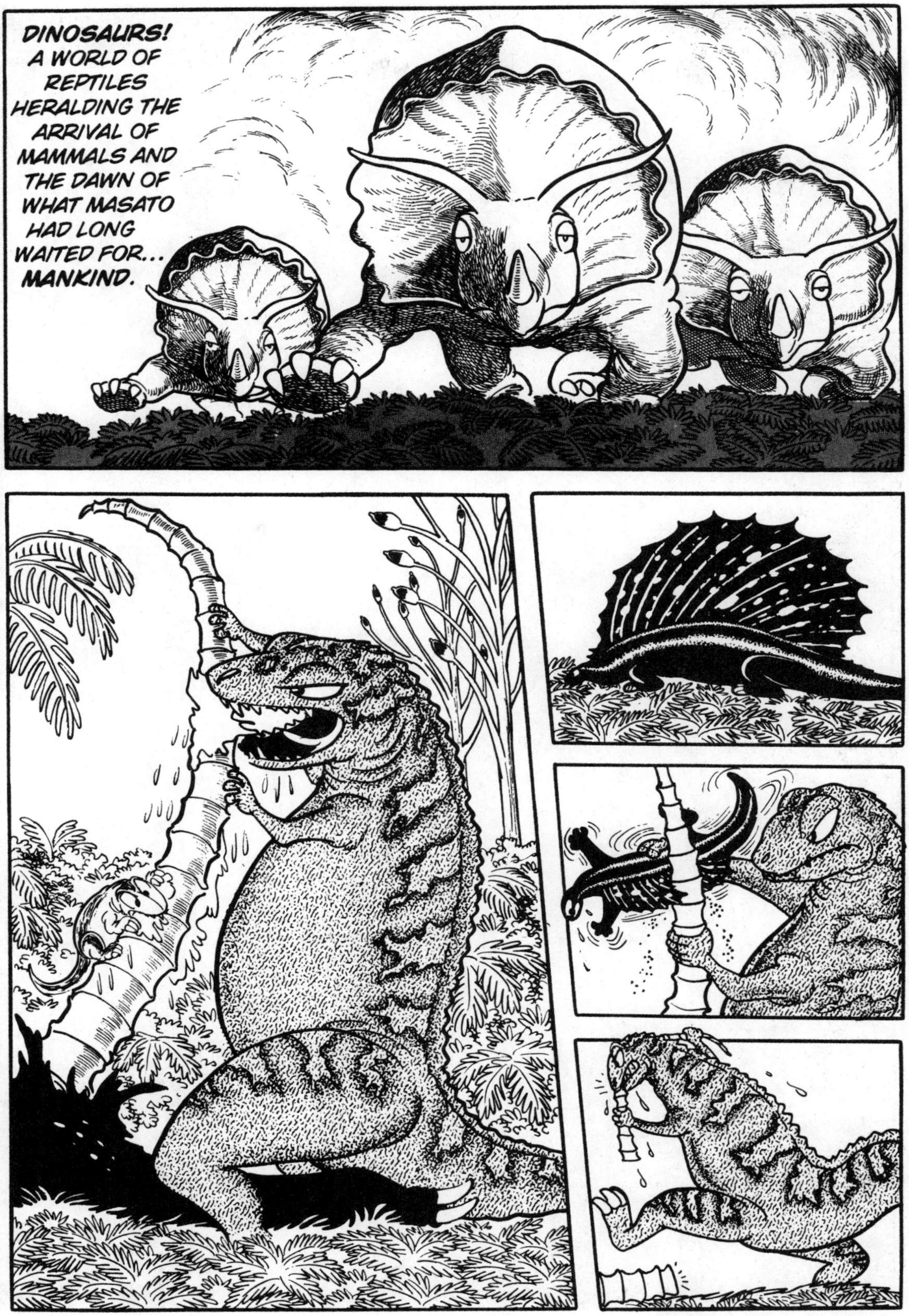
DINOSAURS! A WORLD OF REPTILES HERALDING THE ARRIVAL OF MAMMALS AND THE DAWN OF WHAT MASATO HAD LONG WAITED FOR... MANKIND.

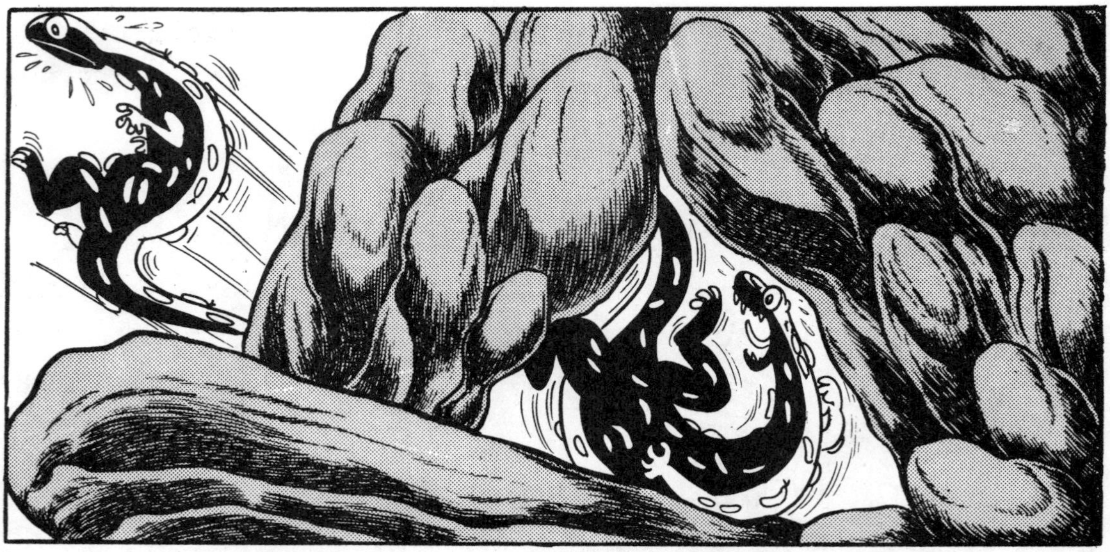

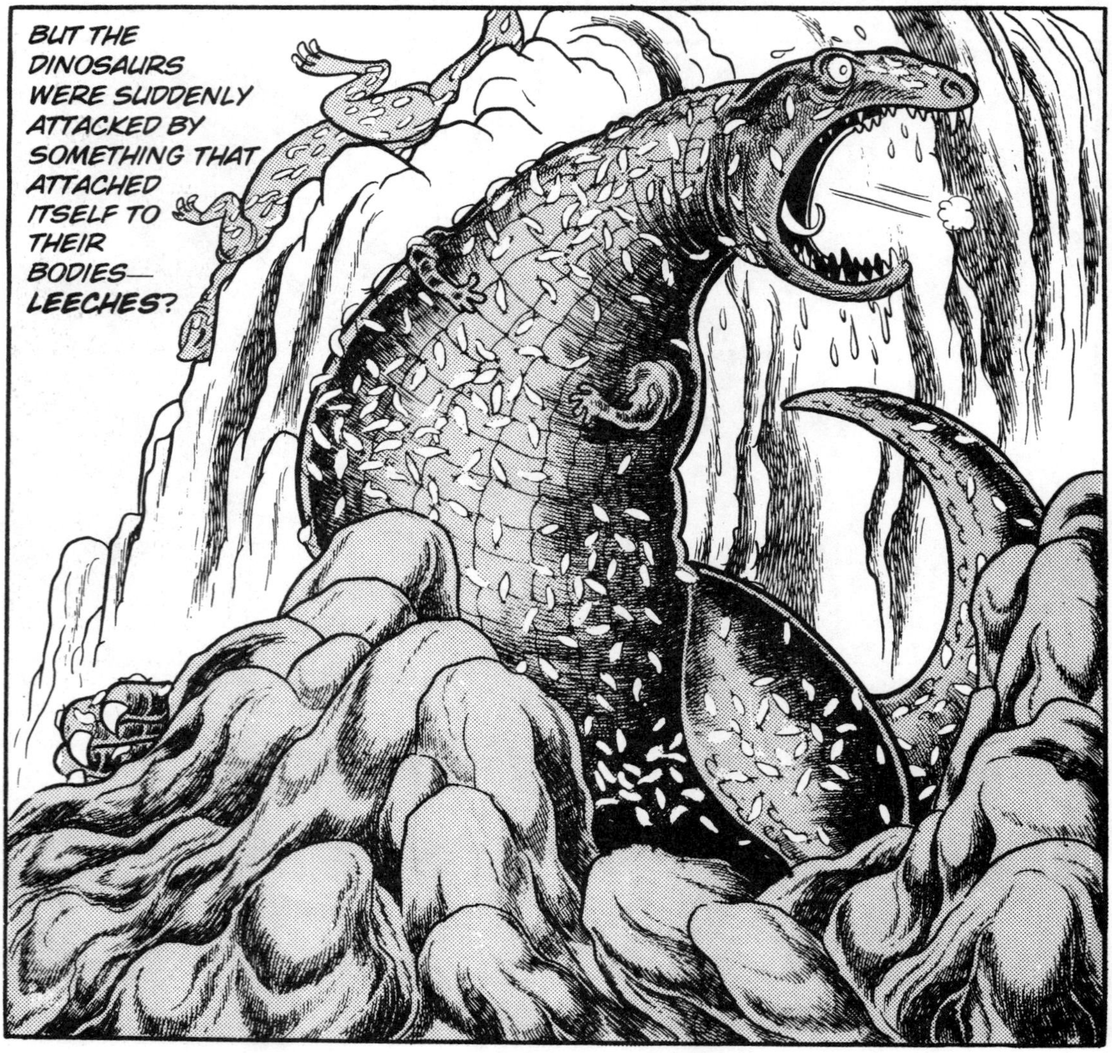
BUT THE DINOSAURS WERE SUDDENLY ATTACKED BY SOMETHING THAT ATTACHED ITSELF TO THEIR BODIES—LEECHES?

NO! SLUGS!

THEY ATTACKED THE DINOSAUR!!

UNTIL THEY BECAME EXTINCT...

AND THE FEW MAMMALS THAT REMAINED WERE ALSO SOON OVER- COME BY THE SLUGS.

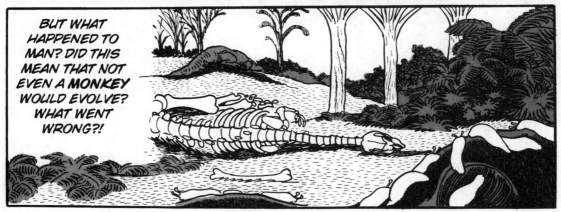

BUT WHAT HAPPENED TO MAN? DID THIS MEAN THAT NOT EVEN A **MONKEY** WOULD EVOLVE? WHAT WENT WRONG?!

THE SLUGS CONTINUED TO EVOLVE.

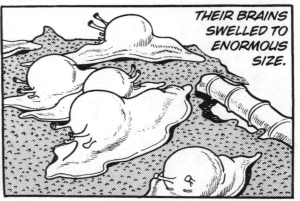

THEIR BRAINS SWELLED TO ENORMOUS SIZE.

FINALLY...

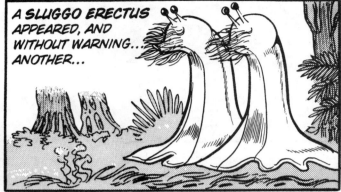

A SLUGGO ERECTUS APPEARED, AND WITHOUT WARNING... ANOTHER...

THESE TWO THEN BEGAN TO REPRODUCE AT AN ALARMING RATE.

FOR LACK OF BETTER NAMES MASATO CALLED THEM ADAM AND EVE!!

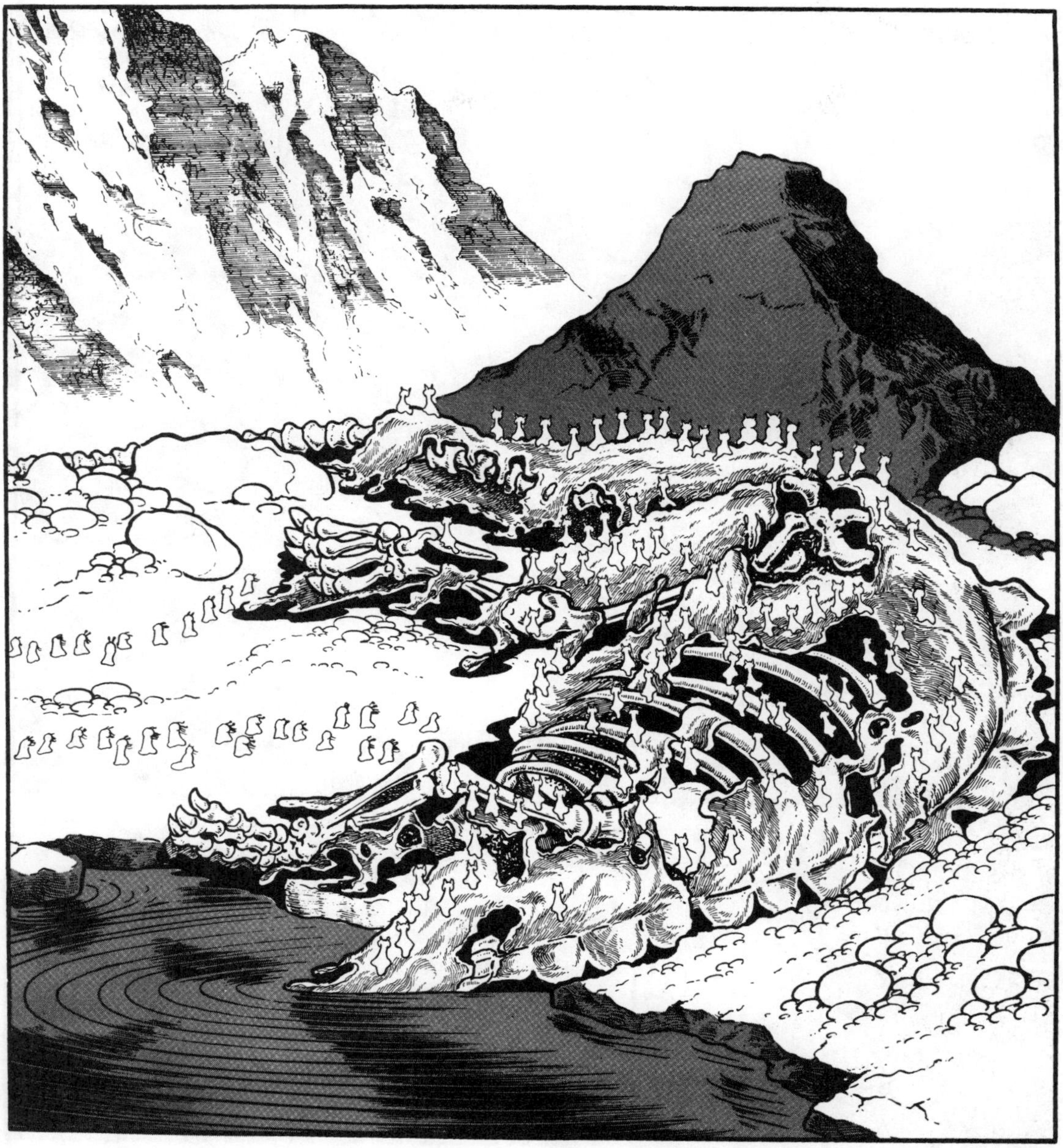
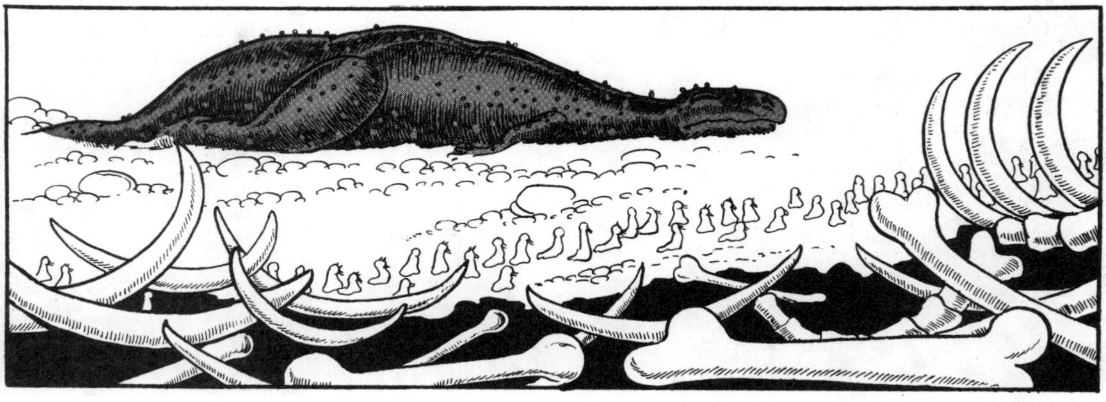

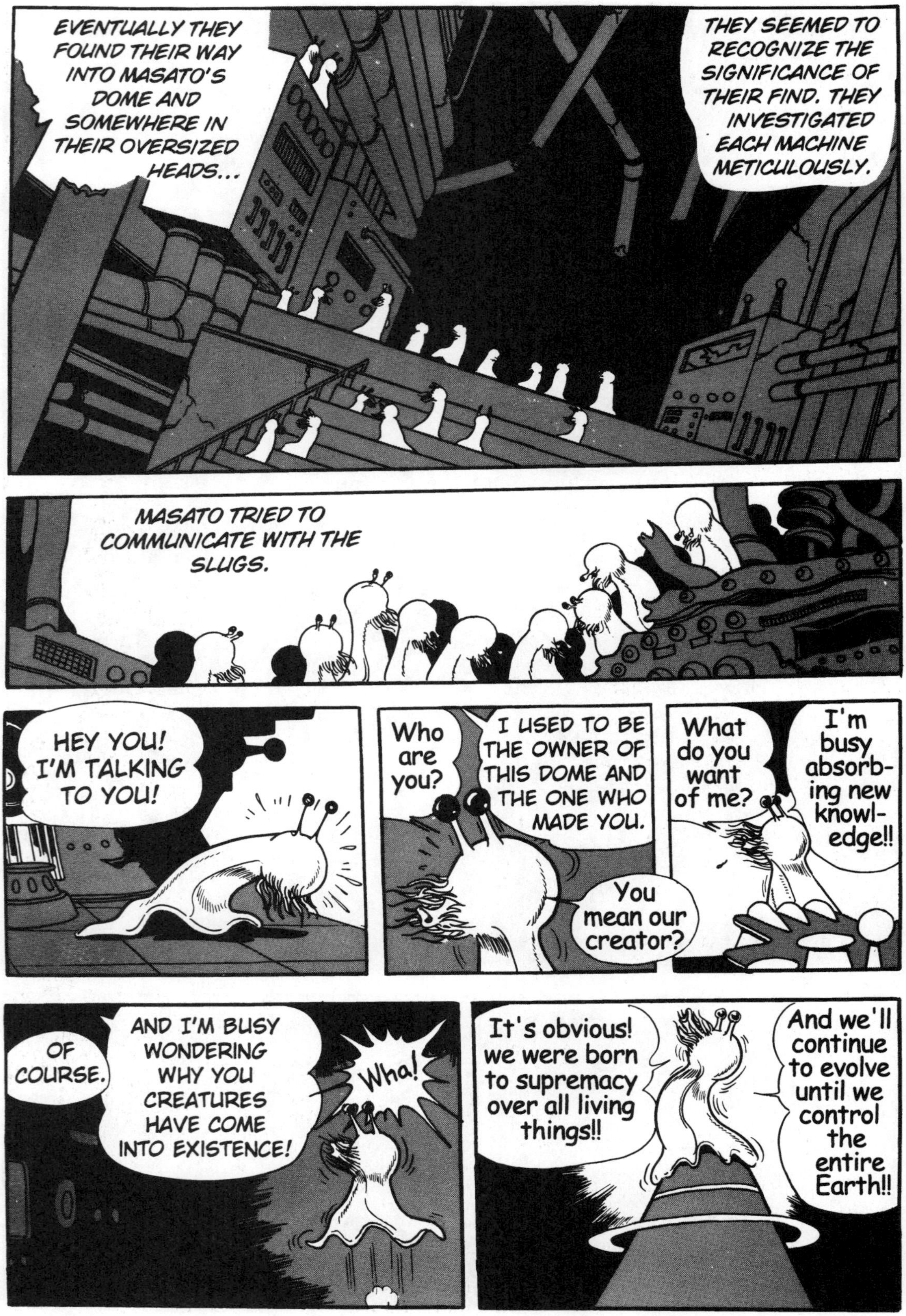
EVENTUALLY THEY FOUND THEIR WAY INTO MASATO'S DOME AND SOMEWHERE IN THEIR OVERSIZED HEADS...
THEY SEEMED TO RECOGNIZE THE SIGNIFICANCE OF THEIR FIND. THEY INVESTIGATED EACH MACHINE METICULOUSLY.
MASATO TRIED TO COMMUNICATE WITH THE SLUGS.
HEY YOU! I'M TALKING TO YOU!
Who are you?
I USED TO BE THE OWNER OF THIS DOME AND THE ONE WHO MADE YOU.
You mean our creator?
What do you want of me?
I'm busy absorb-ing new knowl-edge!!
OF COURSE.
AND I'M BUSY WONDERING WHY YOU CREATURES HAVE COME INTO EXISTENCE!
Wha!
It's obvious! we were born to supremacy over all living things!!
And we'll continue to evolve until we control the entire Earth!!

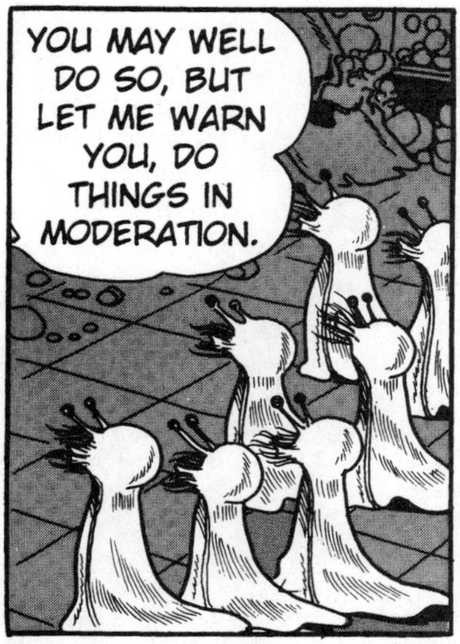
YOU MAY WELL DO SO, BUT LET ME WARN YOU, DO THINGS IN MODERATION.

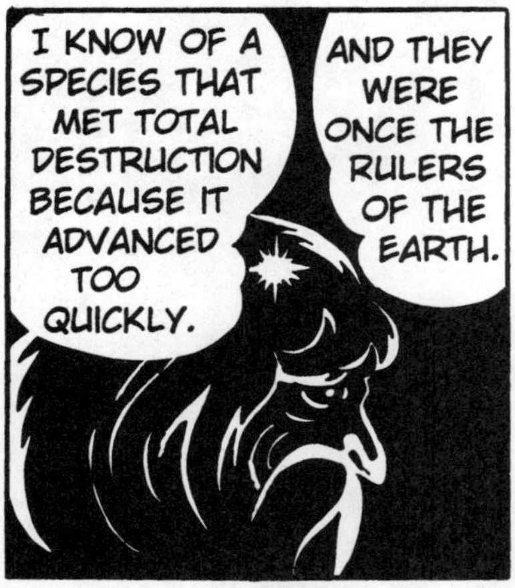
I KNOW OF A SPECIES THAT MET TOTAL DESTRUCTION BECAUSE IT ADVANCED TOO QUICKLY.
AND THEY WERE ONCE THE RULERS OF THE EARTH.

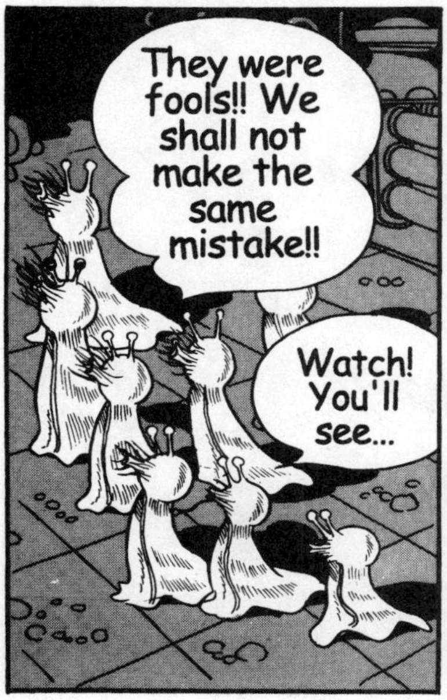
They were fools!! We shall not make the same mistake!!
Watch! You'll see...

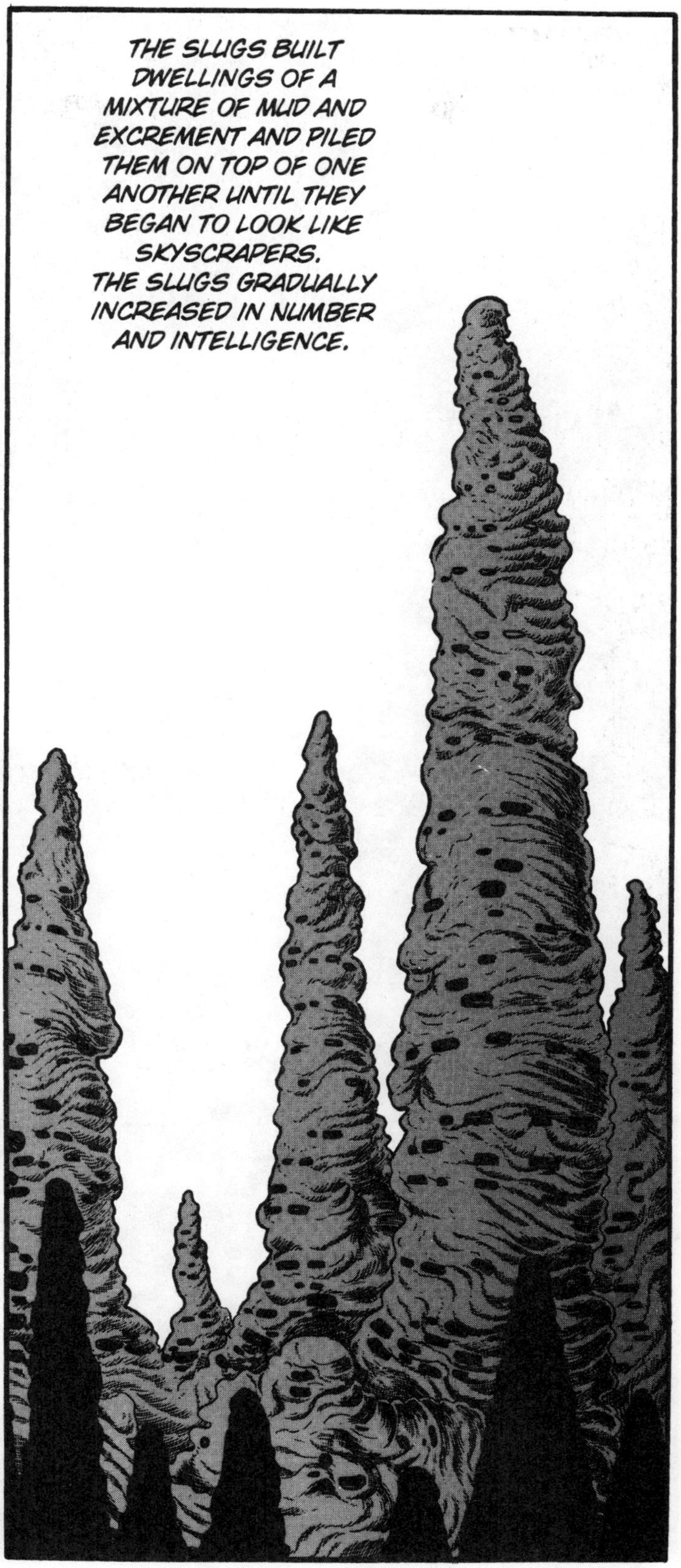
THE SLUGS BUILT DWELLINGS OF A MIXTURE OF MUD AND EXCREMENT AND PILED THEM ON TOP OF ONE ANOTHER UNTIL THEY BEGAN TO LOOK LIKE SKYSCRAPERS.
THE SLUGS GRADUALLY INCREASED IN NUMBER AND INTELLIGENCE.

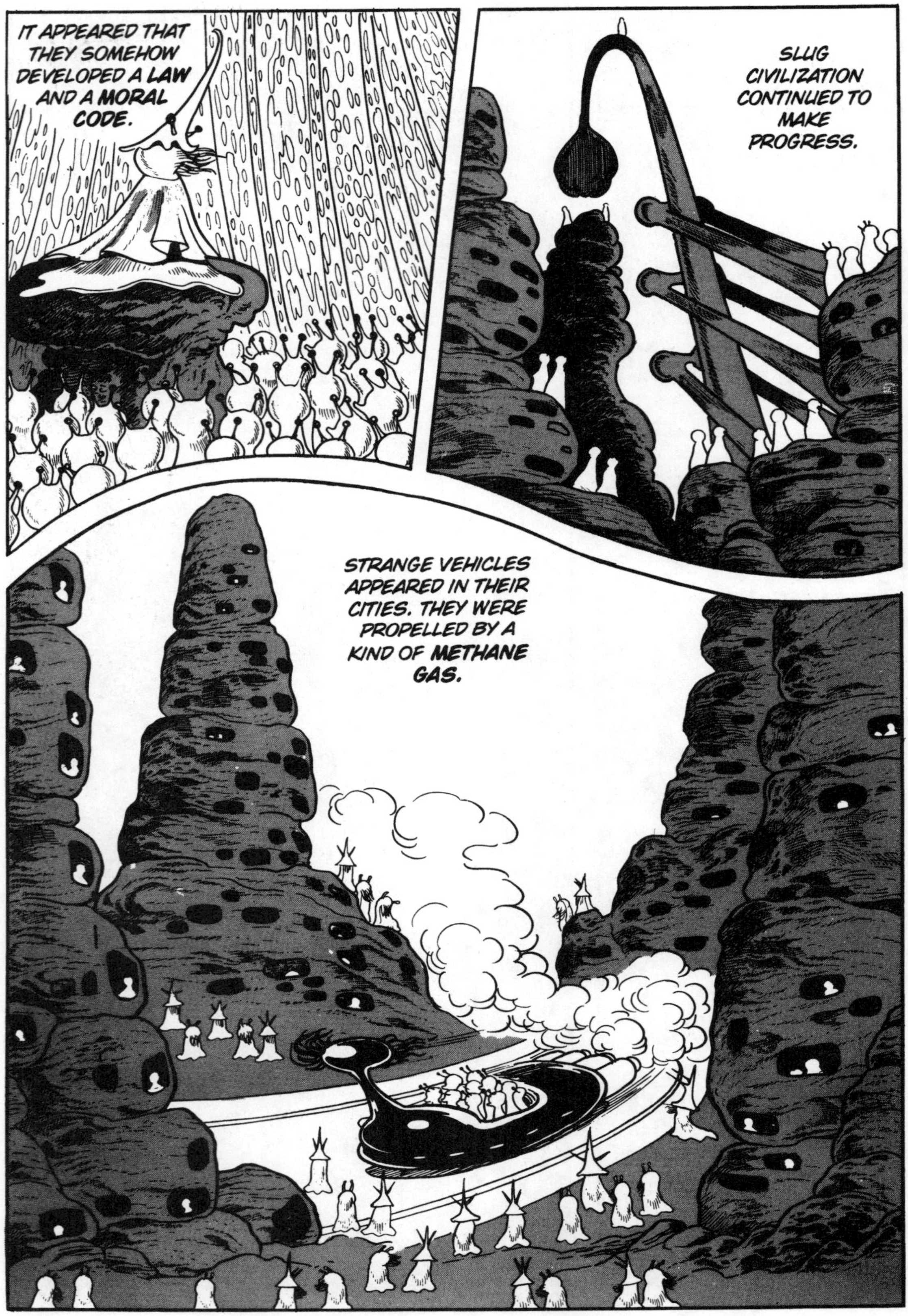
IT APPEARED THAT THEY SOMEHOW DEVELOPED A LAW AND A MORAL CODE.
SLUG CIVILIZATION CONTINUED TO MAKE PROGRESS.
STRANGE VEHICLES APPEARED IN THEIR CITIES. THEY WERE PROPELLED BY A KIND OF METHANE GAS.

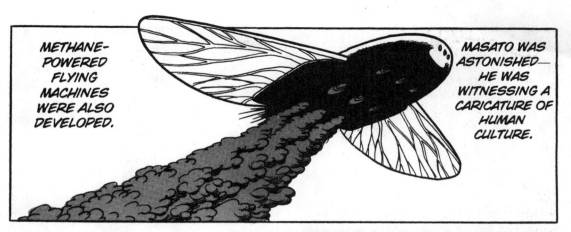

METHANE-POWERED FLYING MACHINES WERE ALSO DEVELOPED.

MASATO WAS ASTONISHED—HE WAS WITNESSING A CARICATURE OF HUMAN CULTURE.

AS TIME PASSED SLUGS DIVIDED INTO TWO DISTINCT TYPES—A HAUGHTY WHITE NORTHERN GROUP AND LARGE BLACK SOUTHERN ONE. BOTH HAD A COMPLETE DIFFERENT CHARACTER, THOUGHT, AND RELIGION.

AND THEY DISLIKED EACH OTHER INTENSELY.

THERE WERE COUNTLESS CONFLICTS.

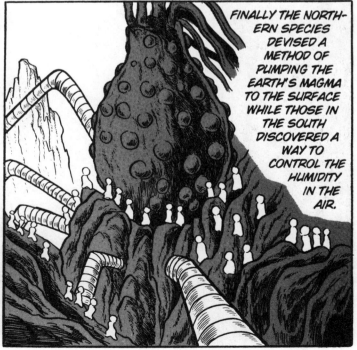

FINALLY THE NORTHERN SPECIES DEVISED A METHOD OF PUMPING THE EARTH'S MAGMA TO THE SURFACE WHILE THOSE IN THE SOUTH DISCOVERED A WAY TO CONTROL THE HUMIDITY IN THE AIR.

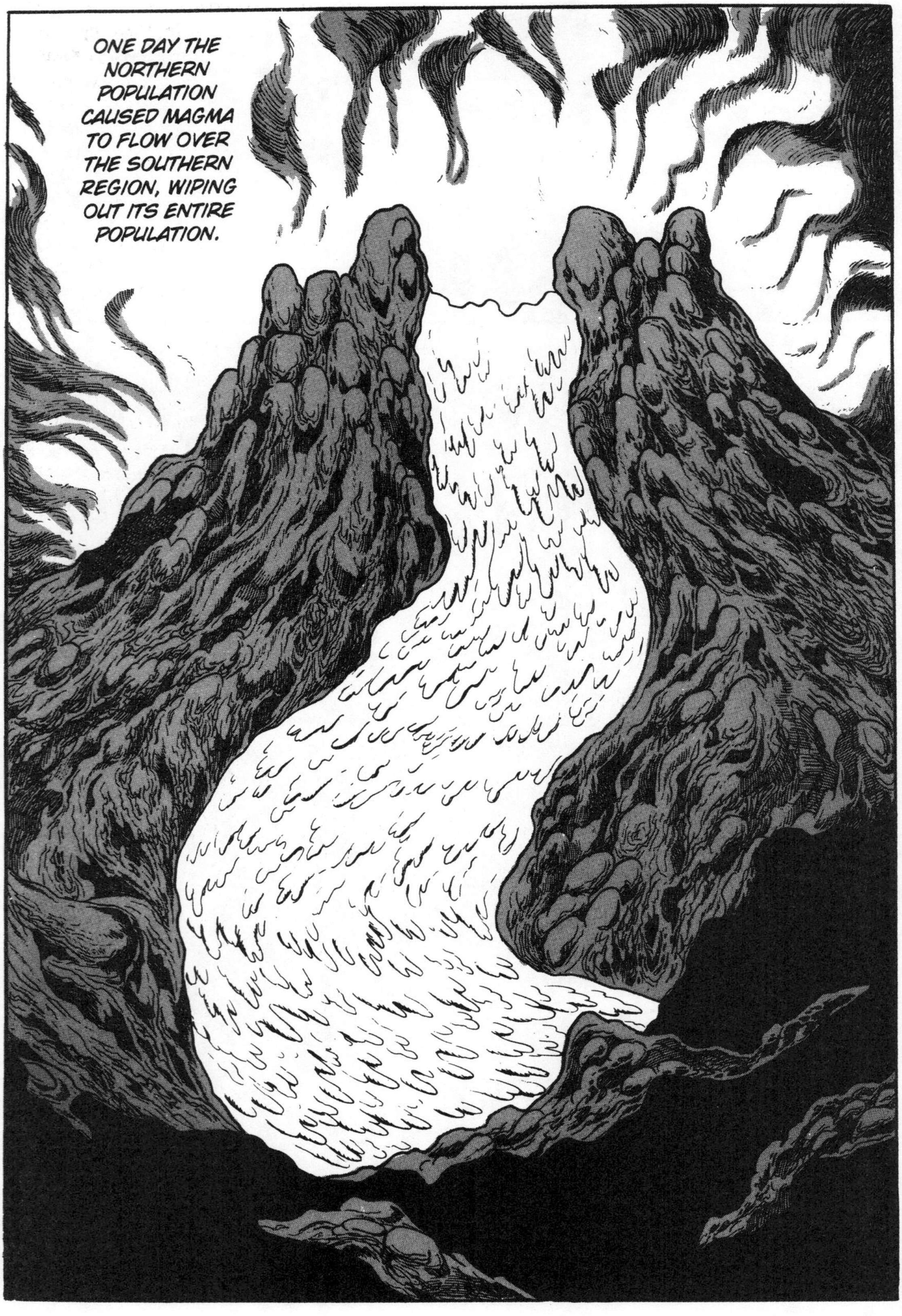
ONE DAY THE NORTHERN POPULATION CAUSED MAGMA TO FLOW OVER THE SOUTHERN REGION, WIPING OUT ITS ENTIRE POPULATION.

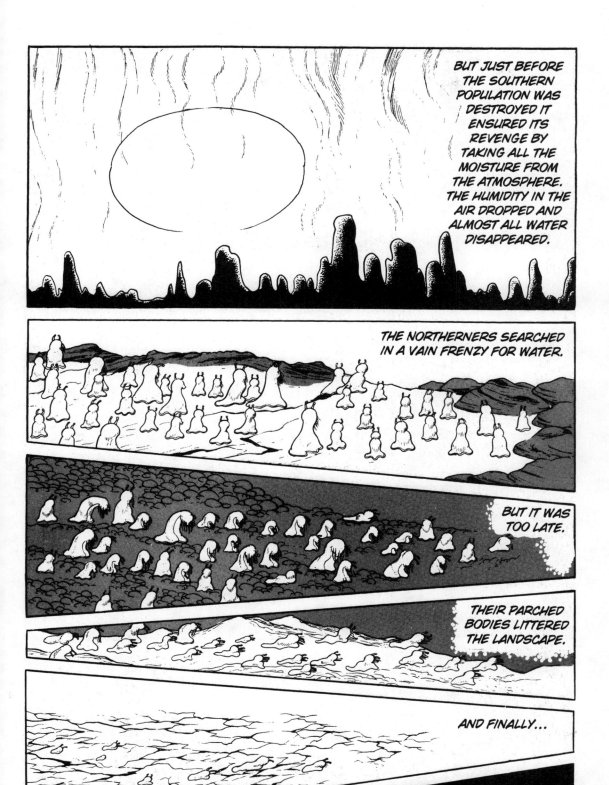

BUT JUST BEFORE THE SOUTHERN POPULATION WAS DESTROYED IT ENSURED ITS REVENGE BY TAKING ALL THE MOISTURE FROM THE ATMOSPHERE. THE HUMIDITY IN THE AIR DROPPED AND ALMOST ALL WATER DISAPPEARED.

THE NORTHERNERS SEARCHED IN A VAIN FRENZY FOR WATER.

BUT IT WAS TOO LATE.

THEIR PARCHED BODIES LITTERED THE LANDSCAPE.

AND FINALLY...

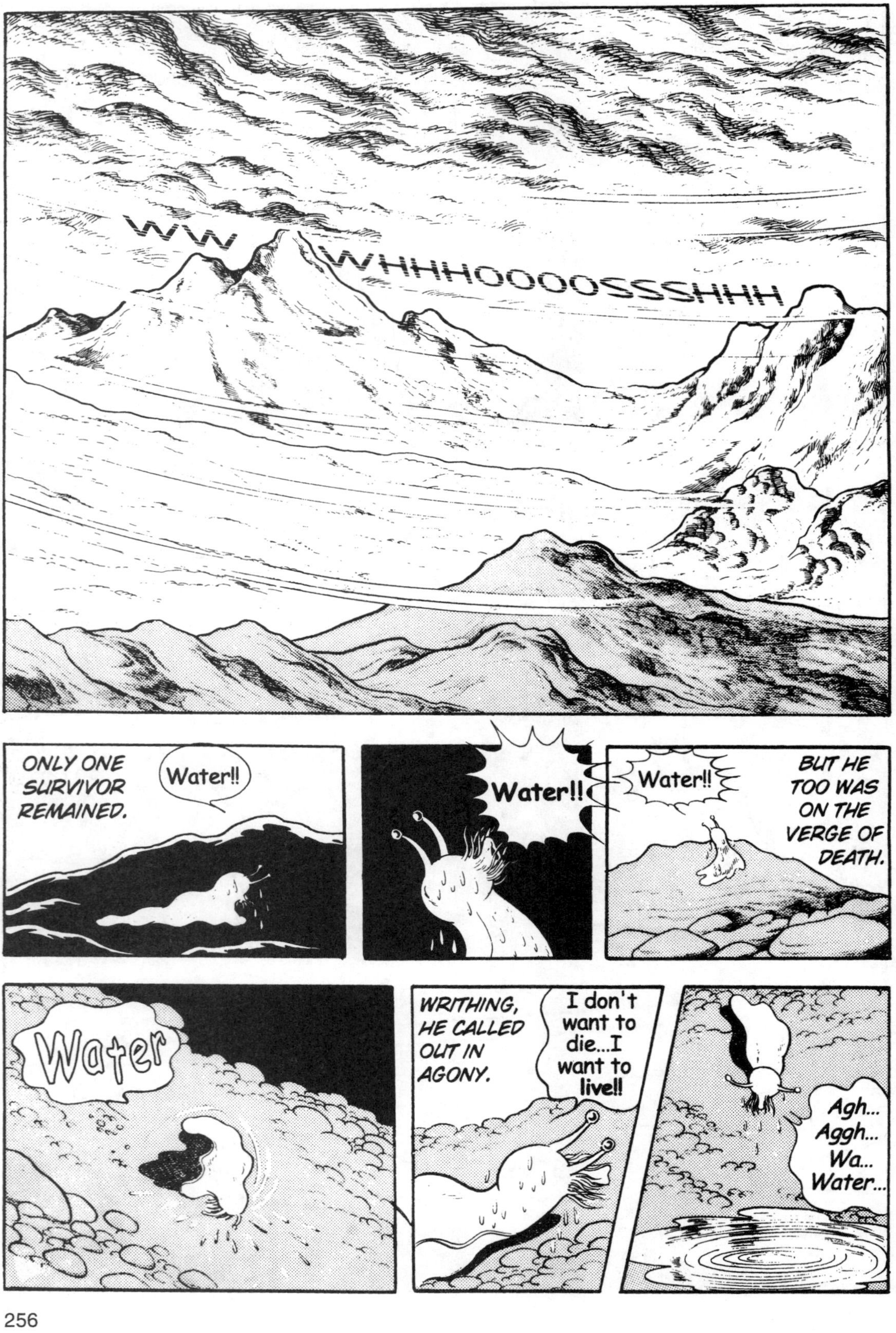
WW WHHHOOOOSSSSHHH
ONLY ONE SURVIVOR REMAINED.
Water!!
Water!!
Water!!
BUT HE TOO WAS ON THE VERGE OF DEATH.
Water
WRITHING, HE CALLED OUT IN AGONY.
I don't want to die...I want to live!!
Agh... Aggh... Wa... Water...

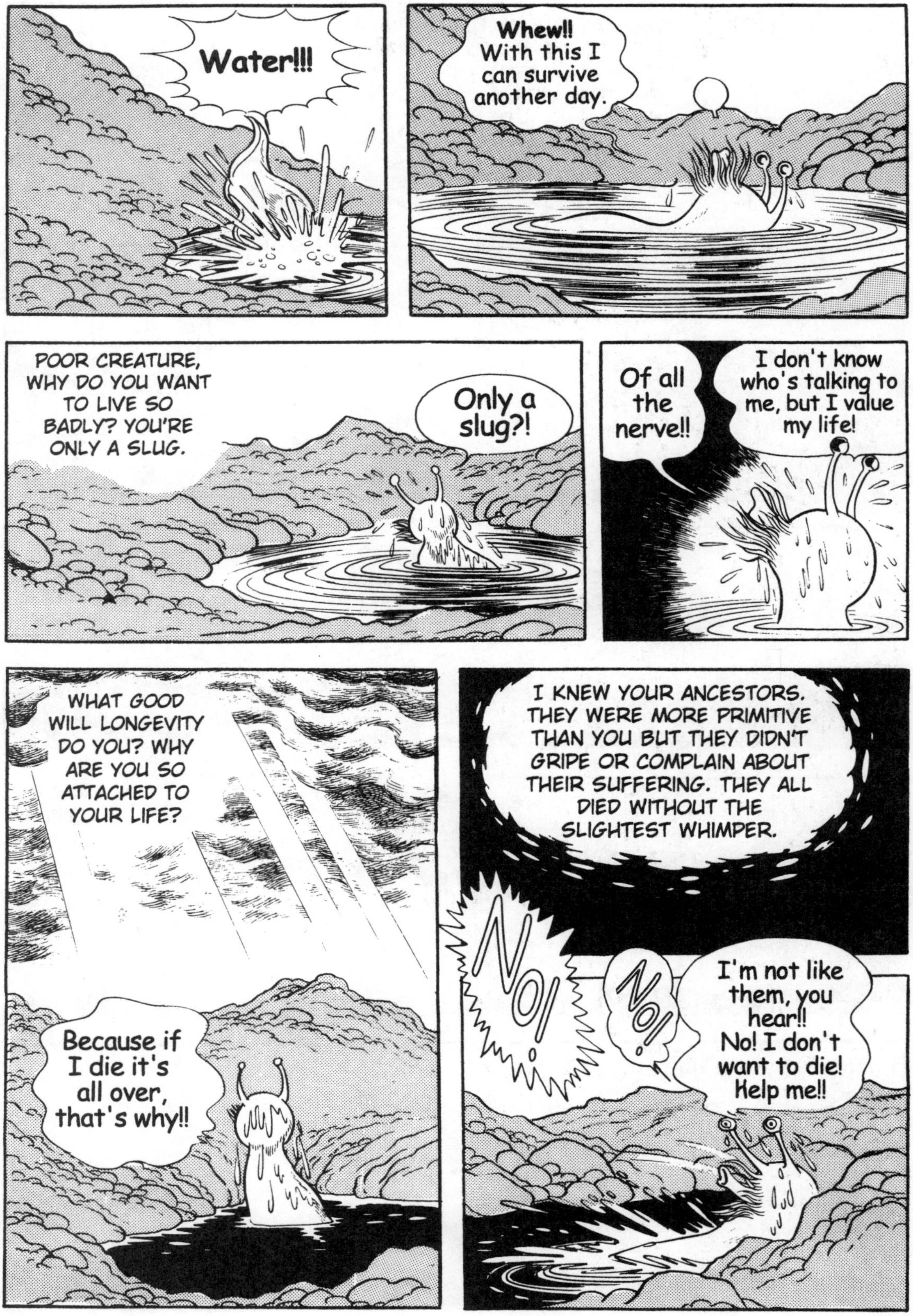
Water!!!
Whew!! With this I can survive another day.
POOR CREATURE, WHY DO YOU WANT TO LIVE SO BADLY? YOU'RE ONLY A SLUG.
Only a slug?!
Of all the nerve!!
I don't know who's talking to me, but I value my life!
WHAT GOOD WILL LONGEVITY DO YOU? WHY ARE YOU SO ATTACHED TO YOUR LIFE?
Because if I die it's all over, that's why!!
I KNEW YOUR ANCESTORS. THEY WERE MORE PRIMITIVE THAN YOU BUT THEY DIDN'T GRIPE OR COMPLAIN ABOUT THEIR SUFFERING. THEY ALL DIED WITHOUT THE SLIGHTEST WHIMPER.
No!
No!
I'm not like them, you hear!! No! I don't want to die! Help me!!

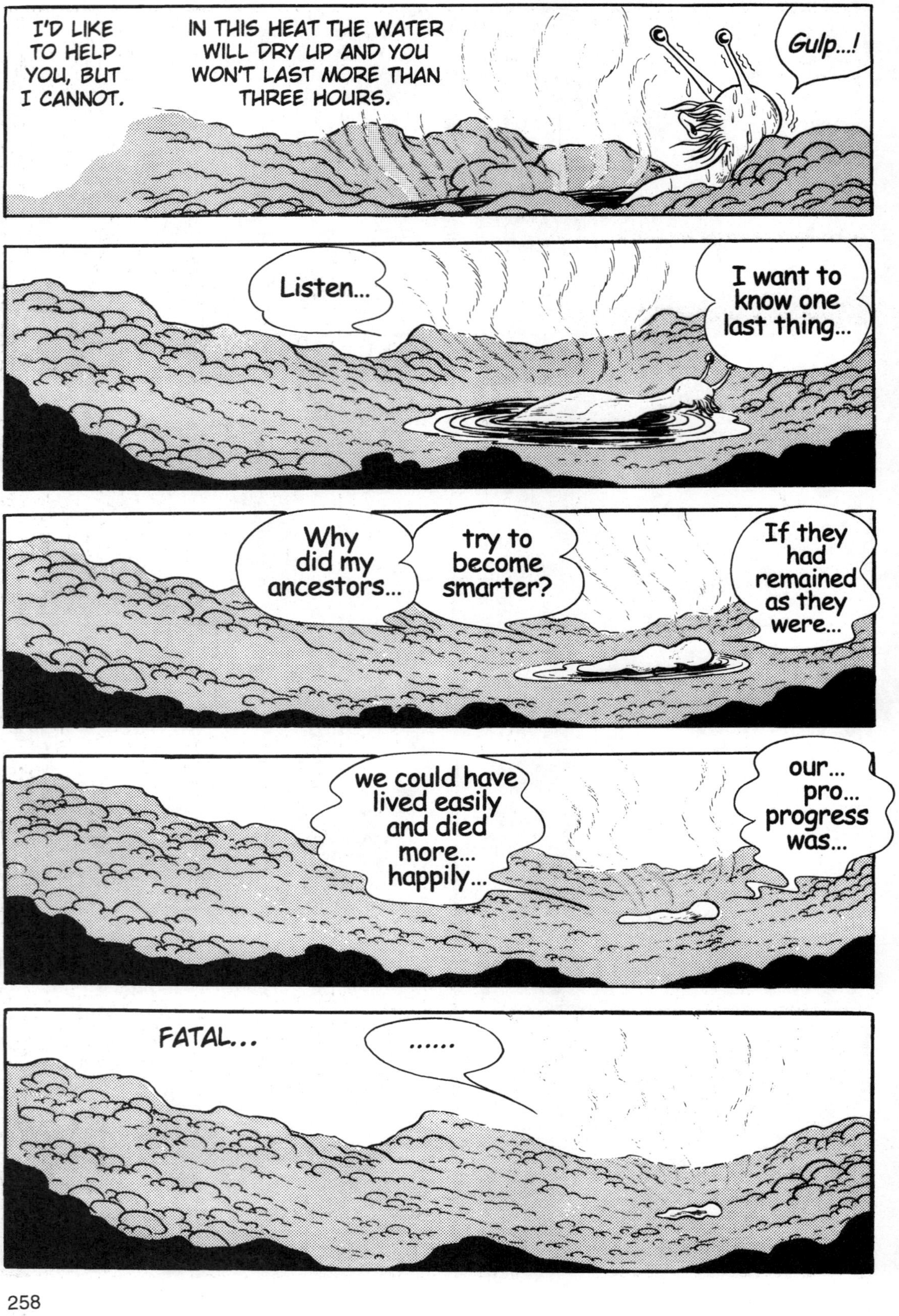
I'D LIKE TO HELP YOU, BUT I CANNOT.
IN THIS HEAT THE WATER WILL DRY UP AND YOU WON'T LAST MORE THAN THREE HOURS.
Gulp...!
Listen...
I want to know one last thing...
Why did my ancestors...
try to become smarter?
If they had remained as they were...
we could have lived easily and died more... happily...
our... pro... progress was...
FATAL...
......

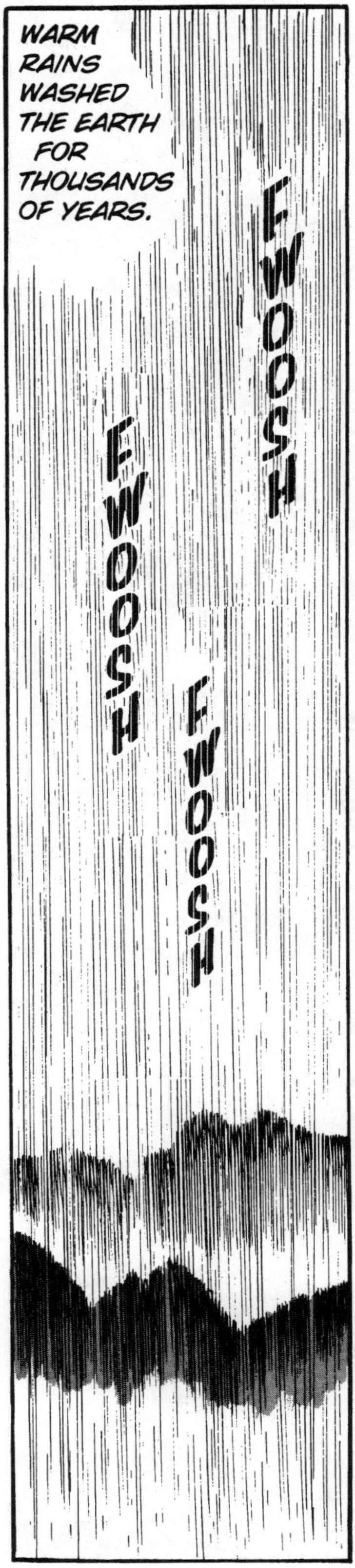
WARM RAINS WASHED THE EARTH FOR THOUSANDS OF YEARS.
FWOOSH
FWOOSH
FWOOSH
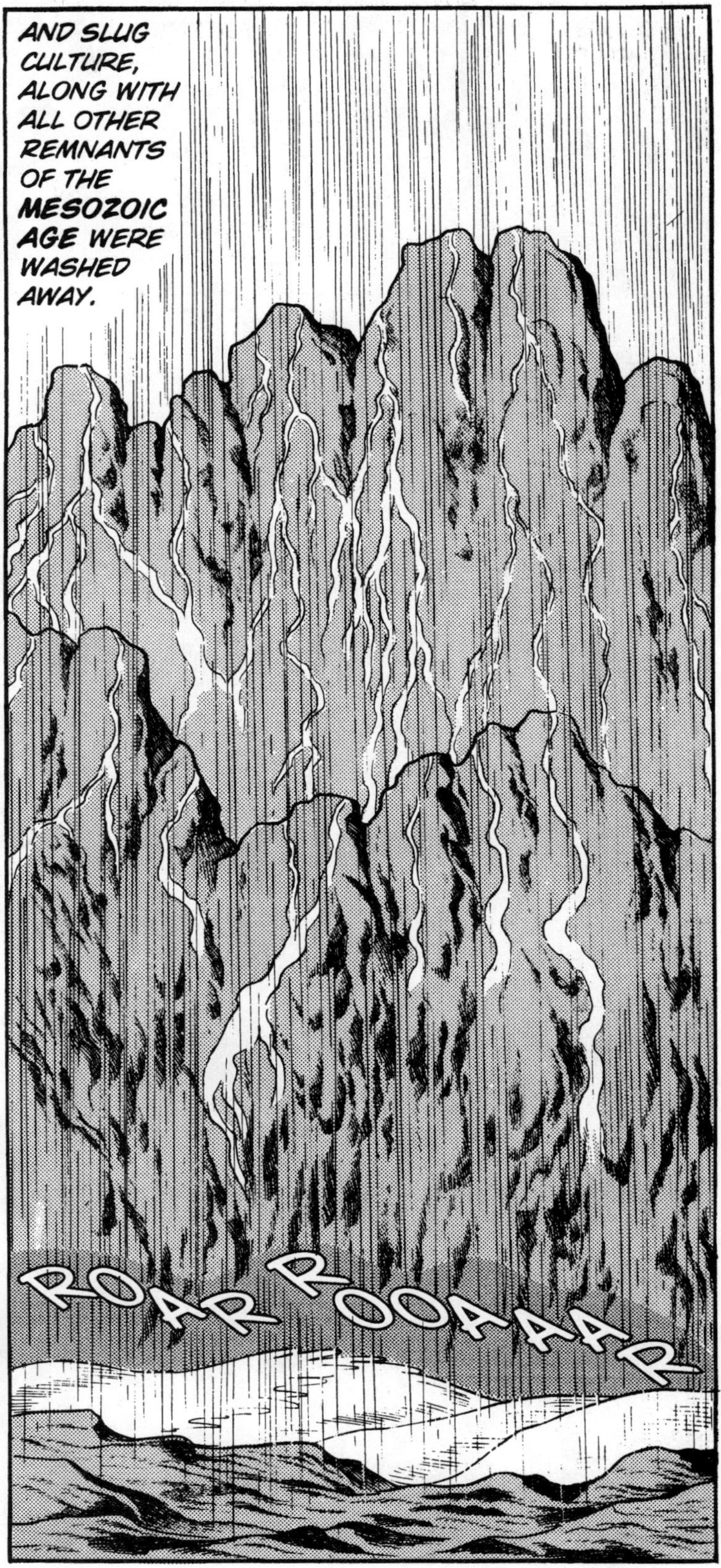
AND SLUG CULTURE, ALONG WITH ALL OTHER REMNANTS OF THE **MESOZOIC AGE** WERE WASHED AWAY.
ROAR ROOAAAR

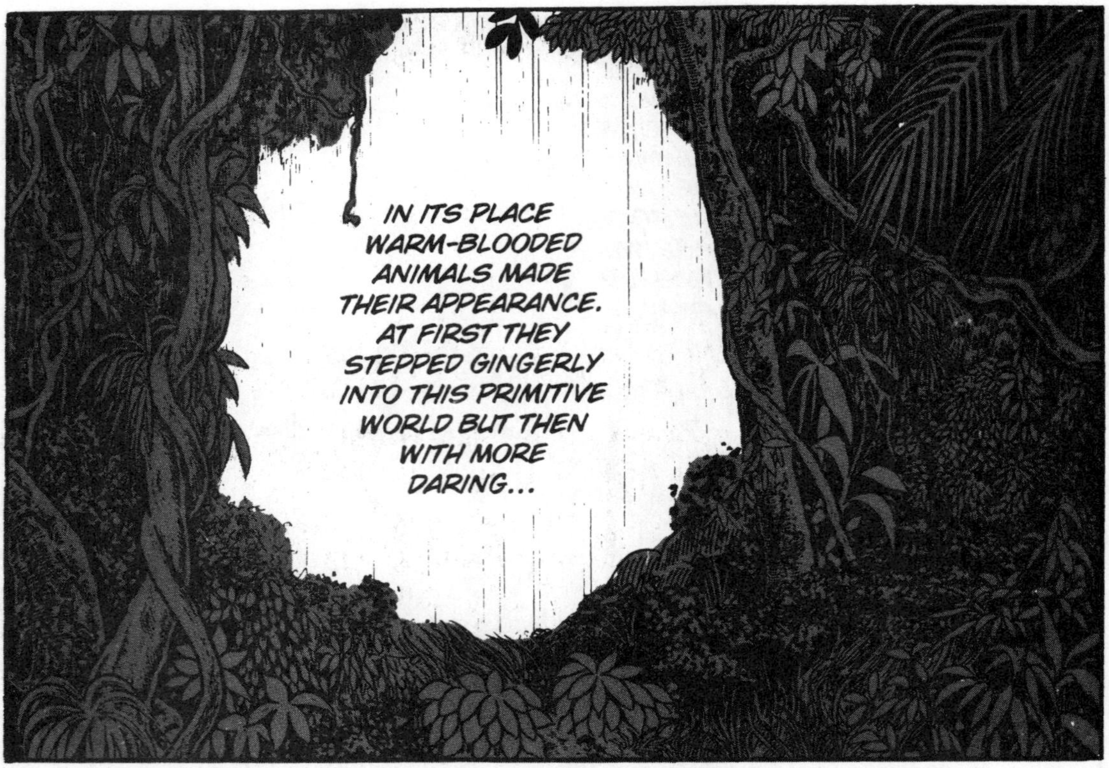
IN ITS PLACE WARM-BLOODED ANIMALS MADE THEIR APPEARANCE. AT FIRST THEY STEPPED GINGERLY INTO THIS PRIMITIVE WORLD BUT THEN WITH MORE DARING...
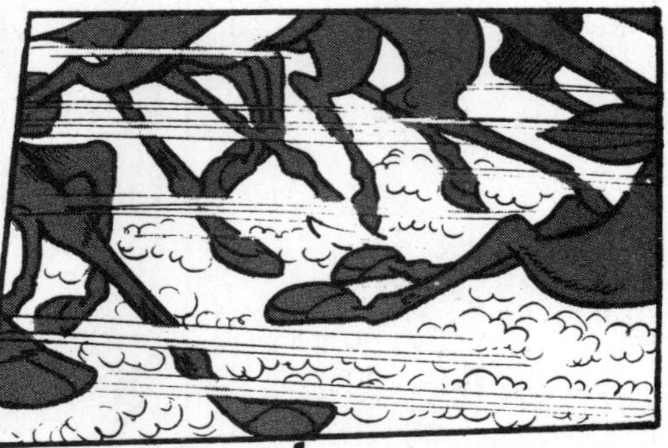
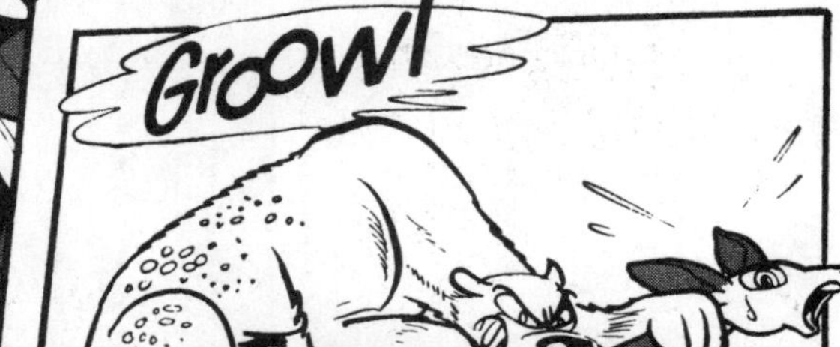
Groowl
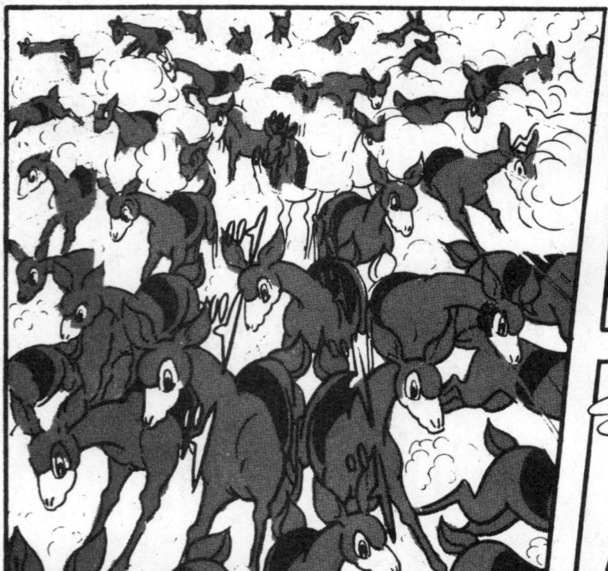

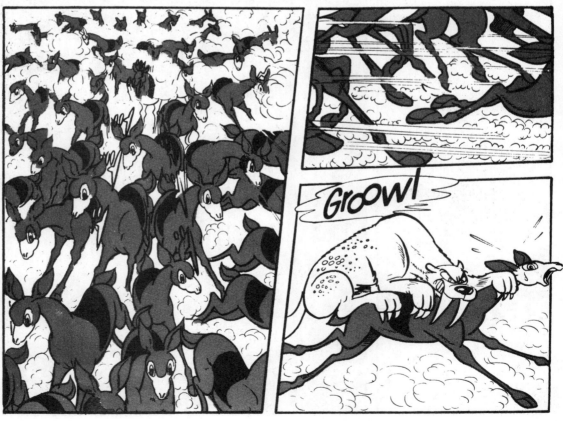

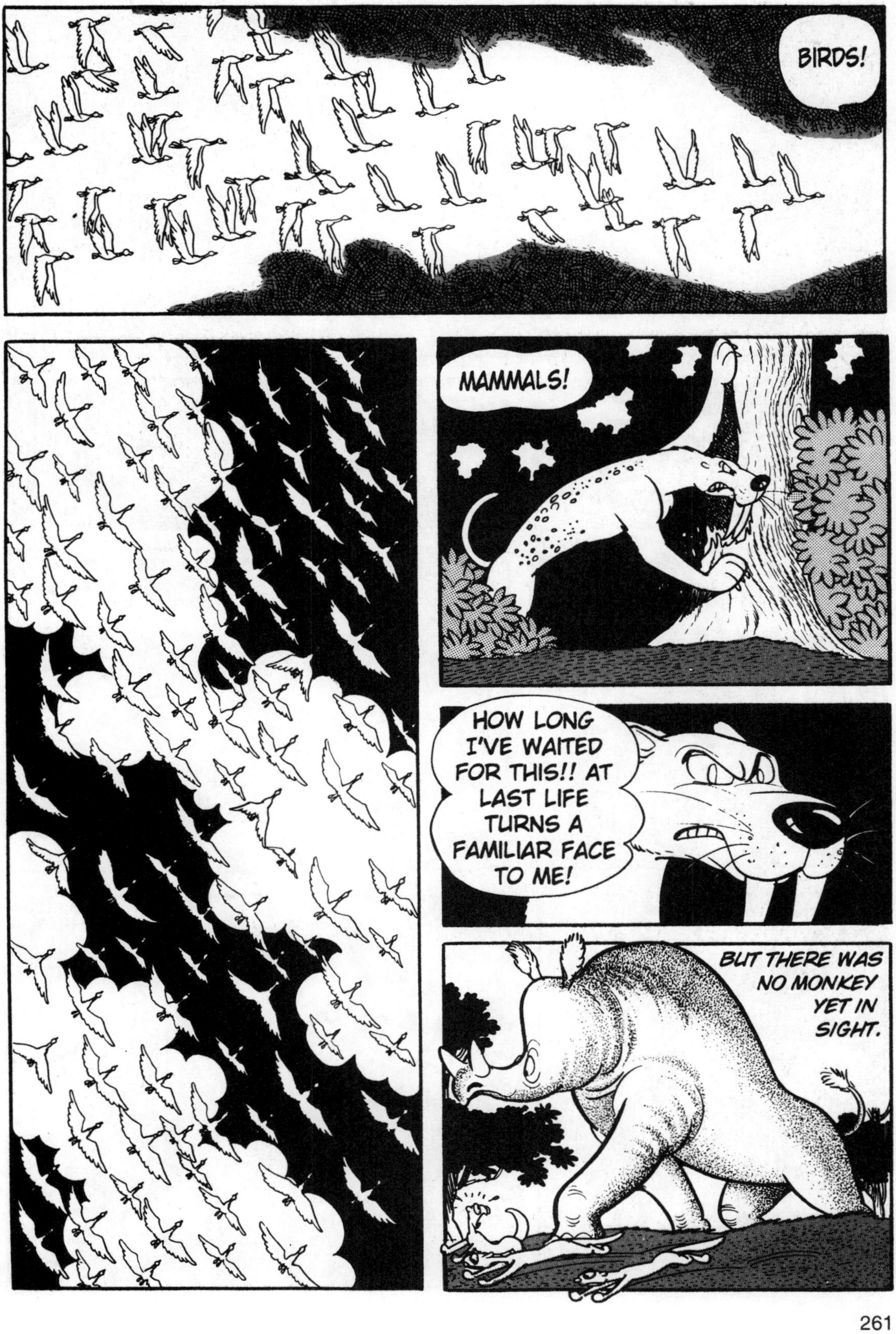
BIRDS!
MAMMALS!
HOW LONG I'VE WAITED FOR THIS!! AT LAST LIFE TURNS A FAMILIAR FACE TO ME!
BUT THERE WAS NO MONKEY YET IN SIGHT.

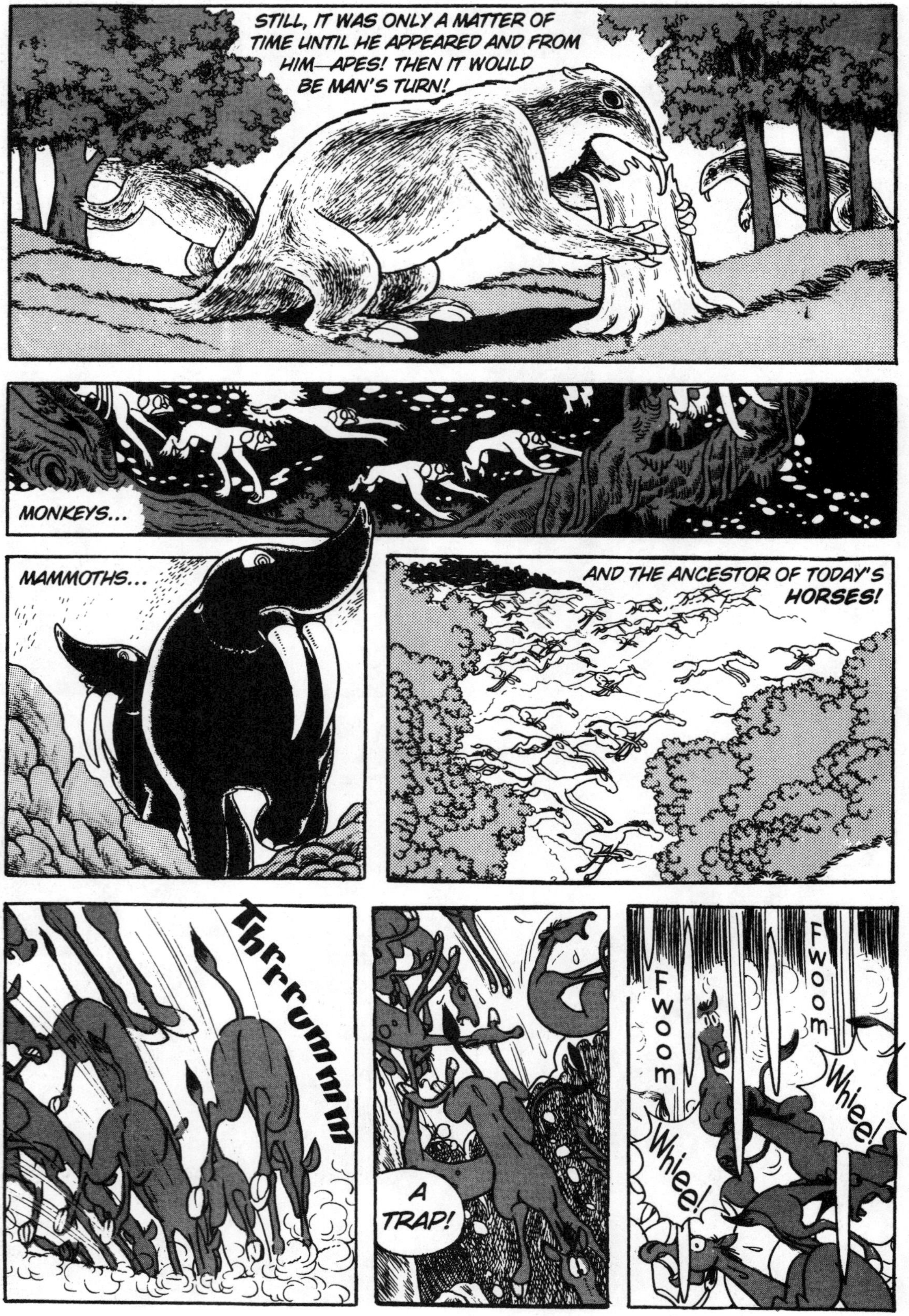
STILL, IT WAS ONLY A MATTER OF TIME UNTIL HE APPEARED AND FROM HIM—APES! THEN IT WOULD BE MAN'S TURN!
MONKEYS...
MAMMOTHS...
AND THE ANCESTOR OF TODAY'S HORSES!
Thrrrummm
A TRAP!
Fwoom
Fwoom
Whiee!
Whiee!

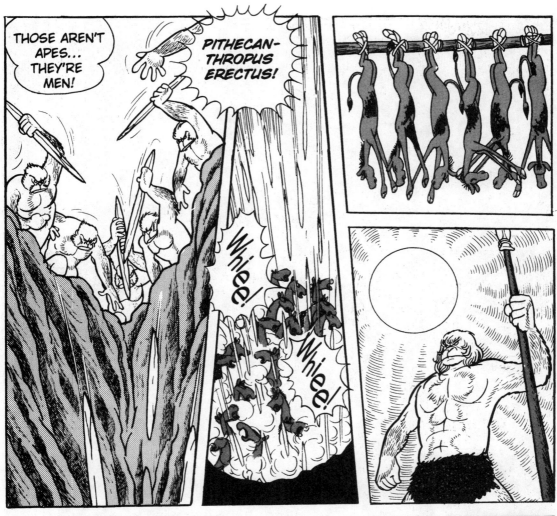

THOSE AREN'T APES... THEY'RE MEN!

PITHECAN-THROPUS ERECTUS!

Whiee!

Whiee!

MAN QUICKLY EVOLVED FROM **NEANDERTHAL** TO **CRO-MAGNON.**

263

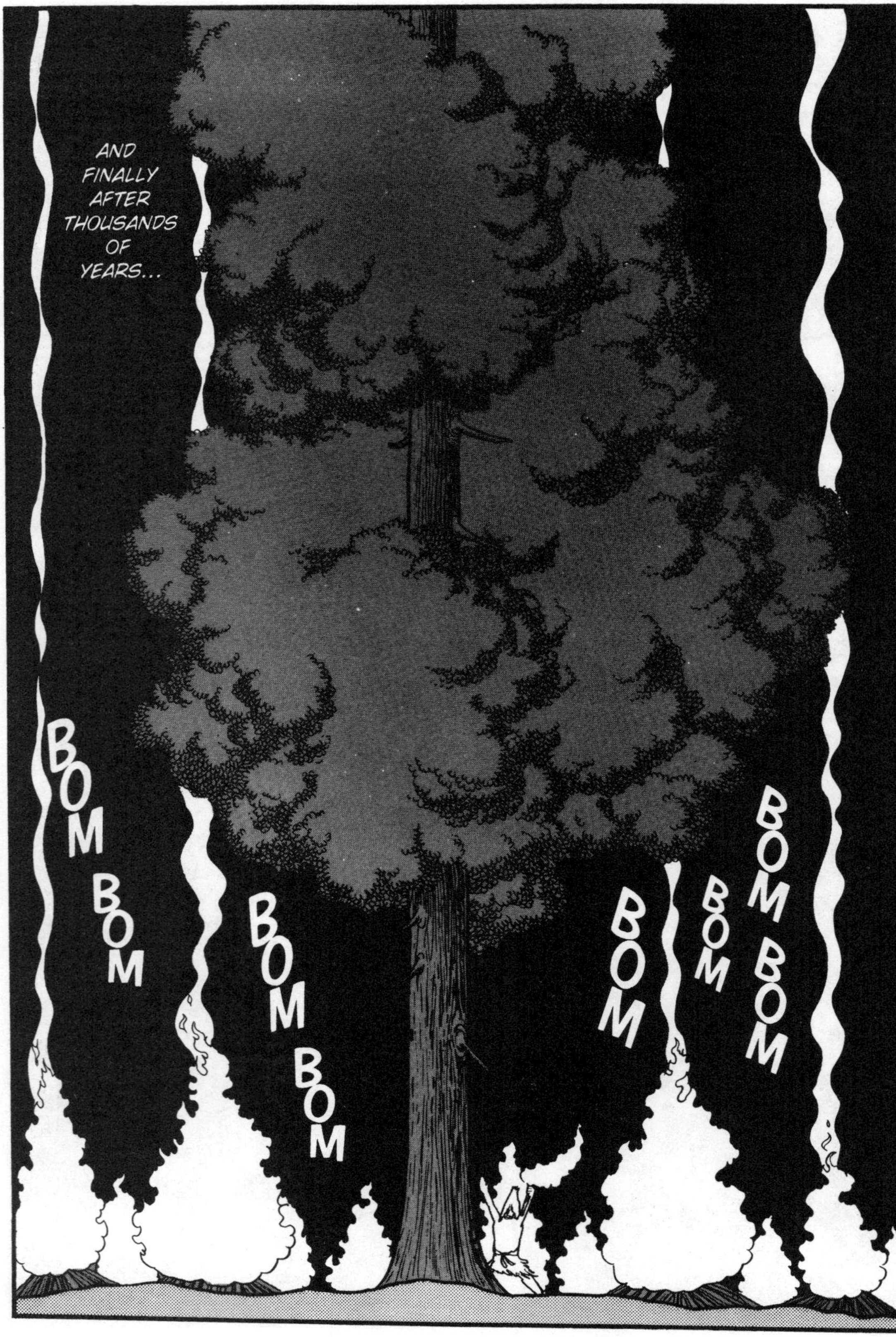
AND FINALLY AFTER THOUSANDS OF YEARS...
BOM BOM BOM
BOM BOM BOM
BOM BOM BOM
BOM BOM
BOM

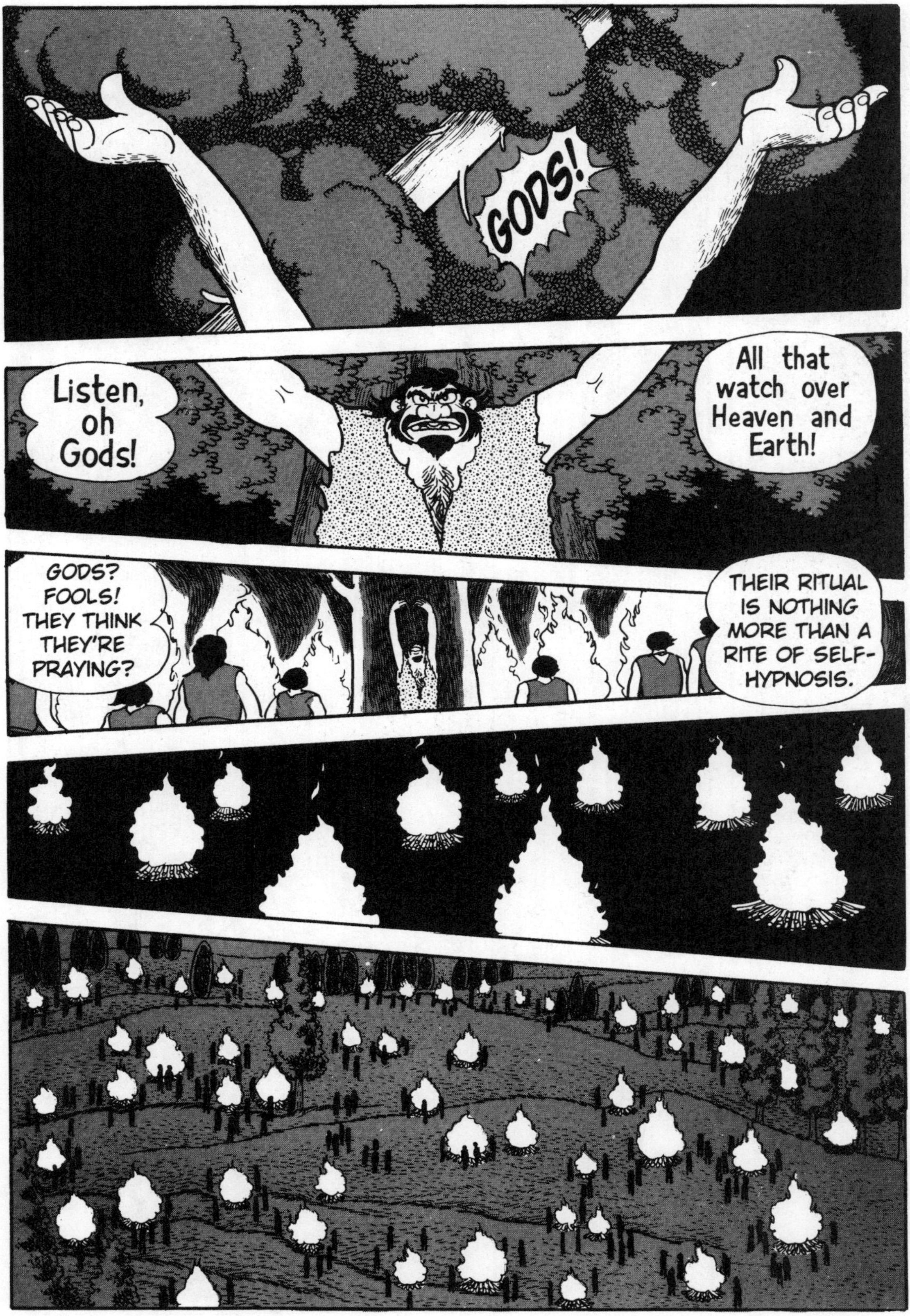
GODS!
Listen, oh Gods!
All that watch over Heaven and Earth!
GODS? FOOLS! THEY THINK THEY'RE PRAYING?
THEIR RITUAL IS NOTHING MORE THAN A RITE OF SELF-HYPNOSIS.

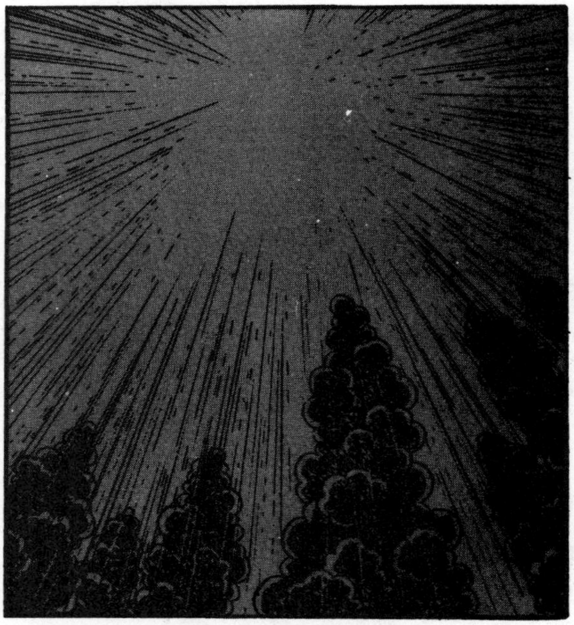
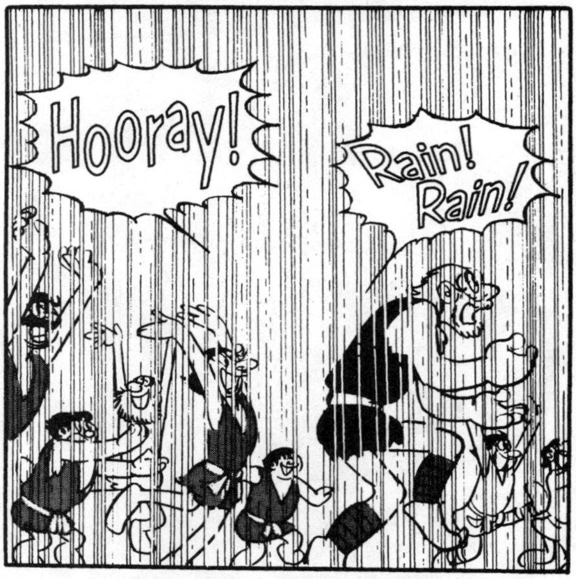
Rain! Rain!
Hooray!
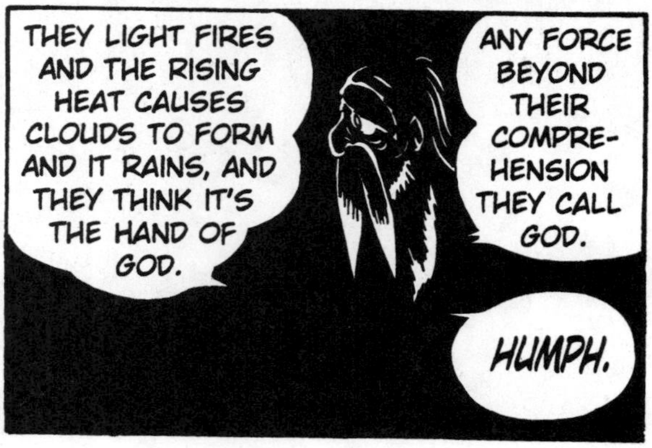
ANY FORCE BEYOND THEIR COMPREHENSION THEY CALL GOD.
THEY LIGHT FIRES AND THE RISING HEAT CAUSES CLOUDS TO FORM AND IT RAINS, AND THEY THINK IT'S THE HAND OF GOD.
HUMPH.
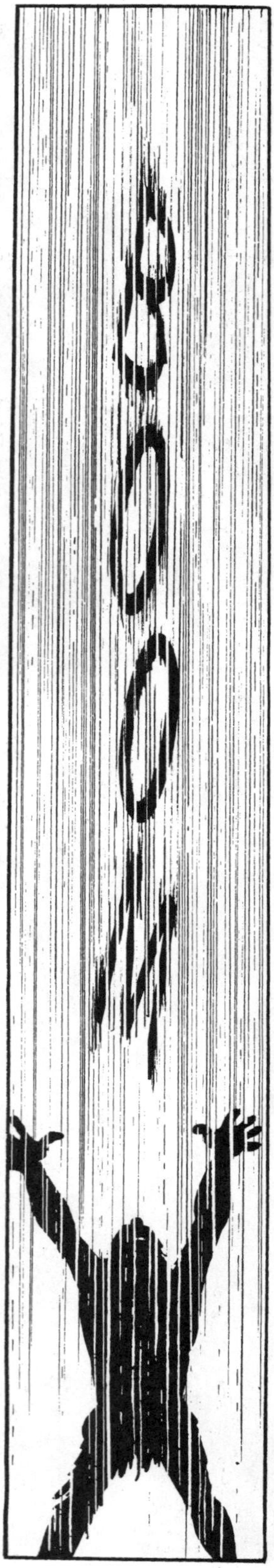
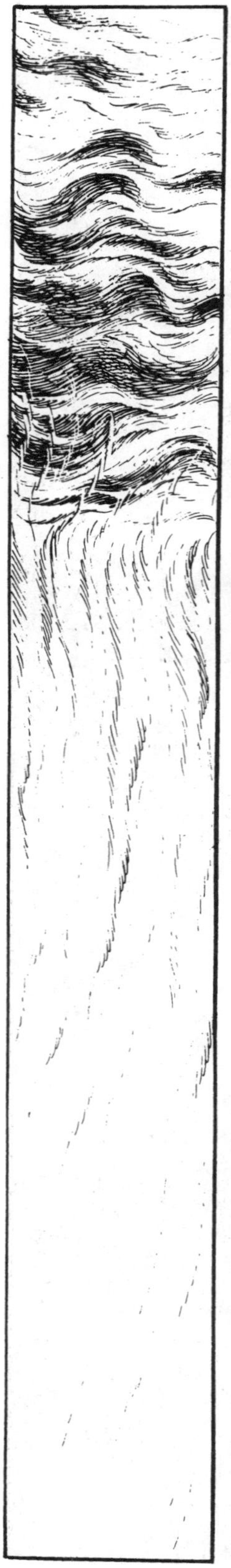

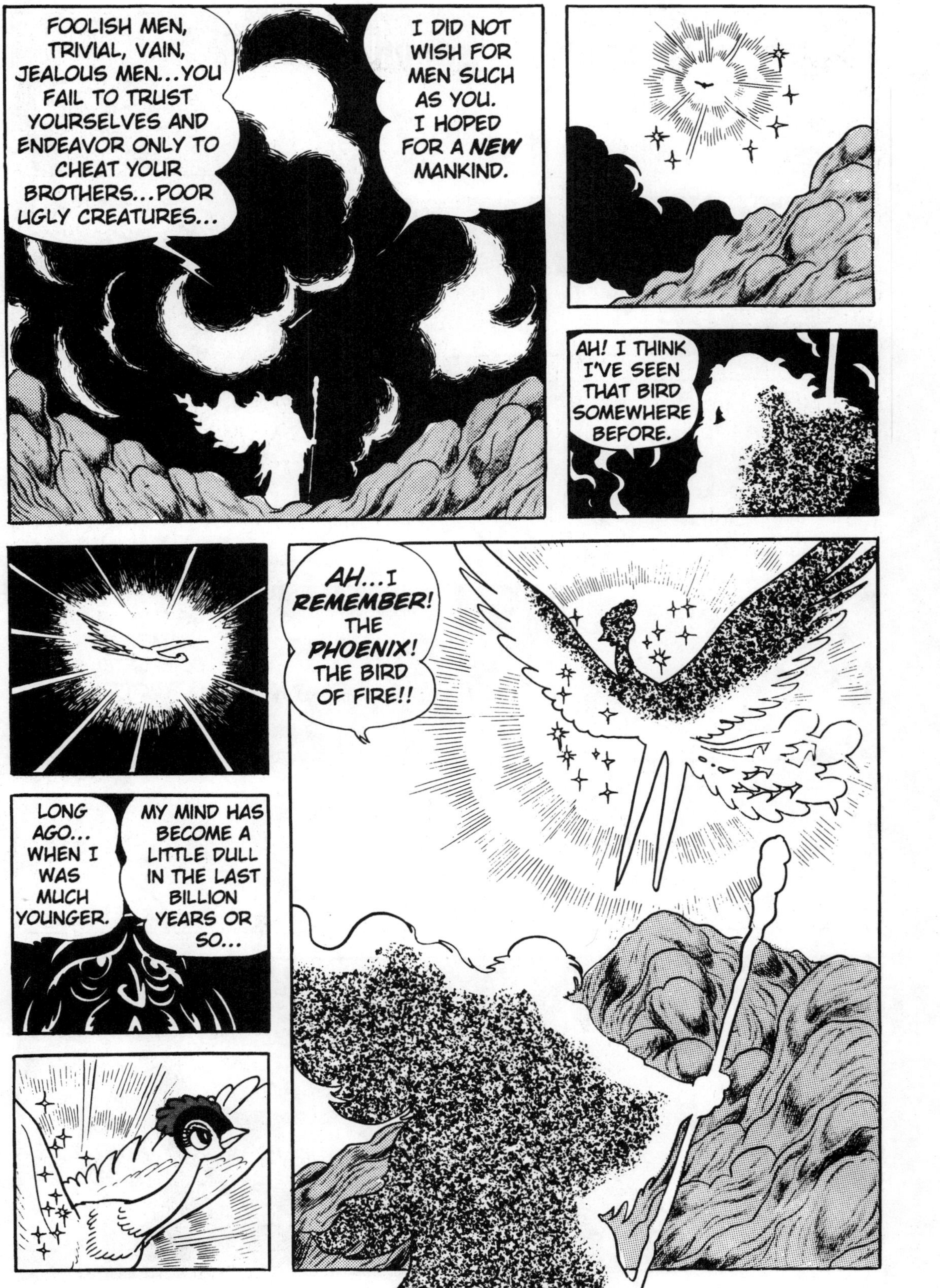
FOOLISH MEN, TRIVIAL, VAIN, JEALOUS MEN...YOU FAIL TO TRUST YOURSELVES AND ENDEAVOR ONLY TO CHEAT YOUR BROTHERS...POOR UGLY CREATURES...
I DID NOT WISH FOR MEN SUCH AS YOU. I HOPED FOR A *NEW* MANKIND.
AH! I THINK I'VE SEEN THAT BIRD SOMEWHERE BEFORE.
AH...I *REMEMBER!* THE *PHOENIX!* THE BIRD OF FIRE!!
LONG AGO... WHEN I WAS MUCH YOUNGER.
MY MIND HAS BECOME A LITTLE DULL IN THE LAST BILLION YEARS OR SO...

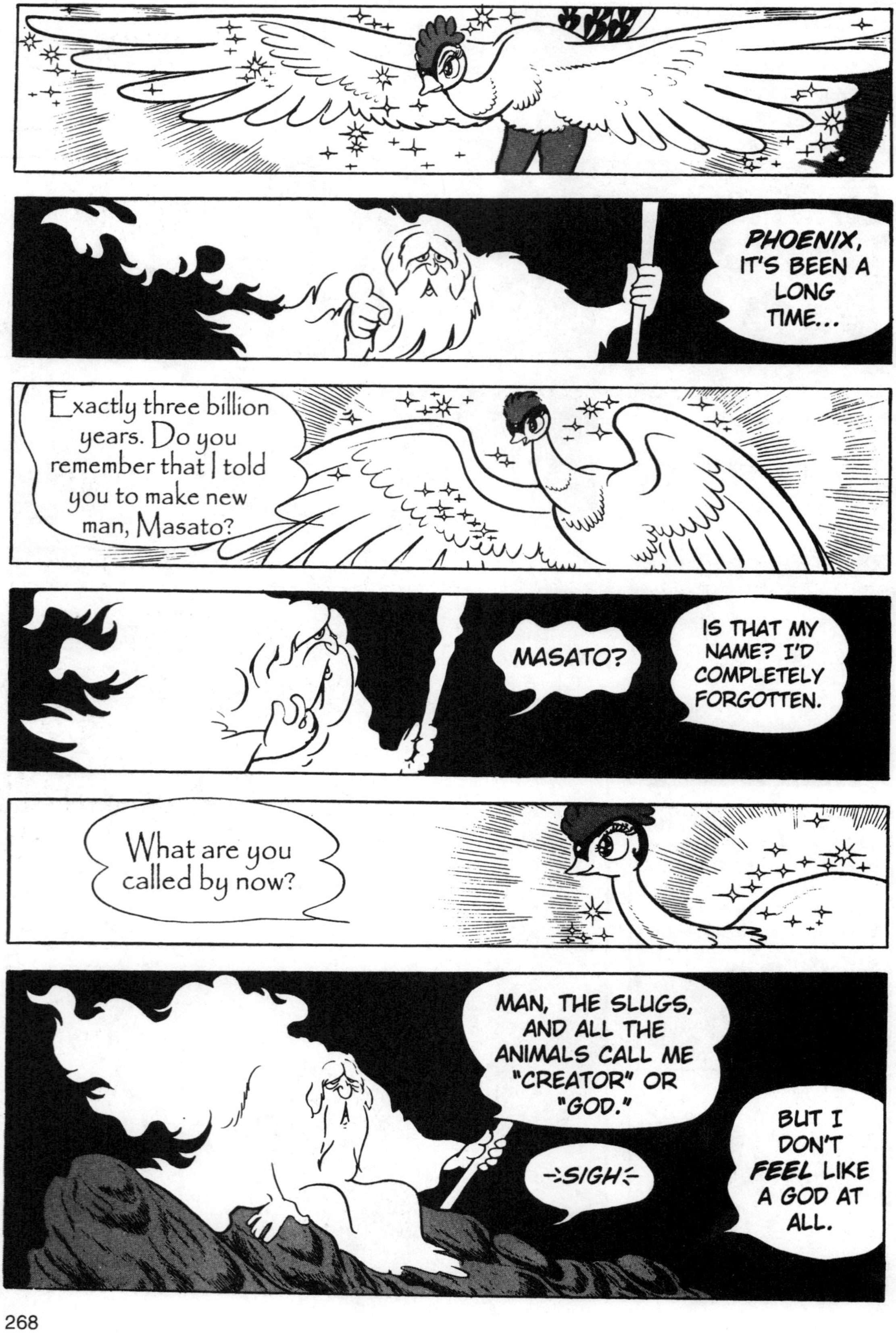
PHOENIX, IT'S BEEN A LONG TIME...
Exactly three billion years. Do you remember that I told you to make new man, Masato?
MASATO?
IS THAT MY NAME? I'D COMPLETELY FORGOTTEN.
What are you called by now?
MAN, THE SLUGS, AND ALL THE ANIMALS CALL ME "CREATOR" OR "GOD."
-SIGH-
BUT I DON'T FEEL LIKE A GOD AT ALL.

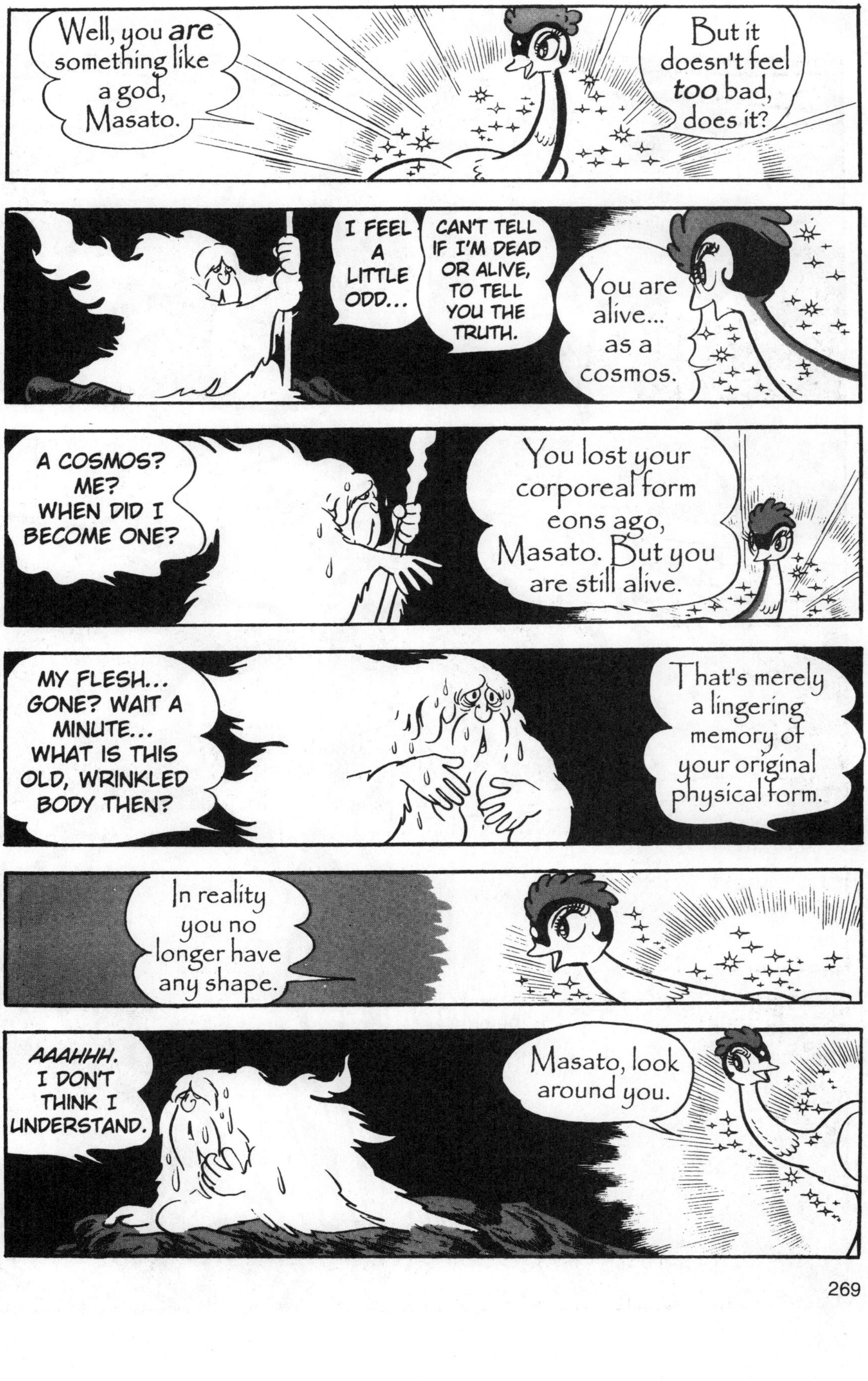
Well, you are something like a god, Masato.
But it doesn't feel too bad, does it?
I FEEL A LITTLE ODD...
CAN'T TELL IF I'M DEAD OR ALIVE, TO TELL YOU THE TRUTH.
You are alive... as a cosmos.
A COSMOS? ME? WHEN DID I BECOME ONE?
You lost your corporeal form eons ago, Masato. But you are still alive.
MY FLESH... GONE? WAIT A MINUTE... WHAT IS THIS OLD, WRINKLED BODY THEN?
That's merely a lingering memory of your original physical form.
In reality you no longer have any shape.
AAAHHH. I DON'T THINK I UNDERSTAND.
Masato, look around you.

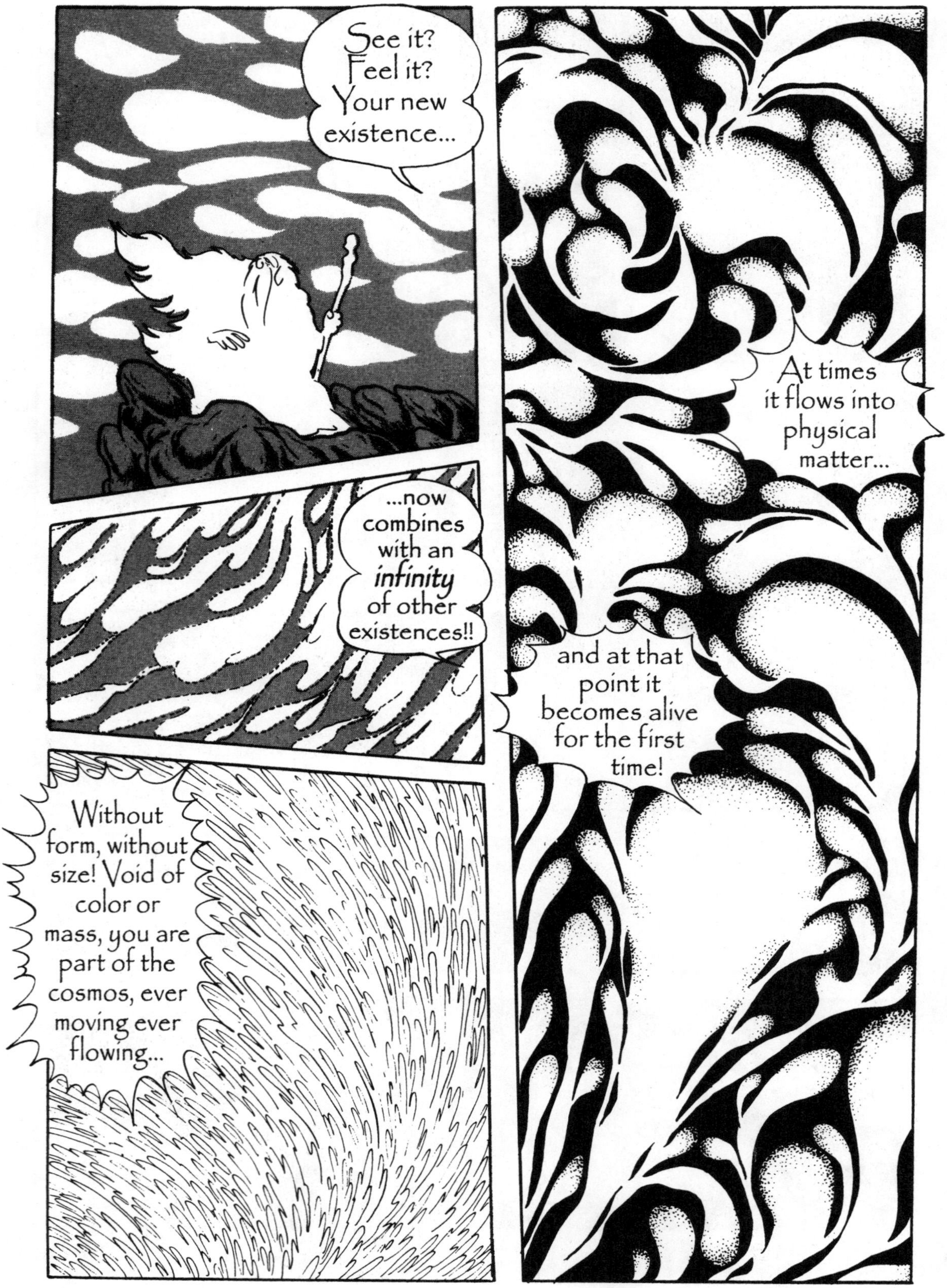
See it? Feel it? Your new existence...
...now combines with an *infinity* of other existences!!
Without form, without size! Void of color or mass, you are part of the cosmos, ever moving ever flowing...
At times it flows into physical matter...
and at that point it becomes alive for the first time!

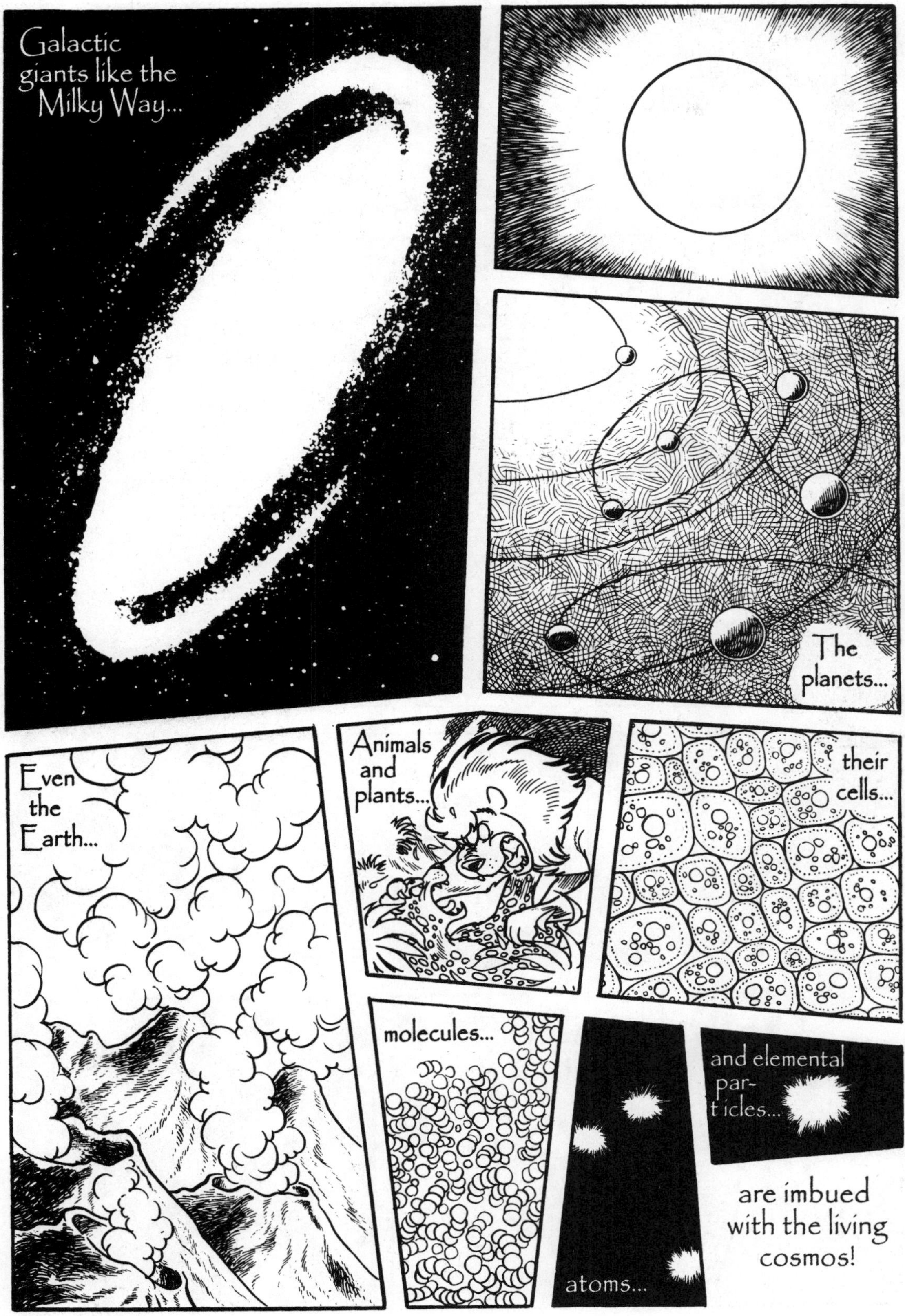
Galactic giants like the Milky Way...
The planets...
Even the Earth...
Animals and plants...
their cells...
molecules...
atoms...
and elemental par- ticles...
are imbued with the living cosmos!

Masato, forget your image of an old, wizened man.
I'M THE COSMOS?
IF... IF I AM...
IS THERE SOMETHING I SHOULD DO?
Yes! You are to watch over the new human race!
And therefore you are in need of a physical form.
You shall become part of me!!
PART OF YOU? HOW? YOU'RE ALIVE!
I am the Cosmos... enter me!
Come, Masato!
Enter me!

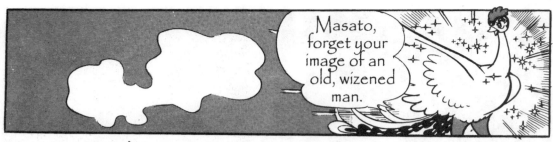

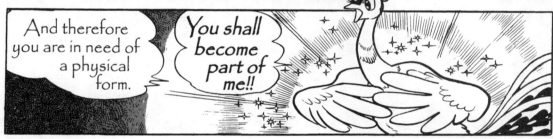

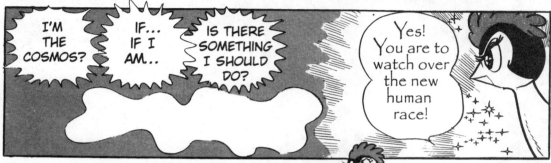

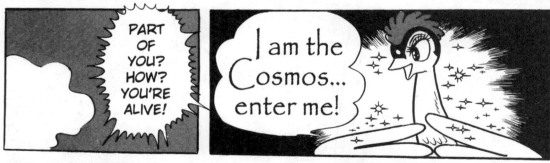

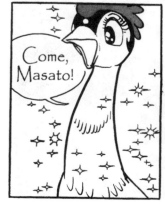

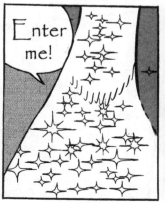

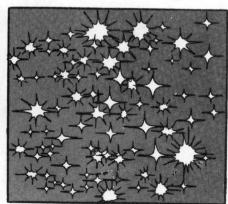

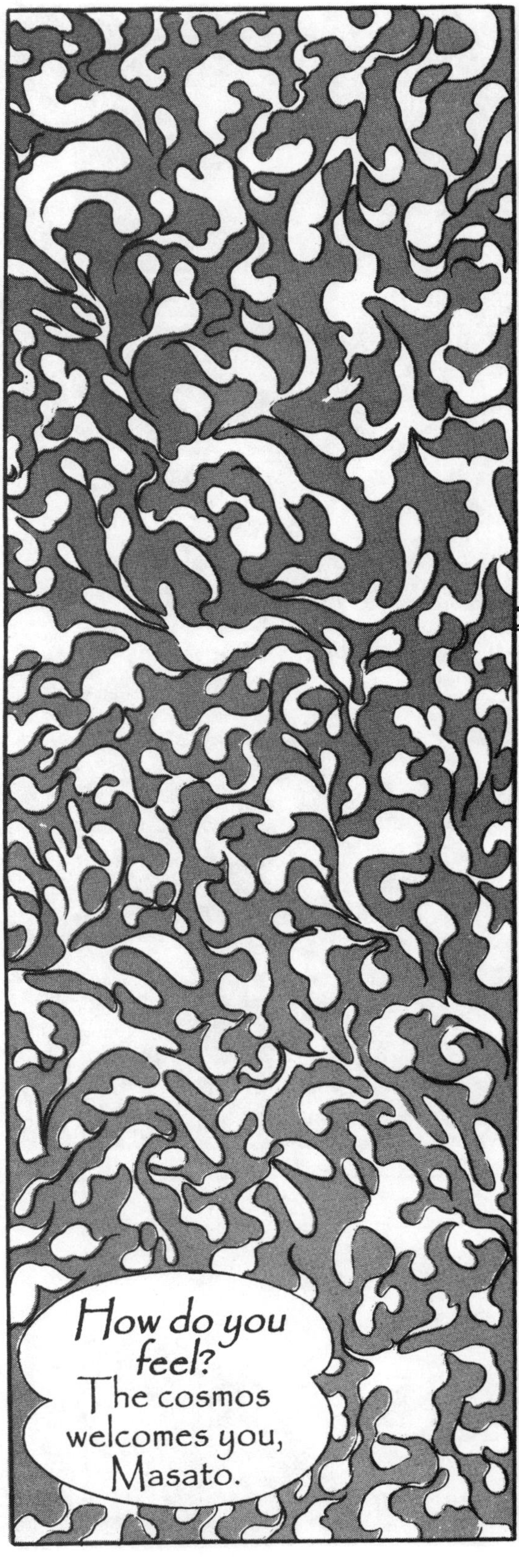
How do you feel? The cosmos welcomes you, Masato.
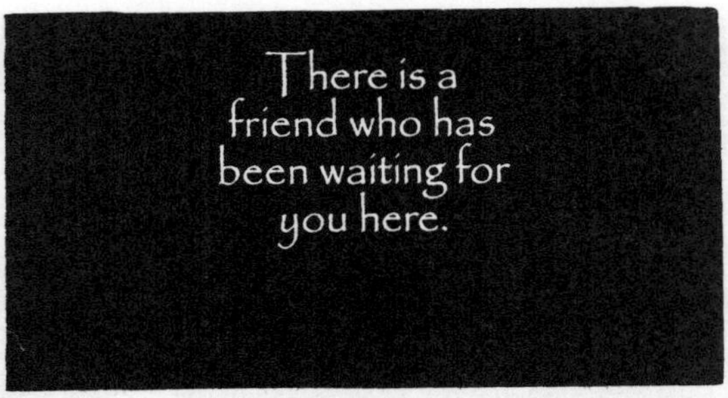
There is a friend who has been waiting for you here.
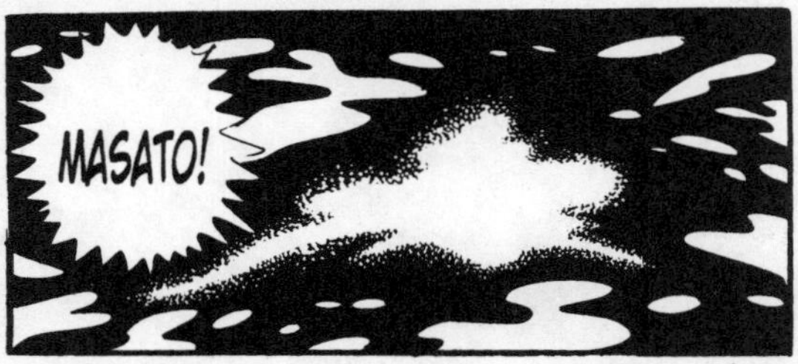
MASATO!
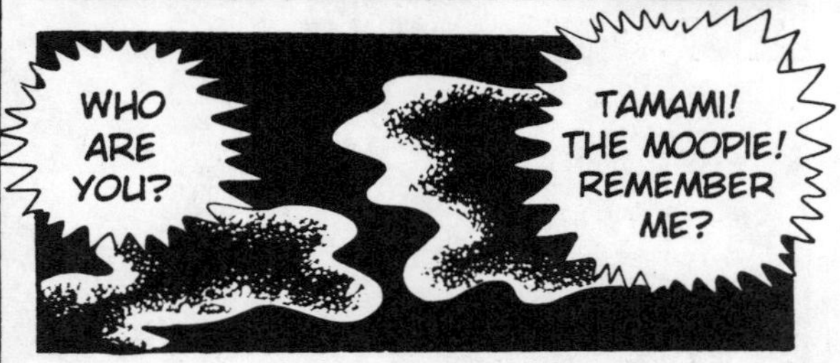
WHO ARE YOU?
TAMAMI! THE MOOPIE! REMEMBER ME?
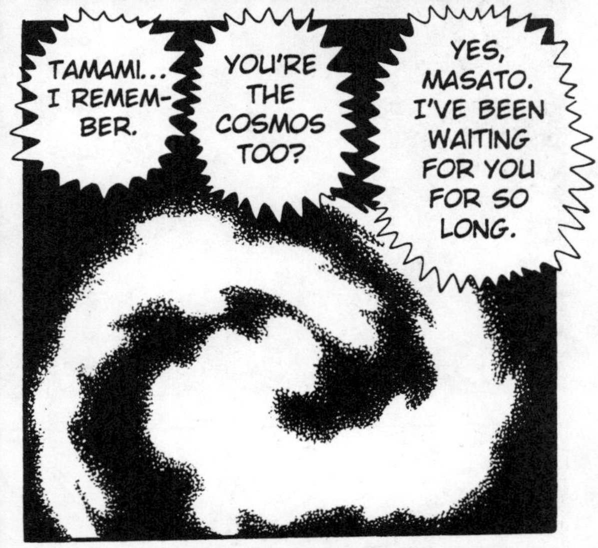
TAMAMI... I REMEMBER.
YOU'RE THE COSMOS TOO?
YES, MASATO. I'VE BEEN WAITING FOR YOU FOR SO LONG.
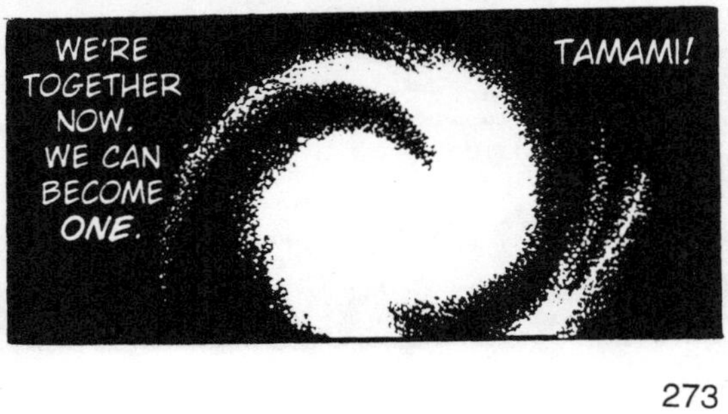
TAMAMI!
WE'RE TOGETHER NOW. WE CAN BECOME *ONE*.

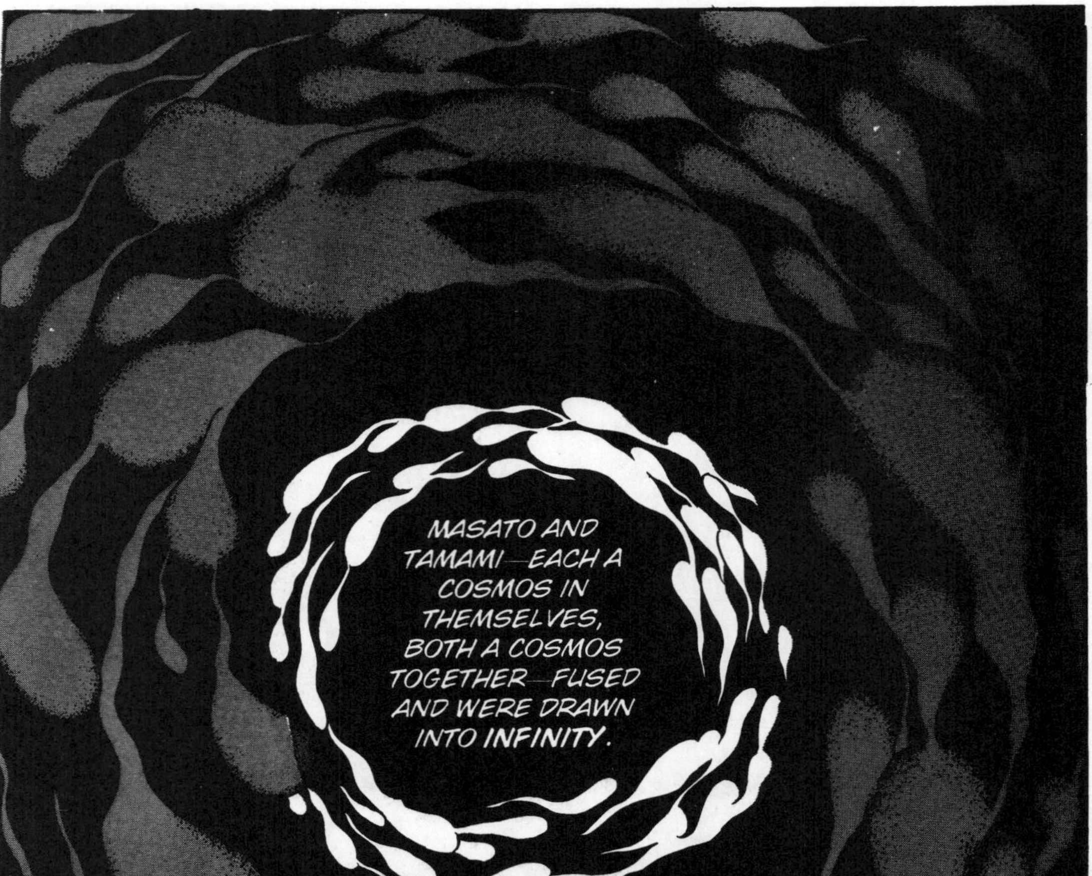
MASATO AND TAMAMI—EACH A COSMOS IN THEMSELVES, BOTH A COSMOS TOGETHER—FUSED AND WERE DRAWN INTO INFINITY.
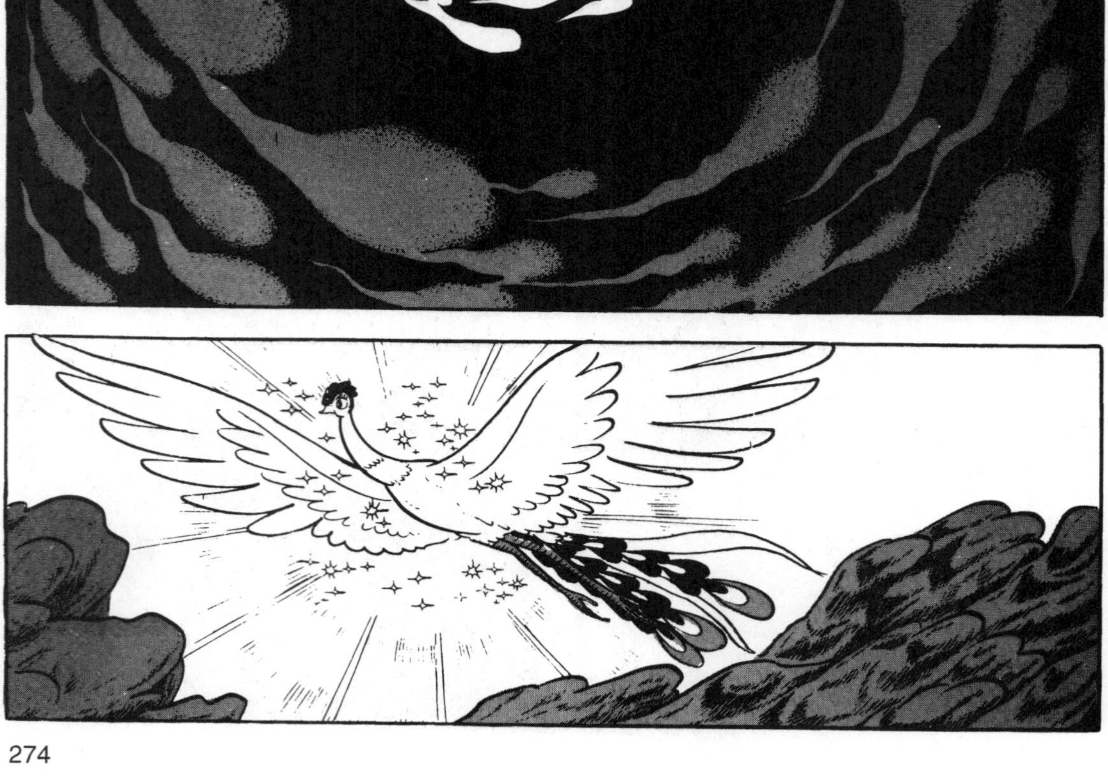

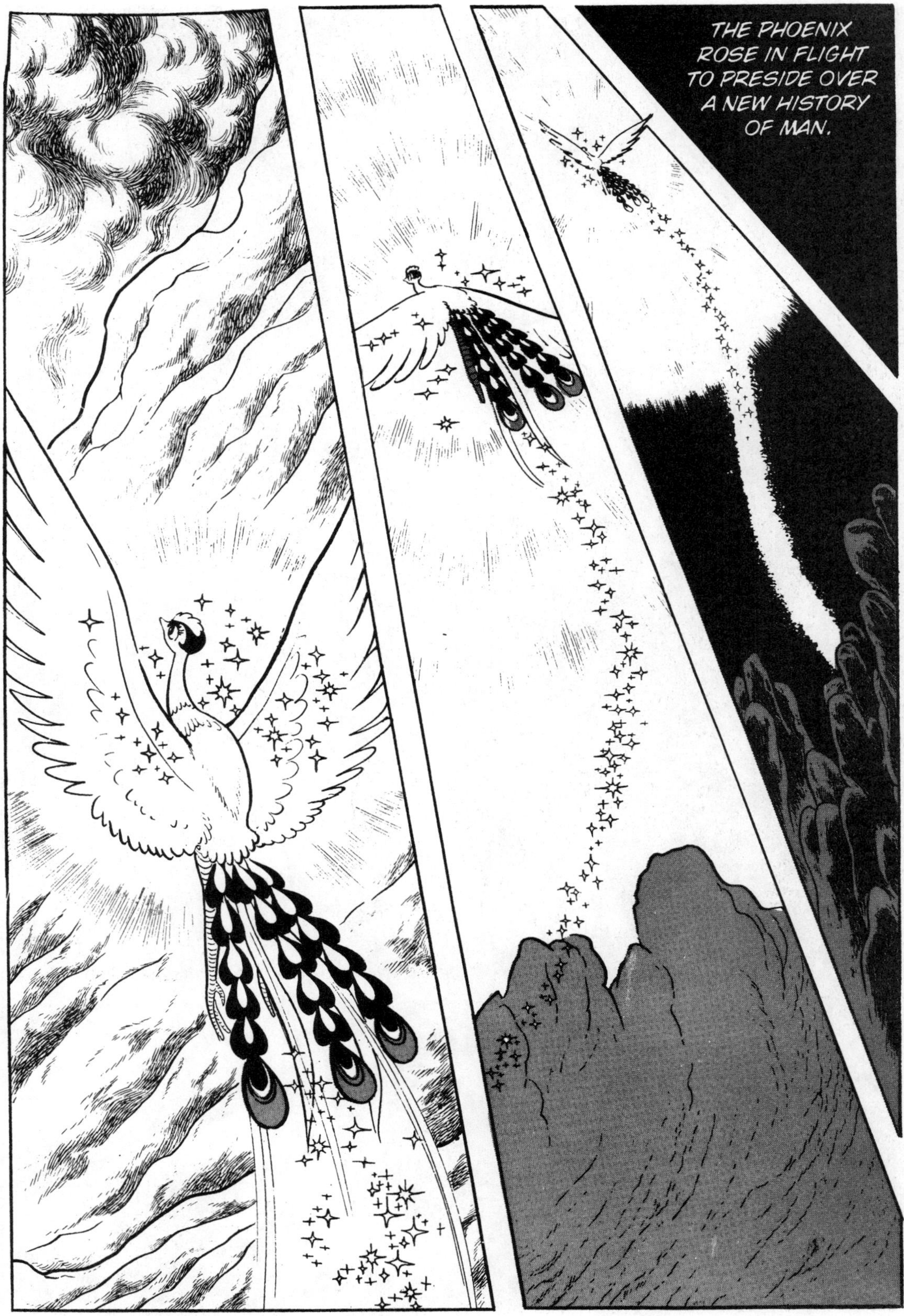
THE PHOENIX ROSE IN FLIGHT TO PRESIDE OVER A NEW HISTORY OF MAN.

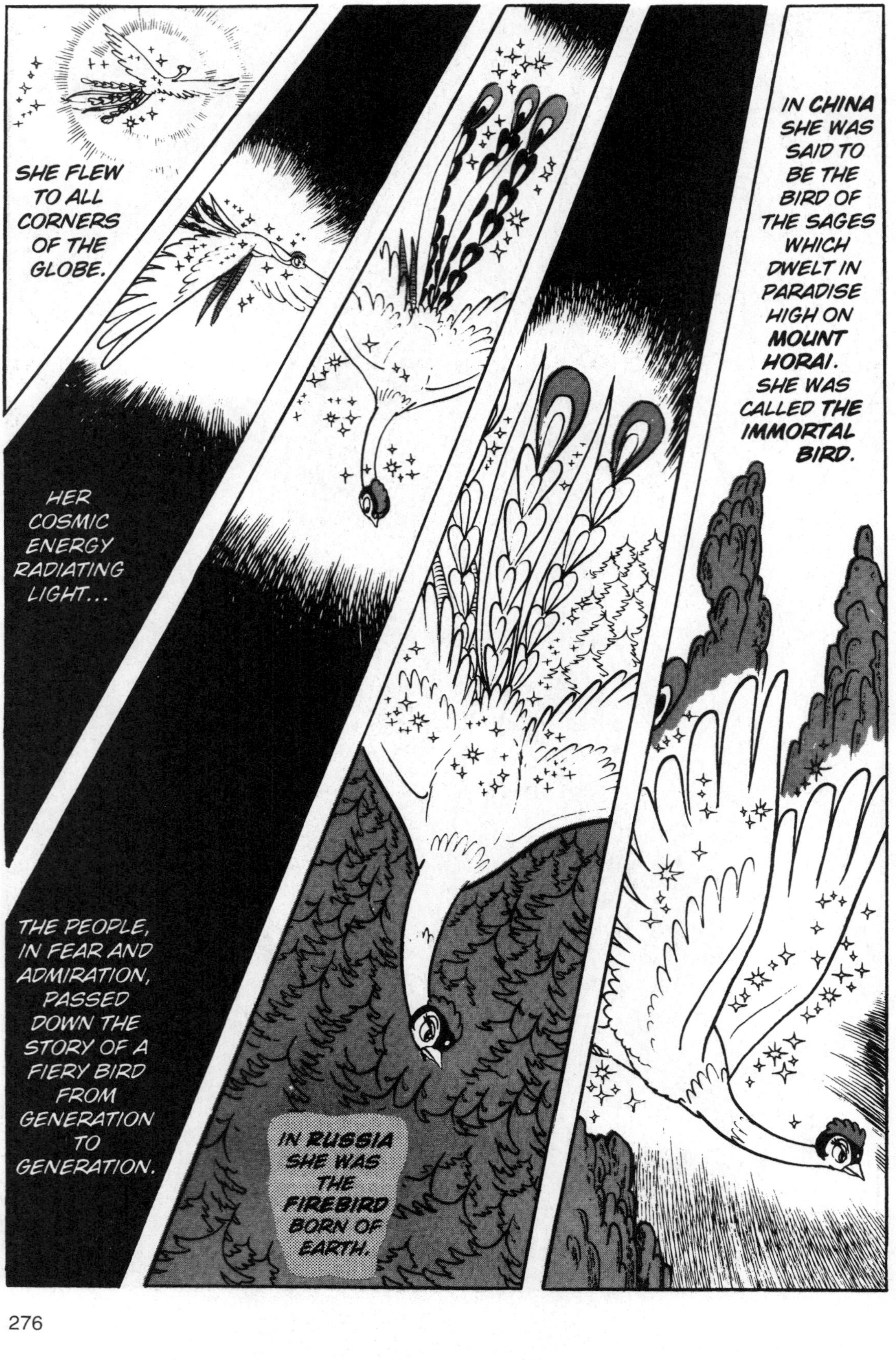
SHE FLEW TO ALL CORNERS OF THE GLOBE.
HER COSMIC ENERGY RADIATING LIGHT...
THE PEOPLE, IN FEAR AND ADMIRATION, PASSED DOWN THE STORY OF A FIERY BIRD FROM GENERATION TO GENERATION.
IN RUSSIA SHE WAS THE FIREBIRD BORN OF EARTH.
IN CHINA SHE WAS SAID TO BE THE BIRD OF THE SAGES WHICH DWELT IN PARADISE HIGH ON MOUNT HORAI. SHE WAS CALLED THE IMMORTAL BIRD.

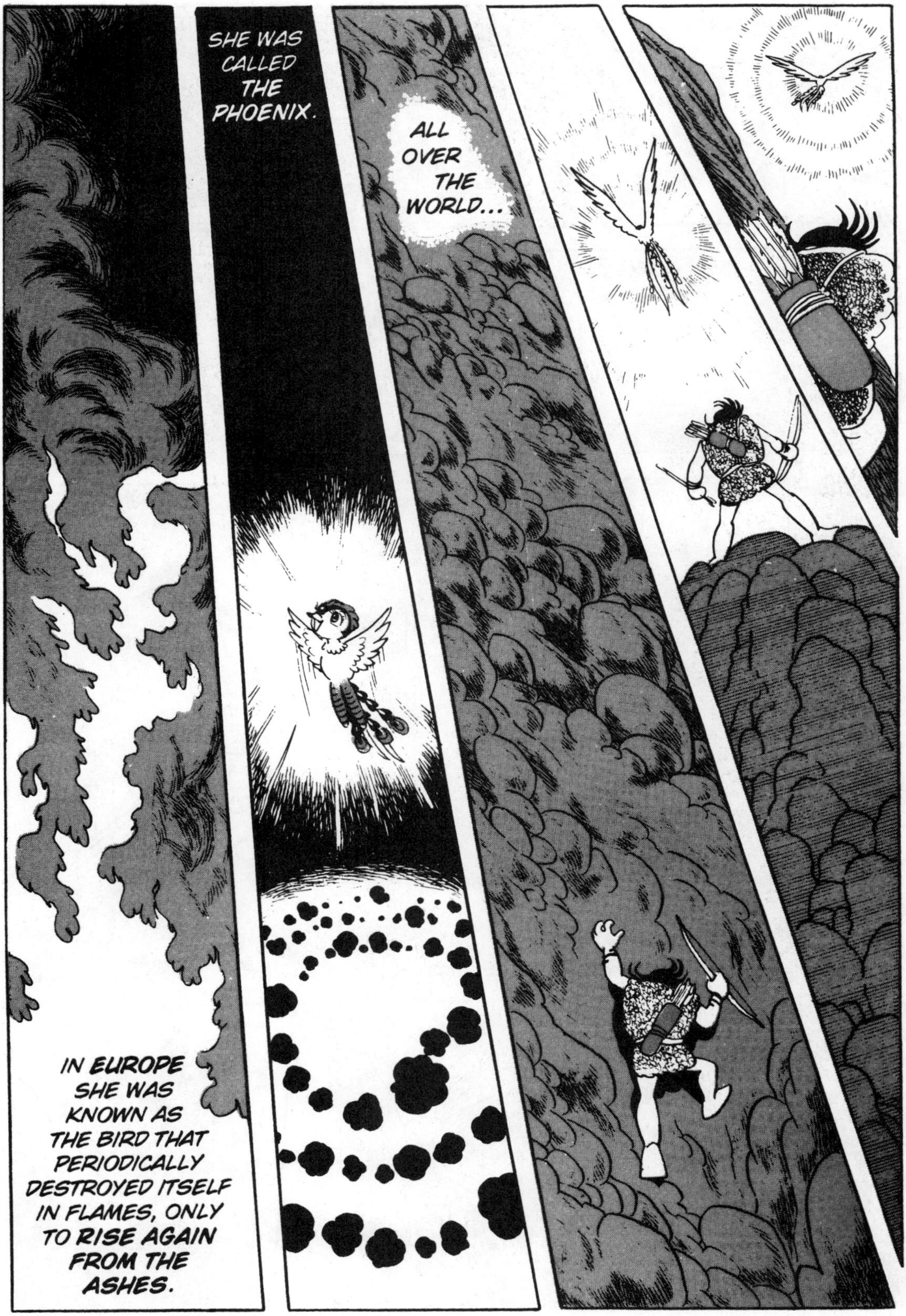
ALL OVER THE WORLD...
SHE WAS CALLED THE PHOENIX.
IN EUROPE SHE WAS KNOWN AS THE BIRD THAT PERIODICALLY DESTROYED ITSELF IN FLAMES, ONLY TO RISE AGAIN FROM THE ASHES.

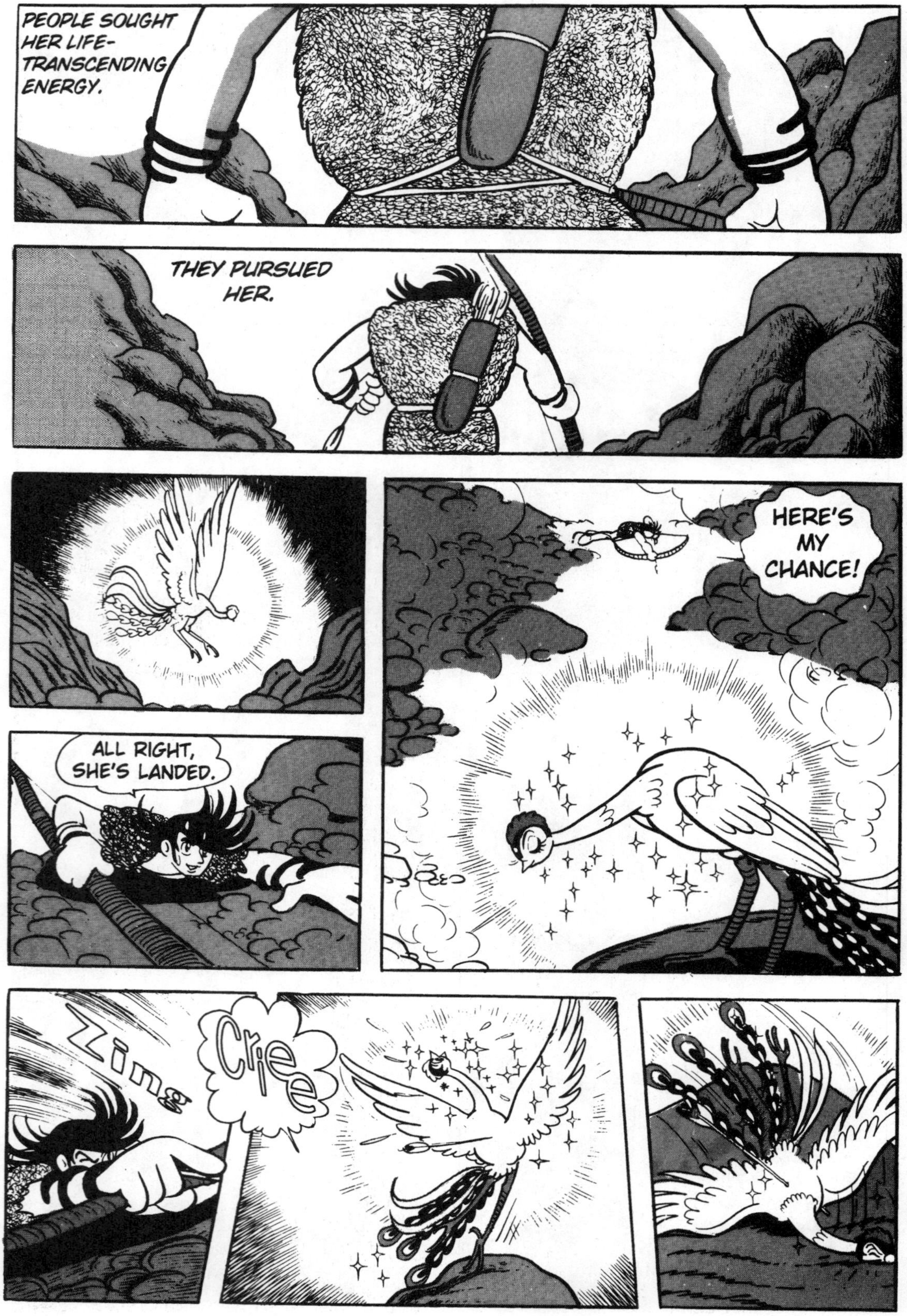
PEOPLE SOUGHT HER LIFE-TRANSCENDING ENERGY.
THEY PURSUED HER.
ALL RIGHT, SHE'S LANDED.
HERE'S MY CHANCE!
Zing
Criee

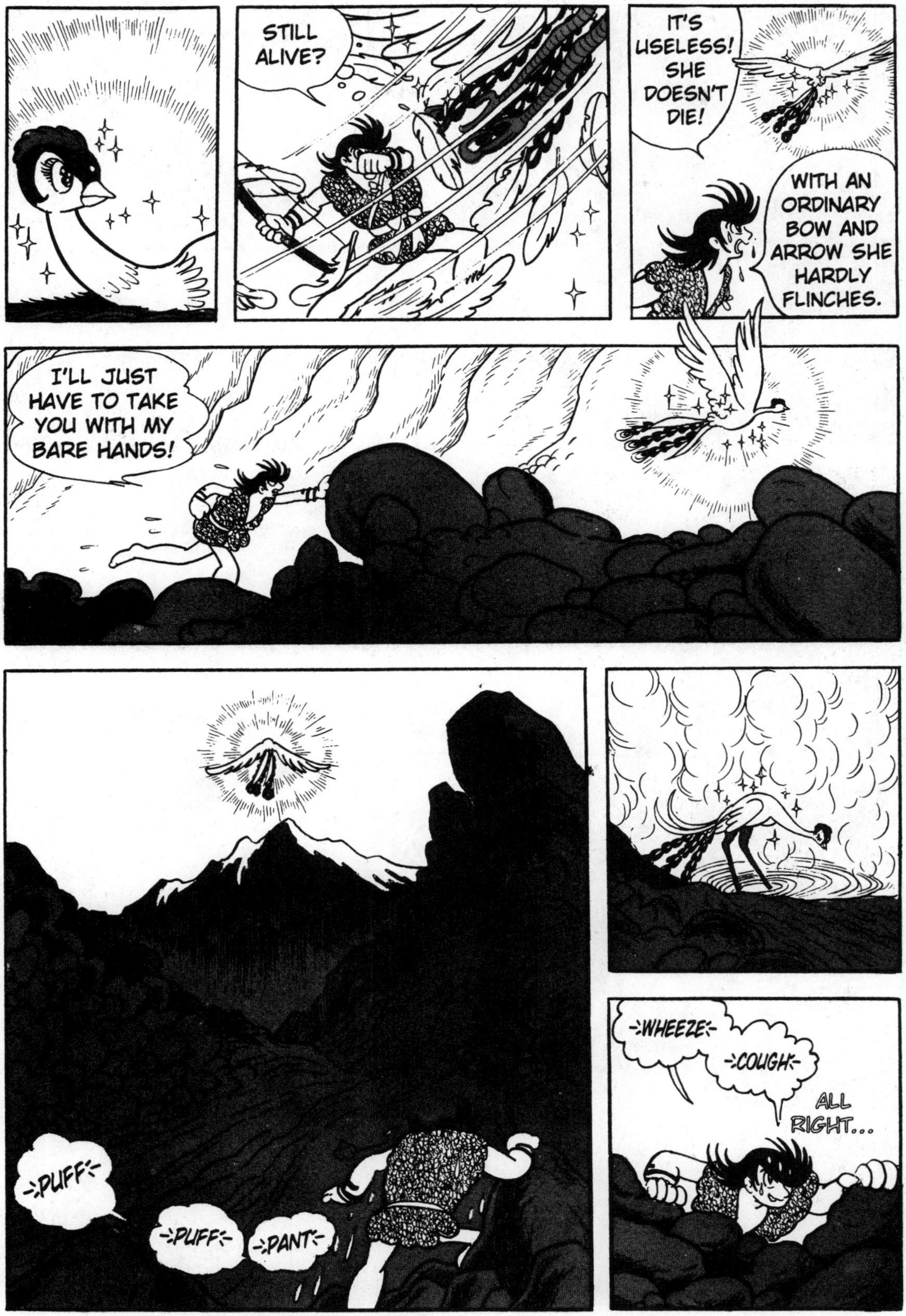
STILL ALIVE?
IT'S USELESS! SHE DOESN'T DIE!
WITH AN ORDINARY BOW AND ARROW SHE HARDLY FLINCHES.
I'LL JUST HAVE TO TAKE YOU WITH MY BARE HANDS!
-PUFF-
-PUFF-
-PANT-
-WHEEZE-
-COUGH-
ALL RIGHT...

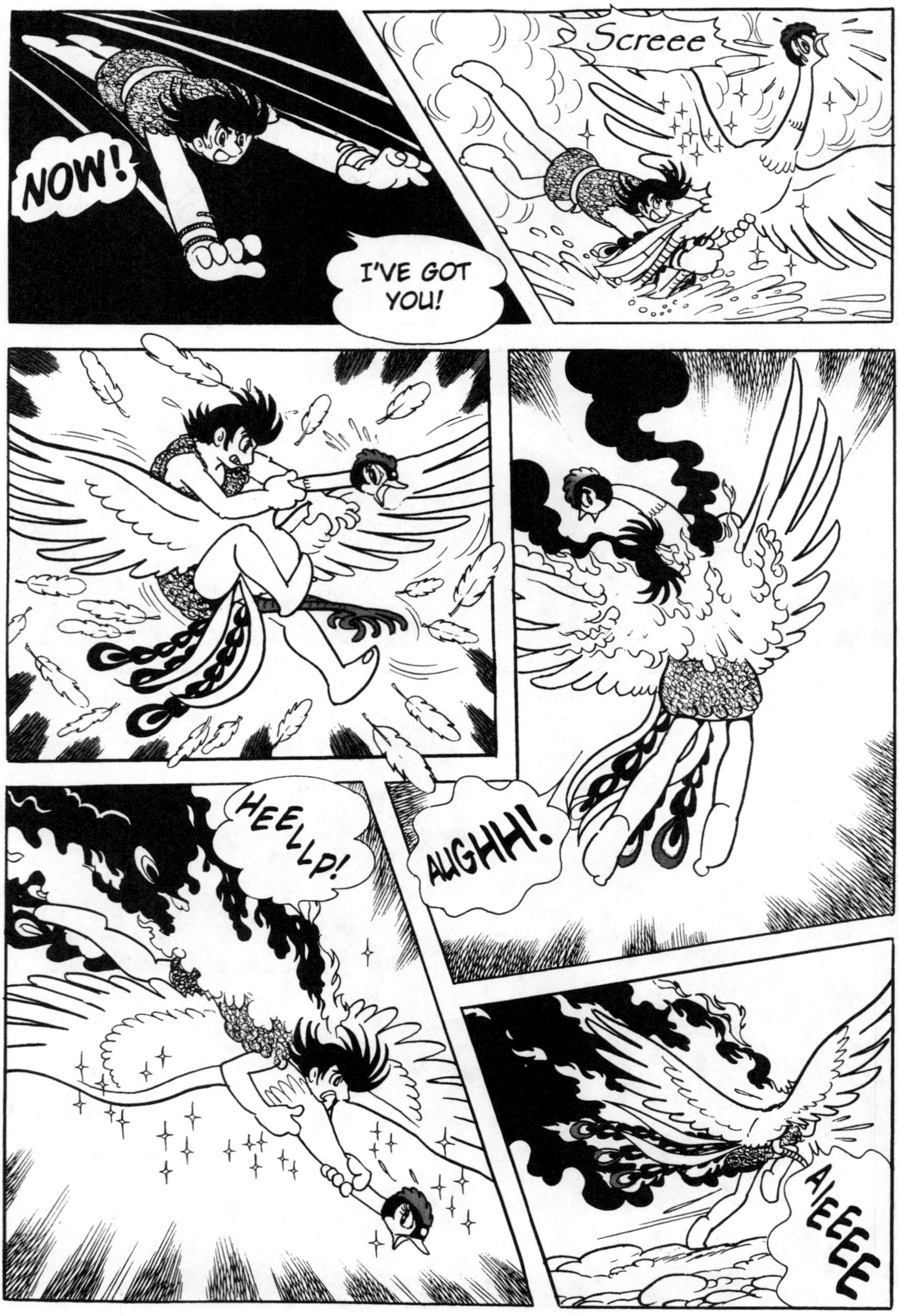
NOW!
I'VE GOT YOU!
Screeee
AUGHH!
HEELLP!
AIEEEE

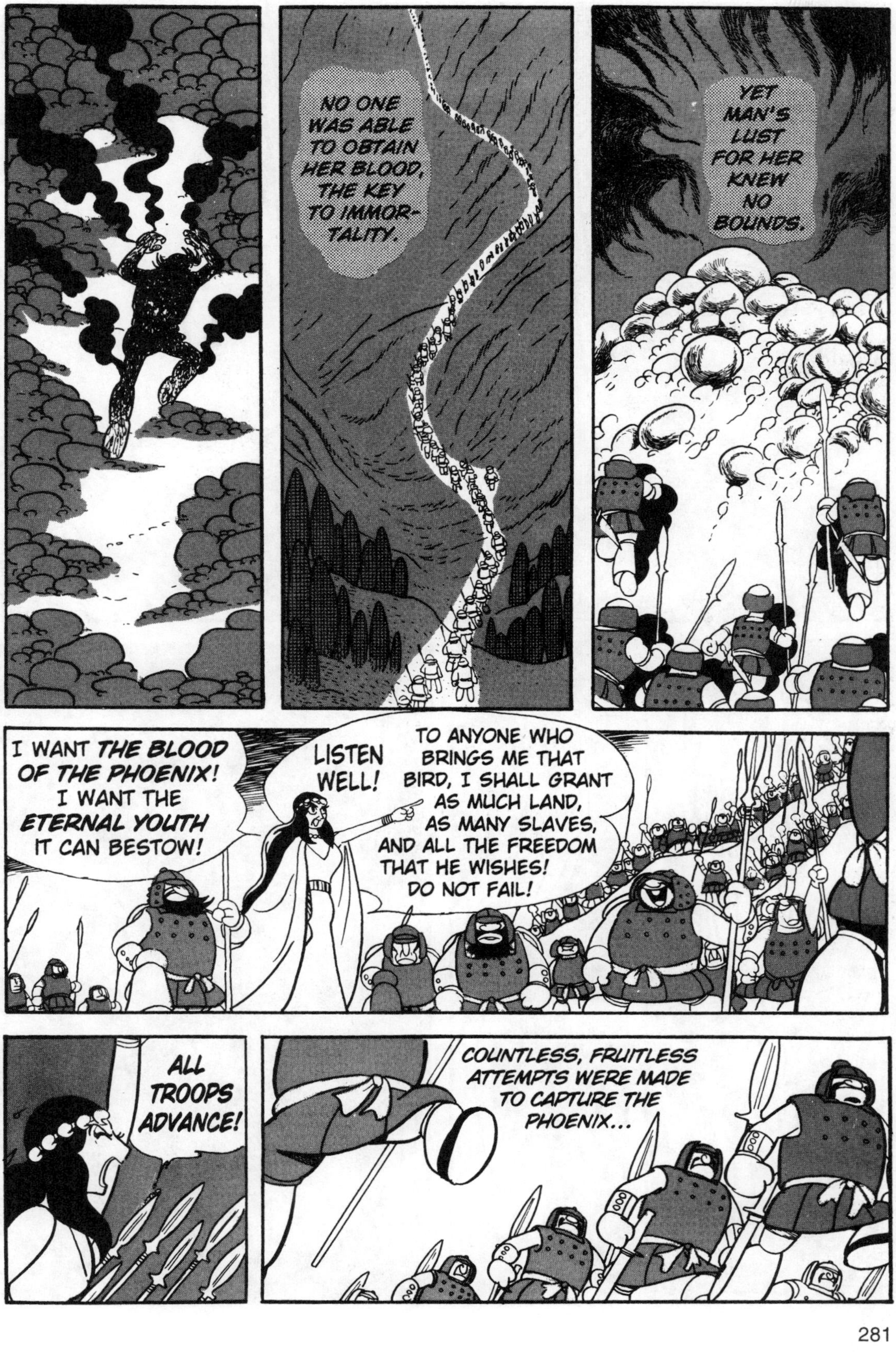

NO ONE WAS ABLE TO OBTAIN HER BLOOD, THE KEY TO IMMORTALITY.
YET MAN'S LUST FOR HER KNEW NO BOUNDS.
I WANT THE BLOOD OF THE PHOENIX! I WANT THE ETERNAL YOUTH IT CAN BESTOW!
LISTEN WELL!
TO ANYONE WHO BRINGS ME THAT BIRD, I SHALL GRANT AS MUCH LAND, AS MANY SLAVES, AND ALL THE FREEDOM THAT HE WISHES! DO NOT FAIL!
ALL TROOPS ADVANCE!
COUNTLESS, FRUITLESS ATTEMPTS WERE MADE TO CAPTURE THE PHOENIX...

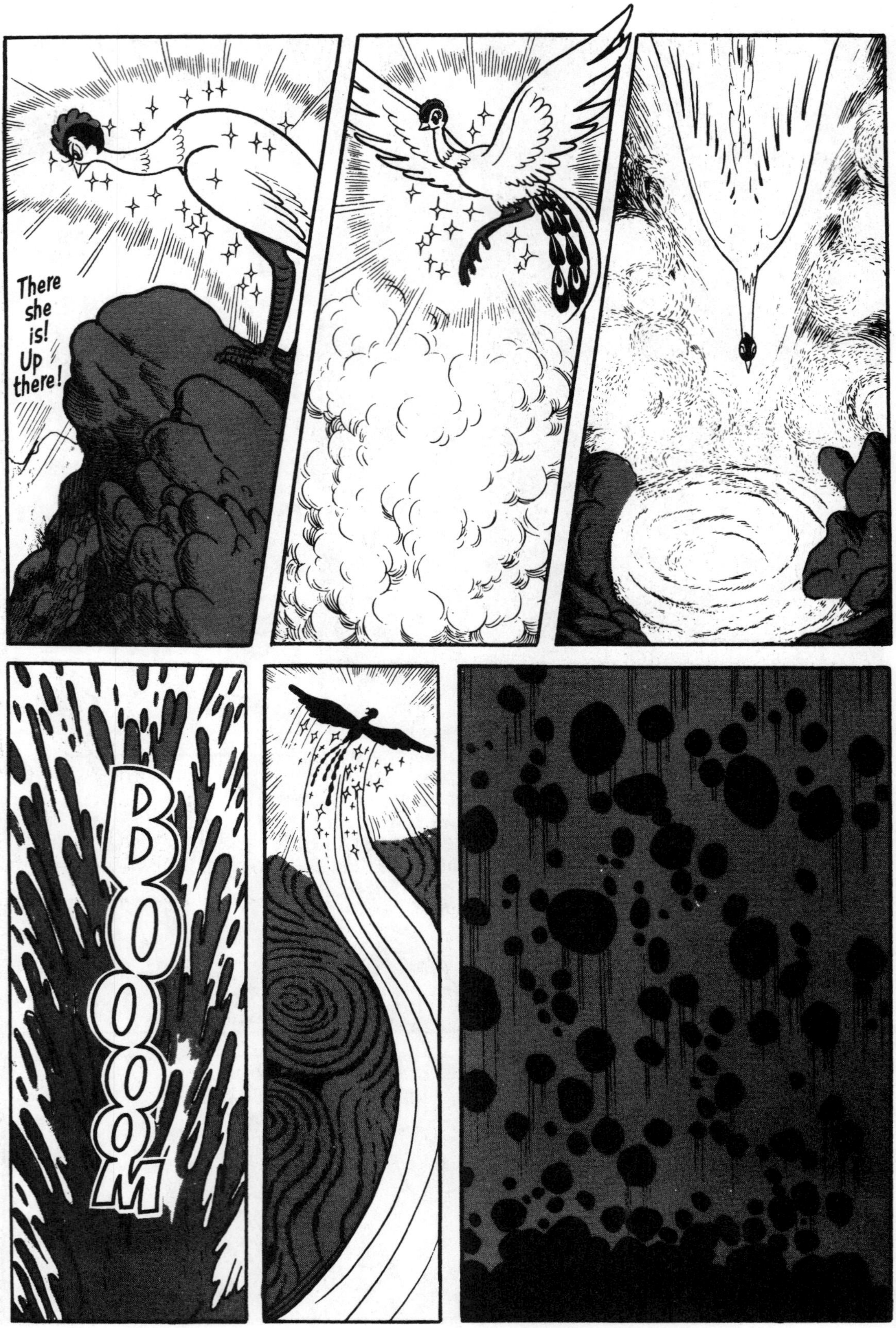
There she is! Up there!
BOOOOOM

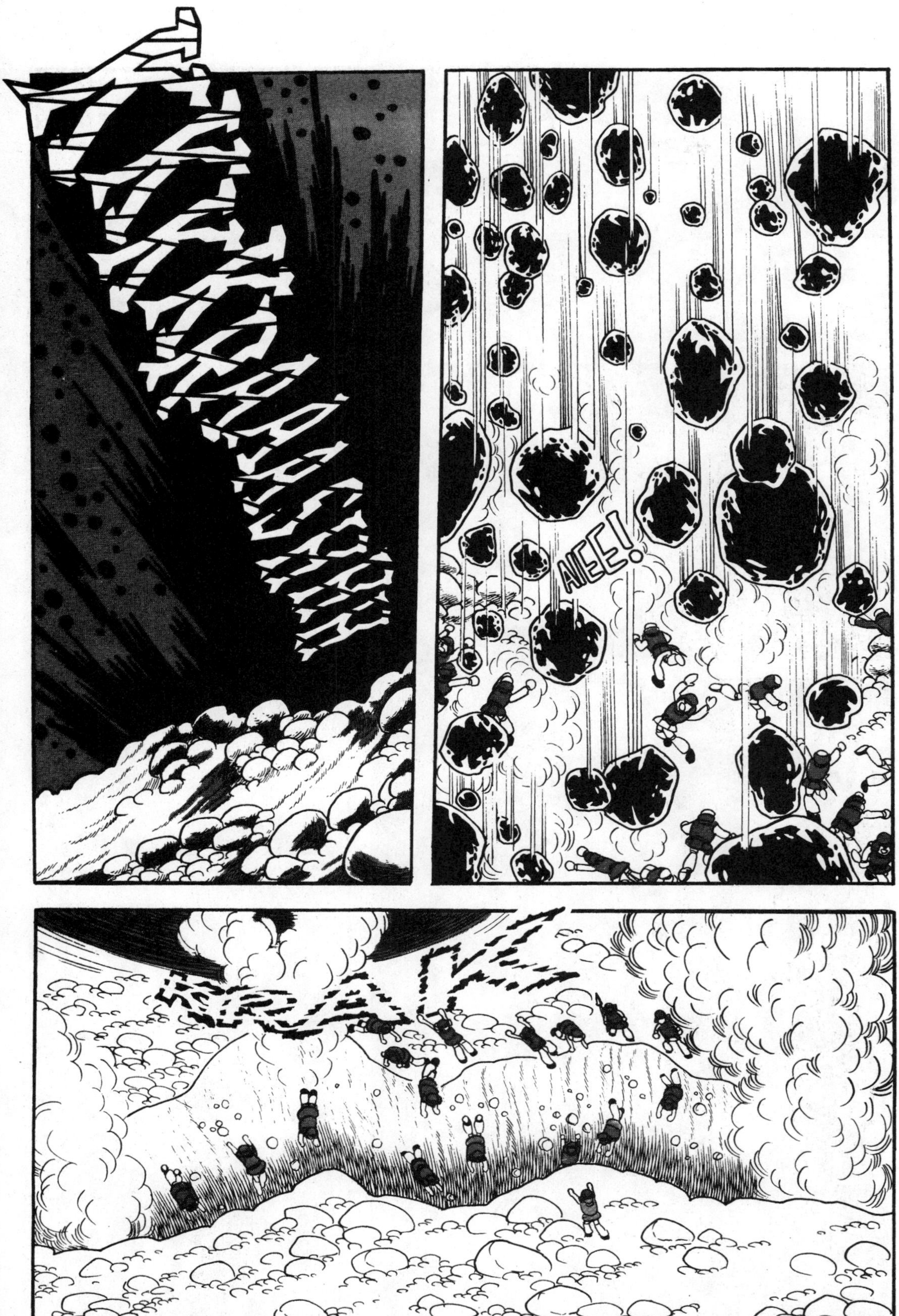
AIEEE!

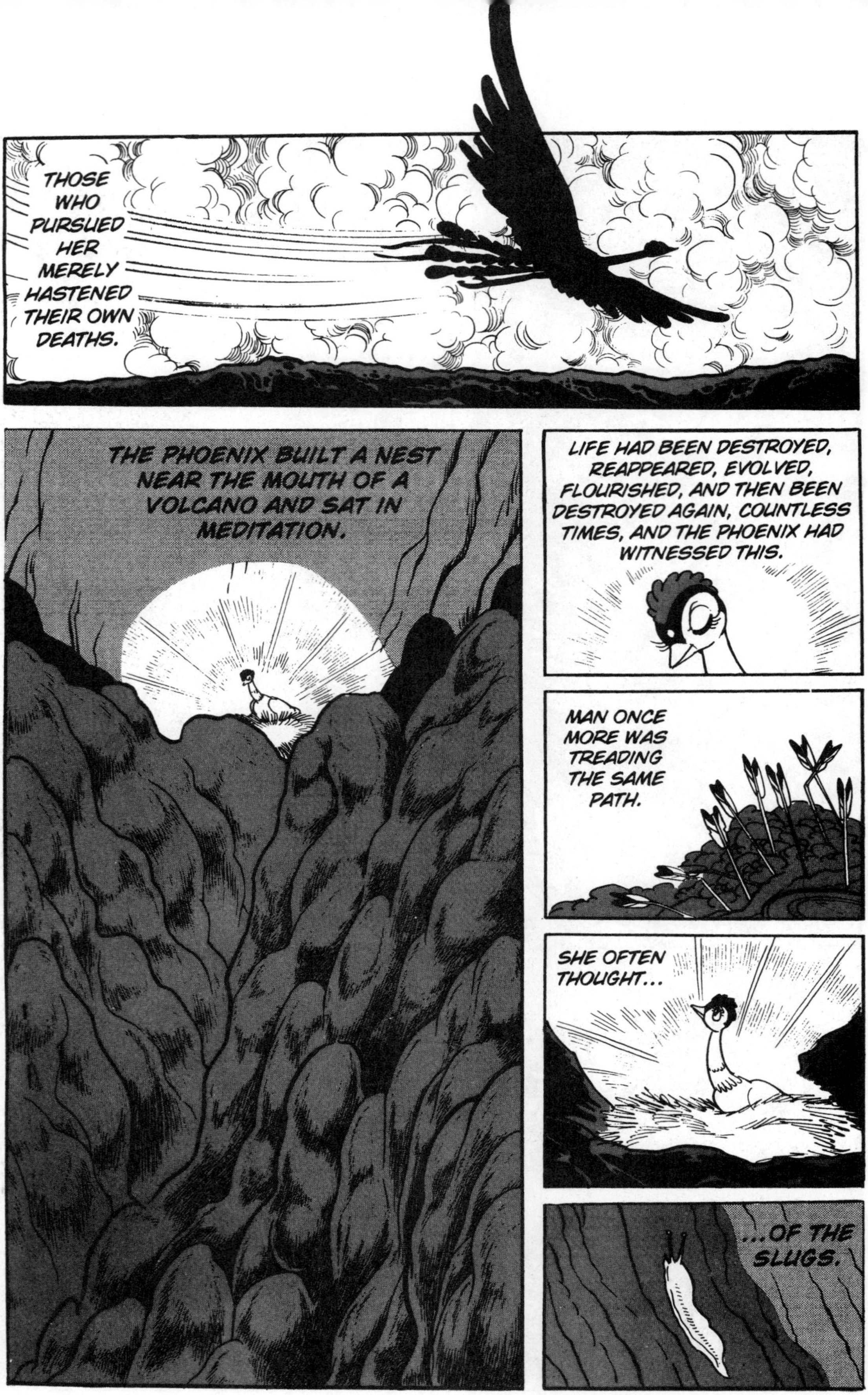
THOSE WHO PURSUED HER MERELY HASTENED THEIR OWN DEATHS.
THE PHOENIX BUILT A NEST NEAR THE MOUTH OF A VOLCANO AND SAT IN MEDITATION.
LIFE HAD BEEN DESTROYED, REAPPEARED, EVOLVED, FLOURISHED, AND THEN BEEN DESTROYED AGAIN, COUNTLESS TIMES, AND THE PHOENIX HAD WITNESSED THIS.
MAN ONCE MORE WAS TREADING THE SAME PATH.
SHE OFTEN THOUGHT...
...OF THE SLUGS.

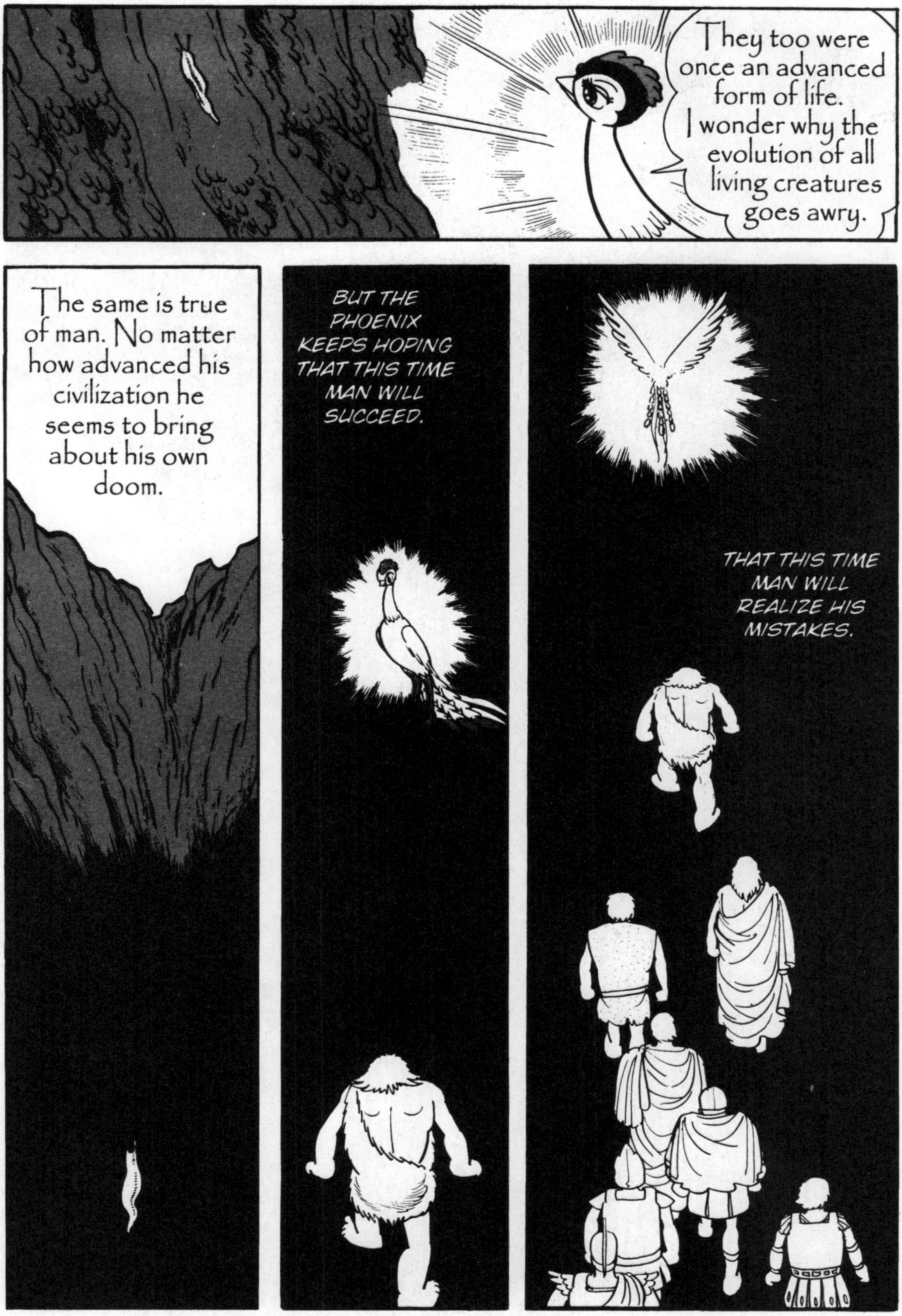
They too were once an advanced form of life. I wonder why the evolution of all living creatures goes awry.
The same is true of man. No matter how advanced his civilization he seems to bring about his own doom.
BUT THE PHOENIX KEEPS HOPING THAT THIS TIME MAN WILL SUCCEED.
THAT THIS TIME MAN WILL REALIZE HIS MISTAKES.

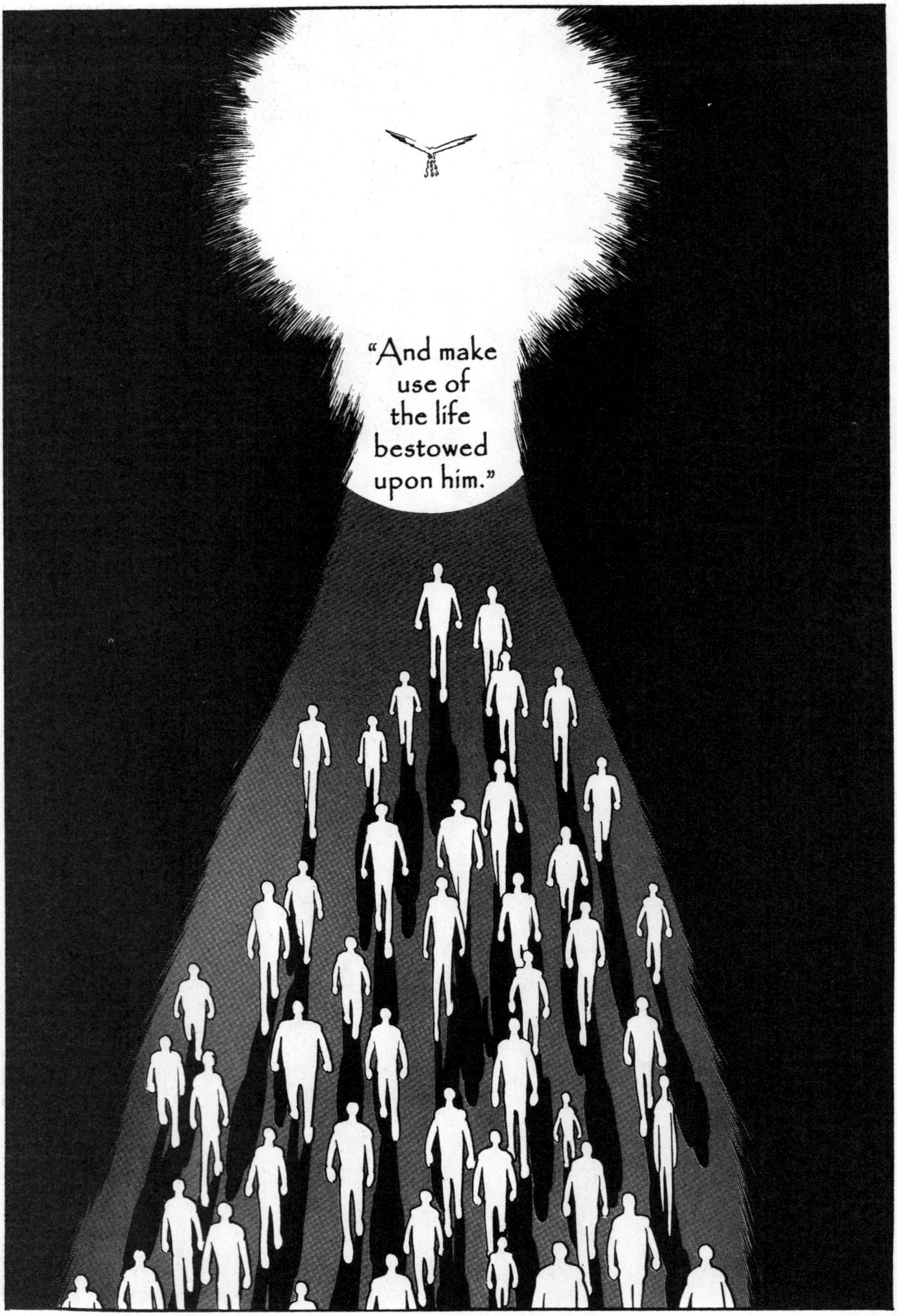
"And make use of the life bestowed upon him."

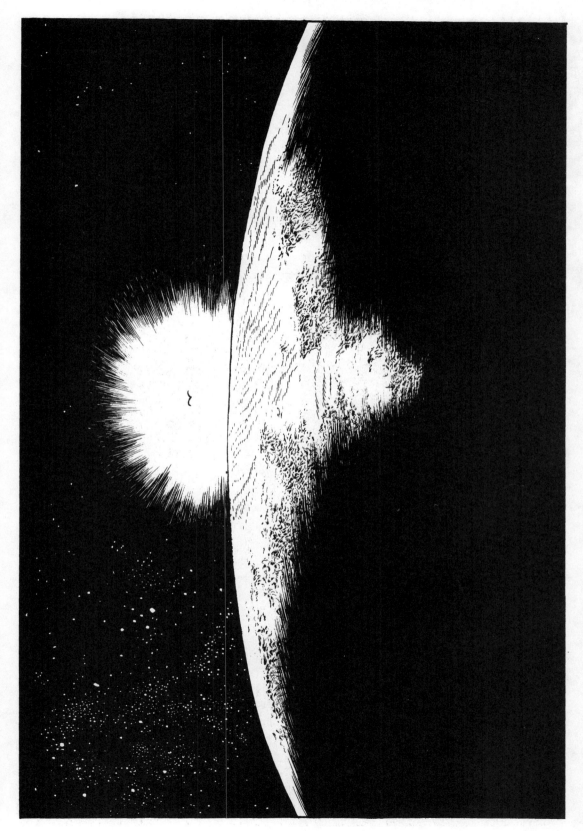

287

ABOUT THIS EDITION OF PHOENIX: A TALE OF THE FUTURE

The twelve self-contained yet interlinked stories that compose Phoenix (Hi no tori in Japanese, literally "Firebird") is considered by many to be the summit of Osamu Tezuka's artistic achievement. Tezuka himself referred to Phoenix as his "life work." Painstakingly composed over a span of decades (initial versions appeared as early as 1954), serialized in a number of venues, and left incomplete with Tezuka's death in 1989, Phoenix represents Tezuka's ambitious attempt to push all he knew about the comics medium to address fundamental questions about existence.

All twelve stories in Phoenix are linked by the presence of the mythical bird, an immortal guardian of the universal lifeforce. Read in order, the separate stories jump across time, alternating between a distant future and a distant past, converging on the present, with characters from one story being reincarnated in another. The existing twelve stories, totaling over three thousand pages of work, are sub-titled "Dawn," "Future," "Yamato," "Universe," "Hou-ou," "Resurrection," "Robe of Feathers," "Nostalgia," "Civil War," "Life," "Strange Beings," and "Sun."

This edition, Phoenix: A Tale of the Future, is an English translation of the second of the twelve Phoenix stories ("Future," or in Japanese, Miraihen). "Future" was first serialized in 1967-8 in the monthly magazine COM, which was published by Tezuka as a venue to feature work too challenging or experimental for inclusion in mainstream manga magazines. The only other portion of Phoenix to appear in English previously is a 27-page excerpt from Dadakai's translation of "Hou-ou," which was printed in Frederik L. Schodt's Manga! Manga! The World of Japanese Comics.

AFTERWORD
By Takayuki Matsutani

"Tezuka-sensei came to Earth from a distant universe, and when his mission here was accomplished, he returned to outer space..." This notion was expressed several times in the tremendous flood of condolences given by intellectuals, artists, and others active in the fields of manga, film, music, and publishing when Osamu Tezuka passed away thirteen years ago. At the time, my grief over his death was so fresh I dismissed the idea as mere science-fiction fancy. Later, however, as I began sorting through Osamu Tezuka's legacy, I truly came to believe "Tezuka was a space alien"—it was the only adequate way of explaining his extraordinary artistry.

Look at Phoenix. I won't go into an analysis of the story; rather, I will just point out that it is one of many manga series he created, that during his career of forty-odd years, Tezuka drew 150,000 pages like those you see here. Simple arithmetic shows this comes out to ten pages a day—without a single day off! That's not all: Tezuka also produced over sixty animation titles (and Astro Boy, for instance, a TV series with two hundred episodes, is counted here as just one title!). Add to this over thirty books of prose, frequent television and radio appearances, lectures, interviews, and travels, not to mention stints as producer or director at various expos and other events...It seems impossible that one person could have done it all, yet Tezuka did. Then consider the breadth of subjects and genres he tackled: historical works, contemporary issues, science fiction, politics, culture, education, character-based drama, epics, short stories, picture books for toddlers, mysteries, psychodramas, fantasy, nonsense, satire, and stories for boys, girls, young adults, and mature readers...in other words, everything under the sun. How could one human being do all that? This is where the "Tezuka as alien" theory comes in handy.

It is extremely unfortunate that Tezuka did not live to see the 21st century, where so many of his stories are set.

In 2001, Japan entered an unprecedented economic recession, while the U.S. was assaulted on September 11 by terrorist attacks that far surpassed our wildest imaginings. These attacks then triggered the retaliatory war in Afghanistan, while in the Middle East the Israeli-Palestinian conflict escalated to new heights of violence. The 21st century has gotten off to a horrific start, and now in 2002, the countdown to Armageddon seems only to have accelerated. As globalization moves forward, the world is getting smaller and smaller. If Tezuka were alive today, how would he feel about all this? What kind of message would he send out to children through his works? Sadly, this is something we cannot know.

Although this *Tale of Future* takes place far beyond our time, in the third millennium A.D., Tezuka set Astro Boy's birthday in the opening years of the 21st century—April 7, 2003, to be exact—only fifty years ahead of the time *Astro Boy* began serialization in 1952. Just seven years after the devastation of World War II, when Japan was still a poor, scrabbling country, Tezuka imagined high-rises and underground cities, expressways snaking between skyscrapers, TV phones, trips to the moon, masses of industrial robots, and even a revolt by robots. Many of these things now actually exist in today's world, lending proof to Tezuka's astounding visionary powers. But even more extraordinary to my mind is the fact that, at a time when Japanese cities were still in ruins, when the Japanese people were living day-to-day and hand-to-mouth, and as such put economic recovery above all else, Tezuka—in such works as *Jungle Taitei* (which began serialization in 1950) and *Astro Boy*—was addressing environmental issues, calling for coexistence between human beings and other animals, and reminding us to take care of our precious planet Earth. These themes, which also dominate the *Phoenix* series, are the most pressing and relevant issues facing humanity today. That Tezuka's imagination could reach so far amidst the reality of 1950s Japan is the mark of genius.

Tezuka continued working up to three weeks before his death. As his strength waned, and he became too weak even to sit up in bed, he would still struggle with all his might to rise.

"I'm begging you, let me work!" were his final words. His wife desperately tried to calm him down, but

Tezuka had always been a workaholic, a man who worked without rest. What made Tezuka so compulsively creative, so urgently obsessive about his work?

Tezuka experienced World War II as a teenager. He spoke of having seen entire neighborhoods turned into a sea of flames by bombs and charred corpses lying on the streets afterwards. He remembered the deeply comforting sight of lights shining brightly in people's homes the night of August 15, 1945—the first night of peace. The war was finally over, the blackouts a thing of the past, and he savored the return of peace with profound gratitude. But at the same time, he swore to himself never to forget the tragic consequences of war, and to pass on his own experiences of war to the children of the future.

The next year, 1946, Tezuka was studying medicine at Osaka University and also made his debut as a professional manga artist. Although he did brilliant manga work and met with success, Tezuka finished his studies as well and obtained a physician's license. Medicine was, then as now, a highly respected and economically stable profession. In contrast, children's manga were dismissed as cheap entertainment; moreover, only a handful of people could make a living from drawing them. Even so, and in spite of the social conditions of the time, Tezuka chose manga over medicine.

Of course he loved drawing manga, probably loved it more than anything else. But I believe he was driven by something more than that: he chose manga because he felt it was his mission to spread the message of peace and respect for life to the children of the future. And Tezuka probably knew, better than anyone else, that he had staked his future on an amazing medium. Today, computer-enhanced Hollywood movies are taking the world by storm. With computer graphics, people can morph easily into different shapes and interact in the same frame with dinosaurs. Some say that manga and animation have lost their advantages and been surpassed. But for those of us who have read Tezuka's works, Hollywood has only now caught up, just barely, with the expressive capacity of manga. Over fifty years ago, Tezuka knew that manga—back then an art form still in its infancy—could express anything and everything the imagination could conjure, from the mundane to the utterly fantastic.

However, and this is probably the same all over the

world, manga has always been viewed as inferior to other art forms, such as painting, prose, music, and theater. Manga was denounced by adults, who claimed it had a bad influence on children. Tezuka battled against the censure of these adults all his life, and this fight for acceptance was another driving force in his passion for work.

Many years ago, Japanese newspapers reported an incident in which children were told to bring all their manga books to school so they could throw them into a big bonfire in the yard. Yes, book-burnings in Japan focused on manga. I don't claim that all manga are good. As with any other art form, there is good work and bad work. But Tezuka, conscious of the average adult's bias toward manga, worked indefatigably to change that bias. Most important, of course, he created high-quality manga, but he also appeared frequently on TV, wrote essays and articles for magazines and newspapers, and did everything else he could in his crusade to bring manga the recognition it deserved as a legitimate art form.

In the year Tezuka died, a national art museum held an Osamu Tezuka exhibition. No museum of that stature had ever mounted a manga-related exhibition before. The culture of manga has been supported by many talented artists, most of them inspired by Tezuka, and today, there are numerous manga works that far outstrip novels and films in popularity, scope, and ambition.

The day after Tezuka passed away, a major newspaper eulogized him in an editorial, "Why do Japanese love manga so much? Foreigners apparently find it very strange to see adults engrossed in weekly comic magazines on the train...One explanation for this is that, in their countries, they did not have Osamu Tezuka." Not only was it extremely unusual for a major newspaper, let alone in an editorial, to discuss manga or a manga artist, but this was praise of the highest sort. Yes, manga in Japan today have earned a secure place as a respectable art form.

Osamu Tezuka devoted his entire life to manga, and *Phoenix* is one of his representative works. I hope you enjoy it.

Takayuki Matsutani
President, Tezuka Productions

Translated from the Japanese by Akemi Wegmuller

PHOENIX AND ME
BY OSAMU TEZUKA

The serialization of *Jungle Taitei* in *Manga Shonen* ended in 1954, and I was at a loss as to what to create next.

Then I saw Stravinsky's famous ballet, *L'oiseau de Feu*. Of course the ballet itself was excellent, but I was especially intrigued by the prima ballerina dancing as the spirit of the phoenix.

The ballet is based on an old Russian legend about a prince that has been captured by a demon. The spirit of the phoenix saves the prince by acting as a guide for his escape. I thought that this passionate, elegant, and mysterious bird would make a wonderful main character comparable to the likes of Leo from *Jungle Taitei*.

Actually, every country has a legend about a mysterious bird such as the phoenix. In these legends, the symbol of supernatural lifeforce takes form as a bird, such as the immortal bird called the *Hou-ou* from the legend of Hourai-san.

I wanted to utilize this phoenix to portray Japanese history in my own way. The theme would be about man's attachment to life and the complications that arise from greed. The phoenix would be the vehicle that would bring it all together.

As a new challenge, I wanted to start by

creating the beginning and then the end of a long story. The story would then return to an ancient period right after the dawn of man. I would then continue to go back and forth, between past and future. In the end, I would set the story where past and future converge—the present. This story, set in the present, would tie all the previous stories together to form a long drama running from the dawn of man all the way to the distant future.

Each story would stand on its own and seem to have nothing to do with the other stories, but the final story would tie everything together—and for the first time, the reader would realize that the structure of the series is such that each story would be just one part of a much longer story. After all, man's history does not have clear divisions or breaks.

Each episode would portray life from various angles and set up different problems. Moreover, the style of each of the episodes would vary from one another, covering a range of genres: science-fiction, war story, mystery, comedy.

I don't know how many more years *Phoenix* will continue, but after it is completed, please go back and read through the whole series again. Otherwise, it will be difficult for me to respond to criticism.

Osamu Tezuka, December 1969

Translated from the Japanese by Andy Nakatani

ABOUT THIS TRANSLATION
An Interview with "Dadakai" —Jared Cook and Frederik L. Schodt

The story of this translation of Phoenix: A Tale of the Future *is an epic tale in of itself. It is twenty-five years old. When Viz Comics licensed the English-translation rights from Tezuka Productions, we were told that translations of the first five volumes of* Phoenix *had already been done. Commissioned a quarter of a century ago—but never published—the translations existed only as dim photocopies of the original Japanese publication, with word balloons whited out and written over in English. When we received the manuscript in the mail, the dust had not yet been completely shaken off. The credit: a mysterious outfit known as "Dadakai."*

Since then two men have stepped forward to identify themselves as former members of Dadakai. Jared Cook is a television producer, primarily of Japanese commercials, running his own film coordination company, the Chiari Cook Co., since 1985. Frederik L. Schodt is an interpreter and author of several books, including the groundbreaking tomes Manga! Manga! The World of Japanese Comics *and* Dreamland Japan: Writings on Modern Manga. *Schodt has translated Tezuka's manga adaptation of* Crime and Punishment *and is working on a book of history, as well as translating the English publication of Tezuka's* Astro Boy *manga for Dark Horse Comics. This interview was conducted by Carl Gustav Horn and Alvin Lu.*

Frederik Schodt: I was thinking the other day about

what Tezuka would have thought about *Metropolis*, because I went to see *Tron* with Tezuka.

Q: What was that like!?

FS: He wasn't so impressed. He was a very competitive man, and he wasn't very impressed with the future of computer graphics. I think that when he saw *Tron* he thought it was too cold and too sterile, that computer graphics would never be able to achieve the warmth of hand-drawn animation. But he was always interested in what was going on and in what other animators were doing. We also went to see Ralph Bakshi's *Lord of the Rings*, for example.

Q: Can you go into the history of your Phoenix *translation? Why didn't the translation get published at the time?*

Jared Cook: We translated *Phoenix* around 1976-77. Fred and I were a little ahead of our time. We knocked on a lot of doors, but the seventies just were not the right time to introduce manga to English speakers. I remember meeting with a rep from Marvel Comics who happened to be in Tokyo. His reaction to our idea of translating Japanese manga into English was not at all inspiring.

I don't think there was much awareness of Japanese culture in America. I visited several animation clubs and groups with Osamu Tezuka in the eighties and became aware of the few but intense followers of Japanese animation, but the phenomenon of Americans starting to collect and appreciate Japanese manga and animation didn't gather steam until the nineties, I think.

I still have relatives that ask me to speak some "Chinese." Americans, in general, don't seem to have a good grasp of geography, except maybe for the areas that we happen to be bombing at the present.

FS: We realized after doing all this work that it was basically too early. People had no idea what Japanese comics were. The attitude was still, "Japanese comics? Are you kidding?" When I wrote my first book, *Manga! Manga!*, I actually had a dispute with

my editor about the title, because I was afraid it would be stuck in library card catalogs with "manganese." At the time there would have been no association with comics at all.

Q: The form of the translation is…unique. It's very carefully handmade.

JC: We were working in an age when copiers were just making their appearance. No computers. The only way we could translate the work and have it live together with the pictures was to white out the dialogue balloons and handwrite the English translation into the boxes. This required some serious editing to make the words fit into their respective "containers," but it also forced us to constantly refer to the pictures and make sure the language was reflecting the drama on the page. It was definitely a hands-on process, requiring the disassembly and reassembly of the books. We regretted that we were unable to flip the pages, so that we could make the English volumes follow the English-style, left-to-right reading direction rather than the right-to-left, Japanese style.

FS: It was all done by hand. With *lots* of Liquid Paper. This was as close we could get at the time to a readable prototype, and it was expensive to make copies. You can tell it's not a real high-quality copy, but we went to a great deal of trouble. I'm embarrassed to say this, but we actually took what we thought was the strongest of the first photocopied five volumes to a printer. We did this because we wanted to conduct a survey of readers, to see what they thought of the story and of manga in general, and we needed multiple copies to do so. But what we took to the printer was one of our rather poor quality originals *[points to manuscript]*, so we wound up with a second-generation bad copy. At that time, it wasn't cheap to take a book of over two hundred pages to a printer, but it was still cheaper than trying to use a copy machine.

Q: Do you draw comics yourself?

FS: I do some cartooning, but I don't claim to be a comic artist. Still, in my book *Manga! Manga!*, where I have an excerpt from of one volume of *Phoenix*, I really tried to do a semi-professional retouch and lettering job. I was crushed because one reviewer at the time said he liked the selections, but thought the lettering wasn't very professional! It was true, of course, but I had just spent ages and ages trying to get it right. There used to be this clear plastic lettering guide which people used with a blue pencil to draw reference lines in the balloons before lettering. It had little holes in it, and by rotating part of it, you could basically adjust the height of the letters, the middle line of the letter, the line spacing, and so forth. All comics artists, or at least all the letterers, used it. You would take a ruler, put it on the page, then put this plastic thingamajig on top of it, and with the blue pencil you would draw three or more guide lines which wouldn't show up when the pages were printed. I spent a lot of time on that. Now nobody letters by hand, right? It's all computers, I suppose.

Q: *What was "Dadakai"?*

JC: Fred came up with the name, a play on the Dada art movement and the Japanese word for fret/nonsense. We had a fellow named Shinji Sakamoto who was our "quality control" guy, who checked our translations and also helped on the business end, negotiating contracts, and making phone calls. There was a Japanese woman named Midori who was also an initial member who helped with translation, but I recall that only Fred, Sakamoto, and myself stayed with the *Phoenix* project until completion.

We had absolutely no experience or credits to bring to Tezuka. Tezuka and Matsutani were kind enough and indulgent enough to take a chance on some crazy college students. I think they realized that we were sincere, however. And I think we understood that *Phoenix* was a work that really should be introduced to English readers.

Q: *What other works did you guys translate?*

FS: *Phoenix* was the first work we did. We did the *Battlefield* series by Leiji Matsumoto after that. I've never asked Matsumoto what he thought of us. Shinji Sakamoto was really into motorcycles, and he knew

Matsumoto was really into motorcycles. In fact Matsumoto was the pioneer of *mecha*; he almost invented the whole concept of *mecha* in manga. He was really into guns and motorcycles and machines— with an aura of romance. That was what the whole *mecha* concept was about. So we went to Matsumoto's place on motorcycles. I had a Honda 750, and I wore a huge sheepskin-lined leather jacket. Sakamoto was into antique motorcycles, and I don't know what motorcycle he went in on, but he was wearing knee-high boots. I can't remember whose bike Jared was on. We roared over to Matsumoto's place and must have looked very strange.

When I was later working at a translating and interpreting firm in Japan, they knew I had this side-thing with manga. Somehow they were approached by a production company in Tokyo. There was a movie being made of Riyoko Ikeda's *The Rose of Versailles*, a live-action film, and they needed the whole manga series to be translated—in a hurry. The film was to be called *Lady Oscar*. It was one of the most convoluted co-productions in the world. Maybe worse than that. It was based on a Japanese manga about the French Revolution, but the manga had androgynous gender-bending Japanese *shojo* manga characters. Since the producers were going to make a live-action film based on this, they needed the whole manga series—which is thousands of pages long—translated and sent to the screenwriters in LA, who would then turn it into an English screenplay, which would then be used by the French director, Jacques Demy, who would use English actors acting on location in Paris and in Versailles. It was kind of a Moebius-strip-Klein-bottle-mirror-image thing. A real happy cultural goulash. And ultimately the film would be shown in Japan for the Japanese market. The actors themselves were British, they all spoke in English, and they were later subbed into Japanese. No one was speaking French to my knowledge. It actually showed in San Francisco at the Castro once. I know because my postman was raving about it.

Most of the stuff I was doing at this company consisted of incredibly boring business and government reports. Since they knew I was into manga they said, "Hey, you're the man, here you go," so Jared and I sat down and in maybe ten days we did the whole thing—the whole *Rose of Versailles* series. It was quite an extraordinary feat. We wrote in pencil right on copies of the pages of the graphic novel. We may have whited out the balloons, or because of the time factor we may have just written in between the lines of the Japanese. I can't remember. Anyway, that was sent to Hollywood and then to England. The readers must have just been flabbergasted. I never heard anything about our translation again. What was really tragic is that I never made a copy. We submitted the only copy. It'd be a true historical artifact today. If anybody finds it, I'd like to have it.

What's really funny is that many years later I was approached by a company in Tokyo and asked to translate *The Rose of Versailles*. Two volumes of the series were published in English in Japan, but I had to do that translation from scratch.

Q: Which of Dr. Tezuka's works are your favorites? What are some of your favorite manga overall?

JC: The first few volumes of *Phoenix* are absolutely the best. I think these are the core of Tezuka's "lifework"…The brilliant way Tezuka jumps through time, while still binding the stories together through reincarnated characters, was at its best in the first six volumes. They introduce a cinematic perspective to Japanese manga that was revolutionary. The manipulation of time and character are still absolute works of genius. Some of the visionary aspects are still remarkable for their accuracy. The architecture of the Tokyo Prefecture office building in Shinjuku existed in a volume of *Phoenix* long before the building was actually built. Maybe the architect was a reader of Tezuka, but I think Dr. Tezuka was also inspired in the way he could envision the future.

My favorite manga when I was rummaging through used bookstores in Tokyo were *Ashita no Joe, Otoko Oidon, Notari Matsutaro,* and the sentimental series *Yuhi no Sanchome.* Leiji Matsumoto's *Battlefield* series was also a favorite of mine. I was also a big fan of *Hagure Gumo,* and even made silk screen T-shirts with the character from *Gaki Deka.* I'm not sure if any of these would translate well into English. They all have very distinct Japanese cultural themes that would be

difficult to render into English. It's almost like trying to translate the information we get from "body language."

FS: I was going to university in Japan in 1970-72. It was a very political time and lots of university students were reading manga. It was a kind of generational badge: "We read manga." Manga were also getting much more interesting. *Gekiga* were appearing; some of them were very political and a lot of the artists were experimenting heavily. A lot of the most interesting stuff around today still comes from that period. Many of my Japanese friends were reading manga, so they started telling me what they thought was great. I had this one friend, Shuichi Okada—he's a Japan Airlines pilot now, flies jumbos and what-not. I remember he came to me and said, "There's this really cool manga. You gotta read it! It's called the *Phoenix*!" I said, "*Phoenix*? Yeah, right! Will you loan some copies?" He presented it almost like this religious thing. You know, like a holy work. And when I read it I just thought it was amazing. I never had read anything in manga that grabbed me like that. So Okada has a lot of responsibility for what he did to my life.

It was a special era. The Vietnam War was still going on, the hippie era was still around and hadn't imploded completely, so something with a cosmic theme like *Phoenix* was pretty powerful stuff for someone 20, 21 years old. I was probably reading Herman Hesse, Kurt Vonnegut, Jack Kerouac, the usual stuff the hippie generation read, and then I read *Phoenix*…

Q: How did you go about approaching the artists for permission to translate their work?

JC: One phone call to Tezuka Pro and a quickly arranged meeting with Mr. Matsutani, Tezuka's manager, started the ball rolling. Tezuka himself was just getting back on his feet after the dissolution of Mushi Pro, his first company. I think Matsutani, who was also fairly new to the new Tezuka Productions, was eager to start a new project and begin the "resurrection" of Tezuka's manga/animation enterprise. We also spoke to Leiji Matsumoto and Go Nagai, but Tezuka was our best and most foremost contact in the manga world.

FS: We made many visits to Tezuka Pro. They had a tiny reception area, and the rest of the place was totally chaotic. There was all this work going on and Tezuka himself was always being besieged by editors, so he was off in a room locked away somewhere. We would talk to Mr. Matsutani initially, and then Tezuka would come out, say hello, and we'd talk to him. He had at that time twelve, maybe thirteen assistants. He had one of the largest manga production studios in Japan. In addition to his assistants, he had his father, who was the president; Mr. Matsutani, who was his manager; and there were office people. Matsutani was his personal manager, which means he sacrificed the best years of his life for Dr. Tezuka. He's the president of Tezuka Productions now. Back then he very rarely slept in his own bed. He usually slept in the office on the sofa. We would go there, and he would be pattering around in his slippers, like everybody else looking really sleepy. He would ward off the editors when they were trying to break down the door, and he would try to take care of Tezuka's schedule to make sure he could get his work done by his deadlines. It's just amazing— he very rarely got a chance to sleep. Anyone who worked with Tezuka very closely, their lives were not exactly made hell, but they didn't sleep a lot.

Q: What was it like meeting and working with Dr. Tezuka?

JC: It was amazing to work with Tezuka. I can recall dinners, plane trips, car rides, conferences…The man had an amazing energy. He was truly driven to create. I don't think he slept more than three hours a day. A typical trip to the U.S. would start with a trip to a local movie theater, directly from the airport, to see a new animated film. From there, a bite to eat, and then directly to a meeting for some new project. After that, perhaps he'd go to a meeting of fans, arranged to coincide with his visit. Tezuka would talk and listen for hours without showing any fatigue. From there, he would return to the hotel to continue drawing manga, usually with an editor waiting outside his hotel room door, preparing to hand carry the finished pages back

to Japan the next morning. He was truly an amazing individual.

I can recall Fred and I interpreting for him at a comic book convention. We'd interpret in shifts because we could not individually maintain the pace and intensity of Dr. Tezuka's dialogue.

FS: He was very polite and very kind. I've never understood completely why, but he once told me that when he first saw me he thought I was a little scary. I think it's because I'm tall, my hair may have been a bit long, and we didn't have very good Japanese business manners then. We must have been kind of a shock. Here, out of the blue, were these two foreigners speaking fluent Japanese. There weren't quite as many foreigners speaking Japanese in those days, and I'm sure in the world of manga, other than a few indirect approaches from American publishers or something, they probably had very few foreigners ever coming to the office.

Tezuka was an extraordinarily kind man when he was dealing with friends, fans, or the general public. To his staff and people who were really close to him, he could throw a fit and make life miserable for them, but to us especially, he was extraordinarily kind.

Tezuka had a huge influence on my life, in every way. If you've ever met one person in your life who changed you, you know what I mean. I never would have done so much with manga if I hadn't known Tezuka, and both Jared and I had a long relationship with him that lasted many years after translating *Phoenix*. Having worked with Tezuka made everything possible, because in Japan human relations are so important. I wouldn't have been able to do *Manga! Manga!* if I hadn't known Tezuka. Knowing him opened the door to interviewing so many artists, not only for *Manga! Manga*, but for *Dreamland Japan* and everything else I've subsequently written. Because of my writings, in 2000 I won the Asahi Newspaper's Special Prize category of their prestigious Osamu Tezuka Cultural Award. I had to give a speech in Japanese on stage in front of hundreds and hundreds of industry and media people and I nearly choked. I was trying to explain what Tezuka meant to me but I couldn't do it justice. He changed my life forever.

A Journey through Time and Space: An Overview of the Complete *Phoenix* Saga

The complete *Phoenix* saga is a story about mankind that features a historical-narrative structure unlike anything that has come before it. The first volume depicts the dawn of civilization. The second volume (see "About this Edition") jumps to the far future. The setting for the third story shifts back to early history, and so on, back and forth, from past to future; the amplitude decreases as past and future converge to meet in the present.

Dawn (1967)
240-270 A.D.

The era of Queen Himiko of the Yamatai Koku. The work quotes from the accounts of the *Gishiwajinden*. Also uses accounts from the legend of *Jinmu Tousei*.

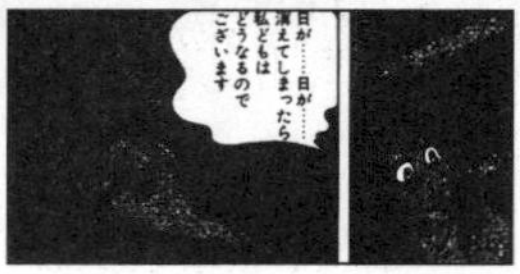
日が……日が……
消えてしまったら
私どもは
どうなるので
ございます

The scene in the Amano Iwato myth where Himiko compares herself to Amaterasu-Oumikami and a solar eclipse occurs.

Yamato (1968-69)
320-350 A.D.

Based on the legend of Yamato-takeru-no-mikoto. The dates above were inferred from the account of Old Man Takeru, and from information in *Dawn.*

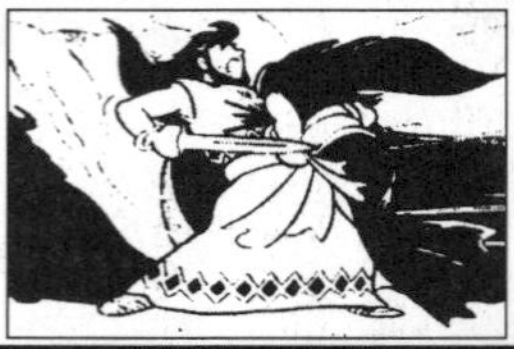

Disguised as a woman, Prince Yamato Oguna approaches the Chieftan of the Kumaso and stabs him. As told in the Kiki myth, the prince gets the name "Takeru" from his opponent right before he dies.

Hou-ou (1969-70)
720-752 A.D.

The complicated drama of the spirit of two Buddhist sculptors. Set in the Nara Period (710-794) during the national enterprise of the construction of the Great Buddha. Here, the Hou-ou (a Chinese myth) is the Phoenix.

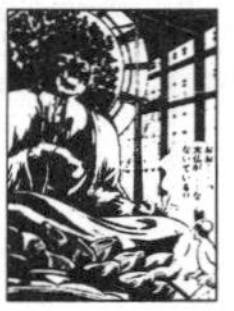

Akanemaru, who has been ordered by the authorities to be in charge of the construction and design of the Great Buddha, is shocked when the statue sheds tears. The workers become frightened, and the bizarre phenomenon halts construction.

Robe of Feathers (1971) 937-941 A.D.

A sci-fi version of the Hagoromo Legend of Miho no Matsubara in Enshu (modern day Shizuoka). Set during Taira no Masakado's rebellion which occurred during the Heian Period (898-1185).

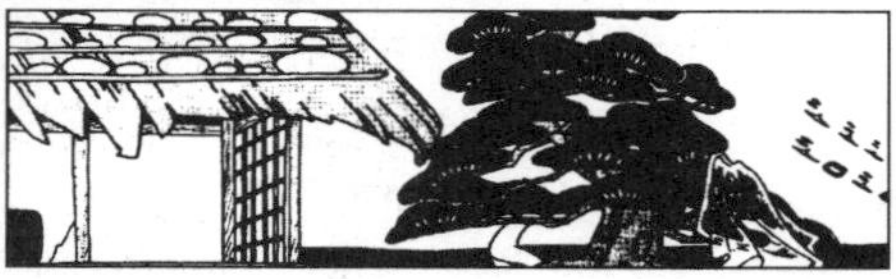

The spirit of a woman swimming in the ocean is captured by the beauty of the white sand and green pine. The spirit of a fisherman is bewitched by the beauty of the woman and he hides her clothes...

Civil War (1978-80)
1172-1189 A.D.

The time of the Genpei Kassen (War between the Taira and the Genji) after the fall of the Heishi (Taira Clan). Using the *Heike Monogatari* and *Gikeiki* as a backdrop, this story depicts "combat" as the fate of living things.

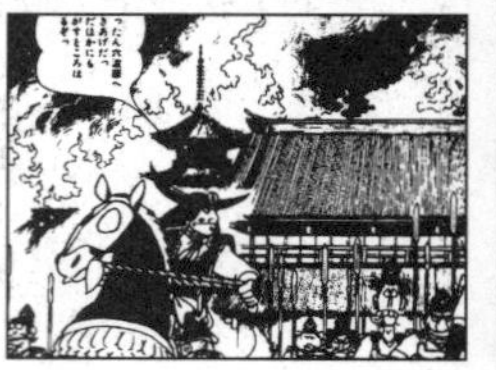

Kiso Yoshinaka defeats the Heishi and takes control of the capital. He cuts down the famous monk Myoun. He came to the capital because he is after the Phoenix.

Strange Beings (1981)1468-1498 A.D.

The Sengoku Period (1482-1558). Sakonnosuke, the heir of General Yagi Iemasa cuts down the nun, Yaobikuni, who seems to be 800 years old. But she doesn't realize the true relationship between herself and the nun.

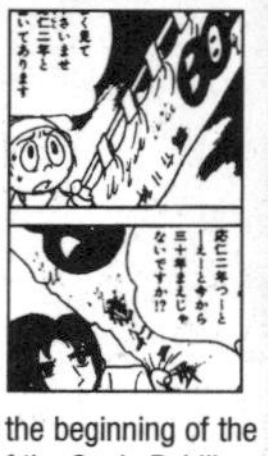
く見て
さいませ
応仁二年と
いてあります
応仁二年っーと
ーえーと今から
三十年まえじゃ
ないですか!?

The banner bearer is saying that "now" is the beginning of the Sengoku Wars and they are in the middle of the Ounin Rebllion. In other words they are in a time before Sakonnosuke was born!

Sun (1986-88)
663-672 A.D.

The story begins after the defeat of the Japan-Kudara alliance at Hakusukinoe and Japan's withdrawl from the Korean peninsula, and ends with the struggle for the imperial throne during the Jinshin Rebellion.

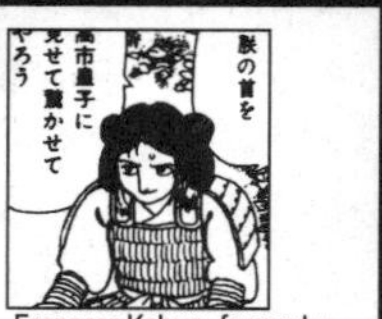
朕の首を
市皇子に
見せて驚かせて
やろう

Emperor Kobun, formerly called Otomo no Miko, is the cousin of Takachi no Miko, who is the son of Oama no Miko.

Future (1967-68)
3404 A.D.-infinity

The end of the future. Mankind is in decline and has become very conservative. The earth is run down and faces devastation. Eventually a nuclear war breaks out causing the end of everything.

The Yamato Central Main Building Megalopolis. Yamato is one of the five remaining underground cities of mankind.

Universe (1969)
2577 A.D.

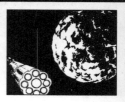

In Orion, a sub-light speed rocket heading towards earth crashes into a meteorite. The ship becomes unable to fly and four people manage to escape, including Saruta and Nana.

Each of the passengers escapes in an individual escape pod. However the pods only have enough food for half a year and enough air for a year and a half. Possibilities of survival are...

Resurrection (1970-71) 2482-3344 A.D.

In the year 3344, Prof. Saruta lands on the moon. He meets and acquires Robita in his final form. Spanning 860 years, the end of this episode goes beyond *Universe* and close to the beginning of *Future.*

Robita and this rocket also make appearances in *Future*, where Robita stops Rock and then gets shot by him.

Nostalgia (1976-78)
Indeterminate (approx. 25th century)

The spaceship is headed for Eden 17. The shiny object in the foreground is its sun. The planet is surrounded by a revolving ring of space dust held there by gravity.

A Japanese woman named Romy establishes a civilization and history for the formerly uninhabited planet, Eden-17. Her husband dies an unnatural death, but the life she carries inside her...

Life (1980)
2155-2170 A.D.

今 企画中なのは 五百人ずつの クローン人間 による 肉弾戦! つまり 殺人 合戦さ

Human clones are being created. It's all for high ratings and a public-killing TV game show called *Clone Man Hunt.*

Animal clones were created for food. Human clones are created for a TV show—the cloning company president speaks as a sponsor. A terrifying plan for a TV show!

Sun (1986-88)
2008 A.D.

The "Light Tribe" acquired the Phoenix in space. However, they turn it into an icon and come to control society through religion. Non-believers are called "shadows" and are chased out to live underground.

The head temple of the "Light Tribe." A young shadow boy named Suguru endeavors to climb the great tower and steal the Phoenix.

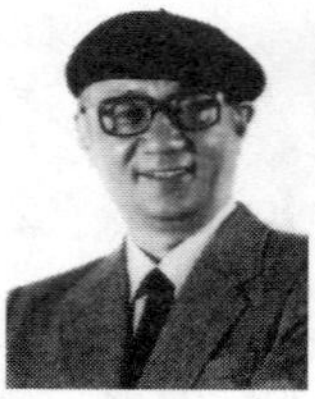

ABOUT THE ARTIST

The Osaka-born Osamu Tezuka (1928-1989) has been long regarded in his native Japan as a cultural icon and the single artist most responsible for the creation of Japan's vast manga and anime culture. He began to draw shortly after WWII, working on short gag strips. In 1947 Tezuka had his first big hit, *Shintakarajima* (New Treasure Island), a 200-page comic drawn when Tezuka was still a medical student that revolutionized the "decompressed storytelling" style that is now the birthright of all Japanese comics.

Tezuka went on, in both short and long narratives, to master and/or invent virtually every genre of the comics form—sci-fi, fantasy, mystery, spy, horror, historical drama, political drama, transforming robots, Shakespearean adaptation, even sex-ed comics—including pioneering the *shojo* (girls') manga genre with *Ribon no Kishi* (aka *Princess Knight,* 1953-6). In 1952 Tezuka created his most beloved work, the robot-boy sci-fi series *Tetsuwan Atom* (aka *Astro Boy*). Other popular Tezuka works include the talking-animal saga *Jungle Taitei* (aka *Kimba, the White Lion,* 1950-4) and the outlaw-surgeon adventure series *Black Jack* (1973-84).

By the mid-sixties Tezuka was a pioneering animator as well as the most popular artist in the history of Japanese comics, yet he continued to fervently reinvent manga forms. The early volumes of *Phoenix,* which began to be serialized in the pages of Tezuka's experimental *COM* magazine in 1967, were Tezuka's bold attempt to expand comics' artistic and demographic reach. Among Tezuka's finest works in this high literary mode are *Buddha* (1972-83), a biography of the religious teacher, and the complex and moving WWII saga *Adolf* (1983-5). In the West, Tezuka's reputation and renown continues to grow. The recent hit anime *Metropolis* (2001) is based on one of Tezuka's earliest works from 1949.